WHAT PEOPLE ARE SAYING ABOUT *A Voice in the Wind*

"With a loving hand, Francin[illegible]f truth and hope in a world filled [illegible] not soon forget Hadassah and [illegible]adfast-ness to the Lord. **A *Voice i*[illegible]earts of all those who read it."

—Rob[illegible] *Ribbon of Years*

"Every one of Francine's books has gone deep inside and changed me."

—**Robin Jones Gunn,**
best-selling author of the Glenbrooke series

"From time to time a novel will appear that changes the course of Christian fiction. I think that **A *Voice in the* Wind** has that power. **A *Voice in the* Wind** is moving and powerful.

"This book is so well-written that it's frightening! The setting—the last days of Rome—is magnificent! The excesses of the emperor, the battles of the gladiators, the hovels of slaves, the pagan temples . . . all are dramatically and colorfully depicted. The psychological facets of the characters are expertly blended with the spiritual aspects. Characters grow stronger—or weaker—but always with skill that makes the reader accept the changes as natural.

"I wish I'd written this book! It is not a 'woman's' book, nor is it a 'man's' book—it is a book that both men and women will read and love. It is a literary gem and a Christian witness such as I've seldom, if *ever*, read."

—**Gilbert Morris, best-selling author**

"The **Mark of the Lion** changed the way I see fiction . . . forever. What is more important, the story changed the way I see life. Thank the Lord for Francine Rivers. What a gift she is to the family of Christ."

—**Stephanie Grace Whitson,**
author of the Dakota Moons series

"As an educational consultant, I selected **A *Voice in the* Wind** for a literary parallel to the Greek world history. The student response was enthusiastic."

—C. H., Port Townsend, WA

A VOICE IN THE WIND

A VOICE in the WIND

FRANCINE RIVERS

TYNDALE HOUSE PUBLISHERS, INC., Wheaton, Illinois

Visit Tyndale's exciting Web site at www.tyndale.com

Check out the latest about Francine Rivers at www.francinerivers.com

Discussion Guide section written by Peggy Lynch.

Designed by Zandrah Maguigad

Library of Congress Cataloging-in-Publication Data

Rivers, Francine, date
A voice in the wind / Francine Rivers.
p. cm — (The Mark of the lion)
ISBN 0-8423-7750-6
1. Church history—Primitive and early church, ca. 30-600—Fiction.
2. Women slaves—Rome—Fiction. I. Title. II. Series: Rivers, Francine, Mark of the lion.
PS3568.I83165V65
813'.54—dc20 93-16608

Printed in the United States of America

08 07 06 05 04
30 29 28 27 26

This book is dedicated with love to my mother,
FRIEDA KING,
who is a true example of a humble servant.

CONTENTS

FOREWORD

In 1992, Tyndale House made a conscious decision to begin publishing excellent fiction that would help us fulfill our corporate purpose—to "minister to the spiritual needs of people, primarily through literature consistent with biblical principles." Before that time, Tyndale House had been known for many years as a publisher of Bibles and of nonfiction books by well-known authors like Tim LaHaye and James Dobson. We had dabbled in fiction before "Christian fiction" became popular, but it was not a major part of our publishing plan.

We began to recognize, however, that we could carry out our purpose very effectively through fiction, since fiction speaks to the heart rather than to the head.

Fiction is entertaining. Well-written fiction is gripping. As readers, we'll stay up until 2:00 A.M. to finish a good novel. But Tyndale has a greater goal than simply entertaining our readers. We want to help our readers grow!

We recognize that authors have something of a bully pulpit for communicating their worldview and values to their readers. But with that opportunity comes a danger. Just what worldview and values is an author communicating? At best, most contemporary novelists present a squishy worldview. At worst, they sow negative values and unhealthy attitudes in the hearts of their readers. We wanted to set a whole new standard for fiction.

So we began looking for novelists who had a heart message that would help our readers grow. And we met Francine Rivers.

Francine had been extremely successful as a writer of romance novels for the general market early in her career. But when she became a Christian, she wanted to use her talents to communicate faith values to her readers. One of her early projects was the Mark of the Lion trilogy.

When I read the manuscript for the first book in the series,

A Voice in the Wind, I was blown away by the power of the story. I was transported back to the first century—to Jerusalem, Germania, Rome, and Ephesus. I lived with Hadassah as she struggled to live out her faith in the midst of a pagan Roman household. I felt the terror of the gladiator as he faced his foes in the arena. Above all, through their experiences I learned lessons in courage.

We are proud to present this new edition of the Mark of the Lion. I trust it will speak to your heart, as it has to mine and to hundreds of thousands of other readers.

MARK D. TAYLOR
President, Tyndale House Publishers

PREFACE

When I became a born-again Christian in 1986, I wanted to share my faith with others. However, I didn't want to offend anyone and risk "losing" old friends and family members who didn't share my belief in Jesus as Lord and Savior. I found myself hesitating and keeping silent. Ashamed of my cowardice and frustrated by it, I went on a quest, seeking the faith of a martyr. *A Voice in the Wind* was the result.

While writing Hadassah's story, I learned that courage is not something we can manufacture by our own efforts. But when we surrender wholeheartedly to God, He gives us the courage to face whatever comes. He gives us the words to speak when we are called to stand and voice our faith.

I still consider myself a struggling Christian, fraught with faults and failures, but Jesus has given me the tool of writing to use in seeking answers from Him. Each of my characters plays out a different point of view as I search for God's perspective, and every day I find something in Scripture that speaks to me. God is patient with me, and through the study of His Word, I am learning what He wants to teach me. When I hear from a reader who is touched by one of my stories, it is God alone who is to be praised. All good things come from the Father above, and He can use anything to reach and teach His children—even a work of fiction.

My main desire when I started writing Christian fiction was to find answers to personal questions, and to share those answers in story form with others. Now, I want so much more. I yearn for the Lord to use my stories in making people thirst for His Word, the Bible. I hope that reading Hadassah's story will make you hunger for the real Word, Jesus Christ, the Bread of Life. I pray that you will finish my book and pick up the Bible with a new excitement and anticipation of a real encounter with the Lord

Himself. May you search Scripture for the sheer joy of being in God's presence.

Beloved, surrender wholeheartedly to Jesus Christ, who loves you. As you drink from the deep well of Scripture, the Lord will refresh and cleanse you, mold you and re-create you through His Living Word. For the Bible is the very breath of God, giving life eternal to those who seek Him.

Francine Rivers, 2002

ACKNOWLEDGMENTS

There are many people I want to thank who have helped me in my writing career: My husband, Rick; my children, Trevor, Shannon, and Travis; my mom, Frieda King; and my second set of parents, Bill and Edith Rivers; my brother and sister-in-law, Everett and Evelyn King; Aunt Margaret Freed—all of you have loved me unconditionally and encouraged me in all I do. I am grateful also to have Jane Jordan Browne as my agent. Without her persistence and expertise, this book might never have found a home, and I might have given up writing long ago.

I offer special thanks to Rick Hahn, pastor of Sebastopol Christian Church, who opened my eyes and ears to the beauty of God's Word; and to members of my church family who have shown me that God truly transforms lives daily. So many of you have encouraged me in ways you will never even guess, and I rejoice that I have so many brothers and sisters.

A note to Jenny and Scott—what would I do without you two? You are very precious to me. May the Lord bless you both always with health and happiness and, of course, children.

Most of all, I want to thank the Lord for all he has done in my life. I pray that he will bless this work and accept it as my humble offering and use it for his good purpose in the lives of others.

Francine Rivers

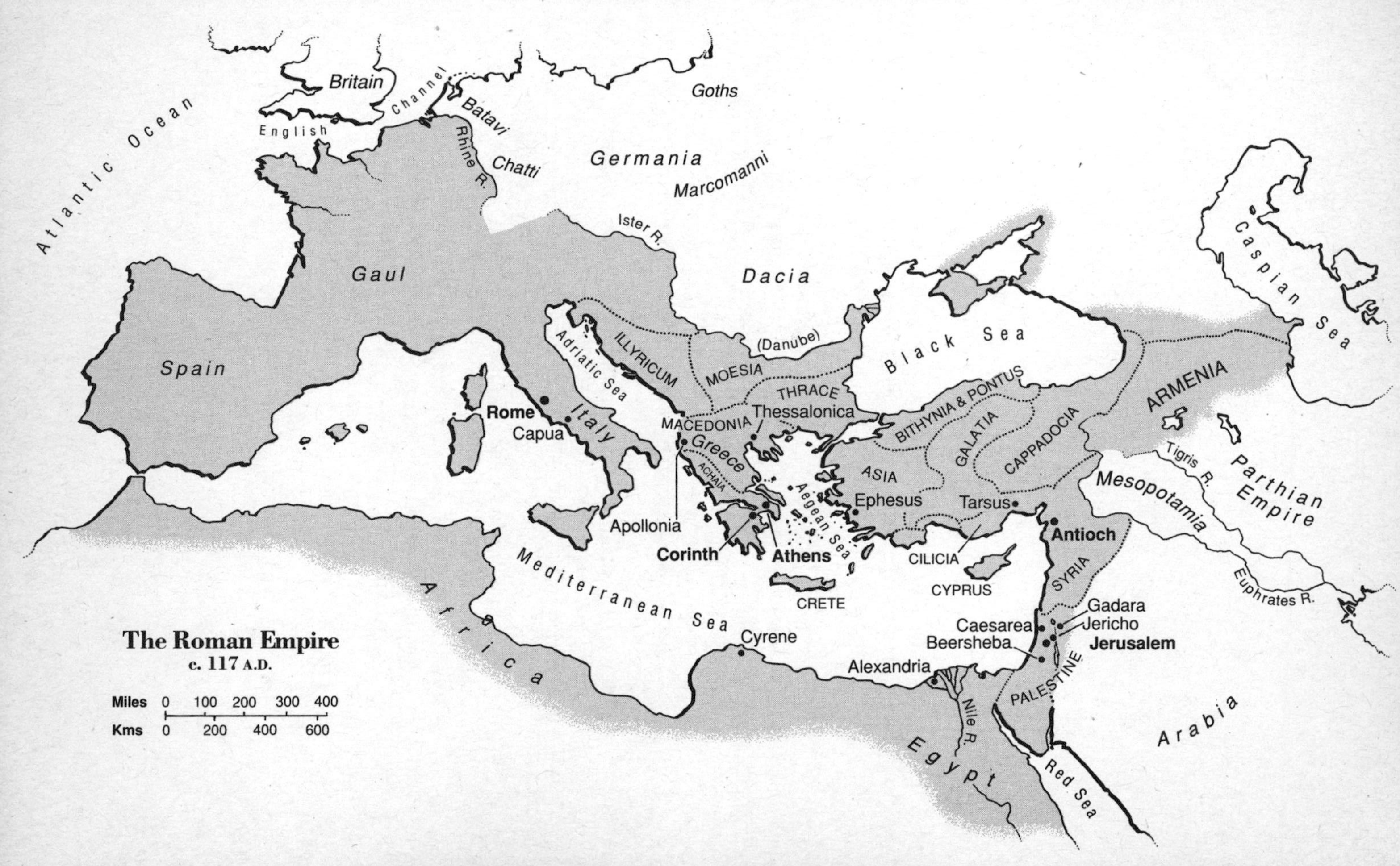
The Roman Empire
c. 117 A.D.
Miles 0 100 200 300 400
Kms 0 200 400 600
Atlantic Ocean
Britain
English Channel
Batavi
Rhine R.
Chatti
Goths
Germania
Marcomanni
Ister R.
Dacia
Gaul
Spain
(Danube)
Black Sea
Caspian Sea
ILLYRICUM
MOESIA
THRACE
Adriatic Sea
Rome
Capua
Italy
MACEDONIA
Thessalonica
Greece
ACHAIA
Apollonia
Corinth
Athens
Aegean Sea
CRETE
BITHYNIA & PONTUS
GALATIA
CAPPADOCIA
ARMENIA
ASIA
Ephesus
Tarsus
CILICIA
CYPRUS
Antioch
SYRIA
Tigris R.
Parthian Empire
Mesopotamia
Euphrates R.
Gadara
Jericho
Caesarea
Jerusalem
Beersheba
PALESTINE
Mediterranean Sea
Cyrene
Alexandria
Africa
Egypt
Nile R.
Red Sea
Arabia

JERUSALEM

1

The city was silently bloating in the hot sun, rotting like the thousands of bodies that lay where they had fallen in street battles. An oppressive, hot wind blew from the southeast, carrying with it the putrefying stench of decay. And outside the city walls, Death itself waited in the persons of Titus, son of Vespasian, and sixty thousand legionnaires who were anxious to gut the city of God.

Even before the Romans crossed the Valley of Thorns and camped on the Mount of Olives, warring factions within Jerusalem's city walls had prepared the way for her destruction.

Jewish robbers, who now fled like rats before the Roman legions, had recently fallen upon Jerusalem and murdered her prominent citizens, taking over the holy temple. Casting lots for the priesthood, they turned a house of prayer into a marketplace of tyranny.

Fast behind the robbers came rebels and zealots. Directed by rival leaders—John, Simon, and Eleazar—the warring factions raged within the three walls. Swollen with power and pride, they sliced Jerusalem into bloody pieces.

Breaking the Sabbath and the laws of God, Eleazar stormed Antonia Tower and murdered the Roman soldiers within it. Zealots rampaged, murdering thousands more who attempted to bring order back to a maddened city. Unlawful tribunals were set up and the laws of man and God mocked as hundreds of innocent men and women were murdered. Houses full of corn were burned in the chaos. Famine soon followed.

In their despair, righteous Jews prayed fervently for Rome to come against the great city. For these Jews believed that then, and only then, would the factions within Jerusalem unite in one cause: *freedom* against Rome.

Rome did come and, their hated ensigns held high, their war cry rang across all of Judea. They took Gadara, Jotapata, Beersheba, Jericho, Caesarea. The mighty legions marched in the very footsteps of devout pilgrims who came from every corner of the Jewish nation to worship and celebrate the high holy days of the Feast of the Unleavened Bread—the Passover. Innocent tens of thousands poured into the city and found themselves in the midst of civil war. Zealots closed the gates, trapping them inside. Rome came on until the sound of destruction echoed across the Valley of Kidron against the walls of Jerusalem itself. Titus laid siege to the ancient, holy city, determined to end Jewish rebellion once and forever.

Josephus, the Jewish general of fallen Jotapata who had been taken captive by the Romans, wept and cried out from atop the first wall defeated by the legionnaires. With Titus' permission, he pleaded with his people to repent, warning them that God was against them, that the prophecies of destruction were about to be fulfilled. Those few who listened to him and managed to evade the zealots in their escape reached the greedy Syrians—who dissected them for the gold pieces they had supposedly swallowed before deserting the city. Those who didn't heed Josephus suffered the full fury of the Roman war machine. Having cut down every tree within miles, Titus built siege engines that hurled countless javelins, stones, and even captives into the city.

From the Upper Market Place to the lower Acra and the Valley of Cheesemongers between, the city writhed in revolt.

Inside the great temple of God, the rebel leader John melted down the sacred golden vessels for himself. The righteous wept for Jerusalem, the bride of kings, the mother of prophets, the home of the shepherd king David. Torn asunder by her own people, she lay gutted and helpless, awaiting her death blow from hated Gentile foreigners.

Anarchy destroyed Zion, and Rome stood ready to destroy anarchy . . . anytime . . . anywhere.

Hadassah held her mother, tears blurring her eyes as she stroked the black hair back from her mother's gaunt, pale face. Her mother had been beautiful once. Hadassah remembered watching her take her hair down until it lay, glistening in thick waves, against her back. Her crowning glory, Papa called it. Now, it was dull and coarse, and her once-ruddy cheeks were white and sunken. Her stomach was swollen with malnutrition, the bones of her legs and arms clearly outlined beneath a gray overdress.

Lifting her mother's hand, Hadassah kissed it tenderly. It was like a bony claw, limp and cool. "Mama?" No response. Hadassah looked across the room at her younger sister, Leah, lying on a dirty pallet in the corner. Thankfully, she was asleep, the agony of slow starvation briefly forgotten.

Hadassah stroked her mother's hair again. Silence lay upon her like a hot shroud; the pain in her empty belly was almost beyond endurance. Only yesterday she had wept bitterly when her mother had uttered thanks to God for the meal Mark had been able to scavenge for them: shield leather from a dead Roman soldier.

How long before they all died?

Grieving in the silence, she could still hear her father speaking to her in that firm but gentle voice. "It is not possible for men to avoid fate, even when they see it beforehand."

Hananiah had spoken these words to her scant weeks ago—though now it seemed like an eternity. He had prayed all that morning, and she had been so afraid. She had known what he was going to do, what he had always done before. He would go out before the unbelievers and preach about the Messiah, Jesus of Nazareth.

"Why must you go out again and speak to those people? You were almost killed the last time."

"Those people, Hadassah? They're your kinsmen. I'm a Benjaminite." She could still feel his gentle touch on her cheek. "We must seize every opportunity we can to speak the truth and proclaim peace. Especially now. There's so little time for so many."

She had clung to him then. "Please, don't go. Father, you know what'll happen. What'll we do without you? You can't bring peace. There is no peace in this place!"

"It is not the world's peace I speak of, Hadassah, but God's. You know that." He had held her close. "Hush, child. Do not weep so."

She wouldn't release him. She knew they wouldn't listen—they didn't want to hear what he had to tell them. Simon's men would slash him to pieces before the crowd as an example of what became of those who spoke for peace. It had happened to others.

"I must go." His hands had been firm, his eyes gentle, as he had tipped her chin. "Whatever happens to me, the Lord is always with you." He'd kissed her, hugged her, then put her away from him so he could embrace and kiss his other two children. "Mark, you will remain here with your mother and sisters."

Grabbing and shaking her mother, Hadassah had pleaded, "You can't let him go! Not this time!"

"Be silent, Hadassah. Who are you serving by arguing so against your father?"

Her mother's reprimand, though spoken gently, had struck hard. She had said many times before that when one did not serve the Lord, they unwittingly served the evil one instead. Fighting tears, Hadassah had obeyed and said no more.

Rebekkah had laid her hand against her husband's gray-bearded face. She had known Hadassah was right; he might not return, probably wouldn't. Yet, perhaps, if it was God's will, one soul might be saved through his sacrifice. One might be enough. Her eyes had been full of tears and she could not—dared not—speak. For if she had, she was afraid she would join Hadassah in pleading that he stay safe in this small house. And Hananiah knew better than she what the Lord willed for him. He had placed his hand over hers and she had tried not to weep.

"Remember the Lord, Rebekkah," he had said solemnly. "We are together in him."

He had not returned.

Hadassah leaned down over her mother protectively, afraid she would lose her, too. "Mother?" Still no response. Her breathing was shallow, her color ashen. What was taking Mark so long? He had been gone since dawn. Surely the Lord would not take him as well. . . .

In the silence of the small room, Hadassah's fear grew. She stroked her mother's hair absently. *Please, God. Please!* Words wouldn't come, at least not any that made sense. Just a groaning from within her soul. Please what? Kill them now with starvation before the Romans came with swords or they suffered the agony of a cross? *Oh, God, God!* Her plea came, inarticulate and desperate, helpless and full of fear. *Help us!*

Why had they ever come to this city? She hated Jerusalem.

Hadassah fought against the despair inside her. It had become so heavy, it felt like a physical weight pulling her into a dark pit. She tried to think of better times, of happier moments, but those thoughts wouldn't come.

She thought of the months long ago when they'd made the journey from Galilee, never expecting to be trapped in the city. The night before they had entered Jerusalem, her father set up camp on a hillside within sight of Mount Moriah, where Abraham had almost sacrificed Isaac. He told them stories of when he was a boy living just outside the great city, speaking far into the night of the laws of Moses, under which he had grown up. He spoke of the prophets. He spoke of Yeshua, the Christ.

Hadassah had slept and dreamt of the Lord feeding the five thousand on a hillside.

She remembered that her father had awakened the family at dawn. And she remembered how, as the sun rose, light had reflected off the marble and gold of the temple, turning the structure into a blazing beacon of fiery splendor that could be seen from miles away. Hadassah could still feel the awe she had felt at the glory of it. "Oh, Father, it is so beautiful."

"Yes," he had said solemnly. "But so often, things of great beauty are full of great corruption."

Despite the persecution and danger that had awaited them in Jerusalem, her father had been full of joy and expectation as they entered the gates. Perhaps this time more of his kinsmen would listen; more would give their hearts to the risen Lord.

Few believers of the Way remained in Jerusalem. Many had been imprisoned, some stoned, even more driven away to other places. Lazarus, his sisters, and Mary Magdalene had been driven out; the apostle John, a dear family friend, had left Jerusalem two years before, taking the Lord's mother with him. Yet, Hadassah's father had remained. Once a year, he had returned to Jerusalem with his family to gather with other believers in an upper room. There they shared bread and wine, just as their Lord Jesus had done the evening before his crucifixion. This year, Shimeon Bar-Adonijah had presented the elements of the Passover meal:

"The lamb, the unleavened bread, and the bitter herbs of the Passover have as much meaning for us as for our Jewish brothers and sisters. The Lord fulfills each element. He *is* the perfect Lamb of God who, though without sin himself, has taken the bitterness of our sins upon him. Just as the captive Jews in Egypt were told to put the blood of a lamb on their door so that God's wrath and judgment would pass over them, so Jesus has shed his blood for us so that we will stand blameless before God in the coming Judgment Day. We are the sons and daughters of Abraham, for it is by our faith in the Lord that we are saved through his grace. . . ."

For the following three days they had fasted and prayed and repeated Jesus' teachings. On the third day, they sang and rejoiced, breaking bread together once more in celebration of Jesus' resurrection. And every year, during the last hour of the gathering, her father would tell his own story. This year had been no different. Most had heard his story many times before, but there were always those who were new to the faith. It was to these people that her father spoke.

He stood, a simple man with gray hair and beard, and dark eyes full of light and serenity. There was nothing remarkable about him. Even as he spoke, he was ordinary. It was the touch of God's hand that made him different from others.

"My father was a good man, a Benjaminite who loved God and taught me the law of Moses," he began quietly, looking into the eyes of those who sat about him. "He was a merchant near Jerusalem and married my mother, the daughter of a poor husbandman. We were not rich and we were not poor. For all we had, my father gave glory and thanks to God.

"When the Passover came, we closed our small shop and entered the city. Mother stayed with friends and prepared for the Passover. My father and I spent our time at the temple. To hear God's Word was to eat meat, and I dreamed of being a scribe. But it would not come to pass. When I was fourteen, my father died and, with no brothers and sisters, it was necessary for me to take over his business. Times were very hard, and I was young and inexperienced, but God was good. He provided."

He closed his eyes. "Then a fever took hold of me. I struggled against death. I could hear my mother weeping and crying out to God. *Lord,* I prayed, *don't let me die. My mother needs me. Without me, she is alone, with no one to provide for her. Please do not take me now!* But death came. It surrounded me like a cold darkness and took hold of me." The hush in the room was almost tangible as his listeners awaited the ending.

No matter how many times Hadassah had heard the story, she never tired of it nor lost the power of it. As her father spoke, she could feel the dark and lonely force that had claimed him. Chilled, she wrapped her arms around her legs and hugged them against her chest as he went on.

"My mother said friends were carrying me along the road to my tomb when Jesus passed by. The Lord heard her weeping and took pity. My mother didn't know who he was when he stopped the funeral procession, but there were many with him, followers, as well as the sick and crippled. Then she recognized him, for he touched me and I arose."

Hadassah wanted to leap up and cry out in joy. Some of those around her wept, their faces transfixed with wonder and awe.

Others wanted to touch her father, to lay hands on a man who had been brought back from death by Christ Jesus. And they had so many questions. How did you feel when you arose? Did you speak with him? What did he say to you? What did he look like?

In the upper room, with the gathering of believers, Hadassah had felt safe. She had felt strength. In that place, she could feel the presence of God and his love. *"He touched me and I arose."* God's power could overcome anything.

Then they would leave the upper room and, as her father walked the family back to the small house where they stayed, Hadassah's ever-present fear would rise again. She always prayed her father wouldn't stop and speak. When he told his story to believers, they wept and rejoiced. To unbelievers, he was an object of ridicule. The euphoria and security she felt with those who shared her faith dissolved when she watched her father stand before a crowd and suffer their abuse.

"Listen to me, O men of Judah!" he would call out, drawing people to him. "Listen to the good news I have to tell you."

They listened at first. He was an old man and they were curious. Prophets were always a diversion. He was not eloquent like the religious leaders; he spoke simply from his heart. And always people laughed and mocked him. Some threw rotten vegetables and fruit, some called him mad. Others became enraged at his story of resurrection, shouting that he was a liar and blasphemer.

Two years ago he had been so badly beaten that two friends had to help carry him back to the small rented house where they always stayed. Elkanah and Benaiah had tried to reason with him.

"Hananiah, you must not come back here," Elkanah had said. "The priests know who you are and want you silenced. They are not so foolish as to have a trial, but there are many evil men who will do another's will for a shekel. Shake the dust of Jerusalem from your shoes and go somewhere that the message will be heard."

"And where else can that be but here where our Lord died and arose?"

"Many of those who witnessed his resurrection have fled imprisonment and death at the hands of the Pharisees," Benaiah had said. "Even Lazarus has left Judea."

"Where did he go?"

"I was told he took his sisters and Mary of Magdala to Gaul."

"I cannot leave Judea. Whatever happens, this is where the Lord wants me."

Benaiah had grown silent for a long moment and then he nodded slowly. "Then it shall be as the Lord wills it."

Elkanah had agreed and laid his hand on her father's. "Shelemoth and Cyrus are remaining here. They will give you aid when you are in Jerusalem. I am taking my family away from this city. Benaiah is coming with me. May God's face shine upon you, Hananiah. You and Rebekkah will be in our prayers. And your children, too."

Hadassah had wept, her hopes of leaving this wretched city dashed. Her faith was weak. Her father always forgave his tormenters and attackers, while she prayed they would know all the fires of hell for what they had done to him. She often prayed that God would change his will and send her father to a place other than Jerusalem. Someplace small and peaceful where people would listen.

"Hadassah, we know that God uses all things for good to those who love him, to those who are called according to his purpose," her mother said often, trying to comfort her.

"What good is there in a beating? What good in being spit upon? Why must he suffer so?"

In the peaceful hills of Galilee, with the blue sea stretched out before her and lilies of the field at her back, Hadassah could believe in God's love. At home, in those hills, her faith was strong. It warmed her and made her heart sing.

In Jerusalem, though, she struggled. She clung to her faith, but still found it slipping away from her. Doubt was her companion, fear was overwhelming.

"Father, why can we not believe and remain silent?"

"We are called upon to be the light of the world."

"They hate us more with each passing year."

"Hatred is the enemy, Hadassah. Not the people."

"It is people who beat you, Father. Did not the Lord himself tell us not to cast pearls before the swine?"

"Hadassah, if I am to die for him, I will die joyfully. What I do is for his good purpose. The truth does not go out and come back empty. You must have faith, Hadassah. Remember the promise. We are part of the body of Christ, and in Christ we have eternal life. Nothing can separate us. No power on earth. Not even death."

She had pressed her face against his chest, the rough woven tunic he wore rubbing against her skin. "Why can I believe at home, Father, but not here?"

"Because the enemy knows where you are most vulnerable." He had put his hand over hers. "Do you remember the story of Jehoshaphat? The sons of Moab and Ammon and Mount Seir came against him with a mighty army. The Spirit of the Lord came upon Jahaziel and God said through him, 'Do not be afraid nor dismayed because of this great multitude, for the battle is not yours, but God's.' While they sang and praised the Lord, the Lord himself set ambushes against their enemies. And in the morning, when the Israelites came to the lookout of the wilderness, they saw the bodies of the dead. No one escaped. The Israelites had not even raised a hand in battle, and the battle was won."

Kissing her head, he had said, "Stand firm in the Lord, Hadassah. Stand firm and let him fight your battles. Do not try to fight alone."

Hadassah sighed, trying to ignore the burning in her stomach. How she missed her father's counsel in the silent loneliness of this house. If she believed everything he had taught her, she would rejoice that he was now with the Lord. Instead she ached with grief, which swelled and spilled over her in waves, spreading with it a strange, confused anger.

Why did her father have to be such a fool for Christ? The people didn't want to hear; they didn't believe. His testimony offended them. His words drove them mad with hatred. Why couldn't he, just once, have remained silent and stayed within the safe confines of this small house? He'd still be alive, here in this room, comforting them and giving them hope instead of leaving them to fend for themselves. Why couldn't he have been sensible this one time and waited out the storm?

The door opened slowly and Hadassah's heart leapt in fright, snapping her back to the grim present. Robbers had broken into the houses down the street, murdering the occupants for a loaf of hoarded bread. But it was Mark who entered. She let out her breath, relieved to see him. "I was so afraid for you," she whispered with feeling. "You've been gone for hours."

He pushed the door closed and sank down, exhausted, against the wall near their sister. "What did you find?" She waited for him to take whatever he had found from his shirt. Whatever food was found had to be secreted or someone would attack him for it.

Mark looked at her hopelessly. "Nothing. Nothing at all. Not a worn shoe, not even shield leather from a dead soldier. Nothing." He started to cry, his shoulders shaking.

"Shhh, you'll awaken Leah and Mama." Hadassah gently laid her mother back against the blanket and went to him. She put her arms around him and leaned her head against his chest. "You tried, Mark. I know you tried."

"Maybe it's God's will that we die."

"I'm not sure I want to know God's will anymore," she said without thinking. Quick tears came. "Mama said the Lord will provide," she said, but the words sounded empty. Her faith was so weak. She was not like Father and Mother. Even Leah, young as she was, loved the Lord wholeheartedly. And Mark sounded so accepting of death. Why was she always the one who questioned and doubted?

Have faith. Have faith. When you have nothing else, have faith.

Mark shuddered, drawing her out of her gloomy thoughts. "They are throwing bodies into the Wadi El Rabadi behind the holy temple. Thousands, Hadassah."

Hadassah remembered the horror of the Valley of Hinnom. It was there that Jerusalem disposed of the dead and unclean animals and dumped the night soil. Baskets of hooves, entrails, and animal remains from the temple were carried there and dumped. Rats and carrion birds infested the place, and the stench frequently was carried in hot winds across the city. Father called it Gehenna. "It was not far from here that our Lord was crucified."

Mark pushed his hand back through his hair. "I was afraid to go closer."

Hadassah shut her eyes tightly, but the question rose stark and raw against her will. Had her father been cast into that place, desecrated and left to rot in the hot sun? She bit her lip and tried to force the thought away.

"I saw Titus," Mark said dully. "He rode over with some of his men. When he saw the bodies, he cried out. I could not hear his words, but a man said he was calling out to Jehovah that it was not his doing."

"If the city surrendered now, would he show mercy?"

"If he could contain his men. They hate the Jews and want to see them destroyed."

"And us along with them." She shivered. "They will not know the difference between believers of the Way and zealots, will they?

Seditionist or righteous Jew or even Christian, it will make no difference." Her eyes blurred with tears. "Is this the will of God, Mark?"

"Father said it is not God's will that any should suffer."

"Then why must we?"

"We bear the consequences for what we have done to ourselves, and for the sin that rules this world. Jesus forgave the thief, but he didn't take him down off the cross." He pushed his hand back through his hair. "I'm not wise like Father. I haven't any answers to why, but I know there is hope."

"What hope, Mark? What hope is there?"

"God always leaves a remnant."

The siege wore on, and while life within Jerusalem ebbed, the spirit of Jewish resistance did not. Hadassah remained within the small house, hearing the horror of what was just beyond their unbolted door. A man was screaming and running down the street. *"They've ascended the wall!"*

When Mark went out to find out what was happening, Leah became hysterical. Hadassah went to her sister and held her tightly. She felt near to hysteria herself, but tending her young sister helped calm her.

"Everything will be all right, Leah. Be still." Her words sounded meaningless in her own ears. "The Lord is watching over us," she said and stroked her sister gently.

A litany of comforting lies, for the world was crumbling around them. Hadassah looked across the room at her mother and felt the tears coming again. Her mother smiled weakly as though trying to reassure her, but she felt no reassurance. What would become of them?

When Mark returned, he told them of the battle raging within the walls. The Jews had turned it and were driving the Romans back.

However, that night, under the cover of darkness, ten legionnaires sneaked through the ruins of the city and took possession of Antonia Tower. The battle had come to the very entrance of the holy temple. Though driven back again, the Romans countered by overthrowing some of the foundations of the tower and laid open the court of the Gentiles. In an attempt to divert them, zealots attacked the Romans at the Mount of Olives. Failing, they were destroyed. The prisoners taken were crucified before the walls for all to see.

Stillness fell again. And then a new, more devastating horror spread through the city as word passed of a starving woman who had eaten her own child. The flame of Roman hatred was fanned into a blaze.

Josephus cried out again to his people that God was using the Romans to destroy them, fulfilling the prophecies of the prophets Daniel and Jesus. The Jews gathered all the dry materials, bitumen, and pitch they could find and filled the cloisters. The Romans drove forward, and the Jews gave ground, luring the Romans into the temple. Once inside, the Jews set their holy place on fire, burning many of the legionnaires to death within it.

Titus regained control of his enraged soldiers and ordered the fire put out, but no sooner had they succeeded in saving the temple than the Jews attacked again. This time all the officers of Rome couldn't restrain the fury of the Roman legionnaires who, driven by a lust for Jewish blood, once again torched the temple and killed every human being in their path as they began plundering the conquered city.

Men fell by the hundreds as flames engulfed the Babylonian curtain, embroidered with fine blue, scarlet, and purple thread. High on the temple roof, a false prophet cried out for the people to climb up and be delivered. People's screams of agony as they burned alive carried across the city, mingling with the horrifying sounds of battle in the streets and alleys. Men, women, children—it made no difference, all fell to the sword.

Hadassah tried to shut it out of her mind, but the sound of death was everywhere. Her mother died on the same hot August day that Jerusalem fell, and for two days, Hadassah, Mark, and Leah waited, knowing the Romans would find them sooner or later and destroy them as they were destroying everyone else.

Someone fled down their narrow street. Others screamed as they were cut down without mercy. Hadassah wanted to jump up and run away, but where could she go? And what of her sister and her brother? She pressed further back into the darkening shadows of the small rooms and held Leah.

More men's voices. Louder. Closer. A door was smashed open not far away. The people inside screamed. One by one, they were silenced.

Weak and gaunt, Mark struggled to his feet and stood before

the door, praying silently. Hadassah's heart beat heavily, her empty stomach tightening into a ball of pain. She heard men's voices in the street. The words were Greek, the tone scornful. One man gave orders to search the next houses. Another door was smashed in. More screams.

The sound of hobnailed shoes came to their door. Hadassah's heart jumped wildly. "Oh, God . . ."

"Close your eyes, Hadassah," Mark told her, sounding strangely calm. "Remember the Lord," he said as the door crashed open. Mark uttered a harsh, broken sound and dropped to his knees. A bloody sword tip protruded from his back, staining the gray tunic red. Leah's high-pitched scream filled the small room.

The Roman soldier kicked Mark back, freeing his sword.

Hadassah could not utter a sound. Staring up at the man, his armor covered with dust and her brother's blood, Hadassah couldn't move. His eyes glittered through his visor. When he stepped forward, raising his bloody sword, Hadassah moved swiftly and without conscious thought. She shoved Leah down and fell across her. *Oh, God, let it be over quickly,* she prayed. *Let it be swift.* Leah fell silent. The only sound was that of the soldier's rasping breathing, mingled with screams from down the street.

Tertius gripped his sword harder and glared down at the emaciated young girl covering an even smaller girl. He ought to kill them both and have done with it! These bloody Jews were a blight to Rome. Eating their own children! Destroy the women and there would be no more warriors birthed. This nation deserved annihilation. He should just kill them and be done with it.

What stopped him?

The older girl looked up at him, her dark eyes full of fear. She was so small and thin, except for those eyes, too large for her ashen face. Something about her sapped the killing strength of his arm. His breathing eased, his heartbeat slowed.

He tried to remind himself of the friends he had lost. Diocles had been killed by a stone while building the siege works. Malcenas had been fallen upon by six fighters when they had breached the first wall. Capaneus had burned to death when the Jews had set fire to their own temple. Albion still suffered wounds from a Jew's dart.

Yet, the heat in his blood cooled.

Shaking, Tertius lowered his sword. Still alert to any movement the girl made, he glanced around the small room. His vision cleared of the red haze. It was a boy he had killed. He lay in a pool of blood beside a woman. She looked peaceful, as though she merely slept, her hair carefully combed, her hands folded on her chest. Unlike those who had chosen to dump their dead in the wadi, these children had lain out their mother with dignity.

He had heard the story of a woman eating her own child and it had fed his hatred of Jews, gained from ten long years in Judea. He had wanted nothing more than to obliterate them from the face of the earth. They had been nothing but trouble to Rome from the beginning—rebellious and proud, unwilling to bend to anything but their one *true* god.

One true god. Tertius' hard mouth twisted in a sneer. Fools, all of them. To believe in only one god was not only ridiculous, it was uncivilized. And for all their holy protestations and stubborn persistence, they were a barbaric race. Look what they had done to their own temple.

How many Jews had he killed in the last five months? He hadn't bothered to count as he went from house to house, driven by bloodlust, hunting them down like animals. By the gods, he had relished it, accounting each death as a small token payment for the friends they had taken from him.

Why did he hesitate now? Was this pity for a foul Jewess brat? It would be merciful to kill her and put her out of her misery. She was so thin from starvation that he could blow her over with a breath. He took another step toward her. He could kill both girls with one blow . . . tried to summon the will to do so.

The girl waited. It was clear she was terrified, yet she did not beg for mercy as so many had done. Both she and the child beneath her were still and silent, watching.

Tertius' heart twisted, and he felt weak. He drew a ragged breath and exhaled sharply. Uttering a curse, he shoved his sword into the scabbard at his side. "You will live, but you will not thank me for it."

Hadassah knew Greek. It was a common language among the Roman legionnaires and so was heard all over Judea. She started to cry. He grasped her arm and yanked her to her feet.

Tertius looked at the little girl lying on the floor. Her eyes were open and fixed on some distant place to which her mind had escaped. It was not the first time he had seen such a look. She would not last long.

"Leah," Hadassah said, frightened at the vacant look in her eyes. She bent down and put her arms around her. "My sister," she said, trying to draw her up.

Tertius knew the little girl was as good as dead already and it would make more sense to leave her. Yet, the way the older girl tried to gather the child in her arms and lift her, roused his pity. Even the child's slight weight was too much for her.

Brushing her aside, Tertius lifted the tiny girl easily and gently slung her over his shoulder like a sack of grain. Grasping the older girl by the arm, he pushed her out the door.

The street was quiet, the other soldiers having moved on. Distant cries rang out. He walked quickly, aware that the girl was struggling to keep up.

The air of the city was foul with death. Bodies were everywhere, some slain by Roman soldiers pillaging the conquered city, others dead of starvation, now bloated and decaying from days of being left to putrefy. The look of horror on the girl's face made Tertius wonder how long she had been cooped up in that house.

"Your great Holy City," he said and spat into the dust.

Pain licked up Hadassah's arm as the legionnaire's fingers dug into her flesh. She stumbled over a dead man's leg. His face was crawling with maggots. The dead were everywhere. She felt faint.

The farther they walked, the more horrifying the carnage. Decaying bodies lay tangled together like slaughtered animals. The stench of blood and death was so heavy Hadassah covered her mouth.

"Where do we take captives?" Tertius shouted at a soldier separating the dead. Two soldiers were lifting a Roman comrade from between two Jews. Other legionnaires appeared with plunder from the temple. Wagons were already loaded with golden and silver sprinkling bowls, dishes, wick trimmers, pots, and lampstands. Bronze shovels and pots were piled up, as well as basins, censers, and other articles used in temple service.

The soldier looked up at Tertius, casting a cursory glance over Hadassah and Leah. "Down that street and around through the big gate, but those two don't look worth bothering with."

Hadassah looked up at the temple's once pristine marble, the marble that had appeared as a snow-covered mountain in the distance. It was blackened, chunks had been gouged out by siege stones, the gold melted away. Whole sections of wall were broken down. The holy temple. It was just another place of death and destruction.

She moved sluggishly, sickened and terrified at all she saw. Smoke burned her eyes and throat. As they walked along the wall of the temple, she could hear a rising, undulating sound of horror coming from within it. Her mouth was parched and her heart pounded harder and faster as they approached the gate to the Women's Court.

Tertius gave the girl a shove. "You faint and I'll kill you where you drop, and your sister with you."

Thousands of survivors were within the court, some moaning in their misery and others wailing for their dead. The soldier pushed her ahead of him through the gate, and she saw the ragged multitude before her. They crowded the courtyard. Most were gaunt with starvation, weak, hopeless.

Tertius lowered the child from his shoulder. Hadassah caught hold of Leah and tried to support her. She sank down weakly and held her sister limply across her lap. The soldier turned and walked away.

Thousands milled around, looking for relatives or friends. Others huddled in smaller groups weeping, while some, alone, stared at nothing—as Leah did. The air was so hot Hadassah could hardly breathe.

A Levite rent his worn blue and orange tunic and cried out in an agony of emotion, "My God! My God! Why hast thou forsaken us?" A woman near him began to wail miserably, her gray dress bloodstained and torn at the shoulder. An old man wrapped in black-and-white striped robes sat alone against the court wall, his lips moving. Hadassah knew he was of the Sanhedrin, his robes symbolizing the desert costume and the tents of the first patriarchs.

Mingled among the crowd were Nazirites with their long, braided hair, and zealots with dirty, ragged trousers and shirts over which they wore short sleeveless vests with a blue fringe at each corner. Divested of their knives and bows, they still looked menacing.

A fight broke out. Women began screaming. A dozen Roman legionnaires waded into the multitude and cut down the adversaries, as well as several others whose only offense was to be in close proximity. A Roman officer stood on the high steps and shouted down at the captives. He pointed out several more men in the crowd and they were dragged away to be crucified.

Hadassah managed to draw Leah up and move to a safer place by the wall, near the Levite. As the sun went down and darkness came, she held Leah close, trying to share her warmth. But in the morning, Leah was dead.

Her sister's sweet face was free of fear and suffering. Her lips were curved in a gentle smile. Hadassah held her against her chest and rocked her. Pain swelled and filled her with a despair so deep she couldn't even cry. When a Roman soldier came over, she scarcely noticed until he tried to take Leah away from her. She held her sister tighter.

"She's dead. Give her to me."

Hadassah pressed her face into the curve of her sister's neck and moaned. The Roman had seen enough death to become hardened by it. He struck Hadassah once, breaking her hold, and then kicked her aside. Dazed, her body laced with pain, Hadassah stared helplessly as the soldier carried Leah to a wagon stacked with the bodies of others who had died during the night. He tossed her sister's fragile body carelessly onto the heap.

Shutting her eyes, Hadassah drew up her legs and wept against her knees.

The days ran together. Hundreds died of starvation, more of despair and lost hope. Some of the able-bodied captives were taken to dig mass graves.

Rumors spread that Titus had given orders to demolish not only the temple but the entire city. Only the Phasaelus, Hippicus, and Mariamne towers were to be left standing for defensive purposes, and a portion of the western wall. Not since the Babylonian king Nebuchadnezzar had destroyed Solomon's temple had such a thing happened. Jerusalem, their beloved Jerusalem, would be no more.

The Romans brought in corn for the captives. Some Jews, still stiff-necked against Roman rule, refused their portions in a last and fatal act of rebellion. More grievous were the sick and weak who were denied food because the Romans did not wish to waste corn on those who would not likely survive the coming march to Caesarea. Hadassah was one of the latter, and so received no food.

One morning, Hadassah was taken with the others outside the city walls. She stared with horror at the scene before her. Thousands of Jews had been crucified before the crumbling walls of

Jerusalem. Scavenging birds feasted upon them. The ground on the siege work had drunk in so much blood it was as red-brown and hard as brick, but the land itself was beyond anything Hadassah had expected. Other than the great, gruesome forest of crosses, there was not a tree, nor a bush, nor even a blade of grass. A wasteland lay before her, and at her back was the mighty city even now being reduced to rubble.

"Keep moving!" a guard shouted, his whip hissing through the air near her and cracking on a man's back. Another man ahead of her groaned deeply and collapsed. When the guard drew his sword, a woman tried to stop him, but he struck her down with his fist, then with one swift stroke, opened an artery in the fallen man's neck. Taking the twitching man by his arm, he dragged him to the edge of the siege bank and pushed him over the side. The body rolled slowly to the bottom, where it took its place in the rocks amongst other corpses. Another captive helped the weeping woman to her feet, and they went on.

Their captors sat them within sight and sound of Titus' camp.

"It would seem we must suffer through a Roman triumph," a man said bitterly, the blue tassels on his vest identifying him as a zealot.

"Be silent or you will be crow bait like those other poor fools," someone hissed at him.

As the captives watched, the legions formed and marched in tightly drilled units before Titus, who was resplendent in his golden armor. There were more captives than soldiers, but the Romans moved as one great beast of war, organized and disciplined. To Hadassah, the rhythmic cadence of thousands of men marching in perfect formation was terrifying to watch. A single voice or signal could make hundreds move as one. How could any people think they could overcome such as these? They filled the horizon.

Titus gave a speech, pausing now and then as the soldiers cheered. Then the awards were presented. Officers stood before the men, their armor cleaned and gleaming in the sunlight. Lists were read of those who had performed great exploits in the war. Titus himself placed crowns of gold on their heads and golden ornaments about their necks. To some he gave long golden spears and silver ensigns. Each was awarded the honor of removal to higher rank.

Hadassah looked around at her fellows and saw their bitter

hatred; having to witness this ceremony poured salt in their open wounds.

Heaps of spoils were distributed among the soldiers, then Titus spoke again, commending his men and wishing them great fortune and happiness. Jubilant, the soldiers cried out their acclamations to him time and time again as he came down among them.

Finally, he gave orders that the feasting begin. Great numbers of oxen were held ready at the altars to the Roman gods, and at Titus' command they were sacrificed. Hadassah's father had told her Jewish law required the shedding of blood as an atonement for sin. She knew priests within the holy temple performed the sacrifices daily, a constant reminder of the need for repentance. Yet her father and mother had taught her from birth that Christ had shed his blood as an atonement for the sins of the world, that the law of Moses had been fulfilled in him, that animal sacrifices were no longer needed. So she had never seen animals sacrificed. Now she watched in grim horror as one ox after another was killed as a thank offering. The sight of so much blood spilling down over stone altars sickened her. Gagging, she closed her eyes and turned away.

The slain oxen were distributed to the victorious army for a great feast. The tantalizing aroma of roasting beef drifted to hungry captives across the night air. Even had they been offered some, righteous Jews would have refused to eat it. Better dust and death than meat sacrificed to pagan gods.

At last, soldiers came and ordered the captives to line up for their rations of wheat and barley. Weakly, Hadassah rose and stood in the long line, sure she would again be denied food. Her eyes blurred with tears. *Oh, God, God, do as you will.* Cupping her hands as her turn came, she waited to be shoved aside. Instead, golden kernels spilled from the scoop into her palms.

She could almost hear her mother's voice. *"The Lord will provide."*

She looked up into the young soldier's eyes. His face, weathered from the Judean sun, was hard, devoid of any emotion. "Thank you," she said in Greek and with simple humility, without even a thought as to who he was or what he might have done. His eyes flickered. Someone shoved her hard from behind and cursed her in Aramaic.

As she moved away, she was unaware the young soldier still watched her. He dipped the scoop into the barrel again, pouring corn into the hands of the next in line without taking his eyes from her.

Hadassah sat down on the hillside. She was separate from the others, alone within herself. Bowing her head, she tightened her hands around the corn. Emotion swelled. "You prepare a table before me in the presence of my enemies," she whispered brokenly and began to weep. "Oh, Father, forgive me. Amend my ways. But gently, Lord, lest you reduce me to nothing. I am afraid. Father, I am so afraid. Preserve me by the strength of your arm."

She opened her eyes and opened her hands again. "The Lord provides," she said softly and ate slowly, savoring each kernel.

As the sun went down, Hadassah felt oddly at peace. Even with all the destruction and death around her, with all the suffering ahead, she felt God's nearness. She looked up at the clear night sky. The stars were bright and a wind blew softly, reminding her of Galilee.

The night was warm . . . she had eaten . . . she would live. *"God always leaves a remnant,"* Mark had said. Of all the members of her family, her faith was weakest, her spirit the most doubting and the least bold. Of all of them, she was least worthy.

"Why me, Lord?" she asked, weeping softly. "Why me?"

GERMANIA

2

Atretes raised his hand high, signaling to his father that a Roman legion was moving into the clearing. Hidden by the forest, the German warriors waited. Each held a *framea*—a spear much dreaded by the Romans, for its strong shaft held a narrow, short head that was razor-sharp and could pierce armor. It could be hurled with accuracy from a great distance or used in hand-to-hand combat.

Seeing the moment was right, Atretes brought his hand down. His father immediately began the war cry. It rose and spread along the horizon as the entire retinue sang out against their shields to Tiwaz, their war god. Marcobus, leader of the Bructeri, unifier of all the Germanic tribes, joined in, along with the rest of the Bructeri and the Batavi tribes—a hundred men in all. The horrifying and chaotic sound reverberated across the valley below like a roar from the demons of Hades. Grinning, Atretes saw the legionnaires lose their rhythm. And it was in that instant that the tribesmen flooded down the hillsides for the attack.

Surprised and confused by the barbarous screams, the Romans could not hear their commanders ordering them to form the tortoise. The commanders knew that this military maneuver—in which the men moved close together and turned their shields outward on all sides and above their heads, thus forming an impenetrable armor similar to a tortoise's shell—was their only true defense against the barbarians. However, seeing a horde of fierce, almost naked warriors armed with spears falling on their flanks, the legion broke ranks just long enough to give the tribesmen a badly needed advantage. Framea flew. Legionnaires dropped.

Atretes' father, Hermun, headed the wedge formation, which began the charge. His chieftain's helmet glistening, he led his clan from concealment in the thick spruce forest as the Chatti warriors ran down the hillside. Long hair streaming, most of the tribesmen wore nothing more than a *sagum*—a short protective cloak that was secured at the shoulder by a simple bronze brooch—and they were armed simply with an iron-and-leather shield and a framea. Only the wealthiest chieftains carried swords and wore helmets.

Screaming his war cry, Atretes threw his framea as he ran. The long-headed spear went through the throat of a Roman tribune and sent the ensign crashing to the ground. Another Roman grabbed it up, but Atretes reached him and broke his back with one blow of his doubled fists. Ripping the spear from the dead man, he thrust it through another soldier.

Tribeswomen and children ran down the hillside and sat, shrieking and cheering for their warriors. The battle would not last long, for the element of surprise was only a momentary advantage. As soon as the Romans came to grips with the situation, the German warriors would retreat. They knew they had little chance in a protracted battle against the highly trained forces of Rome. Over the last months, the tribesmen had used the tactic that worked best: nagging the flanks of the army, striking quickly, then retreating as soon as the battle began to turn.

Atretes' spear snapped as he rammed it through the armor of a centurion. He swore to Tiwaz and slammed his shield into the head of an attacker as he snatched up a dead centurion's *gladius,* or short sword, barely managing to parry the blows from two other Romans. He was unaccustomed to fighting with a short sword and knew he had to fall back before he was overcome.

The legion's initial panic was already gone. Mounted officers were in the midst of the fracas, wielding their swords and shouting orders. The ranks were closing again, and the Romans' training and discipline were taking their toll on their attackers.

Atretes saw his brother Varus fall. Swinging the sword, he amputated a Roman's arm. When he tried to reach his brother another centurion came against him, and he was hard put to stay alive against the man's skill with the gladius. Atretes blocked thrust after thrust. Using brute force, he rammed the full weight of his powerful body into the centurion and sent him back into three others.

"Your back, Atretes!" his father shouted. Atretes ducked sharply as he swung around, bringing the sword down and up swiftly, breaking bone as he sliced upward through the groin and into the abdomen of his attacker. The man screamed and went down before Atretes could pull the sword free.

The centurion Atretes had knocked down had regained his feet and was coming at him again. Swordless, Atretes rolled and caught his attacker's leg, bringing him down. Jumping onto him, he gripped the man's head and made a hard jerk, breaking his neck.

Grabbing the gladius from lifeless fingers, he leaped to his feet and charged a Roman who was pulling his sword out of a fallen clansman. Atretes caught him across the exposed side of his neck and a fountain of blood splattered him in the face. Dropping the sword, he yanked a framea from the body of a dead soldier as he ran.

He couldn't see his father's gilded helmet, and German forces were dwindling as the Roman soldiers regrouped and showed the organized destruction for which they were famous. Marcobus, his left arm hanging useless at his side, shouted for his men to fall back. Contrary to Roman thinking, the tribes saw nothing dishonorable in giving ground when the battle turned. The Batavi followed suit and retreated, leaving Atretes' clan behind and vulnerable. Atretes knew prudence called for the Chatti to fall back into the woods with the others, but his blood was hot, his hand still strong. He charged into two Romans, screaming his war cry.

His uncle fell, a Roman dart through his chest. His cousin Rolf tried to reach him and was cut down by a centurion. Roaring in fury, Atretes hacked right and left, caving in the side of one legionnaire's helmet and slicing through the arm of another. Too many of his clansmen were falling, and finally prudence won. Atretes shouted for the remaining members of his clan to head for the woods. They melted into the forest, leaving the Romans frustrated and ill-equipped to pursue.

A half mile up the hill, Atretes found his sister Marta on her knees cleaning her husband's shoulder wound. His brother was unconscious beside them, his leg wound tightly bound, the bleeding stanched.

Sweat pouring down his pale face, Usipi grimaced beneath Marta's brisk, sure ministrations. "Your father," he said. He raised his hand slightly, pointing.

Atretes ran through the woods to the west and came upon his mother, who held his father. One side of the chieftain's helmet was caved in, the gilded bronze bloody. Atretes uttered a savage cry and went down on his knees.

Face white and contorted, his mother worked feverishly over a gaping wound across his father's naked abdomen. She wept as she pushed his entrails back inside and tried to pull the wound closed. "Hermun," she pleaded. "Hermun, Hermun . . . "

Atretes caught hold of his mother's bloody wrists, stopping her frenzied efforts. "Leave him be."

"No!"

"Mother!" His hands tightened as he jerked her once. "He is dead. You can do nothing more."

She quieted, the stiff resistance relaxed. He let go of her and her bloody hands lay limply against her thighs. Atretes closed his father's staring eyes and placed his hands on his motionless chest. His mother sat very still for a long moment, then, with a sob, leaned forward and drew her husband's bloody head into her lap. Using the edge of his short cloak, she wiped his face as though he were a child.

"I will carry him to the others," Atretes said. His mother raised Hermun's shoulders and Atretes lifted him from the ground. Tears wet his hard face as he stumbled beneath the weight of his father's body, dropping to one knee. Fighting exhaustion, he gritted his teeth and rose, each footstep an effort.

When they reached his sister and Usipi, he laid his father down carefully beside the bodies of Dulga and Rolf, whom the other women of his family had managed to retrieve. Breathing heavily and feeling weakness creeping up his spine, Atretes took the carved talisman his father wore around his neck and pressed the wooden image into his palm. It had been carved from the oak of the sacred grove and had protected Hermun through many battles. Atretes tried to gain strength from it, but he felt a deep despair.

The battle was lost, and his father was dead. Leadership would fall to him if he was strong enough to hold it. But did he want it?

The prophecies of Veleda, the Bructeri seeress who sat hidden in her tower where no man could see her, were proving false. Though Julius Civilis and his rebels had destroyed the frontier legions, the rebellion was now failing. After a year, freedom was no longer within their grasp.

Vespasian had come into power after a twelve-month period that saw three emperors fall. Now, under the command of the ruler's youngest son, Domitian, eight more legions had been sent against Julius Civilis. Veleda had prophesied that Domitian's youth would defeat him, but the boy had arrived on the frontier at the head of his legions, rather than hiding behind them. Reputedly trained as a gladiator, he seemed determined to prove himself as able a commander as his father, Vespasian, and his brother, Titus. And the young maggot was succeeding.

Overcoming the rebel forces, Domitian took them captive. He ordered Julius Civilis' men decimated. Prisoners were lined up and one out of every ten men was crucified. With Julius Civilis chained and on his way to Rome, the unity of the tribes who had supported him was breaking down. Factions were splitting off. Many of the Batavi had been taken captive. One out of three men in Atretes' own clan were now dead.

Atretes felt his anger growing as he looked at his father. Only a week ago, the Chatti leader had thrown pieces of branch and bark from one of the sacred oaks onto a white cloth. He had been unable to read a clear sign from them, but the priest had said the neighs and snorts of the white horse assured a victory.

Victory! Where was their victory? Had even their gods turned against them? Or were the Roman gods proving themselves more powerful than the mighty Tiwaz?

As they carried their dead to the village, other clansmen gathered, reporting that the Romans had marched north.

Atretes cut wood to build a death house for his father, while his mother dressed her husband in his finest furs and prepared the funeral feast. She placed the best of their pottery bowls, cups, and platters beside her husband and filled the bowls with thick grain porridge and the cups with strong mead. Roasted joints of lamb and pork were placed on the platter. When she finished, Atretes set fire to the death house. Other fires flared bright in the darkness.

"It is done," his mother said, tears running down her cheeks. She laid a gentle hand on Atretes. "You will gather the men in the sacred grove tomorrow night."

He knew his mother had assumed he would become chieftain. "It will be up to the priests."

"They have already chosen you, as have our men. Who is better suited? Was it not your command they followed without question when the battle turned? And the Chatti were the last to leave the field."

"Only because Father had fallen, not through any great valor of mine."

"You will be chieftain, Atretes. Hermun knew this day would come. It is why he trained you as he did, driving you harder than his other sons. The signs told us at your birth that you would become a great leader."

"The signs have been wrong before."

"Not in this. Some matters are not of choice. You cannot fight destiny. Do you remember the night your father took you before the council and presented you with your shield and framea?"

"Yes," he said, containing his grief as he stared into the flames, his father's body visible as the walls crumbled. He made a fist. The last thing he wanted was the bondage of leadership.

"You became a man that night, Atretes. And you have grown in manhood ever since. You killed your first enemy at fourteen." She smiled, her blue eyes glistening with tears. "You barely had any whiskers to shave over your dead foe, but you scraped your face raw to follow our tradition."

Her hand tightened. "You were fifteen when you took Ania as your bride, sixteen when you lost her in childbirth, and your son as well. Two years later, you triumphed over Bructeri raiders and were allowed the honor of removing the iron ring from your finger. Your father said you fought better than any warrior he had ever seen. He was proud of you." She gripped his arm. "I am proud of you!"

She fell silent, the tears streaming down her face as she looked into the flames again. "We had peace for two years."

"And then Julius Civilis came to us and told us of the rebellion in Rome."

"Yes," she said, looking up at him again. "And a chance of freedom."

"Vespasian has taken control, Mother."

"Vespasian is a man. We have Tiwaz on our side. Have you not listened to Veleda's prophecies? Freedom will not come to us as a gift, Atretes. We must fight for it."

He raked his hand back through his blond hair and stared up at the stars. If only he had the knowledge of a priest and could read the answer there, in the heavens. He wanted to fight! He wanted it so badly that his muscles grew taut and hard and his heart beat faster. He felt most alive when he was in battle, fighting for victory and for his very life. As a chieftain, he would have other things of which to think, others to consider.

"When you were a boy, you dreamed of leaving the tribe and becoming part of Marcobus' retinue," his mother said quietly.

Atretes looked down at her in surprise. Did she know everything that was in his mind?

She touched his face tenderly. "You never spoke of it out of loyalty to your father, but he knew as well as I. Atretes, you have another destiny. I read the signs at your birth. You will lead your people to freedom."

"Or death," he said grimly.

"Many will die," she said solemnly. "I among them."

"Mother," he said, but her hand tightened on his arm, silencing him.

"It will be so. I have seen it." Her blue eyes became vague and disquieting. "Your name will become known in Rome. You will fight as no other man in the tribe of Chatti has done before you and you will triumph over every foe." Her voice was strange and distant. "A storm is coming that will blow across the Empire and destroy it. It will come from the north and the east and west, and you will be a part of it. And there is a woman, a woman with dark hair and dark eyes, a woman of strange ways whom you will love." She fell silent, blinking as though coming out of a deep sleep.

Atretes' heart beat fast. He had seen his mother like this only a few times before, and each time there was a coldness in the pit of his stomach. Had she been anyone else, Atretes would have discounted her words as those of a mother dreaming of greatness for her son. But he could not, for his mother was a respected seer and diviner, revered by some as a goddess.

Her expression cleared. She let out her breath and smiled bleakly. "You must rest, Atretes," she said. "You must be ready for what is ahead." She looked away into the glowing embers of the death house. "The fire is almost out. Leave me alone with Hermun," she said softly, her face like gold in the flickering light.

It was hours before Atretes could sleep. When he arose from his pallet at dawn and came out of the longhouse, he saw his mother collecting his father's bones from the ashes and placing them in an earthen vessel for burial.

Four more men died of battle wounds before the sun reached its zenith, and new death houses were being built.

Then word was brought to Atretes that a deserter had been caught. Atretes knew the men were looking to him to lead the council. He knew what had to be done, but bringing judgment on a man, even one such as Wagast, sat ill with him.

The men gathered in the oak grove, the high council sitting near the sacred tree. The night air was cool and moist; the sounds of frogs and owls echoed eerily around the gathered men. Atretes took a humble position, half in hopes that leadership would fall to Rud or Holt rather than him. They were able men, older.

Gundrid, the priest, took the images from the hollow trunk of the sacred oak and placed them on the lower branches. Murmuring incantations and prayers, he unwrapped and held high the golden horns, which were adorned with graven symbols.

When he lowered this holy element, Atretes remained motionless. The priest's pale blue eyes moved slowly from one man to the next and came to rest on him. Atretes' heart began to pound. The priest came toward him and he felt the sweat breaking out on his skin. Only the priests and the chieftain were allowed to touch the sacred images and great horns. When the priest held them out to him, Atretes saw that on one horn were the images of a three-headed man holding an ax, and a snake nursing her young. On the other was a horned man holding a sickle and leading a goat. Atretes knew if he touched the sacred horns he would be declaring himself the new high chieftain. The men were already cheering and raising their spears in confirmation.

Steadying his nerves, he placed his framea on the ground beside him and held out his hands, thankful that they were steady. As the priest relinquished the holy idol into his keeping, Atretes rose, holding the great horns high. The men cheered louder and shook their spears in acclamation. Atretes cried out to Tiwaz, his deep voice carrying through the woods.

The priest lit the incense lanterns as Atretes carried the horns to the altar. When he placed the horns there, he knelt for the high priest's blessing. Gundrid called upon Tiwaz to guide the clan's new high chieftain, to give him wisdom and to give his fighting arm strength. Atretes felt his face and body go hot when the priest prayed that a wife would be found for him and that their union would be fruitful.

When Gundrid finished, Atretes rose and took the dagger that was offered to him. With a swift stroke, he opened a vein in his wrist. In the silence, he held his arm out and spilled his own blood over the sacred horns as an offering.

Gundrid gave him a white cloth to stanch the flow. Atretes wrapped it tightly, then untied the thin leather strap which held a small pouch against his loins. His mother had prepared it for him as an offering to the gods. As the priest poured the contents into the incense lantern, a small flame hissed and exploded in brilliant reds and blues, drawing a frightened gasp from the men.

Gundrid swayed and moaned as the air filled with a sweet, heady scent. He threw his hands in the air, worshiping ecstatically, the language he spoke unrecognizable except to Tiwaz and the forest deities. The other priests laid their hands on Atretes, guiding him again to the altar. He knelt and kissed the horns as they cut themselves with sacred knives and spilled their blood over him in blessing.

His heart beat faster and faster; his breath came rapidly. The sweet odor of the incense made his head swim with visions of winged beasts and writhing bronzed bodies locked in mortal combat within the holy flames. Throwing back his head, he cried out savagely, the excitement building within him until he thought he would explode. His deep voice rang again and again through the dark forest.

Gundrid came to him, and when he placed his hands on Atretes they were like fire. Atretes tipped his head back and let the mark be drawn on his forehead. "Drink," Gundrid said and placed a silver goblet to his lips. Atretes drained it, his heart slowing its thunderous beat as he tasted the mixture of strong mead and blood.

It was done. He was the new chieftain.

Rising, he took the place of honor and grimly faced his first task: executing one of his oldest friends.

Wagast was dragged before the council and thrown down before Atretes. The young clansman's face poured sweat; his mouth jerked nervously. As Atretes regarded him, he remembered that Wagast had received his shield and framea a month before Atretes.

"I am no coward!" Wagast cried desperately. "The battle was lost! Atretes, I saw your father fall. The Batavi were running for the woods."

"He dropped his shield," Rud said, his hard, shaven face bronzed and uncompromising in the firelight. There was no baser crime of which a man could stand accused, no matter how young or untried.

"It was knocked from my hands!" Wagast cried out. "I swear it!"

"Did you try to retrieve it?" Atretes demanded.

Wagast's eyes darted away. "I couldn't get to it."

The men murmured rejection of Wagast's claim. Rud glared at him in disgust, his blue eyes fierce. "I saw you myself, running from the field like a frightened dog." He cried out to Atretes and the council. "The punishment for cowardice is set. There is no staying it—our law demands his death!"

Tribesmen brandished their swords, though with no great zeal.

None of them relished executing a clansman. When Atretes raised his own sword, the judgment was set. Wagast tried to scramble away, rolling and kicking at the men reaching for him. Screaming for mercy, he was dragged to the edge of a morass. Digging his heels into the soft ground, he struggled violently, sobbing and begging. Sickened, Atretes struck him down with his fist. Then, hoisting him high, he threw him into the mire himself. Two elders set a hurdle over him and held it down with long poles, trapping him in the bog.

The harder Wagast thrashed, the more quickly he sank. When his head went under, he clawed for any handhold. One elder yanked his pole free and tossed it aside. The others did as well. Wagast's muddy fingers clung to the hurdle. Finally, loosening, they slipped away as a last few bubbles broke the surface.

The men stood silent. There was no triumph in such a death. Better to die beneath a Roman sword than to be lost in the shame and foul oblivion of the morass.

Atretes turned to the lone gray-haired man standing off to one side. He put his hand on Herigast's shoulder and gripped him tightly. "You were my father's friend. We all know you to be a man of honor and do not fault you for your son's cowardice." The man's hard face jerked, then became still and emotionless. Atretes felt pity, but showed only grave respect. "You are welcome at my fire," he said and left the marsh. The others followed him.

Only Herigast remained behind. When all were gone, he hunkered down, pressed his forehead against his framea, and wept.

Severus Albanus Majorian had fought this foul tribe of Germans before. For the past two months, they had dogged various Roman legions, striking suddenly and then melting away, after cutting away a chunk of the ranks, like a deadly mist. Even so, though he had fully expected and counted on an attack by the German tribesmen, the Roman commander was stunned by the ferocity he was now facing.

The instant he had heard the war cry, Severus had signaled a counterattack. These foul Germans played unfair, striking like a venomous snake that appeared out of nowhere then slithered swiftly away to its hole. The only way to kill a snake was to cut off its head.

Unseen, the cavalry moved into position. The ranks began the practiced turn. As the horde of naked warriors ran from the trees, Severus spotted the leader who, blond hair streaming behind him like a banner, ran ahead of his pack of wolves. Rage flashed through the soldier, then was replaced almost immediately by a grim determination. He would have that young barbarian in chains. Driving his horse forward, Severus shouted more orders.

Charging straight into the legion, the young barbarian used his bloody framea with such skill that the frontline Romans fell back from him in terror. Undaunted, Severus signaled again, the trumpets giving a command that brought the Roman cavalry in from behind the tribesmen. Having survived the initial onslaught, the Roman ranks tightened again, moving to take what the barbarians could give, thereby drawing them further into the legion's trap.

Severus rode his horse into the mass of fighting men, swinging his sword to the right and left, knowing enough of German warfare to realize he only had a few minutes before the ambushers headed for the forest. If they broke free of the legionnaires, they would disappear again, only to attack later. Even now Severus saw that their leader had realized the trap and was shouting to his men.

"Take the giant!" Severus roared, driving harder. He ducked as a framea just missed his head. Slashing his sword into another attacker, he swore. "The giant! Take him! *The giant!*"

Atretes let out a piercing whistle, once again signaling his men to fall back. Rud fell with a dart in his back, Holt shouted madly to the others. A few broke through the lines, but Atretes was caught. He drove the point of his spear into one soldier and brought the back of it up beneath the chin of another who attacked him from behind. Before he could pull the spear free, another soldier rammed him in the back. Letting his momentum take him, keeping his hold on the framea, Atretes rolled and came to his feet, freeing the weapon and bringing the razor sharp spear point into the abdomen of an attacker.

He saw a flash to his right and shifted, feeling the sting of a sword wound along his right shoulder. A mounted commander was driving his horse toward him, shouting. A half-dozen soldiers closed in on Atretes, surrounding him.

Letting out a feral war cry, Atretes drove into the youngest soldier coming at him, putting a hard dent into the side of his helmet, then slicing through his groin. When another lunged at him, he ducked sharply and turned, bringing his heel up into the soldier's face. The Roman commander rode right into him, but Atretes was able to roll and come swiftly to his feet, throwing his hands up and letting out a shrill, warbling scream that made the commander's stallion rear. Dodging its hooves, Atretes retrieved his framea.

The Romans drew back as soon as the Chatti's spear was in his hands again. Fighting for control of his horse, the commander bellowed orders at his troops, his face dark red with fury.

Atretes saw no way to escape and resolved to take as many of the foul soldiers with him as he could. Baring his teeth, he swung around, waiting for the attack. When a soldier stepped forward into the circle, he faced him, holding the spear in two hands. The soldier shifted his sword and moved around to the right while the others called encouragement. The Roman attacked first. Parrying the blow easily, Atretes spit in the man's face before shoving him away. Enraged, the soldier lunged. Expecting this, Atretes dodged and brought the end of his framea around and into the side of the unwise legionnaire's head with a hard thud. As the soldier dropped, Atretes made a swift slice through the fallen man's jugular. The legionnaire twitched violently, but briefly, as he died.

Another soldier came at him, sword swinging. Atretes ducked to one side and circled, expecting a sword thrust to his back from someone in the tightening group of men. It didn't come. It seemed these Romans wanted their last kill to be a contest.

The second soldier was quickly disabled with a deep gash across his thigh. Atretes would have killed him had not another entered the circle quickly and blocked the thrust of the framea. The wounded man was dragged back, and Atretes faced a third opponent, at whom he made swift, sharp jabs, driving him back. The circle broke and then closed quickly again. The Roman facing Atretes brought his shield down hard, clanging it against the long metal head of the spear, at the same time swinging his sword. Atretes ducked sharply and spun around, catching the man in the back of the head with the framea's long handle. The soldier fell, face in the dust, and didn't move.

The men were furious and they shouted in fury, encouraging two others as they challenged the barbarian. Atretes moved so agilely they crashed against one another. Laughing, Atretes kicked dust at them and spit. If he was to die, he would die scorning his enemies.

Astride his black stallion, Severus watched the young German fight. Though surrounded by soldiers, death assured, the dog mocked his attackers openly. As Severus looked on, the giant swung his weapon in a wide circle, laughing loudly as the Roman soldiers drew back. When another challenged him, he made swift work of him, using his long spear like a sword and club in one. Stepping over the fallen man, he held the weapon between two hands and grinned fiercely, taunting the others in that heathenish language only a German tribesman could understand. When yet another challenger came at him, he moved so swiftly that the soldier passed him altogether. The man tried to check himself, but it was too late. The barbarian slammed one end of the spear into the soldier's helmet and, bringing the other end around, sliced mercilessly across the exposed neck.

"Enough of this!" Severus shouted, furious. "Do you plan to die one by one? Take him down!" When three entered the circle, intent upon the young German's blood, he shouted again. *"I want him alive!"*

Though Atretes didn't understand the orders, he knew something was changing by the look on his attackers' faces. They used their swords to block his blows, but not to return them. Perhaps they meant to keep him alive long enough to crucify him. Uttering an enraged scream, he lashed out with fury. If death were coming for him, he'd greet it with a framea in his hands.

More soldiers closed in on him, slamming him with their shields. The biggest caught hold of the spear, while another brought the flat of his sword against the side of his head. Crying out in fury to Tiwaz, Atretes brought his framea down and cracked his forehead hard against his adversary's face. As the man dropped, Atretes lunged forward over two other men. He dodged a shield, but, before he could raise his weapon again, the flat of a sword hit and briefly stunned him. He brought his foot up hard into the groin of one attacker, but another blow to his back made his knees buckle. Another blow dropped him.

Instinctively, he rolled and attempted to regain his feet, but four men grabbed his arms and legs. They forced him down while another tried to bang the spear free of his clenched fist. Atretes kept up his savage yell, bucking and struggling. The Roman commander dismounted and stood over him. He gave a quiet order, and the butt of a sword was brought against Atretes' temple. He gripped the framea until blackness overcame him.

Atretes awakened slowly. Disoriented, he didn't know where he was. His vision was blurred and, instead of the clean scent of the forest, the smell of blood and urine filled his nostrils. His head throbbed and he tasted blood in his mouth. He tried to rise and only managed a few inches before the sound of rattling chains sent stabs of pain through his temples and brought back the full realization of his defeat. Groaning, he sank back.

His mother's prophecy mocked him. She'd said he would be undefeated by any foe, yet here he lay, chained on a slab of wood, awaiting an unknown fate. He had failed his people; he had failed himself.

"If we die, let us die free men!" his warriors had cried when he offered them the choice of moving the tribe north or continuing the fight against Roman dominion. How bitterly this pledge stuck in his throat now, for neither he nor they had ever once considered being taken captive. Unafraid of death, they had gone into battle intent on slaying as many of their enemy as they could. All men were fated to die. Atretes and his clansmen always believed their deaths would come in battle.

Now, chained down, Atretes knew the gut-wrenching humiliation of defeat. He struggled violently against his chains and blacked out. Rousing again moments later, he waited for the dizziness and nausea to pass before he opened his eyes.

Turning his head, he tried to evaluate his position. He was in a small room built of thick logs. Sunlight streamed in through a small, high window, making him squint as pain shot through his head. He was stretched out and chained down to a large table. Even his sagum had been stripped from him. He moved sluggishly, testing his bonds as pain licked through his shoulders and back. Short, thick chains were attached to iron manacles around his wrists and ankles.

Two men entered the room.

Atretes rose slightly, jerking at his restraints. He uttered a short, foul curse, insulting them. They stood placidly, savoring their victory. One, dressed in magnificent armor and a scarlet cloak, held a bronzed helmet beneath his arm. Atretes recognized him as the high-ranking officer who had stood over him, gloating at the battle's end. The other man wore a finely woven tunic and dark travel cloak, both bespeaking wealth.

"Ah, so you are conscious," Severus said, grinning down into the fierce blue eyes of the young warrior. "I am gratified to know you are alive and have some wits about you. My men would like to see you flogged and crucified, but I have other, more profitable plans for you."

Atretes did not understand Latin or Greek, but the officer's insolent manner fanned his rebellious nature. He fought the restraints violently, uncaring of the pain it caused him.

"Well, what do you think of him, Malcenas?"

"He growls like a beast and stinks," the merchant said.

Severus laughed softly and straightened. "Take a good long look at this one, Malcenas. I think you'll find him out of the ordinary and the price I have set on him more than fair."

Atretes' rage grew as the merchant moved closer and began an avid perusal of him. When the man reached out to touch him, Atretes lunged, jerking hard against the chains. The explosion of pain in his head and shoulder only incensed him further. He spit on the man. "Foul Roman pig!" He swore and struggled.

Malcenas grimaced and took a small cloth from his sleeve and dabbed his tunic delicately. "These Germans are no better than animals, and what a heathenish tongue he speaks."

Severus grabbed the young man by the hair, forcing his head back. "An animal, yes. But what an animal! He has the face of Apollo and the body of Mars." The German jerked violently, trying to sink his teeth into his tormentor's arm. Severus yanked his head back again, holding him tighter this time.

"You know very well, Malcenas, that one look at this well-formed young barbarian, and the women of Rome will go mad for the games." He looked at Malcenas' flushed face, and his mouth tipped cynically. "And some men as well, I think, if I may judge by the look on your face."

Malcenas' full lips tightened. He could not look away from the young warrior. He knew Germans to be fierce, but one look into this warrior's blue eyes sent a shudder of fear through him. Even with him chained, Malcenas didn't feel safe. It excited him. Ah, but money was money, and Severus was demanding a fortune for this captive. "He is very beautiful, Severus, but is he trainable?"

"Trainable?" Severus laughed and let go of the warrior's blond hair. "You should have seen this barbarian fight. He is a better gladiator now than any you have sent to the arena in the last ten years." His smile flattened out. "He killed more than a dozen trained legionnaires in the first few minutes of battle. It took four seasoned soldiers to hold him down. They couldn't pry that bloody framea from his hand. Not until I had him knocked out." He gave a sardonic laugh. "I don't think he'll need much training. Just keep him chained until you're ready to turn him loose in the arena."

Malcenas admired the straining muscles of the powerful young body. Oiled, he would look like a bronzed god. And that mane of long blond hair. Romans loved blonds!

"Nevertheless," Malcenas said with a regretful sigh, hoping to drive Severus' price down, "what you ask is too much."

"He's worth it. And more!"

"Mars himself is not worth your price."

Severus shrugged. "A pity you cannot afford him." He gestured toward the door. "Come. I will sell you two others of inferior quality."

"You won't bargain?"

"It's a waste of my time and yours. Prochorus will buy him without quibbling over a few thousand *sesterces*."

"Prochorus!" At the mention of his competitor, Malcenas knew an instant of fury.

"He arrives tomorrow."

"Very well," he said impatiently, his face darkening. "I'll take this one."

Severus grinned. "A wise decision, Malcenas. You are a shrewd man when it comes to human flesh."

"And you, my dear Severus, have a merchant's black heart."

"Do you wish to see the others?"

"You said they were inferior. Offer them to Prochorus. I'll put my seal on the contract for this one, and the funds will be transferred to you as soon as I return to Rome."

"Agreed."

Malcenas went to the closed door and rapped on it. A man in a simple tunic entered quickly. Malcenas nodded to Atretes. He knew the journey to the *ludus,* the training school for gladiators, would not be a short one. "See to him, Quintus. He's opened his wounds. I don't want him bleeding to death before we reach the ludus in Capua."

ROME

3

Decimus Vindacius Valerian poured more wine, then thumped the silver pitcher down on a marble table. He looked across the marble table at his son, who was lounging on the couch, an indolent look on his handsome face. The young man was trying his patience. They'd been talking for over an hour and Decimus had gotten nowhere with him.

Marcus sipped the Italian Falernian and nodded. "Excellent wine, Father." The compliment was met with a stony glance. As always, his father was trying to direct him down the course he'd chosen for his son. Marcus smiled to himself. Did his father really expect capitulation? He was part of his sire, after all. When would the elder Valerian realize that his son had his own ideas to carry out, his own way to follow?

His father was a restless man, given to fits of irascibility when he didn't get his way. Doggedly, he continued, his demeanor seemingly calm, which Marcus was well aware was only a veneer concealing the temper boiling beneath.

"Vespasian, for all his brains and tactical ability as a general, is still a plebeian, Marcus. And as a plebeian, he hates the aristocracy that has almost destroyed our Empire. A member of the senate claimed his genealogist had traced the emperor's line back to Jupiter. Vespasian laughed in his face."

Marcus shrugged and rose from the couch. "So I've heard, Father. He removed four senators whose bloodlines go back to Romulus and Remus."

"If you believe in such nonsense."

"It's in my best interest to believe. This Flavian admits openly to being the son of a Spanish tax collector, and that may be his ultimate downfall. He is a commoner who has taken the reins of an Empire founded on royal bloodlines."

"Just because you're the biggest dog doesn't mean you're the smartest or the best. Vespasian may not have the bloodlines, but he is a born leader."

"I share your admiration of Vespasian, Father. Galba was a senile fool and Otho, greedy and stupid. As for Vitellius, I suspect the only reason he wanted to be emperor was to have the wealth to fill his belly with goose livers and hummingbird tongues. I've never seen a man eat with such passion." His dry smile flattened. "Vespasian is the only man strong enough to hold the Empire together."

"Exactly, and he will need strong young senators to help him."

Marcus could feel his smile stiffening. So that was it. He had wondered why his father had given in so easily when Marcus had refused his suggestion of a suitable marriage. Now it made sense. Father had a bigger topic to approach: Politics. A blood sport if ever there was one, to Marcus' way of thinking.

The gods hadn't been kind to his father the last few years. Fire and rebellion had cost him several warehouses and millions of sesterces in goods destroyed. He'd blamed Nero, despite the emperor's efforts to blame the conflagration on the Christian sect. Those close to Nero had been aware of his dream to redesign and rebuild Rome, renaming it Neropolis. Instead, the madman had succeeded in the city's destruction.

Rome staggered in rebellion over Nero's mismanagement.

Emperor Galba had proven a fool. When he ordered all those who had received gifts and pensions from Nero to return nine-tenths to the treasury, he had assured his death. Within weeks, the Praetorian Guard had handed his head to Otho and proclaimed the bankrupt merchant the new emperor of Rome.

Rome stumbled.

Otho served no better. As Vitellius' legions invaded Italy and swept away the northern garrisons of the Praetorian Guard, Otho committed suicide. Yet, once in power, Vitellius worsened the situation by relinquishing his responsibilities to the corruptions of his freedman, Asiaticus. Vitellius, foul pig that he was, retired to the life of a fat, slothful, epicurean gourmand.

As power washed back and forth like a tide, upheaval spread throughout the Empire. The Judean revolt continued. Another started in Gaul. German tribes united under the command of the Roman-trained Civilis and attacked frontier outposts.

Rome was on her knees.

It took Vespasian to bring her to her feet again. As word carried through the provinces the disintegration of government, the generals' legions proclaimed Vespasian their emperor, and they upheld their proclamation by sending General Antonius and a great army into Italy to dethrone Vitellius. Defeating an army at

Cremona, Antonius marched into Rome, killing Vitellius' troops without quarter. Vitellius himself was found hiding in the palace and was dragged half-naked through the streets. The citizenry pelted him with dung and tortured him without mercy. Even with his death, the masses and soldiers were not satisfied. They mutilated Vitellius' body, dragging it by hook through the city streets and finally discarding what remained in the muddy Tiber.

"You say nothing," Decimus said, frowning.

His father's words drew Marcus out of his reverie. He had seen too many die in the past few years to desire a career in politics. Young men, whose only mistake was to support the wrong man, were dead. Granted, Vespasian was an honorable and able man, a man accustomed to battle. However, to Marcus' thinking, that didn't mean that he wouldn't fall prey to a concubine's poison or an assassin's dagger.

"Many of my friends had political ambitions, Father. Hymenaeus and Aquila, for example. And what became of them? They were ordered to commit suicide when Nero suspected them of treason, based on no evidence other than the word of a jealous senator. And Pudens was murdered because his father was a personal friend of Otho. Appicus was cut down when Antonius entered Rome. Beyond that, considering the lives of most of our emperors, and their ends, I don't find politics a particularly healthy or honorable pursuit."

Decimus sat down, forcing himself to a calmness he was far from feeling. He knew the look on Marcus' face. If only his son's powerful will could be appropriately channeled to something other than selfish pleasures.

"Marcus, reconsider. With Vespasian in power, this is an opportune time for political ambitions. It is a good time to find a worthy path for your life," he said. "Times have been turbulent, but they will now come under the reign of a man of intelligence and justice." He saw the wry look on his son's face and came to the point. "One million sesterces will buy you a place in the equestrian order and a seat in the senate."

Marcus stifled his anger and put on an expression of sardonic humor. "So that I can become part of a class you have always mocked and disdained?"

"So that you can become part of the new order of Rome!"

"I am a part of it, Father."

"But on the edge of power." Decimus leaned forward and closed a fist. "You could be holding a good deal of it."

Marcus gave a derisive laugh. "Antigonus has almost impoverished himself in his efforts to court the mob. You avoid the games, Father, but as you well know, financing them is a political necessity. Whatever the cost, the multitude must be appeased. By the gods, would you see your life's work poured out on the sand in an arena you refuse to visit? Or shall we pour thousands of sesterces into feasts for those fat aristocrats you hate so much?"

Decimus curbed his temper, hearing his own oft-spoken words repeated back to him. It was a method of debate Marcus commonly used—and one which Decimus detested. "A time of great upheaval can be a time of great opportunity."

"Oh, I agree wholeheartedly, Father. However, the winds of politics are too swift to change, and I've no desire to be blown away by them." He smiled tightly and raised his goblet. "My ambitions lie in another direction."

"To eat, drink, and enjoy life before you die," Decimus said darkly.

Marcus breathed deeply before giving in to his rising anger. "And to make you richer than you already are." His mouth tipped cynically. "If you want to leave a mark on the Empire, Father, do it in cedar and stone. Nero destroyed us with fire; Galba, Otho, and Vitellius with rebellions. Let the house of Valerian have part in raising Rome again."

Decimus' eyes darkened. "I would rather you sought the honor of becoming a senator than have to see you pursue money like any common merchant."

"I would not call you common, my lord."

Decimus slammed his goblet down, sloshing wine onto the marble table. "You are impudent. We are discussing *your* future."

Marcus lowered his wine goblet and took up the challenge. "No, you are attempting to dictate plans you made without consulting me. If you want a Valerian in the senate, take the seat yourself. I'm sorry to disappoint you again, Father, but I have my own plans for my life."

"Would you mind telling me what those plans encompass?"

"To enjoy what little time I have on the earth. Paying my own way, of course, as you very well know I can."

"And will you marry Arria?"

Marcus felt his blood heating at the dry mention of Arria. His father disapproved of her free-spirited attitude. Annoyed, Marcus glanced away, then saw his mother and sister coming from the gardens. He rose, relieved to have an end to this discussion. He didn't want to say anything he'd later regret.

His mother looked up at him in question when he came out to greet her. "All is well, Marcus?" she asked as he bent to kiss her cheek.

"Isn't it always, Mama?"

"You and Father have been talking a long time," Julia said from behind their mother, subtly prying.

"Just business," he said and pinched her cheek lightly in affection. At fourteen, she was becoming quite a beauty.

Phoebe entered the *triclinium,* a spacious dining room with elegant furnishings and decorations, ahead of her son. Normally this room gave her a sense of pleasure as she entered it. On this day, however, she barely noticed her surroundings; her eyes were fixed on her husband. Decimus looked strained, the gray hair curling on his damp forehead. She sat on the couch beside him and placed her hand on his. "It didn't go well?" she said softly.

Curving his fingers over hers, he squeezed lightly. He saw the concern in her eyes and tried to ease it. They'd been married for thirty years and, though their passion had long since eased, their love had deepened. "Marcus disdains the honorable pursuit of politics."

"Honorable?" Julia laughed gaily in surprise. "You utter honorable in the same sentence with politics, Father? You loathe politicians. You've never had a single good thing to say about them, and now you suggest Marcus become one? You cannot possibly be serious!"

Marcus grinned broadly at his young sister's candid outburst. Leave it to her to say the first thing that came into her mind before considering their patriarch's good humor, or rather, lack of it. "It would seem, despite Father's frequent remarks on the dubious legitimacy of most senators, he has held secret aspirations all along to see a Valerian in the Forum."

"Oh, but wouldn't it be wonderful!" Julia said, dark brown eyes alight. "Marcus, I can just see you standing before the senate." She stood and struck a dramatic pose. Thrusting her lovely chin in the air, she gathered her *palus,* an elegantly embroidered mantle or overdress, and strolled back and forth before her brother and parents, her hand against her chest, an expression of such grave regality on her face that even Decimus smiled.

"Sit down, imp," Marcus said, tugging her onto the couch.

Julia, irrepressible when she was in a gay spirits, took his hand. "You'll make a most beautiful senator, Marcus."

"Beautiful? That is a description better placed upon fair Scorpus," he said, referring to a wealthy merchant who had come from Ephesus to do business with their father. Julia had been quite impressed with his dark eyes and swarthy skin.

"Is it true he has a catamite?"

"Julia!" Phoebe said, shocked to hear her young daughter speak of such things.

Julia grimaced. "I apologize, Mama."

"Where do you hear such things?"

"Father was telling Marcus he didn't trust a man with a catamite, and Marcus said—"

"How long were you standing outside the *bibliotheca?*" Marcus broke in quickly, silencing her before she could chatter on. He was irritated, both because she had eavesdropped on his conversation with his father in the library and because she had embarrassed their mother, who was clearly shocked by such free talking. Julia knew more of the world at fourteen than their mother did at forty-four. Perhaps because their mother didn't want to know.

"I was just passing by." Too late, Julia saw the displeasure on her mother's face. Quickly she changed the subject. "Will you be a senator, Marcus?"

"No." He met his father's look. "If you want to have a hand in politics, assist poor Antigonus."

"Antigonus?" Decimus said. "The pup who hawks statuary to the aristocracy?"

"Works of art, Father, not statuary."

Decimus gave a derisive snort.

Marcus replenished his goblet and handed it to him. "Antigonus told me this afternoon he was ready to open his veins over the cost of the games he sponsored last week. You could have a senator of your own for the bargain price of a few hundred thousand sesterces. He already has the ear of the emperor through Vespasian's son Domitian. He and Antigonus train together as gladiators at the ludus. It's only a matter of time until Antigonus is sitting in the senate, unless he kills himself first, of course."

"I doubt Antigonus would do serious harm to himself," Decimus said dryly. "Except by accident."

"Antigonus admires Seneca, and you know Seneca preached suicide. If Antigonus dies, we will have lost a great advantage," he said, his voice tinged with cynical amusement.

Phoebe was dismayed. "I thought Antigonus was your friend, Marcus."

"He is, Mama," he said gently. "A despondent one, at the moment." He looked at his father. "Political ambition often leads to poverty."

Decimus' mouth tightened. What his son said was true. He knew of more than one senator committing suicide when their fortunes had dissolved under the responsibilities of office. "Courting the mob," as Marcus put it. It was an apt statement. And the mob was like an expensive and unfaithful mistress. He relented. "Find out what his needs are and we will discuss them."

Marcus was surprised at his father's capitulation. He had expected a long and arduous debate before getting a *denarius* out of him. He named a price that brought his father's brows up. "I told Antigonus this afternoon at the baths that my father is a wise and generous benefactor."

"Is that so?" Decimus said, torn between pride and anger at his son's audacity.

Grinning, Marcus lifted his goblet in salute. "You'll find Antigonus a most grateful fellow. We discussed building contracts at some length before I came home this evening. He was very agreeable."

Decimus saw that his son had already begun carrying out his own plans. "And what will you build, Marcus? Temples to the goddess Fortune?"

"Nothing so grand as that, Father. Houses for your new and noble aristocracy, I think. And tenements for plebeians, if you so desire."

Dismayed at the tension between father and son, Phoebe nodded to a Parthian slave standing in the doorway. "You may serve us now." The Parthian signaled, and two young Greek slaves entered silently and sat unobtrusively in the corner. One blew softly into a panpipe, while the other softly stroked a lyre. An Egyptian slave girl carried in a silver platter on which were slices of roasted pork from pigs fattened in oak forests.

"I promised Antigonus I would tell him of your decision this evening," Marcus said, selecting a piece of meat.

"You were that sure I would agree," Decimus said dryly.

"You taught me never to allow an opportunity to pass. It might never come again."

"Some things that I taught you I wish I hadn't," Decimus said.

With the first course finished, another was set before them. Julia picked through the fruit and selected a small cluster of Syrian grapes. Marcus bit into a Persian peach. The Parthian stood tall and motionless in the doorway. When goblets were empty, the Egyptian girl replenished them.

"Marble is easily obtained from Luna and Paros," Decimus said, considering Marcus' idea. "But cedar is growing scarce in Lebanon, driving the price up. We'd do better to import timber from Greece."

"Why not Gaul?" Marcus asked.

"There is still too much unrest in that region. If you're going to have contracts to fulfill, you'll need materials on hand, not en route."

The Parthian signaled the Egyptian girl to bring in the small bowls of warm scented water. As she leaned over to set a bowl before Marcus, she raised her eyes to his, a clear message in them. Smiling slightly, Marcus dipped his hands into his bowl, rinsing his fingers of meat and fruit juices. He took the towel the girl offered him and let his gaze drift over her as she stood waiting for his command.

"That will be all, Bithia," Phoebe said gently, dismissing the girl. The young Egyptian was not the first slave in the Valerian household to fall in love with her son, Phoebe knew. Marcus was handsome and well built, exuding virility. His morals were not what Phoebe wished them to be; they were, in fact, generally in opposition to all she had taught him at her knee. If a beautiful young woman was willing, Marcus was only too ready to oblige. Well, there were already far too many willing young Roman women in Marcus' social circle for him to take unsuitable advantage of an enamored Egyptian slave in their own home.

His mother's disapproval amused Marcus, but he honored her silent plea. He tossed the hand towel on the table and stood. "I'll go and tell Antigonus of your decision, Father. He'll be very relieved. And I thank you."

"You're going out again?" Julia said, disappointed. "Oh, Marcus! You only arrived a few hours ago and you and Father have been talking most of the time. We haven't even had a chance to visit!"

"I can't stay this evening, Julia." He leaned down and kissed her cheek. "I'll tell you about the games when I return," he whispered for her alone to hear.

Decimus and Phoebe watched their son leave. Julia jumped up and followed him. It had always pleased Phoebe to see how devoted Julia was to her older brother, and how deep was his affection for his young sister. There was an eight-year age difference between the two, her other two children between having been lost in infancy.

However, lately, their closeness had worried Phoebe. Julia was high-spirited and passionate, a nature easily corrupted. And Marcus had developed into an outspoken epicurean. He saw little purpose in life other than to make money and take every pleasure he could from it. She supposed she couldn't blame the young men and women who embraced this philosophy, for over the past few years, turmoil and bloodshed had taken so many. Life was uncertain. Yet, she was bothered by such attitudes.

What had happened to decency? What had happened to purity and faithfulness? Life was more than pleasure. It was duty and honor. It was building a family. It was caring for others who hadn't the means to care for themselves.

She looked at Decimus. He was deep in thought. She touched his hand again, drawing his attention. "I would like to see Marcus married and settled. What did he say about an alliance with the Garibaldis?"

"He said no."

"You couldn't sway him? Olympia is a very lovely girl."

"As you just noticed, Marcus can have his choice of lovely young girls, slave or free," Decimus said. "I didn't think marriage would have any great allure to him." He wondered if his son was still foolish enough to think himself in love with Arria. He doubted it.

"His life is becoming so aimless," Phoebe said.

"Not aimless, my love. Self-centered. Indulgent." Decimus rose, drawing his wife up with him. "He's like so many of his young aristocratic friends. He considers life a great hunt; every experience prey to be devoured. There is little thought these days of what is good for Rome."

They walked out into the *peristyle,* a large corridor that encircled the courtyard. They strolled along beneath the white marble columns and went out into the garden. It was a warm evening and the stars shone in the clear sky. The pathway meandered among trimmed shrubs and flowering trees. The marble statue of a nude woman stood in the flower bed, her male counterpart on the other side of the walkway. Perfect forms glistening white in the moonlight.

Decimus' mind wandered to the day Marcus had shaved for the first time. Together they had taken the whiskers to the temple of Jupiter. Marcus made his offering and became a man. It seemed like yesterday—and a lifetime ago. During the intervening years, Decimus had seen the boy through rhetorics and military training. Yet, somewhere along the way, he had lost control. He had lost his son.

"I was hoping to convince Marcus that a new order could bring much-needed changes to the Empire," he said, putting his hand over Phoebe's as it rested on his arm.

"Isn't it a worthy pursuit to want to rebuild Rome?" Phoebe asked gently, putting her other hand over his. He seemed so troubled, and he had not been well lately, though he did not speak of what ailed him. Perhaps it was only concern over Marcus' future. And Julia's.

"Rome needs rebuilding," Decimus said, but he knew Marcus cared little about the Empire, except as it affected him personally. Marcus had no altruistic reasons for wanting to rebuild Roman houses. His only motivation was to increase Valerian wealth. One cannot rape life without the means to do so, and money was what gave one those means.

Decimus supposed he was to blame for Marcus' preoccupation with money. Most of his own life had been spent in building the Valerian fortune through various enterprises. He had begun in Ephesus, part owner of one small ship. Now he made his home in Rome itself, overseer of an entire merchant fleet. His ships traveled all the known seas and returned with cargoes from most every country in the Empire: cattle and wool from Sicily; slaves from Britain; wild beasts from the coasts of Africa; rare essences, gems, and eunuchs from Parthia and Persia; grain from Egypt; cinnamon, aloes, and laudanum from Arabia.

Valerian caravans journeyed as far as China to bring back silk, dyes, and drugs; others traveled to India, returning with pepper, spices, and herbs along with pearls, sardonyx, diamonds, and carbuncles. Whatever Roman markets wanted, Valerian caravans and ships would supply.

From boyhood, Decimus had been aware of Marcus' brilliance. He had a gift for making money. His ideas were shrewd, his intuition solid. Even more important, he could see into men's souls. Decimus took pride in his son's natural abilities, yet he recognized a side of his son's character that grieved him greatly. For all his charm and intelligence, Marcus used people.

Decimus remembered the first time he realized how callous Marcus had become. It'd been three years ago, when Marcus was nineteen.

"There is more gold in sand than grain, Father."

"The people *need* grain."

"They want the games, and you cannot have the games without the sand to soak up the spilled blood."

"There are hundreds starving and in need of food. We must think of what is best for our people."

For the first time, his son challenged him. "Bring in two ships, one loaded with grain and one with sand, and see which cargo is paid for and unloaded first. If it's grain, I'll do whatever you ask for the next year. But if it's sand, you'll give me management over six ships, to do with them as I wish."

Decimus had been so sure need would outweigh want. Or perhaps he had only hoped.

In the end, Marcus had his six ships. It sat ill with Decimus to admit to himself he was relieved now to know that Marcus would fill them with lumber and stones and not more sand or victims for the arena.

The father sighed. Phoebe was wrong to say that Marcus was aimless. Marcus was single-minded in his pursuit of wealth and pleasure—all that he could get.

At the front door, Marcus swung on his cloak and kissed Julia on the forehead. "I'll take you to the games when you're a little older."

Julia stamped her daintily sandaled foot. "I despise you when you patronize me, Marcus," she said. When he opened the door, she quickly clung to his arm. "Please, Marcus. You promised me."

"I did no such thing," he said, amused.

"Well, you sort of promised. Oh, Marcus. It isn't fair. I've never been to the games and I'll simply *die* if I don't get to go."

"You know Mother would have my head if I took you."

"She would forgive you anything and *you* know it. Besides, Mother doesn't have to know. You could say you were taking me out for a ride in your new chariot. Just take me to the theater for an hour or two. Please. Oh, Marcus. It's so humiliating to be the only one of my friends who hasn't seen a gladiatorial contest."

"I'll consider it."

Julia knew he was putting her off. She drew back slightly and tilted her head. "Glaphyra told me you take Arria. She's only three years older than I."

"Arria is Arria," he said.

"It isn't Roman to not attend the games!"

Marcus put a quick hand over her mouth and shushed her. "Any more outbursts like that and you can forget it." Quick tears filled her eyes and he relented. "Whether I agree with you or not, now is not the best time for me to be taking you anywhere."

"Because you disappointed Father with your lack of noble ambition?" she mocked.

"I see nothing noble in politics. Nor in marriage."

Julia's eyes widened. "Father wants you to get married? To whom?"

"He only hinted and made no suggestions." While Julia delighted him with her endless gossip, he didn't want word of his rejection of Olympia arriving at the Garibaldi door via one of Julia's infantile friends. Besides, it was not Olympia he had rejected as much as marriage itself. The mere thought of spending the rest of his life with one woman was daunting.

He had briefly considered marrying Arria during the height of their passionate affair. Good sense had kept him silent. Arria, beautiful exciting Arria. In the beginning, just thinking about her had given him an edge of excitement. Sometimes he felt his blood stir just watching her screaming over two gladiators fighting it out in the arena. Arria was still pleasing, still charming and witty—but for all her considerable charms, she had begun to bore Marcus.

"You and father were together more than an hour. You just don't want to tell me who it is. No one ever tells me anything. I am not a baby anymore, Marcus."

"Then stop acting like one." He kissed her cheek. "I have to leave."

"If you don't take me to the theater, I'll tell Mother what I heard about you and Patrobus' wife."

Stunned, he could only laugh. "You didn't overhear that in this house," he said. "One of your foul little friends, I'll wager." He swung her around and laid a firm slap on her backside. She let out a yelp of pain and jerked free, her dark eyes flashing with fury.

He grinned down at her. "If I do agree to take you . . . " Julia calmed instantly at his capitulation, her pretty face blooming with a triumphant smile. "I said *if*, you little witch. If I agree, it won't be because you threaten to repeat rumors about a senator's wife!"

She pouted prettily. "You know I wouldn't really."

"Mother wouldn't believe you if you did," he said, knowing his parent had never believed the worst of him.

Julia knew, too. "I've wanted to go to the games for so long."

"You'll probably faint at your first sight of blood."

"I promise I won't shame you, Marcus. I won't even flinch, no matter how much blood there is. I swear it. When shall we go? Tomorrow?"

"Not that soon. I'll take you the next time Antigonus hosts them."

"Oh, Marcus, I love you. I love you so much," she said, hugging him.

"Yes, I know." He smiled affectionately. "As long as you get your own way."

4

Marcus stepped out into the street and breathed deeply of the night air. He was glad to be out of the house. He loved his father, but he had new ways of thinking about things. Why work unless you intended to enjoy the fruits of your labor?

He had observed his father's life. The elder Valerian arose at seven and spent two hours in the *atrium,* the central courtyard, doling out pensions to clients, most of whom had not worked in years. He ate a meager breakfast and left for the warehouses. Late in the afternoon, he exercised in the *gymnasium* and relaxed in the baths, conversing with aristocrats, politicians, and other wealthy merchants. He returned home to dine with his wife and family and then retired to his books. The next day was the same as the one before. Day after day after day.

Marcus wanted more from life. He wanted to feel his blood rushing through his veins as it did at the chariot races, or when he witnessed a good gladiatorial contest or when he was with a beautiful woman. He enjoyed the lassitude of being drunk on good wine, or of sharing a night of passion and pleasure. He enjoyed tasting new and rare delicacies. He liked watching dancers, listening to singers, and attending plays.

Life was a hunger meant to be sated. Life was meant to be swallowed, not sipped. But living cost money . . . lots of money.

For all his father's speeches and posturing, Marcus was sure it wasn't honor that ran Rome and the world. It was gold and coin. Money bought alliances and trade agreements; money paid for the soldiers and war machines that expanded the boundaries of the Empire. Money purchased *Pax Romana.*

Marcus walked with purposeful steps down Aventine Hill. The city was full of thieves awaiting a careless victim to fall upon. Marcus was watchful. His reflexes were quick, his dagger sharp. He would almost welcome an attack. A good, bloody fight might vent the frustrations his father aroused with his demands and expectations. Why this sudden disdain on his father's part for money when the man had spent his life accumulating it? Marcus gave a harsh laugh. At least he was honest in his quest for riches.

He didn't pretend to despise that which gave him the life-style he wanted.

The rumble of wheels on stone became louder as Marcus neared the thoroughfares. Carts and wagons laden with merchandise clambered through the city, creating a head-splitting din greater than most battles. He should have left the house earlier, before the ban lifted on wheeled vehicles entering Rome.

Marcus cut through the alleyways and followed the meandering streets, trying to avoid the traffic. He stayed close to the walls so he wouldn't be doused with the slops being dumped from upstairs windows. Crossing a main avenue, he saw a cart overturn. Wine barrels broke free of their ropes and rolled. Men shouted; horses screamed. The Greek driver used his whip on a man who tried to roll a barrel away. Two more men began fighting in the street.

Marcus was jarred by a street seller carrying a flagon of wine and a basket of bread and shouldering a ham. Swearing, Marcus pushed him aside and shoved his way through the crowd. Breaking through, he headed for the Tiber bridge. The stench of excrement was powerful. By the gods, he longed for a breath of fresh country air! Maybe he would invest in land south of Capua. The city was growing and prices would rise.

Striding across the bridge, he walked south toward the Gardens of Julius. Antigonus' home was not far away, and the walk had done him good.

A Negro slave opened the door. The Ethiopian was over six feet tall and powerfully built. Marcus looked him up and down and decided he must be one of Antigonus' new African acquisitions. Antigonus had spoken of purchasing a trained gladiator to serve as his bodyguard. Marcus thought it an unwarranted expense since the young aristocrat was not yet in a position to have his life threatened.

"Marcus Lucianus Valerian," Marcus told the slave.

The Negro bowed deeply and led him toward the large banquet room off the atrium.

A depressing atmosphere hung over the dimly lit room. Two well-built young men dressed in loincloths and wearing laurel leaf crowns played melancholy music on a pan flute and lyre. Antigonus' friends spoke in low voices. Some reclined on couches, drinking and eating. Patrobus was occupying a couch, a platter of delicacies beside him. Marcus didn't see the senator's wife,

Fannia, and wondered if she'd gone to their country estate as planned.

He spotted Antigonus, reclining and enjoying the ministrations of a lovely Numidian slave girl. Marcus approached. Crossing his arms, he leaned casually against a marble column, his mouth curving in a mocking grin as he watched them for a few moments.

"Ah, Antigonus, when I left your august presence this afternoon, you were contemplating a journey across the River Styx. And here I find you worshiping Eros."

Antigonus opened his eyes and tried to focus. Disentangling himself, he dismissed the girl with a light shove and stood shakily, clearly drunk. "Have you come for a funeral or for a celebration, my dear Marcus?"

"A celebration, of course. I gave you my word, didn't I? You'll have what you need within the week."

Antigonus let out his breath in great relief. "May the gods be praised for their generosity." Noting Marcus' sardonic look, the young aristocrat added hastily, "And your family, of course." He clapped his hands, startling half a dozen guests from their lethargy. "Stop playing that dirge and give us something more lively!" He motioned impatiently to a slave. "Bring us more wine and food."

Antigonus and Marcus sat and began discussing their plans for the games Antigonus would hold in honor of the emperor. "We must have something new and exciting to entertain our noble Vespasian," Antigonus said. "Tigers, perhaps. You told me that one of your caravans arrived a few days ago."

Marcus had no intention of selling tigers to Antigonus and being recompensed with funds from his own family treasury. A gift of half a million sesterces was enough without adding valuable animals to it. "The people might better receive a reenactment of one of the emperor's more successful Judean battles."

"Word was received that Jerusalem is destroyed," Antigonus said. "Five months of besieging that forsaken city and thousands of our soldiers killed. Ah, but it is well worth it knowing that foul race is almost obliterated." He snapped his fingers and a slave hurried over with a tray of fruit. Antigonus selected a date. "Titus has marched ninety thousand captives to Caesarea."

"So Judea is finally at peace," Marcus remarked.

"At peace? Ha! As long as there is one Jew alive, there will be insurrection, never peace!"

"Rome's strength lies in her tolerance, Antigonus. We allow our people to worship whatever gods they choose."

"Providing they worship the emperor as well. But these Jews? Part of this trouble began because they refused to accept offerings for our emperor in their temple. They claimed the sacrifices of *foreigners* would defile their holy place. Well, now they have no holy place." He laughed and popped the date into his mouth.

Marcus accepted wine offered by a lovely Parthian. "Perhaps now they will give up their futile faith."

"Some will, perhaps, but those who call themselves righteous will never relent. The fools prostrate themselves before a god they cannot see and refuse to their deaths to bend their necks a fraction to the only true deity, the emperor."

Patrobus shifted his bulk on a couch nearby. "At least they are more interesting than those cowardly Christians. Pit a Jew against anyone and you will see how fiercely he fights, but put a Christian in the arena and he'll kneel and sing to his unseen god, dying without raising a finger to defend himself." He took another delicacy from the silver platter. "They sicken me."

Marcus remembered only too well the hundreds of Christians Nero had ordered put to death. He had even doused some in pitch and bitumen and set them aflame to serve as torches for the games. The mob had been hungry for Christian blood following the emperor's claims that the cult had set fire to Rome, ostensibly to fulfill their prophecy that the world would end in fire. But the mob hadn't known of Nero's own dreams of a new city named after himself.

Watching men and women die without a fight had left Marcus with a vague feeling of unrest, a disquiet that gnawed at him. Patrobus called them cowards; Marcus wasn't sure he agreed with that assessment. A coward would run before a charging lion, not stand firm in facing it.

Antigonus leaned toward Marcus, grinning. "Fair Arria arrives," he whispered.

Arria came in from the gardens, laughing with two other young women. Her white *stola* was elegantly wrapped around her slender body, her narrow waist encircled by a wide gold and jewel-studded belt fashioned after one she had seen a gladiator wearing in the arena. She had taken to bleaching her dark hair with Batavian foam, and her now-blonde tresses were braided and ringed intricately on her proud head. Small curls were left to frame her delicate face. Marcus smiled faintly. Purity and fragile womanhood. How many men had been fooled by that sweet image when beneath lay a voracious and sometimes bizarre appetite?

She glanced around until she saw him. She smiled. He knew that look very well, but he no longer responded to it as he had in the beginning of their affair. Though he smiled back at her, he almost wished that she were absent. The freedom he had felt a moment before dissolved as she crossed the room.

"Marcus, ever loyal," she said, a faint bite in her dulcet voice as she reclined gracefully on his couch. "We heard the music change in the gardens. I take it you have saved our dear Antigonus from financial ruin."

Wondering at her sharp tone, he took her small white hand and kissed it. Her fingers were cold and trembling. Something was amiss. "Only for the time being," Marcus said. "Until he can gain a seat in the senate and begin partaking of the public treasury."

Her mouth softened. "The evening air is refreshing, Marcus."

"Ah, yes, by all means, enjoy it while you can," Antigonus said, mouth curving in wry amusement. Only this afternoon at the baths, Antigonus had been probing about Arria. "Why is it, Marcus, that as a woman's passion for a certain man grows, his for her wanes?" It seemed apparent to all but the lady involved that Marcus was growing weary of her.

Marcus rose and placed Arria's hand on his arm. They went out into the gardens and strolled along the marble pathway in the moonlight. Marcus didn't underestimate Arria. She wouldn't be discarded easily. She'd been with him longer than with all her other lovers. He knew it had less to do with his prowess than his nature. While he had been infatuated from the beginning, he had never completely fallen beneath her spell, an experience to which young Arria was unaccustomed.

"Did you see Antigonus' latest statue?" she said.

"Aphrodite?" Though Antigonus was more than satisfied with the work of his Greek artisans, Marcus had been unmoved by the completed work. He didn't think Antigonus would make much profit from the fulsome creation. His father was right in his evaluation of Antigonus' works of art. A snort of derision was about all they merited.

"Not a god this time, my love. I think this work is the best he has done. He should ask a fortune for it, but he's hidden it away for himself. He showed it to me earlier this evening, but no one else has seen it." She took him along the pathway to the far end of the gardens. "It's back this way, behind the copse."

Set in a bed of flowers near the high marble wall was a statue of a man standing behind a beautiful young girl with long, flowing hair. Her head was tilted to one side, her eyes downcast. The man's hands were on her shoulder and hip. The sculptor had put strength into those hands so that it seemed the man was trying to turn the girl and embrace her. Her youthfully delicate body emanated resistance and innocence. Yet, there was restrained passion in her as well. Her eyes were hooded and her lips parted as though trying to draw breath. The conflict seemed to be less with the man than within herself.

"Look at the man's face," Arria said. "You can feel his desire and frustration. Quite . . . moving, isn't it?" She fanned her face.

Astonished to find anything so magnificent among Antigonus' collection, Marcus stood impassively studying the work. Arria's evaluation was acute. This was a masterpiece and worth a good price. However, he knew that whatever he said now would be repeated to Antigonus and would serve to drive his price up should he decide to sell it. Marcus took in the pure and elegant lines of the white marble with an air of indifference. "It is somewhat better than his usual."

"Have you no eye at all, Marcus?"

"I suppose he will get a better price for this than most of the trash he sells," he said. Were this his, he wouldn't part with it, but then, his income didn't depend upon a crew of carvers creating stone gods and goddesses for rich men's gardens.

"Trash! This is a masterpiece and you well know it."

"I've seen a dozen others exactly like it in half the gardens on Palatine."

"But none so evocative."

True, Marcus had to admit. The girl was so lifelike he felt that if he touched her, she'd be warm.

Arria's mouth curved. "Antigonus said he had the man carved behind her for modesty's sake."

Marcus laughed low. "When did Antigonus become concerned with modesty or with the censors?"

"He doesn't want to offend the traditionalists at such a sensitive time in his political career," Arria said. "You like it, don't you? I can tell by that avaricious gleam in your eyes. Do you own any of Antigonus' statues?"

"Hardly. His artisans have a common eye and my taste has never run toward corpulent women."

"Antigonus never carves corpulent women, Marcus. They are voluptuous. Surely you know the difference." She looked up at him. "Fannia is corpulent."

So little Arria had heard the rumors about his brief encounter with the senator's wife. He didn't like the proprietary look on her face. "Generously curved is a far better description of her, Arria, and far more accurate."

Her dark eyes flashed. "She looks like an overfed pigeon!"

"Arria, my sweet, it is regrettable you believe everything you hear."

Arria's chin rose. "Most rumors don't begin without a basis of truth."

"Isn't it amazing how you know so much more about my activities than I do?"

"Don't mock me, Marcus. I know it's true. Fannia was here and was quite smug about it."

"By the gods," he said, temper rising. "What'd you do? Question her before Patrobus?" It was at moments like this that Marcus found women in general a cursed bother.

"Patrobus was so busy stuffing his mouth with goose livers he paid no attention whatsoever."

"He pays little attention to Fannia. That's part of her problem."

"And one of the reasons she was so ripe for your plucking. Is that it? I suppose you'll tell me that you met with her in the Gardens of Julius only out of pity for her sad plight."

"Lower your voice!" He had done no plucking. It was Fannia herself who had approached him during one of the games. It wasn't until later that he had met her in the gardens and spent a long and ardent afternoon with her.

"She's a sow."

Marcus gritted his teeth. "And you, my dear Arria, are a bore."

Stunned by the unexpected attack, she froze for a brief instant before her pride erupted and she tried to slap him. Marcus caught her wrists easily and laughed at her fit of temper.

"A bore, am I?" Quick tears came, enraging her even more. "You unfaithful dog!"

"You've had your moments of infidelity, my dear. That retiarius, for example. Remember? You couldn't wait to tell me all about it."

"I did it to make you jealous!"

It would please her to know he had burned with fury when she related every detail of her encounter with a gladiator. He let her go, disgusted by her display and his own swift temper.

Arria bit her lip as she studied him for a moment. "What's happening to us, Marcus? There was a time when you couldn't bear to be away from me." And now, she was the one with insatiable hunger for him.

Marcus almost told her the truth and then decided it was better to appeal to her vanity. "You're like the goddess Diana. You love the hunt. You captured me some time ago."

She knew he was trying to pacify her. "But I don't have you anymore, do I, Marcus?" she said quietly, feeling the sharp pang of loss. Her eyes filled with tears. She didn't try to stop them. Perhaps tears would soften him as they had others. "I thought I meant something to you."

"You do," he said and drew her into his arms. He tipped her chin up and kissed her. She turned her face away and he felt her tremble. He turned her face back and kissed her again, feeling her grow less resistant.

"I've always admired you, Arria. Your beauty, your passion, your free spirit. You want to feast on life, and that's the way it should be. You want to try everything. So do I."

"You're the only man I've ever loved, Marcus."

He laughed. He couldn't help it.

Arria pushed out of his arms and glared up at him, tears forgotten. "How can you laugh when I'm telling you I love you?"

"Because you're such a sweet little liar. Have you so quickly and conveniently forgotten Aristobulus, Sosipater, Chuza, and several others? Even Fadus, poor fellow. I think you just wanted to see if you could win him away from his gladiator. There were bets going on over that little episode. Fortunes were lost when you actually succeeded in making him fall in love with a woman."

Her mouth curving, Arria sat on the bench and crossed her legs. Gazing up at him petulantly, she said, "But Fannia, Marcus. I must object. It's simply too humiliating. She's at least ten years older than I and not nearly as beautiful."

"Nor as experienced."

She lifted her head. "Then you weren't particularly pleased with her."

"That's none of your business."

Her mouth tightened. "Are you meeting her again?"

"That's none of your business either."

Her dark eyes flashed. "You are unfair, Marcus. I tell you everything."

"Because you're indiscreet." His mouth tipped wryly. "And cruel."

Her sultry eyes widened. "Cruel?" she said innocently. "How can you accuse me of cruelty when I've done nothing but please you from the beginning?"

"When a man thinks himself in love with a woman, he doesn't want to hear every detail of her affairs with others."

"And were you in love with me?" She rose and came to him. "Did I hurt you, Marcus? Did I really?"

He saw the satisfaction in her eyes. "No," he said frankly, watching her expression fall. She had enraged him, yes. Impassioned him frequently. Yet, she had always missed the mark of his heart. She was not alone, either. He had never felt an all-consuming passion for anyone or anything.

She ran the tip of her fingernail along his jaw. "So you don't love me?"

"I find you a pleasing distraction." Seeing her displeasure, he bent his head and brushed his lips against hers. "At times, more than distracting."

She looked troubled. "Did you ever love me, Marcus?"

He ran his finger lightly down her smooth cheek, wishing the subject of love had been avoided. "I don't think I'm capable of it." He kissed her slowly. Familiar territory.

Perhaps that was what was wrong between them. There was no mystery anymore, no great passion on his part. The feel of Arria's smooth skin, the scent of her hair, and the taste of her mouth no longer drove him mad. Even their conversations had become boring repetitions. All Arria really wanted to talk about was Arria. All the rest was subterfuge.

"I'm not ready for it to end," she said breathlessly, tilting her head back.

"I didn't say it had to."

"I know you better than Fannia."

"Will you forget about Fannia?"

"Can you? Oh, Marcus, no one will be as exciting as I am." Her hands moved over him. "I was at the temple of Astarte today and the priestess let me watch what she did to one of the worshipers. Shall I show you what she did, Marcus? Would you like that?"

Aroused, yet inexplicably disgusted, Marcus pressed her away from him. "Another time, Arria. This is hardly the place." He was too aware of other things. Laughter came from the house. A gay melody was being played on a pan flute. He wanted to drown himself in wine tonight, not a woman.

Arria looked distressed, but try as he might, Marcus could feel nothing for her.

The torchlight flickered, drawing his gaze back to the statue. Watching him, Arria tried to control her tumultuous emotions. Her mouth tightened as she saw Marcus study Antigonus' statue of the young lovers with far more interest than he had looked upon her. She longed to hear him beg the way Chuza did.

But Marcus was not like Chuza, and she didn't want to lose him. He was rich, he was handsome—and there was something about him, a restlessness and deep passion, that appealed to her.

Swallowing her pride, Arria slipped her arm through his. "You do like the statue, don't you? It's quite good. I doubt Antigonus will part with it. He's in love with them."

"We'll see," Marcus said.

They returned to the house and rejoined the party. Pensive, Marcus reclined on the couch near Antigonus. The wine flowed freely as they talked politics. Bored, Arria mentioned Marcus' fascination with the statue of the lovers. Antigonus' brows dropped and he changed the subject. Marcus suggested the possibility of future financial needs, bemoaning the cost of putting on games for the mob, parties for the aristocracy, and other expensive obligations of political office. Antigonus soon saw the need for generosity.

"The statue will be in Valerian gardens by the end of next week," he offered grandly.

Marcus knew the way Antigonus' mind worked. He conveniently forgot promises when he was drunk. Smiling slightly, Marcus poured himself and Antigonus more wine. "I'll take care of the arrangements," he said and signaled one of the slaves.

Antigonus' countenance fell as Marcus gave orders to have the statue removed to the Valerian villa within the hour.

"You *are* generous, Antigonus," Arria said. "Especially to Marcus, who has so little regard for true beauty."

Leaning back indolently, Marcus smiled at her mockingly. "True beauty is rare, and seldom recognized by the one who possesses it."

Flushed with anger, Arria rose gracefully. Smiling, she placed a slender jeweled hand on Antigonus' shoulder. "Go carefully, dear friend, lest you sell yourself to a plebeian's ambition."

Antigonus watched her walk away and then grinned at Marcus. "Fair Arria has heard about your tryst with Fannia."

"One woman is a pleasure, two a curse," Marcus said and turned the conversation back to politics and eventually to building contracts. He might as well make use of Antigonus' advent into the senate. By sunrise, he had all the guarantees he needed to spread his own name as a builder throughout Rome and fill his coffers with gold talents.

His goal would be achieved. Before he reached the age of twenty-five, he would surpass his father's wealth and position.

5

Hadassah stood straight among the long line of Jewish men and women as richly dressed Ephesian slavers walked through the captives, looking for the healthier prospects. Some measure of protection had been offered the Jewish captives as long as they marched with Titus, but now that he had departed for Alexandria, slavers fell upon them, picking over them like vultures looking for carrion to devour.

Seven hundred of the fittest and most handsome men had gone with Titus, marching south again with his legions to see the remains of Jerusalem before the journey to Egypt. From there, they'd sail to Rome. Titus would present his captives in the Triumph and send them into the games in the arena.

One woman cried out as a Roman guard stripped her of her ragged tunic, allowing the slaver a closer examination. When she tried to cover herself with her hands, the guard struck her. Sobbing, she stood still beneath the two men's perusal.

"She isn't worth a sesterce," the slaver said in disgust and moved on. The Roman threw the torn tunic against her.

The most beautiful women had long since been used by the Roman officers and then sold off in the cities through which they marched. It was a motley group that was left: old women and children mostly, and others who were too unattractive to have drawn attention from the Roman soldiers. Yet, though they weren't beautiful, they had a quality about them. They had survived months of grueling marches and hardship. In every city through which Titus passed, games had been held and thousands of captives had died. Yet these few remained alive.

When Titus had taken the Herodian princess Berenice as his mistress, there had been a brief time of hope that the Jews would be spared more games. They prayed that Berenice would deliver them as Queen Esther had done centuries before. However, Titus' love for the beautiful young princess did not bring salvation to her people. Arenas in Caesarea Philippi, Ptolemais, Tyre, Sidon, Berytus, and Antioch ran with Jewish blood. Of the thousands to leave Jerusalem, these few gaunt women remained.

Hadassah had suffered as the others. Death traveled with the captives on the road, taking them through heat, dust, meager rations, sickness, and Roman victory celebrations. When Titus' legions and the captives reached Antioch, less than half of those who had been taken from the Holy City remained alive.

The people of Antioch poured from the city to welcome Titus as a god. Doe-eyed women followed the handsome emperor's son, their children trailing after them. Recently, the free Jews of Antioch had been fighting amongst themselves, fanning the hatred of the Syrians. Clods had struck Hadassah and the others as they walked, while Syrians shouted insults at the captives and demanded they be destroyed. Roman guards finally drove the attackers back. Word spread that the Syrians wanted Titus to take the free Jews of their city along with him, but Titus refused and grew annoyed at their unceasing demands. After all, what was he to do with more Jews on his hands? Their country was destroyed, their Holy City in ruins, and he had all he needed for the games. Who wanted them?

The Syrians demanded that the brass tables on which were engraved Jewish privileges be removed from Antioch, but again, Titus refused. He went one step further and, for reasons known only to himself, made a proclamation that the free Jews of Antioch were to continue to enjoy all the privileges they had always known. If they didn't, the Syrians would answer to Rome.

While the lives of the Jews of Antioch were thus secured, the lives of the wretched captives were increasingly precarious. Determined to avoid any future conflicts in the Roman province of Judea, Titus set about scattering the Jewish survivors throughout all the countries of the Roman Empire. Able-bodied slaves were always in demand, and vast numbers were purchased in lots, roped together, and marched to ships bound for every province in the Empire.

Some Jews were sent down into the bellies of a hundred ships, where they would spend the remainder of their lives manning the oars. Others were sent to Gaul to lumber trees and provide timber for expanding Roman cities. Large groups were shipped to Spain to work cattle or toil in the silver mines. Hundreds more were sent to Greece to cut and carry marble in the quarries. The most rebellious and proud were sold to their ancestral enemies, the Egyptians. They'd die shoveling and loading sand onto barges—sand destined for the arenas of the Empire where it would soak up Jewish blood shed as entertainment for the Roman mob.

The best captives had been sold; the weakest and ugliest now remained. Hadassah was among the last few hundred to be dispersed. The dealer who now surveyed them was purchasing weavers, field hands, household servants, and prostitutes. Clenching her hands, she prayed she'd be delivered of the last.

"What about this one?" a Roman soldier said, yanking a woman from the line.

The dark Ephesian looked at her in distaste. "Ugly beyond anything I've ever seen." He moved on, speaking disparagingly of the women who remained. "Remember that I am buying slaves to serve the shrine prostitutes in the temple of Artemis. They must be somewhat attractive."

Hadassah's heart pounded sickeningly as he approached her. *Lord, let him pass me by. Let me be invisible.* Better to clean slops than serve a pagan goddess.

The slaver paused before her. Hadassah stared down at his feet, shod in fine leather sandals that were stitched with bright colors. The rich linen of his robe was blue and clean. She felt cold and sick as he continued to stare at her. She didn't raise her head. "This one has potential," the man suddenly said. He took her chin and tilted her face up. She looked into his cold eyes and almost fainted.

"She's too young," the soldier said.

"How was she passed over?" The dealer turned her face to the left and to the right. "Let's see your teeth, girl. Open your mouth." Hadassah's chin trembled as she obeyed and he studied her teeth. "Good teeth."

"She's too thin," the Roman said.

He tipped her face again, studying her closely. "Decent food will alter that."

"She's ugly."

The slaver glanced at the young soldier and smiled. "Not so ugly you haven't taken an interest in her. Have you been using her?"

Affronted and repulsed by the suggestion, the Roman legionnaire stiffened. "I've never touched her."

"Why not?"

"She is one of the righteous."

The dealer laughed. "'One of the righteous,'" he sneered. "All the more reason I should buy her. Half the men of Ephesus would like nothing better than to have access to a righteous Jewess." He looked at Hadassah again, his full mouth stretching in a smile that made her stomach turn.

A muscle jerked in the Roman soldier's face. "What's it to me if you pay thirty pieces of silver for a girl who will be dead before you reach Ephesus?"

"She looks healthy enough to me, and she has endured this long. I doubt the rigors of what she'd be required to do in the temple would kill her."

"I'd bet my salt ration she'll kill herself before you reach Ephesus."

"Why would she do that?"

"You obviously know nothing of Jews. This one would rather be dead than serve what she considers a pagan god." He grabbed the front of Hadassah's tunic and yanked her forward. "But here. Take her. One less Jew for me to worry about."

Hadassah went cold as the slaver looked at her again. Sweat broke out on her skin. The blood left her face and she swayed. The Roman's fist tightened roughly on her tunic, holding her up for the Ephesian's continued inspection.

The slaver studied her closely, his eyes narrowing. "Perhaps you are right. She looks ready to drop dead right now." He gave a contemptuous flip of his hand and moved on. "All these foul Jews. I'd rather have Egyptians."

The young soldier released her and started to follow. Impulsively, Hadassah grasped his hand. "May God bless you for your mercy," she said and kissed it.

He jerked his hand from her. "You thanked me once before. Do you remember? I gave you a scoopful of grain and you . . . " He grimaced. "I've watched you pray. Mile after mile, month after month, praying. What good has it done you?"

Tears filled her eyes.

"What good?" he said, angry and seeming to want an answer from her.

"I don't know yet."

He frowned slightly, searching her eyes. "You still believe, don't you? You're a fool. All of you are fools." He started to turn away, then looked at her again, his face rigid. "I did you no favor. Temple slaves are very well treated. Especially the prostitutes. You may have cause to curse me in time."

"Never."

"Get back in line."

"I will never curse you," she said and did as he bade her.

The slaver bought ten women and departed. A Greek slaver came the next day. Hadassah was purchased as a household slave. Roped with ten other women, she was led through the streets of Antioch. Small dark boys ran alongside the women, pelting them with dung and calling them crude names. One Jewess screamed at them hysterically and the dung became stones. The slaver's guards chased the boys off and then stripped and beat the woman who had screamed at them. To worsen her humiliation, they made her walk the rest of the way naked.

Ship masts rose before Hadassah and the smell of the sea washed over her, bringing with it piercing memories of Galilee and her father and mother, her brother and sister. Blinded by tears, she stumbled along with the other women as they were prodded up a gangplank onto the ship.

Hadassah climbed down steep steps and walked the narrow aisle between rows of rank-smelling galley slaves who manned the oars. Black-skinned Ethiopians, blue-eyed Britons, and dark-haired Gauls stared at her without emotion as she passed. A second ladder was lowered into the hull. A sickening stench of feces, urine, sweat, and vomit rose to meet her.

As she descended, she saw shadowy shapes moving. It was a moment before her eyes adjusted to the darkness and she realized she saw the second crew of galley slaves. "Women," a slave said in Greek, the single word telling how many years it had been since he had seen one.

The ropes were loosened and the grate was slammed down. Locks were set. Within seconds the naked woman was grabbed, her scream quickly smothered as other more horrible sounds came. Whimpering, Hadassah scrambled away and tried to shut out the sounds of the desperate struggling in the darkness. A fight broke out between two men. The darkened hull took on the semblance of a roiling Sheol, and Hadassah frantically hid herself in the farthest recesses of darkness.

Finally the struggle ended, and Hadassah heard a woman sobbing hysterically. When someone kicked her and told her to shut up, the woman crawled feebly through the rank mess on the planks. When she came close, Hadassah reached out and touched her. The woman jerked sharply and Hadassah spoke softly. "There is space here, beside me."

She could feel her violent trembling as the woman huddled next to her in the darkness. Her shaking increased. Hadassah touched cold, clammy skin. She had no words to comfort her, though she wanted desperately to do so. The woman started to cry again, stifling the sound this time against her raised knees.

Hadassah's throat closed. She removed her overdress and gave it to the woman, leaving only the long gray tunic to cover herself. "Put this on," she said softly. Shivering violently, the woman did as Hadassah instructed. Hadassah put her arms around the woman and held her close, stroking her foul-matted hair as she had stroked her mother's.

"Blessed is the barren woman who never sees her child come to this," someone moaned.

Silence fell upon the occupants of the hull. Only the creaking of the ship, the boom on the drum as a cadence was beaten out for the galley slaves, and the slide of the oars broke it. The grate was slammed back several times a day, and the rested slaves ordered above, while the exhausted were sent below. Sometimes a whip cracked sharply, drawing a gasp of pain from someone who was sluggish.

Day and night ran together. Hadassah slept, awakening when the locks were released and the grate slammed back as crews changed or meager rations were dispensed. The roll of the ship increased the misery of some as they lay ill in the fetid darkness. The air was close and foul. Hadassah longed for a breath of clean air and dreamed of Galilee.

A storm struck as the ship sailed along the Lycian coast. The ship rose high and crashed down against the waves as the wind moaned and screamed. The slaves panicked, scrambling for handholds and crying out in half a dozen languages for half a dozen gods to save them.

Icy water splashed down into the hull and ran back and forth, soaking Hadassah's ragged tunic as she held onto a ship rib. Shivering, she clung fast and prayed silently amidst the screaming. The ship rose so sharply it seemed it would soar from the water. Then it dropped as suddenly, making her stomach drop with it. The hull struck the sea with a loud crack, and the entire ship shuddered as though it would fall apart.

"We're going to die! Let us out!"

Men clawed frantically at the grate as more water poured down upon them. "Let us out! *Let us out!*"

As the ship rolled again, someone fell against Hadassah and broke her hold. She slid away and slammed against a beam as the ship rose again. The roaring sound of the sea was like a wild beast. The ship rolled to one side, and she felt cold water wash over her. *Oh, Father, help us! Save us as you saved the disciples on the Sea of Galilee.* She sought a hold and found none. Then something struck her heavily in the head, and sound receded. She floated in darkness, past feeling anything.

It was the steady cadence of the drum and of the dip of the oars that awakened her. The sound of the sea hitting the bow and lapping the sides of the ship soothed her throbbing temples. She thought she had been dreaming. Her head ached; her tunic was drenched, her hair as well. The hull was awash with seawater. Two slaves filled skins and hooked them to a rope to be lifted and emptied.

A woman sat beside her and touched her brow. "How are you feeling?"

"My head aches a little. What happened?"

"You hit your head during the storm."

"It's over then."

"Long since. The crews have changed four times since it eased. I heard the guard say we are passing Rhodes." She opened a soiled cloth and held it out to Hadassah. "I saved you some grain."

"Thank you," Hadassah said and took the offering.

"You gave me your tunic," the woman said, and Hadassah knew who she was.

Days and nights melted together in dark silence. While filth, poor food, no privacy, and abuse dehumanized some, these things drove Hadassah to God. Her father had said suffering brought endurance in order that one might be strengthened for whatever lay ahead. She didn't like to think about what lay ahead. There were too many horrible possibilities. Death came in too many ways.

God was all-seeing, all-powerful, all-present, and her father had always assured her that all things worked toward God's good purpose. Yet she could find no purpose in what she and those around her suffered. Like herself, others had merely been in Jerusalem at the wrong time. They'd been trapped like rabbits before a pack of hounds. Zealot or Roman, she could see no difference. They were all men of violence.

Many family friends had believed that the end times of which Jesus had spoken were upon them, that the Lord would return and reign in their own lifetime. Some had even gone so far as to sell everything they owned and give the money to the church. Then they'd sat back to wait for the end. Her father was not one of these. He went on as always, working his trade.

"God will return in his own good time, Hadassah. He told the disciples he would come like a thief in the night. For that reason, I don't think he'll be expected. We only know he will come. It's not for us to know when."

Surely the destruction of the temple and city of Zion were signs that the end of the world was upon them. Surely the Lord would return now. She wanted him to come. She yearned for him. Yet, a deep sense within her warned against quick rescues. God didn't always intervene. Throughout Scripture he had used pagan nations to bring Israel to her knees.

"'Come, and let us return to the Lord;'" the woman whispered, "'For He has torn, but He will heal us; He has stricken, but He will bind us up. After two days He will revive us; on the third day He will raise us up, that we may live in His sight.'"

Voice trembling, Hadassah took up where the woman had stopped, reciting the words of the prophet Hosea. "'Let us know, let us press on to know the Lord; his appearing is as sure as the dawn; he will come to us like the showers, like the spring rains that water the earth.'"

The woman took Hadassah's hand. "Why is it only in darkness that we remember what sustained us even in the light? I have not thought of the words of the prophet since childhood, and now in this darkness they come to me more clearly than the day I heard them read." She cried softly. "Jonah must have felt this same dark despair inside the belly of the whale."

"Hosea was speaking of Yeshua and the Resurrection," Hadassah said, without thinking.

The woman let go of her hand and peered at her in the darkness. "You are a *Christian?*" The word sounded like a curse. Frightened, Hadassah didn't answer. She felt the chill of the woman's animosity. The silence that grew between them was thicker than a wall. Hadassah wanted to say something, but could find no words. "How can you believe our Messiah has come?" the woman hissed at her. "Are we delivered from the Romans? Does our God reign?" She began to weep.

"Yeshua came to atone for us," Hadassah whispered.

"I lived by the law of Moses all my life. Don't speak to me of atonement," the woman said, her face ravaged by bitter emotion and grief. She got up and moved away, sitting near several other women. She glared at Hadassah for a long moment and then turned her face away.

Hadassah put her head against her knees and fought against despair.

When the ship reached Ephesus, the women slaves were brought above deck and tied together again. Hadassah drank in the fresh sea air. After long days and nights in the belly of the ship, it was several moments before her eyes adjusted to the bright sunlight and she could see around her. The docks were alive with bustling activity. Workers were everywhere, plying their trades. Darkly tanned *stuppatores* worked on scaffolding to caulk a ship docked beside the one that had carried Hadassah. To her left was another Roman vessel. *Sburarii* struggled up the ladders, shouldering sacks of sand. Plodding down the planks, they dumped the ballast into a wagon, which would haul the sacks away to an Ephesian arena.

Other workers called *sacrarii* carried grain sacks and dropped them on scales. *Mensores* then weighed them and wrote in ledgers. A man stumbled and a box fell into the sea. A naked *urinator* dove for it.

Orders were shouted in half a dozen languages from as many ships. A whip cracked again and the guard in charge of Hadassah's group shouted for the women to go down the plank. They were led along a street lined with merchant stalls and filled with clamoring patrons. Many stopped and stared. Others shouted insults: "Foul stinking Jews!"

Hadassah burned with shame. Her hair was crawling with lice, her tunic stinking and stained with human excrement. A Greek woman spit on her as she passed and Hadassah bit her lip to keep from crying.

They were taken to the baths. A robust woman roughly stripped her of the ragged tunic and then shaved off all of her hair. Humiliated, Hadassah wished she could die. Worse came when the woman rubbed a foul-smelling salve into every curve and crevice of her body. "Remain standing over there until I tell you to wash," the woman said tersely. The salve burned like fire. After several excruciating minutes, the woman ordered her into the next room. "Scrub yourself thoroughly or I will do it for you," the woman said. Hadassah obeyed, grateful to rid herself of the crusted filth that had accumulated on her body during the long journey and voyage. The salve had killed the vermin.

She was doused with icy water and ordered to the baths.

Hadassah entered a vast room in which there was a huge pool shaped of white and green marble. A guard was present, and she hastened into the water to hide her nakedness. The man scarcely noticed her.

The warm water soothed Hadassah's burning skin. She'd never been in a Roman bath before and looked around in awe. The walls were tiled murals that were so wondrously beautiful that it was a moment before Hadassah realized the scenes depicted pagan gods seducing earthly women. Her cheeks burned and she lowered her gaze.

The guard ordered her and the others from the pool and into another chamber where they were given gray towels to dry themselves. They were handed clothing, and Hadassah pulled the simple tan tunic and dark brown overdress over her head. She wrapped the red-and-brown striped cloth around her waist twice and tied it securely. The long frayed ends hung against her hip. She was handed a light brown cloth to drape over her bare head. She tied it at the back of her neck to secure it. Lastly, the shameful slave necklace was fitted on her and then a slate was hung around her neck.

The owner entered when they were finished. When he came to stand in front of Hadassah, he studied her carefully. Then he lifted the slate and wrote something on it before moving on to the next.

Roped together, they were taken to the slave market. The owner haggled with the auctioneer until a commission was agreed upon. Then a hawker was sent into the thronging quay to attract a crowd. "Jewish women for sale!" the hawker shouted. "Best of Titus' captives at the lowest prices!" When a throng was gathered, the owner untied one woman and ordered her to stand on a huge round table fashioned like a potter's wheel. A half-naked slave stood with a rope over his broad shoulder, awaiting the order to turn it.

Jests and insults were flung at the woman by the onlookers. "Strip her and let us see what you're really selling!" one shouted. "Cursed Jews! Send them to the dogs in the arena!" The woman stood erect, eyes staring straight ahead as the wheel was turned so that those staring at her could see all sides of the merchandise offered.

However, there were those present who were in search of slaves for their households. One by one, the women were sold as a cook, a weaver, two seamstresses, a child's nurse, a kitchen slave, and a water carrier. As each was sold, she was ordered down from the great wheel and led away on a rope by her new master. Hadassah felt bereft watching them go.

She was the last to stand on the wheel.

"She's small and skinny, but she made the march to Antioch from Jerusalem, so she's strong. She'll make a good household slave!" the auctioneer said and opened the bidding at thirty sesterces as he had with the others. No one offered, so he lowered the price to twenty-five, then twenty, then fifteen.

A thin man in a white toga with purple trim finally purchased her. She came down from the wheel and stood before him, her head bowed in obeisance, her hands clasped. The longer he studied her, the tighter seemed the brass slave collar. When he yanked the cloth from her head, she glanced up just long enough to look into his dismayed eyes. "What a pity they shaved your head," he said. "With hair, you might look more like a female." He thrust the cloth at her, and she quickly retied it.

"I wonder which god is playing a joke on me this time," he muttered in great annoyance as he took the rope that tied her wrists and began to walk briskly along the dock. Hadassah took two steps to his one, hurrying to keep up with him. Her side began to ache.

Procopus dragged her along behind him, wondering what to do with her. His wife, Ephicharis, would have his head if he took her home with him. Ephi despised Jews, calling them treacherous and worthy of extermination. Her best friend's son had been killed in Judea. He shook his head. What had possessed him to buy the girl in the first place? And what was he to do with her now? Ten sesterces for this mite. Ridiculous. He had been wandering the docks, minding his own business, dreaming of sailing off to Crete and leaving all his troubles behind when he had followed that hawker. He'd been curious to see the Jewish captives and had felt an unfamiliar pity when this one had had no buyer.

He shouldn't have gone to the docks today. He should have gone to the baths and had a massage. His head ached; he was hungry; he was furious with himself for feeling the least pity for this sprout. Had he kept his hand at his side, someone else would have her on a rope at this moment and he wouldn't have this problem to deal with.

Maybe he would make a gift of her to Tiberius and thus get her off his hands. Tiberius liked young girls, especially those too young to get pregnant. He glanced back at her. Her wide brown eyes flickered up to his and then dropped quickly away. Scared to death. And why not? Most of her race was dead. Hundreds of thousands of them, from what he had heard. Not that the Jews didn't deserve extermination after all the trouble they had been to Rome.

He frowned heavily. Tiberius wouldn't want her. She was all bones and drawn skin and great, dark suffering eyes. Even a satyr couldn't be aroused by such as this. Who else then?

Clementia perhaps. She might need another maid, but he didn't feel like facing his vitriolic mistress today. He doubted the gift of a scrawny female slave would endear him to her, especially as he hadn't had the time to see his jeweler and purchase the needed bauble to dangle before her avaricious eyes. She was still furious over the brooch he had given her. He had not realized she was so astute, nor had he considered the possibility she'd have it so quickly appraised.

"After all your promises, how dare you give me an imitation!" she'd screamed at him, flinging the lovely piece of jewelry at his head. Women were grotesquely unattractive when they wept, especially when the tears were inspired by rage. Clementia's normally lovely countenance had been twisted into a mask of such ugliness that Procopus had retrieved the disparaged bauble and fled the apartment. His wife had accepted it with appropriate appreciation.

Several Roman centurions stood guard over a line of ragged, emaciated slaves who were roped together and boarding a ship. There were forty or more men and women in the group. "Where are you bound for?" Procopus called to the commander who stood at the top of the loading plank.

"Rome," he called down.

Hadassah's heart plunged. She looked at the captives and knew their fate. *Oh God, spare me, please.*

"Are they Jews?"

"What do they look like? Roman citizens?"

"Would you have use of another?" Procopus said, yanking the rope and pulling Hadassah forward. "Fifteen sesterces and you can have her." The Roman laughed derisively. "Ten, then." The Roman ignored him. "She's strong enough to have made the march from Antioch. She's strong enough for whatever you have in mind for those slaves."

"Strength won't be required of them."

"I'll sell her to you for seven sesterces."

"I wouldn't pay one coin for a Jew," the Roman called down. "Be off with you."

Procopus gave Hadassah a shove forward. "You can have her then! For nothing! Take her to Rome with the rest." He tossed her rope out of his hands. "Go on and get in line with the others," he ordered her. "I wash my hands of you."

Hadassah watched him stride away and felt the brief flicker of hope dwindling. "Move along," the legionnaire said and pushed her. When she reached the top of the plank, she looked into the commander's face. He was weathered by years of campaigning and stared back at her with hard, cold eyes.

Festus despised Jews. Too many of his friends had died at their treacherous hands for him to feel pity for even a small girl like this one. He had watched her lips move as she came up the plank and knew she was beseeching her unseen god to save her. She was the only Jew in the bunch who had looked him full in the face, straight into his eyes. He caught hold of her rope and yanked her out of line. She looked at him again. He saw only fear, no rebellion.

"You're bound for Rome," he said. "You know what that means, don't you? The arena. I watched you beseech your god to save you, but you're still bound for Rome, aren't you?"

When she said nothing, he grew angrier.

"Do you understand Greek?"

"Yes, my lord."

Her voice was soft, but held no tremor. Festus' lips hardened. "It would seem your unseen god doesn't mean to spare you after all, does he? What have you to say to that?"

She looked up at him. “If God wills that I die, then I die. No power on earth can change that.”

Simple words, quietly spoken and from a frail girl, but in them lay the seeds of more bloody rebellion. Festus’ lips tightened. “There is only one true power on this earth, girl, and it is the power of Rome.” He jerked his head at the centurion standing by. “Take her below with the rest.”

6

Chains rattling and manacles digging into his ankles, Atretes was forced down off the wagon just inside the gates of the ludus of Capua. Malcenas had purchased nine other men on the way south, several purely for their size. Atretes learned quickly that they had no heart for blood, nor wits for a good fight. Like beasts of burden, they followed every order given. The German warrior held them in contempt.

Atretes moved sluggishly, aching from the beating he'd taken after his latest escape attempt. "Get in line," the guard ordered and swung his whip. Atretes drew in a quick breath as his back was laced with sharp needles of pain. He cursed the guard and was shoved into line.

Malcenas walked down the line of men in chains, issuing orders. "Stand up straight!" he snapped to one, and a guard jabbed the obviously ill slave into compliance. The other captives kept their eyes downcast in proper subservience—except for Atretes, who spread his legs and glared openly at the merchant, showing all the hate he felt pumping through him. A guard lay his whip hard across his shoulders. Other than a flinch, Atretes didn't alter his manner. "Enough," Malcenas said before the whip was used again. "I don't want him marked up any more than he already is."

Consumed with pain, Atretes squinted his eyes against the sunlight, trying to study his surroundings and judge any possibility of escape. High, thick stone walls surrounded him. Iron bars, heavy doors, and alert armed guards boded a grim future of enforced servitude to his enemy. In front of him, men were training for the arena. So, they meant to make a gladiator of him, did they?

The instructor was easy to spot, for he was tall, powerfully built, wore a heavily armored leather tunic, and was the only one carrying a gladius, which remained in the sheath at his belt. It was more for appearance than for anything else. He didn't need it for protection or to enforce his orders.

Malcenas noted where the young German's gaze was fixed and grinned maliciously. "That's Tharacus. It wouldn't do you well to annoy him as you've annoyed me these past weeks. He's been known to slit the throat of a slave for no reason other than to make an example."

Atretes had learned a little Greek during his few weeks of captivity, but he cared nothing about Malcenas' threat. He made a sudden move as though to attack the merchant and laughed at the Roman's quick retreat. It was the only pleasure Atretes had left—seeing a man who called himself "master" recoil in fear of him. "Had you been born a Chatti, we would have drowned you in a bog," he sneered.

Malcenas didn't need to understand German to know he had been grossly insulted. Red-faced with rage, he grabbed the guard's whip and struck Atretes across the chest, ripping away skin. Atretes sucked in his breath, but didn't move. He looked at Malcenas and then spit at his feet.

"Scorpus arrives," one of the guards said when Malcenas again raised the whip.

Lowering it, Malcenas tossed it back to a nearby guard. "Watch him."

"We ought to kill him," the guard muttered.

"He's the only one worth selling," Malcenas said grimly. But remembering he had guests, Malcenas turned away with a confident smile and politic greeting.

Atretes watched a man flanked by two armed guards greet "the master." The guest had the look of a soldier, but was garbed like a soft Roman aristocrat. After a brief perusal, Atretes returned his attention to the men training behind the grid wall. They were a mixed lot, brought from the farthest reaches of the Roman Empire. Tattooed Britons, olive-skinned Gauls, black Africans all moved with each shouted command. Armed only with wooden swords, they went through their drills, every man moving in unison to the deep voice of Tharacus. "Thrust, parry, swing high and round, block, turn, thrust. *Again.*"

Atretes studied the compound, searching again for possible ways of escape. His hopes quickly dwindled. He had never seen a place more fortified. The walls were thick and high, every door heavy-timbered and equipped with double bolts and locks, and there were armed guards everywhere, some looking down at him as though they could sense his mind and were prepared to stop him.

Malcenas' laughter grated, making Atretes' blood heat; he

longed to feel Malcenas' fat neck between his hands. Even if it were the last thing he did in this world, he wanted the satisfaction of killing Malcenas.

"Well, Scorpus? Do you see any that suit your needs?" Malcenas said, smugly aware that the wealthy proprietor of the ludus had fixed his attention on that defiant German. "He is beautiful, isn't he?" He tried not to sound like he was rubbing his hands together.

"I'm not interested in beauty, Malcenas," Scorpus said dryly. "Stamina and endurance are far more profitable."

"He has both."

"Where did you get him?"

"On the frontier of Germania. He was high chieftain of one of the tribes and killed more than twenty soldiers in a single battle."

"A typical exaggeration, Malcenas. He's too young to be a high chief," Scorpus said and walked along the line of men. He noted every flaw from rotting teeth to sallow skin. Malcenas was edgy and argued halfheartedly, his gaze returning frequently to the German. Obviously he was eager to be rid of the barbarian. Scorpus returned to the young man and studied him again. Malcenas looked uneasy, sweat beading his brow and upper lip.

"He's taken several beatings by the looks of him. What cause, Malcenas? Did he object to your advances?"

Malcenas was not amused. "He attempted escape," Malcenas said, motioning his guards closer. "Four times." It wouldn't do to have Scorpus attacked within his own ludus, and that young barbarian was mad enough to do it.

Scorpus noted the movement of the guards. The German did have a certain look about him. Malcenas was sweating in fear of him, and Scorpus found that amusing. The blue eyes staring back at him were fierce and full of open hatred. Untamed ferocity was worth buying. "How much for him?"

"Fifty thousand sesterces," Malcenas said, casting a quick silent prayer to Mars to be free of the heathen.

"*Fifty* thousand?"

"He's worth it."

"The whole lot of them are not worth fifty thousand sesterces. Where did you find them? Picking grapes or building roads? Down in the mines, perhaps? They have all the intelligence and life of stones." Except the German, who appeared to have some intelligence—something that was both desirable and dangerous.

Malcenas haggled a moment over price, but Scorpus shook his head, looking over two others. Malcenas ground his teeth; he wanted to be rid of that young German even if it meant selling him for a lower price than he was worth. The young devil had already killed one of his guards on the way here, and Malcenas knew the German would like nothing better than to kill him as well. He saw it in those cold eyes every time he looked at him. He felt it now, raising the hair on the back of his neck and turning his bowels to water.

"I'll let you have the German for forty thousand sesterces, but that is as low as I can go."

"Keep him then," Scorpus said. "How much for this one?" He stood looking over a Gaul that Malcenas had purchased from a road crew.

As usual, Scorpus was correct in his assessment of the stock Malcenas had brought. Most of the men standing in line had not the wits to last five minutes in the arena. "Ten thousand," Malcenas said, not even looking at the man he was pricing. Instead, he glanced warily back at the German, feeling the chill of those blue eyes right into the marrow of his bones. He wasn't going to travel another mile with that devil. "Match the German against Tharacus if you don't think he's worth the price I've set on him." If he couldn't sell the German, he'd have the satisfaction of seeing him die.

Scorpus glanced at him in surprise. "Tharacus?" He laughed without humor. "Do you mean to see this one slaughtered before he's sold? He wouldn't last one minute with Tharacus."

"Put a framea in his hands and see what he can do," Malcenas said in challenge.

Scorpus smiled mockingly. "I think you're afraid of him, Malcenas. Even with all your guards to protect you."

The taunt smarted. If it weren't for Malcenas, Scorpus would have to leave his lavish quarters and look for stock for his ludus. Gritting his teeth, Malcenas said coldly, "He's attempted escape four times; the last time he killed one of my men. Broke his neck."

Scorpus' brows rose. "Four attempts." He looked at the young German again. "He does have a certain air about him, doesn't he? He looks as though he'd like nothing better than to drink your blood. All right, Malcenas. I'll take him off your hands. Thirty thousand sesterces."

"Done," Malcenas said, far from pleased with the meager profit he'd make. "And the others?"

"Just him."

"The Gaul is strong and well proportioned."

"Just the barbarian."

Malcenas took a step back as he ordered his guards to remove the leg chains from Atretes. "Make sure his hands are securely chained behind him before you remove the ankle restraints," he ordered. Scorpus laughed derisively, but Malcenas was too afraid to take offense.

Heart pounding faster, Atretes stood placidly as the locks were released and the chains pulled through the rings of the other slaves. One chance, that's all he would have—one chance. Tiwaz would see him die a warrior. The guard pulled the chains through the rings on the ankle manacles, freeing four other slaves before he reached Atretes. Another guard breathed down his neck. "You try anything, and I'll club you down like the dog you are." He yanked the chains hard around Atretes' wrists to make sure they were well secured.

As the chain rang free of his ankle manacles, Atretes' blood caught fire and he exploded into action. Ramming the full force of his body back against the guard behind him, he brought his leg up and slammed his foot into the groin of the one in front. Giving his battle cry, he shook off another who tried to take him down and made a run at Malcenas, who screeched frantic orders as he fled madly for cover.

Laughing, Scorpus watched Malcenas' guards attempt to get the German back in control. When it was clear that more than Malcenas were in fear of the German and could not stop him, Scorpus snapped his fingers and his own guards took over the situation. "You can come back now and watch, Malcenas!" he called out mockingly. "Our German is being subdued."

Atretes struggled violently, but Scorpus' men were stronger and quicker. Working together, two set their full strength against him as a third looped a thick cord around his neck. With his hands chained behind him, Atretes couldn't break the hold. His air was cut off and the blood could not get to his brain. The cord tightened. Jerking violently as he choked, he fell to his knees. His vision blurred, and he dropped forward into the dirt as the hard weight of a man's knee bore into the middle of his back. The heavy cord was loosened—but not removed—and Atretes was allowed to drag air into his burning lungs. He gagged on dust and rasped out a curse.

"Stand him up," Scorpus ordered indolently. Malcenas approached cautiously, his face pale and streaked with sweat.

"Sabinus, I want you to translate what I say exactly." The guard nodded and did as he was ordered. "My name is Scorpus Proctor Carpophorus and I own you. You will take the oath of a gladiator to suffer yourself to be whipped with rods, burned with fire, or killed with steel if you disobey me. Do you understand?"

Atretes spit on his feet.

Scorpus' eyes narrowed. "You were right in asking fifty thousand sesterces, Malcenas. A pity you didn't hold out for it." At a signal, Atretes was subjected to a savage beating, but still he glared in silence at Carpophorus, refusing to take the oath.

Scorpus nodded to his officer and the beating began again.

"I consider myself fortunate to be rid of him," Malcenas said with feeling. "You'd do well to take extra precautions where he's concerned. If he doesn't take the oath now, he'll think he's bested you."

Scorpus halted the beating with a small wave of his hand. "There are other ways to make a man like him capitulate. I've no desire to break his spirit, only his will." Scorpus glanced at Sabinus. "Brand him and put him in the Hole."

Atretes understood the command that he be branded a slave of Rome and uttered a cry of rage, struggling violently as the guards half dragged him toward the iron grid door. The door was slammed and locked behind Atretes as his guards shoved him along to the forge, where an iron with emblems on the end was placed in the red coals. He fought harder, uncaring when the cord tightened, choking him. Better to be dead than to bear the brand of Rome.

One man lost hold of Atretes and crashed against a table. The one behind him swore and ordered two more to get a firmer grip. Atretes went down and was held there while the hot iron seared through the layers of skin on his heel. Atretes couldn't hold back a guttural sound of pain as the mark was burned deeply into him, the sickeningly sweet stench of his own burning flesh filling the air. Then he was dragged to his feet again.

Atretes was taken along a stone block corridor, down stairs, and along another corridor. A heavy door was opened, his chains were removed, and he was forced to his knees and shoved forcefully into a tiny dark chamber. The door slammed behind him and a bar dropped solidly into place, the sound echoing in Atretes' brain. He wanted to scream. The walls were tight about him, the stone ceiling so low he couldn't sit up, and the chamber was so short, he couldn't stretch out his legs. He pushed with all his strength against the door, but it didn't move. He cursed and heard the guards laugh as their hobnailed shoes echoed softly by. "I'll make you a bet," Sabinus said. "One day is all it'll take and he'll be screaming for mercy." Another door closed, and then there was silence.

Panic rose. Atretes closed his eyes tightly, struggling for control as the walls of the small chamber seemed to close in on him. Gritting his teeth, he didn't make a sound, knowing if he did, he'd be giving in to the terror filling him. His heart pounded heavily and he could hardly breathe. He kicked at the door with all his strength, ignoring the throbbing pain of the brand, and kept kicking until his heels were bruised.

Atretes panted in fear, sweating profusely. *One day is all it will take and he'll be screaming.* He said the words over and over again to himself until rage overwhelmed the fear.

Hours passed in total darkness.

To keep himself from going mad, Atretes curled on his side and tried to envision himself in the forests of his homeland. He had no water; he had no food. His muscles cramped, and he groaned in pain, unable to stretch out enough to ease them. Lice crawled on him and bit into his flesh. He kicked at the door again and cursed Rome with every breath.

"He'll cooperate now," a guard said. The door opened. As the guard bent down, Atretes kicked him in the face and sent him crashing back. Atretes tried to keep the door open, but the second guard forced it closed and locked it again. He could hear the injured guard swearing in German.

"Two days doesn't seem to have improved his disposition," another said.

"Let him rot in there! Do you hear me? You're going to rot!"

Atretes shouted curses back and kicked the door. His heart pounded and his breath came fast and hard. "Tiwaz!" he screamed, filling the chamber with his war cry. "*Tiwaz!*" He screamed the name of his god until he was hoarse, then lay in a ball, fighting the fear that once again rose in him.

Smothered in darkness and drifting in nightmares, he lost

touch with time. When the door opened, he thought he was dreaming, but knew he wasn't when strong hands gripped his ankles and straightened his legs, sending pain shooting up through his body. His muscles cramped and he couldn't stand. A gourd was held to his lips, and he gulped the water that spilled from it. Hauled to his feet, his arms were slung across the shoulders of two guards. They took him to a large room and dumped him into a stone pool.

"You stink!" the guard said in German and tossed a sponge against Atretes' chest. His nose was swollen and bruised, and Atretes knew him to be the guard he kicked. "Wash yourself or we'll do it for you."

Atretes looked at him in contempt. "How does a tribesman happen to be a menial of Rome?" he said through cracked lips.

The guard's face tightened. "I heard you screaming last night. Another day in the Hole and you'll lose your mind and whatever honor you think you have left, just like I did!"

Atretes clenched his fists and washed, sensing the two guards nearby. They spoke and Atretes learned that the German's name was a Romanized *Gallus*.

Gallus caught Atretes studying him and returned his full attention. "I was taken captive much the same as you and became a slave of Rome," he said. "I made the best of it." He held up a small rectangular piece of ivory with writing on it that hung from a chain around his neck. "It took seven years of fighting in the arena, but I earned my freedom." He dropped the ivory. "You could do the same, maybe even in less time if you put your mind to it."

Atretes glanced pointedly around the stone block walls and at the armed guard at the top of the stairs, then looked into Gallus' eyes. "I see no freedom here." He stood, naked and dripping. "Do I dry myself or is that for your pleasure?"

Gallus took a towel from a shelf and slapped it against Atretes' chest. "Careful, slave. You will learn or you will die. Your choice, which means nothing to me." He nodded toward a shelf of clothing. "Take a tunic, a belt, and a robe, and put them on."

Atretes glanced up the ladder, his mind churning, but he noted another guard had joined the first.

"I wouldn't try anything if I were you," Gallus said, hand on the hilt of his gladius.

Clenching his jaws, Atretes donned the clothing and climbed

the ladder. Two guards walked in front of him and two in back. They were taking no chances. The corridor was long, with one chamber after another on both sides. Gallus stopped and opened one. "Your new home. Until you're sold."

"He doesn't seem overly eager to go in," a guard said derisively and shoved Atretes roughly inside the small room. Atretes flinched as the door was slammed behind him and the bar was dropped into place. "Sleep well," Gallus said through the small grate.

The dark-shadowed and dank chamber was seven feet long and four feet wide. A thin, straw-filled mattress lay on a stone shelf. Beneath it was a clay pot for slops. Graffiti was scratched into the stone walls. Atretes couldn't read, but the pictures were clear enough. Men fighting and dying. Men and women coupling. Lines, one after another, as though a man had counted the days. A niche had been carved into the back wall for an idol—a hideous squatting goddess with a dozen breasts.

Shadows cast by a torch flickered through an iron-grated opening above his head. Atretes heard hobnailed shoes scraping the stone and looked up to see a guard briefly peering down at him before continuing his rounds.

Atretes sat down on the pallet. Raking his fingers back through his hair, he held his head in his hands for a long moment, then leaned back against the cold stone wall. He was shaking again, inside as well as out.

It seemed hours before he heard doors opening and others entering the corridor. Someone whispered and a guard shouted for silence. One door at a time was opened and closed as the men were locked into their chambers for the night. A long silence followed. Atretes heard a man crying.

Lying down on the stone shelf, he closed his eyes and tried to envision the forests of Germania, the faces of his family and friends. He couldn't. All he could see in his mind was the compound and those men going through their practiced movements.

Sounds of the guard walking back and forth above came with grim regularity, beating into Atretes' brain that there would be no escape from this place. No escape but death.

He awakened at the shout of a guard and stood waiting for his door to be opened. His door was passed by. He listened and heard the men filing out of the barracks, and then silence closed about him again. He sat, gripping the edge of the stone shelf.

Finally, Gallus opened the door. "Take off the over robe and follow me," he said. Two other guards fell in behind him as Atretes came out into the corridor. He felt weak from lack of food and wondered if they meant to feed him or let him starve. They took him to the training compound and Tharacus, the *lanista,* or head trainer, of the ludus.

Tharacus' face was weathered and hard, and his dark eyes were shrewd. A scar ran the length of one cheek and half of one ear was cut off, but he, too, wore an ivory rectangle around his neck, signifying he'd earned his freedom in the arena.

"We have a new slave from Germania," he announced loudly to the formation of men. "He thinks he's a fighter. But we know that all Germans are cowards. When they fight, they hide behind trees and rely on the ambush! Then, as soon as the battle turns against them, as it always does, they run for the woods."

Some of the men laughed, but Atretes stood silent and rigid, watching Tharacus walk back and forth before the trainees. The heat built higher inside him with each insult the lanista uttered, but the alert and well-armed guards posted every few feet around the slaves convinced Atretes that there was nothing he could do.

"Yes, we know Germans are good at running," Tharacus said, taunting Atretes further. "Now, let's see if they can stand and fight like men." He stopped in front of Atretes. "What's your name, slave?" He spoke in a German dialect. Atretes looked at him placidly and said nothing. Tharacus struck him hard across the face.

"I'll ask again," Tharacus said, a small tight smile curving his mouth. "Your name."

Atretes noisily sucked the blood from a cut in his mouth and spit it in the sand.

A second blow knocked him off his feet. Without thinking, Atretes lunged up and forward, but the lanista kicked him back and drew his gladius. Atretes felt the tip of that sword at his throat before he could make another move.

"You'll give your name," Tharacus said evenly, "or I'll put an end to you right now."

Atretes stared at the unrelenting face above him and knew Tharacus meant it. Death he'd welcome if he were on his feet and had a framea in his hand, but he wouldn't lose his honor by dying on his back in the dust. "Atretes," he grated, glaring up at the lanista.

"Atretes," Tharacus said, testing the name, the sword still in position for a quick kill. "Listen well, young Atretes. Obey and you'll live, defy me again and I'll slit your throat like a pig and hang you up by your feet so you'll drain before the ludus for all the world to see." He flicked the sword tip just enough to break the skin and draw a few drops of blood to show it was not an idle threat. "Do you understand? *Answer me.* Do you understand?"

"Yes," Atretes said through his teeth.

Tharacus stepped back and sheathed the gladius. "Get up."

Atretes rose.

"I was told you could fight," Tharacus said with a mocking smile. "So far you've shown me nothing but stupidity." He nodded to a guard. "Give him one of the poles." He took one for himself and took a fighting stance. "Let's see what you can do."

Atretes didn't need a second invitation. He weighed the pole in his hands as he moved around the lanista, ducking and parrying and managing a few solid blows before Tharacus made a quick turn and brought the pole up beneath his chin. Another swift blow behind his legs sent him crashing down, then another across the side of his head kept him there. Stunned, Atretes lay on his face, gasping for breath.

"Not good enough to survive in the arena," Tharacus said, contemptuously, kicking Atretes' pole away. He tossed his own to the guard standing by and then stood over him. *"Get up!"*

Face burning with shame, Atretes regained his feet. All muscles rigid, he waited for whatever humiliation the lanista planned next. With a word of dismissal from Tharacus, the others went with their armed guards and instructors to various sections of the compound.

Tharacus returned his attention to him. "Scorpus paid a high price for you. I expected a better performance." Pride smarting, Atretes clenched his teeth and said nothing. Tharacus smiled coldly. "You were surprised to be dropped so quickly, weren't you? Ah, but you were in chains for five weeks, and then in the Hole for four days. Perhaps that accounts for your weakened state and befuddled mind." His demeanor changed subtly. "Arrogance and stupidity will kill you quicker than lack of skill. Keep that in mind and you might live."

Getting back to business, Tharacus looked him over critically. "You need more weight, exercise, and conditioning. And you'll be tested. When I'm convinced you're worth my time, you'll join those I train." He nodded toward a motley group of men who were exercising in the far corner of the compound. "Until that time, you're assigned to Trophimus."

Atretes glanced toward a short, muscular officer shouting at a dozen men who looked as though they'd come from the mines, not a battlefield. Atretes sneered. Tharacus drew his gladius and slammed the flat of it against Atretes, cold steel pressed against his abdomen.

"I was informed you killed a Roman guard on your way here," Tharacus said. "You don't seem afraid to die. I believe only the manner of it disturbs you. That's good. A gladiator who's afraid of death is a disgrace. But I warn you, Atretes, insurrection isn't tolerated here. Lay one hand on a guard and you'll curse the day you were born." Atretes felt the blood draining from his face as Tharacus brought the gladius down and up slightly so that he felt its edge against his manhood. "Wouldn't you rather die with a sword in your hands than be castrated?"

Tharacus laughed softly. "I've got your ear now, haven't I, young Atretes?" He pressed the edge of the sword dangerously closer. The mockery died. "I was told you refused to take the gladiator's oath when Scorpus ordered it. You'll swear it to me now, or become a eunuch. They're much in demand in Rome."

Atretes had no choice. He obeyed the command.

Tharacus sheathed his gladius. "We'll see now if a German barbarian has the courage and honor to uphold his word. Report to Trophimus."

Atretes spent the rest of the morning running through a series of obstacles, but having been chained in a wagon for weeks, and denied food for several days, he tired quickly. Even so, the others fared worse than he. One man accused of laziness was whipped every step of the way through the course.

At the sound of a whistle, Trophimus ordered them into single line. They filed into a dining compound of iron lattice. Atretes took the wooden bowl a woman slave handed him. His stomach cramped painfully at the smell of food. He took his place on a long bench with the others and waited as two women carrying buckets walked along the line of men, ladling out portions of thick meat and barley stew. Everything, including food, was calculated here. Meat would build muscle, and the rich grain would cover the arteries with a layer of fat, which would keep a wounded man from quickly bleeding to death. Another woman handed out thick hunks of bread, followed by other women who poured water into wooden cups.

Atretes ate ravenously. When his bowl was empty, a slender, dark-haired woman ladled more stew for him. She moved to another who clacked his cup against his bowl to summon her. When the woman returned and replenished Atretes' bowl once again, the tattooed Briton beside him whispered in Greek, "Go easy or you'll suffer for it in afternoon exercises."

"No talking!" Trophimus shouted.

Atretes swilled the last of his stew as they were ordered to rise. As they filed out, he dropped his bowl and water cup into a half barrel.

Standing in the sun, Atretes felt drowsy as Trophimus lectured them on the need to build their strength and stamina for the arena. Atretes hadn't had a full meal in weeks, and the heavy weight of food in his belly felt good. He remembered the feasts that always followed a victorious battle and how the warriors stuffed themselves on roasted meat and rich beer until they could do little more than tell stories and laugh.

Trophimus took them to an exercise area where several *pali* were erected within the iron grated wall. The pali, wheels that were laid on their sides and mounted on the ground, had thick posts up through the center. Two leather covered swords protruded from each post, one at the height of a man's head and the other at the level of his knees. A slave-driven crank worked the gears that turned the pali, swinging the sheathed swords around at whatever speed was commanded by the instructor. Anyone standing on the wheel would have to jump the lower sword and duck quickly before the higher one struck him in the head.

Trophimus ordered Atretes and the Briton to demonstrate. They took their places on the wheel first while a Numidian trainee manned the crank. As the post turned, Atretes jumped and ducked the sheathed sword each time. On the sixth time around, the Briton was struck squarely in the forehead and knocked backwards off the wheel. Atretes kept going.

"Faster," Trophimus ordered.

The Numidian turned the crank harder. Atretes was tiring fast, but kept on, muscles burning. The heavy weight of food in his stomach lurched, but around and around the post swung. Trophimus stood by and watched without expression. Atretes' chest heaved, his gorge rose. The high sword brushed his head and he barely made it over the lower one. Sweat poured down into his eyes. He glared at Trophimus and felt an explosion of pain across the bridge of his nose. He flew backwards and hit the ground heavily. Groaning, he rolled over, pushed himself up, and vomited into the dust. His broken nose gushed blood. Not far away, Gallus stood laughing at him. Crawling a few feet away from the wheel, Atretes shook his head, trying to clear it.

Trophimus ordered two others onto the wheel and came over to Atretes. "Kneel and tilt your head back." Tharacus' warning of castration hung over Atretes and he took the subservient position as ordered. Trophimus gripped his head, positioned the length of his thumbs on either side of his broken nose, and worked the cartilage. "Your mistake was looking at me." Atretes clenched his teeth, afraid he was going to disgrace himself further by passing out. Blood poured down over his mouth and chin and stained the brown tunic. Trophimus didn't take his hands away until the cartilage snapped back into place.

"The ladies like something pretty to look at," Trophimus said with a grin. He washed his hands in a bucket of water that a slave held for him. He took the sponge from the bucket and tossed it to Atretes. "You need stamina for a good fight," he said, drying his hands on a towel the slave handed him. "When the bleeding stops, rejoin the others." He dropped the towel in the dust beside Atretes and turned his attention to the next two on the wheel.

Atretes pressed the dripping sponge to his throbbing face. Cool water eased the pain, but not his rage or embarrassment. He heard a thud and groan as another man was quickly struck down. "Next!" Trophimus shouted.

The afternoon wore on. Trophimus didn't move the men to another section of the compound until every one of them had taken several turns on the wheel.

The sun rose higher, beating down on the trainees as they returned to the obstacle course. Even tired, his tunic soaked with blood and sweat, Atretes managed it without too much difficulty. He'd spent his life in the forests of Germania—running through obstacles was nothing new to him. Ducking branches, leaping roots and boulders, and zigzagging through clusters of pine were second nature.

Others who had been purchased from mines and fields stumbled and fell, gasping for breath and rising only when the whip sang through the air and cracked across their backs. But as his overstuffed belly emptied, the obstacles these Romans had set up were child's play to Atretes.

Trophimus was disgusted with the display of some of the trainees. "How many days have we been doing this and still you can't make it through the course! It'd do you all well to observe the German! If there is one thing a German knows, it's how to run!"

Atretes burned with rage as he was ordered through the course twice more while the others watched.

When another whistle blew, the men filed into their building and down a ladder to the baths. Exhausted, Atretes rested his forearms on the stone as he sat in the bath. His nose throbbed and every muscle in his body ached. He filled the sponge and pressed it against the back of his neck. The water felt good, as did the knowledge that he had done well.

The only sound in the torchlit chamber was water running into the baths. No one spoke. Four guards were stationed around the room. As much as he longed to kill one, Atretes knew Tharacus would enjoy carrying out his threatened punishment.

He was handed a fresh tunic. Once dressed, he was ordered up the ladder. Following another meal of meat and barley stew, which Atretes ate sparingly, the trainees were taken to their chambers and locked in for the night. He pulled on the heavy robe he had left on the stone shelf and stretched out on the thin straw mattress.

All his life, he had wanted nothing more than to feel the rush of hot blood, to be a warrior, to fight. There was honor in destroying an enemy who invaded your lands; there was honor in fighting to protect your people; there was honor in dying in battle. But there was no honor in killing your peers to entertain a Roman mob.

Atretes stared up through the iron bars at the shadows flickering on the walls of the corridor above. He was too tired to feel anything except deep shame and futile rage at what lay ahead of him.

7

Julia tried to squeeze past the others ahead of her in order to see the arena below, and she felt Marcus' hand clamp on her arm. "There's no hurry, Julia," he said in amusement. "The *locarius* will show us to our seats when our turn comes," he said, watching for the usher as he spoke.

"I thought you had a special box."

"I do, but it's in use today, and I thought you'd like to sit among the crowd and feel the real excitement of the games."

Spectators were already crowding into the theater, swarming down the steps and into the tiers of seats, called the *cavea*. Three circular walls, the *baltei,* were in four superimposed sections. The highest and least desirable section was the *pullati.* Closest to the arena was the *podium,* where the emperor would sit. The knights and tribunes were behind and above in the first and second *maenianum.* The third and fourth maenianum were reserved for the patricians.

"Why are they taking so long?" Julia said, exasperated. "I don't want to miss anything."

"They're trying to handle the crowd. Don't worry, little sister, you won't miss anything. They haven't even presented the sponsor yet." He handed their ivory passes to the usher and supported Julia with a firm hand beneath her elbow as she went down the steep steps. The usher took them to the proper row and handed the ivory chits over again so Marcus could match the numbers with the stone seats. "The first hours will be tedious," Marcus said as Julia sat down. "I don't know how I allowed you to talk me into this. The real fighting won't begin for a long while yet."

Julia scarcely heard Marcus' complaint, so completely enthralled was she by the crowd. Hundreds were in attendance, from the wealthiest patricians to the lowliest slaves. Her gaze became fixed on a woman coming down the steps, a Syrian slave wearing a white tunic right on her heels. He was carrying a sun guard to shade her and a basket undoubtedly laden with wine and delicacies.

"Marcus, look at that woman. She must have a fortune in jewelry on her! I'll bet those bracelets weigh ten pounds each, and they're set with jewels."

"She's a patrician's wife."

She glanced up at him. "How can you sound and look so bored when it's all so exciting?"

He'd been to the games a hundred times or more. The only part he enjoyed were the death matches, and they wouldn't come for hours yet. "Because I *am* bored. I'd enjoy it more if they'd cut through all these preliminaries."

"You promised you'd let me stay as long as I liked, Marcus, and I'm going to stay for *everything*. Besides, the signs said that Celerus is going to fight today. Octavia said he's wonderful."

"If you like scarred *Thracians* who use their weapons with the skill of a bull in full charge . . ."

Julia ignored his sarcasm. Ever since he'd begun building houses on Aventine Hill, all he talked about was business and how much lumber and stone cost, and how many more slaves he needed to buy in order to complete the contracts. She'd looked forward to this moment too much to allow his moodiness at missing a few hours of work spoil it for her. After all, she was the only one of her friends who hadn't attended the games. She deserved to have fun. She was going to drink in every sound, sight, and moment.

But a flicker of doubt made her frown. Mother and Father thought she and Marcus were on a day's excursion to the country. It was just a small lie; it wasn't really deceit. Marcus had taken her out in his chariot before. What did it matter when Father and Mother were unreasonable? Their rules were unfair and ridiculous. Just because Father despised what the games had become didn't mean she and Marcus had to feel the same way. Father was prudish and traditional and a hypocrite. Even he attended the games on occasion, though he claimed he did so only when social and political reasons demanded it.

"It disgusts me to hear young women screaming for a man who is nothing more than a thief and murderer," he had said only the other day. "Celerus struts around the arena like a cock and fights just well enough to survive. Yet they make him a god."

She thanked the gods for Marcus, who couldn't say no to her. He was just and reasonable, and willing to risk their father's ire to give her the same simple privileges her friends possessed.

"I'm so glad you brought me, Marcus. Now my friends won't

be able to make fun of me anymore," she said, putting her hand over his.

Distracted, he gave her a slight smile. "Enjoy yourself and don't worry about anything."

Marcus was thinking about what his father had said about using slaves rather than free men to complete the labor contracts. Father claimed slaves were the reason Rome was going soft. Free men needed work and purpose. Marcus said free men demanded too high a wage. He could buy a slave, use him until the work was done, and sell him when the projects were completed. That way he saved money while the work was going on and even gained a further profit once it was finished. Father had been enraged by the logic, claiming that if Rome were to survive, she needed to hire her own citizens rather than import slaves from elsewhere.

Julia leaned over and looped her arm through his. "You needn't worry about my telling Father you brought me to the games. I won't say a word."

"That relieves me greatly," he said.

She pulled away, offended by his patronizing tone. "I can keep a secret."

"I wouldn't trust you with one!"

"Isn't this a secret? Father would skin you alive if he learned you brought me here."

"One look at your face this morning was enough to tell him you weren't going for a simple ride in the country."

"He didn't forbid you to take me from the house."

"Perhaps he knows you would find some other way to come. He might prefer you attend with me rather than with one of your flighty friends."

"I could have come with Octavia."

"Ah, yes, innocent little Octavia."

She didn't like his wry tone. "She gets to go to the ceremonial feast the night before the games and see all the gladiators up close."

"Indeed," Marcus said dryly, well aware of the fact. "Octavia does many things I wouldn't want my sister to do."

"I don't see why you disapprove of her. She's escorted by her own father."

Marcus made no comment, certain any information he might give on Drusus would be repeated to Octavia. Drusus was not rich enough to be a threat, but he had enough influence and money to be bothersome.

Julia clenched her hands tightly in her lap. He was trying to make her feel guilty. It was beastly of him and she wouldn't be drawn into a discussion about Father. Not now. She was well aware she was disobeying his wishes, but why should she feel guilty? Marcus had been living for himself since he was eighteen. He didn't bow to their father's ridiculous sense of morality, so why should she? Father was unreasonable and dictatorial and dull. He expected her to study and prepare herself to be a proper wife, like Mama. Well, that was fine for Mama—who seemed to enjoy such a mundane life—but Julia wanted more. She wanted excitement. She wanted passion. She wanted to experience everything the world had to offer.

Marcus shifted his body. His eyes were half-closed already with boredom. Julia's mouth tightened. She didn't care if he was bored. And it annoyed her that he defended Father's attitude, especially when he and Father were so often at odds themselves lately. They argued constantly, about everything.

She glanced at her brother and saw the rigid line of his jaw. His mind was wandering. She had seen that look on his face often enough to know he was thinking about some spat he had had with Father. Well, it wasn't fair. She wasn't going to allow anything to spoil today—not Father, not Marcus, not anyone.

"Octavia said she has seen Arria at the feasts more than once."

Marcus' mouth curved cynically. Julia was not telling him anything he didn't already know. "Arria does many things I wouldn't want you to do."

Why did everyone expect her to be different from everyone else? "Arria is beautiful and rich and she does whatever she wants to please herself. I wish I could be exactly like her."

Marcus laughed without humor. "You are too sweet and uncomplicated to become like her."

"I suppose you mean that as a compliment," she said, and looked away, fuming silently. Sweet and uncomplicated! He might as well have said she was dull. No one really knew her, not even Marcus, who knew her better than anyone. To him, she was his little sister, someone meant to be spoiled and teased. Father and Mother saw her through a cloud of their own expectations and spent every waking moment trying to mold her into those expectations.

Julia envied Arria's freedom. "Is she going to attend today? I'd like to meet her."

"Arria?"

"Yes, Arria. Your mistress."

The last person Marcus wanted his sister to meet was Arria. "If she does attend, she won't arrive for hours yet. Not until the real bloodletting begins. And when she comes, my sweet, she will sit with Antigonus and not with us."

"You mean Antigonus won't be sitting here?" she said in surprise.

"He'll be in the sponsor's box."

"But you always sit with him."

"Not this time."

"Why not?" She grew indignant as she grasped the possibility that the young aristocrat thought himself too important to sit with an Ephesian merchant's son. "We should be sitting in the sponsor's box. Considering it's Father's money paying for all this, I wouldn't think it to Antigonus' interests to exclude us."

"Calm down. It was no slight on his part. I excluded us," Marcus said. He had no intention of putting his sister in the same vicinity as his lascivious friend or his own amoral mistress. He wanted Julia to enjoy herself, not to be completely corrupted after only one hot afternoon at the arena. Antigonus had already remarked once that Julia was growing into a lovely young lady, and that was enough to warn Marcus of his intentions. Julia was far too impressionable and would probably fall easy prey to an attack of Antigonus' experience. Marcus intended to make sure Julia didn't. She'd remain intact until she was married to a man of their father's choosing, and then she could do as she pleased.

A frown momentarily creased Marcus' face. Father *had* chosen, though Julia wouldn't be informed of it until all the arrangements had been made. Father had told Marcus of his choice only an hour ago, just before Julia came into the room. "Arrangements are being made for your sister's marriage," he had said. "The announcement will be made within the month."

Marcus was still stunned. If Father suspected he was taking Julia to the games, he hadn't let on. He had looked at his father cautiously, wondering why he was telling him about the engagement. "I've never given Julia free rein under any circumstances," Marcus had said to reassure him. "She's my sister, and I will see her reputation protected."

"I know that, Marcus, but you and I both know that Julia has a tendency to be excitable. She could be easily corrupted. You must shield her whenever possible."

"From life?" Marcus said.

"From pointless and foul entertainment."

Marcus stiffened, well aware the remark was aimed at his own life-style. He didn't rise to the argument, however. "Who have you chosen for her?"

"Claudius Flaccus."

"*Claudius Flaccus!* A worse mate you couldn't find!"

"I'm doing what I think best for your sister. She needs stability."

"Flaccus will bore her to death."

"She will have children and be content."

"By the gods, Father, do you even know your own daughter?"

Decimus stiffened, his dark eyes flashing. "You are foolish and blind where your sister is concerned. What she wants is not what is best for her. I hold you partly responsible." Marcus turned away, aware that in his anger he might say something he'd later regret. "Marcus, see that Julia is not compromised while in your care!"

Marcus knew Flaccus was a man of impeccable bloodlines, a trait Father disdained openly, but coveted secretly. Flaccus also possessed some measure of wealth and community standing. However, Marcus suspected the real reason behind Father's selection was Flaccus' bronze-cast traditional points of view and morality. Flaccus had had only one wife and, from all accounts Marcus had heard, had remained constant during her lifetime. It had been five years since she had died in childbirth, and yet Flaccus' name had never been linked with any other woman. The man was either celibate or homosexual.

For all Flaccus' assets, Marcus didn't think the marriage would bring happiness to Julia. Flaccus was far older than Julia, and he was an intellectual. Such a man would be dull company for a girl of Julia's temperament.

"You're making a mistake, Father."

"Your sister's future does *not* concern you."

Julia had chosen that moment to come into the room, thus preventing Marcus from venting his opinion on that statement. Who knew Julia better than he? She was like him, chafing under the restrictions of a morality that no longer existed anywhere in the Empire.

On the ride to the arena, he had given Julia the reins and let her send the horses into a wild gallop. *She is barely fifteen years old. . . . Let her feel the wind of freedom in her face before Father hands her over to Flaccus and she is locked behind the high walls of an Aventine Palace,* he thought glumly. The same hot blood that ran in his own veins ran in Julia's, and the thought of her fate sickened him. It was half in his mind to allow his sister any adventure she wanted, but the family honor and his own ambition wouldn't allow it.

His father's warning had been clear, though unspoken: Keep your sister away from your friends, especially Antigonus. The warning was unnecessary. Besides the need of protecting Julia's purity in order to protect the family reputation, Marcus didn't want to further complicate his relationship with Antigonus. He knew his friend, the aristocrat, far too well to trust him with Julia. Antigonus would seduce Julia and marry her just to guarantee himself future access to the Valerian coffers. Marcus was no fool. A substantial investment in Antigonus' career had been necessary to gain the building contracts he coveted, but Marcus had no intention of allowing a marriage that would permanently obligate him.

Now that he had the contracts, he could prove his own abilities on a broader scale. In three or four years, Antigonus would be useless to him. For while Marcus found Antigonus amusing and somewhat intelligent, he was wise enough to know Antigonus wouldn't last in the Senate. He ran through money and wine too quickly and ran off at the mouth too much. One day, Antigonus would have one party too many, get too drunk and speak too freely, seduce the wrong patrician's wife, then end up with an imperial order to slit his own wrists. Marcus intended to have some political distance between them before that time came.

Julia's exclamation drew him back to the present. "Oh, Marcus, it's so exciting, I can hardly bear it!" The stands were filling up with men, women, and children. The noise rose and fell like the ebbing surf. Marcus saw little to interest him and leaned back indolently, resolved to suffer through the morning tedium. Julia sat, back straight and eyes wide with fascination, taking in everything that was happening around her.

"A lady is staring at you, Marcus." His eyes were half-closed against the sunlight.

"Let her stare," he said indifferently.

"Perhaps you know her," she said. "Why don't you open your eyes and look?"

"Because it's pointless. If she is beautiful, I might wish to pursue her, and I must remain and protect my beautiful and innocent sister."

Giggling, she hit him. "And if I weren't here?"

He opened one eye and sought the woman mentioned. He closed it again. "No further discussion necessary."

"There are others looking," Julia said, proud to be sitting by him. The Valerians could claim no royal Roman bloodlines, but Marcus was very handsome and he had an air of masculine confidence about him. Men, as well as women, noticed him. This pleased Julia, because when they looked at him, they ended up looking at her as well. She had made special preparations today and knew she looked her best. She felt the bold look of one man a few rows away and pretended not to notice. Did he suppose she was Marcus' mistress? The thought amused her. She wished she looked sophisticated and aloof, but knew the hot color flooding her cheeks gave her innocence away.

What would Arria do under the circumstances? Pretend she didn't feel the man's open stare? Or return it?

Trumpets blared, startling her. "Wake up, Marcus! The gates are opening!" Julia said excitedly and leaned forward in her seat.

Marcus yawned widely as the tedious preliminary proceedings began. Usually he came late in order to avoid the boring pronouncements of whom to credit for funding the day's games. Today Antigonus would lead the parade with his banners flying. No one really cared who paid, as long as the games went on. In fact, sometimes insults were shouted at sponsors who took too long to advertise their part in the production.

Julia clapped wildly as the chariots bearing the sponsors and duelists appeared. "Oh, look! Aren't they wonderful!" Her excitement amused him.

As primary sponsor of the events to come, Antigonus led the parade. He was splendidly dressed in white and gold with his hard-earned edging of purple denoting his new, but tenuous, rank of senator. He waved to the crowd while his driver struggled to keep the pair of majestic stallions under control. As they made a full circle and a half, the driver turned the chariot and halted it before the emperor's platform. Antigonus, with all the dramatic flare of an actor, presented the speech Marcus had written the evening before. The crowd approved the brevity; the emperor, its eloquence. Antigonus signaled grandly and the duelists climbed down from the chariots to display themselves before the cheering multitude.

Julia gasped and pointed at a gladiator stripping off a brilliant red cloak. Beneath it, he wore polished bronze armor. "Oh, look at him! Isn't he beautiful!" His helmet held dyed ostrich plumes of bright yellow, blue, and red. He marched around the arena so that the spectators could get a good look at him. Marcus' mouth curved wryly. For once, he agreed with Father. Celerus looked like a cock on the walk. Julia, on the other hand, stared in fascination and seemed to think him the most beautiful man she had ever seen—until the next half-dozen gladiators stripped off their cloaks and joined him.

"What is *he?*" Julia asked, pointing.

"Which one?"

"The one with the net and trident."

"He's a *retiarius.* They will put him up against a *mirmillo,* the ones with fish-shaped crests on their helmets, or a *secutor.* You see that man over there, the fully armed one? He is a secutor. They are supposed to chase down their opponents until they are worn down enough to finish off."

"I like the mirmillo," Julia said, laughing. "A fisherman against a fish." Her cheeks were flushed, her eyes shining brighter than he'd ever seen them. He was glad he'd brought her. She clapped her hands as trumpets blared again. "Is that one a *Thracian?*" she asked, pointing to a tall gladiator carrying an oblong shield and wearing a plumed helmet. He had a gladius and lance and a sleeve on his right arm. "Octavia said the Thracians are the most exciting!"

"That one's a *Samnite.* The one with the curved dagger and the small round shield is a Thracian," Marcus said, unable to arouse much enthusiasm for either.

Celerus had stopped before a box of richly dressed women and rolled his hips at them. They shrieked in lustful approval. The more explicit his antics, the louder they laughed and screamed, others around them joining in. Several men clambered down over the rows, pushing past people to reach the ledge, so they could lean over and toss flowers down to the famous gladiator. "Celerus! Celerus! I love you!" One shouted down at the gladiator.

Eyes and mouth wide open, Julia absorbed all of it. Marcus drew her attention away from the *amoratae*, as the devotees of the gladiators were called, and pointed out the finer points of the other gladiators. Her attention kept drifting back however. As Celerus came full circle and passed by their box, women stood and cried out his name over and over again, each trying to outshout the others in order to draw his attention. To Marcus' dismay, Julia rose with them, caught up in the hysteria. Annoyed, he pulled her down beside him.

"Let go! I want a better look at him," she said in protest. "Everyone is standing and I can't see anything!"

Marcus relented. Indeed, why not let her have a little excitement for a change? She'd spent most of her life cooped up in the house under the watchful and overly protective eye of their parents. It was time she saw some of the world outside the high walls and sculptured gardens.

Julia stood on her seat and stretched up onto her toes. "He's looking at me! Wait until I tell Octavia. She'll be so jealous!" Laughing, she waved and called his name along with the others. "Celerus! Celerus!"

The women screamed louder, but suddenly Julia froze, mouth open. Her eyes grew wider, her face bloomed with hot color. Marcus grabbed her hand and she sat quickly beside him, eyes closed tightly as the women's screams rose to a near frenzy.

Marcus laughed at the look on his sister's face. Celerus was notoriously proud of his body and enjoyed showing it off to the crowd—all they wanted. Marcus grinned. "So," he said with all the tactlessness of an older brother, "Did you get a *good* look at him?"

"You might have warned me!"

"And spoil the surprise?"

"I hate it when you laugh at me, Marcus." Tipping her chin, she ignored him. The women were screaming so loudly, she was getting a headache. Whatever was that horrid man doing now? A great protest came from them and then, one by one, they sat down. She caught a glimpse of Celerus again, striding away. He rejoined the others standing before the emperor's platform, who, extending their right arms, called out the creed of the gladiator.

"Ave, Imperator, morituri te salutant!" Hail, Emperor, those who are about to die salute you!

Despite all Octavia had said, Julia didn't think Celerus was handsome at all. In fact, several of his teeth were missing, and he had one ugly scar on his thigh and another across the side of his face. But there was something about him that made her heart pound and her mouth go dry. She was uncomfortable sitting beside her watchful, amused brother. To make matters worse, the young man several rows below was watching her as well, his expression tying her stomach in knots.

"Your face is red, Julia."

"I hate you, Marcus!" she said, near tears of anger. "I hate you when you make fun of me!"

Marcus' brows rose slightly at her vehemence. Perhaps he had become too immune to the coarse displays of some of the *bustuarii,* or funeral men, as they were called. Nothing surprised him anymore, while everything would shock and excite Julia. He put his hand over hers. "I apologize," he said sincerely. "Take a deep breath and calm down. I suppose I'm so used to these spectacles that they've ceased to shock me."

"I'm *not* shocked," she said. "And if you laugh at me again, I'll tell Father and Mother you brought me to the games against my will!"

His own swift temper rose at her imperious tone and ridiculous threat. Julia had been pleading to attend the games for the past two years. Marcus looked at her through narrow, sardonic eyes. "If you're going to act like a spoiled child, I'll take you home where you belong!"

She saw he meant it. Her lips parted, and tears welled and pooled in her dark eyes.

Marcus swore beneath his breath. He had seen that crushed look before and knew her capable of bursting into tempestuous tears and making him look the abusive lout. He clamped his hand around her wrist. "If you cry now, you'll humiliate us both before the entire Roman populace, and I swear I'll never attend the games with you again."

Julia swallowed her tears and protest. Turning her head away, she grew rigid with the effort to regain control of her emotions. Marcus could be so cruel at times. It was fine for him to tease her, but if she defended herself he threatened to take her home. She clenched her hands.

Marcus watched her for a moment and frowned. He'd looked forward to introducing her to Rome's favorite recreation. Julia was high-strung and easily excited, but surely she wasn't like some of these women who became so overwrought they fell into wanton hysteria.

Julia pressed her lips together as she felt her brother studying her. If he was waiting for an apology, he'd wait forever. He didn't deserve one after laughing at her. "I shall behave, Marcus," she said with great solemnity. "I won't shame you."

Marcus' better judgment told him to take her home now, before the bloodletting started. She'd be angry, she'd even avoid speaking to him for a few days . . . but he dismissed the idea. He didn't want to disappoint her. She'd waited far too long for this experience. Perhaps that accounted for her highly emotional state.

He took her hand and squeezed it. "If it gets to be too much for you, we'll go," he said grimly.

Relief flooded her. "Oh, it won't, Marcus. I swear." She looped her arm through his. Leaning against him, she looked up with a bright smile. "You won't be sorry you brought me. I won't even flinch when Celerus slices through someone's throat."

The trumpets blared, announcing the second-rate bloodless displays, which were meant to warm up the crowd. However, Julia was delighted with the *paegniari,* the mock fighters. She clapped and called out encouragement, drawing amused attention from the more experienced attendees who found her more entertaining than the display. Appearing next, the *lusorii* fought in earnest, but could do little vital damage to one another with their wooden weapons.

The sun was already high and hot. No wind stirred in the arena, and Marcus saw perspiration beading on Julia's pale forehead. He touched her hand and found it cool. "I'm going to purchase a wineskin," he said, worried that she'd faint from the heat. She needed something to drink and a sunshade. He'd been so engrossed in his own thoughts that he hadn't made proper preparations. Usually Arria brought along wine, food, and a slave to hold a shade over them. "Stay here and don't talk to anyone."

Within minutes, the young Roman who had stared at her took Marcus' seat. "Your lover has deserted you," he said in Greek, his accent common.

"My brother has not deserted me," she said stiffly, her cheeks burning. "He's gone to purchase wine and will return shortly."

"Your brother," he said, pleased. "I am Nicanor of Capua. And you are . . . ?"

"Julia," she said slowly, remembering what Marcus had said, but wanting to have something to tell Octavia.

"I love your eyes. Eyes like that could make a man lose his head."

She blushed, her heart racing. Her whole body felt hot with embarrassment. He was not dressed suitably for her class, but there was an earthiness about him that excited her. His eyes were brown and thickly lashed, his mouth full and sensuous. "My brother told me not to speak to anyone," she said, lifting her chin again.

"Your brother is wise. There are many here who would wish to take advantage of such a youthful and lovely woman." His deep voice caressed as he went on. "You're a true daughter of Aphrodite."

Flattered and fascinated, Julia listened. He spoke long and fervently, and she drank in his words, deliciously aroused. But when his calloused hand touched her bare arm, the spell was broken. With a soft gasp, she drew back.

Nicanor looked past her and departed quickly.

Marcus sat down beside her and plunked the heavy wine bag in her lap. "Making new friends?"

"His name was Nicanor. He just came and sat down beside me and started talking to me, and I didn't know what to do to make him go away. He said I was beautiful."

"By the gods, Julia, you've been kept under lock and key too long. You are gullible."

"I rather liked him, common though he was." She looked up over her shoulder. "Do you think he'll come back?"

"If he does, Antigonus'll have extra meat to throw to his lions." Marcus poured wine into a small copper cup and handed it to her.

The war trumpets blared, announcing the first contests with sharp weapons. Julia forgot Nicanor, swallowed her wine quickly, and thrust the cup back at Marcus so she could lean forward in her seat. Antigonus had hired musicians and, as the fighters battled, trumpets and horns blasted. Blocking several blows, the defender took the offensive, and pipes and flutes trilled. The crowd shouted encouragement and advice to their favorites. The contest continued for some time, and even Julia grew disappointed. "Do they always take so long?"

"Often."

"I want the retiarius to win."

"He won't," Marcus said, watching the contest without much interest. "He's already tiring."

"How can you tell?"

"The way he's holding the trident. Watch closely. See how it dips and swings to one side. He's leaving himself wide open. The Thracian will end this soon."

One trainer hounded the Thracian, while another whipped the retiarius and shouted for him to fight harder. The crowd was hissing and shouting insults, impatient for a kill. The retiarius' trainer chose the wrong moment to swing his whip, for it tangled across the fork of the trident just long enough to give the Thracian the opening he needed. His sword went true and deep, and the retiarius dropped.

"Oh!" Julia said in dismay as the crowd screamed and cheered. "You were right, Marcus."

The retiarius was on his knees, his hands clutching his middle, blood pouring down over his breechcloth. "He's had it!" people shouted, turning their thumbs down. *"Jugula! Jugula!"* The Thracian looked to the emperor. Vespasian pointed his thumb down, hardly pausing in his conversation with a senator. The Thracian turned back and put his hand on the retiarius' head. Tilting it back, he made a quick slice and opened the man's jugular. A fountain of blood splashed him before the dying man fell back, twitched, and then lay still in a pool of blood.

Marcus glanced at Julia and saw that her eyes were shut, her teeth clenched. "Your first kill," Marcus said. "Did you even watch it?"

"I watched." Her hand clutched the front of her tunic. She opened her eyes again as an African man dressed as Mercury danced across the sand toward the fallen man. As the divine guide of dead men's souls to the infernal regions, he dragged the body through the porta. The victorious gladiator was presented with a palm branch while other African boys raked the bloodstained sand, then darted away as the next pair was presented.

Julia was pale and trembling. Her brother brushed his fingertips across her damp forehead and found it cool. "Maybe we should leave."

"No. I don't want to leave. I was only queasy for a moment, Marcus. It's passed now." Her dark eyes were bright and dilated. "I want to stay."

Marcus assessed her and then nodded, proud of her. Father had said she was too weak for the games. He was wrong.

Julia was a true daughter of Rome.

8

Enoch knew he was at risk in what he had done. While his master had approved the purchase of seven slaves, he'd said nothing about buying Jews. Enoch had made that decision himself, despite the fact that he knew his master preferred Gauls and Britons. But having watched his people brought by the hundreds from Judea to Rome and sent into the arenas to die, Enoch couldn't throw away the one opportunity he had to save even a few.

All Jews suffered, not just those who were part of rebellion. The half-shekel previously collected from Roman Jews for the upkeep of the temple in Jerusalem was now collected to finance the building of a colossal amphitheater. Jewish slaves were carrying the stones, Jewish captives would be among the first to die on the sand, Jewish citizens paid the heaviest share of finance.

Enoch struggled between rage and grief at what had become of his homeland and his people. Up until this morning he'd been helpless to do anything to save even one member of his race. Now, he had seven in his care. But he was afraid. Not one of them was suited for the hard labor that would be required on the estate. Even washed, shaved, and dressed in fresh tunics, they were pathetic and spiritless. Four hundred sesterces each, and not one was worth half that.

He looked at the girl, wondering why he'd risked buying her at all. Of what possible use was she? Yet, one look in her eyes and he'd felt God's hand on him, had heard a still, soft voice: *Save this one.* Enoch had purchased her without question, but now wondered and worried what his master would say. His master was expecting Gauls and Britons, and he was bringing back seven broken Jews, one a small girl with the eyes of a prophetess. Enoch prayed fervently for God's protection.

Opening the lock to the western gate, Enoch brought the seven slaves within the high walls of his owner's property. He led them along the pathway and into the back of the house. Lining the seven up in the receiving room, where his master doled out pensions each morning, he gave them instructions to stand straight and silent, to keep their eyes downcast, to speak only if the master directed a question at them personally.

"You'll wait here while I speak with the master. Pray he will accept each of you. Decimus Vindacius Valerian is kind for a Roman, and if he agrees to your purchase, you'll be well treated. May the God of our fathers protect us all."

Decimus was with his wife in the peristyle, where she twirled a daisy between her graceful fingers and listened to her husband. Enoch thought his master looked drawn and in poor humor, but taking in a deep breath and gathering his courage, he approached them. He waited for his master to acknowledge his presence and nod permission to speak.

"My lord," he said, "I've returned with seven slaves for your inspection."

"Gauls?"

"No, my lord. None were available. Nor were there any Britons." He hoped the lie wouldn't bloom on his face. "They're from Judea, my lord," he said and saw his master's mouth tighten into a hard line.

"Jews are the most treacherous race in the Empire, and you would bring seven into my house?"

"Enoch is a Jew," Phoebe said with a smile, "and he has served us faithfully for fifteen years."

Enoch thanked God she was present.

"In this, he has served himself," Decimus said, staring coldly at his overseer. If the slave thought to defend himself, he changed his mind and remained silent. "Are these slaves suited for hard labor?"

"No, my lord," he said truthfully, "but with food and rest they will be."

"I have neither the time nor inclination to pamper rebels."

The Roman's wife touched her husband's arm. "Decimus, would you fault a man for compassion?" she asked softly. "They are his people. Enoch has served us loyally. At least let us look at them and see if they are suitable for our purposes."

They weren't. "By the gods," Decimus said under his breath. He'd seen many captives from many nations, but none so pathetic as these weak, despondent, and spiritless survivors of the destruction of Jerusalem.

"Oh," Phoebe said, her gentle heart touched with pity.

"They were bound for the arena, my lord, but I swear by my God, they'll serve you as I have served you," Enoch said.

"She's little more than Julia's age," Phoebe said, her attention all on the young girl whose eyes were dark with suffering and a knowledge of things unspoken. "The girl, Decimus," Phoebe said quietly. "Whatever you decide about the others, I want her."

He frowned slightly and looked down at his wife. "For what purpose?"

"To serve Julia."

"Julia? She's not suitable for Julia."

"Trust me in this, Decimus. Please. This girl will do very well for Julia."

Decimus looked at the girl again, studying her more closely and wondering what it was about her that made his wife take her after rejecting so many others. Phoebe had been searching for a maid for their daughter for some time. Dozens of slave girls had been presented, but none had been what Phoebe wanted. And now, without the least hesitation, she selected an emaciated young Jewess who was ugly beyond words and probably the daughter of a murderous zealot.

Marcus and Julia entered the courtyard, laughing and in high spirits. They quieted when they saw the slaves. Marcus looked the seven over with distaste. "Jews newly arrived from Judea?" he said in surprise. "What're they doing here?"

"I need slaves for the estate."

"I thought you preferred Gauls and Britons?"

Decimus ignored him and told Enoch to have the six men sent to the estate in Apennines. "The girl will remain here."

"You actually bought them?" Marcus said, stunned. "Even her?" he said flicking a derisive glance at the girl. "I've never known you to waste money, Father."

"The girl will serve Julia," Phoebe said again.

Julia looked from her mother to the girl and back again. "Oh, Mother, you can't mean it. She's terribly ugly. I don't want an ugly slave to serve me! I want a servant like Olympia's!"

"You'll have no such thing. Olympia's slave may be beautiful, but she's arrogant and deceitful. A slave like her can't be trusted."

"Then Bithia! Why can't Bithia serve me?"

"Bithia won't do for you," Phoebe said firmly.

Marcus smiled wryly. He knew very well why his mother wouldn't have Bithia serve Julia and he suspected he knew her reasons for purchasing this particular slave as well. His mouth curved without humor. Jewish morality didn't amuse him, but a slave to watch over and protect his sister would be good.

"What's your name, child?" Phoebe said gently.

"Hadassah, my lady," she said quietly, shamed by the young Roman's derisive perusal and the whining protest of the young girl. Her life hung in the balance of their conversation. She clasped her hands in front of her and kept her eyes downcast, all too aware that if the lady of the house weakened and had her returned to the slave market, she'd die in the arena.

"Just look at her," Julia said in disgust. "Her hair is cut like a boy's and she's so thin!"

"Proper food will put weight on her and her hair will grow back," Phoebe said calmly.

"It's not fair, Mother. I should be able to choose my own personal maid. Octavia chose hers. She has a very exotic Ethiopian whose father was a tribal chieftain."

Marcus laughed. "Tell fair Octavia this one is related to Princess Berenice."

Julia sniffed. "She would never believe it. One look at that girl and Octavia would know she couldn't be related to the woman who captured Titus' heart."

"Then tell her your slave is the daughter of a high priest. Or say she was born a prophetess for her unseen god and has powers to foretell the future."

Hadassah stole a glance at the mocking young Roman. He was very handsome; his dark hair was cut short and curled slightly on his brow. Broad-shouldered and narrow-waisted, he was dressed in a white tunic with an intricately worked leather-and-gold belt. The leather straps of his expensive sandals wove securely around strongly muscled calves. His hands were strong and beautifully made, their only adornment a gold seal ring on his first finger. Every inch of him bespoke an arrogance of breeding and affluence.

In contrast to the young man's physical strength, his sister was delicate. Hadassah was charmed by her ethereal beauty. Even complaining, the girl's voice was cultured and dulcet, and the angry flush in her cheeks merely added color to her pale skin. She wore a pale blue toga with gold trim. The weight of her dark hair was piled in curls on her head and was held in place by gold-and-pearl prongs that matched her earrings. Around her neck was a heavy pendant of a pagan goddess.

Marcus noticed the slave girl's study of his sister. He saw no bitterness or enmity in her expression, rather an awed fascination. She watched Julia as though his sister was a beautiful creature never seen before. Marcus was secretly amused and thought perhaps his mother was right after all. For all the ravages of a Judean holocaust the girl had survived, there was a sweetness in her face, a gentleness that might soothe Julia's wild and restless spirit.

"Keep her, Julia," he said, knowing a word from him would sway his sister more quickly than anything his mother and father might say.

"Do you really think I should?" Julia said in surprise.

"She has some mysterious quality about her," he said, keeping a straight face. He could feel his father's ire. He kissed Julia and his mother as he took his leave.

As his mocking eyes grazed her, Hadassah's heart lurched. She was relieved when he departed. At his word, the girl capitulated, studying her more closely and bringing hot color into Hadassah's pale cheeks.

"I'll keep her," Julia said grandly. "Come with me, girl."

"Her name is Hadassah, Julia," Phoebe said softly in reproof.

"Hadassah, then. Come with me," Julia said imperiously.

Hadassah followed obediently, taking in the wonders of the great house. The floors were brightly tiled mosaic, the walls of marble. Grecian urns were placed beside the doorways, and Babylonian curtains hung on the walls. They crossed an open court lush with flowering shrubs and plants and adorned by marble statues. The soothing sound of water running in a fountain was close by. Hadassah blushed hotly as she saw the statue of a nude woman standing in the midst of the small pool.

Her mistress led her into a chamber strewn with garments. "All those things need to be put away," Julia said as she reclined on a bed.

Hadassah set to work, gathering togas and tunics and shawls from the floor and low stool. She felt her mistress watching her as she worked, and she folded the garments carefully before putting them away.

"Jerusalem is said to be a holy city," Julia said.

"Yes, my lady."

"Is anything left of it?"

Hadassah straightened slowly and smoothed a soft tunic over her arm. "Very little, my lady," she said quietly.

Julia looked into the girl's dark eyes. Slaves didn't usually look their mistresses in the face, but Julia felt no offense that this girl did. Perhaps she didn't know any better. "My father was in Jerusalem once many years ago," she said. "He saw your temple. He said it was very beautiful. Oh, not as beautiful as the temple of Artemis in Ephesus, of course, but a marvel to see nonetheless. It is unfortunate that it's gone!"

Hadassah turned away and began to straighten the vials and cups on the vanity.

"What became of your family, Hadassah?"

"They're all dead, my lady."

"Were they zealots?"

"My father was a humble merchant from Galilee. We were in Jerusalem for Passover."

"What is Passover?"

Hadassah told how God had taken the firstborn of all the Egyptians because Pharaoh wouldn't let Moses and his people go, but God had passed over all the Israelites. Julia listened and then drew the prongs from her hair.

"If your god is so powerful, why did he not intervene and save your people this time?"

"Because they rejected him."

Julia frowned, not understanding. "Jews are very strange," she said and dismissed the subject with an indifferent shrug. She turned away and shook her hair loose about her shoulders. She raked her fingers into it, loving the feel of its softness. She had beautiful hair. Marcus said so. "It's ridiculous to believe in something you cannot see," she said and picked up a tortoise shell comb. She worked it through her luxuriant black hair and forgot about the slave girl.

When would Marcus take her to the games again? She had loved watching them today and wanted to go again as soon as possible.

"What would you have me do now, mistress?"

Julia blinked, annoyed with the interruption of her sweet thoughts. She glanced at the wretched girl and then around at the room. Everything was put neatly away. Even the bedcovers were smoothed, the cushions arranged. "Do my hair," she said and saw the girl pale as she held out the comb to her. "You do know how to arrange hair, don't you?"

"I-I can braid your hair, mistress," the girl stammered.

"I don't know why Mother bought you. What use are you to me if you can't even arrange my hair?" She tossed the comb at the girl in vexation and stormed to the door. "Bithia! *Bithia!* Come here at once."

The Egyptian girl hurried into the room, a closed look in her eyes. "Yes, my lady?"

"Teach this imbecile to arrange hair. As I am stuck with her, she must at least learn how to carry out her duties."

"Yes, mistress."

"She can braid," Julia said with enough sarcasm to cut to the quick. Hadassah watched the Egyptian girl work expertly. She thought the arrangement wonderful, but her mistress was not satisfied. "Do it again." After the second time, Julia yanked the golden pins from her hair and shook her head angrily. "It's worse than before. Go away! You're worse than this imbecile." Tears of emotion filled her dark eyes. "It's not fair I don't get to choose my own maid!"

"You have the most beautiful hair I've ever seen, my lady," Hadassah said sincerely.

"And no wonder, considering what they've done to yours," Julia said bitingly, thinking the girl only meant to flatter her. She glared at her. The young Jewess looked hurt and lowered her eyes. Julia frowned, feeling a twinge of regret at her harshness. The girl made her uncomfortable. She looked away. "Come over here. I want a maid who can arrange my hair like Arria, my brother's mistress, and you're going to learn how, starting *now!*"

Shocked and blushing at her young mistress's careless words, Hadassah took the comb in shaking fingers and did exactly as she was told.

They went to the bathing room and Julia ordered scents stirred into the tepid water. "I'm so bored," Julia said. "Do you know any stories?"

"Only those from my people," Hadassah said.

"Tell me one then," Julia said, desperate for any entertainment within the confines of her mundane life. She leaned her head back against the marble and listened to the girl's quiet, thickly accented voice.

Hadassah told the story of Jonah and the whale. It seemed to bore her mistress and so, when she finished it, she told of the young shepherd boy David fighting the giant Goliath. That one pleased her mistress far more. "Was he handsome? I like that story," she said. "It'll amuse Octavia."

Hadassah sought to please her young mistress, but it was difficult. The girl was consumed with herself, worrying over her hair, her skin, her clothing, and Hadassah knew nothing about the refined tending of such things. Out of necessity, though, she learned quickly. She had only heard of scented oils and paints used to enhance a woman's beauty, she had never seen them used. It fascinated her to watch Julia rub scented oil into her pale skin. She arranged and rearranged her mistress's hair until Julia tired of sitting. Nothing was ever exactly the way she wanted it.

When the family gathered in the triclinium for their meals, Hadassah stood by Julia's couch, replenishing her goblet with watered wine and holding a bowl of warm water and a towel for Julia to rinse and dry her fingers. The conversation moved from politics to festivals and on to business. Hadassah stood silent and still, listening with avid interest, though she was careful not to show it.

The Valerians fascinated her with their heated discussions and obvious differences of opinion. Decimus was dogmatic and rigid, growing angry easily with his son, who agreed with him about nothing. Julia teased and provoked. Phoebe was the peacemaker. She reminded Hadassah of her own mother: quiet, unassuming, but with a strength that pulled the family together again when the discussions became too heated.

Later on, Octavia came to call. "She's so ugly," Octavia said, looking at Hadassah with distaste. "Why ever did your mother choose her for you?"

Julia's pride was stung and she tipped her chin. "She is ugly, but she tells wonderful stories. Come here, Hadassah. Tell Octavia about King David and his mighty men. Oh, and tell her about the man with six fingers."

Hadassah obeyed, blushing with shyness.

"She knows others, as well," Julia said when she finished. "She told me about a tower of babble that explains where all the languages came from. Utterly ridiculous, of course, but amusing."

"Well, I suppose that's something," Octavia conceded. "My maid speaks only rudimentary Greek." She and Julia walked arm in arm along the pathways. They sat on a bench near a statue of a nude Apollo. Hadassah remained close by in attendance while the two young women leaned together, whispering and laughing. Octavia's beautiful Ethiopian said not a word, but every now and then her haughty eyes would rest with dark loathing on Octavia.

As she listened, Hadassah was embarrassed by Octavia's free talk. However, she was even more distressed over Julia's rapt attention and clear desire to absorb every word and idea the girl had to offer.

"Is it true you're to marry Claudius Flaccus?" Octavia asked after a long description of a festival she had attended and the adventures she had had there.

Julia's gaiety died. "Yes," she said miserably. "It's all arranged. How could Father do such a thing to me? Claudius Flaccus is almost as old as he is."

"Your father is an Ephesian and covets good Roman blood."

Julia's chin tilted and her dark eyes flashed. It was no secret that Octavia's father, Drusus, was distantly related to the Caesars through an illegitimate sister of one of Augustus' offspring. Octavia liked to remind Julia that there was a spoonful of royal blood in her veins—a small stab to make Julia aware how fortunate she was to have a friend with such illustrious connections. "There's nothing wrong with our blood, Octavia." Julia's father could buy Drusus with the snap of his fingers. What the family lacked in royal blood, they more than made up for in wealth.

"Don't take offense at everything, Julia," Octavia laughed. "If my father could marry me off to Claudius Flaccus, he would. Claudius comes from a long line of Roman aristocrats, and he still retains some of his family fortune because he's been cunning enough to avoid political office. It may not be all that bad being married to him."

"I don't care anything about his royal bloodline. It makes me feel sick to even think of him touching me." Blushing, she shuddered and looked away.

"You're such a child." Octavia leaned forward, putting her hand over Julia's. "Just close your eyes and it will be over in a few minutes." She giggled.

Chagrined, Julia changed the subject. "Marcus took me to the games again. It was so exciting. My heart raced and there were moments I could scarcely breathe."

"Celerus is wonderful, isn't he?"

"Celerus! Ho! I don't understand why you are so taken with him. There are others far more beautiful."

"You should attend the feast the night before the games. Up close, he's magnificent."

"I think he's ugly with all those scars all over him."

Octavia laughed. "All those scars are what make him so exciting. Do you know how many men he has killed? Fifty-seven. Whenever he looks at me, that's all I can think about. He's unbearably exciting."

Chilled and shocked by their every word, Hadassah stood silent nearby, head down and eyes tightly closed. She wished she was blind and deaf so she wouldn't see their animated faces and hear their calloused words. How could they speak so casually of men dying, or be so cavalier about their own precious innocence? Octavia seemed proud to have lost hers, and Julia seemed only too eager to throw her own away.

They rose. "Tell me what Marcus is up to these days," Octavia said, looping her arm through Julia's again, seeming only casually interested.

Julia was not fooled. Smiling slightly, she talked of Arria and Fannia as she and Octavia wandered through the garden. For all Octavia's professed adoration of Celerus, Julia knew she would forget him in an instant if Marcus but smiled at her once.

Restless, Marcus rose from his bed and stood in the open doorway to the peristyle. Listening to the sound of crickets in the pale moonlight, he ran his hand over his bare chest and stared out at the courtyard. He couldn't sleep and could put no reason to his disquiet. The building project was going well. Money was pouring in. Arria had gone to the country for a few weeks, freeing him of her cloying presence and jealousy. He'd spent an evening with his friends, enjoying enlightening conversation and the attentions of Antigonus' slave girls.

Life was good, and it was getting better as his wealth grew. So why this gnawing restlessness and vague dissatisfaction?

He went out to take some fresh air. Even the peristyle felt confining, and he went through the arched doorway at the north end of the courtyard to the gardens beyond. He wandered the pathways, his mind leaping from one thing to another—the shipments of timber from Gaul, Arria and her sudden and vastly irritating possessiveness, Father and his disapproval of everything he did. His nerves were stretched taut.

Pausing beneath the rose-covered trellis, he inhaled the sweet scent. Maybe he was worried about Julia, and that was why he was so on edge. She was fighting the marriage arrangements. She had burst into tears this evening and screamed at Father that she hated him. He had ordered her to her room, and she had remained there all evening with that strange maid of hers.

Movement caught his attention and he turned slightly. Julia's little Jewess came out from the doorway of the peristyle. His eyes narrowed as she walked along the pathway not far from the trellis, where he stood unnoticed. What was she doing outside the house? She had no business in the gardens at this late hour.

He watched her walk up the pathway. He knew she wasn't intending to run away, for she was heading in the opposite direction of the door in the western wall. She stopped at the wide junction of two cobbled paths. Drawing her shawl over her head, she knelt on the stones. Clasping her hands together, she bowed her head.

Marcus' eyes widened in amazement. She was praying to her unseen god! Right here in the garden. But why in darkness, hidden from others' eyes? She should be worshiping with Enoch at the small synagogue where he and other Jews gathered. Curious, Marcus moved closer. She was so still, and her profile was clear in the moonlight.

She was distressed. Her eyes were closed and her lips moved, though she spoke not aloud. Tears ran down her cheeks. With a soft moan, she stretched out facedown on the stones, arms outstretched, and he could hear her then, murmuring words in a language he didn't understand. Aramaic?

Marcus moved closer, stirred strangely by the sight of the girl prostrating herself before her god. He had often seen his mother praying to the household deities in the lararium, where her shrines and altars were located, but she had never prostrated herself. Devoted to them, she went each morning to place salt cakes in offering and ask their protection over her loved ones. His father hadn't set foot in the lararium since Marcus' two younger brothers had died of fever. Marcus himself had little faith in gods, though he worshiped money and Aphrodite. Money suited him; Aphrodite appealed to his senses. Marcus believed whatever real power a man possessed came from within himself, from his own will and effort, and not from any god.

The slave girl arose.

She was small and slender, not at all like Bithia with her luscious curves, full mouth, and sultry eyes. The little Jewess stood for a long moment in the moonlight with her head bowed, seemingly reluctant to leave the peaceful garden. She tilted her head back so that the moonlight spilled over her face. Her eyes were closed and a soft smile curved her mouth. Marcus saw in her uplifted face a peace he had never felt, a peace for which he hungered and searched.

"You shouldn't be in the garden at this time of night."

She jumped at the sound of his voice and looked ready to faint when she saw him walk toward her. Her body tensed, and she went very still again, her fingers tightening in the thin shawl that was now down about her shoulders.

"Is this your usual practice?" He tipped his head slightly to one side, trying to read what was in her face. "To pray to your god every night when the household sleeps?"

Hadassah's heart pounded. Had he guessed she was a Christian, or did he still suppose her a Jew? "The lady said it was permitted." Her voice trembled noticeably. It was a warm evening, but she was suddenly cold, then hot again as she saw he wore only a loincloth.

"My mother or Julia told you this?" he said, stopping within a few feet of her.

She looked up at him and then lowered her eyes quickly in obeisance. "Your mother, master."

"Then I suppose it is permitted, as long as your worship does not interfere with your duties to my sister."

"The lady Julia was sleeping well when I left, master. I wouldn't have left her otherwise."

Marcus studied her for a long moment. What was it about these Jews that they could prostrate themselves before a god they couldn't see. It made no sense to him. Except for Enoch, Marcus had no fondness for them anyway, nor did he trust them. He was not sure he trusted this girl or wanted her in the household. She was a product of the destruction of Jerusalem and therefore had reason, if not the right, for enmity against Romans. He wanted Julia safe.

Yet the girl looked harmless enough, even timid. Appearances, however, could be deceiving. He raised one brow.

"Rome tolerates all religions save those that preach rebellion," he said, testing her. "The Jewish cry for Roman blood has been a common one for years and is the reason your Holy City lies in ruin today."

Hadassah did not respond. What he said was true enough.

Marcus saw only dismay in her expression. He moved closer so he could better read her face, and she reacted then. Her chin lifted just a fraction, and he saw his nakedness mortified her. He grinned, amused at her discomfort. How long had it been since he had seen a girl truly embarrassed by anything?

"Have no fear, girl. I haven't the least desire to touch you," he said, though he found himself studying her. She had gained weight over the past weeks, and her hair now lay softly about her small face like a dark cap. She was far from beautiful, but no longer ugly. She glanced up at him when he didn't speak, and Marcus was struck by the darkness of her eyes, the mysterious depth of them. He frowned slightly.

"May I return to the house now, master?" she said, not looking up at him again.

"Not yet." He remained firmly planted in her path. His words had come out more harshly than he intended, and she looked ready to flee from him. To do so, she would have to step into the flower garden to get around him, and he doubted she had the courage to try.

Something about this girl intrigued him. Perhaps it was the heady combination of fear and innocence. She reminded him of the statue he had bought from Antigonus, which now stood barely fifty feet up the hill from where they stood. He thought of fair Bithia stealing whatever time she could to be with him. This girl clearly wished to be anywhere but here in the garden with him. He saw she was afraid of him and wondered if it was only because he was a Roman, an enemy of her people. Or was it something more basic? They were alone, he less than fully attired.

"Your name," he said. "I've forgotten it."

"Hadassah, master."

"Hadassah," he said, testing it.

Hadassah trembled. It sounded strange and foreign the way he said it. And beautiful, somehow. "Hadassah," he said again and, like a caress, the sound of his deep voice aroused emotions in her she had never felt before.

"Why do you persist in worshiping a god who has deserted you?"

Surprised by his question, she looked up at him. Why would he wish to speak with her of anything? He stood before her, virile and beautiful, representing Rome itself: powerful, rich, and full of frightening temptations.

"You should choose another," he said. "Walk up the Sacra Via and take your pick of gods. Choose one who's kinder to you than the unseen one before whom you prostrated yourself a moment ago."

Her lips parted and her face flamed with hot color. How long had he been watching her? She'd sought the solitude of the garden at night, thinking she would have privacy, that no one would see her there. To think of him watching her the whole time made her body go cold.

"Well? Can't you speak?"

She stammered her reply. "My God has not deserted me, my lord."

He laughed sardonically. "Your Holy City is rubble, your people are scattered across the face of the earth, and you're a slave. And you say your god has not deserted you?"

"He's kept me alive. I have food, shelter, and good owners."

Marcus was astounded at her quiet acceptance, her gratitude. "Why do you suppose your god granted you such bounteous favor?"

His sarcasm stung, but she answered simply anyway. "That I might serve."

"Do you say that because you think it's what I expect of you?" She lowered her head. "Look at me, little Hadassah." When she did as he commanded, he was struck again by her eyes, dark and wonderful in that small oval face. "Doesn't it matter to you that you have lost your freedom? Tell me the truth. Come on, now, girl, speak!"

"We all serve someone or something, my lord."

He smiled. "An interesting supposition. And whom do I serve?" When she seemed too timid to respond, he used his charm to cajole. "I mean you no harm, little one. You can answer without fear of retribution from me. Whom do you think I serve?"

"Rome."

He laughed at that. "Rome," he said again and grinned down at her. "Foolish girl. If we all serve something, I serve myself. I serve my own desires and ambitions. I fulfill my own needs my own way without the help of any deity." He wondered even as he spoke why he admitted this to a mere slave girl to whom such things could never matter. He wondered even more why she should look so saddened.

"It is the purpose of life, is it not?" he said mockingly, annoyed that a slave girl should look at him with something akin to pity. "To pursue and grasp happiness wherever you can. What do you think?" She stood silent, eyes once again downcast, and suddenly he wanted to shake her. "What do you think?" he said again, commanding her this time.

"I don't believe the purpose of life is to be happy. It's to serve. It's to be useful."

"For a slave, perhaps that is true," he said and looked away. He felt weary. Weary to his very bones.

"Are we not all bond servants to whatever we worship?" Her words brought his head up and around to her again. His handsome face was rigid with arrogant disdain. She had offended him. Frightened, she bit her lip. How had she dared speak so freely to a Roman, who could have her killed by mere whim?

"So, by your own words, since I serve myself, I am a slave to myself. Is that what you are saying?"

She took a step back, the blood draining from her face. "I plead your pardon, my lord. I'm no philosopher."

"Don't retreat now, little Hadassah. Tell me more that I might be amused." But he didn't look amused.

"What am I that you would ask me anything? Have I any wisdom to impart to you? I am a mere slave."

What she said was true. What answers did a slave have to offer him and why had he stayed in the garden with her? Something nagged at him. He did want to know something from her. He wanted to ask what exchanges she had made with her unseen god to have gone through what she'd been through and still have the look of peace he had seen and envied. Instead, he said briskly, "Was your father a slave also?"

Why was he tormenting her? "Yes," she said quietly.

"And what was his master? What did he believe?"

"He believed in love."

It was so trite, he winced. He had heard it from Arria and her friends often enough. *I believe in love, Marcus.* It was, he supposed, why she spent so much time at the temples, partaking of it, satiating herself with it. He knew all about *love.* It left him exhausted and empty. He could lose himself in a woman, drown in sensation and pleasure, but when it was over and he left, he found himself still hungry—hungry for something he couldn't even define. No, love wasn't the answer. Maybe it was as he always supposed. Power brought peace, and money bought power.

Why had he thought to learn anything from this girl? He already knew the answer for himself, didn't he? "You may return to the house," he said curtly, moving aside so she could pass.

Hadassah looked up at him. His handsome face was deeply lined, reflecting his troubled thoughts. Marcus Valerian had everything the world had to offer a man. Yet, he stood there, silent and oddly bereft. Was all his arrogance and affluence only an outward sign of an inner affliction? Her heart was moved. What if she told him about the love she meant? Would he laugh or have her sent to the arena?

She was afraid to speak of God to a Roman. She knew what Nero had done. She knew what was happening every day in the arena. So she kept what she knew secret.

"May you find peace, my lord," she said softly and turned away.

Surprised, Marcus glanced at her. She had spoken so gently, as though to comfort him. He watched her until she was out of sight.

9

Marcus found himself watching the young Jewess every time he was at home. He wondered what it was about her that fascinated him so much. She was devoted to his sister and seemed to sense Julia's every mood and need, seeing to her with gentle humility. Bithia had served Julia before Hadassah, but the Egyptian had had no fondness for her. Julia was high-strung and difficult. Bithia *obeyed.* This young Jewess *served.* Marcus could see it in the way she put her hand on Julia's shoulder when his sister was in one of her restless moods. He had never seen anyone but his mother touch Julia in that way. What was most amazing was that Hadassah's touch seemed to soothe his sister.

Father's announcement of Julia's marriage had put the home in an uproar, and Hadassah to the test. As soon as the words were out of Father's mouth, Julia had flown into a fit of hysteria, and it had been hovering near the surface ever since.

"I won't marry him! I won't!" she screamed at their father the evening he had told her. "You can't make me! I'll run away! I'll kill myself!"

Father slapped her across the face. He had never done such a thing before, and Marcus was too surprised to do anything but sit up from the couch and slam his goblet on the table.

"Decimus!" his mother gasped, clearly as shocked as he was that Father would do such a thing. Not that Julia didn't deserve it. Even so, to slap her in the face was unpardonable.

Julia stood in stunned silence, her hand pressed against her cheek. "You hit me," she said as though she couldn't believe it either. "You hit me!"

"I will have none of your hysterics, Julia," their father said through his teeth, his face ashen. "You speak to me in that tone of voice, and I will slap you again. Do you understand?"

Her eyes filled with tempestuous tears as she clenched her hand at her side.

"What I do, I do for your own good if you but had the sense to understand it. You will marry Claudius Flaccus. He is well respected and he holds considerable property in the Apennines, which you profess to love even more than Rome. And he was a considerate and faithful husband to his wife before she died. He will be so to you as well."

"He's old and decrepit."

"He is forty-nine and in good health."

"I won't marry him, I tell you! I won't!" Julia cried out again and burst into tears. "I'll hate you if you make me. I swear it. I'll hate you until I die!" She ran from the room.

Marcus started after her, but his mother's gentle voice stopped him. "Marcus, leave her be. Hadassah, see to her." Marcus watched the girl hurry from the room.

"Was that necessary, Father?" Marcus grated, his own temper simmering despite his coldly polite calm.

Decimus stared down at his hand, his face pale and strained. Clenching his fingers into a fist, he closed his eyes, then left without a word.

"Marcus," his mother said, laying her hand firmly on his arm when he started to rise and follow, "leave him alone. It will not help Julia if you take her side in this."

"He had no right to strike her."

"He had the right of a father. Much of what is going wrong with the Empire has to do with fathers who have not disciplined their children. She had no right to speak to your father the way she did!"

"Perhaps not the right, but certainly the reason! Claudius Flaccus. By the gods, Mother! Surely you are against this match."

"Indeed not. Claudius is a fine man. Julia will have no cause of grief from him."

"Or pleasure."

"Life is not about pleasure, Marcus."

Marcus shook his head angrily and left the room. He paused, then turned toward Julia's room. He wanted to see for himself that Julia was all right. She was still crying, but not so hysterically, and the young Jewess was holding her like a mother, stroking her hair and speaking to her. He stood unnoticed in the doorway watching them.

"How could my father think of marrying me off to that wretched old man?" Julia whined, clutching the girl like a talisman.

"Your father loves you, mistress. He desires only your good."

Cautiously Marcus backed out, but remained in the corridor, listening.

"No he doesn't," Julia cried. "He doesn't care about me at all. Didn't you see him hit me? All he cares about is having control over me. I can't do anything without his express approval, and I'm sick of it. I wish Drusus were my father. Octavia can do anything she pleases."

"Sometimes that kind of freedom doesn't come from love, my lady, but lack of care."

Marcus expected another outburst from Julia at that quiet, volatile statement. A long silence followed. "You say the strangest things, Hadassah. In Rome, if you love someone, you let them do whatever they wish. . . ." Julia's voice trailed off.

"What do you wish to do, mistress?"

Marcus eased forward and saw Julia sit quiet for a moment, confused and troubled. "Anything," she said, frowning. "*Everything,*" she amended and stood in agitation. "Except marry flaccid Claudius Flaccus."

Marcus' mouth twitched at her estimation of Claudius. He watched his sister cross the chamber to her vanity. She picked up a small Grecian vial of expensive perfume. "You can't understand, Hadassah. What can you know? Sometimes I feel I'm more a slave than you are." With a soft cry of frustration, she threw the vial across the room, shattering it against the wall. The perfume splattered and ran down the mosaic tiles of children gamboling in a profusion of flowers, filling the chamber with its cloying scent.

Julia sat down heavily and wept again. Marcus expected Hadassah to see him in the doorway when she fled his sister's rage, but she never turned around. She rose and went to his sister. Kneeling down, she took Julia's hands and spoke to her softly, too softly for him to hear.

Julia stopped crying. She nodded as though in answer to something Hadassah asked. Still holding her hands, Hadassah began to sing softly, in Hebrew. Julia closed her eyes and listened, though Marcus knew she didn't understand the language. Nor did he. Yet, standing in the shadows, he found himself listening, too—not to the words, but to Hadassah's sweet voice. Troubled, he left.

"Has Julia calmed down?" his mother asked when he joined her by the fountain.

"So it would appear," Marcus said, distracted. "That little Jewess is casting a spell over her."

Phoebe smiled. "She is very good for Julia. I knew she would be. There was something about her that day Enoch brought her to us." She ran her hand through the clear water of the pool. "I hope you will not fight your father in his decision."

"Claudius Flaccus is hardly exciting for a girl of Julia's temperament, Mother."

"Julia doesn't need excitement, Marcus. She breeds it within herself. It could burn her up like a fever. She needs a man who will steady her."

"Claudius Flaccus will do more than steady her, Mother. He'll put her to sleep on her feet."

"I don't think so. He's a brilliant man and has much to offer."

"Indeed, but has Julia ever shown an interest in philosophy or literature?"

Phoebe sighed heavily. "I know, Marcus. I've thought of the difficulties ahead. But whom would you have your father choose? One of your friends? Antigonus, perhaps?"

"Absolutely not."

She laughed softly at such a quick response. "Then you must agree. Julia needs maturity and stability in a husband. Those traits are not usually found in a younger man."

"A young girl wants things other than maturity and stability in a man, Mother," he said dryly.

"A young girl with any common sense realizes that character and intelligence far outlast charm and handsome features or build."

"I doubt such wisdom will mollify Julia."

"Despite the histrionics, Julia will bend to your father's decision and be the better for it." She folded her hands and looked up at him. "Unless you provoke her to rebel."

His mouth tightened. "She doesn't need provoking, Mother. She has a mind of her own!"

"You aren't blind to the influence you have over your sister, Marcus. If you were to speak with her—"

"Oh, no. Don't drag me into this. If I had any say, Julia would choose whom she pleases."

"And whom would your sister choose?"

His mind flashed to the handsome young rogue at the arena. A peasant most likely. He was annoyed to be reminded of the episode. A muscle tightened in his jaw. All young girls were fools for handsome faces; his sister no exception. Even so, that didn't alter his opinion. "Claudius Flaccus is not suitable for her."

"I think you're very wrong, Marcus. You see, what you have not been told is that your father didn't go to Claudius Flaccus. He came to us. Claudius is in love with her."

Claudius Flaccus and Julia exchanged wafers of wheat called *far* before the watchful eyes of two senior priests of the temple of Zeus. Julia was pale and emotionless. When Claudius took her hand and kissed it lightly, she looked up at him, her cheeks blooming red. Decimus stiffened, expecting an outburst. He saw tears filled her eyes, and he knew his daughter was capable of making a fool of herself before them all.

There was a stillness in the temple chamber, the marble idols seeming almost watchful. Marcus' face was a grim mask, his dark eyes flashing. He had argued long and hard against this marriage. He had suggested *coemptio,* or bride-purchase, a marriage easily dissolved by divorce. Decimus refused to consider it.

"You will *not* make such a suggestion to Claudius and bring shame on our family! Haven't you considered it far more likely he'd want to divorce your sister in the long run? For all of Julia's beauty and delightful high spirits, she is vain, selfish, and volatile. Such a combination quickly wears on any man. Or haven't you learned that with Arria?"

Marcus paled in anger. "Julia is nothing like Arria."

"Marriage by *confarreatio* to a man like Claudius will assure that she doesn't become like her."

"Have you so little confidence in your own daughter?"

"I love her more than my own life, but I am not blind to her faults." Decimus shook his head sadly. He knew that beauty faded quickly when embodied by selfishness, and Julia's charm was a tool of manipulation. Marcus saw only what he wanted to see in his sister—a high-spirited, willful child. He didn't see what she could become if allowed free rein. On the other hand, with the proper husband, Julia could mature into a woman like her mother.

Julia needed stability and direction. Claudius Flaccus would provide both. Granted, Decimus agreed, he was not a young girl's dream, but there were more important things: honor, family, duty. Decimus wanted to assure a respectable future for his daughter, and no amount of rationalization on the part of his hot-tempered son would dissuade him from it. Freedom without license bred destruction. Someday, perhaps both of his children would understand and forgive.

Decimus watched his daughter raise her chin slightly and give Claudius a brave smile. He felt a surge of pride and relief. Perhaps she had the sense to realize what a good man she had just married, and perhaps her adjustment would go more smoothly than anyone expected, himself included. By the gods, he loved her so. Perhaps she wasn't the fool he feared she was. He took Phoebe's hand and squeezed it lightly, satisfied to witness Julia married before the priests by *confarreatio,* the more traditional union, which couldn't be dissolved and would last until death. His eyes burned with tears, remembering his own marriage day and the love he had felt for his frightened bride. He loved her still.

Octavia was the first to embrace Julia after the ceremony as guests surrounded the couple, congratulating them. Their voices mingled and rose in the holy chamber, echoing. The priests approached Decimus, who paid them and took the document declaring the marriage verified. Phoebe pressed several more coins into their hands, quietly asking them to burn incense and make sacrifices to bless the marriage. Decimus had been generous, and they promised to do so. They went on their way, coins jingling in their pouches.

Decimus watched with a twinge of pain as his beautiful young daughter accepted the congratulations and good wishes of their guests. Claudius would take Julia for a brief trip after the feasting tonight. After a few weeks, he planned to take her to his country estate near Capua, where they would live. Of course, Decimus approved, knowing it was best for her. Ensconced there, Julia would be far from the destructive influences of young women like Octavia and Arria with their modern ideas of independence and immorality. She would be far from Marcus.

But, oh, how he would miss her, his only daughter.

"So, it's done," Phoebe said quietly, smiling up at him through her tears. "All the battles are over and the war is finally won. I think they'll prosper, Decimus. You've done well for her. Someday she'll thank you."

They joined their guests and went outside into the sunlight. Claudius was assisting Julia onto the flower-covered sedan chair. Decimus knew Claudius would be an attentive and patient husband. He watched Claudius join Julia and take her hand. That he adored her was obvious, yet she looked so young, so vulnerable.

As their procession moved slowly through the thronging streets of Rome, people called out to the newly married couple. Some uncouth youths shouted ribald remarks that brought stinging color to Phoebe's cheeks as she reclined beside Decimus. Cosseted behind the high walls of their home, she was protected from much of the licentious and ill-mannered behavior of the citizenry.

Decimus longed for the quiet of the country. He longed for the clean blue waters of the Aegean Sea. He longed for the hills of his homeland. He was weary of Rome.

Phoebe sat beside him beneath the canopy, her hip against his. All these years together and he still felt strong desire for his wife, even though thoughts of death depressed him, and the pain that had come intermittently in the beginning was now a constant companion. He took her hand, weaving his fingers through hers. She smiled up at him. Did she suspect what he knew—that his illness was getting worse?

The guests gathered in the triclinium for the celebration feast. Decimus had kept the number small; no less than the Graces, nor more than the Muses. Phoebe had seen to decorating the room with a profusion of colorful aromatic flowers. Decimus held no confidence in her belief that the sweet scent of the blossoms would neutralize the fumes of the lamps—nor the effects of the wine, which would pour freely this evening. He was tired, the ever-present pain sapping him of his strength. The cloying scent of the flowers nauseated him.

Claudius and Julia removed their shoes and reclined on the first couch, while the others took their places on couches around them. Leaning close, Claudius spoke to her softly. She blushed. With the marriage ceremony behind her, Julia seemed in better spirits.

Decimus hoped Claudius would get her with child quickly. With a child at her breast, Julia would settle more easily into being a proper Roman wife. She would see to her hearth fire and run her home as Phoebe had trained her to do. Her mind would be occupied with the early education of her children and caring for her family rather than on the games and lewd gossip.

Enoch stood at the doorway. Decimus nodded for him to have the servants bring in the *gustus,* the hors d'oeuvres.

In the kitchen, Hadassah watched Sejanus arrange the lavish

appetizers on silver platters. The aroma of exotic and delicious foods filled the hot room and made her mouth water. The cook carefully placed each sow udder until there was a starburst pattern, adding generous dollops of jellyfish and roe and sprigs of herbs to expand the design. Another platter displayed a goose-liver sculpture of a nesting bird, and wedges of eggs were arranged to look like white feathers. Hadassah had never seen such food before, nor inhaled such heavenly aromas. The servants chattered about the marriage between Claudius and Julia.

"The master is probably giving a sigh of relief to have her married off."

"Flaccus will have his hands full."

"She can be a delight when she's not in one of her moods."

The conversation went on around Hadassah. Most of the servants hoped that Julia would be unhappy, for they disliked her arrogant manners and outbursts of temper. Hadassah took no part in the gossip. She watched in fascination as Sejanus worked.

"I've never seen food like this," she said, awed by the creations he made.

"Not like the palace cooks, but the best I can do." He glanced up as Enoch came in. He dabbed the perspiration from his brow and looked over the platters with a critical eye, making a few last minor changes.

"Everything smells and looks so wonderful, Sejanus," Hadassah said, feeling privileged to have watched him make the final preparations.

Pleased, he was generous. "You can taste whatever they leave."

"She'll touch none of it," Enoch said tersely. "Pig udders, lampreys, sea urchins, fish eggs, calf boiled in its mother's milk," he said, and shuddered with distaste as he looked over the elegant display. "Our law forbids us to eat anything unclean."

"Unclean!" Sejanus said, insulted. "Your Jewish god would suck the pleasure from the poorest orphan's mouth. Bitter herbs and bread without leaven! That's what Jews eat."

Enoch ignored Sejanus and signaled to several slaves to take platters. He looked down at Hadassah with an air of paternal sternness. "You'll have to cleanse yourself after serving this evening."

Cringing inwardly at such an insensitive remark regarding Sejanus' culinary perfection, she gave Sejanus an apologetic look. His face was mottled red in anger.

"Take that one," Enoch commanded, pointing with distaste to the pig's udders. "Try not to touch any of it." She lifted the platter and followed Enoch from the kitchen.

As Hadassah set the platter before her, Julia was laughing with Octavia. Waving Hadassah away, she dipped her fingers into the jellyfish and roe while Claudius took a sow's udder stuffed with shellfish. Enoch poured the honeyed wine into silver goblets while several musicians played softly on pan flute and lyres.

Hadassah moved back against the wall. She was relieved to see Julia laughing and talking again, though she suspected it was more to impress her friends rather than with any real joy. For all her brightness and gaiety, there was an emptiness in Julia that hurt Hadassah. She could soothe her. She could serve her. She could love her. But she could not fill that emptiness.

God, she needs you! She thinks all the stories I tell her are only for her amusement. She hears nothing. Lord, I am so useless. Hadassah felt such a tenderness toward Julia, a tenderness akin to what she had felt for Leah.

Hadassah soaked in the beauty of the evening as she served silently. The sound of pan flute and lyres drifted sweetly in the room as the musicians played quietly in the corner. Everything was so beautiful, the people in their togas and jewels, the flower-decorated room, the colorful pillows, the food. Yet, Hadassah knew, for all the celebration and lavishness of this evening, there was little joy in the room.

Decimus Valerian looked drawn and pale. Phoebe Valerian was clearly concerned about him, but trying not to annoy him with any inquiries. Octavia flirted boldly with Marcus, who looked bored with her advances, not to mention the gathering itself. There was an edge of overbrightness to Julia's laughter, as though she was determined to look happy for the sake of appearances, more for Octavia's benefit than her own family. No one but Claudius was fooled, and he was in love, oblivious of everything but the beauty of his youthful bride.

Hadassah had grown to care deeply for this family she served. She prayed for each of them unceasingly. In this gathering, they looked so close, and yet they were pulled in opposing directions, each struggling with one another as well as with themselves. Was it in the Roman nature to be constantly at war? Decimus, a self-made man who had built his wealth, strove now to right what his own affluence had wrought upon his children. Phoebe, ever loyal and constantly loving, sought solace and blessing from her stone idols.

Hadassah prayed for Julia more than all the others combined, for God had given her Julia to serve, and Julia lay victim to the strongest character traits of all. She was possessor of a will equal to her father's, a loyalty fiercer though less selective than her mother's, and passion as hot as Marcus was reputed to have.

Reclined on the couch with Octavia, Marcus suffered her flirtation. She moved and brushed her hip against his. He smiled sardonically and took a wedge of egg, dipping it into goose liver. She had all the subtlety of a yowling she-cat.

He wondered what Arria was doing to while away the evening. She'd been angry when he informed her his father refused to invite her to the wedding or to the festivities afterward. She'd been even more furious when she learned Drusus and Octavia would be attending. She thought Drusus nothing more than a plebeian blessed by Fortuna. Like Marcus' father, Drusus had bought his Roman citizenship and respectability.

"Your father doesn't think I'm good enough for you, does he?" Arria had said yesterday as they were together after attending the games.

"He thinks most young women these days are too free-spirited."

"A polite way of saying he considers me little better than a common harlot. Does he think *I* corrupted *you,* Marcus? Could he not guess it was the other way around?"

Marcus laughed. "Your reputation far preceded mine. It was one of the reasons I pursued you so madly, to find out what all the talk was about!" He kissed her lingeringly.

She wouldn't drop the subject, however. "What does Julia have to say to all these arrangements?"

Marcus sighed impatiently. "She has accepted the inevitable," he said, trying to keep the grimness from his voice.

"Poor girl. I pity her." There was a tinge of mockery in her tone that grated on Marcus. "She'll be little better than a chattel once the vows are declared and *far* wafers exchanged before the priests. She'll have no rights whatsoever."

"Claudius won't abuse her."

"Nor excite her."

Marcus watched Claudius and his sister on the first couch. It was obvious Claudius was enthralled. He studied everything Julia did with a raptness that announced to everyone present he was in love. Julia was giddy, not because she was happy over her marriage, but because Enoch was keeping her goblet filled with honeyed wine. Drunk, she'd feel no pain—nor pleasure.

Hadassah stood nearby as she always did, serenity amidst chaos. Her gaze traveled over the family and guests. Watching her, Marcus guessed at her feelings for each—concern for his father, admiration for his mother, tenderness for Julia, curiosity about Claudius.

What did she feel for him?

He hadn't spoken with her since the evening he had watched her pray, although wherever Julia was, Hadassah was there, too. He never heard her speaking more than a word or two, yet Julia said Hadassah frequently told amusing stories about her people. She related a story of a slave's baby who was left in the bulrushes of the Nile, then found and reared by a royal princess. Another tale centered on a Jewess who became queen of Persia and saved her people from annihilation, and yet another told of a man of God who was cast into a den of lions, yet survived an entire night unharmed. Marcus considered the girl's tales nothing more than simple stories to while away a long, dull afternoon. Yet, as he watched her, he almost wished he could escape this celebration and go into the garden with her to hear her stories himself. Would she tell him one, or would she sit in the moonlight trembling in fear of him as she had the last time they had been there?

She felt his gaze and glanced his way, her dark eyes brushing his briefly in question. He lifted his hand slightly and she came to him immediately. "Yes, my lord?"

Her voice was soft and sweet. She wore her slave expression, dutiful, emotionless. He was unaccountably irritated. "Do you still pray at night in the garden?" he said, forgetting Octavia's presence beside him on the couch.

"Jews pray everywhere," Octavia said derisively. "Little good that it does them."

Marcus' mouth tightened when Hadassah's expression became even more veiled. He wished he hadn't asked anything so personal, at least not within the hearing of another. Octavia went on with her derision of Jews. He paid no heed. "What is on the *cena* menu, Hadassah?" he said as though that had been his sole interest in beckoning her. Why had he?

She spoke without inflection, reciting the items that would be brought out for the main course. "Roasted fallow deer, lamprey from the Straits of Sicily, turtle dove stuffed with pork and pine kernels, truffles, Jericho dates, raisins, and apples boiled in honey, my lord." It was the same tone Bithia used when speaking to him in front of his mother. When they were alone, though, Bithia's voice was far richer and deeper.

He looked at the fine shape of Hadassah's mouth, the slender column of her throat where her pulse beat wildly, and then into her eyes again. She didn't move, but he felt her withdraw. Did she see him as a lion and she the prey? He didn't want her to be afraid of him. "You'll be accompanying Julia to Capua?"

"Yes, my lord."

He felt a sense of loss and it annoyed him. He lifted his hand slightly, dismissing her.

"She's very homely. Whyever did your mother buy her for Julia?"

Homely? Marcus looked at Hadassah again as she took her place at the wall. Plain, perhaps. Quiet, certainly. Yet, there was a loveliness about Hadassah he couldn't define. Something that transcended the physical. "She's totally without conceit."

"As any slave should be."

"And is your Ethiopian?" he said dryly.

Octavia felt the barb and changed the subject. Dipping his fingers into the goose liver, Marcus allowed Octavia's conversation to roll over him. Her mind was on the games. She knew more than a lady should about several gladiators. After a few minutes, he tired of her again and listened to the conversation going on around him, but he could feel little interest in Claudius' vineyards and orchards.

The main course was served, and he found himself watching Hadassah again as she removed the platter of sow's udders and placed another of fallow deer before Julia and Claudius. No one seemed to notice her at all—no one except him—and he felt her presence with every fiber of his being.

Was it only that he was bored and looking for distraction? Any distraction? Or was there really something extraordinary about her, something beneath the surface commonness? He wondered every time he saw her.

When she removed the tray of appetizers from his table, he watched her strong, slender hands. As she walked away, his gaze flickered over the gentle sway of her slender hips. Six months in their possession had changed the emaciated little Jewess child into a nubile young woman with beautiful, mysterious dark eyes.

He knew that Hadassah was around the same age as Julia, which would make her fifteen or sixteen. What ran through her mind as she saw her mistress wed? Did she long for a husband and family of her own? It wasn't uncommon for slaves in a household to marry. Was there anyone in this household that caught Hadassah's interest? Enoch was the only Jew, and he was old enough to be her father. The other Jewish slaves Father had purchased had been sent to the country estate.

Hadassah adjusted the tray before Julia so that the choicest morsels were within easy grasp. As she bent over, Marcus looked at her slender ankles and small sandaled feet. He closed his eyes. She had survived the destruction of her country and her people. She had marched a thousand miles over some of the harshest terrain in the Empire. She had seen and experienced things he could only imagine, if he wanted to—and he didn't.

The soothing music was getting on his nerves. He couldn't get it out of his mind that Hadassah would be going to Capua with his sister. What did it matter if she did? What was she to him but a slave in his father's household, a slave who served his sister?

Bithia danced then, distracting him briefly with her undulating movements and the swirling of colorful veils. She aroused Drusus, if not the staid Flaccus, so solicitous of his now tipsy bride. Marcus was bitter. The thought of his sister with her aging husband made him sick; the thought of not having Hadassah's quiet presence in the household depressed him.

Musicians played as a poet recited, and the last course was served—sweet wine cakes and dates stuffed with nuts. It was only in this household that Marcus felt powerless. He was still beneath the auspices of his tyrannical father; he was a son, not a man in his own right. He had a fierce will of his own, cause for their frequent battles, and though Marcus knew death would someday make him victor, it wasn't the sort of victory he eagerly awaited.

Though they seldom got along, he loved his father. They were too much alike, flint against flint. Decimus had clawed his way up from seaman to wealthy merchant. He now had a sizable fleet. Discontent with the status quo, Marcus wanted to go further. He wanted to take the fortune his father had made and diversify, to spread the wealth through other enterprises and provinces so the family fortune didn't rest upon the good will of Neptune or Mars alone. Thus far his father had resisted and held tight rein, even though Marcus had made considerable profits from the six ships his father had given him to manage. He'd invested those profits in lumber, granite, marble, and building construction. And he toyed with the idea of investing in the noble horses that were bred for the races.

At twenty-one, he had been successful and respected by his peers. By twenty-five, he'd surpass his own father in wealth and position. Perhaps then, and only then, Decimus Valerian would see that tradition and archaic values must give way to progress.

Hadassah returned to the kitchen, dismissed by Claudius for the evening. She had seen the look in Julia's eyes: a flicker of anger that he would *dare* dismiss her personal maid . . . and then a wide-eyed virgin's fear.

Sejanus set Hadassah to work washing pots and cooking utensils. He sent the other two slave girls to clear the tables in the dining room now that the guests had adjourned for the night. "I suppose you'll have to cleanse yourself in purer waters after you've washed those pots," he said, still smarting from Enoch's remarks. "Just your hands," he added, "or will you have to wash from head to foot as well, just to make sure you're a nice clean little Jewess again?"

She bit her lip and looked back at him, hearing the hurt behind his cutting question. "I'm sorry you were insulted, Sejanus." She smiled at him, wishing he could understand. "Everything looked and smelled delicious. Julia and the others enjoyed every bite."

Sejanus took the pot she had washed and hung it up. "Why should you apologize for what he said?"

"Enoch is bound by the law. If he hadn't thought I was about to break it, he would have said nothing."

Mollified, Sejanus watched her wash the utensils, then dry and put them away. He liked this young slave girl. Unlike the others, who had to be told what to do, Hadassah saw what needed doing and did it. The others took their time in performing their duties, grumbling over everything. Hadassah grumbled about nothing and served as though it was her delight. She learned quickly and even assisted the others as time permitted.

"There's plenty left," he said. "Bithia and the other girls have had their fill and gone to bed. The musicians and everyone else have eaten—all except Enoch, may he die of constipation. Sit down and eat something. All you've taken tonight is bread. Have some cheese and some wine." He sat down on the bench across the table. "Try a sow's udder. I know you've never had anything so good in your life. What harm can it do?"

None, Hadassah knew, not from the viewpoint of whether it would defile her. It wasn't what she put in her mouth that would defile her, but what proceeded from her mouth, be the words unkind, slanderous, gossipful, boastful or blasphemous. Yet, she couldn't eat of this food because Enoch, who still lived beneath the Jewish law, abhorred it. He had saved her from the arena. He had brought her here to this beautiful house, to these people she had come to love. He was a brother of her race. To eat this would dishonor and insult him; she couldn't do it no matter how much her mouth watered for a small taste.

Yet, she counted Sejanus a friend as well, and to refuse to sample what he had worked so hard to create would hurt him. She looked back into his face and saw this was a test of her loyalty. Enoch was abrasive, proud, and self-righteous at times, but he had proven himself compassionate and brave, risking himself to save her and the six men he had brought back to this house. Sejanus was equally proud and quick to take offense. He was also generous and free-spirited, telling jokes to the slave girls as they worked.

The food smelled so delicious that her stomach cramped from hunger. She hadn't eaten since early morning. The temptation to eat of these delicacies was strong, but Enoch mattered too much to her.

"I cannot," she said in apology.

"Because of your accursed law," he said in disgust.

"I'm fasting, Sejanus." He would understand that. Even pagans fasted.

"For Julia," he said. "Is it not enough that you pray for her constantly? Why forsake your food as well? Fasting won't soften her heart. Not even a dozen blood sacrifices would accomplish that!"

She turned away and washed the remaining utensils, unwilling to listen to his criticism of her mistress. Julia had faults. She was selfish and conceited. She was also young and beautiful and vibrant. Hadassah loved her and was afraid for her. Julia was so desperate to be happy.

Hadassah had never been among people like the Valerians,

who had so much and yet so little. They needed the Lord, and yet she lacked the courage to tell them of the miraculous and wondrous things she knew. She tried, but the words stuck in her throat; fear kept her silent. Every time an opportunity came, she remembered the arenas along the way from Jerusalem; she heard again the screams of terror and pain that sometimes haunted her nights. Not a member in this household would believe her father had died and been raised up by Jesus, not even Enoch, who knew God. What they would do is condemn her to death.

Why did you spare me, Lord? I'm useless to them, she thought in despair.

True, she told Julia stories her father had told her in Galilee. But Julia was merely entertained. She heard no lessons in them. How could Julia choose the truth if she had not the ears to hear it? How could she seek Christ if she felt no need for a Savior? Despite the stories Hadassah had told her, stories from Scripture of God's intervention for his people, Julia didn't understand. She was convinced that each individual was placed on this earth to grasp all she could and do as she wished. Not only did Julia feel no need of a Savior, she did not want one.

Hadassah saw the wealth and comfort the Valerians enjoyed as a curse on them. Because of those things, they felt no need for God. They were warm, well fed, and beautifully clothed and sheltered. They enjoyed rich entertainment and were served by a large retinue of slaves. Only Phoebe worshiped a god at all, and her devotion was to stone idols who could give nothing back to her, least of all peace and joy.

Hadassah shook her head sadly. *How do you reach people who feel no need or desire for a Savior?* she wondered. *God, what do I do to make them see that you are here in their garden, that you dwell in their house, if not in their hearts? I am helpless. I am a coward. I am failing Julia, Lord. I am failing them all. Beneath the smiles and laughter, they are lost. Oh God, how great thou art. Not all the gods and goddesses of Rome can raise one soul from the dead as you have done. And yet they will not believe.*

"I don't mean to hurt you," Sejanus said, coming over to her. He had watched the distressed expressions crossing her face for the last few minutes and felt he was to blame. He had little regard for Julia—too often he had heard her screaming in a fit of rage, her pretty young face distorted by savage emotion. Yet, for some unaccountable reason, this slave girl loved her and served her with fond devotion. "You needn't worry about Julia," he said, trying to sound comforting. "She'll find her own way."

"But will her way bring her peace?"

"Peace?" Sejanus said with a laugh. "That's the last thing Julia wants. She's very much like her brother, except that Marcus far exceeds her in wits. He has his father's shrewdness, but not a particle of his morality. Not that it's Marcus' fault. It's the fault of the rebellions," he said, quick to excuse him. "He saw too many of his young friends murdered or ordered to commit suicide. It's understandable that he has adopted the philosophy of 'Live for today, for tomorrow you die.'"

"He doesn't seem content."

"Is anyone in this world content? Only fools and the dead are content."

Hadassah finished the chores Sejanus had asked of her and looked for something else to do for him. Together they cleaned the counters, disposed of the leftover food, and washed and polished the platters and put them away. Sejanus talked proudly of Greece.

"Romans own the world, but they envy Greeks. Romans only know how to make war. They know nothing of beauty and philosophy and religion. What they don't steal, they imitate. Our gods and goddesses, our temples, our art and literature. They study our philosophers. They may have conquered us, but we've remolded them."

Hadassah heard the pride mingled with resentment.

"Did you know the master was born in Ephesus?" Sejanus said. "He was the son of a poor merchant near the docks. By his own wits, he made himself into a great man. He purchased his Roman citizenship. It was a wise move," he said, excusing the disloyalty. "By doing so, he avoided certain taxes and gained social advantages for himself and his family."

Hadassah was aware of some of those advantages. The apostle Paul had been released from prison more than once because of his Roman citizenship. And, if one must die, it was better to die swiftly by a sword than by hanging on a cross. Roman citizens were executed with mercy. Paul had been beheaded while Peter, a Galilean, had been crucified upside down after having been made to watch as his wife was tortured and murdered.

Hadassah shuddered. Sometimes she could forget the gruesome visage of the thousands of crosses before the walls of Jerusalem. Tonight she saw them again—and the faces of the men who hung on them. "I have some final packing to do for the Lady Julia," Hadassah said and bid Sejanus good night.

The oil lamp was still lit in Julia's empty bedchamber. Four trunks were closed, already packed full. Two more remained open. Hadassah picked up a pale blue tunic and folded it carefully, laying it on top of a yellow one already in the trunk. She removed the rest of Julia's possessions and packed them. Closing the trunks, she locked them. She straightened and looked around the room. With a sigh, she sat down on a stool.

"It's barren, isn't it?" Phoebe said from the doorway and saw the young slave start in surprise. She had looked small and forlorn, sitting with the locked trunks around her. Now she stood and faced her mistress. "I wonder how she fares this night," Phoebe said and came into the room.

"Well, my lady," Hadassah said.

Phoebe smiled. "I couldn't sleep. Too much excitement." She sighed. "I miss her already. You looked as though you were missing her, too."

Hadassah smiled back at her. "She is so full of life."

Phoebe ran her hand along the smooth surface of Julia's vanity, now denuded of her cosmetics, perfumes, and jewelry boxes. She raised her head slightly and looked at Hadassah. "Claudius will send someone to fetch you and Julia's things."

"Yes, my lady."

"Probably by the end of the week," she said, looking around the room. "It's not a difficult journey to Capua. There is beautiful countryside along the way. You'll have plenty of time to unpack Julia's things and prepare for her arrival in her new home."

"All will be ready for her, my lady."

"I know." Phoebe looked at the young girl and felt a deep warmth toward her. She was kind and faithful, and despite how difficult Julia could be, Phoebe knew this young Jewess loved her daughter. She sat on Julia's bed. "Tell me about your family, Hadassah. What did your father do for a living?"

"He was a merchant of earthen vessels, my lady."

Phoebe gestured for Hadassah to sit on the stool near the bed. "Did he make a good living?"

Why was she asking her such personal questions? Of what possible interest was she to this fine Roman lady? "We were never hungry," Hadassah said.

"Did he make the earthen vessels or just sell them?"

"He made many of them, some plain and some very beautiful."

"Diligent and hardworking, but creative."

"People came to him from other provinces." Though they had purchased his wares, she knew they had come more to hear his story. She remembered the many times she had listened to her father speak to a stranger who had come to hear of his resurrection.

Phoebe saw the tears shimmering in the slave girl's eyes and was saddened. "How did he die?"

"I don't know," Hadassah said. "He went out into the street to speak to the people and he never came back again."

"To speak to them?"

"About the peace of God."

Phoebe frowned. She started to say something and then hesitated. "And your mother? Is she alive somewhere?"

"No, my lady," Hadassah said and bowed her head.

She saw the tears the girl tried to hide. "What happened to her? And the others in your family?"

"She starved to death a few days before the Roman legions took Jerusalem. Soldiers were going from house to house, killing everyone. One entered the house where we were and killed my brother. I don't know why he didn't kill me and my sister, too."

"What happened to your sister?"

"The Lord took Leah the first night we were in captivity."

The Lord took . . . what a strange way of putting it. Phoebe sighed and looked away. "Leah," she said softly. "A pretty name."

"She wasn't yet ten years old."

Phoebe closed her eyes. She thought of her own two children who had died of fever. Fevers often ravaged the city, for it was surrounded by marshes and frequently struck by noxious floods of the great Tiber. There were those who survived the fever, like Decimus, only to suffer from bouts of chills year after year. Others coughed until their lungs bled and they died.

Life was so uncertain, as Hadassah's testimony bore witness. She had lost everyone she loved in Jerusalem. She had spoken of the peace of God, yet even with the gods there seemed no guarantees. No matter how many hours Phoebe spent beseeching Hestia, goddess of the hearth, Hera, goddess of marriage, Athena, goddess of wisdom, Hermes, god of travel, and a dozen other household gods to protect her loved ones, might there not be another god or goddess more powerful to snatch them from her?

Even now, Decimus, her beloved, was ill and trying to hide it from everyone. Tears burned in Phoebe's eyes as she clenched her hands. Did he think he could hide anything from her?

"You are distressed, my lady," Hadassah said and laid a hand over hers.

Phoebe was surprised by the girl's tender touch. "The world is a capricious place, Hadassah. We are blown by the whims of the gods." She sighed. "But you know that, don't you? You have lost everything, family, home, freedom." She studied Hadassah in the lamplight, the smooth curve of her cheeks, the dark eyes, her slender frame. She had seen Marcus looking at the girl with curious fascination. Hadassah was no more than a year older than Julia, sixteen at most, yet she was profoundly different. She had a quiet humility gained through suffering. And there was something more . . . a sweet and rare compassion lit her dark eyes. Perhaps, despite her tender age, she possessed wisdom as well.

Phoebe took her hand firmly. "I entrust my daughter to you, Hadassah. I ask that you watch over her and care for her always. She will often be difficult, even cruel perhaps, though I can't believe she would ever be deliberately so. Julia was such a sweet and loving child. Those qualities are still within her. But she desperately needs a friend, Hadassah, a real friend, and she's never chosen wisely. That's why I selected you that day when Enoch brought you to us with the other captives. I saw in you someone who might be able to stand by my daughter in all circumstances." She searched her eyes. "Will you promise me to do that?"

As a slave, Hadassah had no other choice but to do the will of her masters. Yet, Hadassah knew the promise the mistress asked was not one to be given for that reason alone. Phoebe Luciana Valerian spoke, but Hadassah sensed that it was God himself who was asking her to love Julia, in all circumstances, whatever came from this day forward. It wouldn't be easy, for Julia was willful and selfish and thoughtless. Hadassah knew she could say she would try. She could say she would do her best. Either answer would satisfy the lady. But neither would satisfy the Lord. *Shall your will or mine be done?* the Master asked. She had to choose. Not tomorrow, but now, in this room, before this witness.

Phoebe knew full well what she asked. Sometimes it was difficult for her to love her own daughter, especially during these last days when Julia had made life so miserable for Decimus, who acted only for her own good. Julia wanted her own way at all costs, and this time she hadn't gotten it. She saw struggle in the slave girl's face and was pleased she hadn't answered quickly. A quick answer would soon be a forgotten promise.

Hadassah closed her eyes and let out her breath slowly. "Your will be done," she said softly.

Phoebe felt a wave of relief that Julia would be in Hadassah's care. She trusted this girl and, at this moment, felt deep and abiding tenderness toward her as well. A loyal slave was worth her weight in gold. Her instincts about purchasing this little Jewess had been right.

She rose. Touching Hadassah's cheek, she smiled down at her through her tears. "May your god always bless you." She laid her hand against the soft dark hair, like a mother would, then quietly left the room.

10

Atretes ran down the road, keeping up with the grueling pace Tharacus set as he rode horseback beside him. Tharacus alternately insulted and encouraged him, keeping the animal reined in to a steady trot. The sleek stallion snorted and tossed its white mane angrily, wanting its head, while the weights Atretes wore felt heavier with each mile. Gritting his teeth against the pain, the German kept on, his body drenched in sweat, his muscles straining, his chest burning.

Stumbling once, Atretes caught himself and swore under his breath. Much more of this and he would drop and shame himself. He focused his mind on reaching the next milestone and, when he saw it, set his mind on attaining the next.

"Hold up," Tharacus ordered. Atretes took three more steps and stopped. Bending over, he gripped his knees and dragged air into his starved lungs.

"Straighten up and walk it off," Tharacus said tersely. He tossed Atretes a water pouch.

Mouth parched, Atretes tipped it and drank deeply. Before he tossed it back, he squirted water onto his face and down his bare chest. He returned the bag and walked back and forth on the roadside until his breathing slowed to normal and his body cooled from its furnace heat.

"You have gained attention, Atretes," Tharacus said, grinning as he nodded toward the other side of the road.

Atretes glanced across the road and saw two young women in a peach orchard. One wore a fine white linen tunic, the other a brown tunic with paler brown overdress belted with a striped sash.

"She is poised like a hart ready to flee," Tharacus mocked. "It would seem they have never seen a naked man before." He laughed cynically. "See how the lady stares."

Atretes was too tired to be much affected by the rapt attention of a pretty girl or a shocked little Jewess or, for that matter, by the mockery of his lanista. He longed for his bench and the quiet coolness of his cell. He was rested enough to start back, but Tharacus seemed in the mood to amuse himself.

"Take a good long look at her, Atretes. Beautiful, isn't she? You will meet many like her when you enter the arena. Women of aristocratic breeding will clamor for your attentions. And men as well. They will give you anything—gold, jewels, their bodies—whatever you ask and in whatever way you ask."

He smiled faintly, then went on. "I had a woman who used to wait for me while I fought. She wanted me to touch her when my hands were still slick with the blood of a good kill. It drove her nearly mad with passion." His smile twisted into a sardonic sneer. "I wonder whatever happened to her." He swung his horse around.

Atretes looked across the road again, straight at the girl in white who stood in the shade of the tree. He stared at her boldly until she looked away. The little Jew spoke to her, and they turned and walked back through the orchard. The girl in white glanced back over her shoulder at him, then lifted her hem and began to run, her merry laughter drifting back to him.

"Romans are partial to blonds," Tharacus said. "Enjoy the adoration while it lasts, Atretes. Take all you can get!" He rapped Atretes with the butt end of his whip. "She's gone. Begin the run back. Turn left at the crossroads and go back through the hills," Tharacus said, assigning him the uphill road.

Atretes forgot about the girl and started off again. He set an even pace he knew he could keep, but Tharacus shouted at him to pick it up. Steeling himself, Atretes ran up the hill, timing his breathing.

He had undergone four months of grueling training at the ludus. The first month he had been trained by Trophimus. Tharacus had watched him closely and soon taken over his training. Turning the other trainees over to Gallus and the others, Tharacus spent most of his time working with Atretes. He pushed him harder than all the rest, teaching him tricks he didn't share with the others.

"If you listen to me and learn, you may survive long enough to earn your freedom."

"I am honored by your attention," Atretes said through gritted teeth.

Tharacus grinned coldly. "I will make you into a champion. If you succeed in surviving, I succeed in building reputation enough to earn a place at the great ludus of Rome rather than spend the rest of my life in this rabbit warren."

Unlike many of the others, Atretes reveled in the exercises. Having trained all his life as a warrior, to be trained as a gladiator was merely an expansion of his skills. He vowed to someday use all he learned against Rome itself.

To that end, he became expert with the gladius, though Tharacus assigned him more frequently the trident and net of the retiarius. Several times, Atretes tossed the net aside in frustration and attacked his opponent with such ferocity that Tharacus was forced to intercede or lose a trainee.

It was anger that kept Atretes going. He used it to drive himself on the long runs; he used it to drive away the depressions that came upon him in the night, hearing the hobnailed shoes of the guard as he walked his rounds; he used it to give himself the desire to learn every way possible to kill a man, hoping someday to earn his freedom so no one could ever be master over him again.

Atretes made no friends. He kept himself aloof from the other gladiators. He didn't want to know their names. He didn't want to know whence they came or how they had been taken. Someday he might face one of them in the arena. He could kill a stranger without the least regret; to kill a friend would haunt him forever.

He saw the ludus in the distance and got his second wind. His legs ate up the flat stretch of road. Tharacus allowed the horse just enough rein to pull ahead. A guard whistled shrilly from his position on the wall and, in response, the gate of the compound opened.

Tharacus dismounted and tossed the reins to a slave. "To the baths, Atretes, then report to Phlegon for a massage." His mouth tipped. "You did well today. You will be rewarded."

Entering the changing room, Atretes stripped off the damp loincloth, took a towel, and went into the tepidarium chamber. The water was warm and soothing. He relaxed and washed in a leisurely manner, ignoring the others talking in low voices so the guards wouldn't hear. He left the tepidarium and went into the next chamber, the caldarium, the room nearest the boilers. Atretes breathed in the steamy air while a slave rubbed his body with olive oil and then scraped it off with a knifelike strigil.

In the next chamber, Atretes plunged into the frigidarium. The cold water was a pleasant shock, and he swam the length of the pool and back. He swung himself up onto the edge and shook his head, splashing water about like a dog shaking its fur. He returned to the tepidarium for a last few minutes of respite before he was ordered to the massage room.

Phlegon was rough. He pounded and kneaded Atretes' muscles until they loosened. It seemed everything in this foul place was designed to break down the body and then build it up again, turning flesh into steel.

Atretes ate heartily of the meat and barley stew and then marched with the others back to the cell block. Closed in for the night, he stretched out on his bench and put his arm behind his head. He tried not to think about anything. Then the murmur of male voices and a door opening roused him. Someone was coming toward his cell. He sat up and leaned back against the cold stone, his heart pounding heavily.

The iron lock gave way and the heavy plank door opened. Gallus stood outside, a slave girl in front of him. She entered the cell without looking at Atretes, and Gallus locked the door behind her. Without a word, she came forward and stood before him. Atretes rose from the bench, looking at her. He remembered the beautiful girl in white who had watched him from the shade of a peach tree, and he felt a surge of desire and anger. He could have poured his hatred into her and relished it. But this girl was more like the little Jewish slave. When Atretes reached out to touch her, he did so without animosity.

Afterward, Atretes stood on the other side of the cell. He heard a scrape from above and knew a guard had been watching. The stain of humiliation filled his face and he had to stifle the urge to cry out. He had become little more than an animal at which to gawk.

The girl went to the door, rapped twice, and stood waiting. Atretes kept his back turned to her, less because of his own shame and more in consideration of hers. The lock scraped and the door opened, then it closed again and was relocked. The slave girl was gone. The reward Tharacus promised, given.

A deep, debilitating loneliness washed over Atretes. What if he had spoken to her? Would she have answered? She had come to him before, and he had felt the unspoken appeal to say nothing, to not even look into her face. She came to him because she was sent to serve him. He accepted in order to release the unbearable tension slavery built in him, but there was no warmth, no love, no humanity. She gave him a fleeting physical satisfaction, always followed by a drenching shame.

He lay down upon the stone bench and put his arm behind his head, staring up at the grate. He remembered his wife laughing and running through the forest, her blonde braid bouncing against her back. He remembered making love to her in the sunlight of a meadow. He remembered the tenderness they shared. Death had taken her all too soon. His eyes burned and he sat up, fighting against the despondency that made him want to smash his head into the stone wall.

Was he no longer a man? Had six months in this place turned him into an animal who gave in to the basest instincts? He was better off dead. He veered away from the thought of suicide. The guards were always on the lookout for attempts, but men found ways to kill themselves despite all efforts to prevent it. One man had eaten a pottery cup before the guards could stop him. He had died within hours, his insides lacerated. Another had put his head through the spokes of the training wheel, breaking his neck. The last, only two nights before, had torn his cloak and tried to hang himself from the grate.

Atretes believed no honor lay in taking his own life. When he died, he wanted to take as many Romans, or those who served Rome, with him as possible. Finally he closed his eyes and slept, dreaming of the black forests of Germania and of his dead wife.

Tharacus did not run him the next day. Instead, he took him to the small exhibition arena. He joined him in a series of warm-up and stretching exercises. Atretes wondered at the four armed guards who stood at equidistance within the walls, and he glanced up at the viewers' box. Scorpus stood with a tall black man dressed in a red tunic trimmed in gold.

"Let's see if you can best me, Atretes," Tharacus said in German, and tossed Atretes one of two thick long poles. He crouched and moved to one side, flipping the stick over and over expertly, waiting. "Come on," he said, mocking him. "Attack me if you dare. Show me if you have learned anything."

The weight of the oak felt good in Atretes' hands. The ends were blunted by leather. Scorpus had ordered this match for one of two reasons: either the African was wealthy and looking for a little entertainment, or he was buying himself a gladiator. Neither reason suited Atretes' pride. With Scorpus out of reach, he focused all of his hatred on Tharacus.

Moving slowly and cautiously around Tharacus, he looked for an opening. Tharacus made a sharp swing. Atretes blocked it, and the crack of wood on wood resounded in the arena. Tharacus shifted his weight, turned swiftly, and caught Atretes across the side of his head, opening a cut next to his eye.

Hot rage raced through Atretes' blood, but with force of conditioning and will, he subdued it. He took two more blows and then landed two of his own, rocking Tharacus on his feet. Using the heat of his anger to give him strength, he took the offensive. He had learned to watch an opponent's eyes rather than his hands to know what he intended. He blocked two swings and drove the long pole into Tharacus' kidney, catching the lanista's startled look as he stumbled. He swung the stick in a swift circle and aimed the blow at Tharacus' head. The lanista dodged it and rolled to his feet. One word from him and the guards would intercede. But he said nothing.

The swift, sharp cracks of the long poles rang across the small arena. Sweat poured from both, and they grunted with each powerful blow. Seeing they were too evenly matched for him to gain an advantage, Atretes dropped his stick and caught hold of Tharacus', using the full force of his strength to bring it down to the lanista's chin. He knew all the lanista's tricks. Tharacus would try to sweep his feet. When he made the move, Atretes brought his knee up hard. Tharacus expelled a sharp breath, his eyes glazing with pain and his fingers loosening. Atretes brought his knee up again and then used the stick to knock the lanista back.

From the corner of his eye, he saw a guard move as Tharacus fell. He knew he had little time. Releasing the long pole, Atretes dropped onto Tharacus, gripped the helmet with his left hand and brought his right back. Tharacus' eyes widened and he tried to dodge the blow he himself had taught as he cried out an order too late. Atretes drove the heel of his hand against the base of Tharacus' nose, snapping the cartilage and driving it into his brain.

Two guards dragged him back from Tharacus' convulsing body. Atretes threw back his head and screamed out his war cry in jubilation. Adrenaline still raced through his body, and he threw off one guard and drove his fist into the abdomen of the other, yanking the gladius from his scabbard as he fell. The third and fourth drew blades. *"Don't kill him!"* Scorpus shouted from the box.

Swords sheathed, the guards used a net to bring him down. Tangled in it like a thrashing wild animal, he was pinned face-down in the sand, and the gladius was pried from his hand. Wrist and ankle manacles were locked on, and he was dragged to his feet, spitting out profanity in Greek. They stood him before the viewers' box.

Chest heaving, he looked up at Scorpus and his guest and shouted the foulest names he had collected in his six months at the ludus. Scorpus glared down at him, face white and pinched. The black man grinned, said something to Scorpus, and left the box.

Within the hour, Atretes was chained in another wagon with a Gaul, a Turk, and two Britons from other Capuan ludi. The black man rode ahead in a shaded sedan chair carried by four slaves.

The African's name was Bato. He was owned by the emperor Vespasian and held the prestigious position of head lanista at the ludus of Rome.

Atretes was bound for the heart of the Empire.

"Tell him I have a headache," Julia said in dismissive tones, not even looking up at the slave who stood in the doorway with the polite request from Claudius that she join him in the bibliotheca. She didn't even pause in the game she was playing, but dropped the knucklebones from the back of her fingers and watched them clatter on the marble floor. When she did not hear Hadassah speak or the door close, she glanced up crossly and saw Hadassah's beseeching look. "Tell him," she ordered imperiously, and Hadassah had no choice but to repeat her mistress's message.

"I heard," Persis said under his breath and turned away.

Hadassah closed the door quietly and looked at her young mistress. Was she so selfish and foolish as to deny her husband the smallest courtesy? What must Claudius Flaccus feel?

Seeing Hadassah's look, Julia became defensive. "I've no desire to spend another boring evening in the bibliotheca while he talks dull philosophies. How do I know or care what Seneca thought?" She snatched up the bones again and clenched them in her fist. Her eyes smarted with tears. Why couldn't everyone just leave her alone? She threw the bones and they bounced and rolled in wild array. She sat back on her heels.

Hadassah bent and gathered up the knucklebones one by one.

"You just don't understand," Julia said. "No one understands."

"He is your husband, my lady."

Julia's chin jerked up. "Does that mean I must answer his every summons like a slave?"

Hadassah could only wonder what Claudius Flaccus would do when told his young wife refused to come to him on the weak excuse of a headache. In the beginning, Julia had played the joyous bride, more to impress her friends than to please her husband. Once out of Rome, though, she became painfully polite. Settled in Capua, she became petulant.

Claudius Flaccus was a man of monumental patience, but Julia's daring to bluntly refuse him might well shatter that virtue. Over the past six months, Claudius had overlooked Julia's moodiness. However, outright disobedience and rudeness would surely gain his anger. Hadassah was afraid for her mistress. Did Roman husbands beat their wives?

She was also, quite honestly, annoyed. Was Julia so blind she couldn't see that Claudius Flaccus was intelligent, kind, and gentle? He was a worthy husband for any young woman. Claudius did all he could to entertain Julia, introducing her to his friends, taking her on chariot rides through Campania, buying her presents. Yet, Julia gave not even meager consideration in return. Her gratitude was perfunctory, as though whatever he did was her due and his duty.

"He is kind to you, my lady," Hadassah said, searching for a way to reason with her.

"Kind," Julia said with a sniff. "Is it kind to press his attentions on me when I don't want them? Is it kind to demand his rights when the mere thought of him repulses me? I don't want to spend the evening with him." She put her hands over her face. "I hate it when he touches me," she said and shuddered. "His flesh is pale as death."

Hadassah felt the heat pouring into her face.

"Just thinking about him makes me sick." Julia rose and went to the window, gazing out at the courtyard.

Hadassah looked down at her clasped hands, unsure what to say to soothe her mistress. Such blunt talk embarrassed her. What did she know of the intimacies of married life? Perhaps it was unbearable for Julia and she shouldn't be so quick to judge. "Perhaps your feelings will change when you have children," Hadassah said.

"Children?" Julia said with a flash of her dark eyes. "I'm not ready to have children. I haven't even lived yet." She ran her hand down a Babylonian tapestry. "The gods must agree with me, for I am not with child yet, and not for lack of Claudius' trying. Oh, he tries and tries. For all of Father's grand hopes of a royal line, Claudius' seed has probably gone bad."

Her bitterness changed to amusement when she glanced back at Hadassah. She laughed. "Your face is all red." Her smile dimmed quickly, however, and she reclined on a lounge. She gazed at a bright fresco on the wall of men and women gamboling in a forest glen. They were laughing and joyous. Why couldn't her life be like that? Why did she have to have such an old and dull husband? Was she to be locked away in this Capua villa for the rest of her life? She longed for the excitement of Rome. She missed Marcus' wit. She wanted adventure. Claudius wouldn't even consent to take her to one of the gladiatorial ludi to see a training session.

"Do you remember that gladiator we saw?" Julia said dreamily. "He was beautiful, wasn't he? Like Apollo. His skin was the color of bronze and his hair was like the sun." She laid her hand delicately on her stomach. "He made me quiver inside. When he looked at me, I felt as though I was on fire."

She turned, her face pale, her eyes bright with tears of bitter disappointment. "And then there is Claudius, who makes my blood run cold."

Hadassah remembered the gladiator. Julia had insisted upon going through the orchard the next day and the next, but thankfully, the gladiator and his trainer hadn't appeared again.

Julia stood restlessly and rubbed her temples. "I do have a headache," she said. "Just thinking about Claudius gives me a headache." It occurred to her belatedly that Claudius might be angry at her refusal. It wasn't proper for a wife to refuse a husband anything. She thought of her mother and felt guilty. She could almost see her reproving look and hear her reprimand, gentle though stinging.

Julia bit her lip, vexed. She had never seen Claudius angry. Her heart began to beat heavily.

"He probably won't believe it, but I'm *not* feeling well. Go and speak with him for me," she said and waved her hand toward the door. "Give him my fond regards and explain that I'm going to take a long bath and then retire to my bed. Summon Catya for me." That foul Persis had probably told Claudius that she was playing knucklebones.

Hadassah summoned the Macedonian maid and then went along the inner corridor to the bibliotheca. The great house was quiet and still.

Claudius was sitting at his desk, a scroll spread out before him. The lamplight made the gray streaks in his hair shine white. Claudius glanced up. "Persis already brought word that the lady Julia has a headache." His tone was dry, his expression indifferent rather than angry. "Has she changed her mind?"

"No, my lord. The lady Julia sends her fond regards and regrets she is not feeling well. She is going to take a bath and retire for the night."

Claudius grimaced. Thus he was dismissed before the sun was even set. He was neither fooled nor upset by Julia's excuses. In fact, he was relieved. He leaned back slightly and released his breath slowly. Trying to entertain Julia had become tedious. In six months of marriage, Claudius had learned a great deal about his young wife, little of which had endeared her to him. He smiled painfully. She was beautiful and made to be admired, but she was childish and self-centered.

And he was an old fool, flying high with eros.

The first time he had glimpsed Julia, he had been struck by her similarity to Helena, his beloved wife. He had thought, or rather dreamed, that she was perhaps even a reincarnation of her. He had been besotted, drunk on hope, clinging to a nonexistent possibility. The gods had merely been playing with him.

Thinking of Helena filled him with loneliness. He remembered her sweet presence with an aching longing. All the years he had spent with her hadn't been enough. A lifetime would not have been enough.

Helena had been quiet, pensive, tender, satisfied to sit with him in this room by the hour. They talked of everything—the arts, the gods, philosophy, politics. Even the mundane, everyday matters of what he had said to their overseer had interested Helena. Julia was constant motion and scarcely-contained energy. He sensed unruly passions constantly at war within her, passions he could not tap with his possession. She was beautiful, more beautiful than Helena, with fine curves and a smoothness like pure marble. But she was disquieting.

Nothing interested Julia, except perhaps the gladiatorial ludi that populated the Capuan area. She wanted to visit one of those barbarous places and see how the gladiators were trained. She wanted to know everything about them. Whenever he tried to steer the conversation to other avenues of more enlightening thought, she drove the conversation back to those poor wretches behind the high walls and thick bars.

Perhaps he expected too much of her. She was young and inexperienced. She had a quick mind, but her interests were far too narrow. His Helena had been cerebral; Julia was physical. While he took some pleasure in Julia's lovely young body, the pleasure was growing briefer, the aftermath more disheartening. With Helena, he had shared passion and tenderness. Sometimes they even laughed and talked until they slept. Julia suffered his possession in martyred silence. He never remained in her chamber longer than necessary.

The unbearable loneliness of surviving Helena remained with him. He had thought to overcome it by marrying the young and vibrant Julia. How wrong could a man be? They had nothing in common. What he had mistaken for love had only been the physical need of a foolish man.

How Cupid must be laughing, having shot his arrow so straight and true. Claudius had lost his head, but not his heart, and now had the rest of his life to repent his foolishness.

He unrolled the scroll further and lost himself in his studies of religions of the Empire. It was a worthy enough subject to keep him occupied until Hades, the god of the underworld, claimed his soul.

The next morning, he saw his young wife walking through the gardens with her maid. Julia sat on a marble bench and plucked flowers while her maid stood, speaking. Julia glanced up once and made a brief remark, then gestured for the maid to continue. He watched for long moments as the slave girl spoke, then went out to join them, curious to hear what she was saying.

Julia saw him coming and her countenance fell. Hadassah saw him as well and left off telling her story. Julia chewed her lower lip. She wondered if he would reprimand her for refusing to join him in the bibliotheca last evening, but he said nothing of it as he joined her. Hadassah stood in proper silence at the approach of her master. Julia hoped whatever Claudius wanted to say, he would say and go.

He sat beside his wife on the bench. "Your maid was speaking to you." He saw the flush of red spread across the slave girl's face.

"She was telling me another of her stories."

"What kind of stories?"

"About her people." Julia plucked another flower. "The stories help pass the time when there is little else to do." She lifted the blossom to her nose and inhaled the sweet, heavy scent.

"Religious stories?" Claudius said.

Julia glanced at him through her lashes. She laughed softly. "To a Jew, everything is religious."

Claudius looked at Julia's maid with more interest. "I would like to hear some of her stories when you can spare her, my dear. I'm doing a comparative study of religions. It would be interesting to hear what your maid has to say about the foundations of a Jew's faith in an unseen god."

And so it was that the next time Claudius sent Persis to summon his wife, Julia sent her fond regards and regrets—and Hadassah in her place.

11

Marcus held tight to the bridle of his new white stallion as he led it through the crowd near the city gates. The horse was a majestic beast, just recently arrived from Arabia, and the noise and confusion made the animal nervous. Marcus soon saw he was making little headway on foot, so he mounted. "Move aside or be trampled!" he shouted to several men in front of him. The stallion tossed its great head and bounced in agitation. Marcus urged him forward and watched those on foot make way quickly.

Outside the walls of Rome, the road was thronged with travelers wanting to enter the city. The poorest were on foot, carrying everything they owned in a sack on their backs, while rich men were held aloft on fancy sedan chairs or drawn in elaborate gilt carriages with red curtains. Four-wheeled, four-horsed *raeda* were packed tight with passengers, while the faster and lighter *cisium*, with two wheels and two horses, pushed ahead. The drivers of the ox-drawn wagons, which were loaded with merchandise, were in no hurry, knowing they'd have to wait until after sunset before the ban on their vehicles was lifted.

Marcus rode south along Via Appia, proud of his new acquisition. He allowed the animal to canter, its head proud and high as it jerked angrily, wanting to run. The road was busy with ambassadors from far provinces, Roman officials, legionnaires, merchants, tradesmen, and slaves from a dozen conquered principalities. He rode through the suburbs and passed a construction party of slaves, prisoners, and soldiers, all at work improving a section of road that led into new villas in the hills. New developments were cropping up like weeds on every slope around the city.

He breathed easier the further he went. He needed to get away from the rush of the city, from the unceasing noise and annoying obligations. He was almost finished building the *insulae*—huge high-rise tenements, each of which filled a city block—near the Field of Mars and the cattle market. People were already lining up for a place in his apartments, since they were better built than most and less likely to burn down. The rents would soon be pouring in. The villa on Capitoline was only half complete, yet he had already had four offers on it, each better than the one before. He had accepted none. Once completed, he planned to open the villa to a special few affluent guests and then hold a private auction, driving the price up even higher.

Father was putting pressure on him to take more responsibility in the shipping business, but his own enterprises were going so well and taking so much of his time that Marcus balked. What challenge was there in taking over what was already established? He wanted to build his own name and his own small empire within the Empire. And he was doing it. His reputation had grown steadily with the contracts Antigonus had arranged through his political connections.

Antigonus was another reason Marcus wanted to leave Rome for a few days. He was tired of listening to him whine about his troubles and beg for money. And he spoke too freely in criticism of those in power.

He also wanted some distance between himself and Arria. He had ceased seeking her company, but she still sought his. She told him Fannia was divorcing Patrobus and telling everyone she had a lover, and he didn't want that trouble added to his shoulders as well. He grimaced, remembering Arria's hurt and angry tones.

"Is it you, Marcus?"

"I have not seen the fair Fannia since the banquet Antigonus threw before the Apollinare games," he had answered truthfully. "You were there, don't you remember? You swam naked in Antigonus' fountain to the Satyrs." She had been drunk and wildly angry when she saw him in the gardens with Fannia. He had tossed her into the fountain, but doubted she remembered.

Now Arria attended every festival and banquet he did, a constant burr in his side. Piqued by his rejection, she told her friends she had tired of him, though it was all too obvious she still wanted him. Her persistence was embarrassing.

There was a measure of relief in his unattached status. He could do what he pleased, when he pleased, with whom he pleased. For a few brief days, he had enjoyed Mallonia, a woman who was a friend of Titus, the emperor's son. Through her, Marcus had been introduced to Titus. The younger Flavius had been depressed over the termination of his love affair with the Jewish princess, Berenice. Though his captive, she had captivated him. Marcus had wondered at the rumors circulating through the Empire that Titus wanted to marry a Jew. He hadn't believed it until meeting Titus. Were it not for Vespasian ordering the affair ended, Titus might actually have done it.

Titus should never even have considered marrying a woman of such a heathenish race. Perhaps it was a combination of too many months of campaigning and too long a time beneath the hot Judean sun. Women were meant to be conquered and enjoyed, not turn a man's life inside out or set the Empire to rebellion.

Marcus thought of Hadassah and then pressed the image of her gentle face away.

He turned his thoughts to the rock quarries. He had purchased interest in two of them within a day's journey of Rome after hearing a rumor passed on to him by one of his agents. One of Vespasian's palace slaves had overheard a conversation between the emperor and several senators concerning Nero's lake near the Golden House. Vespasian was mulling over the idea of draining the lake and making it the site for an amphitheater large enough to seat more than one hundred thousand plebeians.

Tons of stone would be needed, and where better to buy it than from quarries closest to Rome? Granted, Marcus only owned a very small share in the quarries, but even a small share would be worth a fortune once the colossal project got underway.

Grinning, Marcus gave the stallion his head and galloped down the road. The speed and power of the animal under his control exhilarated him, and his blood raced in response. The stallion slowed his pace after several milestones. Marcus drank in the fresh country air.

He wondered how Julia fared with her aging Claudius. He hadn't seen her in months. She wasn't expecting him, and the prospect of completely surprising her pleased him.

He purchased food from an open-air market in one of the small *civitates* and continued on his way. He passed by a rich traveler ordering his slaves to pitch a tent for the night. With the size of the man's retinue and the frequency of Roman legionnaires on the road, there was less likelihood of an attack in the open. Spending a night at a local inn was an invitation to robbery or worse.

Marcus had friends along the way, but chose not to stop. He wanted to be alone, to hear silence and his own thoughts. He chose a place to bed down well off the road and hidden by a formation of granite.

The evening was warm, and he needed no fire. He removed the saddle and blanket from his horse, then brushed him down. There was a small stream and plenty of grass for grazing. He hobbled the stallion within reach of both and stretched out beneath the stars.

The sweet silence sang in his ears as though sirens were nearby. He drank it in, savoring the peace. However, all too soon, that peace left him as his mind filled with the dozens of business decisions he had to make over the coming weeks. It seemed the more successful he was, the more complicated his life became. Even escaping for a few days took a monumental effort.

At least he was not in the social position of his father. He did not have to sit in a curule chair early each morning and dole out denarii to twenty or more clients who stood with their hats in their hands. They always lingered, asking advice, offering flattery, bowing their insincere thanks.

His father was a generous man, but there were times when even he begrudged the doled-out coin. He said it took away the desire in men to work for themselves. For a few denarii, they sold their self-respect. Yet, what choice did Romans have when the population became glutted from every conquered province and foreign goods dominated the marketplace? Free Roman laborers demanded higher pay than provincial slaves. Romans thought themselves above the common pay. Ephesians like his father had grasped every opportunity.

Born and educated in the Eternal City, Marcus felt himself torn by allegiances. He was more Roman than Ephesian. Yet, his father still felt his roots were deep in Ephesus. A few nights ago, his father had said in wrath, "Roman I may be by purchase, but in my blood I am and always will be an Ephesian—as are you!"

Marcus wondered at his father's vehemence. "Once it mattered to be a Roman, to ensure protection and opportunity," Decimus had said, explaining his reasons for becoming a citizen. "It took time and effort. It was a thing of honor bestowed on a select few who earned it. These days, any man with the price can be a Roman, be he ally or enemy! The Empire has become like a common whore, and like a whore she is diseased and rotting from within."

His father had seemed driven and talked with irritating rapidity of the homeland he had left over two decades ago. Even Vespasian's able leadership of the Empire did not quiet his dire suppositions. It was as though some unknown force within the elder Valerian sought to draw him back to Ephesus.

Marcus sighed and thought of more pleasing and less disturbing things. Mallonia with her green eyes and practiced wiles; Glaphyra and her smooth, voluptuous curves. Yet, when he slept, the woman who filled his dreams was a young Jewess, her hands raised heavenward to her unseen god.

Julia was deliriously happy to see her brother. She threw herself into his arms, laughing and saying how thankful she was that he'd come. He lifted her and kissed her fondly, then set her on her feet again, putting his arm around her as they went out into the courtyard. She had grown up some in the months since he had seen her, and she was more lovely than ever.

"Where is your doting husband?"

"Probably in his bibliotheca poring over his scrolls again," she said with an indifferent shrug and dismissive wave of her hand. "What brings you to Capua?"

"You," he said, proud of how beautiful she was. Her eyes were bright and shining, all for him.

"Will you take me to one of the ludi? Claudius hasn't the time with his studies, and I have been simply dying to see how they train the gladiators. Will you, Marcus? Oh, please. It would be so much fun."

"I see no problem in that. Was there one in particular you wanted to visit?"

"There's one not far from here. It belongs to a man named Scorpus Proctor Carpophorus. I've heard it's one of the best training facilities in the province."

Claudius' gardens were extensive and beautiful. Numerous slaves were pruning and trimming and weeding to keep the pathways manicured. Birds flitted and sang from the high branches of mature trees. Claudius' family had owned this villa for many years. His wife Helena had died here. Marcus saw no sign that her ghost had dampened Julia's marital happiness. She seemed happier now than on the day the vows were said.

"How do you fare with your husband?" Marcus asked with a teasing smile.

"Quite well," Julia said with a sly smile. "Sometimes we walk in the gardens, sometimes we talk." She laughed at the wicked grin he gave her. "That, too, but not often these days, thank the gods."

A quick frown crossed Marcus' face as she ran ahead and sat

on a marble bench beneath the shade of an ancient oak. "Tell me everything about Rome, Marcus. What's happening there? What gossip have I missed? I'm dying to know."

Marcus talked for some time, his sister utterly absorbed with all he said. A maid came with wine and fruit. He'd never seen her before. Julia dismissed her and grinned at him. "Her name is Catya. Lovely, isn't she? Do try not to get her with child while you're here, Marcus. It would annoy Claudius' sense of propriety."

"Did you sell the little Jewess Mother gave you?"

"Hadassah? I wouldn't part with her for anything! She's devoted and obedient, and she's been most useful to me over the past few months."

There was a hidden message in the last part of her statement, for bedevilment shone in his sister's eyes. He smiled wryly. "Indeed?"

"Claudius is quite taken with her," she said and seemed amused.

A sudden hot flood of dark emotion burst inside of Marcus. He couldn't assess his feelings, for what gripped his stomach was far too uncomfortable. "And you're pleased with the situation?" He asked in quiet, controlled tones.

"More than pleased. I rejoice!" Her smile dimmed at the look on his face. She bit her lip like a child suddenly unsure of herself. "You needn't look at me like that. You can't understand how awful it has been, Marcus. I could hardly bear it."

Growing angrier, he caught her wrist as she looked away. "He was cruel to you?"

"Not cruel, exactly," she said and looked up at him with embarrassment. "Just *persistent*. He became tedious, Marcus. He wouldn't leave me alone for even one night. Then I came upon the idea of sending Hadassah. There's nothing wrong with that, is there? She's just a slave. She's to serve in whatever way I decide. Claudius seems perfectly content with the arrangement. He hasn't complained."

The blood was pounding in Marcus' head. "A fine scandal it will be if she becomes pregnant before you."

"I don't care," Julia said. "He can do whatever he likes to her as long as he leaves me alone. I can't stand him touching me." She stood up and moved away from him, wiping tears from her pale cheeks. "I haven't seen you in months, and now you're angry with me."

He stood and went to her. He took her shoulders firmly. "I'm not angry with you," he said gently. "Hush, little one." He turned her and held her close. He knew such arrangements worked in many households. What business was it of his if his sister decided to conduct such practices in her own home? As long as she was happy, what difference did it make what she did?

But it did make a difference. He told himself it was concern for his sister's marriage that made him uneasy. But the thought of Claudius Flaccus having both his sister and Hadassah rankled. More than he would have thought possible.

Claudius joined them then. He looked robust for a man of fifty, and content in his marriage. Marcus watched him with Julia for the rest of the afternoon and into the evening. One thing was clear: Claudius was no longer in love with her. He treated her with polite consideration and diffidence, but the spark was noticeably gone.

Julia was relaxed and went on questioning Marcus about Rome. She made no effort to include Claudius in her conversation, almost blatantly ignoring him. When he did join in the conversation, she listened with an air of boredom and long-suffering that made Marcus cringe inwardly. However, Claudius seldom had anything to say. He listened politely to their conversation, but didn't seem much interested in affairs of state or what had occurred at the various festivals. He seemed distracted and deep in his own private reverie.

They reclined on the couches for the evening meal. A succulent oak-fed pig was served as the main course, but Marcus had little appetite and ate sparingly. He drank more wine than usual, and the tension grew in him rather than dissipating with the drink. Hadassah waited upon Julia.

After a first brief glance at the Jewess, Marcus didn't look at her again. He noted Claudius did, however, several times. He smiled once, a fond smile that made Marcus' hand clench on his wine goblet. Julia seemed perfectly content.

Musicians played on a pan flute and lyre, soothing sounds to ease a troubled heart. Following a final course of fruit, Claudius held up his golden goblet and then turned it over. The red wine splashed onto the marble floor in libation to his gods, thus ending the meal.

Julia wanted to sit in the gardens. "Marcus and I have so much to talk about, Claudius," she said, looping her arm through Marcus' and making it clear that her husband's company was not wanted. Marcus noted that Claudius smiled warmly, relieved.

"Of course, my dear," he said, leaning down to kiss her cheek. Marcus felt her fingers tense on his arm. Claudius straightened and looked at him. "I will see you in the morning, Marcus. Whatever you want, you've only to tell Persis." He left them.

"Would you like a shawl, my lady?" Hadassah said. "It's cool this evening."

Her soft voice cut through Marcus' heart and he felt a rush of unreasoning anger against her. She left the room and came back with a wool shawl, which she placed tenderly over Julia's shoulders. He watched her openly, but her eyes never once lifted to his. Hadassah bowed slightly and took a step back.

As they sat in the garden, Julia wanted him to talk about all the gladiatorial contests he'd seen over the past months. Marcus amused her with various stories of contests gone awry.

"The Briton dropped his sword and began running around and around the arena. He was small and very fast and made the Gaul look like a lumbering ox. The little Briton must have run past his sword three times and never thought to pick it up. The crowd roared with laughter."

Julia laughed, too. "Did the Gaul ever catch him?"

"No, and the contest became so boring, the Gaul was called out of the arena and a pack of trained dogs sent in. The little Briton didn't last long after that. A few minutes and it was over."

Julia sighed. "I saw a gladiator some time ago running with his trainer along our road. He was very fast. He would have caught that Briton easily." She put her hand on Marcus' thigh. "When will you take me to the ludus?"

"Give me a day of rest from my journey. Then we'll discuss it," he said with a distracted smile. Try as he might, he could not keep his mind from wandering back to Hadassah.

"I don't want to discuss it. Every time I discuss it with Claudius, he changes the subject. He says he hasn't the time to take me. He has time. He just doesn't want to go. If you refuse me, I shall find a way to visit a ludus all by myself."

"Still threatening me with dire consequences, I see," he said, grinning at her.

"It's not funny. You can't imagine how boring it is to live in the country."

"You used to love the country."

"For a week or two, when I was a child. I'm a woman now, Marcus. I'm sick of playing knucklebones and dice."

"Then settle down and have some children," he said, tweaking her cheek playfully. "Card wool and weave like Mother."

Her eyes flashed with resentment. "Very well," she said with grave dignity and began to rise.

Laughing, Marcus caught her wrist and made her sit again. "I'll take you, little sister. Day after tomorrow, I'll make the necessary arrangements."

She brightened immediately. "I knew you wouldn't disappoint me." The evening air grew chilly and they returned to the house.

Marcus made use of Claudius' fine bath. He was amused when Julia sent Catya to him. She held the towel as he left the water and offered to rub his body with scented oils and scrape him. However, he dismissed Catya in favor of Claudius' masseur. He had ridden long hours and slept on the hard ground. His muscles ached, and a woman's gentle hand wasn't what he required. Later, perhaps.

He thought of Hadassah as the slave kneaded his muscles.

Somewhat relaxed after the rubdown, he retired to a spacious guest chamber and reclined on the bed. He gazed in bemusement at the prim fresco of children playing in a field of flowers. Perhaps this room had been intended for a nursery.

A dark thought came. What chance was there for Julia to have children if she allowed her maid to usurp her?

The hour was late. Julia would long since have gone to bed and would have no need of her maid now. He wondered if Hadassah still went secretly into the garden at night to pray to her god. Thinking to find her there, he rose and went out. When he didn't find her, he entered the house again and summoned a slave.

"Bring Hadassah to me," he said and saw the brief flash of surprise before the servant's feelings were hidden.

"My apologies, my lord, but she is with the master."

"The master?" he said darkly.

"Yes, my lord. The master summoned her after the evening meal. May I bring you something? Would you like some wine?" He cleared his throat nervously and lowered his voice. "Do you wish Catya summoned?"

"No." The evening meal had been over for hours. Had they been together all this time? Angry blood pounded in his veins. "Where are the master's chambers?"

"The master is not in his chambers, my lord. He is in the bibliotheca."

Marcus dismissed him with a jerk of his head. He was going to put a stop to whatever was between Claudius Flaccus and Hadassah. He couldn't imagine why Julia had been so foolish as to allow it to go this far. He left his room and went along the corridor toward the library. The door was open.

As Marcus came near, he heard Claudius speaking. "Of all these many laws you have told me over the past few days, what then is the most important one, the one that supersedes all the others?"

"'You shall love the Lord your God with all your heart, with all your soul, and with all your mind.' This is the first and great commandment. And the second is like it: 'You shall love your neighbor as yourself.' On these two commandments hang all the Law and the Prophets.'"

Marcus moved into the doorway and saw them sitting close together. Hadassah sat straight-backed on the edge of a stool, hands folded in her lap. Claudius was more comfortable on his sofa, his gaze intent upon her face. Marcus leaned indolently against the frame, trying to keep a cool head against the hot rush of anger. "And if your neighbor is your enemy?" he said indolently.

Claudius glanced up in surprise. Obviously, he did not welcome the intrusion. Marcus didn't care and returned his attention to Hadassah. She was standing, eyes downcast, awaiting her master's dismissal.

"You may go, Hadassah," Claudius said and stood.

Marcus didn't move from the doorway and she couldn't pass. He studied her from the top of her dark head down to her small sandaled feet. He waited for her to raise her eyes and look at him, but she didn't.

"Come in and sit down, Marcus," Claudius said, putting away his ink and quills and rolling up a scroll on his desk.

Marcus straightened slightly, and Hadassah moved by him. He heard the soft tread of her footsteps down the hall. "It always takes me a few days to adjust to the silence after Rome," Claudius said, smiling at Marcus in commiseration.

Marcus entered the room. It wasn't the silence that had kept him awake.

"May I offer you some wine?" Claudius said and poured a goblet of wine before Marcus answered. He held it out to him. Marcus took it and watched him pour another for himself. Claudius was relaxed, his eyes brighter than they had been all afternoon in Julia's company. It would seem Hadassah was stimulating company.

"I'm sorry I interrupted something between you and my sister's maid," he said stiffly.

"No apology necessary," Claudius said and reclined on a sofa. "We can continue tomorrow." He made himself comfortable. "Did you wish to talk about your sister?"

"Your wife?"

Claudius smiled slightly. "When she so pleases," he said ruefully. He took a sip of his wine and motioned for Marcus to sit. "If you want my permission to take her to one of the local ludi, you have it. I will give you a few names."

"I'll make the arrangements tomorrow," Marcus said.

"Was that all that was on your mind, Marcus?" He felt the younger man's tension, even sensed his anger, though he could not fathom the reason for it.

"All is well between you and Julia?" he said.

"Did she say it was not?" Claudius said in some surprise.

Marcus knew he was standing on sandy ground. This was Claudius Flaccus' home, not his own. Julia was Claudius' wife, Hadassah her slave. Marcus had no right to question another man's treatment of his wife or how he used his slaves. "No," he said slowly. "She told me she is content." His eyes narrowed coldly. "Julia is far too innocent."

Claudius studied him more closely. "What is really on your mind, Marcus?"

Marcus decided to be frank. "Your relationship with my sister's maid."

"Hadassah?" Claudius sat up and set his wine aside. "Your sister earned my undying gratitude when she sent her to me. She is the first Jew who has spoken freely about her religion. Most look upon us as heathens. Amusing, isn't it? Every religion looks upon others as heathen, but there is a profound arrogance to the Jews' monotheism. Hadassah, for example. She is a humble servant, devoted and obedient. Yet there is an uncompromising quality about her faith in her god."

He stood and went to his scrolls. "Hadassah fascinates me. I've gained more knowledge about Jewish history and religious culture from her in the last two months than I've been able to glean in years. She knows a great deal about their Scripture, despite the fact that most Jewish women are excluded from studying their Torah. Her father apparently taught her. He must have been a freethinker. Listen to this."

He rolled his scroll out and set a weight upon it. "'My God, My God, why have You forsaken Me? Why are You so far from helping Me, and from the words of My groaning. O My God, I cry in the daytime, but You do not hear; and in the night season, and am not silent.'"

Claudius looked up. "Do you hear the anguish of it? She had tears in her eyes the evening she quoted the passages to me. They were not just poetic words to her." He ran his finger down the columns of writing.

"She said the fall of Jerusalem was foretold because of the unrighteousness of her people. She believes her god has a hand in everything that happens on the earth."

"Like Zeus."

Claudius glanced up. "No. Not like Zeus. Her god is absolute, he doesn't share his rule with myriad other gods and goddesses. She says he is unchanging. He does not think like a man. Wait a minute. I'll read her own words about it." He pulled out another scroll and spread it on the table, searching again.

"Here it is. 'God is not a man, that He should lie, Nor a son of man, that He should repent. Has He said, and will He not do it? Or has He spoken, and will He not make it good?'" Claudius looked up, eyes alight with amusement. "She told me a funny tale along with that Scripture passage. It was about a king named Balak, who hired a prophet named Balaam to curse Israel. On his way to meet the king, Balaam's donkey stopped on the road because an angel with a sword blocked the way."

"An angel?" Marcus said blankly.

"A supernatural being that works for their god," Claudius said quickly. "Hadassah said these beings have appeared to men all through history. Message carriers like Mercury. They are servants of her god." He waved an end to his explanation. "Anyway, the prophet tried to beat the donkey into moving, but the donkey stood firm and finally *spoke* to him." He laughed. "When the prophet reached the king, every time he tried to curse Israel, the curse came out a blessing." He let the scroll go and rolled it up quickly, setting it in a pile with others. Marcus looked at them and imagined the hours of time with Hadassah they represented.

"Hadassah believes her god takes a personal interest in each one of us, whether we be Jew or not. She said that Jewish Scripture is the lamp that lights the path of her life." He gestured to another scroll. "She claims it is impossible for her god to lie. When he makes a promise, he keeps it to the end of time. His loving-kindnesses never cease, and his compassion never fails."

Marcus gave a sardonic laugh. "Titus told me more than a million Jews were killed in the destruction of Jerusalem, countless thousands crucified. If that's the sort of kindness and compassion her god bestows upon his people, it is a wonder the Jews are not flooding the temples of Artemis and Apollo."

"My own thoughts. We've been discussing that, also. She looks upon the destruction of Jerusalem as a just punishment upon Israel for their unfaithfulness. She says her god uses war and affliction and suffering as a means of drawing his people back again. An interesting concept, isn't it? Affliction as a means of protecting and hedging them into their faith! She said something else that was intriguing. Apparently a man named Jesus of Nazareth prophesied the destruction of Jerusalem. His own people crucified him, but she says all the Jewish prophets came to a bad end. Some of the Jews worship this Jesus as the incarnate son of their god. Christians, they call themselves. It's a Jewish cult."

"You will remember Nero tried to annihilate them after the burning of Rome," Marcus said.

"Yes. One of their beliefs is that the world will come to a fiery end, and this Christ will return with an army and create his own empire on earth."

Marcus was little interested in Claudius' comparative study of religious cults of the Empire. "Then am I correct in assuming you are not sleeping with her?"

Claudius looked up from his scrolls. "With Julia?"

"Hadassah."

"Hadassah? She is but a child."

"She's the same age as my sister," Marcus said coolly.

Claudius blushed. It was a long, painful moment before he answered slowly and with grave dignity. "Your sister is my wife,

Marcus. You have my promise I will be as faithful to her as I was to Helena."

Marcus seldom felt embarrassment, but he felt it wash over him at the look on Claudius' face. Not only had he hurt him, he had opened an old wound. "I was concerned for my sister," he said, trying to excuse his unpardonable rudeness. "You have my apologies if I have insulted you."

It was another long, still moment before Claudius spoke. "Apology accepted," he said.

Marcus finished his wine and set the goblet on the table. "I bid you a good night, Claudius," he said quietly and left the library.

"He's gone to Rome!" Julia said, tossing her shawl aside and sinking down onto her lounge despondently.

"Your brother, my lady?" Hadassah said, gathering up the shawl and carefully folding it.

"No. The gladiator we saw on the road five weeks ago. I found out his name is Atretes. He killed the lanista at the ludus and was sold to a man named Bato, who trains the emperor's gladiators. He was taken to Rome a month ago." She looked away, her pretty face lined with bitterness. "And I'm stuck here in Capua. Octavia will see him fight before I do. She'll probably drink wine with him at one of the feasts before the games." Her eyes filled with tears of self-pity.

Though Hadassah schooled her expression to show nothing of what she felt, she was relieved the gladiator was gone. Perhaps now Julia would put him from her mind and turn to her husband. Claudius wouldn't disappoint her. He was kind and intelligent, sensitive and tender. Knowing Julia's feelings, Claudius wouldn't press her for his marital rights. If Julia just gave herself time, she could learn to love him for the man he was.

Hadassah prayed unceasingly for both of them.

She spent long hours in the library with Claudius. It saddened her to do so, for he was a lonely man. His pursuit of knowledge occupied, but didn't satisfy, his mind. She tried to offer God's knowledge to him through the Scriptures her father had taught her. She wanted to tell him of Christ. But how could she? If he didn't believe in a Creator, man's fall, or the necessity for redemption, he would reject the Lord.

Claudius didn't seem to grasp the importance of anything she told him. As with Julia, lessons of truth were merely stories to while away the time, something for him to write down on one of his scrolls. The holy God was stacked on a pile among myriad gods throughout the Empire, just one more interesting cult or religion of Rome.

It grieved Hadassah. Claudius was lost, and she was failing him as she was failing Julia. She was failing the Lord. Her father would have known what to say to open their eyes and ears to Jesus.

Something else bothered Hadassah as greatly as the futility of Claudius' quest for worldly knowledge. Julia withdrew from her husband more and more. And now, rather than reach out to his wife, Claudius continued to summon Hadassah. At first, it had only been in his library during the evening hours after Julia no longer needed her. And they always discussed Jewish culture and religion. But during the last week, Claudius had summoned her twice in midday when she was serving Julia and Marcus. Today he summoned her to the gardens as soon as Marcus had taken Julia from the villa for a ride.

Persis came for her. He managed the household slaves and was devoted to Claudius—and he despised Julia's treatment of his master.

"You have given my lord reason to live again," Persis said as he led her to Claudius. "We all thought he would commit suicide when he lost the Lady Helena. He married Lady Julia because she looks like her. It was a cruel trick of the gods." He paused and put his hand on her arm. "Offering you to the master was the single selfless act the Lady Julia has done since coming here. You've been good for him." He nodded his head toward the open doorway. "He awaits you in the gardens."

Hadassah was mortified with shame. She knew that the household slaves who came into contact with Julia disliked her. Did they hope Claudius would reject his wife in favor of a mere slave? May it not be so! She went to Claudius reluctantly, embarrassed to be in his presence in the open.

Claudius talked about gladiators. Although, like all Romans, he had attended the games, witnessing a man's death was repugnant to him. Julia's fascination for it disturbed him. "Did she attend the games often in Rome?"

"No, my lord. Her brother took her a few times."

"Did Decimus encourage it?"

Hadassah blushed.

Claudius smiled down at her. "You are not breaking a sacred trust by telling me something of my wife, Hadassah. It will go no further than my ears."

"The master did not know," she said.

"I thought not, though I imagine he suspected it. It's difficult to stop Julia from doing as she pleases." He asked if the Jews had any great warriors. Hadassah told him of Joshua taking Jericho and putting the fear of God into the Canaanites. She told him how King Saul's son Jonathan and his armor bearer had climbed a hill and routed a garrison of Philistines, thus turning the tide of an entire war. She told him the story of Samson.

Claudius gave a rueful laugh. "This Samson of yours appears to have had a fatal weakness for unfaithful women. First, a betraying wife, then a harlot in Gaza, and finally the beautiful, but cunning Delilah." He shook his head as he walked along the pathway with her, his hands clasped behind his back. "A pretty face and a beautiful body blind a man more quickly than any poker through the eyes." He sighed. "Are all men slaves to their own passions, Hadassah? Are all men fools when it comes to women?" He looked straight ahead, his thoughts distant. ". . . As I was a fool when I married Julia?"

Distressed by his words and mood, Hadassah stopped in the pathway and, without thinking, put her hand on his arm. He seemed so despondent, so hopeless. She wanted to give comfort. "Do not think so, my lord. It was not a mistake to marry my lady." She searched frantically for a way to explain and excuse her mistress's faults. "Julia is inexperienced. Give her time."

Claudius smiled sadly. "Yes, she is inexperienced. She has never suffered hardship. She has never been hungry or in want of anything. She has never had anything taken from her." He spoke without rancor. "But time will alter nothing."

"All things work for good, my lord."

"Good has come from my marriage to her." He touched her cheek gently. "I have you." He smiled ruefully as hot color poured into her cheeks and she looked down. "Don't be distressed, my dear. After the first few weeks of marriage to Julia, I saw my life stretched out ahead of me like a wasteland. Now, as long as I have you, I can bear all things."

Claudius tipped her chin and gazed down into her tear-filled eyes for a long moment, studying her tenderly. "Passion lasts but a moment, compassion a lifetime," he said quietly. "A man needs a friend, Hadassah. Someone he can talk to and confide in." He bent and kissed her forehead, as her father used to do. Straightening, he slid his hands down her arms and grasped her hands firmly. "I am grateful." He kissed her knuckles and released her, then left her alone in the garden. She sat on a bench and wept.

Now, watching Julia's sullen expression as she stared out the window into the garden, annoyed because a gladiator had gone to Rome, Hadassah wondered again what she could do to encourage and renew Claudius' love for his young wife. It wasn't right that he was turning to her.

"The master is in his library, my lady. You would enjoy his company," Hadassah said gently.

Julia gave her a brittle look. "Claudius bores me to death. Better that he caress his scrolls than me." She sighed and turned away again, looking more like a vulnerable child than a petulant, selfish young wife. "I'm tired and my throat is parched."

Hadassah poured her a goblet of wine. "Your feet are dusty, my lady. Would you like me to wash them?" Julia gave an indifferent nod, and Hadassah went for the basin.

Marcus entered the room. Hadassah's stomach quivered oddly when he greeted Julia. She felt her pulse quicken as he came closer; it was as though his mere presence made her skin tingle and her blood grow warm. She kept her eyes lowered as she knelt and poured water over Julia's dusty feet. She poured scented oil into her palm and began to knead Julia's feet gently as they talked.

"Did you enjoy your visit to the ludus, little sister? Or was it spoiled by the absence of your German?" He was amused, not reprimanding.

"It was fine. The contest between the retiarius and the Thracian was entertaining."

"Don't sound so excited," he said drolly, watching Hadassah massage his sister's feet. Her hands seemed gentle, but firm. "I was talking with Claudius. He has quite a study going on religions in the Empire."

"I'm not the least interested in what Claudius is doing," Julia said, annoyed at the mention of her husband.

"It would be wise to be interested," Marcus said flatly, and Hadassah felt his gaze on the back of her head so intently it was as though he were touching her. She had been aware of his glance more than once during his visit, dark and compelling . . . accusing.

"Claudius is free to do as he pleases," Julia said. "By the gods, that I could be as free as a man." She pulled her feet back abruptly, splashing water into Hadassah's face. "Dry my feet," she commanded angrily. "I'm going to walk in the gardens." She gave her brother a sullen look. "Alone."

"As your heart desires, little sister," Marcus said, mockingly. "Such a sweet disposition deserves solitude."

As Julia left the room, Hadassah gathered up the damp cloth, the vial of scented oil, and the basin of dirty water. She moved to leave, but Marcus blocked her way.

"Don't be in such a hurry. My feet are dirty, too," he said. "Empty the basin in that potted plant over there and come back here."

Hadassah did as she was ordered. As she came back, he sat down on the couch. She knelt at his feet, her hands trembling as she removed his sandals. She took the half-full pitcher and almost dropped it. Gripping the handle tightly, she poured water over his feet and set it aside again. She could feel his attention fixed on her as she poured oil and rubbed her palms together before beginning to massage his feet. He made a deep sound in his throat that caused a burst of strange sensations in the pit of her stomach.

"What is the relationship between you and my sister's husband?" he asked darkly.

His question surprised and confused her. "He is interested in the religion of my ancestors, my lord."

"Only in your religion?" he said, dubious. "Nothing else?" He suddenly reached out, caught her chin roughly, and jerked her head up. Seeing the heightened color in her cheeks, he grew angry. "Answer me! Have you become his concubine?"

"*No,* my lord," she said, blushing painfully. "We talk of my people and my God. Today, he spoke of gladiators and Julia."

His hand gentled. She looked up at him with dark guileless eyes. Innocent. "He has never touched you?" He let go of her and she lowered her head again.

"Not in the way you mean."

Angry heat poured through him. "In what way then?"

"He put his hand on my shoulder today. He held my hands and . . ."

"And?"

"Kissed them, my lord." She looked up at him. "He said every man needs a friend, but it's not right that it be me, my lord. I pray you. Talk to your sister, my lord. Encourage her to be kind to her husband. No more than kind, if she so wishes. He is a lonely man. It's not right that he should have to turn to a slave for companionship."

"Are you daring to criticize Julia?" Marcus said. He watched Hadassah's cheeks flame and then go deathly white. He went on. "By your words, she is neglectful of her wifely duties and unkind to her husband."

"It was not my intention to criticize, my lord. May God do so to me and more also if I lie to you." She looked up at him beseechingly. "The Lady Julia is unhappy. So, too, is her husband."

"What do you expect me to do about it?"

"She listens to you."

"Do you think my speaking with Julia will change anything?" *Less than she might think*. "Finish my feet," he said tersely and Hadassah did so, her hands shaking now. She dried his feet carefully and strapped on his sandals. He stood up and moved away from her, his emotions roiling.

He didn't need Hadassah to point out to him that his sister's marriage was disintegrating, and Julia was doing nothing whatsoever to stop it. That concerned him—but what ate at him even more was the thought of Hadassah spending hours with Claudius in the privacy of the library. She said Flaccus needed a friend. Was that all he needed? Marcus had been telling himself he wanted to set Julia's marriage aright for the sake of his sister's happiness. Suddenly, he saw the truth: he wanted it not for his sister, but so that Claudius would leave Hadassah alone—and that stunning realization struck a raw nerve.

Marcus looked back at Hadassah as she gathered up the towel, oil vial, and basin. She was growing more lovely each time he saw her, not that he could see any great physical change in her. She was still too thin, her eyes too large, her mouth too full, her skin too dark. Her hair had grown down to her shoulders, yet to look at her critically, she was still homely. But there was something beautiful about her.

He could see she was shaking badly, and he felt an odd pang of guilt for having frightened her so. She was just a slave. Her feelings shouldn't matter to him, but they did. They mattered too much. He hated the way Claudius looked at her.

And then, as he watched her and drank in the sensation of her nearness, he was rocked by another realization: he was jealous!

By the gods, what a joke. He was jealous over *a slave*. He, a Roman citizen by birth, stood there intrigued by a skinny little Jewess with big dark eyes who shook in fear of him. How Arria would laugh!

The situation was ludicrous, though not uncommon. Antigonus carried on affairs with his slaves—male and female. Marcus thought of Bithia, seeking him in the secret of darkness, warm and eager. No, it was not uncommon to use a slave for convenient sexual gratification.

He watched Hadassah pour the water into the potted palm and then go back to set the empty pitcher in its basin. All he had to do was command her. His heart beat faster. She straightened with the basin and pitcher in her hands, the damp towel draped over her arm. Crossing the room, she put both away in a small cabinet and set the glass vial on top with half a dozen others. She straightened again, the damp towel now in her hand.

Marcus looked down over her slender body, clothed in a brown woolen dress belted by a striped garment that proclaimed her heritage. A Jew. Jews had a ridiculously rigid sense of morality. Virginity until marriage, fidelity until death. Their restraints defied the nature of man, but he could make her break all her laws by a single word. All he had to do was command her and she would have to obey. If she didn't, he could punish her in whatever way he chose, even unto death if he so desired. He held the power of her life in his hand.

She looked up at him. "Do you wish anything more, my lord?"

Every woman he had ever been with had come to him willingly or sought him out—Bithia, Arria, Fannia, and numerous others before and after them. If he commanded Hadassah, would she melt in his arms or cry copiously that he had defiled her?

He knew. She wasn't like the others.

"Leave me," he said tersely.

It didn't occur to him until he was riding back to Rome that for the first time in his life, he had put another's feelings above his own.

12

Atretes was not prepared for the splendor and magnificence of Rome. In the thick forests of Germania he had seen the well-disciplined, seasoned legionnaires in their armor and leather and brass-studded skirts. He had faced the shrewd ruthlessness of the officers. Yet never had he imagined the teeming population of Rome itself, the cacophony of languages, the mass of citizens and foreigners alike descending upon the city like ants, the glistening marble columns and buildings, the tremendous diversity of Rome itself.

The main artery of the Empire, the Appian Way, was engorged with travelers from a dozen regions within the Empire, all clamoring for entrance. Wagons clogged the roadway, pressed as close together as possible, waiting for the ban to lift with sunset and the gates to open. Bato, in the service of the emperor, was at the head of the line. The Roman guards had already examined his papers and looked over his cargo of gladiators. When the gates opened, Atretes could feel the rush of adrenaline as wagons, carts, oxen, and humanity pressed at their backs to get into the city.

The noise and push within the gates of the city sent Atretes' head spinning. Greeks, Ethiopians, savages from Britain, mustachioed Gauls, peasants from Spain, Egyptians, Cappadocians, and Parthians shoved their way along the crowded thoroughfares. A Roman lounged within a thinly veiled sedan chair borne aloft by four Bithynians. Another carried by Numidians passed by. Arabs in their red-and-white *kaffiyehs* mingled with barbarians from Dacia and Thrace. A Greek cursed a Syrian shopkeeper.

Streets were lined with shops. Wine taverns dotted the streets on both sides, all crowded with patrons. In between, jammed so tightly together they appeared to have common walls, were fruit sellers and booksellers, perfumers and milliners, dyers and florists. Some shouted their wares and services to passersby. A glass-blower drew attention to his shop by performing his art with dramatic flair, while a sandal maker hawked his shoes from atop a crate. A fat woman in a blue toga, followed by two equally fat children in white, entered a jeweler's shop for more of what already bedecked her hair, neck, arms, and fingers. On the other side of the street, a crowd gathered to watch two hardened legionnaires argue with a leatherworker. One laughed while the other shoved the shopkeeper into a pile of leather goods.

Atretes' head pounded as he sat chained in the wagon, taking in the city. Amazed, he could only stare in silence. In every direction he looked were buildings: small shops and grander emporiums; squalid tenements and lavish homes; giant marble temples with gleaming white columns, and the smaller tiled and gilded temples, or *fana,* sheltering the devout.

Rome was aflame with color. Massive buildings were constructed with red-and-gray granite and alabaster, and purple-red porphyry from Egypt, black-and-yellow marble from Numidia, green cipollino from Eubold, and the white stones of the Carrara quarries near Luna. Houses built of wood, brick, and whitewashed stucco rose every day. Even the statues were painted in garish colors, some draped with vivid fabrics.

Amidst the grandeur, the stench of the imperial city made Atretes' head swim and his stomach lurch. He longed for the crisp clean air of his homeland, the scent of pungent pine. He could smell the sweetness of cooking meat mingling with the polluted Tiber and the odious city sewer system, the *Cloaca Maxima.* A woman pitched slops out of a second-story tenement window, barely missing a Greek slave carrying bundles for his mistress. Another pedestrian was less fortunate. Drenched by slops, he stood shouting curses up at the woman, who set her bucket aside and put her basket of clothes on the windowsill. While he continued railing at her, she ignored him and draped several tunics over a wash line.

Atretes longed for the simplicity of his village and the comfort of a log longhouse and cleansing fire. He longed for silence. He longed for privacy.

Men and women of all nationalities gawked at him and the others in the wagon. They made slow progress in the heavy traffic, and there was plenty of time for people to come close, making insulting comments and suggestions. They seemed to find him of particular interest. A man touched him in a way that sent the hair on the back of his neck bristling. He lunged at him, wanting nothing more than to break his neck, but the chains prevented him from doing so. Bato gave an order and several guards moved closer to the wagon to keep admirers back. But that didn't prevent them from following and calling out lewd propositions.

In Germania, men who lusted for men were drowned in a bog, their perversity thus hidden from the world forever. Ah, but in Rome, they spoke openly of their foul passion, shouting it from the roofs and street corners, and in the streets, as they strutted about proud as peacocks.

Atretes felt a burning contempt in his heart. Rome, reputedly pure and majestic, was a stinking bog of base humanity drowning in the filth of depravity. His hatred deepened and an even fiercer pride rose within him. His people were pure, unpolluted by those they conquered. Rome, on the other hand, embraced and absorbed its vanquished. Rome tolerated every excess, accepted every philosophy, encouraged every abomination. Rome joined itself with every comer.

When the wagon rolled through the gates of the Great School, Atretes felt relief to be in familiar surroundings. It was as though, once through the thick gates and within the high stone walls of the gladiator school, he was at home. It was a disturbing feeling.

There was little difference between this ludus and the ludus in Capua. It possessed a large rectangular building with an open court in the middle, where the men were practicing. Around the court ran a roofed passageway with small rooms opening into it. There was a kitchen, a hospital, an armory, quarters for trainers and guards, a prison with shackles, branding irons, and whips. So, too, would this ludus have a small solitary cell where a man had not the room to sit up or stretch out his legs. The only thing missing was a large graveyard. It was against the law to bury the dead within the walls of Rome.

Even after the gates were closed behind him, he could hear the sounds of the city. It was dark now that the sun had gone down, and torches lit their way. Atretes fought against the despair filling him as he was taken to his quarters. Even if he did escape this place, he would have to make his way through the city, past the city gates and guards. And even if he made it outside of Rome, he was so far from his homeland, he didn't know how to get back.

He began to understand why each man was searched before entering his cell, and why the guards walked back and forth overhead through the long, dark hours of night. Death began to look like a friend.

Life fell into a pattern again. In the Great School, the food was better and more abundant than under Scorpus Proctor Carpophorus. Atretes wondered if he would have another equally arrogant and stupid lanista to replace Tharacus.

Bato proved to be a different sort of man from the others Atretes had come across during his bondage. The Ethiopian was intelligent and shrewd. Tougher than Tharacus, he never resorted to mockery, humiliation, or unnecessary physical abuse to gain what he wanted from his trainees. Atretes felt a grudging respect for him, which he rationalized by telling himself Bato was not a Roman and therefore acceptable. He learned by listening to the conversations of others that he shared a commonality with the black man. Bato had been leader of his tribe, the eldest son of a chief who had been slain in battle by a Roman legion.

Beneath Bato's tutelage, Atretes learned to be as skilled with his left hand as he was with his right. To build muscle, Bato had him use weapons that were twice as heavy as the ones Atretes would use in the arena. Bato put him in bouts with other gladiators who were far more experienced, several of whom had already fought in the arena. Twice, Atretes was wounded in practice fights. Bato never stopped the fight at first blood. He waited until a life hung in the balance before he blocked a killing blow.

Atretes worked harder than the rest. Silent, he listened and watched, studying each man carefully, knowing his life depended on what he learned in this foul place.

Sometimes women came to the ludus—Roman women who found it entertaining to go through the paces of a gladiator. Beneath the watchful eyes of several armed guards, they exercised with the trainees. Dressed in short tunics like the men, they exposed their legs. Atretes looked upon these women with disdain. They were arrogant in their insistence that they were as good as any man, all the while demanding they be pampered.

Atretes' mother had been a strong woman, capable of entering a battle when necessary. Yet never once had he heard her claim she was better than or even equal to any man, even the least among the tribesmen. Her husband was Hermun, chief of the Chatti, and there was no one to equal him. His mother was sorceress and seer, and no one had equaled her either among all the Chatti. She was considered a goddess in her own right.

Atretes thought of Ania, his young wife. Her sweetness had roused a tender protectiveness in him. He had wanted to keep her from harm, but the forest gods had taken her from him, and his son as well.

He looked at a young Roman woman exercising with the men. No woman of his tribe would stride about dressed as a man and brandishing a sword as though the mere mention that she was a woman would inflame rage and shame. Atretes' mouth twisted in contempt. These Roman women came to the ludus disdainful of men, then strove to become one.

He noticed they never challenged the well trained. They chose instead the smallest novice on which to test their blade, strutting about when they drew blood. They believed they had proven themselves equal. What a joke! All with whom they sparred were constrained by unspoken laws—only free Roman women came to play games with the gladiators, and one scratch on a pretty white Roman hide could cost a man his life, unless the woman was fair-minded and spoke quickly enough to spare him.

Other women came to the ludus as well, not to fight, but to watch from the safe confines of the balcony. Bato allowed it because there were gladiators who worked harder beneath the eyes of a woman, especially if she was pretty. The men flexed and preened and made fools of themselves while the women giggled from the lounges overlooking the courtyard. Others, like Atretes, ignored their presence, training their minds on lessons yet to be learned.

Roman men also came to the ludus to train, but Atretes was kept away from them. He had been training for three months when one young aristocrat who considered himself a skilled gladiator spotted him and told Bato he wanted to spar with him. Bato tried to talk him out of it, but the young Roman, confident of his own skill, insisted.

Bato called out to Atretes and signaled him over. "Give him a good fight, but don't draw his blood," he said. Atretes looked the young aristocrat over as he was making practice swings with his gladius, then grinned at Bato.

"Why would I want to draw a Roman's blood?"

Atretes kept a measured distance, allowing the young man to advance and show his mettle and skill. Watchful and cautious at first, the barbarian tested his opponent until he knew his weaknesses. Within a few minutes, it was apparent even to the foolish young man who was the master. Atretes toyed with him until sweat beaded on the Roman's face and body, and fear shone vividly in his eyes. "Back off, Atretes," Bato called out.

"Is this the best Rome has to offer?" Grinning, Atretes made a swift move and nicked the Roman's face. The man gasped and jerked back, dropping his gladius, and Atretes left a thin line of blood down the Roman's chest. At the sight of the blood, a rush of heat burst in the barbarian's brain and he uttered a war cry as he brought the sword up and around. It rang against steel as Bato blocked the blow.

"Another day," Bato said quietly, gripping Atretes' sword arm with fingers as strong as a vice. Breathing heavily, Atretes looked into the lanista's dark eyes and saw complete understanding.

"Another day," he agreed between his teeth and relinquished his weapon.

The Roman, having salvaged enough of his pride to dust himself off, strode back into the small arena to pick up his gladius with an air of dignity. "You're going to regret cutting me," he said, glaring at Atretes.

"Bravely said," Atretes laughed derisively. The man walked toward the door. "Come back if you can find your courage!" he called after him in Greek, the common language of Rome. "I thought you Romans had a taste for blood. I'll give you blood! Your own, little boy. In a cup, if you so desire." He laughed again. "A libation for your gods!"

The door slammed. Atretes felt the still silence that fell on the courtyard. Bato was grim. The two guards said nothing as Atretes was led away to his quarters. He expected to be whipped and put in solitary confinement for his actions. Instead, Bato sent him a woman. This one was not a tired kitchen slave, but a young prostitute with imagination and a sense of humor.

The door opened and she stood looking in at him, a guard just behind her. She was young and beautiful and dressed in finery fitting for a Roman feast. "Well, well," she said, smiling and looking him over from head to foot as she entered his cell. "Bato said I would like you." She laughed as he stood frozen with shock, staring at her, and the sound was like long-forgotten music.

The guard didn't come back until dawn.

"My gratitude," Atretes said to Bato the next day.

Bato grinned. "I thought you should have one good thing before you died."

"There are worse things than death."

Bato's grin died. He nodded grimly. "The wise man and the fool alike die, Atretes. What matters is that one die well."

"I know how to die well."

"No one dies well upon a cross. It's a lingering foul death without honor, your body stripped for the world to see." He looked him in the eyes. "You didn't listen to me yesterday. A foolish mistake and one you may not survive. To best a Roman in a fair match is one thing, Atretes. To deliberately mock and humiliate him is another. The young man you took such pleasure in defeating yesterday is the son of a respected senator. He is also a close and personal friend of Domitian, the emperor's younger son." He let his words sink in.

Atretes' blood turned cold. "So, when am I to be crucified?" he said flatly, knowing he would have to find a way to commit suicide.

"At the emperor's pleasure."

A few days later, Bato took Atretes aside. "It seems the gods have smiled on you. The emperor said too much time and money have been invested to waste you on a cross. He's ordered you scheduled for the games next week." Bato put his hand on Atretes shoulder. "Two months short of completing your training, but at least you will die with a sword in your hand."

Atretes was fitted with elaborate gilded armor. He scorned the red cape and gilded helmet with ostrich plumes, throwing both aside when they were handed to him. A slave picked them up again and held them out to Atretes, who told the man in no uncertain terms where he could put them. Bato's face was rigid.

"You won't be wearing these things for the fight," he said in annoyance. "They are for the opening ceremonies. You remove the cape before the crowd. It's part of the show."

"Let someone else strut in feathers. I will not."

Bato jerked his head and the slave left with the finery. "Bearskins then. They better suit a barbarian. Unless you would prefer to wear nothing at all. It is your German custom to fight naked, is it not? The mob would like that very much."

For the next several days, Bato spent extra time with him, teaching him tricks and moves that might save his life. The lanista worked him until they were both exhausted, then ordered him to the baths and masseur. No more women were sent to his quarters, but Atretes didn't care. He was too tired to take pleasure in one.

At this rate, he would not have strength left to fight in the arena, let alone survive the ordeal.

Two days before the games, Bato exercised him, but allowed him plenty of rest. On the last night, he came to Atretes' cell. "You will be taken to other quarters in the arena tomorrow. A feast is always held before the games. It will be unlike any you have ever seen, Atretes. Take my advice. Eat and drink moderately. Forgo the women. Focus your mind and save your strength for the games."

Atretes raised his head. "No pleasure before I die?" he asked mockingly.

"Heed what I say. If the gods are merciful, you will survive. If not, at least you will make a good fight of it. You will not shame your people."

Bato's words struck Atretes' heart. He nodded. Bato extended his hand and Atretes clasped it firmly. The lanista looked grim. Atretes' mouth tipped into a lopsided grin. "When I come back, I look forward to my reward."

Bato laughed. "If you come back, you shall have it."

Six men from the Great School were to fight in the Ludi Plebeii, games held for the plebians, commonly called the Roman mob. They were brought into an anteroom, where they were to wait until a contingent of guards would arrive and take them to the quarters beneath the arena. The other five gladiators in the room had fought before. One was credited with twenty-two kills. Atretes was the only newcomer. He was also the only man with shackles on his wrists and ankles.

The Thracian was big and strong. Atretes had been paired against him once and knew he was mechanical, his moves predictable. Brute strength was his greatest threat, for he used it like a battering ram. The Parthian was another matter. Leaner and more agile, he struck fast. The two Greeks were good fighters, but Atretes had sparred with both and knew he could beat them.

The last man was a Jew who had somehow managed to survive the destruction of his homeland at Titus' triumph. Caleb was his name, and he was handsome and powerfully built. Credited with twenty-two kills, he was the greatest threat. Atretes studied him carefully and wished he had had the opportunity to be paired with him at the ludus. Then he would know how the man fought—he would know what to expect, what to watch for, and how to counterattack to best advantage.

The Jew had his head bowed and his eyes closed, seemingly deep in some sort of strange meditation. Atretes had heard that Jews worshiped an unseen god. Perhaps their god was like his own forest gods. Present, but elusive. Atretes watched the man's lips move in silent prayer. Though relaxed and deep in concentration, Atretes sensed he was alert to his surroundings. This was confirmed as the Jew raised his head and looked straight into Atretes' eyes, having sensed his perusal. Atretes stared back at him, trying to peel away whatever bravado there might be. What he saw, though, was courage and strength.

They stared at one another for a long moment, assessing one another without animosity. The Jew was older and vastly more experienced. His steady unblinking gaze warned Atretes he would be deadly.

"Your name is Atretes," he said.

"And you are Caleb. Twenty-two kills to your credit."

A flicker of emotion shadowed the man's features. His mouth curved without humor. "I heard you tried to kill a guest of the ludus."

"He asked for it."

"I pray God will not pair us, young Atretes. We share a common hatred of Rome. It would grieve me to kill you."

Caleb spoke with such deep sincerity and simple confidence that Atretes' pulse quickened. He did not respond. Better to let Caleb believe youth and inexperience made him an easy kill. Overconfidence might be the man's one weakness, and the only tool Atretes could use in surviving a match with him.

The emperor's legionnaires arrived. Two were assigned to each gladiator, an extra to Atretes. Grinning coldly, Atretes stood, the bite of his fetters sending a rush of anger through him. Was he to shuffle along the corridor while the others strode? He saw Bato in the open doorway. "Tell these dogs I will not run away from a fight."

"They know that already. They're worried you'll eat one of the Roman guests at the pregame feast."

Atretes laughed.

Bato ordered his ankle fetters removed so he could walk without restraint. Flanked by the guards, Atretes followed the others through a torchlit tunnel of several hundred yards in length. The heavy plank door closed behind them. At the end of the tunnel was a lighted chamber. When they entered it, the second door was closed and locked. Another opened into a maze of chambers beneath the amphitheater and arena.

Lions roared from somewhere within the darkness, and the hair on the back of Atretes' neck rose. There was no greater shame than to be fed to the beasts. Gladiators with their guards walked through the narrow, cold stone corridors and climbed stairs into the lower chambers of a palace. Atretes heard music and a burst of laughter as they entered a marble hall. Huge, elaborately carved double doors stood at the end of the room; two slaves, dressed in white tunics trimmed in red and gold, stood ready to open them.

"They are here!" someone cried out excitedly, and Atretes saw the room was thronged with Roman men and women in rich, colorful togas. A young woman in a jeweled belt and little else stopped dancing as Atretes and the others were marched to the center of the great room, the center of all attention. Men and women assessed them like horseflesh, commenting on their height, breadth, and attitude.

Atretes watched the other gladiators with casual interest. The Thracian, the Parthian, and the Greeks all seemed to be enjoying the situation. They moved toward the dais at the far end of the room, grinning and making comments to several of the young women who watched them. Only Caleb remained aloof. Atretes followed his example, his gaze focusing on the honored guests to which they were being ceremoniously presented. His heart leaped as he recognized the man in the center.

The guards lined them up before the platform, and Atretes stood face-to-face with the Roman emperor, Vespasian. On his right was his elder son, Titus, conqueror of Judea; on his left, Domitian.

Atretes focused on Vespasian. The emperor had the powerful build and bearing of a soldier. His gray hair was closely cropped, his face weathered and deeply lined from years of campaigning. Titus, no less impressive, sat nearby, three beautiful young women draping themselves over him. Domitian seemed less commanding by comparison, though it stabbed Atretes' pride to admit it was this teenage boy who had shattered the unity of the Germanic tribes. He judged the distance he would have to leap to take one of them and knew it was impossible. But just the thought of breaking the neck of one made his blood pound.

Vespasian studied him without expression. Atretes stared back coldly, wishing his wrists were unshackled and he had a gladius in his hand. Before him on the dais sat the almighty power of Rome itself. Guards lined the walls of the chamber, and two stood behind Atretes. One more step toward the dais would be his last.

He paid no heed to the grandiose announcement made by the centurion, nor did he follow suit with the other five gladiators who raised their fists in salute as they hailed Caesar. Vespasian was still staring at him. Whispering buzzed. Atretes raised his shackled wrists and offered a sardonic smile. For the first time, he was glad of his chains. They saved him the humiliation of giving honor to a Roman. He let his gaze move from Vespasian to Titus to Domitian and back again, letting them see the full force of his hatred.

The two guards took him by the arms as he and the others were led from the great hall into a lesser chamber. He was pushed onto a couch. "You are to be honored this evening," one said dryly. "Tomorrow you die."

Atretes watched the other gladiators ushered to couches of honor. Some of the emperor's guests had followed them into the room and surrounded them. A lovely young Roman girl was laughing and stroking the Parthian as though he was a pet dog.

Several men and women approached Atretes as well, looking him over and discussing his strength and size. Atretes glared at them with contempt and loathing. "I don't think he likes being discussed," a handsome, well-built man remarked dryly.

"I doubt he understands Greek, Marcus. Germans are reputed to be strong, but stupid."

The man named Marcus laughed. "By the look in his eyes, Antigonus, I'd say he understood you very well. I'll put my wager on this one. He has a certain look about him."

"I'll still put my wager on Arria's Greek," the other said as they walked away. "She said he has tremendous stamina."

"No doubt she's tested it," Marcus said as he strolled over to take a closer look at the Parthian.

Atretes wondered how long he was to endure being "honored." Trays of delicacies were brought to him and he scorned them. He had never seen or smelled such food before and did not trust it. He drank the wine sparingly, his blood warming at the sight of scantily clad dancing slave girls twirling and swaying, rocking and undulating in an erotic dance.

"A pity, Orestes," a man said, standing in front of him with another. "The German seems to prefer women."

"A pity indeed," the other sighed.

Atretes' jaw locked and his hand whitened on his goblet. He felt their foul perusal and swore if one laid a hand on him, he would kill him.

A burst of laughter caught Atretes' attention. One of the Greeks had pulled a slave girl onto his lap and was kissing her. She was screaming and struggling to get away while the Romans around him laughed and encouraged him to take further liberties. On the couch a few feet away, the Parthian stuffed himself with all manner of delicacies and swilled wine without restraint. *The fool had better enjoy himself, because it's the last meal he'll ever eat if I have the good fortune to face him on the morrow,* thought Atretes.

Caleb reclined on a couch well back from the others. He held no wine goblet and the platter before him was untouched. A woman was standing behind him, speaking with him and caressing his shoulder. He paid her no attention. His eyes were half closed, his expression withdrawn and grim. She persisted for some time, and then, annoyed, left.

No one sat on the cushions of Atretes' couch. Vespasian had ordered his wrist restraints removed, but the guards stood alert and ready should he try anything, warning guests to keep a safe distance. "Germans are like berserkers," he overheard someone say. It seemed that half of the gathering was watching him, hoping to witness a mindless rage. Several young women in rich finery kept staring avidly at every part of him. He gritted his teeth. Were all Roman women so bold? Trying to ignore them, he lifted his wine goblet and sipped. They moved toward him until they were close enough for him to hear plainly what they were saying about him. Did they think him deaf or stupid?

"Domitian said his name is Atretes. He's beautiful, isn't he? I just love blonds."

"He's too savage for my taste. Those blue eyes give me chills."

"Oooh," one said, fanning herself dramatically. "They give me a fever."

Several laughed softly, and one asked, "How many men do you suppose he's killed? Do you think he'll have a chance tomorrow? Domitian told me he's matched against Fadus' Thracian, and he's every bit as good as Caleb."

"I'll put my bet on this one. Did you see the look in his eyes when he was brought into the room? And he didn't hail Caesar."

"How could he? He was in chains."

"They say Germans enter battle naked," another said in a hushed voice. "Do you think Vespasian will have him stripped bare for the contests tomorrow?"

One laughed huskily, "Oh, I do hope so." The tittering laughter of the others joined hers.

"I'll suggest it."

"Arria! I thought you liked the Parthian."

"I'm tired of him."

Atretes was tired of them. Turning his head slightly, he stared straight into the brown eyes of the prettiest of the five young women, the one who'd said she would suggest he fight naked. The mass of braids and curls of improbable blonde hair seemed too much weight for her slender neck, which was encircled by rare pearls. She was beautiful. Taking full note of his attention, she raised a smug brow at her friends and smiled at him. His bold stare didn't make her blush.

"Do you think we should stand so close?"

"What do you think he's going to do? Grab me?" Arria said in a purring tone, still smiling into his eyes as though challenging him to do exactly that.

Atretes continued to stare at her. She was wearing a jeweled belt designed like one the rapacious Greek was wearing. His gaze lingered for a moment, then he lifted his goblet, took a slow swallow of wine, and returned his attention to the dancing slave girls as though they were far more alluring.

"I think you've just been insulted, Arria."

"So it would seem," came the cold response. They moved away, relieving Atretes of their irritating presence. He wondered again how long he would have to endure this evening of "pleasure." He allowed his wine goblet to be refilled and tried to close his mind to the merriment that assaulted his soul.

Finally they were taken from the feast and, one by one, they were locked into small holding cells beneath the amphitheater. Atretes stretched out on the stone shelf and closed his eyes, willing himself to sleep. He dreamed of the forests of his homeland, of standing among the elders as his mother prophesied he would bring peace to his people. The confusion of a battle made him writhe and moan, and one of the guards rapped loudly on the door, awakening him. He slept again, fitfully, dreaming he was in the bog. He could feel it sucking at his ankles and, struggling to get free, he sank deeper, the weight of the moist earth pressing around him and pulling him down, down, until he was beneath it and couldn't breathe. He could hear his mother and the others from his village crying out as the ring of steel sang out through the forest. The air was filled with the screams of his people dying. He couldn't free himself from the weight of the earth.

With a harsh cry, Atretes sat up, coming out of the nightmare with a sharp jolt. It was a moment before he realized where he was. Sweat streamed down his chest despite the chill of the stone walls. Letting out his breath, he raked shaking hands back through his hair and dragged in air.

His mother had said he would bring his people peace. What peace had he brought them? What peace but death? How many Chatti were still alive and free in the forests of Germania? What had become of his mother? What of the rest? Were they, like he, all now slaves of Rome?

Full of rage, he clenched his fists. Trembling with it, he lay back, trying to relax, trying to rest for the battle ahead, even as his mind roiled with images of violence fed by his longing for vengeance.

Tomorrow. Tomorrow he would die with a sword in his hand.

13

The guards came for him at midmorning, bringing a heavy bearskin. He was taken along the torchlit corridor as the others were brought out to the confusion behind the Porta Pompae, the central door for processions leading into the Circus Maximus. The sunlight was like a physical blow.

"The emperor has arrived and the opening ceremonies have begun," a guard shouted, his contingent hurrying them to the chariots that waited to carry them into the arena so they could be displayed before the thousands of spectators crowded into the tiered seats.

Atretes was ordered into a chariot with Caleb. "May God be with us both," the Jew said.

"Which one?" Atretes said through his teeth as he braced himself for the ride. The crowd screamed wildly as they appeared along with a dozen other chariots carrying gladiators from other schools. The sight and sound of so many thousands filling the Circus Maximus made Atretes' hands sweat and his heart pound. Trumpets blared, whistles trilled, and thousands of voices rose until the earth itself seemed to shake.

The track was over two hundred feet wide on one side, and stretched out before him more than eighteen hundred feet in length. Down the center of the track rose a huge platform, the *spina.* Made of marble, it measured at least 233 feet in length and 20 feet in width. The spina served as a platform for marble statues and columns, fountains that gushed perfumed water, and altars to a dozen Roman gods. Atretes rode past a small temple of Venus where priests were burning incense paid for by charioteers. At the center of the spina, Atretes stared up at the towering obelisk brought from Egypt. Squinting against the brilliant glare, he looked up at the golden ball mounted on top, which shone like a sun.

Near the end of the spina rose two columns, on top of which were mounted marble crossbars. Situated atop the crossbars were seven bronze eggs—the sacred symbols of Castor and Pollux, heavenly twins and patron saints of Rome—and seven dolphins, sacred to the god Neptune.

The driver brought the chariot around sharply, narrowly missing the *metae,* turning posts with cones that rose like cypress trees to protect the spina from being damaged during the races. The cones were twenty feet high and carved in reliefs of Roman battle scenes. Atretes took all of this in as his chariot headed down the other side of the track, in line with two other chariots.

They came round one more time and stopped before the tribunal where the emperor sat with the other officials of the games. Caleb stepped down. Atretes did as well, feeling the heat rising from the sand. The sun beat down and Atretes longed to throw off the bearskin. Brightly colored awnings were being unrolled along rope cables, shading the top rows of spectators. His mouth was dry. He wished for one of the thin wool tunics of the ludus.

Caleb strode along the rim of the arena, arms outstretched to accept the cries of his admirers. The other gladiators did the same, showing off breastplates inlaid with silver and gold. Some wore swords set with precious jewels. Glistening helmets were topped with ostrich and peacock feathers. Brassards and cuisses were engraved with battle scenes. Bedazzled, the spectators shouted their delight, calling out to their favorites and mocking the others, especially Atretes in his barbarian furs, standing silent, legs splayed, feet planted. Some spectators were calling out to him and laughing.

The mob was awash in red, white, green, and blue as spectators wore the colors of the factions, denoting which chariot team they backed. Those with the emperor wore predominately red. The editor, as the organizer and master of ceremonies for the games was called, came back before the emperor's tribunal. As the editor stepped down off the chariot, spectators jumped up and waved placards. Diocles Proctor Fadus: A Friend of the People! Smiling and bowing, the man in the purple toga waved to the people and made a brief speech before the emperor.

The gladiators presented themselves before the emperor, Atretes among them. He raised his hand in stiff salute with the others and called out, "Hail, Caesar! Those about to die salute you." The loathsome words stuck in Atretes' throat and his hand closed into a fist, which he held a little longer in the air than the others.

Climbing back onto the chariot with Caleb, Atretes braced

himself again for the last circle of the track before the chariot shot through the gates. "The waiting begins," Caleb said as he stepped down.

"How long?" Atretes asked, walking beside him toward the quarters where they were to be held until they were called for their matches. Groups of women pushed against the guards surrounding them, crying out for Celerus, Orestes, and Promethius.

"There's no way to know. An hour. A day. The real spectacle isn't the games at all. It's the spectators. When a race is going, they tear at their clothes and themselves, faint from excitement, dance about like madmen, and bet every sesterce they have on a team. I've seen losers sell themselves to a slave dealer just for a few more coins to bet. Hippomania, they call it. Romans are horse-mad."

Atretes gave a bitter laugh. "So, we're just the entertainment between races."

"Be angry. It'll give you extra strength. But don't let anger overpower your thinking. Not unless it's your will to die." He glanced at Atretes as they walked. "I have seen men deliberately drop their guard so a killing blow could be struck."

"I won't drop my guard."

Caleb smiled without humor. "I have seen you fight. You are full of rage, blinded by it. Look around you at the mob, young Atretes. These conquerors of the world are slaves to their passions, and someday their passions will bring them down." The guard opened one of the cells in the torchlit corridor and Caleb stepped inside. Turning, he stared straight into Atretes' eyes. "You have much in common with Rome." The door closed, blocking him from view, and the lock was set.

Atretes was not summoned until early afternoon. When he stepped out of his cell, he was given a two-handed broadsword and no armor. Slaves were clearing away the remains of two mangled chariots and raking the sand. Roasted partridges were being catapulted to the crowd. Most of those watching were drugged by sunlight and wine and lounged back eating bread they had brought for the day.

Shrugging off the heavy bearskin, Atretes strode out onto the sand to meet his opponent, a mirmillo, equipped as a Gaul, a fish insignia on his helmet. *Boo*s and catcalls from the crowd greeted Atretes as he walked forward, and partridge bones were flung at him. Ignoring them, Atretes stood beside the Gaul and faced the emperor, raising his weapon in salute. Then he turned to face his opponent.

They moved around one another, looking for an opening. The Gaul was heavyset and made the first rush. He favored his right arm and used his bulk to ram Atretes when the German barbarian blocked his sword thrust. Atretes ducked the Gaul's move and brought his fist up, knocking his opponent's helmet askew. He took the split second of advantage to drive his sword through the Gaul's side. He let go of the weapon and the man dropped to his knees. Raising his head sluggishly, the wounded man fell backward. He braced himself up on one elbow for a few seconds before he died. Atretes stepped away as the crowd burst into shouts of derision; they felt cheated by the brevity of the fight.

Snatching up the Gaul's weapon, Atretes raised it into the air and gave his war cry to Tiwaz. Lowering his arms, he strode back and forth before the tribunal.

"I killed ten of your legionnaires before I was captured!" he shouted up at the emperor and officials. "It took four to hold me down and put me in chains." He raised his sword to the crowd. "The weakest German is worth a legion of yellow-bellied Romans!"

Amazingly, the crowd roared with approval. Clapping and laughing, they cheered his nerve. He spit in the dust.

"Give him Celerus!" shouted a tribune surrounded by members of his regiment.

Atretes pointed his gladius straight at him. *"Coward!* Come down yourself! Or is Roman blood water?" The tribune started to shove his way along the aisle, but hands pushed him back. Atretes laughed loudly. "Your men are afraid for you!" he taunted. Two others rose.

"Celerus! Celerus!" Hundreds took up the chant, but another young officer jumped down into the arena and demanded armor and a weapon. "For the honor of Rome and those who died on the German frontier!" he shouted, striding forward onto the sand to meet Atretes.

They were evenly matched physically and the crowd was silent at the clash of swords. Neither gave ground for several moments as they blocked blows and tried for advantage. Atretes ducked one swing and drove his shoulder into the Roman's chest, flinging him back. Following quickly, he beat the young officer to his knees. The Roman managed to roll away and scramble to his feet.

Atretes leaped back as the gladius flashed, opening a six-inch gash on his chest. Slipping in a pool of blood where the Gaul had fallen, Atretes went down heavily.

The crowd rose en masse, screaming wildly as the officer drove forward and straddled him. Atretes saw the gladius rise for the death stroke and brought his fist up between the man's legs, doubling him over in agony. Rolling away, he bounded to his feet and swung his sword with all his strength, cutting through the gorget that protected his opponent's neck.

The headless body sagged forward in the dust and the crowd went silent.

Chest heaving, Atretes turned and raised his bloody sword in challenge to the officer's regiment. The crowd screamed again in excitement, but two other legionnaires were prevented from leaping into the arena by the emperor's soldiers. Vespasian made a signal and a retiarius came forward.

Atretes knew he was expected to play the part of the secutor, or "chaser," and catch the net man. He also knew that the retiarius had the advantage. His net was edged with small metal weights so that it would open in a wide circle when thrown. If caught in it, Atretes would have little chance of defending himself. He was already tired from the first two contests, so he made no advance.

"I seek not you," the retiarius said loudly, reciting the traditional chant, "I seek a fish!" He made a tentative cast of his net, snapping it back.

Atretes stood his ground, waiting for the retiarius to come to him. Cocky, the net man made sport of him, dancing around and calling him a barbarian coward. The crowd shouted at him to fight. The legionnaires called him "Chicken!" Atretes ignored them. He had no intention of exhausting himself by running after the net man. He would watch and wait for his chance.

The retiarius showed off with fancy casts. He flung the long net toward Atretes' feet, intending to tangle him, but Atretes jumped back.

"Why do you flee?" the retiarius taunted, swinging the net back and forth as he advanced. When he pitched it, Atretes caught hold, blocking the thrust of the trident and bringing his knee up into the retiarius' stomach. He looped the net around the man's head, kicked him to his knees, and brought the butt of his gladius down on the back of his head, killing him.

The crowd was on its feet again, cheering wildly. Breathing heavily, Atretes stepped away from the fallen retiarius. His muscles were trembling from exhaustion and loss of blood. Dropping to one knee, he shook his head and tried to clear his vision.

Vespasian nodded, and Atretes saw a Thracian come out onto the sand. *Celerus.* Gripping his gladius tighter, Atretes rose to his feet and made ready to fight again, knowing this time he would die.

Thousands of spectators rose to their feet waving white handkerchiefs—an unexpected show of favor toward Atretes. Vespasian looked from the crowd to the German barbarian. Titus leaned toward his father and spoke. The roar of humanity rose until the stadium seemed to tremble with the sound. White swatches of cloth waved in every direction, giving the emperor a clear message: spare the barbarian, let him fight another day.

Atretes wanted no mercy from a Roman mob. Anger pumped through him, giving him added strength. He strode toward the Thracian shouting, "Fight me!"

"You are so eager to die, German!" Celerus shouted back, making no move toward him. He looked up at the emperor for some sign and received none. When Atretes continued to advance, Celerus turned to face him, sword ready. The sound of the mob turned menacing, white handkerchiefs moving in unison like a drum beat. Vespasian made a signal, and Celerus' lanista ordered him at rest. Bato and four guards from the Great School came out onto the sand.

"I will die as I choose!" Gripping his sword in both hands, Atretes took a fighting stance.

Bato snapped his fingers and the guards spread out as they advanced. Two shook out whips. At Bato's nod, one whip was snapped around Atretes' sword and the other snaked around his ankle. Hands slick with blood, Atretes couldn't hold the gladius. Releasing it, he brought his elbow up against the side of one guard's head and kicked another back. The other pulled the whip taut, pitching him off-balance long enough for the other guards to get a firm hold of him. Thrashing, he tried to shake them off. When he couldn't, he screamed his war cry. Bato forced the handle of the whip between his teeth to silence him and they took him fighting from the arena.

"Get him on the table!" Other hands helped Bato's men, and

Atretes was slammed onto a wood frame, his arms and legs shackled. He arched up against the restraints.

"Stanch the wound," a man in a bloodstained tunic said, gesturing impatiently to another washing his hands in an earthen basin. "He's lost a lot of blood," he told Bato and then shouted at another. "Leave that one. He's as good as dead. Tell Drusus he can have him for dissection if he hurries. Once he's dead the law forbids it. Hurry up about it, and then get over here. I need help with this one!" He looked across Atretes at Bato. "Is he fighting again?"

"Not today," Bato said grimly.

"Good. That makes it easier." The doctor took up a pitcher and poured blood into a cup. He mixed opium and herbs into it. "This'll give him strength and cool the bloodlust. Hold his head down. He'll either drink it or drown in it." The surgeon pulled Atretes' cheek away from his gums and poured the brew into his mouth.

Atretes gagged, but the surgeon kept pouring. A man screamed behind them; neither the doctor nor Bato flinched. The lanista leaned down, but Atretes could barely see his face through tears of rage. Cup drained, the surgeon stepped away. Atretes gave a heaving sob and swore in German. His body shook violently. The doctor leaned over him again, looking into his eyes. "The opium is taking effect."

"Sew him up," Bato said.

The surgeon worked quickly and then moved on to another gladiator who had been carried in on his shield. Bato stood beside the table. His mouth curved in a mirthless smile. "Better death than Roman mercy. Isn't that it, Atretes? You don't want to owe your life to a Roman mob. That's what drove you mad with rage."

Grabbing his hair, Bato held Atretes' head back. "You throw away your only chance for vengeance. It's within your grasp," he hissed through his teeth, dark eyes blazing. "Only in the arena can you get your revenge on Rome! You want to be a conqueror. Then be one! Take their women. Take their money. Let Rome grovel at your feet and worship you. Let them make you one of their gods!"

He released him and straightened. "Otherwise, you and the rest of your clansmen will have died for nothing."

14

"They all think it's my fault," Julia said, tears streaming down her cheeks as she lay pale on her bed. "I see the way they look at me. They blame me for Claudius' death. I know they do. It's not my fault, Hadassah. It isn't, is it? I didn't want him to come after me." Her shoulders shook as she sobbed again.

"I know you didn't," Hadassah said gently, holding back her own tears as she tried to comfort her distraught mistress. Julia never intended harm. She simply never thought of anyone but herself, nor did she consider what the results of her actions might be.

The tragic morning of Claudius' death began with Julia whining about how bored she was. She wanted to go to a private showing at a gladiatorial ludus and she needed Claudius to accompany her. Accustomed to her complaining, Claudius hardly bothered listening to her. He was deep in his studies. Julia pressed him and he refused, politely informing her he was finishing a thesis on Judaism. Julia left the study in a silent rage. She changed her clothes and ordered a chariot.

Persis, more worried about his master's reputation than his mistress's, informed Claudius that Julia had left the villa unescorted. Claudius was angry to be interrupted yet again because of Julia. A cup of wine calmed his nerves. He supposed in Rome it was permissible for a young married woman to go about the countryside unchaperoned, but in Campania it was not proper. Persis offered to send someone after her, but Claudius said no. It was time he and Julia spoke plainly. He ordered a mount from the stables.

An hour later, his horse came home without him.

Alarmed, Persis gathered several others and went out to look for his master. They found Claudius two miles from the ludus, his neck broken from a fall.

Crying over Claudius' death, Hadassah was frantic with worry for Julia. The house was in chaos, and no one would go after her. Persis said she could be damned.

Julia arrived just after sundown, dusty and disheveled. When no one came to assist her, Julia left the chariot untended and slammed into the house, shouting for Hadassah. Hadassah ran to her, relieved that she was all right and not knowing how she was going to tell her of Claudius' accident.

"Have the bath filled with warm, scented water, and bring me something to eat," Julia ordered tersely, striding toward her room. "I'm covered with road dust and I'm famished."

Hadassah passed on the instructions quickly, almost certain they would not be fulfilled, then hastened after her mistress.

Julia paced about the room like an angry house cat. Her face was flushed and dirty, except for the white streaks left by tears. She noticed nothing amiss about Hadassah's ashen face and nervous manner.

"I've been worried for you, my lady. Where have you been?"

Julia turned on her imperiously. "Don't you dare question me!" she cried out in frustration. "I won't answer to a slave about my behavior!" She sank down miserably on her couch. "I won't answer to anyone, not even my *husband.*"

Hadassah poured her some wine and gave her the goblet.

"Your hand is shaking," Julia said and glanced up at her. "You were so worried about me?" She set the cup aside and took Hadassah's hand. "At least someone loves me," she said.

Hadassah sat down beside her and took her hands. "Where have you been?"

"I was on my way home to Rome, and then knew it was no use. Father would just send me back. So, here I am, a prisoner again in this dreary place."

"Then you never went to the ludus?"

"No. I didn't go," Julia said wearily. Her mouth twisted bitterly. "It wouldn't be proper for me to arrive unescorted," she said derisively. She gave a soft, self-mocking laugh. "Marcus would say I'm plebeian in my thinking." She stood up and moved away. Hadassah could see the tension gathering again, the storm coming. How was she going to tell Julia about Claudius? Her mistress's emotions were already a shambles. Her own were no more under control.

Julia drew several pins from her hair and threw them on the vanity. They bounced off onto the floor and Hadassah stooped to pick them up. "I should have gone and seen the match," Julia said. "A little scandal might wake Claudius up to his duties as my husband. Am I to do nothing but sit around for the rest of my life while he buries himself in his boring studies of religions of the

Empire? Who will read them? Tell me. No one is interested." Her eyes filled with angry, self-pitying tears. "I despise him."

"Oh, my lady," Hadassah had said, biting her lip, unable to keep the tears back.

"I know you are fond of him, but he is so *dull*. For all his supposed intellect, he is the most boring man I've ever met. And I don't care if he knows it." Flying to the door, she flung it open and cried out across the open garden of the peristyle. "Can you hear me, Claudius? You're a bore!"

Mortified by her behavior, Hadassah was overcome. She rushed to the door, pushed Julia aside, and closed it.

"What are you doing?" Julia cried shrilly.

"My lady, please be quiet! He's dead! Do you want everyone hearing you?"

"What?" Julia's response was faint, disbelieving, and her face paled.

"He went after you. They found him on the way to the ludus. He fell from his horse and broke his neck."

Eyes wild, Julia drew back as though she had been struck. "By the gods, he's such a fool!"

Aghast, Hadassah stared at her, her own emotions in turmoil. Did Julia think Claudius a fool for having fallen from his horse or a fool for having gone after her? For an instant, Hadassah had loathed her, and then swift shame filled her. She had failed in her duty. She should have stopped Julia from leaving the villa. She should have gone after her.

"He can't be dead. What will I do?" Julia cried and dissolved into hysteria.

Word was sent to Decimus Valerian of Claudius' death. Hadassah knew arrangements had to be made for the funeral, but Julia, the only one with authority, was incapable of making any decisions in her present state. Claudius' body lay in his chambers, washed, wrapped, and decaying.

Persis grieved Claudius as a son would grieve the loss of a father. Even the maids wept. The gardeners were silent and grim. The slaves gathered and talked, and no work was done.

Julia was right. They did all blame her. In small part, they even blamed Hadassah, for she served Julia and was completely loyal to her. Granted, she had served Claudius well, spending hours helping him with his studies, but she was not one of them.

Julia's grief was guilt inspired, and her hysteria took the form of irrational fears that the slaves wanted her dead. She refused to leave her chambers. She wouldn't eat, she couldn't sleep.

"I should never have married him," Julia said one day, pale and distraught. "I should have refused no matter what Father said. The marriage was a disaster from the beginning. Claudius wasn't happy. I wasn't the wife he wanted. He wanted someone like his first wife who was content with studying dull scrolls." She wept again. "It's not my fault he's dead. I didn't want him to come after me." Her tears turned to irrational rage. "It's Father's fault. If he hadn't insisted I marry Claudius, none of this would have happened!"

Hadassah did her best to soothe away Julia's fears and make her see reason, but Julia wouldn't listen. She refused to eat, terrified one of the kitchen slaves would poison her. "They hate me. Did you see how she looked at me when she brought the tray in? Persis runs the household and he hates me as much as he loved Claudius."

When she finally slept, she awakened with nightmares. Hadassah was frightened by her mistress's unruly passions and her wild flights of imagination. "No one wants to harm you, my lady. They are worried about you."

That was true, the slaves *were* worried; they had overheard some of Julia's wild, unfounded accusations that they were intent on killing her. If Valerian heard and believed, they were all at risk of execution.

Decimus Valerian didn't come. He had sailed to Ephesus on business just before Claudius' accident. He wouldn't learn of it until his return. Phoebe Valerian arrived with Marcus on the afternoon of the third day. Catya came running and knocked on the locked door of Julia's chambers announcing their arrival.

"Don't unlock the door!" Julia said, eyes wild from lack of sleep. "It's a trick."

"Julia," Phoebe said a few minutes later. "Julia, let me in, darling." When Julia heard her mother's voice, she flew from her bed to the door and unbolted it. "Mama!" she cried, throwing herself into Phoebe's arms and sobbing. "They all want to kill me. They all hate me. They wish I'd been killed, and not Claudius!"

Phoebe drew her daughter into the room. "Nonsense, Julia. Come and sit down now." She glanced at Hadassah. "Have someone bring my cases in here immediately. I have something I can give her to calm her nerves."

Hadassah saw Marcus standing in the doorway, his face darkened with anger and concern. Not a single word Julia had said was true, but the rash accusations were enough to destroy the lives of an entire household of slaves if Marcus believed her. Julia was weeping copiously and clinging to her mother.

As soon as Hadassah returned, one of the men carrying two cases behind her, Phoebe told her to take a small amphora from her cosmetics box. "Mix a few drops in a glass of wine."

"I won't drink any wine in this house!" Julia cried out. "They've poisoned it!"

"Oh, no, my lady," Hadassah said in distress. With trembling hands, she poured some in a glass and drank half. She held the glass out to show Julia, and looked at Phoebe in tearful appeal. "I swear no one means to harm her."

Marcus took the glass from her. "Where did you say the amphora was, Mother?" He found it and poured the drops into the wine, handing it to his mother, and watched as his weeping sister drank it. "If you don't need me, Mother, there are arrangements that should be made," he said grimly. She nodded, understanding.

Marcus took Hadassah firmly by the arm and half-pushed her into the corridor, closing the door behind him. "You look dead on your feet," he said, taking in her white face and the dark shadows beneath her eyes. "How long has Julia been like this?"

"Three days, my lord. Since she learned of Claudius' death."

Marcus was struck by the familiar way Hadassah said *Claudius*. Had she come to love him? "An unfortunate accident by the report we received," he said. Her eyes filled with the tears she clearly was trying to hold back. They spilled over and ran down her cheeks. "Go and rest," he said tersely. "I will speak with you later."

While his mother comforted Julia, Marcus took command of the household. He was appalled at the state the house was in. It appeared nothing had been done in days. Claudius had not even been buried. Marcus ordered it done immediately. "Is his wife buried here?" he demanded of Persis, who said she was. "Then bury your master beside her. And quickly!" All the furnishings from Claudius' fouled chambers were burned and the room scoured and aired.

Closeting himself in the library, Marcus went over the meticulous records and journals concerning the villa and surrounding estate. He smiled cynically as he sipped wine and made calculations. Julia would be well consoled when she realized Claudius' death had left her with a fortune, though she would have little say in the dispensation.

In his father's absence, Marcus had full authority to make whatever decisions he thought necessary. Julia had made no secret of her dislike of Capua, and Marcus knew she wouldn't want to remain here. He made arrangements for a solicitor to come and review the property. The price Marcus set made the man choke. Marcus remained firm. "I'll give you the names of two senators who covet an estate in Campania," he said, and the solicitor gave in.

With her mother in residence, Julia was calmer. She was eating and sleeping again. Marcus told her of his decision to sell the villa, and her grief was entirely forgotten in the joy of knowing she was returning to Rome. "And what of the slaves? What will you do to them?"

"What would you have me do?"

"I want them scattered. Except for Persis. He was always disrespectful. He should be sent to the galleys. I insist," she said.

"It's not your place to insist anything," Marcus said, annoyed. "You're now beneath Father's care again, and I'm executor of the estate in his absence."

Julia's eyes flashed. "I've nothing to say about anything? I was Claudius' wife."

"Not much of a wife from what you've told me."

"You accuse me, too!" Julia said, quick tears coming again.

"I had to set my own affairs aside in order to come and sort out yours. Grow up, Julia! Don't make matters more difficult than they already are," he said, his patience with her tears and self-pity coming to an end.

He went out into the gardens alone each evening, wandering aimlessly, restlessly. He wondered if Hadassah came out to pray in the darkness as she used to. To what god should he pray to unravel this mess? What was he to do concerning the slaves? He knew he had to make a decision, but was loath to do so.

He went up onto the hill and sat beneath a *fanum,* one of the small temples. Leaning back against a marble pillar, he stared up at the starlit night. He had known the marriage was a mistake from the beginning, but he certainly had never wished ill upon Claudius. Julia had said enough in the last few days to reveal what a disaster things had been. Most of the blame he knew lay at her own feet. Now, she had brought up another matter he had to consider.

No one had gone to look for her. After a few days of observation, he began to wonder if some of her accusations were true. The slaves may not have actively sought her death, but they hadn't provided for her protection either.

"My lord?"

Startled, he sat up. His heart quickened as he saw Hadassah standing nearby in the shadows. "So you have not given up coming out to pray to your unseen god," he said lightly, relaxing back against the pillar again.

"No, my lord," she said, and he heard the smile in her voice. She came closer. "May I speak with you freely?" He nodded his assent. "I don't believe Master Claudius would have wanted Persis or the others taken from this home."

His mouth tightened. He had come up here to get away from the problem for a while, and now here was the last person he expected to mention it bringing it up. "Did Persis blame Julia for Claudius' death?" he asked bluntly.

Silence hung. "My lord, no one is to blame for another's actions."

He rose, angry now. "You didn't answer the question, which is answer enough. Julia's accusations are not so farfetched as I first thought."

"No one ever sought to harm her, my lord. May God do so to me and more also if what I say isn't true. Persis grieves his master like one grieving a beloved father. His only thought was for him. Lord Claudius brought him here when he was a small boy. Persis served with love and devotion, and Master Claudius trusted him in everything, treating him as fondly as a son. Persis never meant harm to come to your sister."

"I've only your word for what you say," he said tersely.

"As God lives, my lord, I wouldn't lie to you."

Marcus believed her, but it didn't alter anything. He felt weary. "Sit with me and tell me what happened that day." He patted the marble beside him. She sat down slowly, her hands clasped tightly in her lap. He wanted to take her hand and encourage her to trust him, but knew such an action would do the opposite. "Tell me. You needn't be afraid."

She told him the bare facts. Julia wanted to go to the ludus;

Claudius didn't. Julia went by herself, and Claudius went to bring her back. He knew all that from Julia herself.

"When Claudius was found and brought back, who went for Julia?" he said pointedly, knowing already no one had. He spoke before she could answer. "She told me she was on her way to Rome." He had been furious when Julia told him that. Her temper always did overcome her common sense. "Do you know what can happen to a woman alone on the Appian Way? She's open game for robbers and worse. Who went to search for her, Hadassah?"

"The fault lies with me," she said. "May God forgive me, but I didn't search for Lady Julia any more than the others did. I didn't know where to look or what to do, so I did nothing. I watched and I waited. It's more my fault than anyone's because her good is my responsibility."

He was angry that she had come to plead their cause and offered herself in sacrifice. "You blame yourself for the inaction of an entire household staff? Your thoughts have always been trained on her. You didn't leave her alone for a moment after she learned of Claudius' death. You were exhausted from caring for her when I arrived."

He got up. "Perhaps there was another possibility I've been hesitant to accept, but which Julia has insisted upon since my arrival. Were you afraid for her life?"

"No, my lord!" she said, alarmed and frightened by the direction of his thoughts. "No one was ever a threat to her. Not ever."

"Neither were they a help," he said and moved away from her.

"They loved Claudius. They love him still."

"Enough!" He cut her off. "Don't come to me and plead their cause."

"They are innocent of what she has accused them," she said, showing an uncharacteristic boldness in defying him.

He glared at her. "Where is the innocence in a slave discarding duty, Hadassah? Julia's appeal to send Persis to the galleys has more mercy than what I know should be done. Persis should be killed for not seeing to his mistress's safety."

Hadassah stood with a soft gasp. "I knew that was what you were thinking." She came close to him. "Please, Marcus, I beg of you. Don't bring the sin of innocent blood upon your head."

Astonished at what she said and at her use of his familiar name, he stared down at her. Her eyes were shimmering with tears and he wondered at her words. Had she come to plead for Persis, or for *him?* "Give me one practical reason why I should spare him," he said, knowing there was none.

"Persis can read and write and cipher," she said.

"So can others."

"Lord Claudius trained him to manage all the estate matters."

He frowned. "Why would a master do that?"

"So that he could be free for his studies. My lord, Lady Julia said you will sell the villa to a senator who would make this an occasional resting place. Wouldn't a slave with Persis' knowledge and abilities prove invaluable to an absentee owner?"

He laughed softly. "Neatly argued, little Hadassah." He considered it and then shook his head. "Julia's feelings must be taken into account."

"She needs direction, not vengeance for a wrong never committed against her."

He knew she was right, but why should the life of one slave matter so much? Carrying out Julia's wishes in respect to the slaves would give her some peace, but in doing so, he would hurt Hadassah—something he realized he was loath to do.

"This entire tragic fiasco was created by her doing," he said, rubbing the back of his neck. He needed a long soak in the baths and a massage.

"You mustn't think she's to blame," Hadassah said.

He was surprised that she defended his sister so readily. "She defied her husband and he went after her. That makes it her fault in the eyes of some."

"She wasn't to blame for the wine Claudius drank before he left. She wasn't to blame that he wasn't a good rider and fell from his horse. She wasn't even to blame for his decision to go and find her. Each person answers for their own actions, and even then, it is God who decides."

"So by the mere whim of an unseen god, Claudius is dead," he said dryly.

"Not by whim, my lord."

"No?" he said with a curt laugh. "All gods act upon their whims. How is yours any different from the others?"

"God is not like the idols men create and credit with their own actions and passions. God doesn't think and act as men do." She took a step toward him as though being closer would make him understand. "We're each single threads woven together in a tapestry God has created. Only he sees the full picture, but not even a sparrow falls without his knowing."

She spoke not as a slave, but as a woman who believed every word she said. "All those hours you spent talking with Claudius in the privacy of his library have loosened your tongue," he remarked. She lowered her head, and he reached out to tip her chin up. "You think Claudius' death is part of some divine plan?"

"You mock me."

He let her go. "No. I wonder at this god of yours who so freely wipes out his people and kills a man whose only crime was to bore a young wife. I wonder that you would still worship this cruel god of yours and not be wise enough to choose another."

Hadassah closed her eyes. She failed at every turn to explain. She failed even to drive the doubts from herself.

Why did you take Claudius, Lord? Why, when I felt so close to him? Why now, when I was finally able to gather the courage to speak of you? He was so full of questions, and I tried to explain. But Lord, I hadn't reached him. He didn't understand. He didn't fully believe. Why did you take him? And now I can't make Marcus Valerian understand, either. He's bent upon destruction.

"God makes all things work to the good," she said more to herself than Marcus.

He gave a soft, cynical laugh. "Ah yes. Good has come from this already. Claudius' death set Julia free." He saw Hadassah's hand go to her throat at his callous words. With a pang, he wished he could recall them, knowing he had hurt her, for her grief over Claudius Flaccus' death was sincere. "A harsh reality," he said flatly.

She said nothing for a long moment, then spoke softly. "The Lady Julia will have less freedom in Rome than she has had here, my lord."

He studied her face in the moonlight, more curious about her than ever. "You're very perceptive." When Julia realized she would have no control whatsoever over the money she had inherited from Claudius, she would balk. Rebellion would swiftly follow when Father took command of her social affairs as well. Marcus knew he could expect to be drawn into the mess that would soon develop. His mother would plead that he use his influence with Julia, while Father would order him to do nothing. As for Julia, she would use any means she could to get her own way.

Owning a villa in Campania had a certain appeal.

Marcus let out a weary breath. At least one burden had lifted. He knew what he would do about Persis and the others. Nothing. Nothing at all. "You may go to bed now, Hadassah. You've accomplished what you wanted, lay your fears at rest. Persis and the others will be spared."

She spoke so softly that he knew she hadn't meant for him to hear: "It was you I feared for most, Marcus."

He watched her walk down the path and he knew that all the evenings he had spent in the garden, he'd been waiting for her and the inner peace she would bring with her.

15

Decimus took Phoebe's hand and looped it through his arm as they walked along the cobbled pathway of the gardens adjoining the emperor's palace. Painted marble statues stood in the tended grounds, and fountains bubbled with soothing waters. Young people laughed and ran past Decimus and Phoebe, while other couples strolled as they did, taking in the glory of the day.

A marble statue of a nude maiden pouring water from a jug stood among a profusion of spring flowers. The sound of the running water soothed Decimus. "Let's sit here awhile," he said and relaxed onto a stone bench in the sunshine.

The trip to Ephesus had been hard, for he tired easily. Business had always consumed his mind, but these days he was distracted by so many strange and interconnected thoughts. His illness brought with it a crisis of his spirit—a sickness of his very soul, if he had one.

Why had he worked so hard all these years? To what purpose? His life seemed so futile, his accomplishments empty. His family was established, wealthy, assured of comfort. He had position in Roman society. Yet, rather than basking in the glory of his achievements, his family was torn by opposing ideologies. There was no unity anymore—he and his son argued about everything from politics to how to rear children, and his daughter clawed for independence. He had worked a lifetime to build an empire, to give his children all the things he had never had, and he had succeeded beyond his wildest expectations. But what had it brought him except an empty triumph?

Marcus was handsome, intelligent, well-spoken, shrewd. Julia was beautiful, charming, full of life. Both were well educated and admired by their peers. Nevertheless, Decimus felt a gnawing despair, a sense of failure as their father.

Who would think the mind could of itself be a battlefield? If not for Phoebe, he would open his veins and end the despair of his soul and the physical pain that was beginning to consume his every moment.

Perhaps it was the approach of death that had opened his eyes wide and made him see so clearly. Oh, that he had only been blind to it all and so been spared this emotional anguish. He had hoped visiting Ephesus, his place of birth, would bring him some peace. But peace was not to be found.

A slave came forward to shade Decimus, but he waved him away impatiently. He needed the warmth of the sun to take away the chill of foreboding that grew in him. Phoebe took his hand and pressed it to her cheek.

"I have failed," Decimus said flatly.

"In what, my love?" she said gently.

"In everything of any importance." He clutched her hand like a lifeline.

Phoebe lowered her head, remembering the latest confrontation between Julia and Decimus. Julia had wanted to attend the games, and Decimus refused permission, reminding her that she was in mourning for Claudius. The ensuing scene had shocked Phoebe as much as Decimus. Julia had cried out that she didn't care about Claudius, and why should she mourn a fool who couldn't sit a horse? Decimus had slapped her, and Julia stood for a moment in stunned silence, staring at him. Then her expression had altered so dramatically that she was scarcely recognizable. It was as though thwarting her desires had roused some dark presence within her, and her eyes had burned with such wild fury that Phoebe was afraid.

"It's *your* fault Claudius is dead," Julia hissed at her father. "You mourn him, for I will not. I'm glad he's dead. Do you hear me? I rejoice that I'm free of him. By the gods, I'd like to be free of you as well!" She ran from the peristyle and remained in her chambers for the rest of the morning.

Phoebe looked up at Decimus' lined face. "Julia didn't mean what she said to you, Decimus. She will apologize for it."

Yes, she had apologized later, much later, after Phoebe had spoken with her and roused whatever conscience was left in their daughter. Decimus thought of Julia's tearful pleadings and her excuses for her abominable accusation and behavior, yet it was the expression in her eyes during the outburst that remained burned into his mind. She had hated him, hated him enough to wish him dead. It was an appalling realization that the child he had created and loved so much held in contempt both him and all he held sacred.

"How is it possible that you and I have two children so

opposed to all we believe in, Phoebe? What has happened to virtue and honor and ideals? Marcus believes nothing is true and anything is permitted. Julia thinks the only thing that matters is her own pleasure. I've worked my entire life in order to give my children everything I never had at their age—wealth, education, position. And now I look at them and wonder if my life is simple vanity. They are selfish, without the least restraint upon their appetites. They haven't the smallest fiber of moral character."

His words hurt, and Phoebe sought some way to defend her children. "Don't judge them so harshly, Decimus. It's neither your fault, nor mine, nor theirs. It's the world they live in."

"A world of whose making, Phoebe? They want complete control over their lives. They want to be free of the old standards. Whatever feels good is right. Whoever stands in the way of their pleasures, they want destroyed. They demand the moral chains be removed, never understanding that it's moral restraint that keeps man civilized." He closed his eyes. "By the gods, Phoebe, I listen to our daughter and I am ashamed."

Tears filled Phoebe's eyes and she bit her lip. "She is young and thoughtless."

"Young and thoughtless," he repeated flatly. "And what excuse do we find for Marcus? He's twenty-three, not a child anymore. He said to me yesterday that Julia should be free to do as she wishes. He said mourning Claudius is a farce. Phoebe, a man is dead because of our daughter's willful defiance and selfishness, and she doesn't even care! Is Marcus also too young to have some sense of honor and decency about what happened in Campania?"

Phoebe looked away, hiding her tears, hurt by his harsh appraisal of their daughter. Decimus tipped her chin back. "I don't blame you. You've been the gentlest of mothers."

She searched his troubled face, so lined with fatigue. "Perhaps therein lies the problem." She touched his temple. He had a new streak of gray in his hair. Couldn't Marcus and Julia see their father was ill? Must Marcus argue about everything? Must Julia plague him so with her endless demands?

Decimus sighed heavily and took her hand again. "I am afraid for them, Phoebe. What happens to a society when all restraints are removed? I see our children consumed with watching blood be spilled in the arena. I see them seeking an unending diet of sensual pleasure. Where does it all lead? How can intemperate minds be free when they're slaves to their own passions?"

"Perhaps the world will change."

"When? How? The more our children have, the more they want, and the less conscience they have about how they get it. We aren't the only ones facing these crises. I overhear it every day at the baths. The same problems plague most of our friends!" Restless, Decimus stood. "Let's walk."

He and Phoebe wandered along the pathway, passing a young couple worshiping Eros beneath a flowering tree. A little further along two men were kissing on a bench. Decimus' countenance was rigid with revulsion. Greek influence had permeated Roman society, encouraging homosexuality and making it acceptable. While Decimus didn't condemn the behavior, he didn't want his face rubbed in it, either.

Rome tolerated every abominable practice, embraced every foul idea in the name of freedom and the rights of the common man. Citizens no longer carried on deviant behavior in private, but pridefully displayed it in public. It was those with moral values who could no longer freely walk in a public park without having to witness a revolting display.

What had happened to the public censors who protected the majority of citizenry from moral decadence? Did freedom have to mean abolishing common decency? Did freedom mean anyone could do anything they wanted anytime they wanted, without consequences?

Decimus ordered the litter. He was eager to return home and close himself inside the walls of his small villa, thereby shutting out a world in which he no longer felt he belonged.

Julia dropped the knucklebones onto the mosaic tiles of her bedroom floor, then laughed triumphantly. Octavia groaned. "You have all the luck, Julia," she said and straightened. "I quit. Let's go down to the markets and browse."

Leaving the knucklebones scattered on the floor, Julia rose. "Father won't give me any money," she said glumly.

"None?" Octavia said in consternation.

"I like pearls, Octavia, and Father says they're extravagant and unnecessary when I already have gold and jewels," she said, in a sneering imitation of her father.

"By the gods, Julia. All you have to do is charge what you want. What choice will your father have then but to release some of Claudius' money? Either that or taint the reputation he holds so dear."

"I wouldn't dare do that," Julia said flatly.

"It's your money by rights, isn't it? You were married to that silly old man. You deserve some compensation for your time in Campania!"

"Marcus had the estate sold. He's invested most of the proceeds for me."

"In what?" Octavia said with brightened interest. Marcus was noted for his financial acumen. Her father would welcome any information where Julia's brother was concerned.

"I haven't asked."

Octavia rolled her eyes. "Shouldn't you be aware of where your money is going?"

"I trust Marcus' judgment implicitly."

"Did I say you shouldn't? I'm only suggesting that it's wise for a woman to be informed." She poured herself some wine. "I've a friend you should meet. Her name is Calabah. She was married to Aurius Livius Fontaneus. Do you remember him? Short, fat, ugly, and very rich. He used to sit with Antigonus and your brother at the games sometimes."

"No, I don't remember him," Julia said, bored.

Octavia waved her hand airily. "It doesn't matter, darling. He's dead. Died of natural causes, though what causes I couldn't tell you. You'd like Calabah," she said, sipping her wine as she sifted her fingers through Julia's jewelry box. She took a gold brooch and examined it. It was simple but exquisite, rather like its owner. Dropping the brooch back in the box, Octavia turned. "Calabah goes to the ludus to exercise with the gladiators."

"Women do that?" Julia said, shocked.

"Some women. I wouldn't. I much prefer attending the pregame feast. There's something very exciting about being with a man who might die in the arena the next day." She swished the wine around in the goblet and gave Julia a catlike smile. "You should come sometime."

"Father would never allow it. He knows what goes on at those feasts."

"Delicious fun, that's what goes on. When are you going to exert yourself, Julia? You've been married and widowed and you still bow to your father's every dictate."

"What would you have me do? My father isn't as malleable as yours, Octavia. And I have to live beneath his roof."

"Fine. He's gone today, isn't he? And still we loll around here, bored out of our minds, waiting for your twelve-month mourning period to be over." She finished her wine and set the goblet down. "I've had enough. I'm going."

"Where?"

"Shopping. Strolling through the park. I may visit Calabah. I don't know. Frankly, Julia, anything is better than sitting here with you and listening to you whine about your fate." She picked up her shawl.

"Wait," Julia cried out.

"Why?" Octavia said with a haughty air. "You've become a dull little house mouse since your marriage to Claudius." She draped the shawl carefully over her elaborate coiffure. "How long have you left to mourn him? Three months? Four? Send me a message when you're free of your social obligations to that farce you claim was a happy marriage."

"Don't leave, Octavia. I thought you were my friend."

"I am your friend, you silly little fool, but I'm not going to sit around bored to death just because you haven't the courage to take command of your own life!"

"Very well," Julia said. "I'll go with you. We'll shop and visit your friend Calabah, though what sort of name that is, I can't imagine. Maybe we'll even go by Marcus' apartments and see if he'll take us to a party. How's that? Is that taking command of my life enough for you, Octavia?"

Octavia gave a mocking laugh. "We'll see if you've the courage to go through with it."

Julia glared at her and clapped her hands. "Hadassah, hurry! Bring me my lavender palus and the amethyst earrings and necklace," she said, well aware Octavia coveted her jewelry. She stripped off the white mourning tunic she wore, wadded it up, and threw it on the floor. "Oh, and don't forget the wool shawl. I'm going out with Octavia and we might be late coming home." She laughed merrily. "I feel better already."

"How long will it take you to get ready?" Octavia said, smiling slightly and feeling in full control of the situation—which was exactly the way she liked it.

"Just give me a moment more," Julia said and sat before her mirror, quickly and expertly applying makeup. She paused and looked at Octavia in the mirror, her eyes bright. "Forget shopping, Octavia. Let's go to the ludus and watch the gladiators exercise. Didn't you say you could do that whenever you liked because your father has connections at the Great School?"

"Father has to notify the lanista in advance, and Father left for Pompeii yesterday. He'll be there on business for several days."

"Oh," Julia said, setting down her pot of rouge. Atretes was at the ludus and she wanted to see him again.

"Now, don't go all glum on me again. If you've a mind to watch men, we can go to the Field of Mars. The legionnaires are there."

"I was hoping to get a glimpse of a gladiator I saw in Campania. I only saw him at a distance once when he was running near Claudius' villa, but he was very beautiful." She dabbed on some more cream and rubbed it into her cheeks. "I was able to find out that his name is Atretes and he was sold to the Great School."

"Atretes!" Octavia laughed.

"You know about him."

"Everybody knows about him! He appeared in the games a few weeks ago and turned a crowd eager for his blood into a mob wanting to worship him."

"What happened? Tell me everything!"

Octavia did, beginning with the pregame feast and Arria being insulted and ending with Atretes' performance in the arena. "You wouldn't see him even if we went to the ludus. He's kept well away from Roman visitors."

"But why?"

"He almost killed a senator's son who wanted to be paired with him. Apparently, Atretes didn't realize it was just an exercise. He was out for blood."

"How exciting! But surely Atretes wouldn't kill a woman," Julia said.

"He looks capable of anything. He has the coldest blue eyes I've ever seen."

Jealousy burned through Julia, followed by swift anger against her father for denying her the opportunity to attend pregame feasts as Octavia did. "You were with him at the feast?"

"I was with Caleb the evening Atretes was first presented. You've heard of Caleb. He's up to twenty-seven kills now." She tipped her head. "Atretes is a bit too barbarian for me."

Hadassah held the palus for Julia and let it slide down over her while the two young women talked. She hooked the gold belt and made a few adjustments so that the long tunic flattered Julia's slender figure. Then she hooked the amethyst necklace as Julia put on the pierced earrings.

"Would you like me to redo your hair, my lady?" Hadassah asked.

"She's done nothing to muss it," Octavia said, impatient.

"I would give anything to have Atretes comb his fingers through it," Julia laughed. Turning, she rose from her stool before the vanity and took Hadassah's hands, her mood suddenly serious. "Don't say anything to Father, even if he demands an explanation. Tell him I went to worship at the temple of Diana."

Octavia groaned. "Not Diana, Julia. Hera, the goddess of the hearth and marriage."

"Oh, I don't care," Julia said, letting go of Hadassah. "Tell him whatever god you choose." She snatched the shawl from Hadassah and twirled happily toward the door, letting the soft woolen fabric float about her. "Even better, tell him I went to the apothecary to find a fast-acting poison for myself. He would like that."

They hurried from the house and down the hill into the throng near the stalls of merchandise.

Julia loved walking through the crowded streets, seeing how heads turned as she passed. She knew she was pretty, and the attention heightened her spirits after having been so long behind the high walls of her father's house. He would be furious with her, but she wasn't going to think about that now. It would only spoil the rest of her day.

Father was bent upon spoiling her whole life if she let him. He was too old to remember what it was like to be young and so full of life you felt you would burst. He didn't believe in the gods anymore; he didn't believe in anything except his ancient standards and archaic morality.

The world was moving away from the old ideas, and he was determined to stand still. Worse, he was determined to make her stand still with him. He had tried with Marcus and failed, and now he was crushing her beneath his expectations. She had to be strong like her brother and not allow Father to dictate her life. She was not going to be like Mother, content to live behind high stone walls and wait upon her husband like he was a god. She had her own life to live, and she was going to do with it as she pleased. She was going to attend pregame feasts and drink and laugh with the gladiators; she was going to attend the Ludi Megalenses next week and celebrate Cybele with her friends. She was going to find some way to meet Atretes.

"How many lovers have you had, Octavia?" Julia said as they walked along, pausing here and there to look at baubles from foreign lands.

Octavia laughed. "I've lost count."

"I wish I could be like you, free to do what I want with whomever I choose."

"Why can't you?"

"Father—"

"You're such a goose, Julia. You have to take control of your life. They've made their choices and done what they wanted. Why shouldn't you do the same thing?"

"The law says—"

"The law," Octavia broke in derisively. "You married Claudius because your father wished it, and now Claudius is dead. Everything that he had belongs to you. Marcus controls it, doesn't he? Well, your brother adores you. Use that."

"I'm not sure I could do that," Julia said, troubled by the way Octavia expressed it.

"You do it all the time," Octavia laughed. "Only you do it over unimportant things like sneaking off to the games once or twice, rather than taking control of the money that rightfully belongs to you. Is it fair that your father and brother have use of that money when you were the one who had to sleep with that dreary old man?"

Julia blushed and glanced away, well aware she had been a poor wife. "He wasn't that dreary. Claudius was quite brilliant."

Octavia laughed. "So brilliant he bored you to death. You told me so yourself in a letter, or don't you want to remember what you wrote about him?"

Suddenly Julia found it hard to breathe. She trembled slightly, wondering how many other horrible things she had said about Claudius that were remembered so vividly. Octavia knew he had been riding after her. Why did she bring him up at all when she was aware it upset her so much? "I don't want to talk about him, Octavia. You know that."

"He's dead. What's to talk about? The gods smiled on you."

Julia shivered. To distract herself from her grim thoughts, she stopped at a stall that displayed crystal pendants. The proprietor was a swarthy and handsome Egyptian. He spoke fluent Greek, but it was heavily accented, giving him an aura of mystery. Julia examined one of the pendants with interest. It was cold in her hand and encircled by a serpent that served to hold the long crystal and allow a loop for a heavy chain.

"My name is Chakras and I bring these crystals from the farthest reaches of the Empire." The Egyptian watched Julia pick up a pendant. "It is lovely, isn't it?" he said. "Rose quartz eases sexual imbalances and helps soothe away anger, resentment, guilt, fear, and jealousy."

"Let me see it," Octavia said and took it from Julia to look at it more closely.

"It is also known to increase fertility," Chakras said.

Octavia laughed and handed it back to Julia quickly. "Here, you hold it."

"Something less dangerous, perhaps?" Julia said, laughing at Octavia. She pointed to another necklace. "What about that one?"

"A good choice," the man said, picking it up reverently. "Moonstone has healing powers for the stomach and it relieves anxiety and depression. It also aids in the birthing process and helps female problems." Noting Octavia's grimace, he added, "A good gift for a woman about to be married."

"I like it," Julia said, setting it aside. "What about that one over there?"

He picked up a beautiful lavender crystal and set it on the cloth-covered pedestal. "It is alexandrite, my lady, a variety of chrysoberyl known to heal internal and external degeneration."

"It keeps you from getting old?" Octavia said.

"Indeed, my lady," he said, watching her finger it. He turned away, cautious to keep an eye on Octavia as he picked up several other pendants. "Alexandrite also helps to align the emotions and reflects the highest potentials of unfolding joy." He set a pale turquoise-colored crystal before them. "This aquamarine is a rare variety of beryl and is known to strengthen the viscera and purify the body," he said. "It enhances the clarity of one's mind and aids in creative expression. It will bring you into balance with the gods."

"My father would like this one," Julia said and set the aquamarine aside. "Mama thinks he's sick."

"Oh, my lady, then you must see this carnelian crystal. It is a highly evolved healer, opening the heart and encouraging communion with the spirits of the underworld, thus finding the many ways to escape death."

"What a pretty red," Julia said and took it. She rolled it over and over in her hand. "I like it, too," she said and set it aside with the aquamarine, moonstone, alexandrite, and rose quartz crystal pendants. Octavia grew pale, her mouth pressed tight, her eyes glittering with burning envy.

Chakras smiled faintly. "Try this one on, my lady," he said, holding out a clear crystal spear about three inches long.

"It's much too big," Julia said.

"This crystal enhances and stimulates the body and mind. It allows you to commune with the god of your choice. From the instant you put it on, you will feel the power in the crystal. It awakens the senses and increases your charms."

"Very well," Julia said, intrigued more by his mesmerizing singsong voice than by the crystal. He placed it around her neck with reverence.

"Do you feel the power of it?"

Julia glanced up at him, and he looked straight into her eyes with a dark, burning intensity. She felt uneasy and then very calm. "I do feel the power," she said in awe. She fingered the pendant distractedly, unable to look away from Chakras. "It's lovely, isn't it, Octavia?"

"It's a piece of rock on a chain."

Chakras did not look away from Julia. "The crystal is the residing place of ancient Egyptian gods. Your friend invites their wrath."

Octavia glared at him. "Are you ready to leave, Julia?" she said testily. She watched the Egyptian reach out and gently take the crystal in his hand, his knuckles brushing against Julia.

"Only those who deserve the power have it," Chakras said, smiling in a way that made Julia's face grow warm.

Octavia gave a dry laugh. "Julia, you can afford pearls. Don't waste a sesterce on glass."

Julia drew back slightly from Chakras' touch, the weight of the crystal dropping between her breasts again. "But they're beautiful!"

Chakras studied the expensive amethyst necklace she wore. "The clear crystal pendant is worth one aureus," Chakras said, knowing she could well afford that and more.

"So much?" Julia said in dismay. One denarius was worth a day's pay, and twenty-five denarii equaled one aureus.

"Ridiculous," Octavia said, glad that it was more than Julia would be willing to pay. The pendants were lovely, and if she could not have one, she didn't want Julia having one either. "Let's go."

"Power doesn't come cheaply, my lady," Chakras said in his melodic, heavily accented voice that bespoke the mysteries of ancient Egypt itself. "These are rare gems created by the gods."

Julia looked at the pendants she had selected. "I'm not allowed to carry money with me in a public market."

"You can fill in my ledger and I will take care of it as you say, my lady."

"I'm a widow," she said shyly, "and my brother manages my estate."

"It is a small matter," Chakras said, producing a ledger.

"She didn't say she wanted to buy those things yet," Octavia said angrily.

"But I do," Julia said and watched Chakras write in each pendant. She gave him Marcus' full name and address. He asked if she resided with her brother and she said no. "I live with my father, Decimus Vindacius Valerian."

"A very great man," Chakras said and asked no more questions. "Sign here, please." He dipped the quill in ink and handed it to her. As she signed, he wrapped the four necklaces in white wool and put them into a leather pouch. He held it out to her with a solemn bow. "May the clear crystal you are wearing bring you all you desire and more, my lady."

Julia was full of excitement at her purchases and insisted upon stopping at several other stalls. She bought perfume in a fancy vial, a small sealed amphora of scented oil, and a painted box of powder.

"I swear by Zeus, Julia, I will not carry another package for you," Octavia said angrily. "You should have brought your little Jewess with you." She shoved the things into Julia's arms and walked off, weaving through the crowd and wishing she had not baited Julia into defying her father and going on this outing.

Laughing, Julia hurried after her. "You were the one that wanted to go shopping!"

"To look. Not to buy everything in sight."

"You haven't bought a thing!"

Octavia gritted her teeth at Julia's remark, annoyed that her friend could afford to buy so many things without the least thought, while she had no money whatsoever. She ignored Julia's pleas for her to slow down. She had no intention of admitting the truth to Julia. All she could think about were the necklaces in Julia's little leather pouch. With all Julia's money, one would think she would buy a gift for her friend. But no, she thought only of herself!

"Octavia!"

Stifling her resentment, Octavia paused and waited. She lifted her head grandly. "Everything is so cheap and tawdry down here. I haven't seen a thing I want."

Julia knew very well that Octavia had admired the crystal necklaces, but she was not going to be coerced into giving her one after having to push her way along the crowded street to reach her. She looked at her as coolly as she could. "A pity. I was thinking of giving you one of the pendants," she said, knowing Octavia had wanted, but could not afford, one for herself. Marcus said Drusus was one step ahead of financial ruin. Suicide would be the only way to save what little honor he had left.

Octavia glanced at her. "You were?"

Julia kept walking. "Well, not anymore. I wouldn't want to give my best friend something tawdry and cheap." She glanced back, satisfied by the expression on Octavia's face. She was tired of her patronizing ways. "Maybe we'll find something to your liking later."

They were both tired when they reached the Field of Mars. Julia didn't want to sit beneath a shady tree. She wanted to sit out in the open, as close to the drilling soldiers as possible. Octavia wished she hadn't suggested coming to watch the legionnaires. They all seemed to notice Julia in her lavender palus and paid little attention to her in blue. Annoyed, Octavia pretended to be bored. She didn't like being overshadowed by Julia. She used to be the one people looked at when they were together. Perhaps she should lose weight or change her hairstyle or wear more cosmetics. Then Julia would fade into the background again. She glanced at Julia and knew that wouldn't happen. The differences between them were widening.

Life wasn't fair. Julia had been kissed by the gods. She had been born into a family with wealth and all the power and prestige a fortune could buy. Then she was married off to a rich old man who conveniently broke his neck before their first year of marital bliss was over, leaving poor little Julia with a fortune—though she was too much of a fool to know how to take control of it. Octavia would know.

Looking at Julia having such a good time, Octavia was torn by envy. Bitterness ate at her. Her father was always making excuses to his creditors. He was spending more and more time with his patrons and searching for others who would add to his depleted coffers. She knew his journey to Pompeii was an excuse to get away for a while. He had shouted at her yesterday, accusing *her* of spending too much money. He said he hated "begging" from patrons. What did he suppose she felt every time she had to beg her own father for money? If they were so poor, perhaps, he should give up betting at the games. He never had been able to pick a winning charioteer.

Why did she have to be the daughter of a fool? Didn't she deserve all the things that Julia had? The one thing she had been able to boast of was her personal maid, the daughter of an African tribal king. She remembered the first time she brought her to Julia's home and saw Julia so ashamed of her ugly little Jewess. It grated now that even that one small triumph had gone awry. Her African princess was arrogant and intimidating and needed constant beating to make her obey, while Julia's humble little Jewess served as though it was her sole delight.

Octavia's gaze fell upon the exquisite amethyst necklace circling Julia's slender neck. The matching earrings caught the sunlight. Envy twisted Octavia's stomach again and turned the beautiful day into an ordeal. She almost hated Julia, whose leather pouch of jewelry purchased for so dear a price only a few hours ago lay forgotten on the grass.

A young centurion rode by on a sorrel stallion and grinned roguishly, not at her, but at Julia, who blushed like a virgin, which made her look even prettier. Octavia's irritation grew.

"Did you see the way he looked at me?" Julia breathed, dark eyes glowing with excitement. "Wasn't he handsome!"

"And probably as dumb as an ox," Octavia said. Piqued at

being ignored by a man, she rose. "I'm hot, hungry, and bored, Julia. I'm going to Calabah's."

Julia came quickly to her feet, dismayed that she wouldn't be able to watch the soldiers any longer, but eager for whatever Octavia had in mind. "I'll go with you."

"I'm not sure you'd like her. She's much too sophisticated for you."

"But you said earlier—"

"Oh, I know what I said," Octavia interrupted with a wave of her hand. "But you'll be quite out of your element, Julia." It was true, though it was not the entire reason she was dismissing Julia. Of course, it might be fun to let Julia come along. Calabah would probably make fun of Julia's provinciality. Octavia looked forward to that. Perhaps Caius Polonius Urbanus would be visiting as well. The intensity of his dark eyes and touch of his cool hands made her insides shiver. She had heard the rumors about him, but they only made him more intriguing and dangerous. She was certain he was growing interested in her.

Julia picked up her leather pouch of necklaces and the packages of perfume, oil, and powder. Octavia seemed determined to exclude her from everything exciting. "If you take me to meet Calabah, I'll give you one of the necklaces I bought."

Octavia turned on her angrily, her cheeks on fire. "What sort of a friend do you think I am?"

"You wanted one, didn't you?" Julia said, just as angry, but covering her feelings with a practiced smile of tearful vulnerability. "Well, I'm offering you whichever one you want." Juggling her purchases, she held out the leather pouch. "I was going to give you one earlier, but you were being so cruel, going on and on about Claudius," she said.

Octavia hesitated, and then took the pouch. "You were really going to give me one?"

"Of course." Chakras had many more necklaces. Whichever one Octavia chose, she could send Hadassah back to get another to replace it.

"Well, then," Octavia said, opening the pouch and taking the necklaces out. "I want the alexandrite." It had been the most expensive. She took it out, unwrapped it, and put it on, discarding the white cloth.

She would take Julia to Calabah's. It would be fun to watch Calabah subtly mock her. She frowned for a moment, considering again how beautiful Julia was and the way the centurions had reacted to her earlier. Caius loved beautiful women, and Octavia certainly didn't want any interference with what she was sure was the beginning of something between herself and Caius. Then she shrugged . . . surely Caius wouldn't be interested in a cosseted child like Julia.

She turned to smile indulgently at Julia. "Calabah's isn't far from here. She lives just up the hill from the baths."

16

Marcus entered the house and found it thankfully quiet and cool. Enoch took his red cape. "Are my father and mother resting?"

"No, my lord. They went to walk in the park."

"And the Lady Julia?"

"She left with the Lady Octavia."

Marcus frowned. "With my father's permission?"

"I don't know, my lord."

Marcus looked at him through narrowed eyes. "You don't know," he said dryly. "Come, come, Enoch. You know everything that goes on in this household. Did she ask my father's permission and, if so, where did she go with Octavia?"

"I don't know, my lord."

Marcus grew impatient. "Did her slave go with her?"

"No, my lord. Hadassah is sitting on a bench in the peristyle."

"I'll speak with her."

Marcus smiled slightly when he saw Hadassah sitting quietly on a marble bench near the wall. Was she listening to the fountain and the birds singing? She looked troubled, and her hands were clasped tightly in her lap as she sat on the marble bench. He watched her for a few seconds longer and realized she was praying again. Because of her devotions, he was hesitant to approach her.

His mouth tightened in anger at himself. What was the matter with him? Hadassah was a slave. Why should he care if she was disturbed from her prayers or anything else? It was his will that mattered, not hers. He strode toward her purposefully. She heard him and rose. When she looked up at him, he felt an odd sensation in his chest. Annoyed, he spoke harshly. "Where is my sister?"

"She is out, my lord."

"Out where?" he demanded and saw the slight frown flicker across her brow. He could almost read her thoughts. She didn't want to betray Julia. Silent, she lowered her head. Her loyalty to his sister made him want to be more gentle with her. "I'm not angry with you. I'm concerned about Julia. She's supposed to be in mourning for another three months, and I doubt Father gave her permission to leave the villa with Octavia. Am I correct?"

Hadassah bit her lip in indecision. She didn't want to lie and she didn't want to disobey Julia. She let out her breath softly, troubled. "She said she was going to the temple of Hera."

Marcus gave a dry laugh. "Octavia wouldn't be caught dead in the temple of Hera. She worships Diana or any other god or goddess that promotes her promiscuity." Even as he said it, he faced the hypocrisy of it, for he did much the same thing himself. Anger flooded him. It was different for a man than it was for a woman. It was especially different when it concerned his sister.

"Tell me where they went, Hadassah. I know you want to protect her, but is it protection to allow her to do something rash and stupid? Octavia is known for both. Tell me where they went! I'll find Julia and bring her home. I swear it." Even as he said it, he wondered why he was explaining himself to a slave girl, or even swearing an oath to her.

She looked up at him. "They were going shopping, and then to the Field of Mars."

"To watch the legionnaires," Marcus said in disgust. "That's just like Octavia, though her taste runs more to gladiators. Did they say anything else?"

"The Lady Octavia said she wanted to visit a friend."

"Do you remember the name of this friend?" he said, thinking it was probably some man.

"I think her name was Calabah."

"By the gods!" Marcus exploded in anger. Calabah was worse than any disreputable man Octavia might take Julia to meet. He paced angrily, rubbing the back of his neck. "Julia doesn't even know what she's walking into." He had to bring her back—quickly.

He stopped before Hadassah and gripped her shoulders. "Listen and obey me. When my father and mother return, avoid them. Hide in the kitchen. Do whatever you have to. If they summon you and ask where Julia is, you will tell them she went to worship Hera just as she probably told you to say. That's all. Don't mention Octavia. Don't mention the Field of Mars or anything else. Do you understand?"

"Yes, my lord, but what about Enoch?" Hadassah said, knowing he would be only too willing to tell Decimus Valerian everything. He had no great affection for Julia, nor did any slave in the household. "He will feel duty-bound to tell your father she's left the villa," she added quickly, not wanting to bring trouble on his head.

He let her go. "You're right," he said and swore under his breath. "I'll send Enoch on a long errand. An important errand that demands his personal attention." He glanced back at her and saw her relief.

"My lord, you came in answer to my prayers."

He laughed. "You prayed for me to come to you?" She blushed and lowered her head, stammering a reply. "What did you say, Hadassah? I couldn't hear you."

"I was praying for help for Julia, my lord, not for you specifically."

His mouth tipped ruefully. "A pity. And here I thought I was the answer to a maiden's prayers," he said, amused at her embarrassment. He tipped her chin up and saw the color heighten even more. "How am I the answer to your prayers, Hadassah?"

"You'll bring my lady back safely."

"I'm pleased to know you have such confidence in me." He chucked her lightly under the chin the way he did his sister and smiled mockingly. "Maybe between the two of us, we'll find a way to keep Julia out of too much trouble."

His platonic manner broke her tension and, with a soft exhalation, she laughed. "From your mouth to God's ears, my lord," she said.

Marcus had never heard her laugh before. Looking down into her small, happy face and hearing the sweet sound, he almost cupped her face and kissed her. The change in her filled him with disturbing warmth. It wasn't lust; he was all too familiar with that emotion. This was something else. It was something deeper, more mysterious, something that had less to do with his senses than his spirit—or his soul as she would call it. She tugged at his heart.

He realized how little he really knew about her. "I've never heard you laugh before," he said and regretted his words immediately when her light mood fell away.

She lowered her head, once again the slave girl. "I'm sorry, my lord. I—"

"You should laugh more often," he said gently. When she glanced up at him in surprise, he looked into her eyes. A hundred questions came to mind, followed by impatience. He didn't have time for this and he didn't need any more complications in his life! Hadassah wasn't Bithia. She wasn't simple to understand, easy to dismiss.

"Stay out of sight of my parents until my return. If you're unavailable, they can't ask questions."

Hadassah watched him go. Why had he looked at her that way? Hands pressed to her racing heart, she sank down on the bench and closed her eyes. What was this she felt every time he came near her? She could hardly breathe. Her palms grew damp, her tongue sluggish. He had only to look at her and she trembled. And just a moment ago, she had felt so relieved at his manner that laughter had bubbled out of her. What must he think of her?

Even when Marcus Valerian didn't look at her, she was in turmoil when he was present. She wanted him to glance her way, and when he did, she was clumsy and embarrassed. Sometimes she wished he would stay away from the villa. But when he did, she longed to see him again just to know he was well.

Her father had spoken of a girl's infatuation for physical beauty. He warned her even as a child to look at the man behind the handsome face, to seek the soul. "A beautiful face can mask great evil," he said.

Marcus was beautiful, like one of the statues near the marketplace. Sometimes she looked at him and forgot all about his soul. Marcus didn't believe he had one, nor did he believe in an afterlife as his father and mother did. She had overheard him say to his father that when a man died, he died. He said that was the reason he wanted to have as much from life as he could.

The only god in Marcus' life was his own intellect. He laughed at Hadassah's faith and scoffed at her "unseen god." He believed a man made himself by grasping whatever opportunity came his way.

Bithia boasted she had power over Marcus, that with the right incantation and sacrifice, she could make him want her. Hadassah didn't believe her, but she had seen Bithia in the garden early in the morning, standing in the scented smoke drifting from her incense burner. And Marcus did go to her. Often.

Hadassah pressed her hands to her hot cheeks. She had no right to feel anything for Marcus Valerian. She had prayed that God would remove the confusing feelings she had for him and open her eyes that she might better serve. But Marcus had only to appear for her heart to feel as though it would jump from her chest.

Bithia said Marcus was the best lover she had ever had. The Egyptian girl said many things that Hadassah didn't want to hear. She didn't want to know what went on between the slave girl and her master.

She prayed Marcus Valerian would fall in love and marry a good woman like his mother. She didn't want to see him fall beneath Bithia's black spells. Bithia was like Egypt in the Scriptures, seductive and beguiling, beckoning a man to his destruction. Bithia seemed wise in the ways of the world, but she was completely ignorant of what she brought upon herself. Commerce with the powers of darkness might gain her what she desired for the moment, but at what cost in the end?

Phoebe Valerian believed Bithia had healing powers and often summoned the slave girl to the master's bedchamber. Yet, even after all these weeks, Decimus Vindacius Valerian was no better.

The master believed in religious tolerance and, therefore, everyone in the household was allowed to worship their gods in their own way. Many of the slaves worshiped at various shrines and temples. Bithia was allowed to go daily to the shrine of Isis near the Field of Mars, just as Enoch was allowed to go to morning prayers in a small synagogue near the river where many free Jews lived and worked. The unspoken rule between the slaves in the Valerian household was live and let live. However, when Bithia began using her spells and potions on the master, Enoch's tolerance evaporated like rain in a desert.

"I pray God strikes her dead before she can do more harm to the master with her black arts," he said as he accompanied Hadassah to the marketplace one morning.

"Enoch, she really believes in her heart that what she is doing will cure the master. She fasts and prays and meditates in order to earn powers she believes have been promised to her."

"And that's an excuse for what she is practicing on him?"

"No, but—"

"She is a deceiver and a sorceress."

"She is the one deceived, Enoch. She believes in false gods and false teachings because she has never heard the truth."

"You are too young to understand the evil that's in the world."

"I have seen evil in the midst of Jerusalem, long before the Romans ever ascended the walls."

His eyes narrowed. "What are you saying?"

"If Bithia knew the Lord, things would be different for the master and for her."

His eyes flashed in astonishment. "What are you suggesting? That I make an Egyptian harlot a proselyte?"

"Scriptures say Ruth was a Moabitess, and yet through her came our King David and from the line of David, the Christ."

"Ruth had a heart for God."

"How do we know Bithia does not? How would Ruth have come to know God unless her husband and her mother-in-law first told her of him?"

"I will not stand here and argue Scripture with an ignorant child, Hadassah. What can you know? Forgive me if I seem abrupt, but your tender heart will not change the ways of the world, or of a harlot like Bithia!"

She laid her hand on his arm. "I don't mean to argue, Enoch." She looked up at his dear face, knowing that if God hadn't sent him to buy her that day in the slave market, she would have long since perished in the arena. "Israel is God's chosen witness to the world. How can we be witnesses of the one true God if we hold the truth as our own possession? God meant his truth for the world."

"You would give away what is holy even to unclean Gentile dogs?" Enoch said and shook his head in sad disbelief. "Listen well to me, Hadassah. Stay away from Bithia. Stop up your ears against her. She is evil. Do not forget that tolerance of evil is what destroyed our nation. Be careful it doesn't destroy you as well."

Hadassah had wanted to weep. Not once had she spoken of Jesus. Not one word had she uttered of how the Lord had raised her own father from the dead. It was as though her tongue were a heavy weight in her mouth, and now her heart was even heavier for having kept silent. Would Enoch have listened? She told herself he wouldn't have. Yet, the question lay unanswered. Bithia didn't know God; Enoch didn't know his Messiah. And why? Because her fear of rejection and persecution kept the truth locked in her heart. The knowledge she had was hidden treasure meant for both of them, and she clung to it, gaining her strength from it, but too afraid to give it away.

Now, a small bird flittered into the peristyle and perched on the statue Marcus called "Passion Spurned." Hadassah pressed her fingers against her temples and rubbed gently. The open courtyard was full of light and color and the soothing sounds of the fountain, and yet she felt the darkness all around her, closing in. She longed for the company of others who shared her beliefs. She ached for someone to talk to about God the way she used to talk to her father.

She felt so alone. Enoch had his law and tradition, Bithia her false gods and rituals. Julia had her hunger for life, Marcus his ambition. Decimus believed in nothing, while Phoebe bowed down to stone idols. In a sense, they were all alike, each using religion to give them what they thought they needed—power, money, pleasure, peace, righteousness, a crutch. They obeyed their individual laws, made their sacrifices, performed their rituals, all the while expecting to have their desires fulfilled. Sometimes it seemed as though they succeeded, and then she would see the empty longing in their eyes.

God, why can't I cry out the truth from the rooftops? Why don't I have the courage to speak as my father did? I love these people, but I haven't the words to reach them. I'm afraid to speak out and say they are wrong and I'm right. Who am I but a slave? How do I explain to them that I'm really the one who is free, and they are the captives?

She thought of Claudius and all the hours they had spent together as he had asked about God. Everything she had said had only tickled his ears, not a word had changed his heart. Why did the Word sink in and transform some and seem to bounce off of others? God said to sow the seed, but why didn't he soften the soil?

Lord, what must I do to make them hear?

Phoebe came out into the peristyle. She looked so tired and strained that Hadassah forgot Marcus' admonition and approached her. "May I bring you something, my lady? Cool wine or something to eat?"

"Some wine, perhaps," Phoebe said in a distracted tone. She trailed her fingers through the water.

Hadassah went inside quickly and brought the wine out to her. She was still sitting the same way. Hadassah set the tray down and poured some wine for her. Phoebe took the goblet and set it down untouched on the bench. "Julia is resting?"

Hadassah froze. She bit her lip, wondering what to answer. Phoebe glanced up at her and understanding was clear in her eyes. "Never mind, Hadassah. Where is Bithia?"

"She went to the temple of Isis just after you and the master left."

Phoebe sighed. "Then she won't be back for hours." Her hand trembled as she took the goblet. "My husband needs distraction. His illness . . . " She set the goblet down again and took Hadassah's hand. Hers were cool. "I heard you singing to Julia the other evening. Something in Hebrew, I think. It was beautiful. Your master is tired, but he can't sleep. Perhaps if you sing to him, he'll be able to rest."

Hadassah had never sung for anyone in the household but Julia and was nervous. Phoebe led her inside, where she handed her a small harp. "Don't be afraid," she whispered and crossed the room to her husband. Decimus Valerian was reclined on his couch and looked older than his forty-eight years. His face was drawn and pale, even after a morning in the sunlight. He hardly noticed Hadassah as she obeyed Phoebe's silent command to sit near him. "All is well?" he said quietly.

"Everything is fine. Julia doesn't need Hadassah at the moment and I thought it would be pleasurable to hear her sing." She nodded to Hadassah.

Hadassah's mother had taught her to play. She caressed the instrument, allowing the memories of her family to rise up and bring back the melody of their worship and praises together. Plucking several simple chords, she established the notes and began to sing softly. "The Lord is my shepherd, I shall not want . . . " She sang in Hebrew first and then again in Greek and finally in Aramaic, the language she had spoken all her life. When she finished, she lowered her head and thanked God silently for the peace King David's psalm gave her.

When she looked up again, she found Phoebe watching her. "He's asleep," she whispered. Touching a fingertip to her lips, she made a gentle gesture of dismissal. Hadassah placed the small harp on a stool and quietly left the room.

Phoebe placed a blanket over Decimus. Then she went to the stool and picked up the harp Hadassah had played. She clutched it to her and went back to sit near her husband, tears slipping down her cheeks.

Calabah Shiva Fontaneus was the most fascinating woman Julia had ever met.

"All life is but a stage of becoming a new being," Calabah said to her small gathering of women. "As women, we have the greatest potential for godhood, because it is the female who is the procreator of life."

Julia listened raptly to Calabah's rebellious ideas. Calabah spoke eloquently, presenting new and enticing philosophies that tickled Julia's imagination.

Octavia had told her a great deal about Calabah on their way from the Field of Mars. "She's rich, has several lovers, and conducts all her own financial affairs, which include several lucrative businesses."

"What sort of businesses?"

"I don't have any idea, and it would be rude to ask. Whatever she does, she does well because she lives a lavish life-style."

Julia wasn't sure what she expected to find when she met Calabah, but everything about her seemed unique. She was tall and athletically built. Rather than wear her hair up in an intricate style as most Roman women did, she wore hers, which was a lovely shade of auburn, down in a simple braid. She wasn't beautiful. Her eyes were a murky shade of green, her skin too tan, and her jaw too firm, but her vitality and personality made her stunning. She seemed to fill a room with her presence.

Octavia said no one really knew anything about her background. Rumor claimed she met Aurius Livius Fontaneus at a feast where she was a dancer. He was taken with her gymnastic abilities; she, with his money.

Whatever the woman's history, within a few minutes of meeting Calabah, Julia admired her greatly. Here was a woman who was everything Julia longed to be: rich, sought-after, independent.

"All life is born through woman," Calabah said to her guests and received soft *ayes* in response. "When a man dies, does he cry out for his father? No! He cries out for his mother. In each of us is the untapped possibility of who we really are, goddesses who have forgotten our true identities in our prelife. Woman is the fountain of life and only she has the seeds of divinity that can grow and lift her to heavenly plains. We are the bearers of eternal truth."

Julia could imagine what Marcus would say to such ideas. It made her smile slightly thinking of it. Calabah looked her way and raised a dark brow in question. "You don't agree, Sister Julia?"

Julia felt uneasy beneath Calabah's steady stare and asked a question to avert it. "I haven't decided, but I'd like to hear more. How do we attain this godhood of which you speak?"

"By not giving away our power to men," Calabah said simply, her smile patient rather than patronizing. She rose and moved around the occupied couches in the room. "We must achieve our full potential in all spheres to earn our godhood," she said. "We must train our mind, exercise our body, commune with the gods through meditation and sacrifice." She stopped beside Octavia and caressed her shoulder. "A little more time marching and less pursuing pleasure."

Octavia blushed as the others laughed. Her hand whitened on the golden goblet. "You mock me, Calabah? I'm not a chattel like others I know," she said and looked pointedly at Julia. "I have a life of my own and am free to do as I please. No one tells me when I shall get up and when I shall get down."

"We've all been chattels at some time, dear Octavia." Calabah smiled slightly. "Do you control your own purse strings?"

Octavia's eyes glittered as she glanced up at the older woman. Calabah was well aware of her true financial situation. They had discussed it during a private moment a few days before. How could Calabah bring it up now in front of Julia and the others? "A kind and cutting question," she said, feeling betrayed.

Calabah gave her a condescending smile. "Better that you use your head and marry than waste yourself on barley men," she said, referring pointedly to Octavia's numerous alliances with gladiators.

Octavia blushed. "I thought you were my friend."

"I am. Doesn't a friend speak the truth? Or do you prefer lies and flattery?"

Octavia glared up at her. She had come expecting Calabah to be delighted to see her and equally delighted to verbally dismember Julia. Instead, Calabah had welcomed Julia and aimed her biting words at Octavia's undeserving self. Her anger at the injustice of the situation loosed her tongue. "Better a strong young gladiator than a weak old man."

The others gasped at her insult, but Calabah laughed softly. "Dear Octavia, you're still far too sensitive. Men will use that as a weapon against you. Be warned, fair sister. If you go on living by your emotions, you'll end up with nothing but a remembered pleasure in the arms of a man long dead."

Octavia sipped her wine and said nothing more, but her resentment burned within her. It was all very well for Calabah to say one should marry. It was not so simple for Octavia. Her father had no money to offer as dowry, and no man would step forward with a bride's price when all she had to offer was a father so deeply in debt that he would probably be required to commit suicide to save his honor.

She glanced at Julia, who watched Calabah with the open fascination of a child. She was swallowing every idea Calabah spewed forth, her eyes aglow with what could be rather than what was. And Calabah seemed to be speaking only to her. Octavia's lips tightened.

Life was unjust.

"Our gods and goddesses have come down to earth to show us that we can raise ourselves to their heights by the pure power of our minds," Calabah continued. "It is true that men are stronger than women physically, but they are ruled by their passions. It isn't Jupiter that controls the heavens with his might, but Hera with her mind."

Julia sipped her wine. It had a cloying aftertaste and made her head feel fuzzy. One of the others asked a question then, and the discussion veered off into politics. Momentarily distracted, Julia gazed about the room and realized the walls were covered with erotic murals. The one straight across from her was a scene of a man and woman entwined. Behind them was a winged creature with frighteningly grotesque features and a body that was both man and woman. Julia couldn't take her eyes from it until laughter drew her startled attention. They were all watching her.

"A god of fertility?" she asked, trying to salvage some dignity.

"My husband's depiction of Eros," Calabah said with a sardonic smile.

Two ladies rose to leave. One kissed Calabah on the mouth and whispered something to her. Calabah shook her head and ushered them toward the courtyard, where a slave waited to show them to the door.

"We should go as well," Octavia said, rising. The day had been a disaster from the onset. Her head throbbed. All she wanted to do was get rid of Julia and go home.

Calabah turned back to them and looked disappointed. "You mustn't leave now that we're alone. I've had no opportunity to become acquainted with your friend, Octavia."

"It's late, and she wasn't supposed to go out in the first place," Octavia said brittlely.

"I'm in mourning," Julia said and laughed uneasily. "Or I should say, I'm supposed to be in mourning."

Calabah laughed also. "She's delightful, Octavia. How good of you to bring her to me." She took Julia's hand and drew her back to the couch. "Sit a while longer and tell me all about yourself."

"Julia," Octavia said in annoyance. "We must leave."

Calabah sighed wearily. "You leave, Octavia. I'm tired of your testiness."

Octavia's eyes smarted. "I've a headache," she whined.

"Then by all means, go home and rest. You needn't worry about Julia. I'll see that she's returned safely to her home. Now, go. Julia and I have much to talk about. And the next time you come, Octavia, please come in a better mood."

Calabah apologized to Julia as Octavia stormed out of the room. "Would you like some more wine?"

"Yes, thank you. It's very good."

"I'm glad you like it. I added some special herbs to it to open the mind." Calabah asked questions and Julia answered, feeling more relaxed as time passed. Calabah was easy to talk to, and she found herself confiding her frustrations.

"Fighting your father will not gain you what you want. You must use logic and reasoning to win his respect," Calabah advised. "Deal kindly with him. Bring him small gifts and sit with him and listen to his woes. Spend some time with him. Flatter him. Then ask what you want and he won't refuse you."

A slave entered the room and remained standing silently nearby until Calabah acknowledged his presence. "Marcus Lucianus Valerian is here asking for his sister."

"Oh, by the gods," Julia muttered in quick distress and rose. "Oh," she said and sank down again, her head swimming. "I think I've had too much wine."

Calabah laughed and patted Julia's hand. "Do not worry about anything, Julia." She nodded to the slave. "Bring her brother here." She took Julia's hand and squeezed it lightly. "You and I are going to become good friends, Julia." She let go of her and rose as the slave escorted Marcus into the room. "How nice of you to come visit me, Marcus," Calabah said, her tone full of sardonic amusement.

"Julia, we're leaving."

"Alas, Julia. Your brother doesn't seem to like me," Calabah said. "I think he's afraid I might corrupt you with new ideas about womanhood and our role in society."

Julia looked between them. "You know one another?" she said, slurring slightly.

"Only by reputation," Calabah said. Her smile was full of venom. "I know Arria. I know Fannia. I know a great many women who have known your brother."

Marcus ignored her and went to his sister. She swayed as she stood up. "What's the matter with you?" he demanded softly.

"She's had a little too much wine," Calabah said casually.

Marcus took Julia by the arm. "Can you walk, or must I carry you out of here?"

Julia pulled free angrily. "Why must everyone order me about? I've been enjoying myself for the first time in months, and you come barging in and spoil it."

Calabah clucked her tongue at the two of them and came to Julia. She put her hand on Julia's arm and spoke soothingly. "There's always another day, little sister. Go peacefully or Marcus will give in to those passions we discussed earlier and carry you out over his shoulder like a sack of grain." She kissed Julia's cheek, her eyes sparkling with laughter at the look on Marcus' face. "You're welcome to come to see me anytime."

Seething, Marcus took Julia by the arm and firmly escorted her from the room. She was half-running by the time they reached the front door. He lifted her into the covered litter waiting outside and sat beside her. Calabah's slave quickly followed, handing Julia her packages. The four slaves hefted the support bars to their shoulders and started the journey home.

"You're worse than Father," Julia pouted, glaring at him briefly before staring out through the thin veiling. "I've never been so embarrassed in my life!"

"You'll survive it," he said dryly. He knew Julia well enough not to forbid her from seeing Calabah again. To do so would guarantee she would. "I suggest you start thinking of a good story to tell Father and Mother, unless you want to spend the rest of your mourning period locked in your room with a guard at the door."

Julia gave him a mutinous look. "I thought you were on my side."

"I am, but all the headway I've made with Father you obliterated with this foolery today. Shut up and start thinking about what you're going to say to them when we get home."

"How did you know where to find me?" Julia said, and then her eyes flashed. "Hadassah!"

"She did not betray you," he said harshly, seeing it was not unlikely that Julia would lay all blame at the little Jewess's feet. "She told me nothing until I forced her, and then only because she wants you protected. Hadassah knows as well as I what will happen if you're found out."

Julia lifted her head. "I told her to tell Father and Mother I went to worship at the temple of Hera."

"That's exactly what she told me. The temple of Hera!" He gave a sarcastic laugh. "I knew better, and so will Father if Hadassah gives that lame story to him. Enoch told me Octavia came visiting, and everyone in Rome knows your friend isn't interested in bowing down to a goddess of hearth, home, or childbirth!"

"She's not my friend anymore."

"What do you mean?"

"Just that," Julia said with a jerk of her chin. "I'm tired of her always patronizing me and putting on airs. Besides, Calabah is far more interesting."

A muscle jerked in his cheek. "You liked her idea of women being superior to men, I take it. You liked the idea of eventually being able to become a goddess."

"I liked the idea of having control of my own life."

"That's not likely to happen any time soon, dear sister. Not unless we can get you back into the house unseen."

They didn't. Phoebe was waiting for them. "I went to your chamber a while ago and you weren't there. Where have you been, Julia?"

Julia launched into her story about worshiping Hera, then added that she went to the marketplace afterward to look for a healing amulet for Father. Surprising Marcus, she produced a carnelian pendant from a leather pouch. "The merchant assured me that the stone is a highly evolved healer." She handed it over to Mother. "Perhaps if Father wore it, he might feel better."

Phoebe held the carnelian crystal in her hand and looked at it for a long moment. Phoebe didn't want to ask any more questions; she wanted to believe that Julia's motivation for leaving the villa had been a desire to worship and buy a gift for Decimus, but she knew in her heart that it wasn't so. The carnelian pendant came from a pouch filled with other pendants Julia had bought for herself. The "gift" was, in truth, a bribe—or an afterthought.

She let out her breath slowly and handed the carnelian crystal back to her daughter. "Give this to your father when your mourning ends, Julia. If you give it to him now, he'll want to know when and where you purchased it."

Julia clenched it tightly in her fist. "You don't believe me, do you? My own mother thinks the worst of me!" she said, full of angry self-pity. She stuffed the carnelian pendant back into her hoard, expecting her mother to protest. When she didn't, tears sprang to Julia's eyes. She lifted her head and saw the disappointment in Phoebe's eyes. Guilt made her blush, but rebellion made her stubborn. "I'd like to go to my room. Or must I ask your permission to do that as well?"

"You're excused, Julia," Phoebe said quietly.

Julia stormed through the room and down the hallway. Phoebe watched her beautiful young daughter stalk away in anger. She was weary of trying to make Julia see reason. Sometimes she wondered if either of her children possessed a conscience. They never seemed to comprehend the consequences of their actions on those around them, especially on Decimus. She looked up at Marcus.

"Did she go to the temple to worship?" she said, then shook her head and turned away. "Never mind. I don't want to put you in a position of having to lie for her." She moved across the room and sank down onto a chair.

Seeing his mother so dejected concerned Marcus. "She's young, Mother. This mourning period Father has set upon her is unreasonable."

Phoebe said nothing for a moment. She struggled with her own feelings. She frequently agreed with her son, for Decimus could be harsh in his dictates, not taking into account youthful zeal and individual differences. Yet, neither Marcus nor Julia understood where the real issue lay. She lifted her head and looked at him solemnly. "Your father is the head of the household."

"I understand that only too well," Marcus said. It was one of the reasons he spent so little time at the villa and had purchased his own apartments.

"Then respect and obey him."

"Even when he's wrong?"

"That's a matter of opinion, and Julia is his daughter. Your interference only worsens the situation."

He clenched his hand. "You blame me for what happened today?" he said, angry. "I have never encouraged her to disobey Father."

Phoebe stood. "Indeed you have, though you are too blind to see it for yourself. Every time you argue openly with your father and accuse him of being unreasonable and unfair, you encourage Julia to defy him and please herself. And where did she go today, Marcus? What pleases Julia?"

"You have so little confidence in the morals of your children?"

Phoebe's smile was pained. "Of what morals do you speak, Marcus? The old ones that say children are to obey their father, or the new ones that tell you to do whatever pleases you?"

"I'm of age, Mother. Julia is sixteen and a widowed woman. Neither of us are children, though you and Father seem determined to see us as such. We are each individuals, and we have the right to pursue happiness in our own ways."

"No matter the cost to others? Even to yourselves?" She stood before him, saddened and distraught. "You walk blithely along the path you've chosen, pulling Julia along with you, and you don't see what's ahead. You only see the pleasure of the moment, not the future pain."

Marcus' mouth tipped in a faint smile. "You've forgotten what it's like to be young, Mother."

"I haven't forgotten, Marcus. Oh, no, I haven't forgotten. Youth is no panacea for any generation. But the world today is so much more complex, so filled with destructive influences. Julia is too easily swayed." She put her hand on his arm. "Can't you see your father doesn't want to destroy her pleasure, only protect her from harm?"

"What harm is there in a young girl going out with a friend to buy trinkets and watch the soldiers practice drills at the Field of Mars?"

Phoebe had no more words to explain. She lowered her head, knowing further argument was useless. At her defeated gesture, Marcus leaned down and kissed her cheek. "I love you, Mother, and I see your point, but I don't think you give Julia enough credit."

"She's far too strong-willed."

"Would you and Father be happier with a weak-minded daughter? I doubt it. Up to now, Julia has had no freedom whatsoever. How can she learn to handle it if she's never had it?"

"Too much freedom can sear a conscience."

"Too little can wither a mind."

"And if your father was to agree to shorten her mourning period and allow Julia more freedom, what do you suppose she would do with it?"

Marcus thought of Calabah Shiva Fontaneus. "You could make conditions," he said. "Certain people are acceptable, certain people are not."

"I'll discuss it with your father later this evening," she said. Freeing Julia might be the only way to attain any peace in the household. Even better, though, would be finding her another husband. . . .

17

Atretes lifted his head from the massage table and looked skeptically at Bato. "The proprietor wants to pay me twenty aurei to spend one night in his inn? What does he want me to do while I am there?"

"Nothing but sit in his dining room and sleep in one of his beds," Bato said. "You'll get many such offers, Atretes. You have moved into the ranks of the favored few—those whose kills continue to increase. Twenty-one now to your credit, isn't it? And the more kills you have, the more your fame will grow. Fame brings fortune."

Atretes laid his head down again and closed his eyes. "Will it bring freedom?" he said as the masseur pounded his muscles and kneaded them expertly.

"Eventually, perhaps. If the gods continue to smile upon you."

Atretes swore. "Gods are fickle. What will it take for me to gain my own freedom? How much will it cost? What do I have to do?" He shoved the masseur back as he sat up. The masseur glanced at Bato, but the lanista jerked his head toward the door, dismissing him.

"You may never gain your freedom," Bato said frankly. "As you increase in reputation, so increases the price of your freedom. The best you can hope for is retirement and a position as a lanista."

"So I will become a butcher," Atretes said, translating the word to its literal meaning.

Bato took no offense. "Where is the difference in what I do and what you did in your homeland? I prepare men to fight and die with honor." He put his hand on Atretes' shoulder. "Take my advice and live well while you can. Take whatever is offered. The day you killed Celerus, you became the reigning king of the Roman arena. An enviable position, as long as you can hold it."

Atretes gave a humorless laugh.

"I understand your bitterness, Atretes. My own almost destroyed me until I found balance. You will train continually, but fight only four to six times a year. That is not a bad life. Between games, you have plenty of time for other pursuits."

"Like making money? For what purpose if it will not buy freedom?"

"Money can buy many things. Celerus didn't live in the barracks of a ludus. He owned his own house and had a staff of servants."

Atretes glanced at him in surprise. "I thought he was a slave."

"A slave who owned slaves. Celerus was a better fighter than you," Bato said with his usual brutal frankness. "What defeated him was his own arrogance. He underestimated your intelligence, and for the first time since I've known you, you didn't lose your temper."

Atretes grew thoughtful. Having someplace other than a rank, stone cell to live in appealed to him. He rose from the bench and bent down over a bowl of water. He splashed his face. Maybe Bato was right. He should get what he could while he could. He had narrowly missed being disemboweled by Celerus two weeks before. He remembered the look in Celerus' eyes as he drove the sword into his side. He hadn't managed a killing wound, only a disabling one. It was the Roman mob who had killed Celerus. The sound of the masses screaming *"Jugula! Jugula!"* still rang in his ears.

Blood pouring from his side, Celerus had dropped to one knee before him. "Listen to them screaming for my blood! They were in love with me an hour ago." The mob screamed louder, the swelling noise making the ground itself vibrate. "They'll turn on you, too." Celerus lifted his head and Atretes saw his eyes through the visor the man wore. "Get it done," he said.

Atretes put his hand on Celerus' helmet, tipped his head back slightly, and made the swift dagger slash that opened the jugular. The mob went mad as Celerus' blood splashed across Atretes' chest. Celerus fell back, bracing himself feebly on his elbows, dying with a look of confused bitterness in his eyes as the mob chanted ecstatically, "Atretes! Atretes!"

Atretes closed his eyes and splashed more water on his face and chest. No matter what he did, he couldn't wash away the blood of his kills. Twenty-one men dead at his hand. . . .

He took a towel from the pile and dried himself. "I'll sleep in the man's inn, but tell him thirty aurei or no deal."

"Thirty it will be. I keep twenty, five for myself for having arranged it, and fifteen to be sent to the emperor as a goodwill offering."

"Goodwill offering?" Atretes glanced back at him coolly. "Tell Vespasian to sleep in the man's inn, and may the gods infest his bed with fleas!"

Bato laughed, then grew serious again. "Be wise for once, Atretes. The emperor owns you whether you like it or not. You can't change what the gods decree. The emperor has the power of life and death over you, and you've done everything in your power to irritate him. One word from Vespasian and you'll find yourself pitted with lions or wild dogs. Is that the way you want to die?"

Atretes threw the towel aside. "If I give him more than I get, I honor him," Atretes said.

"As is his due. He is leader of the empire that defeated Germania. Need I remind you? You don't stand before him as a victor."

Atretes lifted his head. "I am not defeated."

"You're still leading your clan? You're still living in the wilds of your black forest? You fool! Have you ever asked yourself why you're matched against men like Celerus and not other captives brought from the frontier?"

It was a common practice for owners to match their best gladiators with nonprofessionals, thus assuring wins and protecting their investments. Vespasian, however, had ordered Atretes matched against the best professionals with the most impressive kill records. The intent was obvious. He wanted him dead, but in a way that turned a profit and pleased the mob, thus furthering his own political popularity.

"I know why," Atretes said.

"Push too hard, and the emperor will feed you to the lions."

Atretes' mouth tightened. To die the prey of beasts was a death as shameful as crucifixion, perhaps more so. "Give Vespasian his fifteen aurei," he said, giving a scornful bow. As he turned away, he added softly, "And may every one of them bring a curse on him."

Bato came for Atretes late that night. Drowsy, Atretes arose. Bato tossed him a red tunic with gold trim and handed him a handsome leather-and-brass belt. Last, he gave him a voluminous cape. "Cover your hair. It's safer for all of us if you aren't recognized when we're outside."

Guards waited in the corridor. Atretes gave Bato a questioning look. "Am I so dangerous, I need six guards?"

Bato laughed. "Pray to your gods we don't need them."

The guards surrounded him as they went out into the city. The narrow streets were thronged with wagons and people. Friends gathered around fountains, drinking wine and talking. "Keep your head down," Bato ordered when a group of young men passed by and stopped to stare at Atretes. "Cut through that alley." They hurried along. In the shadows again, they slowed. "We don't have far to go. Luckily, Pugnax's inn is close to the Circus Maximus."

The soldiers fell into a march, the sound of their hobnailed shoes on the cobblestones reminding Atretes of the legion he had faced in Germania. Bato nudged him and pointed to a stone wall with words painted on it. "See what it says?"

"I don't read."

"You should learn. The writing proclaims you a young girl's dream. Over there is an announcement for the next games." He read it aloud as they passed it. "'Weather permitting, twenty pairs of gladiators, furnished by Ostorius, together with substitutes in case any get killed too quickly, will fight May first, second, and third at the Circus Maximus. The famous Atretes will fight. Hurrah for Atretes! The fights will be followed by a magnificent wild beast hunt. Hurrah for Ostorius.'"

"I'm impressed," Atretes said drolly. "Who is Ostorius?"

"He's running for some political office. I've heard he was a merchant. Vespasian approves of him because he came up from the plebeian class, but Ostorius still has to get the vote of the people. Financing games could do that for him."

"Is he a good leader?"

"No one cares as long as he finances games and gives out a little bread to stave off starvation. Once in office, Ostorius can do what he pleases."

"We're almost there," one of the guards said, "and I think we're in for trouble."

At the end of the street was an inn alight with lanterns and revelry. The place was overflowing with people, and even more clamored to get inside. Bato paused and studied the situation. "It would appear our friend mentioned you're coming," he said grimly. "We'll try going in the back way."

They skirted the crowd and came in by another narrow street

behind the inn. Men and women were standing in line at the back door, shouting to be let in. A woman turned and saw the guards. Her eyes went wide and she pulled at the man with her. "Atretes! Atretes!" she cried and several other women began to scream when they spotted him. "Atretes! *Atretes!*"

Atretes laughed, excitement quickening his blood.

Bato wasn't amused. "We'd better run!"

"From women?" Atretes said in disbelief and then saw the crowd break from around the door and rush at him en masse, shoving and pushing to be first. The guards moved into position to block them, but the tide swept over two. One woman threw herself upon Atretes, wrapping her arms and legs around him. Digging her fingers into his hair, she kissed him as half a dozen others grabbed at him, screaming hysterically. A wave of panic caught him and he threw the woman off, struggling to get free of the others. His cape was shredded and their hands fell upon him, grabbing with careless abandon. Enraged, he didn't care whom he hit or how hard.

"Get out of here or they'll tear you to pieces!" Bato shouted, grabbing one woman by the hair and flinging her back. His swift action gave Atretes enough of an opening to escape.

Atretes ran and kept running until the sound of hysterical screaming and pursuing footsteps were lost behind him. Soon Bato caught up with him. "Duck in here," he ordered, and they pressed themselves into a doorway to catch their breath. Bato leaned out and looked back down the street. "No one coming. I think we lost them," Bato said. He glanced at Atretes. "Well, how does it feel to be the object of so much affection?" he asked, laughing.

Atretes gave him a disgruntled look and leaned his head back, his heart still racing.

"Any serious damage done?" Bato inquired, grinning.

Atretes rubbed his head. "Some of my hair got yanked out, and it felt as though they were trying to rip me apart so they could take the pieces home with them. But I think I'm still intact."

"Good," Bato said. "Let's hope we can keep you that way." He stepped out into the street. "I know a place not far from here where we can go. The sooner we get there, the better. With your height and build and that blond hair, you're too easily recognized. And those women are probably scattered all through the streets hunting for you."

"This was all your idea. Remember? Thirty aurei!" He swore roundly. "You didn't warn me what would happen. Are all Romans crazy?"

"When they have their idol in arm's reach, they get a little excited. Relax. I'll get you safely back to the ludus. And Pugnax got his money's worth. You'll get your ten aurei and then some. I'll see to it myself."

They entered a narrow alleyway that led into a large court surrounded by tenement buildings. "I used to spend a lot of time here," Bato said, pausing before a door and knocking on it. When no one answered, he pounded. A muffled voice demanded who was there. Bato identified himself, and the door was opened. Atretes entered the darkened room after him. The door closed behind them and a bar was dropped into place.

A tall, slender black woman appeared in the back doorway. She held a small terra-cotta lamp in her hand. "Bato?" she said, and there was a catch in her voice. Bato spoke to her in his native tongue. She said nothing, and he crossed the room to her, took the lamp from her hand, and set it on a table. Cupping her face with one large hand, he spoke again in a voice tender and tentative. She answered softly, and Bato glanced back at Atretes.

Bato turned slightly. "This is Chiymado," he said to Atretes. "An old friend. She's agreed to let us stay here until morning. There's a small room in the back," he said. "You can sleep there. One of the servants will bring you something to eat. We'll return to the ludus midmorning, when most of the city is asleep."

Atretes nodded and followed the servant out of the room. A tray was brought to him. Sitting on the straw pallet, he leaned against the wall and drank the wine. Though he was hungry, he left the stale bread. The room was no bigger than his cell and just as cold. He wondered if the inn that had his name painted over the door was any better. Never having been inside, he wouldn't know. The more he thought about it, the more angry he became.

Eventually Bato came to lean against the doorjamb. "It's almost morning. We'll leave soon."

"Before we go back to the ludus, I want to pay a visit to Pugnax." Atretes thumped the empty bottle of wine down on the floor and stood up. "All those Roman harpies would have flown by now."

It was near dawn and the streets were empty, all the revelers of the night before having returned home to their beds. Bato led

Atretes through the maze of alleys and streets until they reached the inn. No one was outside. The curtains were drawn and the shutters closed. Debris was scattered around in the street. Bato knocked loudly.

"Go away!" A man shouted from inside. He cursed them roundly. "I told you before, Atretes isn't here! Go on home!"

Temper fired, Atretes stepped forward to break the door down. Bato shoved him back and banged on the door again. "It's Bato, you idiot. Open the door or the two of us will burn this inn down around your ears!"

As soon as Atretes heard the bar removed and the latch lifted, he slammed his way into the inn. "You owe me thirty aurei for the use of my name over your door!"

"Bank your fire," retorted Pugnax, unintimidated. "You'll have what I promised." He was a solid man of Bato's height and boasted a massive chest and arms. His hair was gray and cropped short, and he wore the rectangular piece of inscribed ivory around his neck that proclaimed him a freed gladiator. He grinned at Atretes' surprise, and gaps showed where several teeth had been chipped or knocked out completely. "You should've brought a few more guards with you," Pugnax said and glanced at Bato. "A good thing this pretty fellow can run so fast, eh, old friend?"

Bato laughed. "I've never seen him faster."

"Sit down," Pugnax said, and it sounded more an order than an invitation. He shoved Atretes toward the center of the room.

"You should have waited to put up your sign." Atretes took a seat near the brazier to warm himself. He fingered his tattered tunic. "You owe me a new set of clothes."

"Anything else, your lordship?" Pugnax said dryly.

"A decent meal and bed would improve his disposition," Bato said. "And a woman, if one's available."

"I sent them all home." Pugnax nodded toward a long table where a sizable picked-over feast was congealing. "As for food, that was laid out in his honor," he said. He picked up a peach and tossed it to Atretes. "Eat it in good health. I promise you better the next time you come."

"What makes you think I'd come back to this rat hole?"

"You like your cell so much better?" Pugnax mocked him. He grinned at Bato. "I think he's afraid of a few women." He laughed when Atretes rose from his chair, livid with rage.

"Sit down," Bato commanded. "Pugnax was fighting men better than you before you were born."

Pugnax laughed deeply. "Seeing him run reminded me of my own glory days. Remember the Ludi Apollinare, Bato? The women were after me that day." His smile dimmed. "Everyone knew my name in those days." He spread his arms. "Now, look what I have."

"Freedom and property," Bato said.

"Ha! Taxes and debts. I lived better when I was a slave." He poured wine into three goblets, handed the first to Bato, the second to Atretes, then held up the third. "To the games," he said and drank deeply.

Pugnax and Bato talked over their younger years. They relived their exploits in the arena, discussing the tactics of gladiators long since dead. Pugnax recounted several of his own battles and showed off the scars he had earned. "Emperor Nero gave me the wooden sword," he said. "I thought it was the greatest day of my life. It wasn't until later that I found my life was really over. What is left for a retired gladiator?"

"When I earn my freedom, I will return to Germania," Atretes said. "Then my life will begin again."

Pugnax gave Atretes a grim smile. "You don't understand yet, but in time, you will. You'll never be as alive as you are right now, Atretes, when you face death every day."

Bato rose from his stool and said they had to head back before light. Pugnax gave Bato the pouch of aurei. He handed Atretes another tunic and cape to wear and slapped him on the back as they walked him to the door. "I'll make the ladies line up proper next time," he said, giving him a gap-toothed grin. "No more than two or three on you at a time."

With the city gates closed to wagons and carts, the streets were quiet. While the citizenry slept, shopkeepers were busy storing the goods delivered during the night and laying out merchandise for the coming day.

"Pugnax is a fool," Atretes said. "He is free. Why doesn't he return to his homeland?"

"He tried, but he no longer belonged in Gaul. His wife was dead, his children adopted and raised by others. His people welcomed him for a while, but later avoided him. Pugnax was taken from Gaul a simple herdsman. He returned a warrior."

"I was not a herdsman."

"What is there for you in Germania? A young wife who holds your heart? Do you think she will wait ten years, maybe twenty for you to return to her?"

"I have no wife."

"A village then? What's left of it? Rubble and ash? Your people? Dead? Taken as slaves? Scattered? There's nothing left for you in Germania."

Atretes didn't answer. The old futile rage filled him as he remembered all that was lost. Bato stopped at a baker's stall and purchased bread. He tore off a hunk and offered it to Atretes. "There is nothing left for either of us, Atretes," he said grimly. "I was a prince. Now I am a slave. But sometimes a slave of Rome lives better than a prince of a defeated country."

They returned to the ludus in silence.

Caius Polonius Urbanus was the most handsome man Julia had ever seen. The first time she met him at Calabah's, he had done nothing more than smile at her and take her hand, but she had felt almost faint from the rush of excitement that raced through her blood.

Now she looked at him across the room, and then at Calabah as she spoke to the women gathered there. This was what she wanted, where she wanted to be. True, her father had relaxed the restrictions he set on her, but it was not enough for Julia—especially when one condition of her father's leniency was that she was not to visit Calabah. Far from giving in, Julia's visits to Calabah increased. She simply lied about where she was going and with whom she was visiting, all the while being careful to give every appearance of following her father's wishes. Thus she avoided the conflict—and the lecture—she would receive if her father knew she continued her friendship with Calabah.

Marcus didn't approve of Calabah, either. In fact, he despised her. Thankfully, he was traveling in northern Italy on business and would be gone for several months. With him away, Father occupied with business, and Mother unaware of life beyond the walls of the villa, Julia could do as she wished. To be considered Calabah's friend was a great honor and one that gave Julia a heightened sense of importance. Calabah made it clear to all who attended her that she favored Julia. Yet, Julia found Calabah's gatherings nowhere near so diverting as Caius Polonius Urbanus.

Caius was often at Calabah's villa, and Julia was in awe of his powerful, virile presence. He had only to look at her and her mind turned to forbidden thoughts. Octavia told her he was Calabah's lover, but that bit of unwelcome information only added to his charisma. What sort of man could satisfy a woman like Calabah? Surely one far more male than any other. And if he belonged to Calabah, why did he stare at her? Then, too, there was the fact that Octavia was obviously smitten with the man—a fact that only spurred Julia's interest in Caius.

Even now, his dark eyes teased and caressed Julia until she longed to escape the tumultuous feelings he aroused in her. She fanned herself and tried to concentrate on Calabah's diatribe, but her mind kept wandering to the most sensuous thoughts. Caius rose from his couch. As he came toward her, her body flooded with warm tingling. Her heart beat so fast and hard she feared he would hear it.

Caius smiled slightly as he sat down on her couch. He could see she was nervous and half-frightened; her innocence drew and excited him. "You agree with everything Calabah says?"

"She's brilliant."

"No wonder she likes you."

"You don't think she's brilliant?"

"Indeed, she is far ahead of her time," he said. As they talked about Calabah's ideas, Caius realized how little Julia really knew Calabah. He could tell Calabah's young friend was limited in her perception of those outside her world, and, of course, Calabah only revealed what she wanted people to see. She was shrewd. Caius had no doubt Calabah had plans for the young Valerian, but he didn't know what they entailed. He did know Calabah never groomed anyone without a purpose, and she was drawing Julia into her inner circle, treating her with a warmth that roused jealousy in others of longer acquaintance.

"I would think Octavia more to your liking, Calabah," he had said to her the other evening, mindful of the fact that he had begun pursuing Octavia as a diversion. "She's pliable."

But Calabah wouldn't be drawn. She merely smiled secretively and pointed out the practical aspects of why he should think about pursuing Julia. "Her family has money and position, Caius. They have no real political connections, except through Marcus' friend Antigonus. You will remember he gained a position in the curia a year ago. A liaison with her might do you good."

"If Marcus Valerian disapproves of you, I hardly think he would approve of one of your discarded lovers."

She laughed at his sardonic humor. "I haven't discarded you, Caius. I've freed you. You know very well you were becoming restless. Have you noticed the way Julia looks at you?"

His mouth curved in a predatory smile. "How could I not? She's quite delectable." Changing his attention from Octavia to Julia Valerian would not be a difficult task.

"Julia's family could be quite helpful to you."

"Trying to get rid of me, Calabah? Did I frighten you the other evening with my passion?"

"I've never been frightened of anything, Caius, least of all a man. But what excites you doesn't excite me. I'm trying to be generous and think of what's best for a dear, dear friend. I'm not the woman for you, Caius. I think Julia Valerian is."

Caius knew Calabah never did anything without ulterior motives, and he wondered now why she was so ready to hand him one of her lovely young followers like an offering on an altar. He was intrigued.

"What do you know about her?"

"Watch her at the games. She has depths of passion no one even suspects. Not even Julia herself. For you, she is unbroken ground just waiting for the till. She's hungry for life. Plant whatever seeds you desire, Caius, and watch them grow."

Calabah was never wrong about people. He watched Julia with new interest. She was young and beautiful. She attended Calabah's gatherings in secret, which meant she acted in disobedience to her parents and brother. She was also bored by tedious intellectualism and was dying for excitement, a heady combination when Caius could give her more excitement than she could even imagine. He had felt desire grow as he watched her, knowing she felt his perusal. She looked at him and he smiled. Her lips parted softly, and he almost felt the heat of her reaction across the room.

She was attracted by him, but she didn't accost him as Octavia did, nor brood like Glaphyra, nor pretend indifference like Olivia. Julia Valerian looked at him with unveiled curiosity. When he looked back at her, she waited expectantly rather than playing coy games like the others.

Caius wanted to see if Calabah was right about her. He wanted to see how far she would go.

"Walk with me in the garden," he said.

"Would Calabah approve?" she said, blushing, though the darkness in her eyes was promising.

"Do you need Calabah's permission to do as you wish? Perhaps we should test the sincerity of her philosophical outlook. Doesn't she say a woman must make her own decisions, take her happiness from where it emanates, create her own destiny?"

"I am her guest."

"Not her slave. Calabah admires a woman with a mind of her own. One who takes what she wants." He ran his hand lightly up her arm. Her skin was warm beneath the soft wool of her pale yellow palus. He heard her soft inhalation and felt the telltale tension of her body. He smiled into her doe brown eyes. "Oh, and you, sweet Julia, want to take the bull by the horns, don't you? Come out into the garden and see what magic we make together."

Color swept her cheeks again.

"I can't," she whispered.

"Why not?" he whispered back, teasing her. He saw she was too embarrassed to say, and said it for her. "Calabah might become jealous and then you wouldn't be welcome here again."

"Yes," she said.

"You can rest easy. I'm only one of Calabah's many diversions. We have an understanding."

Julia frowned slightly. "You're not in love with her?"

"No," he said simply and leaned down until his lips were almost against her ear and whispered. "Come out into the garden with me, so we can be alone and talk."

The darkness of his eyes held a frightening passion, but still she wanted to go with him. She relished the swirling heat that flooded her and the rush of blood through her veins. His touch made her forget where she was even as her mind warned her there was something dark and hidden about him. She didn't care. A sense of danger only made her excitement that much greater. But still, she worried over Calabah. She didn't want to offend her and make a powerful enemy.

She looked at her and saw that Calabah had noticed Caius' defection. For the briefest instant, Julia felt a wave of some powerful emotion flooding from Calabah's being, and then it was gone. She was smiling as though to encourage them. Julia saw no sign of jealousy or even annoyance darken those mysterious eyes or harden the serene features. Julia gave her a half-pleading, half-questioning look.

"Julia needs a breath of fresh air, Caius. Would you escort her into the garden?" she said, and Julia felt relief bursting inside her, which was replaced by a wave of heat as Caius took her hand and said it would be his pleasure.

"So you received her blessing," he said as they went outside. "Come over here under the arbor."

When Caius took her in his arms, Julia stiffened instinctively. Then he kissed her and the rush of pleasure drowned all resistance. His hands were strong, and she melted against him. When he drew back slightly, she was weak and trembling.

"With me, you'll feel things you never dreamed you could feel," Caius said hoarsely and grew bolder. Some small cry of conscience rose within her at the liberties he was taking.

"No," she gasped softly. "You mustn't touch me like that."

Caius only laughed softly and pulled her back. He kissed her again, silencing her protest and inflaming her passion.

Julia spread her hands against the fine wool of his toga and felt the firm ridges of muscles beneath. The brush of his spice-scented breath raised goose bumps along the curve of her neck. She moaned softly, helplessly, as he kissed her again.

He was hurting her, but Julia didn't care.

"Did Claudius Flaccus make your heart race like it's racing now?" Caius asked. Julia thought she would faint with the intensity of what she was feeling. "If he were alive now, I'd take you from him, even if it meant killing him," he rasped. The tone in his voice both thrilled and terrified her.

Julia knew as she looked up into his dark, glowing eyes and felt the fever in her blood that she had to be with him, whatever the cost. "Oh, Caius, I love you. I'll do anything you want, anything . . ."

With that, Caius had his answer of how far Julia would go. Of course, he wouldn't push her now. Time enough for that when she was within his full power and retreat was impossible.

He smiled. Calabah was right about Julia Valerian. This girl was made for him.

18

Hadassah felt foreboding as Julia's wedding day approached. From the moment Decimus Valerian agreed to a *coemptio* marriage, Julia seemed more settled and happy. Even as Hadassah wondered why the master suggested bride-purchase rather than the binding *confarreatio,* Julia stood before the gathering of friends and made the traditional statement, *"Ubi tu gaius, ego gaia."* "Where you are master, I am mistress." Upon her pronouncement, Caius Polonius Urbanus kissed her and sealed the engagement with an iron ring.

Hadassah could understand why Julia was in love with him. Urbanus was a handsome man with a vital presence and charming manner. Decimus and Phoebe both approved of him. Still, though Hadassah had no facts or foundation for what she felt, she was convinced something dark and sinister was beneath the man's smooth facade. Whenever Caius looked at her, she felt chilled by that dark, unblinking stare.

She had no one in whom she could confide her feelings. Marcus had gone away on business and wasn't due home for another month. If he were here, she might gather the courage to talk to him about it. But by the time he returned, it would be too late. The priests had already been consulted and a lucky day set for the wedding. Julia would be married before her brother returned home.

"Surely you want your brother to be at your wedding," Hadassah said.

"Of course I would like him to be at my wedding," she said. "But the priests said the second Wednesday of April is our lucky day. Delaying the wedding would defy the gods and risk disaster. Besides, I can't wait another week, let alone a month. Marcus could be delayed. Or he could change his plans." She sank down into the warm water of her scented bath and smiled. "Besides, Marcus has seen me get married once already. He was bored at my last wedding. I don't imagine he would find this one any more interesting."

Everyone seemed so pleased with the arrangements that Hadassah began to wonder if she was misjudging Urbanus. He spent hours with Decimus, discussing foreign trade and politics. They seemed to agree about almost everything. As for Phoebe, she was charmed by her future son-in-law. Even the household slaves thought the gods had smiled on Julia by making Urbanus fall in love with her.

Yet, it was as though Hadassah's soul caught a glimpse of something malevolent and dangerous hidden beneath the polished manners and good looks.

The morning of the wedding, Julia was tense with excitement and determined to look more beautiful than she had ever looked before. Hadassah spent several hours arranging her hair in an elaborate style of curls and braids interwoven with a strand of rare and expensive pearls. Julia's wedding palus was of the finest white flannel, and encircling her small waist was a woolen girdle fastened with a Herculean knot for good luck. Hadassah slipped the orange shoes on her mistress's small feet.

"You are very beautiful," Phoebe said, and her eyes misted with tears of pride. She took her daughter's hand and sat with her on the bed. "Are you afraid?"

"No, Mother," she said, amused at the worry she saw in her mother's eyes. If only she knew. She was eager for Caius, so eager she could hardly bear it. It was not her unwillingness that had kept her from his bed, but Caius' own sense of honor.

With tender care, Phoebe arranged the orange veil over Julia's head so that only the left side of her face was revealed. She gave her three copper coins. "One for your husband and two for your household gods," she said and kissed her daughter's cheek. "May the gods bless you with children."

"Oh, Mother, *please*. May the gods wait on that blessing." Julia laughed happily. "I'm too young to be tied down by children."

Hadassah stood at the back of the gathering in the temple as Caius and Julia's hands were joined. She could hear the keening squeal of the terrified pig as it was dragged before the altar. It thrashed violently as its throat was slit, and its blood poured down over the altar as a holy sacrifice for the bride and groom.

Feeling faint with nausea, Hadassah fled outside. Shaking, she sat down upon the high step near the door, where she could hear the marriage contract read, but not see or smell the blood. She put her head on her raised knees and listened to the droning voice of the priest as he read the documents that had more to do with dowry obligations than a lifetime commitment to love one another. Hadassah was saddened. Clenching her hands, she prayed fervently for her mistress.

As the procession of guests passed she rose to follow. Most of those attending the wedding were there purely out of social obligation to Decimus Valerian, their patron. Few who knew Julia had any fondness for her.

The guests accompanied the couple to Caius' villa on the far side of the Palentine, where his slaves had prepared a feast. Julia rubbed oil on the doorposts and hung up a garland of wool. She presented Caius with one of the copper coins. He gave her an offering of fire and water, thus relinquishing control of his household to his new wife.

Hadassah helped serve at the elaborate feast that followed, marveling at how different the atmosphere was from the celebratory meal of Julia's first wedding. Caius' friends made ribald comments, and there was much laughter. Julia was radiant, blushing and laughing when her new husband leaned close and whispered in her ear. Perhaps everything would be all right. Perhaps she was wrong about Urbanus.

Summoned to the kitchen, Hadassah was handed a silver tray of goose liver molded into a horrific beast with exaggerated genitals. Mortified at the obscene offering, she clanged the tray back onto the counter and drew back from it in revulsion. "What's the matter with you? If you've done damage to my work, I'll have the hide flogged off of you. The master asked expressly for that dish. Now take it out and serve it to your mistress."

"No!" she said without thinking, horrified at the very idea of offering something so grotesque to Julia. The blow the cook gave her sent her back against the cupboard.

"You take it," he ordered another who obeyed with alacrity. He turned on her again and she drew back with a gasp of fear, her face throbbing with pain. "Pick up the tray over there and serve it to the guests, *now.*"

Trembling, she went, relieved to see it was only a large tray of a dozen small partridges, browned and glistening with a honey and spice glaze. Her head was still ringing when she entered the large banquet room. Guests laughed and encouraged Julia as Caius dipped his fingers into the dragon and offered it to his bride. Julia laughed gaily and licked it from his fingers. Sickened,

Hadassah turned to the guests farthest away from the scene and offered the partridges.

Several men called for the bride and groom to be sent off to bed. Caius caught Julia up in his arms and carried her out of the room.

With Caius and Julia gone, some of the guests began departing. Drusus helped an ashen and tearful Octavia from her couch. She was drunk and scarcely able to walk. Decimus rose from a couch of honor and helped Phoebe to her feet. She beckoned Hadassah.

"You're returning to the villa with us. Caius told us he's arranged for servants for Julia already and has released you from your duties to her." She touched her arm. "You needn't look distressed, Hadassah. If Julia needs you, you know she will send for you. In the meantime, I've duties in mind for you."

Hadassah settled quickly into her new duties, and she delighted in serving Phoebe. They enjoyed spending hours in the gardens working in the flower beds or in the weaving room with the looms. Hadassah loved working in the garden the most, for she enjoyed the pathways and trellises that were budding with the coming spring. She loved the feel of the soil beneath her hands and the scent of flowers drifting in the fresh air. Birds flitted between the trees and pecked at the seed Phoebe placed on open feeders for them.

Decimus joined them occasionally, sitting on a marble bench and smiling wearily as he talked with Phoebe and watched her work. He seemed somewhat improved, for which Bithia claimed credit. However, he was not regaining his strength. Phoebe felt he was improved because he was under far less strain now that Julia was happily settled with a husband. But he was not cured from whatever ailed him. Phoebe lost faith in the Egyptian girl's healing arts and stopped summoning her to minister to Decimus. She called upon Hadassah instead.

"Sing to us, Hadassah."

Hadassah stroked the small harp and sang psalms her father had taught her back in Galilee. Closing her eyes, she could pretend she was back there again, with the smell of the sea and the sounds of the fishermen calling to one another. For a brief time, she could forget all the horror of the things that had happened since that last journey to Jerusalem.

Sometimes she sang lullabies her mother had sung to her and

her little sister, Leah. Sweet Leah, how she missed her. At times, when the night was dark and silent, she would think how Leah had closed her eyes and mind to the horrors of this cruel world and gone peacefully to be with God. She would remember the piercingly sweet memories of running free through the lilies of the field with her little sister, laughing at how Leah bounded through the high grasses like a rabbit.

Hadassah found pleasure in serving the Valerians, especially Phoebe, who reminded her somewhat of her own mother as she saw to the needs of the household with simple efficiency. Just as her own mother had spent an hour in devotions to Jesus upon first arising, Phoebe went into her lararium and worshiped her household gods. She placed fresh wafers on the altars, replenished the incense, and lit the burners to send up a pleasing aroma to her many stone gods. Her prayers were no less sincere, however misplaced her faith.

Marcus entered Rome with a powerful feeling of homecoming. He was well satisfied with the results of his weeks of travel, having made agreements with several of the merchants with whom his father had dealt in the past. Before going home, he went to the baths, eager to wash away the road dust and have a masseur knead away the ache of weeks of travel.

Antigonus was in the tepidarium, soaking in the warm water, with a retinue of sycophants. Marcus ignored them as a slave rinsed him with warm water. He went down into the water with a sigh and leaned back against the edge, closing his eyes and allowing the water to soothe him.

Antigonus waved his friends away and joined him. "You've been gone a long time, Marcus. Was your journey profitable?" They talked a few moments about trade and the Roman demand for more goods.

"I saw Julia the other evening with her new husband," Antigonus said.

Marcus' eyes shot open. "Her what?"

"By the gods, you don't know," he said. "I take it you haven't seen your family yet. Well, let me enlighten you about events that occurred while you were away. Your lovely sister married Caius Polonius Urbanus several weeks ago. I wasn't invited, since I don't know the gentleman. Do you know him? No? A pity. Everyone is curious about Urbanus, but no one knows much about him other than he appears to have a lot of money. How he gained it is a great mystery. He spends most of his time at the games. Rumor has it that he was Calabah Shiva Fontaneus' lover."

"You will excuse me, Antigonus." Marcus left the pool hastily.

He went straight home and found his father in the triclinium with his mother. With a soft exhalation of joy, his mother came and embraced him. He was shocked at the new gray at his father's temples and at his lack of weight.

"I stopped at the baths and saw Antigonus," he said, taking a couch and accepting a goblet of wine Enoch poured for him.

"And he told you Julia is married," Decimus said, seeing the glitter of anger in his son's eyes. "It's unfortunate you didn't come home first and hear it from us."

"When did all this take place?"

"Several weeks ago," Phoebe said, turning the tray of sliced beef so the choicest pieces were nearest him. "Eat something, Marcus. You look thinner than last we saw you."

"What do you know about this man?" Marcus said, uninterested in food.

"He deals in foreign goods and arranges trades with the northern frontiers," Decimus said. He poured himself some more wine. "Other than that, my agents could find out very little about him."

"And you allowed Julia to marry him with so little information?"

"We inquired about Caius and learned what we could. We invited Caius here numerous times and found him to be intelligent, charming, educated. Your sister is in love with him, and, for all appearances, he is equally in love with her."

"Or her money."

Decimus raised an eyebrow. "Is that what's really angering you about all of this? Not that you missed Julia's wedding, but that you'll have to relinquish control of Claudius' estate?"

Stung, Marcus set the goblet down with a thump. "If you'll remember," he said tightly, "I took on the responsibility because you were in Ephesus. When you returned, you told me to continue administering the estate. I've not taken one denarius profit from anything I've done for her."

Decimus sighed. "I apologize. Your concern has always been noted. I left you in control because your decisions were sound. Julia's estate was safe in your hands. But the burden of that responsibility is now lifted."

"Not so fast, Father. I won't relinquish control until I'm certain this husband of Julia's isn't a wastrel."

"You've no legal right to retain control of her estate," Decimus said firmly. "When Caius Polonius Urbanus took your sister as his wife, he took possession of everything she owns as well, and that includes Claudius' estate."

Marcus thought of Hadassah and felt an uncomfortable feeling coil in his stomach. She was one of Julia's possessions. Who was this Urbanus, and what would he feel toward his new wife's Jewish maid? Embarrassed by his feelings for a slave girl, he hid behind his concerns for Julia. "And if she wants to leave the financial arrangements as they are?"

"It's no longer Julia's right to make that decision."

Phoebe rose and went to Marcus. "Once you've seen how happy she is with Caius, you'll feel easier about your father's giving approval to the marriage."

Marcus went to see Julia the next afternoon. She was still in bed when he arrived at Urbanus' villa, but upon being told her brother had come, she wasted no time in joining him. "Marcus!" she cried, flinging herself into his arms. "Oh, I'm so glad to see you!"

He was surprised to see her so disheveled. Her waist-length hair was unbrushed, her face devoid of makeup. She looked tired and was trembling, as though suffering the aftereffects of heavy drinking. A small, round red mark showed on her neck, disturbing evidence of passion.

He looked down at her, concerned. "Imagine my surprise when I returned to the news that you were married."

Julia laughed gaily. "I'm sorry, but I couldn't wait for you. You'd already been gone two months and sent no word back about how soon we could expect you. You'll like Caius. You have much in common with him. He adores the games."

"How did you meet him?"

Her smile turned mischievous. "Calabah introduced us."

His mouth tightened at her ready admission of defying him and Father. "That's hardly a recommendation."

Julia let go of his hands and moved away from him. "I'm sorry you don't approve of her, Marcus, but it makes absolutely no difference to me." She turned and faced him, angry and defensive. "I can do as I wish now. I no longer need Father's permission, or yours, to choose my friends."

Marcus could see Calabah's influence. "I didn't come to argue with you. I came to see if you were happy."

Her chin jerked up. "I assure you I am. I'm happier now than I've ever been in my life."

"Indeed. I'm joyous to hear it," he said with unveiled annoyance. "You have my congratulations for escaping our clutches and my apologies for intruding on your newfound freedom."

Julia's defiance evaporated at his anger and she hurried to stop him from leaving. "Oh, Marcus, don't be so impossible! You've only just come to see me. Don't stalk off. I couldn't bear it." She hugged him as she always had from the time she was a small child who idolized him. He softened for a moment. She went on, drawing back slightly, "You only disapprove of Calabah because you don't know her as I do." She took his hands in hers. "I'm not like Mother. You know that. I'm not content to weave and see to everyone else's needs above my own. I want excitement the way you do, Marcus. The gods brought Caius and me together."

He searched his sister's face, looking for the radiance of a young bride—and saw along with it the exhaustion of a debauched life-style. He caressed her cheek. "Are you really happy?"

"Oh, I am. Caius is so handsome and exciting. When he's not here, all I can think about is him and when he'll be back again." She blushed. "Don't look at me that way," she said laughing. "Come and sit with me in the peristyle. I haven't eaten yet and I'm starving." She snapped her fingers and ordered one of the servants to have a meal brought to her.

Julia talked about the parties she and Caius attended, the sort that had always appealed to Arria. "I saw Arria the other evening," Julia said as though reading his thoughts. "She asked who you were seeing. She had a gladiator in tow. He had scars all over him and was quite ugly."

She complained about what the servant brought her, telling her to go back for fresh fruit and bread. "I miss Hadassah," she said in annoyance. "She always knew what I wanted. These maids are so stupid and slow."

"What did you do with her?" Marcus asked as carefully as he could. His heart was beating fast and a cold sweat was breaking out over his body.

"Caius doesn't like Jews because they're so prudish. Besides that, he didn't like her because she was homely."

Urbanus arrived before Marcus could ask any questions. Julia rose quickly when she saw him and raced to him. He kissed her briefly, looking her over with a wry smile, and whispered in her ear. Julia shrank slightly and then turned back. "Marcus, this is Caius. I'll leave you two alone and make myself more presentable." She hurried off, leaving Marcus alone with her new husband.

"You must wonder at the life we lead when your sister greets you straight from our bed," Caius said, strolling toward him.

It was obvious to Marcus why Julia had fallen in love with Urbanus. He was the sort of man many women went mad over—dark, well-built, exuding sexuality. His enigmatic smile was challenging. Marcus met it with a smile of his own, stifling the urge to demand what he had done with Hadassah.

"Julia speaks of you often," Urbanus said. "One would think you were descended from the gods." He leaned against one of the marble pillars, his gaze cool.

"Younger sisters have a way of idolizing older brothers."

"There's a considerable difference in your ages."

"We lost two brothers to fevers."

"She doesn't mention them."

"She didn't know them. Have you any family, Caius?"

Caius straightened and walked along the edge of the pond. The only sound for a long moment was the sprinkle of the fountain. "No," he said simply. "Not until I married Julia." He smiled, and Marcus wasn't sure he liked what he saw on Caius' face. "Your mother and father welcomed me with open arms," he went on, looking at Marcus steadily.

"I'll reserve my welcome until I know you better."

Caius laughed. "An honest man," he said. "Refreshing." A servant entered the peristyle and offered Urbanus wine. At his nod, the slave turned to Marcus. He declined. Urbanus sipped his wine for a moment, studying Marcus over the rim of his silver goblet. "I understand you've been managing Julia's estate."

"Would you like an accounting?"

"At your convenience." Caius lowered his goblet. "From all I'd heard about you, I thought you wouldn't be so agreeable about it."

"You're my sister's husband. The burden of her estate now falls upon you."

"Indeed. It's a lot of money." His dark eyes lit with amusement.

Marcus wondered how Caius knew what was involved. Even Julia didn't know. Perhaps Father had laid out the details, but Marcus doubted it. Father would have left it to him.

"Perhaps we could work something out between us," Caius said slowly. "You could continue to manage the estate and pay over an established portion each month."

Very neat, Marcus thought cynically. "I usually charge a fee for my services," he said dryly, having no intention of becoming Urbanus' lackey.

"Even to your own family?" Caius said mockingly.

"A percentage of the profits," Marcus returned smoothly. "A sizable percentage."

Caius laughed softly. "I was just curious to see what you'd say. I'm fully capable of managing things myself. You know, Marcus, you and I have a great deal in common."

"So Julia said a little while ago." He liked hearing it from Urbanus even less.

Marcus stayed only as long as was polite. Julia returned to the peristyle dressed in an expensive fine wool palus. She wore pearls around her neck and woven into the curls piled high on her head. "Aren't they beautiful?" she said, fingering her pearls and showing them off to him. They were the most expensive baubles a woman could have. "Caius gave them to me on our wedding night."

The dark circles beneath her eyes were covered skillfully by makeup, and pink blushes had been added to her pale cheeks and her mouth. Had he not seen her an hour before, he wouldn't have known she was tired and hung over from whatever party Urbanus had taken her to the night before. Her animated chatter grated, and Urbanus' teasing was full of innuendo, which made her laugh. Unable to stomach any more, Marcus made his excuses and left.

Returning home, he was depressed. When he entered the house, he handed his cloak to Enoch. He heard his father's voice in the common room where he met with his patrons each morning, and went to join him. "Hadassah!" he said, seeing her standing before his father and mother. As soon as he said it, he was embarrassed. "What's going on?"

Decimus glanced up at his son and saw an expression on his face that he had never seen before. "Bithia has accused Hadassah of stealing." Decimus had been unable to make sense of the accusation until now. He noted with increasing interest that Marcus scarcely noticed the Egyptian slave; indeed, he seemed to have eyes for none but Hadassah.

"Stealing?" Marcus said, pulling his gaze away from Hadassah as he entered the room. His heart sank. He looked at Bithia and saw her dark eyes glittering with emotion. He had seen that look often enough in Arria's eyes to recognize it. She was burning with jealousy over something. "Has Bithia any proof?" he said coldly.

"We were just getting around to that," Decimus said. Phoebe sat pale and distraught in the seat next to him. Hadassah stood silently before him, her head bowed. She had made no outburst of defense. In fact, thus far she had said nothing at all. "What proof do you have against Hadassah?" he demanded of the Egyptian girl.

"I saw her with my own eyes," Bithia said insistently and named two other household slaves who could corroborate her story. Decimus called them in and they said, yes, they had seen Hadassah giving coin to a woman in the marketplace.

Marcus couldn't believe what he was hearing. Bithia looked smug and unpleasant as the other testimonies agreed with hers. He felt a rush of deep dislike for her and wondered what he had ever found desirable about her in the first place.

"Hadassah," Decimus said grimly. She looked up, frightened and pale. "Is this true? Did you give coin to someone in the marketplace?"

"Yes, my lord."

Decimus wished she had lied. He sighed heavily. He was going to have to flog her and he wondered if her slender body could stand up to the punishment. He didn't like the look on Bithia's face. He suspected the Egyptian resented Hadassah being called to serve them now, instead of her. "Leave us, Bithia." If he was going to be forced to punish Hadassah, he wasn't going to do it before a gloating slave. He dismissed the others as well.

"You know the penalty for theft is flogging," Decimus said. Hadassah seemed to shrink, though she made no defense. Phoebe was growing more and more distraught.

"Decimus, I can't believe she's stolen from us. She's always given a full accounting—"

He raised his hand imperiously, and she fell silent. He was furious to be placed in this position and addressed himself to Hadassah. "We warn every slave that comes into our home what the penalty is for theft. What possessed you to give away money your mistress entrusted to you?"

"I only gave away the coin you gave me, my lord."

"Coin I gave you?" he said, frowning.

"The peculium, my lord."

Decimus blinked. Each morning he sat in his curule chair and doled out coin to his dozens of patrons. He also gave a quadrans to each of the least of the slaves, more to Enoch and the cook. He could scarcely believe a slave would give her peculium away.

Phoebe leaned close again and laid her hand on his arm. "Hadassah has always accounted for every coin I've given her."

Frowning, he studied Hadassah intently. "Have you ever given away any of the money your mistress has given you?"

"No, my lord. Only what you've given me as peculium."

"But why would you give your peculium away?"

"I had no need for it, my lord, and the woman did."

"What woman was this?"

"A woman on the street."

Marcus came closer, astonished by what she was saying. "You're a slave with nothing. The peculium is all the money you'll ever have. Why didn't you keep it for yourself?"

She kept her eyes properly lowered. "I have food to eat, my lord, a warm place to sleep, clothes to cover me. The woman had none of these things. Her husband died a few months ago, and her son is a legionnaire on the frontier of Germania."

Decimus stared. "You, a Jew, gave money to a *Roman?*"

She looked up at him then, tears in her eyes. She was trembling in fear of him, but wanted him to understand. "She was hungry, my lord. The quadrans you gave me was enough to buy her bread."

Decimus leaned back, amazed. That a slave with a few coins would give it all to an enemy of her people was inconceivable to him. "You may leave us, Hadassah. The peculium is yours to do with as you like. Give it to whomever you please."

"Thank you, my lord." He watched her leave the room, then glanced at Phoebe and saw her eyes were filled with tears. He took her hand.

She looked at him. "If Bithia makes further accusations, Decimus, I would like your permission to sell her."

"Sell her now if you wish," he said, and then glanced at Marcus. "Unless you'd like to take her along to warm the bed at your villa."

Marcus hadn't realized his father was so aware of his private affairs, nor that he was willing to discuss them openly before Mother. "Thank you, but no. I want nothing more to do with her."

"Do as you wish," he told Phoebe. She rose and left the room.

Father and son looked at one another. Marcus' mouth tightened. "Bithia came to my room of her own volition the first time."

"I'm sure she did, but I doubt Hadassah will ever behave in the same manner."

Marcus stiffened, his eyes flashing. "Meaning what?"

"You know very well what I mean," he said. He sighed again. "Julia returned her to us—"

"Because Urbanus dislikes prudish Jews," Marcus interrupted with sarcasm.

Decimus' eyebrows flickered, but he made no comment to that surprising disclosure. He had wondered why Hadassah had been sent back. "I seem to remember your having similar reservations when your mother bought her. You said she might hold a grudge against all Romans. You also said she was ugly, as I remember." It was clear Marcus didn't like being reminded. Decimus smiled tightly. "The fact is, Julia has returned her, and Hadassah is now beneath my protection."

Marcus laughed at the amazing declaration. "And you want me to keep my hands off of her," he said, attempting humor but failing to conceal the edge in his voice.

Decimus said nothing for a moment, his gaze steady and coolly assessing. "Your emotions are running high over her," he said and saw that his choice of words discomforted Marcus even more. "I don't believe you've used Hadassah." He raised his brow, half in question.

"No," Marcus said firmly. "I haven't *used* her, Father." It was a disquieting choice of words. "I've never forced a woman to do my will."

"There are other means of force besides physical, as well you know. You are master; she is slave. Your mother has never approved of your dalliance with Bithia or the others you had before her. And frankly, I never thought much about it before now. You're young and vital, Marcus. Women have always been attracted to you. It seemed only natural that you'd take your pleasure."

He rose from his curule chair and stepped down from the dais to stand before his son. "But this girl is different." He shook his head, still amazed and perplexed. "After all Hadassah has been through, she gives everything she has to a Roman woman, the mother of a legionnaire." He shook his head again and let out a soft breath.

He looked at Marcus. "Hadassah isn't like the others, Marcus. She's not like anyone we've ever owned before." She was not like anyone he had ever known.

Reaching out, Decimus gripped Marcus' arm, at once commanding and appealing. "Take your pleasure with the others, but leave this girl alone."

After his father had left the room, Marcus sat on the edge of the dais and raked a hand back through his hair. He had made no promises.

How could he when Hadassah was all he thought about?

19

Julia shook as she spoke with Calabah. Calabah always understood. She always listened and gave suggestions that she could try. She agreed with her and showed compassion. Julia trusted her enough to tell her everything that was happening in her marriage. There was no one else she could talk to about Caius and his increasingly cruel and bizarre demands.

"He slapped me again last night." She put her fingers against the tender spot on her cheekbone. She tipped her chin slightly to show off the swelling. "Can you see? Right here. I've become quite skillful with makeup in the last few months." Her mouth trembled. "Calabah, all I said was 'Did you have luck at the races?' and he shouted the most horrible obscenities at me and blamed me because he lost. He said I bring him luck when I'm there and it was because I stayed home that he lost. I was feeling ill. It wasn't my fault. He frightened me and I tried to leave the room, but he grabbed me and swung me around and hit me. He said no one ever turns his back on Caius Polonius Urbanus."

Calabah took her hand and patted it. "It's your right to know what he's doing with the money from your estate, Julia."

"Not according to him. And my father would agree with him." Her eyes welled up with tears. "After all," she said bitterly, "I'm only a woman, a possession to be used." Biting her lip, she looked away and regained some control over her emotions. "Sometimes I tremble when he looks at me because I still love him so much. He makes me feel things that are so heavenly, Calabah, the way he touches me and kisses me. Then at other times, I'm afraid, so afraid I want to run away from him." She looked at Calabah, her dark eyes wide and troubled. "Caius is always so wild after the games. He hurts me, Calabah, and he seems to enjoy it. He makes me do things I don't want to do." She lowered her head, embarrassed and tearful.

Calabah tipped her chin up. "You can tell me anything." She smiled with tender amusement. "I don't shock easily, Julia. I've seen and done too much in my own life to be surprised by anything in yours." She frowned as she lightly traced the swelling on

Julia's cheek. "A little rough play is one thing, but he's a beast to hurt you like this." She rose from the couch. "I'll get you some wine."

Julia relaxed slightly. Calabah was always so understanding. Julia couldn't go to anyone else. She couldn't tell Marcus anything about Caius because the two men already disliked one another. Marcus would be furious if he knew Caius had ever hit her. A confrontation would undoubtedly make matters worse. She couldn't talk with her mother, either. She didn't *want* to talk to her. Mother would be horrified to know the dark direction of Caius' appetites, if she even believed it. She was too innocent. Julia didn't expect her father to help her, either. Whatever Caius did, Father would deem it her fault. He would say something like, "What did you do to bring this upon yourself?"

Tears welled again and spilled down her cheeks. Calabah wouldn't like her being so weak. She wiped her face quickly as she saw her returning.

"I don't know what I would do without you, Calabah. I've no one else I can talk to."

"You'll never have to do without me, and you know you're always welcome here." Calabah smiled and handed her a silver goblet. "I put some herbs into the wine to calm your nerves." Her expression lighted with rueful amusement. "You needn't look so uncertain, Julia. It's nothing that'll harm you. Drink up." She put her finger beneath the goblet and tipped it slightly. "Drink and feel better."

Julia drank deeply, wanting to be at peace. The drugged wine took effect quickly and she sighed, the tension going out of her.

"That's better, isn't it?" Calabah said, sitting beside her again. "Now, tell me everything Caius has done to you. Every little detail. Perhaps I can offer some advice."

Julia told her everything. The words came pouring out of her like the lancing of a boil. She told Calabah every disgusting, cruel act, and was satisfied to see anger burning in her friend's eyes. Anger began to burn in the pit of her stomach as well. Caius had no right to treat her this way. She had learned fairly quickly that his show of riches was an act and that her estate had changed his circumstances. It was her wealth through Claudius on which they lived. Caius should be grateful! He should treat her with respect.

"I'm ill each morning when I get up just thinking about what he might do to me."

"And you say you still love him?" Calabah said.

Julia closed her eyes and lowered her head, ashamed. "Yes," she admitted softly. "That's what's so terrible about it all. I love him so much. When he walks into a room, my heart, oh, my heart . . . "

"Even when he treats you like this?"

"He isn't always cruel. Sometimes he's the way he was in the beginning. Oh, Calabah, he can make me feel as though I'm flying through the heavens," she said. She wanted her friend to understand.

Calabah did. She knew Caius very well. She knew Julia even better. They were both selfish and passionate. Right now, the excitement of their relationship was keeping them together, but it wouldn't be long before their discontent with one another would lead them to seek excitement elsewhere.

Caius was already wandering, though Julia wasn't aware of it. Six months into the marriage, he had spent several hours relieving his darker passions on an unfortunate prostitute from an exclusive brothel. Calabah had heard of it from Caius' own lips. He had described what he did in detail, expecting her to be titillated and entertained. In fact, she was disgusted, though she didn't show it. He said he used a harlot because he didn't want to hurt his wife, that he *loved* Julia and didn't want his other nature to get out of control. Calabah encouraged his clandestine visits and she encouraged him to talk for one reason: Julia.

If she were to tell Julia now of Caius' infidelity, it would shatter Julia's confidence. Calabah didn't want to see that happen. Better to leave their relationship alone and allow things to develop naturally and let Caius destroy her love instead. Eventually, Caius would become less discreet in his affairs. Eventually, he would boast of his amorous exploits.

Perhaps, before that time, she would drop a few hints for some well-meaning friend like Octavia to overhear. Octavia was petty and jealous. She would gloat over his infidelity and no doubt take pleasure in telling Julia that Caius was seeking the company of other women. Julia would hate her for it, but she would be wiser more quickly.

But, until Julia was fully aware of Caius' foul nature, Calabah wanted to protect her from serious harm.

"You mustn't antagonize Caius or rouse his vile temper, Julia," she said. "It's foolish to ask questions. You've learned already it infuriates him. Never confront him. Find other means of learning what you need to know about what he's doing with his time and your money."

"You mean have spies?"

"Spies," Calabah said mockingly. "How dreadful you make it sound. I prefer to think of them as friends who, for a few sesterces, are willing to look out for your interests."

"I don't know," Julia said, frowning.

"Just a thought," Calabah said and changed the subject. The seed was planted and would take root in time. Caius' abhorrent behavior would see to it. Distrust was a breeding ground that needed tilling before other things could be planted and given time to grow. The harvest would be well worth her patience. She patted Julia's thigh maternally. "Take what you need from me, Julia, and forget all the rest. I love you as you are and wouldn't change you for the world. I admit not all my suggestions are appropriate to your situation, but it hurts me to know you're in such pain."

Julia relaxed beneath Calabah's assurances and finished her wine. She felt deliciously content, though sometimes she became vaguely uncomfortable beneath Calabah's unblinking stare. "I'm tired," she said. "I'm tired all the time lately."

"Poor dear. Lie back and rest."

"I should go home," Julia said dreamily. "We're going out this evening."

Calabah ran her fingertips over Julia's pale smooth brow. "Do you want to go out?"

"I don't care," Julia said, her eyes drifting closed. "I just want to sleep . . . "

"Then do so, sweet child. Do whatever you want."

Julia dreamed Hadassah was stroking her brow and singing songs to her about her strange god. No one served her as well as the little Jewess. She missed her serene presence and her tender care. She missed her stories and songs. Hadassah had always anticipated her needs, while Caius' slaves had to be commanded. Even in her dream, his slaves stood staring at her with cold, unblinking snakelike eyes, eyes that looked familiar and disturbing. Eyes like Calabah's.

Calabah awakened her late in the afternoon. "I've a sedan chair waiting to take you home," she said. "You mustn't be late."

But it was already too late.

When Julia arrived, Caius was waiting for her, angry and suspicious, his mind having created all manner of scenarios to rouse his jealousy. "Where have you been?" His heart beat rapidly and he could feel the rage growing within him—though whether it was at Julia or himself, he couldn't tell. Why had he allowed his temper to get out of control last night? He couldn't forget the look in her eyes after he had slapped her. What if she left him? "Who have you been with all afternoon?"

"I've been visiting with Calabah," Julia said, straining away at his touch. "You're hurting me!"

Caius let go of her immediately. "Calabah," he said, wondering what Julia had heard from her. His eyes narrowed.

"We had some wine and I slept for a while." She flinched as he reached out again, but when he touched her this time, he was gentle.

"I was afraid you'd left me," he said. He tipped her face up and turned it to one side. Caius knew she had been crying. Her eyes were slightly puffy and her makeup was washed away by tears. Even so, she was beautiful. He looked at the mark on her cheekbone and grimaced. He had never meant to hurt her. Sometimes, it was as though some beast within him took control and made him lash out at the things he prized most. "I'm sorry about last night." Tears filled her brown eyes and he felt even worse. "I love you, Julia. I swear it by all the gods. If you don't forgive me, I'll go mad . . . "

He kissed her and felt her resistance. He grew desperate. "I love you, I love you so much," he whispered and kissed her again the way she liked. After a long moment, she began to melt into him, and his sense of power returned along with a wave of pleasure. He still owned her as long as he could arouse her passions. Eros always reigned with Julia, as it did with him. They were so much alike. He caught her up in his arms, his blood pounding. "I'll make it up to you."

She loved Caius when he was like this, his passion focused on pleasing her. It was only when their lovemaking was over that the feeling of emptiness came upon her again, pulling her down into a pit of depression. If only all the pleasurable sensations lasted.

Caius, however, standing across the room now, was content. He knew how much she needed him, how she watched him. He knew she loved to look at him—another confirmation of the power he held over her.

His mouth tipped with a teasing smile and he moved to kiss

her. "I love it when you look at me like that, as though I'm a god," he said, gazing at her as though she were a prized possession.

Julia hid her irritation at his conceit. "Do we have to go out tonight? Antigonus can be such a bore."

Caius put on his tunic. "True enough, but he's useful."

"Marcus thinks he's a fool."

"I thought they were friends."

"They are, but that doesn't mean Marcus isn't aware of Antigonus' many faults. All he can ever talk about is politics or his lack of money."

"Spend the evening with Arria. You like her."

"She's always asking questions about Marcus. She's become tedious and pathetic."

"Arria is a woman of remarkable talents. I'm amazed Marcus lost interest in her." He turned and saw Julia's expression. He laughed at her. "You needn't look at me like that. I've only heard from others, not found out for myself."

"But you want to?"

He came over and bent down to tease her. "Not as long as you continue to please me," he said and noticed the bruise on her cheek. He straightened, frowning slightly. Marcus wasn't coming tonight, but if Antigonus noticed the mark on her cheek, he'd tell him. Marcus could cause all manner of trouble if he wanted, and there was trouble enough already. "You look tired," he said. "Stay home and rest."

Julia warmed at his solicitous concern, but his remarks about Arria were still fresh in her mind. "I am tired, but perhaps I should go."

He kissed her again, lightly this time. "No. I'll suffer the evening without your company and tell Antigonus you're visiting your parents."

Julia sat up and pushed her long tangled hair back over her shoulders. "It has been weeks since I've seen them. Perhaps I'll go tomorrow."

"Rest a day or two, and then go," he said. "You look worn out. I wouldn't want them getting any wrong ideas about the way we live." Nor seeing the bruise he had put on her.

He was in such an agreeable mood, Julia decided to risk more. "I want to bring Hadassah back with me after I see them."

"Hadassah?" he said blankly. "Who's Hadassah?"

"The slave mother gave me."

"What's the matter with the slaves you have?"

If she said they failed to serve her, he would probably bring them in now and beat them in front of her, and she didn't want that. "Hadassah always anticipated my needs. I've never had a maid who could do that except her."

His countenance darkened. "You're talking about the little Jew, aren't you? You know I don't like Jews. They're prudish. They put too much importance on purity."

"Her religion never got in the way of her serving me. And as for purity, I used to send her to Claudius."

Caius glanced back at her in surprise. "He wanted her? As I remember, she's ugly."

"Well," she said, seeing her lie wouldn't be convincing, "Claudius wasn't interested in her that way. He wanted to talk."

Caius laughed. "That's what happens when you marry an impotent old man."

His laughter grated and Julia wished she hadn't mentioned Claudius. Her first marriage amused Caius. At one of the first feasts they attended together, he had told his friends her entire personal history, humorously, as though it were an entertaining tale—she, Youthful Beauty, forced to wed Foolish Old Age. Caius wove a hilarious tale for his friends of an impotent old man pursuing a ripe young maiden through the countryside and never quite catching up to her, until he finally broke his neck in the attempt.

At first, Caius' tale had taken away the guilt and made the marriage seem as utterly ridiculous as one of the farces they saw at a theater. After a while, however, the amusement wore away with the retelling. Now, each time he mocked Claudius, Julia felt shamed. Claudius hadn't been that old, nor had he been a fool. He had been smart enough to increase his family fortune, while Caius appeared only able to lose money at the races.

"I'm going to bring Hadassah back with me," she said.

"Why do you want her so badly?"

"The maids you've given me plod about their duties like mindless animals. When you're not here, I'm bored to death with nothing to do. Hadassah always told me stories and sang songs to me. She always knew what I wanted before I asked."

He raised his brow and considered her request. "Very well," he said. "You may have her."

As soon as he left, Julia decided to go home immediately, see

Mother and Father, and bring Hadassah home with her. She pushed the rumpled blankets aside, summoned her maids, and ordered a bath prepared. "I'll wear the lavender palus," she told one, "and the amethysts and pearls," she said to the other.

Washed and scented, she carefully applied her makeup. It was best if her parents thought everything was perfect. She hoped Marcus wouldn't be home. He knew her too well to be fooled.

Her mother was delighted to see her, embracing her and asking all manner of questions as she ushered her into her father's presence. Julia was even gratified to see a smile of welcome on his face. He embraced her as well and lightly kissed the cheek she turned to him. He was thin and drawn. She wondered if he really was seriously ill, but pressed the thought quickly away.

"I've missed you both so," she said, realizing she had. How strange that she hadn't noticed it until she was back in their presence again. They were so dear to her, her heart swelled. And they did love her after all.

Excited and happy, she talked about the parties and feasts she and Caius had attended. She talked of the games and gladiators she had seen. She talked of the expensive presents Caius brought her, showing off her new pearls. Not once did she notice their disquiet or see their exchanged looks or their increasing dismay at what she disclosed about her new life and her husband.

She asked them questions about what had happened in the household, but as soon as they mentioned anything, it reminded her of something else she had to tell them.

"Enoch, bring me some wine. I'm quite parched," she said and drank half a goblet when he brought it to her. "Hmmm, it's not as good as what Caius buys for us, but it's refreshing," she said and finished the rest. She saw her mother's expression and giggled. "I'm not a child anymore, Mother. One goblet of wine doesn't make me drunk."

Decimus asked careful questions about Caius.

Phoebe ordered the evening meal be served. "Lie down, Julia," she said, patting the couch beside theirs.

Julia nibbled at the simple meal of sliced beef, fruit, and bread, and told them about the feasts of delicacies she had eaten. "Sometimes I eat until I think I'll pop," she laughed. "More wine, Enoch."

"You look as slender as always," Phoebe said.

"Thank you," Julia said, smiling happily. She didn't tell them

Calabah had taught her how to disgorge her stomach so she wouldn't gain weight. It had been unpleasant to begin with, but now was easily accomplished when she had a few minutes of privacy. She wouldn't eat enough of this meal to bother about it. She tossed a sliver of beef back onto the silver tray and took a grape instead.

Hadassah entered with two small bowls of warm water and a cloth draped over each forearm. She smiled brightly when she saw Julia, but went to serve Decimus and Phoebe instead. Julia was annoyed when Bithia brought the bowl to her so she could wash. Hadassah was *her* slave, not theirs. She had only loaned her to them.

She washed and dried her hands and flipped the damp cloth back at Bithia in dismissal. "Hadassah, collect whatever you have. You'll be returning with me." She felt the stillness in the room as soon as she spoke the words. "Is something wrong?" she asked in challenge.

"Leave us, Hadassah," Decimus said softly.

"Do as I said, Hadassah," Julia called after her and then looked at her father.

"It was my understanding you had more than enough maids already and had no need of her anymore," he said.

"Julia," Phoebe said more carefully, "what need do you have of Hadassah with so many others?"

"The others don't serve me the way I like."

"Then teach them," Decimus said tersely, annoyed. He had seen the flicker of emotion in Hadassah's eyes. She was happy here. She served them better than any other slave before her. He had no wish to give her back to his selfish, willful daughter, not when Julia had more slaves than she needed already.

"I would teach them if they had any intelligence," Julia said angrily. "Caius only cares that they're beautiful. Most of them are like Octavia's Ethiopian. Absolutely worthless. I've had one whipped twice and she's still too slow. Caius didn't want Hadassah serving me because she's ugly and a Jew."

"She's still a Jew," Decimus said dryly.

"She's never been ugly," Phoebe said defensively.

Julia glanced at her. "You've become very attached to her, Mother."

"What does Caius dislike about Jews?" Decimus asked, and

Julia realized she had said too much. She could hardly tell her parents why Caius objected.

"Several of his friends were killed in the siege of Jerusalem," she hedged quickly.

"In that case, I think it's best if Hadassah stays here," Phoebe said.

Julia's mouth dropped open. "How can you say that? She's mine. You gave her to me."

"You gave her back to your mother," Decimus said.

Julia rose up on her couch. "I did not! I only loaned her. I never once said you could have her, Mother."

"She's served us very well over the last six months," Phoebe said weakly. "I don't think it's fair to her to be passed back and forth."

Julia stared in disbelief. "Fair? Fair! She's a slave! And what about me? Don't you care about *me?*"

Marcus entered the room and gave his sister a wry smile. "I thought it sounded like old times. Welcome home, Julia." He came to her and bent to kiss her. "What's all the fuss about, little sister?"

"They want to keep Hadassah," she said, glaring at her father. "She's mine and Mother talks about fairness. They care more about a slave than they do about their own daughter."

"Julia!" Phoebe said in dismay.

"It's true!" Julia said, near tears, her heart pounding frantically. She needed Hadassah, she needed her nearby. "Did Father once ask me if everything was fine? Does he know what I have to endure?"

Decimus frowned, wondering at the intensity of her emotions. "What do you have to endure?" he asked sardonically, and Phoebe laid a hand over his and gave him a pleading look for silence.

Marcus studied her face. "What's happened to you?"

"Nothing," Julia said, shaking. "*Nothing!*" She looked at her mother. "You gave her to me."

"Yes, I did," Phoebe said, rising and going to her daughter. "And, of course, you can have her back." She put her arm around Julia's waist and felt a significant change in her. Suddenly she thought she knew the reason Julia was so emotional. "Oh, my dear, we had no idea you had such need of her. You may take her back with you." She felt Julia relax. "She has served us very well, but we have others." She kissed Julia's temple. "I'll go speak with Hadassah."

"No," Julia said, catching her hand. She didn't want to be alone with her father, and she could feel her brother's acute gaze boring into her, full of questions, latent with suspicion. "Send Marcus," she said. "He can tell her to get ready. I've only a few more minutes before I must return home and I want to spend them with you . . . and Father."

Marcus found Hadassah sitting on a bench in the peristyle. His pulse quickened as he came close to her. She stood, and her posture spoke of obedience. He thought of how many times he had wanted to talk with her. Sometimes he would rise early just to watch her go out at sunrise to pray to her god. At those times, the temptation to go out to her had been almost too great. But he knew his father was right. She was different from all others. To take her as he had taken others would ruin her. Odd that it mattered to him, but it did, and he had kept his word to leave her alone.

"Mother said you're to get your things. You're going with Julia."

"Yes, my lord," Hadassah said and started to turn away.

"Wait," he said huskily. "Hadassah, look at me." When she lifted her eyes to his, he saw her sadness and wanted to reach out and hold her. Instead, he spoke harshly. "You don't want to go, do you?" It sounded like an accusation and she looked frightened. It had been a long time since he had seen that look in her eyes and, full of remorse, he impulsively cupped her face. "I meant no accusation. You have served us well. You can tell me the truth." Her skin was so soft, he wanted to trace all her features and comb his fingers through her hair. His hands tightened. How long would it be before he saw her again? He didn't want to let her go.

Hadassah drew back from him slightly, disturbed by his touch. Had she a choice, she would stay here with Phoebe and Decimus. She would remain close to Marcus. He was so troubled. Life was a war to him, each accomplishment a battle to win. It was best that she be sent away. Her love for him was impossible, and yet it was growing each day. Besides, there was her promise to Phoebe about caring for Julia. And, of course, there was Julia to consider. Something was wrong. She had known it the moment she saw her—life with Urbanus was not as wonderful as Julia portrayed. "Lady Julia needs me, my lord."

Marcus felt her withdrawal and took his hands from her. He turned away, frustrated. "No more than my father needs you." *Or I,* he thought, realizing how her presence had served him.

Hadassah lowered her head. "Your mother is always here for him, my lord."

He glanced back at her sharply. "Julia has Urbanus and half a dozen slaves to take care of her."

"Then why has she come for me?" Hadassah said softly.

Marcus turned fully. "You don't trust Urbanus any more than I."

"I can't judge, my lord," she said cautiously.

"But you sense something, don't you? Are you afraid of him?"

"He doesn't notice me."

"He noticed you, and you know it. He refused to have you serve Julia," he said. Suddenly he was more uneasy about this than before. "What if Julia sends you to him the way she sent you to Claudius? Urbanus won't want to talk."

Her face was hot with embarrassment at his obvious suggestion. "She didn't love Claudius, my lord. She does love this man."

He let out his breath. She was right, of course, and he was faintly relieved at the reminder of Julia's lack of affection for her first husband. In fact, Julia had loathed Claudius. In contrast, she was mad for Caius. It was unlikely she'd send a slave in her place. And even if some pique or misunderstanding roused her anger and she did so, it was equally unlikely Urbanus would accept a substitute when he had summoned his wife. Marcus doubted Caius was as understanding as Claudius had been, or as weak and pliable.

Besides, Caius was as obsessed with Julia as she was with him. That had been more than obvious on the few occasions he had been at the same event with them and had had opportunity to observe them. In fact, the depth of their obsession made him uncomfortable. It didn't resemble the love his father and mother had for one another. It was something dark and powerful.

And Hadassah would now be in the middle of it.

Hadassah looked up at him and saw his worry. She knew how much Marcus loved his sister. He was a loyal and devoted brother. She took his hand in both of hers. "Please, my lord, try to trust me. I love her, too. I'll watch over your sister as best I can."

"And who will watch over you?"

She looked up at him in surprise and color poured into her cheeks. She let go of his hand.

Angry that he had revealed so much, he turned away and went back into the house. Julia was drinking another goblet of wine and looked up as he entered. "Where is Hadassah?" Julia demanded in an imperious tone that grated on his already raw nerves.

"Don't use that tone with me. I'm not your lackey."

Julia's eyes widened. "I can see I should never have come home," she said, setting the goblet down so hard that the wine sloshed over the side. A few droplets splashed on her lavender palus, and she uttered a small cry of dismay. "Now look what has happened." She tried to rub the wine drops away, but they were already soaking into the delicate wool. "Caius just gave me this a few days ago!"

Marcus had seen Julia's tantrums before, but this show of emotion was something else. His anger vanished. "It's just a few drops of wine, Julia."

"It's ruined. It's *ruined!*"

Hadassah entered the room with a small tied bundle—one change of clothes. Seeing the state Julia was in, she dropped it and went to her mistress. Leaning down, she caught Julia's hands from their frantic scrubbing. "It's all right, my lady. I know what to do to remove the stain. It will be like new." Julia glanced up at her and Hadassah saw the bruise she had so carefully tried to hide. She looked into her young mistress's eyes and saw more there as well. "I'm glad you came for me, Lady Julia," she said softly. "It will be my pleasure to serve you again."

Julia grasped Hadassah's hands tightly. "I've missed you so," she whispered, her eyes filling with tears. "I need you." She blinked them away, aware her parents and brother were watching her. She let go of Hadassah's hands and rose regally from the couch, smiling brightly again.

It wasn't until after Hadassah and Julia were gone that Marcus noticed the small tied bundle by the door. "Hadassah forgot her things. I'll take them tomorrow."

Decimus looked at him. "Do you think that wise?"

"Perhaps not," Marcus conceded, "but I'd like to know what's going on in that house to put Julia in such a state. Wouldn't you?"

"And you think Hadassah will know after one night?"

"No, but Julia might feel more free to talk with me if we're alone."

Decimus nodded. "Perhaps you're right."

"It would be better if you waited to talk with her, Marcus," Phoebe said. She sank down on her couch, smiling brightly. "I think you're both worrying for nothing. I don't think there's anything wrong with Julia that a few months won't bring to rights."

Decimus frowned at her lack of concern. "What brought on such an emotional outburst then? A tiff with Caius?"

"No." Eyes shining, Phoebe took his hand. "I think our daughter is with child."

He gave a short laugh. "I'm sure she would have said something if that were so."

"She's still very innocent, Decimus. Perhaps she doesn't even know herself, and I'm only guessing. I'll go see her tomorrow. There are questions I need to ask her to be sure."

Decimus looked at his wife in surprise. She was serious! "A child," he said wonderingly. By the gods, that was something worth living for.

Marcus hoped his mother was wrong. While news of a baby brought smiles to his parents' faces, he seriously doubted his sister would be pleased with such news.

In fact, he was sure she would hate it.

20

Julia wept bitterly. "Caius hasn't touched me since I told him about the baby. He refuses to take me to the games or any of the parties or feasts we've been invited to attend. He acts as though it's entirely my fault that I'm pregnant—as if he had nothing to do with it!"

Calabah soothed her with soft words.

"He finds me repulsive," Julia said tearfully.

"Did he tell you that?" Calabah said, knowing Caius was more than capable of such cruelty.

"He didn't have to tell me, Calabah. I feel it every time he looks at me." She clenched her hands. "I know he's been with other women," she said and stood. She turned away so Calabah couldn't see her face and wrapped her arms around herself as though that would stop the pain. "Octavia came to visit me yesterday."

Calabah leaned back slightly, her smile sardonic. "Dear, sweet Octavia. And what did she have to say?"

"She took the greatest delight in telling me she saw Caius flirting with Senator Eusebius' daughter. She said they disappeared for about an hour, but she imagined they were talking about politics." Her tone was bitter and sarcastic. "Can you believe she would come to me with a story like that? I hate her, Calabah. I tell you, I hate her. By the gods, I hope some wretched curse befalls her. You should've seen her gloating face.

"Not only that," Julia continued angrily, "but she was bragging about going to the ludus again and seeing Atretes." She turned, Caius forgotten. "I saw him first. Did you know that? I saw him on the road near Capua before he was famous, but now *she's* the one who sees him almost every day, while I'm locked away in this house like a prisoner. She said—"

"She said, she said, she said . . . " Calabah rose from her couch, wanting to shake Julia. She had seen the gladiator Julia mentioned. All brawn, beauty, and passion. Completely barbarian. How could Julia be attracted to *him?* It was beneath her. It was unthinkable. "What do you care what Octavia says, Julia?

Or who she sees. She's nothing but a stupid, shallow little whore who's jealous of you. Haven't you realized that yet? She was in love with Caius, and he's never looked twice at her. The minute you walked in the room, he was captivated."

"Not anymore," Julia said, full of angry self-pity.

"All isn't lost, Julia, and stop pacing like a madwoman. You're making me dizzy. Come and sit down and let's discuss this intelligently." Julia came obediently, and Calabah took her hand. She squeezed it gently. "Do you want this child?"

Julia jerked her hand away and stood again. "Want it? I hate it. It's ruined my life. I'm sick in the morning. I've dark circles under my eyes because I can't sleep for worrying about what Caius is doing when he's not with me. And I'm getting disgustingly fat."

"You're not fat," Calabah said, glad Atretes was so quickly forgotten. She smoothed the fine wool of her red-trimmed toga and watched Julia surreptitiously. She was so lovely, so graceful in her movements, like a work of art. She could sit and gaze at her all day. The thought of a baby distorting her was repugnant. "How far along are you?"

"I don't know. I can't remember. I never stopped to think much about it when I missed my flux. Three months, I think, maybe four. You really don't think I'm fat?" she said, looking down at her hands spread over her abdomen. "You're not just saying that to make me feel better?"

Calabah studied her critically. "You do look a little tired and drawn, but no one would guess you were expecting a baby. Not yet."

"Not yet," Julia said grimly. "Why did this have to happen just when I was happy? It's not fair. Mama said the gods were smiling on me. Smiling! They're laughing at me! I can almost hear them."

"Then end it," Calabah said in her most reasonable tone, a beatific smile curving her lips.

"End what?" Julia said blankly, wiping her eyes again and blowing her nose delicately. "My life? I might as well. It's already over."

"Nonsense. I mean terminate the pregnancy. You needn't have this child if it's making you so unhappy."

Julia raised her head in surprise. "But how?"

"You really are ridiculously innocent, Julia. I don't know why I waste my time with you. Have you never heard of abortion?"

Julia paled and stared at her in alarm. "Are you saying I should kill my own baby?"

Calabah uttered a soft gasp and stood, insulted and angry. "Do you think so little of me as that? Of course, I would never suggest such a thing. Right now, in the early stages of your pregnancy, what's inside you is merely a symbol of human life, not actual life. It doesn't possess any humanness whatsoever and it won't for another few months."

Julia was uncertain. "My father and mother were so happy with the news. To them, what I carry now is a child."

"Of course. It's a subtle way of pressing you to do what they want. They want you to have grandchildren for them."

She looked away from Calabah's compelling dark eyes. "Neither of them would approve of abortion."

"What has this to do with them?" Calabah said. She stood regally and approached Julia. "It's this kind of thinking that infuriates me. Don't you see the trap, Julia? Don't you understand? By denying you your right to choose, they deny you the right to protect your physical, mental, and emotional health. They take away your humanness for the sake of a mere symbol."

She put her arm around her. "Julia, I care about you. You know that. It's your life we're discussing, not your mother's. Certainly not your father's. Your mother made her choices, and they were good for her." She let her go. "Now it's time for you to make yours. Who are *you?* What do *you* want? Julia, look at me. Look at me, dear. You're clearly miserable over this pregnancy. Caius doesn't want a child. He's made that perfectly obvious. If he doesn't want a child and you don't want one either, why are you going through all this?"

"Because I didn't think I could do anything about it," Julia said, shaking beneath Calabah's stare.

"It's your body, Julia. It's your decision whether you have a child or not. It has nothing to do with anyone else."

"Yes, but my father would never forgive me . . . "

"Why should your father even know about it? It's not his business, is it? If they question you, if you must tell them something, tell them you had a miscarriage."

Julia sighed wearily. "I don't know, Calabah. I don't know what to do." She peered out into the garden and watched Hadassah cutting flowers. How could anyone look so peaceful with all that was going on in this household? She wished she could go out in the sunshine and sit with her and listen to her songs and forget everything else. She wished she could forget the look on Caius' face when she had told him she was carrying his child.

"How could you be so stupid!" His words still rang in her ears, along with the news Octavia had brought her so gleefully. *"I don't know for certain they made love, but they were gone for a very long time."*

Caius was having affairs. Julia was certain of it. He hadn't been to her bed in weeks, and his sensual nature would have driven him to find release elsewhere. Willing partners would pose no difficulty. Like they did with Marcus, women flocked around Julia's husband.

Julia bit her lip to keep from crying again. She didn't want to be pregnant and have her life turned upside down. She didn't want to get fat and ugly and lose Caius. All she wanted was to be out of this situation, to have the problem gone and her life back the way it was. She couldn't stand the thought of Caius making love to anyone else, though she didn't think she could stand to have him touch her again, not now that she knew he'd betrayed her. All she knew was she wanted him to look at her the way he had before, as though she were the most beautiful woman in the world and he wanted to devour her.

Julia stared out at Hadassah. What would she say to all this? Julia longed to talk to her.

Calabah moved, somehow shadowing the garden and recapturing Julia's attention. "Lovely child, does it only take a few weeks for you to forget all I taught you? You, and only you, are the master of your destiny. No one else."

Julia trembled slightly as though a chill wind had blown over her. Calabah was right. It was the only way. Still, she hesitated; some inner voice cried out to her not to do it. "Would the abortion hurt very much?" she said quietly.

"Not as much as having a baby," Calabah said.

Fear took the place of uncertainty. "You speak as though you know."

"One needn't suffer death to know it's something to avoid." She smiled. "I've always been very careful to prevent getting pregnant. I never wanted to be so fat I couldn't see my own feet and have nothing to look forward to but pain. I've witnessed childbirth, Julia, and I can tell you it's excruciating, undignified, and bloody. It takes hours. Some women die giving birth to their babies. Those who don't are in servitude for the rest of their lives. Do you know what a tremendous responsibility it is to rear a child? Men don't help. They don't have to. Caius certainly won't. The care and educating of your child will be up to you."

Julia sank down onto a couch and closed her eyes against the picture Calabah created. Horrible pain followed by a life of drudgery. "My mother never told me there were ways to keep from getting pregnant."

"She wouldn't," Calabah said, her tone full of pity. "It's beyond the realm of her thinking, Julia. Your mother is still mired in ancient traditions foisted upon her by the unthinking generations before her. Children are her sole purpose for existence." She sat down and took Julia's hand. "Don't you see yet? Traditions have imprisoned women for centuries. It is time we were free, Julia. Break your chains! This is a new age."

Julia sighed. "I lack your wisdom, Calabah, and your confidence."

Calabah smiled and kissed her cheek. "Will you ever come to understand the great truths I've taught you over the past months?"

"Tell me what I must do," Julia pleaded.

"You must make your own decisions, dear heart." She rose and went to the window to look out into the garden. She seemed so majestic and beautiful, yet somehow shadowed even with an aura of sunlight around her. "Julia, you must plan your life the way you want it to happen. Visualize it. See it in your mind, happening as you make it happen." She looked back at her. "Happiness springs from within you, from your own inner power."

Julia listened, the confidence and cadence of Calabah's words giving her hope. "I know you're right." She sighed and looked away, pensive and shaken. "Abortion is the only answer." She clenched her hands. "Is it difficult to find someone who can do it?"

"Not at all. It's a common practice. I know at least half a dozen physicians who perform it daily."

"But will it be painful?"

"There will be some discomfort, but not a great deal and not for long. It'll be all over in a few hours, and you'll have your life back again, just the way you want it to be." She came to Julia and sat beside her, placing her hand over hers. "When do you wish to have it done?"

Julia glanced up, pale. "Maybe in a week or two."

"Very well," Calabah said with a soft sigh, taking her hand away. "But you must understand, Julia. The longer you wait, the more risk you take."

Fear swept through Julia. "Then I should have it done now?"

"It would be wise to have it done as soon as possible. Tomorrow morning, if it can be arranged."

"Where must I go?"

"Nowhere. I know a physician who is very discreet and will come to you."

Calabah stood, and Julia clutched her hand even tighter, looking up at her with huge, frightened eyes. "Will you stay with me until it's over?"

Calabah touched her cheek tenderly. "I'll do whatever you want, Julia."

"I want you with me. I'll feel better about this if you are."

Calabah bent and kissed her lightly on the lips. "I won't betray you like the others. I'm not your father or Caius." She straightened and smiled down at her. "You've made a wise decision. After the abortion is over, you can forget it ever happened and start over. I'll teach you what you need to do to keep from getting pregnant again."

Julia watched her walk from the room. As soon as she was alone, she buried her face in her hands and wept.

Hadassah knew she was to leave Julia alone when she had guests. She found other things to do while she waited to be summoned. Today, she worked in the garden alongside Sergius, a slave from Brittania. When Julia came out, Sergius found work far up the path and well away from her, safely out of reach of her swift temper.

Dismayed, Hadassah saw Julia had been crying again. Ever since Octavia had visited, her mistress had been agitated and emotional, given to bouts of tears and rage. Apparently Calabah's visit hadn't improved matters. Julia sat in the sunshine and complained she was cold. Hadassah fetched her shawl, but saw she was still shivering. "Are you feeling all right, my lady? Is it the baby?"

Julia stiffened. The *baby*. It wasn't a baby yet. Calabah had said so. Calabah knew. "Sing to me," she ordered tersely, nodding to the small harp beside her. It had a leather strap, so Hadassah could carry it with her at all times, only setting it aside as she worked or slept. Julia watched Hadassah pick it up and begin strumming it gently. A soft melody soothed her frayed nerves.

Hadassah sang, but noticed Julia scarcely listened. She was distracted, distraught. Hadassah watched her hands pleat the wool of her palus and then clench into white-knuckled fists. Removing the small harp, she went to her. She knelt and took her hands. "What distresses you so?"

"This . . . this pregnancy."

"Are you afraid? Please don't be, my lady," she said. "It's the most natural thing in the world. The Lord has smiled on you. Having a child is the greatest blessing God can give a woman."

"A blessing?" Julia said bitterly.

"You're nurturing new life . . . "

Julia pulled her hands away. "What do you know about it?" She stood and moved away from her. Pressing her fingers against her temples, she tried to regain control of her turbulent emotions. It was time she stopped reacting like a child to everything. Calabah was right. She must take control of her life.

She looked back at Hadassah, still kneeling beside the marble bench, her brown eyes full of compassion and concern. Julia pressed her hand against her heart and felt an unspeakable regret. Hadassah loved her. It was why she needed her so much. It was why she had taken her back from her mother and father. Her mouth curved bitterly. How pitifully ironic that it had to be a slave who loved her unconditionally. It should be her parents. It should be Caius.

"You can't understand what I'm going through, Hadassah. You don't know what it's like being sick, feeling tired all the time, having your husband discard you. What can you know about loving a man the way I love Caius?"

Hadassah stood slowly. She searched her face, wondering at the desperation she saw. "You carry his child."

"A child he doesn't want, a child that's driven us apart. Don't talk to me of this being a blessing from the gods," Julia said angrily.

"Give yourself time, my lady." Why couldn't Julia have the eyes to see and ears to hear the Lord and realize she was blessed?

"Time won't change anything," Julia said. "Other than to

make matters more difficult." Calabah was right. She must take control. She must make things right again. But she was afraid of the decision she had made. Doubt attacked her. Just because it was a common practice, did that make it right? If it was right, why was she assailed by doubt?

Was there such a thing as right and wrong? Didn't it all depend on circumstances? Wasn't happiness the primary thing to achieve in life?

She wanted Hadassah to understand what she was going through. She wanted her to say everything would be fine, that her decision to have an abortion was rational. She wanted her to say that what she was about to do was the only thing she could do to make things as they used to be between her and Caius. But when she looked into her little Jewess's eyes, she couldn't utter a word. She couldn't tell her anything. What Calabah saw as only a symbol, she knew Hadassah saw as a life.

What did it matter what a slave thought? She knew nothing. She was nothing. She was a slave, dispossessed by her own unseen god.

"You say it's a blessing because someone told you it was a blessing," Julia said, in angry defense. "You're just repeating what you've heard. Everything you sing, everything you say is just a repeat of someone else's words and thoughts. Isn't that what you always did with Claudius? Recite your Scriptures, tell him your stories? You haven't a thought of your own. How could you understand what I have to endure, the choices I have to make?"

Speaking harshly to Hadassah gave her no relief. In fact, she felt worse. "I'm tired. I'm going inside to rest."

"I'll bring you some mulled wine, my lady."

Hadassah's gentleness was salt on a raw wound, and Julia reacted in blind pain. "Don't bring me anything. Don't come anywhere near me. Just leave me alone!"

Caius came home late in the afternoon. He was in a rage and Julia knew he had lost at the races again. Her resentment grew until she couldn't resist taunting him a little. "Your luck always held when I accompanied you," she said.

Caius turned slightly and looked at her with fierce, dark eyes. "A good thing you were rich, my dear, or I never would've given you a second look."

His cruel words were like a physical blow. She could hardly breathe past the constriction of pain at his words. Was it true? It couldn't be. He was drunk. That's why he spoke so cruelly. He was always cruel when he was drunk. She wanted to lash back, to draw his blood, but could think of nothing strong enough to accomplish it. He smiled at her, a cold, mocking smile that lacerated her. He was impenetrable and knew it.

Pouring himself a full goblet of wine, Caius drank it straight down. His temper erupted and he heaved the empty silver goblet across the room. It clattered against a mural of frolicking maidens and satyrs and made Julia flinch. "You better hope my luck at the races improves," he said cryptically and left her.

Calabah came early the next morning. Accompanying her was a small Roman woman in a pristine white toga trimmed with gold. A male slave accompanied her and held an ominous carved box beneath his arm.

"You needn't look so frightened, Julia," Calabah said, putting an arm around her. "Asellina is very good at this. She's done it many, many times before." She guided her along the marble-tiled hallway to her chambers. "Her reputation is impeccable and she's highly respected among her peers. She wrote about abortion techniques for the medical community last year, and her work on the subject is widely circulated. You don't have to worry about a thing."

Asellina ordered one of Caius' slaves to replenish the brazier and keep it well-stoked so the room would be warm. Her slave set the carved box down. She opened it and removed an amphora. Pouring some of the contents into a goblet, she added wine and brought it to Julia. "Drink this."

The sweet wine had an aftertaste as bitter as gall.

"All of it," Asellina said, pressing the goblet back to her again. "Every drop." She stood watching and then took the empty goblet from Julia's shaking hands and gave it to her slave. "Remove your clothing and lie back."

A wave of panic gripped Julia. Calabah came to her and helped her. "It will be all right," she whispered, assisting her. "Trust me. Try to relax. It'll make it easier."

Asellina examined her carefully, inserting something inside her and leaving it. She straightened and washed her hands in a bowl of water her slave held for her. "She is further along than you said."

"She wasn't sure," Calabah told her softly.

Asellina took a towel and came to stand over Julia. She smiled down at her. Handing the towel to her slave, she placed her hand on Julia's brow. "You'll feel cramping soon, my dear. The discomfort lasts until your body expels the mass of tissue. A few hours, nothing more." She moved back slightly and glanced briefly at Calabah. "A moment of your time . . . "

They spoke in hushed voices near the door. Calabah sounded angry. "Your fee has increased," Julia heard her say.

"My skill is in greater demand, and you insisted it be done swiftly. I had to reschedule to come here."

Calabah came back and bent down to Julia. "I'm sorry, Julia, but I must ask. Have you any money on hand?"

"No. Caius manages everything."

"You must change that," Calabah said, annoyed. "Well, there's nothing to be done about it now. I'll have to give her your pearls until we can get cash."

"My pearls?" Julia said.

"Only until I can speak to Caius and get from him what's due Asellina for her services. Don't look at me like that. You needn't worry whether you'll get your pearls back. You'll have them by tomorrow afternoon. I promise. Where are they?"

Asellina left the villa with the pearls in her possession.

Julia's contractions began an hour later, and when they did, they came strong and fast, one rolling into another. She writhed in pain, and her body was soon drenched in sweat. "You said it wouldn't hurt," she moaned, digging her fingers into the covers and twisting them.

"You're fighting it, Julia. You must relax and it won't hurt as much. Stop bearing down. It's too soon."

Julia heaved with sobs as the contraction ended. "I want my mother." She rolled her head back and forth on the pillows, groaning again as another came. "Hadassah. Get me Hadassah."

Hadassah came immediately upon the summons. As soon as she entered Julia's chambers, she knew something was terribly wrong. "Your maid's here, Julia. Now, try to calm yourself," Calabah said.

"My lady," Hadassah said, bending over her, frightened. "Is it the baby?"

"Hush, you fool," Calabah hissed, her eyes black as she pushed her aside. "Bring a basin of warm water and a cloth." She bent to Julia again, her tone soothing and sweet again. She placed her hand on her white abdomen and smiled. "It's almost over, Julia. Only a little while longer."

"Oh, Juno, be merciful . . . " Julia moaned through gritted teeth, her shoulders rising from the bed as she bore down.

"Shall I send for a physician?" Hadassah said, sloshing water into the basin.

"She's had a physician," Calabah said.

Julia groaned as another pain gripped her. "I wouldn't have done it if I'd known it'd be like this. Oh, *Juno,* mercy, mercy . . . "

"Do you think carrying a child full term and having it is easier? Better to get rid of it now."

The blood drained from Hadassah's face. She uttered a soft cry, the basin slipping from her hands and shattering on the floor. Calabah glanced at her sharply and Hadassah stared back at her in horror.

The older woman stood and came to her swiftly, slapping her across the face. "Don't stand there while she suffers. Do as you're told. Give me that other basin over there and go get warm water."

Hadassah eagerly fled the room. She pressed herself against the cold marble wall outside the room and covered her face. She heard Julia scream behind the closed door and was galvanized by the sound of her agony. Hadassah ran and filled a big jug with warm water from the bath spout and returned.

"It's all over, Julia," Calabah was saying when Hadassah entered. "You were further along than you thought. That's why it was so difficult. Shhh, no more weeping now. It's done. You'll never have to suffer like that again."

She saw Hadassah standing in the doorway. "Don't stand there, girl. Bring the water here. Put the jug down by the bed. Take what's on the floor and dispose of it."

Unable to look at Julia, Hadassah knelt and carefully took up the small bloody bundle from the floor. She rose and left the room silently. Calabah followed her to the door, closing it firmly behind her.

Hadassah stood outside in the hallway. *Dispose of it.* Her throat closed as she pressed the tiny bundle against her heart. "Oh, God . . . " she whispered brokenly. Blinded by tears, she stumbled out into the garden.

She knew the pathways well and followed one to the flowering plum tree. Sinking down, she held the bundle cradled against her and rocked back and forth, weeping. She dug a hole with her bare hands in the soft soil and placed the discarded child in it. She covered it and patted the earth down gently. "May the Lord raise you up in heaven to sing with angels . . . "

She didn't go back to the house.

Marcus stopped by Julia's villa for a visit. The hush in the house was tense, and when he was taken to Julia's chamber, he found her still in bed. She smiled, but there was no gaiety in it. Her eyes were dull with unhappiness. "What's the matter, little sister?" he said and crossed the room. Perhaps she had heard rumors about Caius' infidelities or heard about his most recent losses at the races. She was pale and seemed depressed. "Are you ill?" A maid stood near her bed, waiting to serve her, but it wasn't Hadassah.

"I lost the baby this morning," she said, avoiding his gaze as she smoothed the blanket across her abdomen. There was no pain anymore, just this listlessness that seemed to suck her down. She couldn't rid herself of the terrible sensation of emptiness and loss, as though more had been taken out of her than tissue. It was as though a part of her had been taken as well, and now she realized she'd never get it back again.

Marcus tipped her chin and searched her face. "You had an abortion, didn't you?"

Her eyes shimmered with tears. "Caius didn't want a child, Marcus."

"Did he tell you to do this?"

"No, but what else could I do?"

He touched her cheek gently. "You're all right?"

She nodded dully and lay back. "Calabah said I'll feel better in a few days. She said it's normal to feel depressed afterwards. It'll pass."

Calabah. He should have known. He brushed the hair back from her temple and kissed her lightly. He moved away, rubbing his hand around the back of his neck. If he said anything against Calabah, it would only drive Julia into further involvement with her. Julia was too much like him in some ways. She didn't want her life dictated.

"It's all right, isn't it, Marcus? There's nothing wrong with what I did, is there?"

He knew she wanted him to say he agreed with her decision to abort the child, but he couldn't. He had always avoided the subject when it arose because it left him feeling uncomfortable. But

Julia needed comfort. He came back and sat with her. "Hush, little one. You didn't do anything that hundreds of other women haven't done before you."

"Caius will want me again, now. I know he will."

Marcus' mouth tightened. He had come to talk with her about Caius, but today wasn't the day to add to her troubles. She didn't need to know her husband's betting losses were mounting at an alarming rate. Even if she was aware, what could she do if she had no influence over him?

"I'll tell Mother and Father you lost the baby and you need time to rest and recuperate." She was far too vulnerable and transparent now to face them. One look at her face and Father would see she was full of guilt over something. That would begin the questioning, which would lead to a hysterical confession. The rifts in the family were already wide enough without adding this to them.

Marcus took Julia's hand and held it tightly. "Everything will be all right." He blamed Caius for making her think she had to abort her child to regain his love. He brushed a tear from her cheek and rubbed it between his fingers. He wanted revenge on Caius, but anything he did would only harm Julia. He felt helpless. "Get some sleep, Julia." He kissed her hand. "I'll visit you again tomorrow."

She clung to his hand with both of hers as he stood. "Marcus? Please. See if you can find Hadassah. Calabah sent her from the room to . . . " She stopped, her eyes shadowed. "She hasn't come back and I want her to sing to me."

"I'll find her and send her to you."

He went out to the peristyle. Several slaves were standing and whispering among themselves near the fountain. As soon as one noticed him, they scattered to their chores. "Have you seen the slave girl Hadassah?" he said to one washing the pool tiles.

"She went into the gardens, my lord. She hasn't returned."

Marcus went out beneath the arches to find her. When he did, she was sitting with her knees drawn up tightly against her chest, her face hidden.

"Julia needs you," he said. She didn't raise her head. "Did you hear me? Julia needs you."

She said something then, but the words were muffled against her knees. She put her hands up over her head and he saw her fingers were caked with earth. He closed his eyes. "I know about it," he said, realizing what she had been sent to do. "It's over now. Try to forget it. She'll be fine in a day or two, and Caius won't be angry with her. Neither of them wanted a child."

She looked at him then. Tears streaked the smudges of dirt staining her ashen cheeks. Her eyes were full of grief and horror. She came to her feet and he grimaced at the blood stains on her soiled tunic. She spread her hands out in front of her, staring at them, her body trembling. "'Dispose of it,' she said. A tiny child balled up in a cloth and dumped on the floor like garbage. A child . . . "

"Put it from your mind. Don't think about it anymore. Besides, Julia wasn't far enough along for it to matter. It wasn't really a child—"

"Oh, God . . . " Her fingers dug into her soiled tunic. "Not a child," she repeated his words in a moan of grief and then looked at him with a fierce despair. "'For You have formed my inward parts; You have covered me in my mother's womb. . . . My frame was not hidden from You, when I was made in secret, and skillfully wrought in the lowest parts of the earth. Your eyes saw my substance, being yet unformed, and in Your book they all were written, the days fashioned for me, when as yet there were none of them . . . '"

The hair rose on Marcus' neck. She spoke like one of the temple oracles, and the look in her eyes pierced him. "Stop it!"

She only wept more, speaking now in Aramaic, her head thrown back. "*Yeshua, Yeshua, saloch hem kiy mah casu lo yaden,*" she said brokenly. "Jesus, Jesus, forgive them for they know not what they do."

Marcus caught hold of her shoulders. "Stop it, I tell you!" He wanted to shake her from her trance, but she looked up at him clear-eyed.

"Are you Romans so foolish you have no fear? God knows when a sparrow falls to earth. Do you think God doesn't know what you do? Do you care so much for shallow pleasures that you would kill your own children to have them?"

Marcus let go of her and drew back. She stepped forward, clutching his white tunic in her blood- and earth-stained hands. "Have you no fear?"

He grasped her wrists and freed himself. "Why should I fear?" He cared nothing about her god, but her accusation stung, angering him. "But you should. You speak rash words for a slave.

Have you forgotten Jerusalem so soon? I've never heard of a Roman woman murdering her nursing infant so she could roast it for dinner!"

She didn't back away from his anger. "No less an abomination before God, Marcus! But is one woman driven mad by starvation the same thing as what's been done here? What excuse has Julia, surrounded by comfort? She is sane. She thought this through. She made this *choice.*"

"What else could she do? She didn't want a child and neither did Caius. Her marriage is disintegrating."

"And killing her child will help put things right again? Do you believe because you don't want something, it's your right to destroy it? Is human life so cheap to you? Do you think Julia won't be judged?"

"Who will judge her? You?"

"No," Hadassah said, her face crumpling and tears coming again. *"No!"* She shook her head, her eyes closed. "It's not for me to condemn anyone, no matter what they do, but I fear for her. God knows." She covered her face with her hands.

Her god and his infernal laws again, Marcus thought, pitying her. "Hadassah, you needn't be afraid for her. This isn't Judea. She won't be taken out and stoned. Rome is civilized. There's no law against a woman having an abortion, if that's her choice."

Her eyes flashed as he had never seen them. "Civilized! What of God's law? Do you think he won't judge?"

"You worry too much about what this god of yours might think. I doubt he cares."

"You think because you don't believe, he doesn't exist. You worship gods you create with your hands and imagination, and deny the Most High God who created you from dust and gave you life. In the end, it won't matter whether you believe or not, Marcus. A higher law than man's does exist, and not your emperor nor all your legions nor all your worldly knowledge can stand against—"

Marcus clapped his hand across her mouth before she was heard. "Be silent!" She struggled and he shoved her back out of sight of the house. "Are you such a fool, Hadassah? Speak no more of this accursed god of yours!" he ordered, his heart pounding. What she spoke was blatant subversion and could get her killed.

He held his hand clamped firmly over her lips, shaking her

once to make her stop fighting him. "You will listen to reason! What power but Rome, Hadassah? What other power is there on earth that can compare? You think this almighty god of yours is so powerful? Where was he when you needed him? He watched Judea torn by war, his city and temple turned into rubble, his people made into slaves. Is this a god with power? No. Is this a god who loves you? No! Is this a god I should fear? *Never!*"

She stilled, looking up at him with an oddly pitying expression. He gentled, wanting her to see reason. His hand was wet with her tears. He spoke softly. "There's no power on earth but that of the emperor and of Rome. It's the Empire that holds the peace together. *Pax Romana,* Hadassah. It comes at high cost. Believing there's anything else is a slave's dream for freedom, and an invitation to death. Jerusalem is gone. There's nothing left of it. Your people have been scattered across the earth like chaff. Don't cling to a god who doesn't exist, or, if he does, who clearly wants to destroy his chosen people."

He took his hand away slowly and saw the marks his fingers left on her skin. "I didn't mean to hurt you," he said. She was so pale and still.

"Oh, Marcus," she said softly, looking straight into his eyes as though to beseech him.

His name never sounded so sweet on a woman's lips. "Give up this faith you have in an unseen god. He isn't there."

"Can you see air you breathe? Can you see the force that moves the tides or changes the seasons or sends the birds to a winter haven?" Her eyes welled. "Can Rome with all its knowledge be so foolish? Oh, Marcus, you can't carve God in stone. You can't limit him to a temple. You can't imprison him on a mountaintop. Heaven is his throne; earth, his footstool. Everything you see is his. Empires will rise and empires will fall. Only God prevails."

Marcus stared at her, mesmerized by what she said and speechless with frustration that she could speak with such conviction. Nothing he had said had reached her. A sudden, swift fear for her rolled over him like a wave, and in its wake came a fierce anger at her stubborn faith in her invisible god.

"Julia sent me to find you," he said tautly. "Will you serve her as you always have, or shall I find another to replace you?"

Her demeanor changed. It was as though she drew a veil down over her face. She lowered her head and clasped her hands in front of her. Whatever feelings and beliefs she embraced so passionately were now carefully hidden within her. Better that they stay there. "I'll go to her, my lord," she said quietly.

My lord. He was once more master; she, the slave. Marcus felt the chasm between them like an open wound. He straightened and looked down at her coldly. "Wash yourself and throw away that tunic before you go to her. She needs no reminders of what she's done." He turned and left her.

Hadassah watched him go, her eyes burning with tears. A soft breeze blew through the garden. "Yeshua, Yeshua," she whispered, closing her eyes. "Have mercy on him. Have mercy on Julia. Oh, Lord, have mercy on them all."

21

Atretes raked his hands back through his hair. He had grown so accustomed to the sound, he hardly heard the hobnailed shoes of the guard passing by on the iron bars above his head. Unless he had had the dream. Then he heard the heavy footsteps and saw the shadow of the guard. Restless, he rose in the darkness of his cell, wondering how near dawn it was. Better to be in the courtyard going through the rigorous exercises. Better to have a sword in his hand. The dream left a memory of the black forests of his homeland so strong that he thought he'd go mad in the confinement of this cell.

He picked up the stone idol from its corner alcove. He ran his fingers lightly over the dozen pendulous breasts that covered her chest and belly. Tiwaz had deserted him in Germania, and he needed a god to worship. Perhaps this one would do. Artemis appealed to Atretes' sensuality. Bato said that for an offering of money, the temple priestesses assisted devoted followers in "worship." Atretes had visited the temple of Isis and come away sated, if vaguely disquieted by his visit. Women worshiped as well, with priests available to them for a fee. Rome had its pleasures.

Torchlight flickered overhead and he heard the guards talking. He set the idol back in its alcove and sat on his stone bench. Leaning back against the cold stone, he closed his eyes and dreamed of his mother again, prophesying before a burning pyre: *"A woman with dark hair and eyes . . . "* He hadn't had the dream in months, not since the night before he killed Tharacus and saw the two young women in the orchard beside the road to Capua. Yet tonight it had been so powerful and so real that it lingered like an echo in the darkness. The woman of whom his mother spoke was near.

Rome was full of women with dark hair and eyes. Many who attended the pregame feasts were incredibly beautiful. Some offered themselves to him. As a means of insult, he ignored them. That he tried the emperor's patience was only a matter of satisfaction. Atretes no longer feared being crucified or thrown to the animals: the Roman mob would never allow it. With eighty-nine kills to his credit, thousands poured into the Circus Maximus just to see him fight. The emperor was no fool. He wouldn't waste such a valued commodity over a matter as insignificant as pride.

Yet Atretes gained no pleasure from his fame. In fact, he found it served to further enslave him. More guards were assigned to him, not to prevent the escape which he now knew was impossible, but to prevent an adoring populace from tearing him apart.

His name was splashed across walls all over the city. Flowers and coin were thrown down to him before and after he fought, and gifts from amoratae poured into the ludus daily. He couldn't appear anywhere outside the ludus without a dozen trained guards around him. Visits to Pugnax's inn were no longer allowed because of the riots they caused. His mere presence at a feast often made women faint. When he was on the sand, his name was shouted over and over by thousands until it sounded like the deep pulsing heartbeat of a primeval beast.

Only in his dreams did he have the vague memory of what it was like to be a free man in the forests, to know the tenderness of his woman, to hear the free laughter of children. His humanity was slowly being taken from him each time he faced an opponent and won.

Atretes looked at his hands. They were powerful and callused from hours of practice with a weighted sword . . . and they were weighted even more by the blood on them. He remembered Caleb's face as he waited without fear for the killing stroke as the blood-maddened mob screamed, *"Jugula!"* Sweat had poured down Atretes' forehead into his eyes. Or had it been tears?

"Free me, my friend," Caleb had said, swaying from loss of blood. He had placed his hands on Atretes' thighs and tipped his head back. When Atretes made the stroke, the mob rose with exultant screams.

Atretes opened his eyes, trying to obliterate the memory, but it remained, like a cancer eating at his soul.

Now the door was unbolted and he filed out into the courtyard for exercises. He gained some relief from the activity, concentrating on the rigorous physical training.

Bato stood on the balcony, guests of the ludus with him. It was not uncommon for visitors to view the gladiators during training sessions. Some came to buy, others to watch. Atretes paid them no attention until two young women appeared beside Bato. He recognized Octavia immediately, for she was frequently at the feasts given before the games and was known to have a passion for any gladiator willing to give her a second look. It was the other girl who attracted his attention. She was dressed in a blue palus with yellow-and-red trim. She was young and very beautiful, with pale skin and dark hair and eyes.

He tried to focus his attention entirely on his training, but he could feel the girl staring at him so intently it made the hair on the back of his neck prickle. *A woman with dark hair and eyes . . .* His mother's words in the dream. He glanced up at her again. Octavia was whispering to her, but her attention was so fixed on him that she seemed not to be listening. She was Roman, and his mother's prophecy came to him like a blow.

What decent woman would come to a ludus? Was she, like Octavia, inflamed by lust for men who drew blood? His mind cried out against her even as he found himself attracted to her.

She stood like a goddess above him, uncaring and untouchable. Desire and anger filled Atretes. He stopped his practice. Turning, he faced her boldly, his eyes meeting hers. Raising one eyebrow, he held her gaze, then, mockingly, held out a hand to her. His meaning was clear, but rather than laugh and call down encouragement as Octavia did, the girl in blue put a hand to her heart and drew back in embarrassment. Bato spoke to the two women and they turned away and went inside the main building.

Bato joined Atretes in the baths. "Octavia was delighted that you noticed her today," he said, leaning against a stone pillar, one towel wrapped around his waist, another slung over his powerful shoulder.

"The gesture was not meant for her," Atretes said, coming out of the water and taking a towel from a shelf.

"The Lady Julia is beautiful enough to make a man forget himself and his hatred of Rome," Bato said with wry humor.

A muscle tightened in Atretes' cheek, but he made no answer.

"She's married to Caius Polonius Urbanus, a man who hovers on the edge of high circles. I've heard he has a questionable bloodline and even more questionable character. His fortune came through her. Her first husband was old and died within months of their marriage. Her father relinquished his rights to her inheritance and turned the management over to his son, Marcus, a shrewd investor, but now Urbanus is said to be donating her fortune to the chariot races."

Atretes pulled a fresh tunic over his head and glowered at him as he tied a belt around his waist. "Why regale me with the lady's private life?"

"Because it's the first time I've seen a woman turn your head. A Roman woman." He straightened and smiled sardonically. "Don't let it dismay you, Atretes. Her father is an Ephesian who bought his citizenship with gold and influence."

He dreamed of his mother again that night and, as she prophesied, it was the Lady Julia in blue who came to him through the mists of the black forest.

Hadassah returned to the marketplace, seeking out a particular stall she had visited yesterday with her mistress. The Roman proprietor sold fruit, and Julia had purchased grapes to eat on her walk to the temple of Hera. Hadassah had noticed a small symbol carved in the counter. She had traced the fish and looked up. The proprietor had looked straight into her eyes and nodded once as he continued his bargaining with Julia. Hadassah had felt a surge of joyous hope swell within her.

Eager to return to the stall, she wove her way among the throng of people. When she found it, she stood aside while the merchant sold apples to a Greek servant. "I will have plums for you tomorrow, Callistus."

"At a better price than last week, I hope, Trophimus."

Trophimus waved him off good-naturedly and smiled at her. "Have you returned for more grapes for your mistress?"

She hesitated, searching his eyes. Had she misunderstood yesterday? He waited without pressing her further. She looked at the counter and didn't see the sign. Then, moving a basket of figs to one side, she found it. She glanced up at him and traced the small carving of the fish. Her heart pounding, she whispered, "Jesus Christ, Son of God, Savior."

Warmth filled his expression. "Jesus is Lord," he said and put his hand over hers. "I knew the moment you came yesterday that you were of the body."

She let out her breath, the rush of relief so great it almost overwhelmed her. Tears filled her eyes. "Praise God. It has been so long . . . "

Trophimus glanced around and then leaned closer. He told her the place and time believers gathered together each night. "Knock once, wait, and then three times. The door will be opened to you. Your name?"

"Hadassah, slave of Julia Valerian, wife of Caius Polonius Urbanus."

"Hadassah. I will tell our brothers and sisters to expect you."

Filled with joy and anticipation, Hadassah returned to the villa in renewed spirits. Julia always went out, leaving her free to pray in the garden. Tonight, she would worship among friends.

Late in the afternoon, Caius entered Julia's chambers as Hadassah helped her prepare to go out for the evening. A heated argument began.

"If you've time enough to spare Octavia, you can spare me a few hours of your precious time tonight!" Caius said. "Anicetus will be insulted if you don't attend his birthday celebration."

Julia sat before her mirror watching Hadassah arrange her hair, pretending indifference to her husband's anger. Only the rigidness of her back acknowledged his demands.

"I don't care if Anicetus is insulted," she said. "Make whatever excuse you like, Caius. Calabah has invited me to attend a play."

"To Hades with Calabah!" he said, furious. "I have asked very little of you lately. I *need* you tonight."

Julia met his gaze in her mirror. "You need me? How exquisite." Fueled by information agents had brought her only that afternoon, Julia turned slowly, hands folded lightly in her lap. Let him beg. "Why tonight, Caius?" she said, daring him to tell her the truth. She knew why he needed her at the feast. She wondered if he had the audacity to admit it himself.

"Anicetus admires you," he said, avoiding her eyes. "He's a business associate of mine. It wouldn't harm you to offer him a smile or occasional harmless flirtation." He poured himself some wine.

She smiled faintly, enjoying his torment. It wasn't her fault he was such a fool. Let him boil in his own blood. "I'll not have that foul cretin pawing me because you owe him money."

Caius turned and stared at her. "You've been spying on me." His hand whitened on the goblet. "Calabah's suggestion, my sweet?" he said dryly.

"I've a mind of my own, Caius. It was a simple matter to learn what was going on." She gave a mocking laugh. "Your lack of luck at the races has become legend. It seems everyone in Rome knew of your losses. Everyone but me, that is." Her voice rose.

"You've gone through two hundred thousand sesterces of *my* money in less than a year!"

Caius set the goblet down slowly. "Leave us," he ordered Hadassah in a tone full of venom. As she started for the door, Julia spoke. "And if I don't wish her to go?"

"Then let her stay and see what I do to her."

Julia gestured for her to leave. "Wait in the corridor. I'll summon you in a few minutes."

"Yes, my lady." Hadassah closed the door quietly behind her, thankful Julia hadn't tested Urbanus' patience any further. She doubted her mistress knew the level of his brutality. Their angry voices could be heard clearly in the corridor.

"Seeing as you are so well informed, Julia, you'll understand why it's paramount for you to attend this evening!"

"Let Anicetus have his pound of flesh, Caius. Your heart might weigh that much!"

"You will attend tonight whether you like it or not. Now go get ready!"

"I will not!" Julia stormed in response. "Take one of your *other* women if you are so eager for someone to take to Anicetus' feast. Or even another *man* if you so prefer. I do not care what you do! But I will go nowhere with you, tonight or any other night!"

Glass shattered and Julia screamed in rage. "How dare you break my things!"

She cried out again, this time in pain. Caius spoke again, his tone dripping with mockery, taunting her. Her response was full of defiance. She cried out again.

Biting her lip, Hadassah clenched her hands, feeling helpless, wanting to flee their madness.

Urbanus spoke again, low and cold this time. More glass shattered, and then the door burst open and he stormed out, his face livid with rage. He grabbed Hadassah and flung her toward the open door. "See that your mistress is ready to leave in an hour or I'll have the skin flogged off of your back."

Hadassah hurried into the room, afraid of what he had done to Julia. "My lady . . . "

Julia was sitting with amazing calm on the end of the big bed she had shared with Caius during the first months of their marriage. Blood trickled from the corner of her mouth.

"My lady, are you all right? Your mouth . . . you're bleeding."

Julia raised shaking fingers to her lips and dabbed at the blood. She stared at it. "I hate him," she said with a chilling intensity. "I wish he were dead!" She clenched her fist, staring darkly into space. "May the gods curse his black heart."

Hadassah was horrified at such words, almost as horrified as she was by the look in Julia's eyes. "I'll get you water."

"Get me nothing!" Julia said fiercely, rising to her feet. "Just be silent and let me think!" Face white and rigid, she began to pace. "He's not going to get away with treating me like this." She waved her hand impatiently. "Go and have a message sent to Calabah that I can't attend the play with her this evening. I'll visit her tomorrow and explain everything."

When Hadassah returned, Julia was standing at her cosmetics table, running her fingers along the colored glass pots. More than half lay shattered on the floor, along with expensive amphoras of scented oils. Julia looked at the destruction in silence, her eyes burning with a fierce anger. She looked over what remained and picked up one.

"Anicetus finds me desirable," she said, her knuckles whitening on the small pot. "Caius used to be jealous at the way he stared at me. He used to say if Anicetus ever so much as touched my hand, he would slit his throat." She ran her fingertip around the rim of the pot, a faint smile curving her mouth. "Bring me the red palus with gold-and-jeweled trim. Caius says I look like a goddess when I wear it for him, and I will look like a goddess this evening. Bring me the gold brooch he gave me as a wedding present."

"What do you mean to do, my lady?" Hadassah said, afraid for her.

She dipped her finger into the pot of red. "Caius wants me to be charming and beautiful this evening," she said and ran the rich, sensual color along her full lower lip. She pressed her lips together and looked at her reflection. "I'm going to give him what he wants, and more."

By the time Caius came back, Julia was more dazzling than Hadassah had ever seen her. When Caius saw her, his mood changed. He looked her over with unconcealed admiration. "So you've decided to help me as a wife should," he said, sliding his hand down her arm.

Julia turned before him coquettishly. "Do you think Anicetus will approve?"

"He will be panting at your heels." He caught hold of her and kissed her. "Had we time, I'd keep you here with me all night . . . "

"As you used to," Julia purred and then turned her face away when he tried to kiss her. "You'll smear my makeup."

"Later. We'll put in an appearance, charm Anicetus out of his foul mood, and come home."

She kissed him lightly on the throat. The mark of her lips was like a slash of blood. Moving out of his arms, she stood for Hadassah to rearrange the folds of her veils and clasp the gold broach securely. Hadassah looked into her eyes and again felt a stab of fear for her. Surely she knew whatever vengeance she planned on Urbanus would rebound on her.

Praying under her breath, Hadassah watched them go down the stairs. She returned to Julia's chambers. She swept up and discarded the shattered amphoras. Opening the doors into the peristyle, she aired the room while washing the scented oils from the marble floor. When her work was done, she draped her shawl over her hair and went out into the night to find the house where believers in Jesus gathered.

The streets of Rome were like a maze, made even more confusing by the darkness. She knew many of the streets well since her sojourns to the marketplace for Julia were frequent. She found the house without much difficulty. Ironically, it was not far from the temple of Mars, Rome's god of war.

She knocked once, waited, and then knocked three times. The door opened. "Your name, please."

"Hadassah, slave of Julia Valerian, wife of Caius Polonius Urbanus."

The woman smiled and opened the door for her to come in. "You are welcome. Trophimus is here with his family. He said to expect you. Come." She ushered her into a room crowded with people of all ages and social stations. Hadassah saw the merchant among them. Smiling, he came to her, took her firmly by the shoulders, and kissed her on both cheeks in greeting. "Sit with my wife and me, little sister," he said. He took her arm and led her between other curious guests to his family. "Eunice, this is the girl I told you about." Eunice smiled and kissed her in greeting. "Brothers and sisters," he addressed those assembled, "this is Hadassah, of whom I spoke."

Others greeted her. Geta, Basemath, Fulvia, Callistus, Asyncritus, Lydia, Phlegon, Ahikam . . . their names ran together. Hadassah felt embraced by their love.

Asyncritus took control of the gathering. "Silence please, brothers and sisters. Our time together is brief. Let us begin by singing praises to our Lord."

Hadassah closed her eyes, letting the music and words of a hymn she had never heard wash over her and renew her. It spoke of hardship and faith, of God's deliverance from evil. She felt revived and far removed from the troubled lives of Decimus and Phoebe, Marcus and Julia. Caught in the mire of gods and goddesses, in the quest for happiness and the satiation of their own ambitions, they were dying. Here, in this small, modest room, among these people, Hadassah felt the presence of God's peace.

Hadassah saw freemen among slaves, rich sitting beside the poor, the old with small children on their lap, all raising their voices in harmony. She smiled and wanted to laugh with joy. Her heart was so full, her sense of homecoming so powerful, she could only rejoice.

One hymn among the many was familiar to her, a beloved psalm of David that she had sung often to Decimus and Phoebe during her brief time as their servant. Eyes closed, hands open with palms up in offering to God, she sang from her heart, unaware of others around her stopping to listen. Only when she finished did she realize. Blushing, she lowered her head, embarrassed that she had drawn attention to herself.

"God has blessed us with a sister who can sing," Trophimus announced in good humor, and others laughed. Eunice took her hand and squeezed it gently.

Asyncritus spread his hands, *"Make a joyful shout to the Lord, all you lands!"* he said with a great gladness, and the others joined in, *"Serve the Lord with gladness; come before His presence with singing. Know that the Lord, He is God; it is He who has made us, and not we ourselves; we are His people and the sheep of His pasture . . ."*

Hadassah raised her head again and spoke the well-remembered words of David's psalm, *"Enter into His gates with thanksgiving, and into His courts with praise. Be thankful to Him, and bless His name. For the Lord is good; His mercy is everlasting, and His truth endures to all generations."*

A worn scroll was unrolled by an elder. "We will continue our reading of Matthew's memoirs tonight." Hadassah had never heard the memoirs of the apostles before, for she had been reared on the Jewish Scriptures and her father's memory of Jesus' teachings. To hear the written words of Matthew, who had walked for three years with the Lord, made her tremble. She drank in the Word and took sustenance from it.

After the reading, the scroll was rolled again and placed carefully in the hands of another elder. Unleavened bread and a cup of wine were passed among those gathered. Christ's words were whispered over and over as each partook of and passed the Communion feast from hand to hand. "This is my body . . . This is my blood . . . Take and eat in remembrance of me. . . ." When all had been served, they sang a solemn hymn of the redeeming love of Christ, the deliverer.

"Are there any new believers among us who would share their testimony?"

Hadassah felt people glancing at her and blushed again, lowering her head, her heart beating fast and hard. Trophimus leaned over and patted her clasped hands paternally. "There, there," he teased. "We expect no polished oratory. Only an encouraging word from a little sister who is new among us."

"Leave her be, Trophimus," Eunice said in her defense. "We're new to her. You said nothing for a full year."

"I'm always at a loss for words."

"I want to speak," Hadassah said and rose. She looked shyly at those around her. "Forgive me if I stumble. It's been so long since I've been able to speak freely among people who know God." Her throat closed and she swallowed and prayed God would give her words and courage.

"I am not new to the faith. My father told me of Jesus from the time I was born. He knew the Scriptures and taught me all he remembered of the Torah and the fulfillment of the prophets and God's promises in Jesus. When I was very young, Father took me to the River Jordan and baptized me in the same place where John had seen the dove come down on Jesus and heard God's voice say, 'This is my Son, in whom I am well pleased.'"

"Praise the Lord," someone said.

Asyncritus sat down slowly. "Your father knew the Lord when he walked on this earth?"

Would they believe her if she told them the full truth? She looked around again, into each face so open and filled with anxious expectation. How could she not tell them when they so hungered for any word of their risen Lord?

"My father was the only surviving son of a widow who lived in Jerusalem. When he was a young man, he was taken by fever and died. The Lord heard his mother weeping and came to comfort her. He touched my father and raised him from Sheol."

"Praise God," several murmured raptly. An excited hum of whispers spread through the room and a man near the back stood excitedly, "What was your father's name?"

"Hananiah Bar-Jonah of the tribe of Benjamin."

"I have heard of him!" the man said to those around him. He looked at her again. "He had a small pottery shop in Galilee."

She nodded, unable to speak.

"The man who brought me to the Lord met him many years ago," another said.

"Where is your father now?" someone else asked.

"He is with the Lord."

There was a hush of reverent silence and Hadassah told them the rest. "We always went to Jerusalem during Passover to meet with other believers of the Way. Each year, we gathered in an upper room and my father told how Jesus fulfilled each of the elements of Passover. But the last time we went, a revolt had begun and the city was in chaos. Many of our friends left the city because of the persecution. My father wouldn't go. And then, the zealots closed the gates and thousands were trapped. Father went out among his people. He never came back."

"And your family, little sister?" Eunice said, cupping Hadassah's hand with her own. "What became of them?"

Her voice trembled as she told them. She lowered her head, almost ashamed that she stood before them, the only survivor of her family, the least deserving of life. "I don't know why the Lord spared me."

"Perhaps for this moment, little sister," Asyncritus said solemnly. "Your words have encouraged me in a time of doubting." His eyes were full of tears. "God answers our needs in all things."

Hadassah sat down again as others spoke of answered prayers and changed lives. Needs were mentioned and provisions made. Requests for prayer were raised and the names of brothers and sisters imprisoned or under threat mentioned.

Hadassah rose again. "May I make a request also?" They

encouraged her to do so. "Please pray for my masters, Decimus Vindacius Valerian, his wife, Phoebe, and their son, Marcus Lucianus. They are lost in a wilderness. Most of all, I beseech you to pray for my lady, Julia. She is on the road to destruction."

22

Hadassah returned to the villa spiritually replenished, unaware that disaster awaited.

She heard Julia screaming when she entered the peristyle. Racing up the steps into the triclinium, she ran through it into the open corridor that led to her mistress's chambers. A maid was crying hysterically outside Julia's door.

"He's going to beat her to death. What are we going to do?"

Julia's screams propelled Hadassah to act without thought of consequences. When she grasped the door handle, the other maid was galvanized as well. She tried to stop her. "You can't go in! He'll kill you!"

Hadassah shook her off, frantic to get to her mistress even as the other maid fled from the scene. When she entered the room, Julia was on the floor trying to scramble away from Urbanus as he whipped her. She screamed in pain as the whip tore the red fabric and reddened her skin.

"Stop, my lord!" Hadassah cried out, but, enraged, he went after Julia again. Hadassah tried to block him, but he knocked her aside. She scrambled to get in his path again and Julia tried to scurry away. He hit Hadassah a stunning blow, knocking her from her feet. "Get out!" he bellowed, kicking her hard in the side before turning on Julia again. "I'm going to kill you, you foul witch. By all the gods, I swear it."

He cornered Julia and she cowered, covering her head with her arms and screaming as the whip came down across her back.

Hadassah rose shakily, her vision blurred. Urbanus' violence was like a malevolent presence in the room, and she heard Julia's screams of terror and pain. Stumbling across the room, Hadassah threw herself over Julia to protect her. The bite of the whip made her gasp and flinch. Sobbing hysterically, Julia curled into a quivering ball beneath her.

Enraged, Urbanus spent his fury on Hadassah. When lashing her failed to satisfy him, he overturned Julia's desk, toppled a favored statue, and smashed her mirror. "I'm not done with you, Julia," he said and left.

Julia's heart slowed. "He's gone. Let me up." Hadassah didn't move. "Let me up before he comes back!" Julia struggled and Hadassah rolled to one side. Julia saw her face, ashen and still. "Hadassah!" Frightened, Julia put her ear near Hadassah's parted lips. She was barely breathing. Gathering her maid into her arms, Julia wept. "You saved me from him," she whispered, rocking her. She stroked the hair from her slave's white face and kissed her brow. "You'll be all right. You *will.*" She held her tightly and rocked her, the anger building inside her.

No more. No more of this, Urbanus!

The door opened slowly and a maid peered cautiously around the edge. Julia glared at her. "Where is my husband?" she said in a cold voice. The slave girl stood in the open doorway, another two behind her.

"Master Caius has left the villa," the first said.

"And so now you come to my aid," she said bitterly. "Coward. You're all cowards!" She saw their fear of her. It was right that they fear her. Every slave in this household was going to the arena for leaving her at the mercy of Caius. She held Hadassah closer, stroking the hair back from her white face. Every one of them, except this one who had protected her. She could feel Hadassah's warm blood soaking into the sleeve of her dress.

Raising her head, she glared at the slaves standing in the doorway awaiting instructions. Cowards! Fools! They deserved death. She hated every one of them. "Come and see to her," she ordered, and two rushed into the room and bent to take Hadassah. "Salt her wounds and bind them and keep her hidden from my husband." She dug her fingernails into the arm of one of them. "If she dies, I'll have the skin stripped from your backs. Do you understand?"

"Yes, my lady," she said quickly, terrified.

"Hurry!" Julia knew she had to leave the villa before Caius returned. Until Caius spent his rage and found his reason, her life was in danger. If he couldn't find her, he would have time to think and regain control of himself. Without pausing to change her tattered clothing, Julia drew a voluminous cloak around herself and fled into the night.

She ran all the way to Calabah's and pounded on her door. A handsome Greek slave admitted her. "Tell Calabah I'm here," she said, standing just inside the door. He made no move to obey her, and she pushed him aside and entered the larger room where

Calabah held her gatherings. "Tell Calabah I'm here," she said again, eyes flashing.

"Lady Calabah is occupied."

Julia turned and glared up at him. "This is a matter of grave importance."

"She said she wasn't to be disturbed."

"She will understand!" she said, exasperated. "Stop just standing there and gawking at me and do as you're told!"

He left the room and Julia paced in agitation. She hugged the heavy cape around her, but could not ward off the chill that was seeping into her bones. The Greek returned after several long moments.

"Lady Calabah will see you in her chambers in a few minutes, my lady."

"I have to see her *now!*" Julia brushed past him again impatiently. She came to an open doorway and saw a maid holding a light robe as Calabah stood naked beside the bed. "Oh," she said and blushed. Calabah glanced toward her, her expression enigmatic. She seemed unembarrassed, standing with her arms slightly outstretched so the maid could drape a toga around her.

"Another emergency, Julia?" she said ruefully, a hint of annoyance in her manner.

Julia was dismayed at such a cool greeting. She never thought that Calabah would be angry with her over her cancellation. "I'm sorry I missed the play, Calabah. Caius forced me to go with him. There was simply nothing I could do—"

"Nonsense," Calabah said. "I'm growing very tired of your histrionics, Julia," she said with weary patience. "What momentous thing happened to you this time that you felt impelled to interrupt my evening?"

Julia entered the room and dropped the heavy cloak, turning so Calabah could see the tatters of her red palus and the welts on her back. She was satisfied to hear her gasp.

"Caius did this to you?"

"Yes," Julia said. "He went mad tonight, Calabah. He would've killed me if Hadassah hadn't intervened."

"Your maid?"

"She threw herself over me and took the rest of the beating." She started to weep again. "I think he's killed her. She—"

"Never mind your slave. Sit a moment and get control of yourself," Calabah interrupted and led her to the bed. She put her hands on Julia's trembling shoulders and forced her to sit. "I'll have salve brought for your back." She spoke with one of her slaves. Closing the door, she turned toward her. "Now tell me what happened to make Caius lose his temper so completely?"

Tense, Julia got up. "Nereus told me yesterday how many thousands of sesterces Caius owed Anicetus. He said Caius has been trying to sell some of the investments Marcus made on my behalf, but couldn't."

"Couldn't?"

"Apparently, Marcus arranged to be informed immediately upon the event of certain properties being placed on the market," she said as she paced restlessly. "Caius knew Marcus would tell me what was going on. That left him in the position of trying to buy time until he could arrange for enough money to repay Anicetus."

She glanced at Calabah. "Anicetus had a birthday celebration this evening, and Caius *insisted* I go." She stopped and shivered. "I'm cold, Calabah." Calabah got her cloak and put it around her shoulders. Julia felt wretched.

"Anicetus finds me beautiful," she said. "He's made his desire for me all too obvious. Caius was always jealous before and told me to sit as far away from him as possible so as not to encourage him. This evening, Caius wanted me to *smile* and *flirt* with that despicable cretin. He said Anicetus would be insulted if I didn't attend his birthday celebration. Of course, after Nereus told me the truth, I knew why Caius was so insistent. He wanted Anicetus in a good mood when he pleaded for additional time to repay his debt."

She sat down on the bed again, her face rigid. "Well, his debt is canceled."

"Canceled," Calabah said dully and turned away. She sighed heavily. "How did you manage that?"

"I made arrangements with Anicetus."

"What sort of arrangements, Julia?"

"I spent an hour entertaining him in his private chambers," she said and immediately rebelled against the shame her admission caused. She came to her feet. "Caius has been unfaithful to me often enough!" she said defensively. "It's time he knew what it felt like."

Calabah looked oddly pained. "Did you enjoy yourself?"

"I enjoyed the look on Caius' face while I smiled and flirted with Anicetus as he asked me to do. I enjoyed the look on his face when I left the feast without him. I enjoyed imagining what he was going through the entire time I was gone. Oh, yes, I enjoyed every minute of that."

"And it never once occurred to you that Caius would retaliate?"

"I didn't care!" Julia said and looked away as her eyes filled with tears. "But I've never seen him so enraged, Calabah. He was like a madman."

"You humiliated him before his peers."

Julia looked up angrily. "You're defending him? After all the times he's made me suffer?"

"I wouldn't think of defending him. I despise him for the things he's done to you for his own pleasure. But think, Julia! You know Caius. You know his pride. You know his rages. He'll kill you for this."

Julia paled. "Then I won't go back."

"You'll have to go back or lose everything." Calabah sat down beside her and took her hand. She let out her breath slowly and squeezed Julia's hand. "You're going to have to protect yourself."

"But how?" Julia said, her eyes swimming in frightened tears.

Calabah tipped Julia's chin toward her and searched her eyes intently. "I'm going to tell you something I've never shared with anyone else. Can I trust you to keep my confidence?"

Julia blinked as she stared into the depths of Calabah's dark eyes. They seemed fathomless and mysterious, full of secrets. "Yes," she said, trembling slightly.

Calabah leaned forward and kissed her softly on the lips. "I know you will." She laid the palm of her hand lightly against Julia's cheek, her eyes beautiful and mesmerizing. "I've known from the beginning you and I would be very close friends." Her touch lingered briefly and then slid away, leaving Julia with a strange sensation of uneasiness.

Calabah stood and moved gracefully away. "Everyone believes my husband Aurius died of apoplexy." She turned and looked back at Julia, wanting to judge her reaction when she told her the truth. "In fact, I poisoned him." She watched Julia's eyes widen with surprise, but not disapproval. She was curious, wanting explanations, and Calabah continued.

"Marriage to him had become intolerable. He was old and repulsive when I married him, but I remained a constant wife. I managed his financial affairs, his appointments, his estate matters. I gave him sound political advice. I rebuilt his dwindling fortune. Then, after one small indiscretion on my part, Aurius threatened to divorce me."

Calabah smiled cynically. "We live in a man's world, Julia. Our husbands can commit adultery as often as desire comes upon them, but one offense on the part of a woman can cost her her life. Not that Aurius would have had the courage to threaten me with death. No, he hated me, but he was afraid, too. He used to say it was my intellect that made him fall in love with me, that and my sensuality. Later, he was threatened by both." She gave a soft, cold laugh. "All he said was he wanted to be free again. Had he been, he would have destroyed everything I'd built. He would have left me with nothing for all my effort, and Roman law would've blessed his right to do so."

She looked at Julia. "His death was quick and merciful. I didn't want him to feel any pain. I planned a feast and entertainment. Those who were present the evening Aurius died were convinced he'd had a brain seizure." Her mouth curved. "I arranged for a physician to confirm their supposition, in case questions arose later. None did."

Calabah sat down beside Julia again. "Of course, your situation is different. Caius is young. You'd have to use something slower acting in order for his death to appear natural. There are little-known poisons that cause high fevers very similar to the ones so common around Rome during the flood season these days." She took Julia's hand. It was cold and clammy. "You're afraid. I understand. Believe me, I was, too, but after all he's put you through, and with the way he now threatens you, what choices have you? I know an old woman who served Augustus Caesar's wife, Livia. She has great knowledge and can help us."

"But must I *murder* him?" Julia said, pulling her hand away and rising. She wanted to flee.

"Is it murder to defend yourself? Do you know what becomes of a woman without family and connections? She's destitute and at the mercy of a very cruel world. Aurius held a sword over my head, and I chose to fight back."

Julia felt faint and dizzy. "Isn't there another way?" she said shakily and touched her forehead, feeling beads of perspiration break out.

Calabah let the silence fill the room for several moments

before she spoke again. She knew all of Julia's weaknesses, and now was the time to use them. "You could go to your mother and father and tell them what's happened."

"No, I couldn't do that," Julia said quickly.

"Your father has power and influence. Tell him how Caius has beaten you and let him crush him."

"You don't understand, Calabah. My father would demand to know why my husband beat me. He thinks I'm to blame for Claudius' death. If he found out about Anicetus, he wouldn't take my side."

Satisfied, Calabah moved to Julia's next ally. "What about your mother?"

"No," Julia said, shaking her head. "I don't want her to know about any of this. I don't want her to think ill of me."

Calabah smiled faintly. Julia's pride was as great as Caius'. "What about Marcus?" she said, moving to eliminate the last possibility.

"Marcus would give Caius some of his own medicine, then threaten him on top of it," Julia said, finding some solace in this potential solution.

"All of which would only put you in more danger," Calabah said with cool rationale. "However, there is another possibility you might consider. Encourage Marcus to destroy Caius financially. Once your money is all gone, Caius will undoubtedly agree to a divorce," she said smoothly, watching Julia's expected response in private amusement.

"And where will that leave me? No, that's no solution, Calabah. I'd be without an aureus to my name, back in my father's household with him dictating my every movement. I swore I'd never allow that to happen ever again."

Calabah fell silent, knowing Julia would eventually agree with her about what must be done. She had known from the very beginning when she had fanned the lust of Julia and Caius' relationship that it would end this way.

Julia paced, searching for justifications and rationalizations. She found them, along with a wave of violent and confusing emotions. "He's used me in ways that are abominable. He's been unfaithful. He's thrown my money away on gambling and other women. Then he tries to use Anicetus' desire for me to his own advantage. I save him, and is he grateful when his debt is canceled? No! He beats me and swears he'll kill me." Trembling violently, she sat down and buried her face in her hands. *"He deserves to die!"*

Calabah put her arm around her shoulders. "Hush, now, Julia. Caius has brought all this upon himself," she said, neatly absolving her of guilt.

"But how can I accomplish it? I'd have to live with him again, and I'm terrified of going back."

"I still have some influence over Caius. I'll speak with him over the next few days and make him realize that abusing you would bring certain disaster down upon his head. He's not a complete fool, Julia. He'll exercise control in order to protect himself from your brother and your father, but only for a time. We both know Caius. He'll be thinking of ways to hurt you, and time will erode what control he has over his temper. Don't look so frightened. Trust me. A few doses during one week, and his health will decline. During the weeks that follow, Caius will be no real threat to you."

Julia's heart beat like a trapped bird before a snake. "And if he becomes suspicious?"

"Julia, darling, forgive me for telling you this, but Caius wouldn't think you capable of such cunning. He's always thought you intellectually unremarkable. He doesn't appreciate you as I do. It was his lust for you that brought him to his knees. You needn't worry about his becoming suspicious. It'd never occur to him that you'd be capable of saving yourself from him." She squeezed her hand softly. "But you must act wisely."

"What do you mean?" Julia stammered.

"Tend him with care. Weep for him. Sacrifice to the gods in his behalf. Consult with several physicians. I will supply you with names of those you can trust. Above all, Julia, no matter what he says, what accusations he makes, do *not* answer in kind. Never lose your temper with him or all is lost. Do you understand? Let those around you see you behave as a loving and devoted wife. And finally, Julia, *grieve* for him when the time comes."

Julia nodded slowly, her face ashen. She raised her head, her cheeks already streaked with tears.

"Don't look so sad, my sweet little friend. There's no such thing as right and wrong in this world, no black and white. Life is filled with gray areas, and the most primal instinct of all is survival. The strong survive. Not necessarily the strong of body, but the strong of mind. You will come through this."

The maid arrived with the salve. "I'll see to her," Calabah told the slave and closed the door. "Remove your palus, Julia, and lie face down on my bed," Calabah said. "I'll be as gentle as I can."

Julia drew a gasp at the first touch. It was like fire. Then the sensation cooled, and she relaxed and allowed Calabah to tend her wounds. "What would I do without you, Calabah?"

"Haven't I said from the first? I'm always here. You'll never have to do without me." Calabah's dark eyes glowed with black fire. "When all this unpleasantness is over, you must set your mind to put it behind you and forget it ever happened. Only then will you be able to grasp true happiness. I'll show you the way." She ran her hand slowly down over Julia's back. "You have so much yet to learn. Life is like a play, Julia, and we are the writers who create it. Think of this as merely one act . . . one small act with many more to come. . . ."

23

Hadassah roused when someone touched her forehead. "She's perspiring," Julia said.

"She has a fever, my lady. It's not severe. We're watching over her closely," Elisheba said timidly.

Hadassah opened her eyes and found she lay facedown on a pallet. The floor was dark stone like the floors in the small chambers in winding corridors beneath the villa, where household supplies were stored. Someone had lifted the blankets from her and now slid them gently up to cover her to the shoulders. "The wounds look raw," Julia said.

"We packed them with salt to prevent infection, my lady," Lavinia said in a tone so meek and frightened, Hadassah knew something was wrong. She moved and sucked in a soft gasp as the searing pain made her wish for oblivion again.

"Try not to move, Hadassah," Julia whispered, a firm hand on the girl's trembling shoulder. "You'll make the pain worse and open your wounds again. I've only come to see that you are being properly tended," she said.

Hadassah heard the edge in her mistress's voice and sensed she was speaking more to Lavinia, the maid who had tried to stop her from entering Julia's room and interfering with Urbanus, than to herself. It must be that Lavinia now nursed her. Elisheba was crying and Julia told her coldly to hush.

Hadassah heard a soft rustle of movement as Julia rose. She gave a curt order to the maids to bring food and wine and be quick. Steeling herself against the pain, Hadassah pushed herself into a sitting position. She was very weak, and her stiff, scabbing back stung and throbbed in protest of even that small effort. Julia's face was too shadowed to see clearly. Had Urbanus marked her? When Julia turned, Hadassah saw he hadn't and let out her breath. "You are well," she said in relief.

Julia's face softened. She knelt down and took Hadassah's hand. "A few bruises, nothing more. Caius would've killed me if not for you." She put Hadassah's hand against her own pale cheek, her eyes moist as they looked into hers. "What will I do without you?"

"Then I am to be sent away," Hadassah said bleakly. Urbanus could order her death for disobeying his command, even when his command would have meant her mistress's death.

Julia avoided her eyes. She didn't want Hadassah in the villa when she returned. It would be difficult enough to do what Calabah instructed without Hadassah present. "You're not safe here," she said, which was true enough. "Caius will kill you if he can get his hands on you. So I'm sending you back to my mother. When circumstances change, I'll send for you."

What circumstances could change? Hadassah wondered. Urbanus had always despised her. It was strange, considering the instinctive revulsion she had felt toward him from the beginning as well. Perhaps his hatred of her was in response to that. She couldn't say.

"But what about you, my lady?" Hadassah said, afraid for Julia. Urbanus was a violent, unprincipled man with dark passions. "He said he would kill you." And Hadassah had no doubt he would do it when next his temper erupted in such madness.

Julia's eyes flickered, but she remained firm in her conviction. "I'm out of his reach. I'm staying with Calabah. She's with him right now. She has influence with Caius, and she'll make him regret what he's done to me. By the time she's finished telling him the risks he's taken, he'll be begging forgiveness from me and pleading to have me back again."

Hadassah searched her mistress's face and saw no sign of compassion or hope. But there was something shining in Julia's eyes that was frightening in its intensity. She wanted revenge. "My lady . . . ," Hadassah said, reaching out with her free hand to touch her cheek.

Julia let go of Hadassah's hand and stood abruptly. Sometimes Hadassah made her very uncomfortable. It was as though the slave girl could look into her soul and see her thoughts. "It'll all work out for the best," she said and forced a smile. She didn't want Hadassah to guess what she intended to do, for if she did Hadassah would try to dissuade her, and Julia didn't know if she was strong enough to ward off Hadassah's reasoning. She thought of Calabah and felt even more determined. Caius was a threat to her life and he must die. She had done nothing to deserve such foul, brutal treatment at the hands of her husband.

Lavinia entered the room with a tray laden with bread, fruit, sliced meat, and a jug of wine. The slave girl was trembling violently as she set the tray down before Hadassah. She gave Hadassah a pleading look. "Leave us," Julia said contemptuously, and Lavinia fled the chamber.

Julia's demeanor changed when they were alone again. She came and knelt down before Hadassah, her expression full of uncertainty. "Tell Mother and Father and Marcus nothing of what's happened. It would only make things more difficult with Caius. I must try to work things out with him and return to the villa. If Marcus hears what he did to me, I fear what he would do in retaliation."

The possibilities were too grim to contemplate. "I understand, my lady."

Julia bit her lip and appeared to want to say more, but when she did, she revealed nothing. "I've problems enough without Marcus adding to them," she said, more troubled than Hadassah had ever seen her. "I must go." Her eyes welled. "I'll miss you," she whispered hoarsely and leaned forward to kiss Hadassah's cheek. "I'll miss you more than you can know."

Hadassah captured her hand in both of hers, frightened for her and wanting to stay close. "Please don't send me away from you!"

For a brief moment, Julia looked ready to give in to her plea. Then her eyes narrowed in even harder determination. "If you want to make things easier on me, you must go, and as soon as possible."

Hadassah blushed, ashamed. Urbanus had never concealed his dislike of her. Perhaps her presence during the past months had only served to add tension to an already volatile relationship. "Then I will pray for you, my lady. I will pray God protects you."

"I can protect myself," Julia said as she stood and drew her hand firmly from Hadassah's clasp. She paused in the doorway. "I've left orders that you be served whatever you want."

While Hadassah was healing, she learned through Elisheba and Lavinia what was happening in the household. After meeting with Calabah, the master came home and ordered wine be brought to him. He drank the jug dry, staring at nothing, his countenance so dark the servants were terrified. Marcus came to see his sister the next morning and was told she was visiting friends. "He asked to speak with you then," Elisheba told her, "but we told him you'd left the villa on errands for your lady."

Just the mention of Marcus made her stomach tighten strangely. "Did he look well?"

"Indeed, yes," Lavinia said with a dreamy smile. "If I were fortunate enough to be slave to a man like that, I'd serve him in whatever way he asked."

Julia returned to Caius' villa with Calabah at the end of the week and the three of them spoke at length in the bibliotheca. Elisheba brought wine to them and was dismissed. The two women left together an hour later. Elisheba recounted the visit to Hadassah. "The Lady Calabah said, 'We'll return tomorrow afternoon when you've had time to think things over carefully, Caius. Hopefully, you will have come to your senses by then.'"

"He was ill this morning," Lavinia said.

"And no wonder. He's been drunk all week."

Elisheba brought Hadassah a new tunic, but even the soft wool felt torturous on her back. "You should stay a few more days," Lavinia said.

"Lady Julia wanted me to leave as soon as possible," Hadassah said. If Julia was returning tomorrow, then her presence might well put her mistress in jeopardy again if Urbanus found out she still was there. She slowly wound the Hebrew sash around her waist, securing it as gently as possible.

She had to stop several times on the way to the Valerian villa. Urbanus' villa was built in the affluent area of the city, and the Valerians were in the older section on the other side of the Palentine. She took her time, stopping to buy something to eat on her way. Weak and tired, she sat down near a fountain to rest. The sound of the water was soothing and she longed to doze in the sunshine. She ate the fruit and bread she had purchased and felt strengthened.

Enoch was surprised to see her. "The master is at his office on the Tiber, but the Lady Phoebe is in the gardens. I'll take you to her." He didn't ask why Julia had sent her home. He only seemed pleased she was there. "My lady," he said when they reached Phoebe sitting on a bench beneath the rose lattice. "Hadassah has returned to you."

Phoebe glanced up and her face, quiet and calm, lit with a smile. She rose, and Hadassah saw she meant to embrace her. Before she could do such an inappropriate thing before Enoch, Hadassah knelt quickly and bent forward, touching Phoebe's feet in an act of humble obedience. "My Lady Julia has returned me to your service."

"Rise, child." She cupped Hadassah's chin as she did so, looking upon her with open affection. "May the gods be praised. Your master and I have sorely missed your songs and stories these past months." She took her hand and began to walk along the pathway. "But tell me about my daughter! We've heard little from her lately."

Hadassah answered her questions as vaguely as possible, while at the same time trying to reassure her. Phoebe seemed content and didn't pursue the subject, leaving Hadassah grateful she hadn't been put into the position of having to lie.

"You will be relieved of your duties for this evening, Hadassah," she said. "Lord Decimus and I are spending the evening with his business associates."

Marcus entered the villa during the early evening hours. He was tired and depressed. Enoch informed him that his parents were out for the evening, and he felt the added burden of loneliness. When asked if he wished something to eat, he declined. Nor did he partake of wine. He had been given disturbing information today and wasn't sure how best to handle it.

He went out into the gardens to try to clear his mind, but his troubled thoughts obliterated what peace he had hoped to find among his mother's trees and flowers. His heart quickened sharply as he saw someone sitting on a bench near the end of the pathway.

"Hadassah?"

She rose slowly, oddly stiff, and faced him. "My lord."

The rush of emotion he felt at seeing her made him defensive. "What are you doing here?"

"Lady Julia sent me back."

"Why?"

She looked hurt by his curt question. "Her husband prefers someone else attend her needs, my lord."

Marcus leaned against the marble column. Trying to appear calm when he had received the information that afternoon had made his mind roil, and now Hadassah's unexpected presence sent his heart racing. "Just what are my sister's needs these days?" He strove to see her face in the starlight, but she kept her head down. "Rumors are rampant," he said after a long moment. "The latest story is that my sister spent an hour in Anicetus' private chambers, returning with signed papers canceling her husband's debts."

Hadassah said nothing.

"I know half a dozen men who owe Anicetus money. They're all afraid of ending up face down in the Tiber if they can't repay during the time allotted. Now, tell me, Hadassah. How did my sister *talk* Anicetus into *canceling* Caius' debts?"

Still Hadassah said nothing, but he could sense her tension.

Marcus straightened from the column and came toward her. "I want to know the truth and I want to know it now!"

"I know nothing of what you're saying, my lord."

"You don't know," he said and grabbed her arm as she drew back from him, "or you won't say." He jerked her toward him and she gave a sharp gasp of pain, then fell. Surprised, he caught her up in his arms before she hit the cobbled pathway. "Hadassah!" he said, dismayed. She was limp in his arms.

He carried her back quickly into the villa, alarmed that she had fainted, angry with himself for taking his frustrations out on her. Enoch glanced at him in surprise. "Bring me some wine, Enoch. She's fainted." The servant hastened to do his bidding as Marcus laid her down upon a couch. She moaned as he slid his arm from beneath her. He frowned. A spot of blood was seeping through the pale wool of her tunic. Turning her on her side, he drew the cloth back. Seeing a red welt on her shoulder, he cursed.

"She didn't look well when she returned this afternoon," Enoch said as he entered the room with a tray. "I'll see to her, my lord."

"Leave the wine and go," Marcus said tersely. "And close the doors behind you."

"Yes, my lord," Enoch said in surprise.

Marcus ripped open the back of her tunic from neck to waist. When he saw her back, he began to shake. How had a girl so small and seemingly fragile taken such a beating? And what could she have done to deserve it? He stared at the lash marks that had bruised and cut her flesh. A dozen strokes at least, and with a heavy hand. Even in high temper, Julia was incapable of such violence. It had to have been Urbanus.

Hadassah roused. Disoriented, she sat up and her tunic slid off of her shoulders. Eyes going wide, she caught it against her breasts and glanced up at Marcus. Her pale cheeks bloomed with color.

"Did Caius do that to you?" Marcus had never felt such a surge of hatred against any man, nor such a burning desire for vengeance.

She paled again and looked ready to faint. "It was my fault."

"Your fault?" he said, angry that she would defend him. "And what horrible thing did you do to deserve such a beating?"

She clenched the wool of her ruined tunic and lowered her head again. "I disobeyed him."

Marcus knew of men who beat their slaves for minor infractions, such as moving too slowly or being clumsy. Disobedience was another matter. If what Hadassah said was true, it was within Urbanus' right to kill her. Yet he knew Hadassah would do nothing without cause. "What was Julia's part in it?"

She looked up at him in dismay. "She would have stopped the beating if she could have, my lord. She saw that I was tended afterwards and sent me here for my safety."

It was uncharacteristic of Julia to do such a kindness without some ulterior motive of her own. Besides, Hadassah's answer came too quickly, as though she'd known she'd face the question and had prepared an answer beforehand. There was more to it than what she said, and Julia had something to do with it. He didn't press Hadassah, knowing her loyalty would keep her silent.

When he went to Julia's villa the next day, he half expected to be told again that she was visiting friends, but she was home, looking more beautiful than he had seen her. "Blue becomes you."

"So I've been told," she said, pleased by his compliment. "I love colors, myriad colors. I designed this palus myself," she said, turning so he could admire the rich blue wool and the trims of bright reds and yellows. A rose among wild flowers. The wide leather-and-brass belt reminded him of something Arria had worn. The thought made him uneasy.

"Caius isn't well," Julia said. "Let's walk in the garden so we won't disturb him." She looped her arm through his. "I've missed you so much, Marcus. Tell me what you've been doing lately. Tell me everything. It's been weeks since I've seen you."

"Not that I haven't tried, little sister. Every time I stop by, you're visiting friends."

She laughed a bit too brightly, but there was little change in her expression. She told him about the plays she'd seen with a friend and the feasts she'd attended. She didn't mention Anicetus and talked little of Caius. Marcus tired of playing games.

"There's a rumor abroad about you and Anicetus," he said and saw her cheeks turn red.

"What sort of rumor?" she said cautiously, avoiding his eyes.

"That you let him use you in order to cancel Caius' debts," he said bluntly.

Her eyes sparked. "I would say it was the other way around," she said defiantly. "He didn't use *me*. I used *him.*"

"For a few sesterces?"

"For fifty thousand sesterces," she said with a tip of her chin.

"The price hardly matters, little sister. An aureus or a talent of solid gold—you sold yourself. Will Caius allow you to handle his other debts in the same manner?"

"Who are you to question my behavior? You know nothing of my life. You know nothing of what's happened!"

"Then tell me what brought you to this!"

She turned her back on him, rigid with anger. "It's none of your business what I do with my life. I'm sick of people imposing their will on me."

He jerked her around to face him. "I want to know what happened to Hadassah," he said, unable to keep the hard edge from his tone.

Her eyes narrowed warily. "So your concern is not for me at all, but for a slave."

"What happened to her concerns you," he said, growing angrier.

"What did she tell you happened?"

"Nothing."

"Then how do you know she was beaten?"

"I saw her back."

She smiled faintly, mocking him. "Do you use her like Bithia?"

Marcus let go of her. He glared at her, feeling a sudden uncomfortable dislike for what his sister had become. She met his look for a moment, stiff and rebellious, then her face dissolved into a tremulous smile, and he saw his beloved little sister again.

"I didn't mean that. I'm sorry. Hadassah is nothing like Bithia," she said, a hand to her temple. She looked up at him beseechingly. "I had to send her away, Marcus. If she remained here, Caius would kill her. And she means more to me than I can explain. I don't know why . . . "

Marcus thought he understood. Perhaps Hadassah affected everyone the way she affected him. Her serene presence somehow became essential. "What happened?" he said more gently.

Julia sighed. "Caius didn't approve of my methods in handling his debt to Anicetus anymore than you do. He lost his temper. Hadassah intervened and took the punishment meant for me."

Marcus felt a burst of heat so intense he felt he was burning up inside. "Has he ever laid a whip to you?"

"Do I look as though he has?" When he turned toward the house, she put a hand on his arm. "You mustn't think of revenge, Marcus. Swear to me you'll do nothing. Don't interfere in any way. Believe me, you'd make matters a hundred times worse." She dropped her hand to her side again. "Besides, it's over. Caius is no threat to me as sick as he is."

"Don't expect me to feel sorry for him."

She looked up at him with an expression he couldn't fathom—satisfaction, pain, uncertainty, resignation—they all seemed to be there in the depths of her eyes. She looked away again. "I wish I could tell you everything." She began to walk again along the pathway. She paused and picked a flower.

"Do you still love him?"

"I can't help myself," she said and glanced at him with a rueful smile. "Perhaps I'm like Arria. She's never stopped loving you, you know."

Marcus smiled sardonically. "Is that what she claims?"

Julia plucked a white petal from the flower and let it float to the ground. "Have you ever thought her promiscuity a sign of desperation? Or despair?"

Was she speaking of Arria or herself? He watched her pluck petal after petal until the flower was destroyed.

"I had such great hopes, Marcus. Life is so unfair."

"Life is what you make of it."

She looked at him with a bleak smile. "I suppose you're right. Up to now, I've allowed others to run my life. Father, Claudius, Caius. Not anymore. I'll do what's necessary to be happy." She looked at the pollen on her hands and then lightly brushed it away. "I should look in on Caius." She looped her arm through his as they headed back. "Perhaps a little wine will bring some improvement."

24

The May celebrations brought with them a jubilation in Rome. Priests called *pontifices*, or bridge builders, threw bundles of rushes resembling men bound hand and foot into the River Tiber. Spring festivals abounded one after another in an orgy of revelry. During Lupercalia, aristocratic youths ran nude up and down the Via Sacra, striking bystanders with strips of goatskins in a rite hinting at fertility. Liberalia, honoring Liber, the god of wine growing, coupled festivities with Dionysus—or "Bacchus," as the god was more commonly called in Rome—culminating in a drunken celebration. Bacchus, represented by a handsome, effeminate young man, rode with a debauched Silenus in a cart drawn by leopards, while boys of sixteen all over Rome officially donned the *toga virilis* and assumed the authority of men free of parental authority.

Games were held. The Ludi Megalenses opened with trumpets for Cybele—the Phrygian goddess of nature and consort of Attis, the god of fertility—and was followed swiftly by the Ludi Cereales, which opened with a ceremony for Ceres, goddess of agriculture. Atretes made his hundredth kill at the Ludi Florales, while hundreds of amoratae cried out his name and threw flower garlands down to him.

At the ludus, Bato poured wine into a silver goblet. Atretes was always deeply depressed following the pulse-pounding excitement of the arena. The fire in his blood grew cold as ice. In the silence of the ludus, his mind cleared of bloodlust, he grew morose and bitter. Unlike Celerus, who had reveled in his fame and position, Atretes felt chaffed. Some men never adjusted to slavery, no matter how golden the cage. Atretes was such a man.

"Sertes is in Rome to see you fight," Bato said and handed Atretes the goblet.

Atretes lounged back on the couch, a seemingly relaxed pose that didn't hide his tension. The room fairly crackled of it. "Who is this Sertes, that I should be impressed?" he asked dryly, drinking his wine, his blue eyes burning. His knuckles were white.

"An extremely wealthy and powerful Ephesian who deals in

gladiators. He's come specifically to see you, and at a time when the emperor's patience has reached its limits. If you survive the games this week, he may sell you to Sertes and see you shipped off to entertain the Turks."

"Is a slave in Ephesus any better off than one in Rome?" Atretes asked sarcastically.

Bato poured himself a goblet of wine. He admired Atretes. Though he was sleek and had the polish of a professional Roman gladiator, the heart of a barbarian still beat strongly within him.

"It depends on what you want," Bato said. "Fame or freedom." He saw he had Atretes full attention. "Last year, during the Ludi Plebeii, Sertes held elimination matches. They started with twelve pairs and pitted the last three men against one another." He sipped his wine, Atretes' eyes riveted to him. "The survivor received his freedom."

Atretes sat up slowly.

"It will all depend on what you do during the next games. Vespasian has turned them over to Domitian."

Atretes knew the threat that information held. "How many will I have to fight?"

"One. A captive."

Surprised, Atretes frowned. "A captive? Why such an easy kill? So I won't make a good enough show to gain Sertes' interest?"

Bato shook his head. "You underestimate your adversary," he said grimly, knowing more of the details than he could share with Atretes. Domitian was shrewd. He was also cruel.

"Why would Domitian pit me with a captive, knowing I'll have the advantage?"

For all his time in Rome, Atretes still did not know the subtlety of a Roman mind. "It's not always training or the strength of a man's body or even the weapon in his hand that gives a man the advantage. It's how he thinks. Every man has his Achilles' heel, Atretes."

"And what is mine?"

Bato looked at him over the rim of his goblet, but didn't answer. He couldn't without risking his life. Domitian would know if he had prepared Atretes beforehand.

Atretes frowned heavily, thinking tactically, wondering where his weakness lay.

"Remember the young Roman aristocrat you almost disemboweled the first few weeks you were here?" Bato said finally, risking all he dared. "He has not forgotten his humiliation at your hands, nor lost the ear of Domitian. Between them, they think they've found an amusing way to destroy you."

"Amusing?"

Though friendship was not possible between them, they had developed a mutual respect. Atretes knew Bato had revealed all he could about the upcoming games and tried to grasp what wasn't spoken.

"Don't forget that Domitian's greatest accomplishment was a successful campaign on the Germanic frontier," Bato said.

Atretes gave a sardonic laugh. "Whatever he chooses to think, we're not defeated. The rebellion will live as long as a single German draws breath."

"A single German can do nothing, and what unification you had between your tribes was short-lived," Bato said pointedly.

"We are brothers against a common enemy, and we'll rise up again soon. My mother prophesied a wind from the north will bring the destruction of Rome."

"A wind that may never blow in your lifetime," Bato said. He set his goblet down and put both hands flat on the table between them. "Spend the next few days praying to whatever god you believe in. Ask for the wisdom to prevail. Domitian has read you well, Atretes. Freedom may come at a price higher than you're willing to pay." He dismissed him.

Decimus relaxed on the couch and took Phoebe's hand. He listened to Hadassah strum the small harp and sing of cattle on a thousand hills, of a shepherd tending his flock, of the sea and sky and a voice in the wind. All the tension seeped from him and he found himself drifting. He was tired, tired of the struggles of life, tired of pain, tired of his illness. In a few months, he and Phoebe would return permanently to Ephesus, where his holdings would support the two of them quite well for the remainder of their lives. All of the assets he had in Rome he'd turn over to Marcus. He worried about Julia, but there was nothing he could do. She had a husband to look after her, her own life to live. She was beyond his reach any longer.

Phoebe sensed his mood and wanted to relieve him of his depression. The sweet music only seemed to make his reverie deeper this evening. "Tell us a story, Hadassah," she said.

Hadassah laid the small harp in her lap. "What kind of story would you like to hear, my lady?" Julia liked stories of battles and love, David and the mighty men, Samson and Delilah, Esther and King Ahasuerus.

"Tell us a story about your god," Phoebe said.

Hadassah bowed her head. She could tell them of Creation. She could tell them of Moses and how God used him to give his people the law and bring them out of Egypt to the Promised Land.

She could tell them of Joshua and Caleb and the destruction of Jericho. She raised her eyes and looked at Decimus. A rush of compassion filled her as she noted the deep lines in his face, his troubled countenance, and heartsick spirit.

The words came to her as clearly as though her father spoke them, as he had done so many times at his small shop in Galilee, clay on his potter's wheel, repeating a parable the Lord had told. *Lord, speak through me that they might hear your voice,* she silently prayed.

"A certain man had two sons," she began, "and the younger of them said to his father, 'Father, give me the share of the estate that falls to me.' And the father divided his wealth between them. And not many days later, the younger son gathered everything together and went on a journey into a distant country. There he squandered his estate with riotous living."

Phoebe moved uncomfortably, thinking of Marcus. She glanced at Decimus, but he was listening intently.

"Now when he had spent everything, a severe famine occurred in that country, and he was in need. So he attached himself to one of the citizens of that country, who sent him into the fields to feed the swine. He longed to fill his stomach with the pods that the swine were eating, for no one was giving anything to him. Then he came to his senses and said, 'How many of my father's hired men have more than enough bread, but I am dying here with hunger! I'll get up and go to my father and say to him, "Father, I have sinned against heaven, and in your sight; I am no longer worthy to be called your son. Make me as one of your hired men!"' And he got up and went to his father."

She paused and folded her hands, then went on. "While the son was still a long way off, his father saw him and felt compassion for him. He ran to him, and embraced him, and kissed him. And the son said, 'Father, I have sinned against heaven and in your sight; I am no longer worthy to be called your son.'"

Hadassah knew it was against every unspoken rule of slavery to look into the face of her master, but she couldn't help herself. She raised her eyes and looked straight into those of Decimus Vindacius Valerian. She saw his pain and felt it as her own. "But the father said to his slaves, 'Quickly! Bring out the best robe and put it on him, and put a ring on his hand and sandals on his feet; and bring the fatted calf, kill it, and let us eat and be merry; for this son of mine was dead, and has come to life again; he was lost, and has been found . . . '"

Stillness fell over the room. Hadassah lowered her head again.

Phoebe looked at Decimus and was dismayed at the look on his face. His eyes were moist with tears. In all their years of marriage, she had never seen him cry. "You may leave, Hadassah," she said, wishing she hadn't asked her to tell a story. This one had pierced her heart and filled her with a terrible, inexplicable yearning. The girl rose gracefully.

"No, wait," Decimus said slowly, and gestured for her to sit again. "The father is your god," he said.

"Yes, my lord."

"Your country is destroyed and your people enslaved."

Hadassah felt a swelling warmth for her master; he was so much like his son. She remembered Marcus speaking the same words in the garden so many months ago. If only she was wiser. If only she knew the Scriptures as her father had. "Calamity is blessing when it brings one to God."

Enoch entered the room with a tray of wine and fruit. He set it down before the Valerians and began to pour the wine.

"But what of the older son who remained with his father?" Phoebe said.

She glanced shyly at Enoch. "He was in the field and when he came in, he heard music and dancing. He summoned one of the servants and asked what had happened. The servant said, 'Your brother has come home, and your father has killed the fatted calf, because he has received him back safe and sound.' The older son became very angry and was not willing to go in, and so his father came out and began entreating him. But he answered and said to his father, 'Look! For so many years I have been serving you, and I have never neglected a command of yours, and yet you have never given me a kid, that I might be merry with my friends; but when this son of yours came, who has devoured your wealth with harlots, and you killed the fatted calf for him.' And he said to him, 'My child, you have always been with me, and all that is mine is yours. But we have to be merry and rejoice, for this brother of yours was dead and has begun to live, and was lost and has been found.'"

Enoch handed a goblet to Phoebe and poured another. Decimus glanced up at his rigid face as he took it. "Which son are you, Enoch?" he said.

"I am not familiar with this story," Enoch said stiffly. "May I bring you anything else, my lord?"

Decimus dismissed him and smiled faintly as he watched him leave the room. "I would guess the older son to be a righteous Jew who obeys the law."

"Then the younger is the Jew who has turned away from his religion," Phoebe said. She glanced at Hadassah for confirmation.

"*Mankind* was created in God's image, my lady. Not only the Jew." Hadassah looked at Decimus. "We are all God's children. He loves us equally, whether Jew or Gentile, slave or free. We cannot earn his love, we can only accept it as a gift—a gift that he will give to each one of us."

Decimus was amazed at her words, amazed even further that she had spoken them aloud. The mask had slipped and the true face of her religion was before him. He wondered if Hadassah even understood the implications of what she offered, or the threat of her ideology to the very structure of the Roman Empire. "You may go," he said, watching her rise gracefully and leave the room.

The Jews were despised for their morality, their separatism, their rigid adherence to their laws, their stubborn belief in one god. Even as a slave, Enoch had a certain arrogance about him, believing he was a member of a chosen race. What Hadassah said about her god went beyond even that. Her words broke down the walls of bloodline and tradition. *Every* man a child of God, *all* equal in his sight. No righteous Jew would agree with—nor Roman emperor tolerate—such a claim, for it broke the pride of one and the power of the other.

But something more disturbed Decimus. He'd heard words like hers before, cried out in a strong voice to a multitude who'd gathered near the Egyptian obelisk. The man who had said them was crucified upside down. A man called Peter.

"It would seem our little Hadassah is not a Jew after all, Phoebe," he said solemnly. "But a Christian."

Atretes' despair grew with his hatred as he stood on the sand and saw what revenge Domitian had planned. Facing him was a powerfully built young man with a beard and long, flowing blond hair. He wore a bearskin and held a framea. *A captive,* Bato had said, giving him as much warning as he could. A *German* captive, and by his markings one of his own tribe, though he didn't recognize him.

"Atretes! Atretes!" the mob cried out, their chant only dying down gradually as he made no move to attack. Others in the mob shouted derisive insults. How swiftly the tide changed. Another wave began among the throng who but moments before had loved him. "Whip them! Burn them!" Atretes saw one of the trainers come out with a hot iron and knew he meant to prod the young captive into battle. On his own side, Bato appeared near the wall, looking grim. He glanced pointedly toward Domitian's box. Turning his head, Atretes looked up. Domitian and his friend were laughing!

As the German warrior let out a whelp of pain, Atretes unleashed his fury on the Roman trainer. The gasp of the crowd could be heard as he cut the man down with a swipe of his gladius. Stunned, the arena rang with silence.

Atretes faced the warrior and took up a defensive stance. "Kill me if you can!" he ordered in German.

"You are Chatti!" the man said in amazement.

"Fight!"

The warrior lowered his framea. "I will not fight a brother. Not for the pleasure of a Roman mob!" He looked around at the mass of people and spat on the sand.

Atretes saw himself five years before. His knuckles whitened on the gladius. He had to make him fight or they would both die ignobly. And so Atretes taunted the younger man as he had been taunted, mocked his pride, rubbed his face in the defeat that had brought him captive to a Roman arena. He knew where the fire in a German's heart lay and fanned the flame until the point of the framea came up again and the young man's eyes were blazing.

"You look Roman, you smell Roman . . . you are Roman!" the warrior said, cutting deeper wounds in Atretes than he could ever know.

The captive fought well, but not well enough. Atretes tried to make the fight last, but the mob wasn't fooled and began to shout angrily. Atretes took the next opening and, when he pulled his blade free, the warrior dropped to his knees, gripping his midsection. Blood oozed between his fingers as he raised his head with an effort.

"I never thought to die at the hands of a brother," he said thickly, the contempt still all too clear.

"Better me than to be thrown to wild animals or nailed to a Roman cross," Atretes said. He bent down and picked up the framea, steeling himself for what he had to do. He handed it to the warrior. "Let them see how a German can die." When the man just looked at him, he shouted, "Get off your knees!"

The man used his weapon to rise. As soon as he was on his feet, Atretes drove the gladius through the warrior's sternum, piercing his heart. He held him upright and spoke into his face, "I send you home to Tiwaz." He let go of his sword and let the man fall straight back, arms outstretched as the mob screamed approval.

Breathing heavily, Atretes didn't retrieve the Roman gladius. Instead, he bent and picked up the framea. Tears blurring his eyes, he turned and glared up at Domitian. Even in victory, Atretes knew he'd been defeated. Thrusting the framea high, he called curses down upon them all in German.

Bato had Atretes brought to him before he was returned to his quarters for the night. "Vespasian sold you to Sertes. You sail for Ephesus in two days," he said.

A muscle jerked in Atretes' cheek, but he said nothing.

"This opportunity was bought at a high price. Don't waste it," Bato said.

Atretes turned his head a fraction and looked at him. Bato had never seen such cold eyes before.

"May the gods continue to smile on you and give you the freedom you justly deserve," Bato said, jerking his head in silent command for the two guards to take Atretes away.

In the darkness of his cell, Atretes buried his face in his hands and wept.

25

Hadassah sat on the floor with fellow believers and listened to Asyncritus speak of problems they all faced.

"Ours is a struggle to live a godly life in a fleshly world. We must remember we are not called upon by God to make society a better place to live. We are not called upon to gain political influence, nor to preserve the Roman way of life. God has called us to a higher mission, that of bringing to all mankind the Good News that our Redeemer has come . . . "

Bowing her head, Hadassah closed her eyes and prayed for the Lord's forgiveness. She was ashamed. She had brought the Good News to no one. When opportunities presented themselves, she shied away from them out of fear. Her master and mistress asked her to tell them about God, and she cloaked the truth within a parable. She should have told them about Jesus, of his death on a cross, of his resurrection, of his promises to all who believed in him.

Asyncritus went on speaking, remembering what Peter and Paul had taught him before they were martyred. He read again from the apostle's memoirs, and Hadassah fought tears.

How could she withhold the truth from those she loved so much? She prayed for each of them unceasingly. And yet, was prayer all she was required to give? How could they ever turn to God if she merely entertained them with stories and not facts? How could they ever understand the deeper meaning behind the stories if they didn't know God? She pressed her fist against her chest over and over again, wanting ease from the pain she felt. God had placed her in their household for a purpose, and she was failing to fulfill it.

Why were the Valerians so obsessed with unimportant things? A week didn't pass that she didn't hear Marcus and Decimus arguing politics and business. "The national budget must be balanced and the public debt reduced!" Decimus insisted; Marcus argued that the authorities had too much control and must be limited. Decimus blamed Rome's problems on the imbalance of foreign trade, saying the Roman people had forgotten how to work and had become content to live on public assistance.

"You've been importing goods for the last thirty years and getting rich on the proposition," Marcus was quick to point out. "Now that you have the protection of your Roman citizenship, you want to deny others the same opportunities." He laughed. "Not that I don't agree in part. The less competition, the higher the price!"

On only one issue did both agree: The nation was headed for bankruptcy.

Following many such arguments, Phoebe summoned Hadassah to play her harp and soothe their troubled spirits. Hadassah's own heart was full of sorrow. What did it matter whether Rome fell? What did any nation matter when measured against the eternity of a single human soul? But how could she, a simple slave girl, open the eyes of these Romans she had come to love to what was truly important?

She sought answers in congregating with other Christians. Sometimes answers were there. Sometimes they weren't.

Oh, God, help me, Hadassah prayed fervently, her fist pressed against her aching heart. *Give me courage. Give me your Word. Burn it into my mind, carve it into my heart, show me the way to reach them!*

How could she begin to explain to the Valerians about a Savior when none of them felt a need for one? How could she explain they belonged to God, who created them, when they believed in ridiculous stone idols and not in an almighty Creator? How could she begin to tell them who God is or prove to them God existed, other than by her own faith, the meager faith of a slave? And what *was* faith but the assurance of things hoped for, the conviction of things not seen?

Oh, Yeshua, Yeshua, I love you. Please help them.

She didn't even know the right words to ask for what she needed. Why else had God placed her in the Valerian household if not to bring them the Good News of Christ? She sensed the hunger in them and knew she had the bread that would fill them for eternity. They never needed to hunger again . . . but how could she get them to eat of it?

The serenity she found in meeting with other believers lingered all the way through the streets of Rome. She could pour out her love for God and be understood among the others. She could rejoice in singing and communal prayer. She could partake of Communion and feel close to God. If only she could hold on to that feeling of renewal all through the night and coming day.

She slipped silently inside the side door to the villa's gardens and lowered the bar again. She hurried along the pathway and entered the back of the house. She closed the door quietly, then gasped as a strong hand caught hold of her arm and spun her around.

"Where have you been?" Marcus said. His fingers tightened, demanding a response, but she was too frightened to speak. "We're going to talk," he said and propelled her along the corridor, into a lamplit room. Releasing her, he closed the door and turned to her.

"Jews don't meet at night nor in secret," he said, his eyes glittering with anger.

She drew back from the intensity of his emotions.

"I'll ask you again! Where have you been?"

"Worshiping God with other believers," she said, her voice trembling.

"By *believers* you mean other *Christians,* don't you?" Her face went ghastly pale at his accusation. "Aren't you going to deny it?" he demanded roughly.

She lowered her head. "No, my lord," she said very softly.

He jerked her chin up. "Do you know what I could do to you for being a member of a religion that preaches anarchy? I could have you killed." He saw the fear come into her eyes. She *should* be afraid. She should be terrified. He took his hand from her.

"We don't preach anarchy, my lord."

"No? What would you call it when your religion demands you obey your god above an emperor?" He was furious. "By the gods, a Christian in my father's household!" He wondered why he hadn't guessed sooner. His father only had to make some offhand remark suggesting the possibility, and all the pieces of the puzzle fell together. "You'll listen to me and obey. Here it ends, Hadassah. As long as you remain with us, you won't leave the villa unless *ordered* to do so. Under no circumstances will you meet with these Christians, nor will you so much as speak to one of them on the street in a chance meeting. Do you understand me?" His eyes narrowed on her pale, shocked face. She lowered her head. "Look at me!"

She lifted her head again and looked up at him. Her eyes were brimming with tears. Seeing how deeply he had hurt her, he became angrier. "Answer me!"

"I understand," she said very softly.

He felt a pang of remorse at his harshness and a muscle jerked in his jaw. "You don't understand. You don't understand a thing." She didn't know the risk she took. "These people have to hide in the darkness. They have to conceal their ceremonies. They can't even put a likeness of their god into a temple to worship like ordinary people. I don't know how you became enmeshed with these people, but your involvement with them stops and it stops *now.*"

"Is Rome so afraid of truth she must destroy it?"

Marcus struck her across the face, a blow that rocked her and surprised a gasp of pain from her lips. She raised a trembling hand to her cheek.

"You forget to whom you speak!" Marcus rasped. He had never struck a woman under any circumstance, and the fact that he had struck this one made his heart twist inside him. But he would strike her again if it would make her listen to him and heed his warning and his command.

She recovered quickly and bowed her head in subservience. "I apologize, my lord."

The palm of his hand burned, but that was nothing to the burning in his conscience. She'd never done anything but serve each member of the family with eager devotion and love. He thought of the whip marks on her back and knew she had taken them for Julia. He remembered her reasoning with him in Claudius' garden, convincing him to spare the slaves, because she feared her god would punish him.

Belief in that god was the cause of this.

Belief in that god was going to get her killed!

He had to make her understand.

Marcus tipped her chin and saw the pink imprint of his fingers on her pale cheek. Her eyes didn't meet his, but he could see they were carefully expressionless. He felt as though someone had punched him in the stomach. "Hadassah," he whispered, "I don't want to hurt you. I want to protect you." He laid his hand over the mark, wanting to cover it and make it go away.

Her eyes flickered to his and he saw an infinite sorrow and compassion in them. She gently laid her own hand over his as though to comfort *him.* He cupped her face, drawing her close and filling his lungs with the scent of her.

"Hadassah . . . oh, Hadassah . . . " He bent and kissed her. Hearing her soft gasp, his heart raced, and he dug his fingers into her hair, kissing her again. Her hands pressed palm-flat against his chest, but he pulled her fully into his arms and slanted his mouth over hers. She stiffened, and then, for one brief, heady moment, she melted against him, her mouth softening beneath his, her hands clinging rather than resisting. Then, as though suddenly realizing what was happening, she struggled in panic.

He released her, and she jerked back from him, her eyes wide and dark. Her breath came in soft gasps that made his heart race. She stepped back.

"I want you," he said softly. "I've wanted you for a long time."

She shook her head and stepped back further from him.

"Don't look at me like that, Hadassah. I'm not threatening you with a beating. I want to love you."

"I'm a slave."

"I don't need to be reminded. I know who and what you are."

She closed her eyes tightly. No, he didn't. He knew nothing about her, not really. Nothing that mattered. "I must go, my lord. Please."

"Go where?"

"To my quarters."

"I want to come with you."

She looked at him again, her hand clutching the wool of her tunic. "Have I a choice?"

Marcus knew what she'd say if he gave her one. Against all natural human instincts, her cursed god demanded purity of his followers. "What if I said no?"

"I would beg you not to violate me."

He flushed hotly. "*Violate* you?" The word cut him and roused his already heightened anger. "My family *owns* you. It's no violation to take what I want from something that belongs to me. It's a sign of the respect I have for you that I'd even—"

He stopped, hearing himself. For the first time in his life, Marcus was filled with an unspeakable shame. As he stared at her, for just an instant he saw himself as she must see him, and he winced. *Something,* he had called her. *Something!* Was that how he really thought of her? As a possession to be used without consideration of her feelings?

Marcus stared at her bleakly and saw how vulnerable she was. She was white and tense, a pulse throbbing in her throat. He longed to hold her, to comfort her.

"I didn't mean that." He came close to her and saw her body tense even more, but by obligation she had to remain. Running the back of his knuckles down her soft cheek, he sought some way to make amends. "I will not violate you," he said. He tipped her chin. "I want to love you. You want me, too, Hadassah. Maybe you're too innocent to realize it, but I know." He ran his finger down her cheek. "Sweet little Hadassah, let me show you what love can be. Say yes."

She trembled, her body responding to the touch of his hand, the gentle huskiness of his voice, the sense of his growing desire—and her own. She could hardly draw breath at his closeness. . . .

But what he spoke of was wrong. What he asked her to do would not be pleasing to God.

"Say yes," he whispered. "One little word could make me so happy . . . "

She shook her head, unable to speak.

"Say yes," he said heavily.

She closed her eyes. *God, help me!* she cried within her heart. She had loved Marcus for so long. The feelings he roused in her now were melting her inside, burning away her reason, making her forget everything but the feel of his hands. He kissed her again, his lips parting. She turned her face away. *Yeshua, help me resist these feelings!* Marcus' hand touched her gently, and the shock of sensation made her draw back.

He closed his eyes, a strange sense of loss filling him at her withdrawal.

"Why must you, of all the women I've wanted, worship a god who demands purity?" He reached out again and cupped her face. "Give up this god of yours. All he does is deny you the few pleasures life has to offer."

"No," she said in a soft, but intent voice.

"You want me. I can see it in your eyes."

She closed them, shutting him out.

He gave a harsh laugh of frustration. "Let's see if you can say no one more time." He pulled her into his arms and took her mouth again, releasing all the passion that had been pent up in him for weeks. She tasted like ambrosia and he drank of her until his own desire was nearly too heavy to bear. Then he finally let her go.

They were both shaking. Her eyes were full of tears and her face was white and strained.

Marcus looked down at her and knew he had done as he hoped. She wanted him. Yet the heavy ache within his body didn't compare to the greater ache in his heart. He had made her want him in order to gain her willingness. Instead, he had erected an even higher wall between them. Would she ever trust him again?

"Very well," he said with a mocking twist of his lips. "Go sleep on your cold little pallet and be warmed by your unseen god." He made a dismissive gesture with his hand and turned away. Shutting his eyes, he listened to her soft, hurried footsteps as she left him.

Swearing, he let out a harsh breath, already paying physically for his folly. He crossed the room and poured himself wine. His body was shaking violently. He knew it was in reaction. He hadn't been with a woman in weeks. Unbidden, Arria entered his thoughts and he grimaced. To think of her in the wake of his feelings for Hadassah sickened him.

Hadassah.

A *Christian!*

A scene came back to him of a dozen men and women tied to pillars and drenched in pitch, screaming as they were set aflame, acting as torches for Nero's circus. Shuddering, Marcus drained his goblet.

Six trained bodyguards saw Atretes safely to the ship where Sertes was waiting for him. The gladiator dealer looked him full in the face. "The chains won't be necessary," he said, addressing the guards.

"But my lord. He's—"

"Remove them."

Atretes stood still as the shackles were taken from his wrists. A crowd of amoratae had followed him from the ludus through the city streets and now gathered on the dock. Some were calling his name. Others wept openly, grieving at his departure.

Atretes noticed Sertes had his own guards on board. The gladiator dealer smiled shrewdly. "For your protection," he said smoothly. "In case you think about diving overboard and drowning yourself."

"I have no intention of committing suicide."

"Good," Sertes said. "I've invested a fortune in you. I wouldn't want to see it wasted." He held his hand out. "This way."

He entered quarters below deck that were smaller than his cubicle at the ludus. It smelled of wood and lamp oil rather than stone and straw. Atretes entered and removed his cape.

"We sail in a few hours," Sertes said. "Rest. I'll send one of the guards for you so you can have your last look at Rome and those who love you."

Atretes looked back at him coldly. "I've seen all of Rome I ever want to see."

Sertes smiled. "You'll find Ephesus a city of unsurpassed beauty."

Atretes sat on the narrow bunk when Sertes left. He leaned his head back and tried to see his homeland in his mind's eye.

He couldn't.

All he could see was the face of a young German warrior.

Phoebe summoned Hadassah to the peristyle. "Sit beside me," she said and patted a space beside her on the marble bench. She crumpled a small piece of parchment as Hadassah sat down. "Caius is dead. He died early this morning. Decimus has gone to help Julia make the arrangements for his burial." She looked at her sadly. "She'll need you soon."

Hadassah's first thought was that she would be away from Marcus. Her heart sank. It must be the will of God. She couldn't remain here if she was to be unscathed. What Marcus wanted, she should never give—not to any man but the one she would one day marry, if it was God's will she ever marry. Perhaps this was the Lord's way of protecting her from herself; she could not deny that from the moment Marcus had touched her, weakness had washed over her. She had forgotten God . . . she had forgotten everything but the wild sensations filling her. "I will go to her whenever you say, my lady."

Phoebe nodded. Rather than feeling pleased, though, she was troubled. "Tragedy seems to pursue Julia. First Claudius, then she loses her child, and now her young husband."

Hadassah lowered her head, thinking of Julia's baby, discarded in the garden.

"I should feel more sorry for Julia than I do," Phoebe said and rose. She walked along the pathway into the garden. Hadassah followed. Phoebe paused beside a flower bed and bent down to run her fingertips along the blooms. She glanced up with a smile. "I've enjoyed your company, Hadassah. We share a love of flowers, don't we?"

Her smile fell away as she straightened, and she moved to sit on a nearby marble bench. "Your master's illness is getting worse. He's tried hard to hide it from me, but I know. Sometimes the pain in his eyes is so great . . . " She looked away, blinking back tears. "For so many years, he's been obsessed with his business. I used to be jealous of how it consumed his time and his thoughts. It was as though something mattered more to him than I or the children ever could."

She looked at Hadassah, motioning for her to sit beside her. "His illness has changed him. He's grown so restless. He said to me the other day that nothing he's ever done in his life matters or will last. That it's all been vanity. The only time he seems to find any peace is when you sing to him."

"Perhaps it's less the music than the message, my lady."

Phoebe looked at her. "The message?"

"That God loves him and wants him to turn to him for comfort."

"Why would a Jewish god care about a Roman?"

"God cares about everyone. All men are his creation, but those who choose to believe become his children and share in the inheritance of his Son."

Phoebe leaned forward and then started at the sound of another voice in the garden. Marcus was home. "Mother!" He came striding into the garden. "I just heard about Caius," he said, his gaze flickering to Hadassah briefly.

Phoebe laid her hand over Hadassah's. "You may go," she said. She set her attention upon Marcus again and saw him watching Hadassah as she hurried down the path. A muscle moved in his jawline. Phoebe frowned slightly. "Your father went to Julia as soon as word came," she said.

Marcus sat beside her on the bench. "Don't send Hadassah back to her."

Surprised, she searched his eyes. "I don't want to send her back, Marcus, but I have little choice." She watched his expression closely. "Hadassah belongs to your sister."

Marcus felt his mother's intent perusal and turned away, debating whether to tell her Hadassah had taken a beating for Julia and almost died from it. If he did, his mother might change her mind, but Julia would never forgive him. He had no wish to hurt his sister, but he wanted Hadassah here, close to him. He knew the circle of friends Julia had formed since marrying Caius. He knew as well what they thought of Christians.

"Julia has more than enough personal servants already, Mother. If she asks for Hadassah, send her Bithia instead."

"A thought that's entered my own mind," Phoebe admitted. "But it's not my decision to make, Marcus." She reached out to touch him. "Speak with your father."

Decimus returned to the villa late in the afternoon. All the arrangements had been made for Caius to be entombed in the catacombs outside the city walls. Roman law forbade burial within the gates of the city, even if there was land enough on a private villa. Phoebe went to spend the night with Julia; Marcus had already been to see her early in the afternoon. Decimus thought his daughter amazingly calm under the tragic circumstances. Caius had been young and vital. The fever had ravaged him over the past weeks.

Now, as he rested, Enoch brought him wine. The room was cold and Decimus had him replenish the brazier with wood. Marcus joined him. "She's taking Caius' death well, isn't she?" Marcus said and reclined on the couch, watching without much interest as the slaves served the evening meal.

"I think she's in a state of shock," Decimus said, sampling the beef, but finding he had little appetite for it.

Marcus' mouth tightened. His sister was either in shock or relieved, he thought, but kept his thoughts to himself. His father and mother knew nothing of Caius' jealous rages or brutality. Julia had proven so secretive, he might never have known if he hadn't seen the stripes on Hadassah's back and confronted his sister about it. He couldn't grieve the fiend's passing; for once, the gods had proven kind.

Marcus sought an opening to discuss Hadassah and her remaining with them, but his father was so preoccupied he found no opportunity. Decimus summoned Hadassah and, as she quietly entered the room carrying the small harp beneath her arm, Marcus' senses quickened. He willed her to look at him, but she didn't raise her eyes once as she took her place on the stool. He wanted desperately to talk with her alone.

"Sing to us, Hadassah," his father said.

Marcus tried not to watch her, but every fiber of his being seemed focused on her. Seemingly casual, he watched the graceful movements of her fingers on the strings and listened to the sweetness of her voice. Then he remembered the softness of her mouth and had to look away. When he did, he encountered his father's gaze.

"That will be all," Decimus said and lifted his hand slightly. As she rose, Decimus spoke again. "Hadassah, you've heard of the Lady Julia's bereavement?"

"Yes, my lord."

"When I saw her today, she asked me to send you back. Pack your things and be ready at dawn. Enoch will take you to her." Decimus felt his son's reaction.

"Yes, my lord," she said, no inflection in her voice to hint at her inner turmoil.

"You have served us well these past weeks," Decimus said. "I will miss your music and stories. You may go." Bowing her head, she whispered a tremulous thanks and was gone.

Marcus glared at his father in consternation. "Julia has no right to her!"

"And you have?"

Marcus bolted up from his couch. "You don't know everything that's gone on in that villa!"

"I know enough of what goes on in this one! If this unfortunate tragedy hadn't occurred, I would have sent Hadassah back to Julia by tomorrow morning anyway. Your feelings for her are inappropriate."

"Why? Because she's a slave or because she's a Christian?"

Decimus was amazed that Marcus didn't deny his infatuation. "Both reasons suffice, but neither concerns me. What does matter is that Hadassah belongs to your sister. I doubt Julia would appreciate the irony of your falling in love with her slave. And what would happen if you succeeded in seducing Hadassah and got her with child?"

Seeing his son's expression, Decimus frowned. "When we purchased Hadassah, your mother made a gift of her to your sister. Julia is my daughter, and I love her. I won't jeopardize what little influence I still have with her over a slave on whom she has a strange dependence. Other than you, whom has Julia trusted? Hadassah. This little Jewess serves your sister with a single-minded devotion that's rare. Hadassah loves your sister no matter what her faults may be. A slave like her is worth her weight in gold."

"That love and devotion almost got her killed a few weeks ago."

"I know Caius beat her," Decimus said.

"Did you know the beating was meant for Julia?"

"Yes. Your sister and mother were blinded by Caius' charm. I was not."

"Then why didn't you prevent the marriage?"

"Because I didn't want to lose my daughter completely! I forced her into an unwanted marriage, and that turned out to be a disaster. I couldn't interfere with one she chose for herself." He winced in pain as he rose from the couch. It was a moment before the pain subsided and he could speak.

"Sometimes, no matter how much you want to protect your children, you have to let them make their own mistakes. All you can do is hold on to the hope that they'll turn to you when they need you." He thought of Hadassah's story of the Prodigal Son and grimaced.

"Much of Julia's trouble was brought on by her own actions."

"I know that! It's always been that way, Marcus. But have you stopped to think? If not for Hadassah, your sister might be dead."

Marcus went cold. Torn by his love for Hadassah and his concern for his sister, he stared bleakly at his father.

Decimus looked old and drawn, but he gave his son a level look back that asked for silence. Some things were best left unspoken. Though he would never speak of it, he knew a great deal of what had happened in Urbanus' villa. Closing his eyes, he saw Julia as a child again, beautiful, innocent, winsome, running through the garden and laughing gaily. Then he remembered her as she had been today, withdrawn and pale, suffering so much he could hardly bear to see it.

She had taken her father's hand, looking up at him with dull eyes. "Just before he died, he looked at me and asked me to forgive him . . . ," she said, seemingly in some terrible torment. "I loved him, Father. I did. I swear I really loved him."

Her nerves were stretched taut. She would tremble as she wept and then, suddenly, she would be very still, tears spilling down her pale cheeks, her thoughts inward. Calabah Shiva Fontaneus had come to call, having heard the news of Caius' death, but Julia didn't want to see her. "Just make her go away! Please! I don't want to see her. I don't want to see anyone!" It was the closest she came to losing complete control.

Decimus hoped Phoebe would be able to give their daughter the comfort she needed, but somehow he doubted it. Something deep and hidden gnawed at Julia. He wasn't sure he wanted to know what it was. He knew too much of what she had done already. His grandchild aborted, paying her husband's gambling debts by prostituting herself. Whatever else she had done, he didn't want to know. What he knew already hurt him worse than the disease that was eating away at his insides.

"Don't interfere in this, Marcus. I'm asking you to let it go. Hadassah has a goodness in her that slavery hasn't ruined. She serves from her heart. Julia *needs* her, Marcus. What you want from Hadassah you could find on any street corner in Rome. Please, for once in your life, don't take from others to serve yourself."

Heat filled Marcus' face as he stared at his father for a moment, then a coldness swept over him. Lowering his eyes, he nodded silently, feeling as he did so that he was sentencing Hadassah to death.

Wordless, unwilling that his father should witness the shaking that was taking him, he turned and left the room.

26

For the fourth time that week, Julia told Hadassah to make preparations to go to Caius' tomb outside the city walls. The journey took several hours, and Hadassah made sure there were provisions for a meal, blankets in case the day turned cold, and wine to soothe her mistress's nerves on the way home. Julia had had constant nightmares since Caius' death. She made gifts to the household gods, as well as to Hera, but nothing helped her. She couldn't stop seeing her husband's face as it had looked a few minutes before he died. He had opened his eyes and looked at her, and she was sure he *knew*.

She was afraid to go to his tomb alone and so invited Octavia to accompany her today. Her mother thought it unhealthy to go so often. Marcus had gone with her once, but was so preoccupied that he was no good to her. She needed someone who could keep her from her thoughts. Octavia always had gossip to share.

Four slaves bore the curtained conveyance aloft. Julia peered out as she and Octavia were carried through the crowded city streets to the gates. Hadassah had gone on ahead with several other slaves so that everything would be laid out when they arrived. Julia could feel Octavia studying her, but said nothing. She was nervous, her palms sweating. She felt nauseated and cold.

Octavia looked Julia over. Dressed in a white stola, her face ashen, her eyes dull and lifeless, her hair combed into a simple style, she looked tragic and vulnerable. Octavia was no longer jealous of her. She had heard rumors about Caius' gambling and affairs. She smiled smugly. Julia deserved everything that he had done to her. If Caius had turned away from Julia and married *her,* things would have been different. Octavia cast another glance at Julia's face. Apparently, she still loved him. Octavia relished her feelings of pity.

"You've lost weight since I saw you a few weeks ago," she said. "And you've cut yourself off from most of your friends. Calabah is very worried about you."

Calabah. Julia's eyes flickered. She wished she had never met Calabah. If not for her, she would never have murdered Caius.

She cast an uneasy look at Octavia. How much did she know about Caius' illness? How much had Calabah said to her? "Do you see her often?"

"Daily. I attend her gatherings as always. She misses you."

"What does she say about me?"

"Say about you? What should she say?" Octavia frowned at her tone. "Calabah isn't one to gossip, if that's what you're implying. You should know that, you being closer to her than I've ever been."

Julia heard the twinge of envy in Octavia's voice and turned her face away. "I just haven't felt up to seeing her lately. I can't think of anything right now but Caius." She drew the curtain aside slightly so she could peer out at the grassy, tree-studded landscape along the Appian Way. "I don't know what Calabah expects from me." She saw a bird take wing into the clear blue sky and wished she could be like that. She wished she could fly far, far away . . . so far away she would never have to see or hear of Calabah again. Just thinking about her made her so afraid. Calabah knew *everything*. "She would think me very foolish to be taking Caius' death so hard. Just tell her I'm fine," Julia said dully.

"You should tell her yourself. You owe her that much."

Julia shot her a half-frightened look. "What do you mean? Why should I owe Calabah anything?"

"Well, aren't you the grateful one? She introduced you to Caius."

There it was again, that hint of anger behind Octavia's smile. Did she still hate her for stealing Caius' love, though Caius had never been the least bit interested in Octavia? Surely she knew that. Surely it had been obvious. But Julia couldn't bear to have anyone dislike her right now.

"If I'd never met Caius, I wouldn't have all this grief, would I, Octavia? And he gave me plenty of grief before he died, too!"

"I know. I heard rumors."

Julia gave her a brittle smile and looked out the curtain again. She wished she hadn't invited Octavia.

Closing her eyes, she tried to think of something else, but she kept remembering Caius as he'd been the day before he died, telling her how much he loved her, how he'd wanted her from the moment he'd seen her, how sorry he was for his abuse and his affairs and his foul luck. He had made her feel so guilty she had almost stopped giving him the poison, but by then he'd been so sick it wouldn't have mattered. Continuing to give it to him ended his suffering more quickly.

Caius had terrified her the night he had tried to kill her. She had thought his death would be the end of her fear. It was more like the beginning. She was more afraid now than ever before. It was as though she carried a dark presence everywhere with her, as though she couldn't get away from him.

Caius had been so vital and full of health. People asked questions about his illness, and she wondered if they suspected anything. What would happen to her if they did? She remembered watching as a woman, who had been convicted of murdering her husband, was torn to shreds by wild dogs in the arena. Her heart beat wildly. No one knew except Calabah. *Calabah*. She had given her the poison and told her how to use it. She had admitted murdering her own husband when he threatened to divorce her. Surely Calabah wouldn't say anything. She clenched her hands in her lap.

Calabah had not told her how awful it would be to watch Caius decline week by week, day by day, hour by hour. She hadn't said there would be pain.

Julia closed her eyes tightly, trying to block out the image of Caius, pale and shrunken. His once mesmerizing eyes had been glassy, like dull marbles. Nothing showed in them near the end but darkness and death. Maybe, if she'd known how awful it would be to watch him die little by little, she wouldn't have done it. She would have left him and gone home to her mother and father and Marcus. She would have found some other way.

Yet all of Calabah's reasons for killing him were still valid. He had betrayed her with other women. He'd tormented her emotionally, beaten her physically. And he would have used up all her money. What other choice had she had but to kill him?

The rationalizations and self-justification roiled in her mind, but guilt tore her reasons to shreds.

"Are you angry with Calabah for some reason?" Octavia asked, studying her.

How could Julia explain that seeing Calabah only reminded her of what she'd done? She didn't want to be reminded.

"No," she said bleakly. "It's just that I don't feel like seeing too many people right now."

"I'm flattered you asked me to come with you today."

"We've been friends since we were children." A sudden rush of tears filled Julia's eyes. "I'm sorry if I've hurt you at times, Octavia. I know I can be dreadful." She knew Octavia had been in love with Caius. Taking him away from her had given Julia the most immense pleasure, but now she wished she hadn't done it. By all the gods, she wished Octavia had won him.

Octavia leaned forward and kissed her cheek. "Let's forget the past," she said and dabbed tears from Julia's face with the edge of her shawl. "I've forgotten it, anyway."

Julia forced a smile. Octavia had forgotten nothing. She could feel it in the chill touch of her hand. She had come along today to see her pain and to relish it. "What have you been doing with yourself these days? Do you still visit the ludus?"

"Not as often as I used to now that Atretes is gone," she said with a shrug.

Julia's heart sank with swift disappointment. "He was killed?"

"Oh no. I think he's invincible. But he's also been a thorn in the emperor's side, so he was sold to an Ephesian who promotes games in Ionia. I saw him fight during the Ludi Florales. He was matched against another German. Unfortunately, it wasn't a very exciting match. It was all over in a few minutes and he didn't even look to see if Domitian's thumb was up or down. He made his opponent stand up and dispatched him like that." She snapped her fingers.

"I wish I could have met him," Julia said, remembering how flushed with excitement she'd been the day he looked up at her. She remembered his gesture and felt the first rush of warmth in weeks.

"Have you noticed that some of the newer statues of Mars and Apollo bear a resemblance to him?" Octavia said. "He was the most beautiful gladiator I've ever seen. Just watching him stride out onto the sand made me hot all over. You know, they're still selling little statuettes of him outside the arena, even though he's no longer in Rome." She had purchased one, but would rather die than admit it to Julia.

Before long, they were lowered from the slaves' shoulders and assisted from the curtained litter. Hadassah and another maid had already laid out the meal, but Julia showed no interest. She stood looking at Caius' tomb. "It's not very big, is it?" she said.

Octavia was famished, but she didn't push; she didn't want to seem inconsiderate of Julia's mood. "It's big enough," she said.

Julia wondered if erecting a larger monument to Caius would have made her feel better. Father suggested she place Caius' ashes in the family mausoleum, where her two siblings were entombed, but the thought had horrified her. When her time came to die, she didn't want to be placed beside a husband she had murdered. She shuddered.

"Are you cold, my lady?" Hadassah said.

"No," she said tonelessly.

"I'm starving," Octavia said impatiently, walking over to survey the sliced meat, fruit, bread, and wine. Julia joined her, but only picked at the food. Octavia ate ravenously. "There's something about traveling that increases my appetite," she said, breaking off more bread. "And everything tastes so wonderful." She glanced at Hadassah. "Why don't you have your little Jew sing to you?"

"Caius hated her," Julia said and got up. She stood near the tomb again, clasping her arms around her as though to ward off a chill in spite of the warmth of the summer day. Hadassah went to her. "Try to eat something, my lady."

"I wish I knew if he was at peace or not," Julia whispered.

Hadassah lowered her head. Urbanus had been an evil man with dark, cruel appetites. Those who rejected God's grace and were cruel to their fellowman were destined to spend eternity in a place of suffering, where there was great weeping and gnashing of teeth. She couldn't tell her mistress that. What could she say to comfort her mistress when she appeared to have loved him so much?

"Leave me alone with him for a few minutes," Julia said, and Hadassah obeyed.

Julia's heart beat dully as she looked at the marble tomb. *Caius Polonius Urbanus* was chiseled into the pristine white stone, *beloved husband* just below. Flowered vines were cut all around, two plump winged cherubs at the top. She knelt slowly and leaned forward to run her finger over the letters one at a time. "Beloved husband," she said, her mouth twisting into a tormented smile. "I'm not sorry I did it. I'm not sorry." But tears filled her eyes and poured down her pale cheeks.

"Will you remain in Caius' villa?" Octavia said when Julia came back and sat down with her again.

Other dismal thoughts entered Julia's mind and depressed her even more. With Caius' death, she found herself again under her father's control. Marcus was reinstated as overseer of her estate. That she didn't mind—for he would give her whatever she asked—but she did mind being treated like a child again and having to ask for money and permission to do as she pleased. Still, what other choice had she short of marrying again? After her two matrimonial experiences, she was not eager for another.

"No, I can't remain there," she said. "Father insists I must return home."

"Oh, how dreadful," Octavia said with her first real sense of sympathy. Julia would have little freedom once she was beneath Decimus Valerian's roof again.

Julia gave her a bleak smile. "Sometimes I long for the days when I was a child running through my mother's garden. Everything was so fresh and wonderful then, the whole world stretching out in front of me. Now everything looks so . . . dark." She shook her head, fighting back tears of disillusionment.

"Give yourself time, Julia," Octavia said. "In a few weeks I'll take you to the games again. They'll help you forget your troubles." She leaned close. "Did you really send two of your slaves to the arena?" Octavia whispered, glancing at Hadassah and the others.

Julia gave Octavia a warning look. Hadassah had grieved when she heard. Julia would never have imagined that punishing the two slave girls would hurt her little friend, but it had. But then, Julia hadn't even thought to consider Hadassah's feelings. All she had wanted was revenge. "Disobedience can't be tolerated," Julia said loudly enough for Hadassah to hear. "Their loyalty was entirely to Caius, and when he died, they couldn't be trusted."

"Well, I imagine your decision will keep the rest of your slaves in line," Octavia said with a soft laugh. She saw the little Jewess's face was white.

"I'd appreciate it if you never mentioned it again," Julia said. It hadn't given her the pleasure she expected. She rose. "It's getting chilly." She ordered Hadassah and the others to get ready to depart. Octavia wore on her nerves with her endless talking and her sharp little prying questions. Julia looked over at Caius' tomb one last time and felt an acute pang of regret. If only things had been different, she wouldn't have had to do it.

On the return journey to Rome, Julia decided she would never go back to Caius' tomb again. She found no peace there. In fact, she felt worse each time she stood before it. Caius was dead, and that meant an end to the unhappiness he had caused her.

She just wished she knew what to do with her life now. She felt so empty and alone. She'd expected Hadassah's songs and stories to be as pleasurable as they'd always been, but they disturbed her now, leaving her with a disquiet she couldn't dispel. So did the slave girl. Her purity and pristine beliefs were a constant affront to Julia. Even more irritating was the sense of contentment Hadassah seemed to have—something Julia had never in her life experienced. How could a slave with nothing be happy when she, with everything, was not?

Sometimes she would be sitting and listening to Hadassah's sweet voice and a wave of violent hatred for the girl would sweep over her. Yet, just as quickly, in its wake would come a deep sense of shame and longing, leaving her confused and yearning for something she couldn't define.

Her temples throbbed. Pressing her fingertips to them, she closed her eyes and rubbed, but the pain remained. So, too, did Caius' expression just before he died—and his final gasped words.

"Don't think it's over . . ."

He had *known*.

"Everything's signed and ready for delivery to my representatives," Decimus said, nodding toward a pile of rolled scrolls on his desk in the bibliotheca.

"I can't believe you've actually gone through with it," Marcus said.

"I've been thinking of moving my headquarters for some time. All of my financial assets will be officially transferred to bankers in Ephesus," Decimus said dogmatically. "Ephesus is the most powerful seaport in the Empire and it's closer to the eastern caravans, where I've made good money over the years. Centered in Ephesus, Valerian Imports will continue to provide Rome with the foreign goods she demands."

"How could you do this, Father? Have you no gratitude toward the city that gave you prosperity in the first place?"

Decimus said nothing for a long moment. Rome had taken more from him than she had given. The great and respectable Republic of Rome had long since passed away. For all the beauty and magnificence that remained, he found himself living atop a rotting corpse. He could no longer endure the stench or stand by and watch how the corruption and decay of the Empire affected his own son and daughter. Perhaps by leaving, he could draw them away as well.

"It grieves me that we've never seen things the same way, Marcus. Perhaps that's as it must be between a father and his son. I didn't agree with my father, either. Had I done so, I'd be a shopkeeper near the docks of Ephesus."

Marcus stood. "How can I make you see reason? Sentiment isn't enough to relocate a thriving business or uproot a family born and bred in Rome. Every road leads to Rome. We are the hub of civilization!"

"May the gods preserve us if that's so," Decimus said grimly.

Marcus saw he was getting nowhere. His father had talked so often of returning to Ephesus Marcus had almost become deaf to it, dismissing it as the dreaming of a disillusioned old man. When his mother had posed the question of returning to Ephesus, Marcus had told her that leaving Rome was unthinkable from a business and personal standpoint. She had been unaccountably dismayed by his vehemence, and now he understood why. The decision had already been made, and he had had no part in it. He'd gain no help from her in dissuading his father. She wanted whatever would make him happy, and if his father thought returning to his homeland would do so, his mother would go without a whisper of dissent.

"What of Julia?" he said, knowing he would have an ally in her. "What has she to say to this plan of yours? Or have you bothered to tell her yet?"

"She's coming with us."

Marcus gave a sardonic laugh. "Do you really think so? You'll have to drag her to the ship. She's struggling enough with having to be here under your roof again!"

"I spoke with your sister this morning and told her of my plans. She seemed almost relieved at the idea of leaving Rome. Her grief over Caius' loss, I expect. She wants to be away from all reminders of him." Or perhaps it was the result of a visit from that Fontaneus woman that had left Julia pale and reticent, and eager to leave Rome.

Marcus stared at him, dumbfounded.

"Speak with her for yourself if you don't believe me," Decimus said.

Marcus frowned, wondering about Julia's capitulation. Was

she so bereaved, or was there more to her acquiescence than met the eye? But even more than his concern for Julia's problems were his own feelings about his father's decision. "What if I were to tell you that *I* have no desire to leave Rome? Would that postpone this decision you've made without consulting me?"

"Is it necessary for a father to consult a son about anything?" Decimus said, his face rigid. "I will do as I must without seeking your approval. You can make your own decisions. Remain in Rome if it pleases you."

Marcus felt the shock of abandonment. He looked into his father's eyes and saw the determination and stubborn will that had built his business empire.

"Perhaps I will," he said. "I'm a Roman, Father. By birth. I belong here."

"Half the blood that runs in your veins is Ephesian, whether you're proud of the fact or not."

Was that what he thought held him back? "I'm proud to be your son, and I've never been ashamed of my heritage."

Decimus felt deep regret that the relationship between him and his son had become so strained that he hadn't felt able to confide in him his decision to move. "It's my hope you'll decide to come with us, but, I repeat, it's your choice." He took a scroll from the pile. "I knew it would be a difficult choice for you." He held it out to his son.

Marcus took it. "What's this?" he said as he broke the seal and unrolled it.

"Your inheritance," Decimus said simply, his expression filled with an unfathomable sorrow.

Marcus stared from his father to the document in his hand. He read several lines and went cold. A son was never given such a document while the father was still living . . . not unless the son was being cast out of the family. In Marcus' mind, there could only be two reasons his father had given him such a thing: either Decimus had given up on his son, or he had given up on himself. Marcus could accept neither option. He glanced up, hurt and angry.

"Why?"

"Because I don't know how else to tell you I've no desire to force you to do anything against your will. You proved yourself a man a long time ago." He sighed wearily. "Perhaps if you came with us, you'd long for Rome as I've longed for Ephesus. I can't say, Marcus. You must decide for yourself where you belong in this world."

Full of powerful, conflicting emotions, Marcus stood silent, the document clenched in his hand.

Decimus looked at his son sadly. "Despite my Roman citizenship and the prosperity this city has given me, I am an Ephesian." He spread his hand palm down on his desk. "I want to be buried in my own country."

He's dying. The sudden realization hit Marcus, driving the air from his lungs. Stunned, he sat down, the unfurled scroll in his hand. He should have realized sooner. Maybe he had, but he'd refused to face it until now, when he had no choice. His father was mortal after all. He looked at him and saw him as he really was—gray, old, and very human. It hurt.

"Then this illness that's plagued you isn't passing," he said.

"No."

"How long have you known?"

"A year, maybe two."

"Why didn't you tell me before now?"

"You've always seen me as a powerful force in your life, something with which to contend. Maybe it was pride," he said flatly. "A man doesn't like to be diminished in the eyes of his only son." He withdrew his hand from the desk. "But we all must die, Marcus. It's our destiny." He saw the expression in Marcus' eyes. "I didn't tell you now to make you feel guilty or in any way obligated."

"No?"

"No," Decimus said firmly. "But you have a decision to make. It's best if you have all the facts before you when doing so."

Marcus knew if he didn't go with his family to Ephesus, he'd never see his father alive again. He stood, rolled it up again, and held it out. His father didn't take it.

"Whatever your decision, all that's listed in that document is yours as of now. Stand at its helm or break it up and sell it piece by piece. Do with it as you will. With proper management, Julia has more than enough to keep her comfortably for life, and I've seen to arrangements for your mother."

Marcus glared down at him. Had his father simply given up? Wasn't he going to fight this at all? For Decimus Vindacius Valerian to simply *concede* to death was unthinkable. And yet, there it was, staring Marcus in the face, along with the fact that even by surrendering and lying down to die, his father held an iron control.

"Ah, yes, Father, as always, you've seen to everyone. Julia's estate in my hands, Mother's life arranged to the moment of her death, and even *my life* all neatly tied up!" He held the scroll up. "In one breath, you tell me you're dying and then strip away my freedom by handing me all you've built and worked for, handing me *your life,* in a document." He crushed it in his hand. "And then you have the unmitigated gall to tell me I have a choice in what I will do!" He tossed the crumpled scroll on the desk among the others.

"What choice?" he said and left.

Trophimus smiled as Hadassah stepped up to his booth with her basket. "We've missed you, little sister."

"I'm back at the Valerian villa," she said quietly, her eyes shadowed. When she had been sent to Julia, she had returned to the night meetings. As soon as Julia moved in with her parents again, she obeyed Marcus' command not to leave the villa unless ordered to do so.

Trophimus understood. Hadassah had brought her dilemma before the others, and they had tried to help her decide what the Lord would have her do. To worship God with the others, she would have to defy her masters. As a slave, Hadassah must serve and obey them. Marcus hadn't said she couldn't worship God, only that she couldn't worship with the others. She had decided she must obey him and pray and worship as she had done before meeting Trophimus.

"Are you on some mighty errand today?" Trophimus said, wondering if she had changed her mind and needed to be with others who shared her faith.

"My mistress had a sudden craving for apricots."

The merchant could tell she was troubled, but he didn't press her. "A craving she will have to suffer, I'm afraid. None of the fruit vendors have had apricots in weeks. A blight on the crop in Armenia."

"Oh," she said too bleakly.

"Does your mistress always crave what's unavailable?" Hadassah looked up at him and he frowned. He patted her hand. "Such is the restless spirit, little sister. We'll give her figs instead—choice, delicious African figs." He picked the best and placed them in her basket. "And I've just gotten cherries from Pontic Cerasus. Here, taste a few. I'll give you a good price."

"You always give a good price," she said, trying to match his mood. She ate one of the cherries. "Lady Julia would like these, I think. They're very sweet."

Trophimus selected only the best cherries. He could contain his curiosity no longer. "What troubles you, little sister?"

"The master is dying," she said softly. "He thinks returning to his homeland will bring him peace." She looked up at Trophimus, her dark eyes wide and troubled. "He was born in Ephesus."

Trophimus hesitated. Words of concern and caution sprang to his lips. But she needed encouragement, not dark stories about an even darker city. "I've heard Ephesus is the most beautiful seaport in all the Empire. The streets are white marble and lined with columns and fanes."

"They worship Artemis," Hadassah said.

"Not everyone," he said. "There are Christians in Ephesus. And the apostle John."

Hadassah's eyes lit up. John the apostle! For as long as she could remember, John had been part of her life. To others, he was one of the exalted, one of the blessed who had been chosen by the Lord to walk with him during his last three years on earth, and therefore he was treated with reverence, even awe by believers. John was among the first chosen by the Lord. He had been present at the wedding in Cana, where Jesus turned the water into wine. He had seen Jesus raise Jairus' daughter. He was on the mountain when Jesus was transfigured and Elijah and Moses came to speak with the Lord. John was nearest Jesus during his agony in the Garden. It was John who had occupied the place of intimacy at the Lord's last supper. John overheard the trial. He stood at the cross with Mary. He had been at the tomb and saw the empty grave clothes, and he had been one of the first who *believed.*

And John was her last link to her father, for he had been with Jesus the day the Lord had touched her father and raised him from the dead.

She loved John almost as much as she had loved her own father. She could remember sitting on her father's lap in an upper room in Jerusalem during the celebration of the Last Supper during the city's Passover. She had fallen asleep in her father's arms, listening to John and her father and the others talk about the

Lord—what he had said, what he had done. John had been a friend of her father's. If only she could get in touch with him . . . but Ephesus was a large city. The chances of finding John were almost negligible. The small glimmer of hope that Hadassah had felt sputtered and died.

Trophimus went on. "I heard once that Jesus' mother, Mary, came with him to Ephesus. Oh, what a blessing it would have been to meet the woman who bore our Lord." He looked at Hadassah with a smile, then noted her trembling. His eyes filled with concern, his large hand covered hers. "What do you really fear, little sister?"

She drew in a quivering breath. "Everything. I'm afraid of what this world holds dear. I'm afraid of suffering. Sometimes I'm afraid of Julia. She does terrible things without thought of the consequences. Trophimus, my courage fails with every opportunity the Lord gives me. Sometimes I even wonder if I am a true believer. If I were, wouldn't I be willing to risk my life to speak the truth? Would suffering a painful death matter?" Her eyes glistened with tears. Most of all, she was afraid of the feelings Marcus roused in her. They grew more and more powerful.

"Was Elijah brave in the face of Jezebel's threat?" Trophimus said. "No. He had just destroyed two hundred priests of Baal, but he ran from a woman and hid in a cave. Was Peter brave when our Lord was taken by the guards? Fear made him deny three times that he knew the Lord. Hadassah, Jesus himself sweated blood in the Garden and prayed the cup would pass from him." He gave her a gentle smile. "God will give you courage when you need it."

She took his hand and kissed it. "What will I do without all of you to encourage me?"

"You have the Lord. He sustains the soul."

"I will miss you and the others so much. Even when I couldn't be there with you, I could stand in the garden and worship with you. Ephesus is so far away."

"We are part of the same body, little sister. Nothing can separate us from the Lord, and in him we are all one."

She nodded, taking strength in what he said, though it didn't take away her sadness. "Please keep praying for the Valerians, especially for Julia."

Trophimus nodded. "And we'll pray for you." He placed his

hands on her shoulders and gave her a gentle squeeze. "We will see each other again when we're with the Lord."

He watched Hadassah disappear into the crowd. He would miss her. He would miss her sweet voice and the look on her face when she sang psalms. Her humble spirit had touched him and his wife and the others deeply, more deeply than she could ever know.

God, protect her. Put angels around her. She will come against all the powers of evil in that city. Guard her from the evil one. Hedge her in and empower her with your Spirit. Make her a light on a hilltop.

For the rest of the day, Trophimus prayed for her as he worked. He would call on the others to pray for her as well.

If Rome was corrupt and dangerous, Ephesus was the very throne of Satan.

EPHESUS

27

Hadassah stood on the deck of the Roman *corbita,* filling her lungs with the salt sea air. The high arc of the bow dipped and rose again, sending a splash of cool spray into the air. A strong wind blew, filling the square sails. Sailors worked the ropes. Everything reminded her of the Sea of Galilee and the sounds of the fishermen as they came in with their catches at the end of the day. She and her father had often walked along the shore near the docks and heard the men shouting back and forth.

Hadassah glanced at the sailors working around her and remembered her father's words. "Peter was such as these. And James and John. Sons of Thunder, the Lord called them. They were sometimes profane and often full of pride."

God chose men like these; Hadassah found hope in that. Jesus hadn't chosen men the world would have chosen. He had picked ordinary men, with obvious faults, and made them into something extraordinary through the indwelling of his Holy Spirit.

Lord, I am so weak. Sometimes I feel so close to you I want to weep, and sometimes I can't feel your presence at all. And Marcus, Lord . . . why am I so drawn to Marcus?

The wind caressed her face as she turned again to watch the sparks of light reflecting off the deep blue of the water. It was all so beautiful—the sights, the smell, the sense of freedom as the ship moved on the broad expanse of water. Pushing the disturbing thoughts and longings from her mind, she closed her eyes and gave thanks for her life, for the beauty God had created, for God himself.

You are here, Lord. You are here and all around me. Would that I could always feel your presence so profoundly. Oh Lord, that I may one day bow before you and worship you forever.

Marcus came up from below decks and saw her at the bow. He hadn't seen her in four days, and his senses quickened. As he approached, he took in the slender curves of her body and the way the strands of dark hair fluttered around her head. He stood right beside her, drinking in the sweetness of her serene profile. She didn't notice him, for her eyes were closed and her lips moved. Entranced, he watched her. She seemed filled with the purest kind of pleasure, as though she were breathing it in deeply.

"Praying again?" he said and saw her start. She didn't look at him, but he was sorry he had shattered her serenity. "It seems to me you pray unceasingly."

She blushed and lowered her head, still saying nothing. What could she say when he had caught her in the act of worshiping God again when he had commanded her not to do so?

He wished he hadn't spoken, but had stood, instead, beside her, drinking in the peace of her contentment—especially since it seemed he could have none of his own. Marcus sighed. "I'm not angry with you," he said. "Pray as you like."

She looked at him then, the tender sweetness of her expression piercing him. He remembered how it felt to kiss her. He lifted his hand and tucked a wayward strand of hair behind her ear. Her expression altered slightly, and he lowered his hand.

"Mother said Julia was being very difficult," he said as casually as he could, wanting her to relax with him. "I take it she is improved?"

"Yes, my lord."

Her quiet, subservient response made him clench his teeth in irritation. He looked from her out to sea as she was doing. "I never noticed how a properly respectful attitude in a slave could put such distance between two human beings." He looked at her again, direct and commanding. "Why do you build walls between us?" He wanted to rip down her defenses and take hold of her. She didn't answer, but he saw she struggled. "Is it always to be *my lord,* Hadassah?"

"As it should be."

"And if I want it otherwise?"

Feeling thrown off-balance by his words, Hadassah reached out and gripped the bulwark. Marcus put his hand over hers and the heat of his touch shocked her. She tried to withdraw her hand, but he clasped it and held it where it was, captive. "My lord," she said, imploring.

"Have you stayed below decks with Julia because she needs you, or in order to hide from me?" he demanded roughly.

"Please," she said, wanting him to release her, frightened by the rush of sensations his touch aroused in her.

"Please *me.* Call me 'Marcus' the way you did in Claudius' garden so long ago. Do you remember? *Marcus,* you said, as though

I meant something to you." He hadn't meant to speak so boldly nor reveal so much of his feelings for her. It was as though he could no longer keep the words buried inside. She stood very still, looking up at him with those beautiful dark eyes—and he wanted her. "You told me once you pray for me."

"I always pray for you." She blushed vividly at that admission and lowered her head again. "I pray for Julia and your mother and father as well."

Hope restored, his thumb rubbed along the smooth skin of her wrist, feeling the wild pulse. "What you feel for me is different from what you feel toward them." He raised her wrist and pressed his lips against it where her pulse beat. When he felt her muscles jerk, he released her. She stepped back from him.

"Why do you do this, my lord?" she said on a soft catch of breath.

"Because I want you," he said and she looked away, embarrassed. "I have no intention of hurting you."

"You would hurt me without even knowing you were doing so."

Her words annoyed him. "I would treat you well." He turned her chin back so that she looked at him. "What do you fear most, Hadassah? Me or this nonexistent god of yours?"

"I fear my own weakness."

Her answer surprised him and sent a rush of heat through his body. "Hadassah," he said in a hoarse whisper, spreading his hand against the silky smoothness of her cheek. She closed her eyes and he felt her longing as intently as his own. But she raised her hand and pressed his away, opening her eyes to look at him in quiet pleading.

"When a man and woman come together with the blessing of God, it is a holy covenant," she said, looking out at the surrounding sea. "Such would not be the case with us, my lord."

His mouth tightened. "Why not?"

"God doesn't bless fornication."

Astonished, he felt the heat pour into his face. He couldn't remember the last time he had blushed, and he was angry that such a ridiculous statement by a naive slave girl should embarrass him. He hadn't been embarrassed by anything in years. "Does your god disapprove of love?"

"God *is* love," Hadassah said softly.

He gave a soft laugh. "Words of a virgin who knows not of

what she speaks. Love is pleasure, Hadassah, the ultimate pleasure. How can this god of yours be love when he sets laws against the purest natural instinct and act of man and woman? What is love other than that?"

The wind changed directions and the sailors shouted at one another. Marcus gave a soft sardonic laugh and looked out at the rippling water, the small flashes of light and color, never expecting her to answer.

But words came to Hadassah, words read by Asyncritus many times to the gathering of believers, words written by the apostle Paul, inspired by God, and sent to the Corinthians. A copy of his precious letter had found its way to Rome. She could hear those words now so clearly it was as though God himself had engraved them upon her mind, and those words applied to this man and to this moment.

"Love is patient, Marcus," she said softly. "Love is kind. Love doesn't act unbecomingly or seek its own. It is not provoked, nor does it take into account a wrong suffered. Love doesn't rejoice in unrighteousness, but rejoices in truth. Love bears all things, believes all things, hopes all things, endures all things. Love never fails . . . "

Marcus gave her a mocking smile. "Love like that is impossible."

"Nothing is impossible for God," she said with such certainty and gentle conviction that he frowned.

"Marcus," Decimus' bland voice came from behind them, and Marcus stiffened. He turned and saw his father standing a few feet away, looking between the two of them. Marcus straightened and smiled faintly. It was obvious his father was wondering what he and Hadassah had been discussing so intently.

"Is Julia better today?" Decimus said, addressing Hadassah.

"She's sleeping well, my lord."

"Has she eaten anything?"

"A bowl of soup and some unleavened bread this morning. She is much improved."

"Did she dismiss you?"

Hadassah blinked. "She—"

"It's the first time in three days that Hadassah's been out of those fetid quarters," Marcus cut in. "Should not even a slave have one breath of fresh air and a moment of rest?"

"As your sister is still in those quarters, it is proper for Hadassah to be there with her, tending to her needs."

Hadassah's eyes pricked with hot tears of shame. "I beg your forgiveness, my lord," she said and took a step. Julia had sent her from the cabin with soiled linen and dishes, and she had thought to linger only a moment or two in the fresh sea air. She should have returned directly rather than so selfishly enjoy herself.

Marcus caught hold of her wrist. "You've done nothing wrong," he said to her. Seeing her distress and knowing he was part of it, he let go of her. He watched her until she was below decks before he spoke.

"She hasn't left Julia since we boarded the ship a week ago," he said, glaring at his father. "Did you have to berate her for standing in the sun and breathing fresh air for one brief moment?"

Decimus was surprised by Marcus' passion. *Berate* was a strong word for the gentle reminder he had given Hadassah. Yet he had hurt her. He had seen that as well as Marcus when she turned away. How deep, he wondered, were Hadassah's feelings for his son? "I'll speak with her."

"To what purpose?" Marcus said, rigid with anger.

"To whatever purpose I deem appropriate," Decimus said warningly. His son stepped past him. "Marcus," he said, but Marcus strode across the deck and went below.

A storm blew the ship off course and renewed Julia's seasickness. She moaned with every dip of the vessel, cursing when her stomach lurched and emptied. Her sleep was fitful at best and filled with nightmares. Listless and pale, she complained constantly when awake.

It was cold and damp in the small cabin. Hadassah tried to keep Julia warm by covering her with heavy woven blankets. Shivering herself, she soothed her mistress.

"The gods are punishing me," Julia said. "I'm going to die. I know I'm going to die."

"You won't die, my lady." Hadassah stroked the limp hair back from Julia's pale brow. "The storm will pass. Try to sleep."

"How can I sleep? I don't want to sleep. I don't want to dream. Sing to me. Make me forget." When Hadassah obeyed, Julia cried out, "Not that one! It hurts me. I don't want to hear songs about your stupid god and how he sees and knows everything! Sing something else. Sing something to amuse me! Something about the affairs of the gods and goddesses. Ballads. Anything."

"I don't know any songs such as those," Hadassah said.

Julia wept bitterly. "Then go away and leave me alone!"

"My lady . . . ," Hadassah said, wanting to comfort her.

"Get out, I tell you," Julia screamed. "Get out! Get out!"

Hadassah went quickly. She sat in the tight, dark corridor, the cold wind seeping in from above. Pulling her knees up against her chest, she tried to keep warm. She prayed. After a long while, she dozed to the dip and sway of the ship. She dreamed of the galley slaves moving back and forth in unison to the pounding of the drum. Dip, *swoosh,* lift, dip, *swoosh,* lift. *Boom. Boom. Boom.*

Marcus almost tripped over her as he came down from helping the sailors. He hunkered down and touched her face. Her skin was icy. He swore softly and smoothed the tendrils of dark hair back from Hadassah's forehead. How long had she been sitting in the corridor with the wind blasting down from above? She didn't awaken as he lifted her in his arms and made his way to his cabin.

He laid her down carefully on his sea bunk and covered her with fur blankets from Germania. He brushed the dark strands of wet hair back from her pale face. "Is this the way your god of love takes care of his own?"

He sat on the edge of the bunk and watched her sleep, an aching tenderness welling up inside and choking him. He wanted to hold and protect her—and he didn't welcome those feelings. Better the fierce passion he had felt for Arria, passion that burned hot and then went cold . . . better that than these new and disquieting feelings he had for Hadassah. They had come gradually, growing slowly, spreading like a vine that worked its way into the mortar of his life. She was becoming part of him; his thoughts were consumed with her.

His mind kept going back over all the things she had said about her god. He couldn't make sense of any of it. She said her god was a god of love, and yet he let his people be destroyed and watched his temple turned to rubble. She believed the Nazarene was the son of her god, a Messiah to her people, and yet this same god-man, or whatever he was, had died a felon's death on a cross.

Her religion was full of paradoxes. Her faith defied all logic. Yet she clung to it with a quiet stubbornness that surpassed the devotion of any temple priestess.

He had grown up on stories of gods and goddesses. His mother worshiped half a dozen. From the time he could remember, he'd watched her place wafer offerings beside her idols every morning and make her visits to the temple once a week.

Devotion wasn't limited to his mother. There was Enoch, the Jew his father had bought upon arrival in Rome. Good old faithful Enoch. More than once, Marcus had seen him turn away with a shake of his head as Marcus' mother went into her *lararium* to take offerings to her idols. Enoch had disdained Roman idols, though he hadn't shared his own beliefs with the Valerians. Was Enoch's silence out of respect and tolerance for the religious practices of others, or was his silence a mark of possessiveness and pride? He had heard it said that the Jews were the chosen race. But chosen for what and by whom?

He looked at Hadassah sleeping peacefully and knew that if he asked, she would open herself to him. Rather than remain a sealed jar, she sought only to pour herself out to others. Everything she did mirrored her faith. It was as though every waking hour of every day she was devoted to pleasing her god by serving others. This god that she worshiped consumed her. It didn't ask for a brief visit to a temple, or a small votive offering of food or coin, or a few prayers every now and then. This god wanted all of her.

And what did she get from him? What reward had she received for her devotion? She was a slave. She had no possessions, no rights, no protection other than what her owners gave her. She couldn't even marry without her master's permission. Her life depended on the goodwill of her owners, for she could be killed for any or no reason at all. She received one small coin a day from his father, and that she frequently gave away.

He remembered the peace on her face as she had stood with her face to the wind. Peace . . . and *joy.* She was a slave and yet she seemed to possess a sense of freedom he had never felt. Was that what drew him?

The storm was dying down. With a shake of his head Marcus knew he needed to be away from her to think more clearly. He left his quarters.

Standing at the bow where he had talked with Hadassah two days before, Marcus gazed out at the dark sea before him. Neptune's dominion. But Neptune wasn't the god he needed now.

With a wry smile, he uttered a prayer to Venus that she would send a winged Cupid to strike Hadassah's heart with love for him.

"Venus, goddess of eros, let her burn as I do."

A gentle wind rippled through the sails. *Love is kind. Love seeks not its own.*

Marcus grimaced, annoyed that Hadassah's words should come back to him now, in the wake of his own appeal to Venus, like a soft whisper in the wind. He looked out at the vast expanse of sea and felt an aching loneliness. A vast darkness closed around him, pressing in on him from all sides, heavy, oppressive.

"I will have her," he said into the stillness and turned to go below.

Julia was standing in the corridor. "I told Hadassah to sit out here and wait until I called her, and she's gone! She's probably with Mother and Father, singing to *them.*"

He caught her arm. "She's in my quarters."

She jerked her arm from him, glaring up at him as though he had betrayed her. "She's *my* slave, not yours."

Marcus held his temper. "I'm only too aware of that, and she's not lying on my bunk for the reasons you suppose. You should take better care of what belongs to you, little sister." He tried to remember that Julia had been suffering from constant seasickness and couldn't be expected to be herself. "I tripped over Hadassah outside your door. She was wet to the skin and half-frozen. A sick slave is hardly of much use to you."

"Well, who's going to attend to my needs?"

The arrogance of her selfishness struck him on the raw. "What do you need?" he said brittlely.

"I need to feel better. I need to get off this ship!"

"You'll feel better as soon as your feet touch dry land," he said, curbing his impatience, ushering her back into her cabin.

"And when will that be?"

"In two or three days," he said, helping her lie back on her rumpled bunk. He drew a blanket over her.

"I wish I'd never agreed to this voyage! I wish I'd stayed in Rome!"

"Why did you agree?"

Her eyes filled. "I didn't want to be surrounded by reminders of what's happened over the last two years. I wanted to get away from all of it."

Marcus felt sudden pity for her. She was his only sister and he loved her, despite her petulance and dark moods. He had pampered and indulged her from the time she was a newborn. He wouldn't stop now. Sitting down on the edge of her bunk, he took her hand. It was cold. "Time will take the bad memories away, and other things will come along to occupy your mind. Ephesus is supposed to be an exciting city, little sister. I'm sure you'll find something of interest there."

"Atretes is in Ephesus."

He raised his brows. "So that's the star that guided you. It's fine to ogle the gladiators, Julia, but don't even think about getting involved with one. They're a different breed of men."

"Octavia said gladiators make the best lovers."

His mouth curved cynically. "Octavia, giver of great wisdom."

"I know you never liked her."

"Rest," he said and rose. She caught his hand.

"Marcus? What star guided you?"

Marcus saw a coolness in her expression that was far removed from the sister he dearly loved. "You," he said, "Mother, Father."

"Nothing else?"

"What other reason might there be?"

"Hadassah." She looked back at him, frowning slightly and studying him intently. "Do you love me, Marcus?"

"I adore you," he said sincerely.

"Would you still love me if I did something horrible?"

Leaning down, he tipped her chin and kissed her lightly on the mouth. He made her look into his eyes. "Julia, you could never do anything so terrible I would stop loving you. I swear it. Now rest."

Julia searched his eyes and then leaned back, still troubled. "I want Hadassah."

"When she awakens, I'll send her to you."

Her face tightened. "She belongs to me. Awaken her now."

Marcus' temper roused as he remembered Hadassah lying in the damp, cold corridor.

"I'm here, my lady," Hadassah said from the doorway, and Marcus glanced back. She was still very pale and drawn with weariness. It was on his tongue to tell her to go back to bed until he saw Julia's face. "I had another bad dream," Julia said, forgetting he was there at all. "I awakened and you weren't here. I remembered you were outside, but I couldn't find you."

Marcus had never seen that look in his sister's eyes before. The minute she had seen Hadassah, a wave of relief seemed to sweep away the anger and fear and trembling desperation.

He spoke quietly, tenderly. "She's here with you now, Julia."

Julia held out her hands to the slave girl, and Hadassah took them, kneeling beside the narrow bunk and pressing her forehead to her mistress's hands. "You should've been here when I called to you," Julia said petulantly.

"Don't take Hadassah to task for something over which she had no control or knowledge," Marcus said.

Julia glanced at him, a question in her eyes—a question that burned him. With a wry smile, Marcus went out, closing the door behind him. Leaning against it, he put his head back and shut his eyes.

28

Two guards brought Atretes above deck and to the bow, where Sertes waited for him. The trader smiled in greeting and made a grand gesture, drawing Atretes' attention beyond him to a glittering temple at the head of the harbor.

"The temple of Artemis, Atretes. She was born in the woods near the mouth of the Cayster and has been worshiped here for over a thousand years. Your goddess, Atretes, the goddess whose image you have in your cell."

"The idol was in my cell in Capua when I arrived." It was bad luck to throw a stone idol away, whether you worshiped it or not.

"However you came by her, I knew when I saw her shrine in your chamber at the ludus that she had chosen you to come to Ephesus." Sertes turned, holding his hand out with great pride. "What you see before you is the greatest temple ever built for any god. It houses a sacred stone hurled to us from the heaven, which was a sign that Artemis chose our city as her *neocoros.*"

"Neocoros?" Atretes said, the word unfamiliar.

"'Temple sweeper,'" Sertes said. "The term once referred to the most menial of laborers, who was devoted to the care of the sacred temple. A term of humility that has become a title of honor." Sertes took a coin from a pouch at his waist and turned it over for Atretes to see. "Neocoros," he said, thumbing the writing on it. "Our city is thus exalted."

Atretes raised his head and looked at Sertes with cold eyes. "The idol was in the cell in Capua when I arrived."

Sertes' smile became sardonic. "And you think that was by accident? Nothing happens by accident, Barbarian. However you came by her image doesn't matter. The gods of your father deserted you in the forests of Germania, but Artemis has kept you alive. Pay homage to her as she deserves and she will continue to protect you. Disdain her, and she'll turn on you and watch as you are destroyed."

He waved his hand again. "Artemis is not the virgin huntress Diana, as the Romans think she is. Artemis is the sister of Apollo, daughter of Leto and Zeus. She is a mother-goddess of the earth who blesses man, beast, and our land with fertility. The stag, the wild boar, the hare, the wolf, and the bear all are sacred to her. Unlike Diana, who is a goddess of chastity, Artemis is sensuous and orgiastic, not prudish and purely athletic."

Atretes looked across the harbor at the great temple. All the beasts Sertes mentioned were plentiful in the Black Forests of his homeland. The temple—a magnificent structure, more magnificent than even the most glorious temples of Rome—glistened in the sunlight. Atretes felt it was almost beckoning him.

"The marble came from Mount Prion," Sertes told him. "All the Greek cities of Asia sent offerings to help build the temple honoring our goddess. There are 127 columns, each 60 feet high, each the gift of a king." Sertes' dark eyes glowed with pride. "Embellishments are added continually by the greatest artists of our time. What other goddess can make such a claim?"

Atretes wondered if Artemis was related to Tiwaz, for she shared some of his attributes. "Will I be allowed to worship her?" he asked, wondering what form celebrating the goddess might take.

Sertes nodded, pleased. "Of course. As is proper," he said magnanimously. "Go below. Water and a clean tunic will be brought to you. Prepare yourself. I will take you to the temple myself so that you may bow down before the sacred idol before you are taken to the ludus."

As soon as the ship docked, Sertes sent two guards for Atretes. Two more waited above decks. The colonnade that led to the Artemision, as the temple was called, was paved with marble and interspersed with shaded porticoes. People turned to stare and whisper as Atretes walked the course. Sertes was obviously well known, and his presence, as well as that of four armed guards, made it clear that the blond giant was a gladiator of importance. Atretes ignored the awed stares he received while wishing Sertes hadn't chosen to march him down the main thoroughfare of the city during the busiest time of day. Clearly, the merchant had done it to create a stir among the populace.

The number of shops that sold wood, silver, and gold shrines increased as they came closer to the Artemision. Small replicas of the temple were everywhere to be seen, and it appeared that every visitor wanted to buy a memorial of Artemis and a model of her temple to take home as a reminder of his or her pilgrimage.

Atretes noted that small idols were in the hands of almost everyone who passed by him.

He stared up at the edifice ahead of him, awed by its immensity and grandeur. Columns of green jasper and white marble rose to the horizontal entablatures, which were intricately carved in every manner of scene. Many of the columns were painted in vivid colors and pictures, some explicitly erotic.

Huge folding doors of cypress stood open and, as Atretes passed through them to enter the holy shrine, he saw that sections of the cedar roof were open to the sky. The gladiator looked around slowly, his trained eye missing little.

"I see you have noticed the guards," Sertes said. "The temple houses the treasury; the lion's share of wealth for all of western Asia is stored here and in the surrounding buildings."

The inner temple was swarming with priests and priestesses, all humming like worker bees around their queen. Sertes inclined his head toward them. "The *megabuzoi* are the priests who conduct the ceremonies within the interior of the temple. They are all eunuchs and in subjection to the high priest."

"And what of the women?" Atretes asked, his mouth tipping at the sight of so many beautiful girls.

"Virgins, all of them. The *melissai* are priestesses consecrated to service of the goddess. They are divided into three classes, all of which are subject to one head priestess. There are also temple prostitutes who await your later pleasure . . . but first, the Most High Goddess."

They entered the smoky chamber that held the sacred image of Artemis. She stood in a haze of incense, hands extended outward, a surprisingly rude and rigid image of gold and ebony. Her upper body was festooned with sagging breasts with extended nipples, her hips and legs covered with carved reliefs of sacred beasts and bees. Her base was shapeless black stone, probably the one Sertes said had fallen from heaven.

As Atretes studied the goddess's image, he saw the engraved symbols upon her headdress, girdle, and base. Suddenly he drew in his breath—the symbol crowning Artemis' headpiece was the rune for Tiwaz! With a hoarse cry, Atretes prostrated himself before the image of Artemis and gave thanks to her for her protection through four years of bloody games.

Incantations of the megabuzoi and the melodious chanting of the melissai surrounded him and pressed down upon him. The scent of incense had become so overpowering that he felt sick. Gagging, he rose and half stumbled from the cloistered chamber. Leaning heavily against one of the massive columns, he dragged in a deep breath of air, his heart pounding in beat with the drums and cymbals behind him.

After a moment, his head cleared, but the heaviness within his spirit remained, dark and suffocating.

"She called to you," Sertes said, eyes glowing with satisfaction.

"She bears the rune for Tiwaz," Atretes said in amazement.

"The 'Ephesian Letters,'" Sertes said. "Pronounced aloud they will be a charm for you. The Letters have great power and, if worn as an amulet, will ward off evil spirits. The building you see over there houses an archive of books about the Letters. The men who write them are the most brilliant minds of the Empire. Which Letter was of special significance to you?"

Atretes told him.

"You can purchase an amulet when we finish our devotions," Sertes said and nodded toward several beautiful, richly garbed young women who moved in the cool shadows of the columned corridor. "Take your pick," Sertes said. "The women are beautiful and skilled, the young men strong and vigorous. There's no faster or better way to achieve connection with Artemis than by enjoying the many erotic pleasures she gives us."

Four years of brutality and being treated like a pampered animal had crushed the gentler side of Atretes. Without embarrassment, he looked over those soliciting and stared at a voluptuous girl dressed in veilings of red, black, and gold.

"I'll take her," Atretes said, and Sertes gestured to her. She walked toward them, every step a movement of provocation. Her voice was low and husky. Two denarii, she said. Atretes handed her the coins and she took him down the steps, across the white marbled plain, and into the cool shadows of a brothel.

He had found his goddess. And yet, long after he came back out into the sunlight, darkness lay heavy upon his soul.

Hadassah thought the Valerians' new home was even more beautiful than the villa in Rome. It was built on a slope facing out onto Kuretes Street, the most privileged section near the heart of Ephesus on the declivity of Mount Bulbul. Each house served as a covered terrace for the one next to it, offering a view of the beautiful city.

The villa had three floors, each opening around a columned central peristyle that allowed sun and moonlight into the inner rooms. A well was in the center of the peristyle, paved round in white marble and decorated by mosaics. The inner chambers also had mosaic floors, and walls covered with appallingly erotic frescoes.

Julia's spirits rose the moment she saw them. Laughing, she spread her arms and turned about in her chamber. "Eros wearing a crown!" she said in delight. In the western corner was a statue of a man, naked except for a wreath of laurel leaves on his head. In one hand he held a bunch of grapes, in the other a goblet. Julia went to it and ran her hands over it. "Perhaps the gods will be kind to me after all," she said, laughing as Hadassah turned her head away in embarrassment. "Jews are so prudish, it's a wonder they beget so many children," Julia said, taking pleasure in teasing her.

The family gathered in the triclinium. Hadassah served the meal, all too aware of the licentious frescoes covering the three walls—Greek gods and goddesses in various amorous escapades.

During the first weeks in Ephesus, Decimus seemed much improved in health. He even took Phoebe and Julia for carriage rides along the western slopes of Mount Panayir Dagi. Marcus went to the Valerian offices near the harbor to make certain that all of the arranged transfers of money had been conducted according to his specifications.

Hadassah remained in the house with the other slaves, unpacking and tidying Julia's possessions. When her duties were complete, she went out to explore the city an hour at a time; Julia wanted to know where jewelry and cloth shops were located. As Hadassah walked along the marble-paved streets, she passed one fane after another, all dedicated to one god or another. She saw baths, public buildings, a medical school, a library. She turned a corner, and there ahead of her, on a street lined by idol vendors, loomed the Artemision. Despite its amazing beauty, Hadassah felt her spirit recoil.

Yet, curious, she approached and sat in a shady portico to watch people mill about the temple. Many who passed her carried small shrines and idols they had purchased. Hadassah shook her head in disbelief. Hundreds of people were going up and down the steps to worship a stone idol that was without life or power.

The young Jewess felt an aching sadness and loneliness. She looked up at the beauty and immensity of the Artemision and felt small and helpless by comparison. She looked at the hundreds of worshipers and was afraid. Rome had been frightening enough, but something about Ephesus oppressed her spirit.

Closing her eyes, she prayed. *God, are you here in this place that is teeming with pagan worshipers? I need to feel your presence, but I don't. I feel so alone. Help me find friends like Asyncritus and Trophimus and the others.*

She opened her eyes again, gazing at the crowds without really seeing them. She knew she should return to the villa, but the quiet voice within her bade her stay a few minutes longer. So she obeyed and waited. Her eyes casually scanned the milling people . . . then she frowned. She had glimpsed someone among a group of men—someone familiar—and her heart leaped. She rose and stood on tiptoe, peering intently. She had not been mistaken! Filled with joy, Hadassah ran, pressing her way through the crowd with a boldness she had never shown before. When she broke through the last followers, she cried out his name and he turned, his face alight with surprise and joy.

"Hadassah!" cried John, the apostle, and opened his arms.

Hadassah went into them weeping. "Praise be to God!" she said, clinging to him and feeling she was home for the first time since she had left Galilee five years before.

Marcus returned early from meeting with solicitors and merchants. The house was cool and quiet. Brooding, he stood outside his bedchamber on the second floor and leaned against a column, staring down into the peristyle. A maid was at work scrubbing the tiles of the mosaic depicting a satyr in pursuit of a naked maiden. The girl looked up at him and smiled. She was new to the household, one of his father's purchases upon their arrival. Marcus suspected his father had bought the girl in the hopes that her dusky beauty and full curves would distract him from his obsession with Hadassah.

His father might as well have saved his money.

Straightening, Marcus went back into his chamber to pour himself some wine. Taking a drink, he went out onto the terrace, looking below at the people thronging the street. With an uncanny sense of swift recognition, Marcus saw Hadassah weaving her way up Kuretes Street. Her hair was covered with the striped shawl she habitually wore, and she carried a basket of peaches and grapes on her hip; fruit to satisfy Julia's whim while his own needs went unanswered. Hadassah lifted her head slightly, but if she saw him watching her, she gave no outward sign.

Marcus frowned. She'd seemed different over the past few days. Elated. Full of joy. A few nights ago, he'd come in late and heard her singing to his father and mother, and her sweet voice had been so rich and pure it had made his heart ache. When he went in to sit with them, she'd been more beautiful to him than ever before.

Leaning against the wall, Marcus watched Hadassah come up the street to the house. She glanced up once and then not again. She disappeared below him as she reached the entryway.

His mood darkening, he went back inside the villa and stood in the coolness of the corridor on the second floor, listening for the door to open. Quiet voices murmured in the lower hall, then one of the kitchen servants crossed the peristyle with a basket of fruit. He waited.

Hadassah came into the stream of sunlight below him. She removed the shawl that covered her hair, leaving it draped loosely back over her shoulders. Dipping her hands slowly into the basin of water, she pressed the moisture to her face. Odd how such an ordinary act could show her grace and simple dignity.

The house was so quiet, Marcus heard her sigh.

"Hadassah," he said, and she stilled. His hand clenched the iron railing. "I want to talk to you," he said rigidly. "Come upstairs to my chambers. Now."

He waited for her in the doorway of his chambers, sensing her reluctance to enter. When she did, he closed the door firmly behind her. She stood subservient, her back to him, waiting for him to speak. For all her seeming calm, he felt her tension like the cut of a knife. It hurt his pride that he had had to command her to come into his presence. He walked past her and stood between the columns to his terrace. He wanted to say something, but couldn't find the words.

Turning slightly, he looked back at her. His own longing was mirrored in her eyes, mingled with confusion and fear. "Hadassah," he breathed, and everything he felt for her was in her name. "I have waited—"

"No," she said in a soft cry and moved to flee.

Marcus caught her before she could open the door. Forcing her around, he pressed her back against it. "Why do you fight your feelings? You love me." He cupped her face.

"Marcus, don't!" she said in anguish.

"Admit it," he said and lowered his mouth to take hers. When she turned her head away, he pressed his mouth to the warm curve of her throat. She gasped and tried to struggle free.

"You love me!" he said fiercely and this time captured her chin and lifted her face to him. He covered her mouth with his, kissing her with all the intense passion that had been growing in him for months. He drank of her like a man dying of thirst. Her body melted gradually into his, and he knew he couldn't wait any longer. Catching her up in his arms, he carried her across the room to his couch.

"No!" she cried and began to struggle again.

"Stop fighting me," he said hoarsely. He saw the darkness of her eyes and the flush of her skin. "Stop fighting yourself." He caught her wrists. "I left Rome to be with you. I've waited for you longer than I've ever waited for any woman."

"Marcus, don't bring this sin upon yourself."

"'Sin,'" he sneered and took her mouth again. She clutched at his tunic, half-pushing, half-clinging. She kept begging him to stop, and her pleas only made him more determined to prove her desire was no less than his own. She trembled beneath his touch, and he could feel the heat of her skin—but he also tasted the saltiness of tears.

"God, help me!" she cried.

"God," he said, suddenly furious. All gentleness was forgotten in an explosion of frustration. "Yes, pray to a god. Pray to Venus. Pray to Eros that you might behave like a normal woman!" He felt the neckline of her tunic tear in his hand and heard her soft, frightened cry.

Swearing, he suddenly drew back. Breathing heavily, he stared down at the damage he'd done, the ripped tunic still clenched in his hand. A coldness swept over him and he let go of it. "Hadassah," he groaned, filled with self-loathing. "I didn't mean—"

He broke off, stunned into silence by the sight of her still, white face. Her eyes were closed and she was not moving. All the breath went out of him as he looked at her still form. "Hadassah!" Cradling her in his arms, he brushed the hair back from her face and laid his hand over her heart, terrified that her god had struck her dead to save her purity. But her heart beat against his palm, and relief flooded him—until it came to him with a sickening blow that he had been about to rape her.

She began to rouse and, unable to face her, he laid her back on the couch and stood. He went to the decanter and poured wine, tossing it down his throat. It tasted like gall. Shaking violently, he looked back and saw her sitting up. Her face was ashen. He poured more wine and brought it back to her.

"Drink this," he said, pushing the goblet into her hand. She took it with unsteady hands. "It would seem your god wants you to remain a virgin," he said, wincing inwardly at the callousness of his words. What was he becoming that he could rape the woman he loved? "Drink all of it," he said bleakly and felt the tremor in her fingers as they brushed his. Full of remorse, he put his hands around hers and knelt in front of her.

"I lost control . . . ," he said, his voice choked with pain, knowing it was no excuse. She didn't look at him, but tears slipped down her pale cheeks—a silent river of them—and his heart twisted. "Don't cry. Hadassah, don't cry. Please." He sat beside her wanting to pull her into his arms, but afraid to. "I'm sorry," he said, touching her hair. "Nothing happened. You needn't cry." The goblet dropped on the floor, splattering red wine like blood across the marble tiles. She covered her face, her shoulders shaking.

Marcus rose and moved away from her, cursing himself. "My love is neither kind nor patient," he said in self-condemnation. "I never meant to hurt you. I swear! I don't know what happened. . . . I've never lost control like that before."

"You stopped," she said.

He glanced back at her, surprised she had even spoken to him. Her gaze was steady, despite the trembling in her body.

"You stopped, and the Lord will bless you—"

Her words roused a fury in him. "Don't speak to me of your god! A curse upon him!" he said bitterly.

"Don't say that," she whispered, her heart full of fear for him.

He came back and forced her to look at him. "Is this love I have for you what you would call a blessing?" He saw his grip was hurting her and let her go. He moved a few feet away, fighting his emotions. "How is it a blessing to want you as I do and not be able to have you because of some ridiculous law? It's unnatural to fight our basic instincts. Your god takes pleasure in inflicting pain."

"God wounds that he might heal."

"So you don't deny it," he said with a harsh laugh. "He plays games with people just like any other god."

"No games, Marcus. There is no other God but the Almighty God, and what he does, he does according to his good purpose."

He closed his eyes. *Marcus.* She blessed his name as she said it, and his rage evaporated—but not the frustration. "What good purpose can come from my love for you?" he asked hopelessly, looking at her. Her eyes shimmered with tears. He thought he would drown at the look of hope in her eyes.

"It may be God's way of unlocking your heart for him."

He stiffened. "For him?" He gave a harsh laugh. "I'd rather be dead than bow down to this god of yours." He had never seen such a stricken look of hurt and sorrow on her face and was sorry he had spoken. He saw how he had ripped the seam of her slave dress with his hands and knew now that he had torn at her heart as well with his angry words. And as he looked into her eyes, he knew that in doing so he had torn himself apart.

"I want to know what it is in you that makes you cling to this unseen god of yours. Tell me."

Hadassah looked up at him and knew she loved him as she would never love another. *Why, God? Why this man who doesn't understand? Why this man who willfully rejects you? Are you cruel, as Marcus says?*

"I don't know, Marcus," she said, deeply shaken. She still trembled with a strange, heavy longing for him and was afraid at how easy it would be to surrender to the sensations Marcus stirred in her. God had never made her feel this way.

Oh, God, give me strength. I have none of my own. The way he looks at me makes me melt inside. He makes me weak.

"Make me understand," Marcus said, and she knew he would wait until she answered.

"My father said the Lord chose his children before the foundation of the world, according to his kind intention."

"*Kind* intention? Is it kind to keep you from enjoying what's natural? You *love* me, Hadassah. I saw it in your eyes when you looked at me. I felt it when I touched you. Your skin was so warm. You were trembling, and it wasn't with fear. Is it kind that your god makes us suffer this way?"

When he looked at her like that, she couldn't think. She lowered her eyes.

Marcus came to her and tipped her chin up. "You can't answer, can you? You think this god of yours is everything. That he's enough. I tell you he isn't. Can he hold you, Hadassah? Can he touch you? Can he kiss you?" His hand spread gently against her cheek, and when he saw how her eyes closed, his pulse jumped. "Your skin is hot and your heart is pounding as fast as mine." He looked into her eyes, beseeching her. "Does your god make you feel the way I do?"

"Don't do this to me," she whispered and took his hand between both of hers. "Please don't do this."

He knew he had hurt her again, but he didn't know why. He couldn't understand anything and it filled him with grief and frustration. How could someone so gentle, so fragile, be so unbending?

"This god can't even speak to you," Marcus said raggedly.

"He does speak to me," she said softly.

Marcus took his hand from hers. Searching her face, he saw she spoke the truth. Others had made such claims before: the gods said this, the gods said that. Whatever the gods said was to their own purpose. But now, as he looked into Hadassah's eyes, he had no doubt—and he was suddenly, inexplicably, afraid. "How? When?"

"Do you remember the story I told once about Elijah and the Baal prophets?"

He frowned slightly. "The man who called down fire from the heavens to burn his offering and then afterwards butchered two hundred priests?" He remembered. He had been amazed that Hadassah could tell such a bloody tale. He straightened and put distance between them. "What of it?"

"After Elijah destroyed the priests, Queen Jezebel said she would do the same to him, and he ran away because he was afraid."

"Afraid of a *woman?*"

"Not just any woman, Marcus. She was very evil and very powerful. Elijah ran away into the wilderness to hide from Jezebel. He asked God that he might die, but God sent an angel to minister to him instead. The food the angel of the Lord gave him enabled Elijah to travel forty days until he reached Horeb, the mountain of God. Elijah found a cave there and lived in it. It was then that the Lord came to him. A strong wind came and broke the rocks, but God wasn't in the storm. Then an earthquake and a fire came, but the Lord was not in them, either. And then, as Elijah was protected in the cleft of a rock, he heard God speak."

She looked up at Marcus, and her eyes were soft and radiant, her face strangely aglow. "God spoke in a gentle whisper, Marcus. A still, small voice. A voice in the wind . . . "

Marcus felt a strange tingling sensation down his spine. Defensive, his mouth curled. "A wind."

"Yes," she said softly.

"There's a breeze today. If I stand outside on the terrace, could I hear the voice of this god of yours?"

She lowered her head. "If you opened your heart." *If your heart was not so hardened.* She wanted to weep again.

"He would speak even to a Roman?" he said mockingly. "More likely this god of yours would want my heart on his altar," he said dryly. "Especially after what I was about to do to one of his most devoted followers." He stood in the open doorway to the terrace, his back to her. "Is it your god I must blame, then, for this desire I have for you? Is it his doing?" He turned to face her again.

"Shades of Apollo and Daphne," he said bitterly. "Do you know of them, Hadassah? Apollo wanted Daphne, but she was a virgin and wouldn't surrender. He pursued her madly and she fled from him, crying out to the gods to save her." He gave a harsh laugh. "And they did. Do you know how? They turned her into a bush with sweetly scented flowers. That's why you'll see statues of Apollo with a wreath of daphne crowning his head."

Marcus' mouth twisted wryly. "Will this god of yours turn you into a bush or a tree to protect your virginity from me?"

"No."

A long stillness hung between them. The only sound in Marcus' ears was his own heartbeat. "You were fighting yourself more than you were fighting me."

She blushed and lowered her eyes again, but she made no denial. "It's true you make me feel things I've never felt before," she said softly and looked at him again. "But God gave me free will and he warned of the consequences of immorality—"

"Immorality?" Marcus said through his teeth, the word like a slap across his face. "Is it immoral for two people who love one another to take pleasure together?"

"As you loved Bithia?"

Her softly spoken question was like a dash of cold water and further roused his anger. "Bithia has nothing to do with my feelings for you! I never loved Bithia."

"But you made love to her," she said very softly, embarrassed to speak so plainly.

He looked into her eyes and his anger evaporated. He felt a sense of shame and couldn't fathom why. There was nothing wrong with what he had done with Bithia. Was there? She had come to him freely. After the first few times, Bithia had come to him in the night even when he hadn't summoned her.

"I would have to command you, wouldn't I?" he said with a rueful smile. "And if I did demand your surrender, you'd feel compelled to throw yourself off the terrace."

"You won't command me."

"What makes you so sure?"

"You're an honorable man."

"Honorable," he said with a bitter laugh. "How easily a single word can wash away a man's ardor. And hope. Your intention, no doubt." He looked at her. "I'm a Roman, Hadassah. Above all else, I am that. Don't count too heavily on my restraint."

The silence hung between them. Marcus knew nothing could destroy his love for her, and he felt a moment of despair. If not for this belief she held so tightly, he could claim her for his own. If not for her god . . .

Hadassah rose. "May I go, my lord?" she said very softly, once more a servant.

"Yes," he said without inflection and watched her walk to the door and open it. "Hadassah," he said, his love for her tearing at him. The only way he could have her was to shatter this stubborn faith of hers. In doing so, would he shatter her? "What has this god of yours ever really done for you?"

She stood very still for a long moment, her back to him. "Everything," she said softly and left, closing the door quietly behind her.

Marcus told his father that evening that he intended to look into buying a place of his own. "Our sudden relocation to Ephesus has raised some speculation concerning the security of our assets," he said. "An outlay of gold talents for a second villa and some lavish entertaining of important Roman officials will dispel the speculations quickly enough."

Decimus looked at him, well aware that Marcus' true reasons for leaving had nothing to do with "outside speculation."

"I understand, Marcus." And, indeed, he did.

29

"Hadassah!" Julia called as she entered the house. Lifting the hem of her palus, she hurried up the stairs. "Hadassah!"

"Yes, my lady," she said, hastening to her.

"Come, come, come, quickly!" Julia said and closed the door of her room behind her. She laughed and spun around happily, stripping off the thin veil that covered her hair. "Mother and I went to the Artemision this morning, and I almost fainted when he came in."

"Who, my lady?"

"Atretes! He's even more beautiful than I remember. Like a god come down from Olympus. Everyone was staring at him. He was within a few feet of me. Two guards were with him while he worshiped. I thought I'd die, my heart beat so fast." She put her hand against her chest as though to still it for a moment and then began rummaging through her things. "Mother said we should leave him in private to worship," she said glumly.

"What are you looking for, my lady? Let me help you find it."

"The red carnelian. Remember it? Not the simple one, but the big one with the heavy gold claw. Look for it. Hurry! Chakras said it enhances the imagination, and I'm going to need all the imagination I can get if I'm going to figure a way to meet Atretes."

Hadassah found the pendant and held it out to her. For all the pure natural beauty of the carnelian itself, the gruesome claw made it a loathsome piece of jewelry, a talisman meant to perform magic. "Don't put faith in a stone, my lady," she said, obediently handing it to her mistress.

Julia laughed at her and put it on. She clutched the carnelian. "Why not? If it's worked for others, why not for me?" She held the carnelian tightly in both hands between her breasts and closed her eyes. "I must center my thoughts and meditate. Leave me until I call for you."

The carnelian seemed to work for Julia. Within an hour, she knew exactly how she would meet Atretes. It wasn't an idea she could share with Hadassah, nor with anyone else in the household. Even Marcus would make objection to her methods, but she didn't care. Her eyes glittered with excitement. No, she didn't care what anyone thought. Besides, no one had to know . . . it would be a secret known only to herself—and Atretes.

Hadassah had said not to put her faith in a stone, but the carnelian had worked! Julia knew she'd never have been able to imagine an idea so outrageous and so thrilling without it. Tomorrow she would make all the necessary preparations.

And the following day, she'd meet Atretes at the temple of Artemis.

Atretes remembered his mother's prophecy the moment he saw Julia Valerian amidst the scented haze of incense smoke within the inner sanctuary of the Artemision. He had been waiting for her to come back into his life, and now she stood before him like a conjured vision, even more beautiful than he remembered her. Wearing a gauzy red palus that was trimmed with gold embroidery and floated about her slender body, she walked toward him. He heard the soft tinkle of bells and saw the anklets she wore.

He frowned slightly as he watched her. How had the shy girl who had blushed at the ludus come to be a temple prostitute in Ephesus? Surely it was the work of the goddess, preparing the way to bring her to him. But then, what did he know of Julia Valerian but what he had been told? He had only seen her once above him in the balcony at the ludus. Now she stood so close to him that he could see the soft flush of her skin as it heated beneath his scrutiny. And he saw her eyes, dark and hungry.

She hadn't the coldness of a prostitute's feigned ardor. Her desire for him was real, so real that Atretes wanted her more than he had ever wanted a woman. But something within him made him wait and hold his silence.

Standing beneath his enigmatic regard, Julia felt nervous and uncertain. She moistened her lips and tried desperately to remember the words she had practiced.

She'd been waiting for him at the temple for hours, warding off the propositions of a dozen others, wondering if he would come at all. And then he had appeared. Heavily guarded, he had placed his offering in the hands of the priest and prostrated himself before the image of Artemis. When he rose, she moved into his line of vision, feeling a wave of heat as he turned and saw her.

Now he cocked his head slightly, his mouth tipping in mock

amusement, challenging her. She spoke in a nervous rush. "Join me in celebration, so that we may delight the Most High Goddess." She knew she sounded breathless, and she blushed.

"At what price?" he said, his voice deep and heavily accented.

"At whatever price you're willing to pay."

Atretes let his gaze move from the top of her head down to her sandaled feet. She was breathtakingly beautiful, but he felt a vague disquiet. Was this the woman of whom his mother had prophesied? A woman who dressed up and sold herself as a harlot? Desire made him disregard his misgivings. He nodded.

She led him to an inn that catered to wealthy foreign visitors rather than to one of the brothels close by the temple. Once inside, she turned eagerly into his arms.

When it was over, Atretes felt a disquieting repugnance at what had passed between them. He stood and moved a few feet away. Startled by his abandonment, she blinked up at him. The handsome lines of his godlike face were hard and cold. What was he thinking as he looked down at her? She tried to judge his expression and couldn't.

"What game are you playing, Julia Valerian?"

Her eyes went wide, her cheeks hot. "How do you know my name?"

"You came once to the Roman ludus. With that Roman whore, Octavia. I asked. Bato told me you were married."

"My husband died," she said, embarrassed.

His brow lifted in mockery. "How did the daughter of one of the richest merchants in the Roman Empire become a temple prostitute?"

She stood shakily, feeling better able on her feet to face his sardonic manner. "I'm not a prostitute."

He smiled coldly and reached out to touch her hair. "No?"

"No," she said, trembling. "It was the only way I could think to meet you."

Atretes was shaken again by the desire that stirred within him when he touched her. "All this subterfuge to be with a gladiator?" he said coldly.

"No," she replied breathlessly, her hands spreading worshipfully against his chest. "No. I wanted to be with you. Only with you, Atretes. I've wanted to be with you since the first day I saw you running on the road near Capua."

"I remember. You had a little Jewess with you."

"You remember? I didn't think you noticed me," she said, searching his face with hungry eyes. "Then it's destiny. . . ." With surprising strength, she pulled his head down.

Atretes fed her hunger. He savored it, wanting to stretch it out and make it last. Julia Valerian wasn't a slave sent to his cell in the ludus as a reward, nor was she a prostitute he had paid on the temple steps. She came to him of her own free will, the daughter of a powerful Roman citizen, a captive of her own passions.

And Atretes used her as balm for the scars inflicted on his soul. Or he thought he did.

Finally, replete, Atretes dressed to leave, keeping his back to her. Part of him wanted to walk out the door and forget what had happened between them.

"When can I see you again?" she said poignantly, and he turned to regard her. She was beautiful, so beautiful she made him catch his breath. His flesh was weak, and her hungry eyes fed a deeper hunger of his own.

He smiled coldly. "Whenever you find a way." He removed the money pouch from his belt, tossed it into her lap, then left her sitting on the floor.

Marcus entertained frequently at his new villa, widening his circle of newly established Ephesian friends. He also cultivated the friendship of the proconsul and other Roman officials, several of whom he had previously known in Rome. His father readily agreed when he suggested having Julia act as hostess at formal feasts and gatherings. Thus Marcus accomplished two ends with the arrangement: he gave his sister some of the freedom she had lost with Caius' death, and he saw Hadassah.

This evening, as on so many others, Marcus' villa was filled with guests and activity. He glanced at Julia as she lay stretched out on a cushioned couch beside him watching the African dancers with only lukewarm interest. Her eyes met his and she smiled.

"The proconsul's daughter was asking all manner of questions about you this evening, Marcus," she said, leaning closer to him. "I think she's in love with you."

"Eunice is a sweet child."

"That sweet child you dismiss so easily has her father's ear, and her father has the ear of the emperor."

He grinned condescendingly. "If I ever marry, Julia, it will be for reasons other than gaining political influence."

"Who said anything about marriage?" Julia said with a mischievous smile.

"You're suggesting I corrupt the daughter of the proconsul of Rome," Marcus said, selecting a delicacy from a tray set before him.

"Corrupt?" Julia said with a slight rise of her brows. "A curious term for an epicurean. I always thought you took your pleasure where you found it." She selected a ripe plum. "Eunice is ripe for the plucking." Her dark eyes sparkled with amusement as she took a bite of the succulent purple fruit. She rose from the couch. "Wasn't your reason for leaving Father's villa so you could entertain and gain influence among the elite? So, garner it where it comes." With that, she rose and moved into the crowd.

Marcus watched Julia thoughtfully. Her year with Caius had changed her. She *worked* a room, talking with various men, laughing, lightly touching, moving away with a teasing glance over her shoulder. It disturbed him. He had always thought of her as his naive, lovely little sister, whom he pampered and adored.

He remembered Arria as he watched his sister turn heads and leave broken hearts in her wake. She was hunting, and no one in the room seemed to be the breed of animal she wanted.

She beckoned Hadassah, and they went out onto the terrace alone. Marcus frowned slightly. Whatever command Julia had given, Hadassah had had something to say about it. Julia was agitated and spoke again, intently. She slipped a gold bracelet from her wrist and gave it to Hadassah before coming back inside. At Julia's curt nod of dismissal, Hadassah left the banquet hall.

Marcus rose to follow her and find out what was going on. Eunice stepped gracefully into his path, bumping him slightly in a coy attempt to gain his attention. "Oh, I'm sorry, Marcus. I wasn't looking where I was going," she said and gazed up at him with such adoration that he cringed.

"My fault entirely," he said, aware that her expression fell with disappointment as he stepped by her. By the time he reached the corridor, Hadassah was gone.

Moonlight reflected off of the white marble streets and fana as Hadassah found her way to the ludus. She knocked at the heavy main gate and waited. When a guard opened it, she asked to speak with Sertes. She was taken across the courtyard and down a darkened corridor to Sertes' office. He was expecting her. When he held out his hand, she gave him the gold bracelet. He weighed it critically and looked at the work, then nodded, locking it in a strongbox inside his desk. "This way," he said and led Hadassah down the stone steps into the cold, granite corridor lit by torches.

Stopping at a heavy door, he found the right key. As he opened the door, Hadassah glimpsed a man sitting on a stone bench. She recognized him from the one time she had seen him on the road to Capua, for he was powerfully built and breath-catchingly handsome. When he rose and turned to face them, she thought of the statue in her mistress's possession. The sculptor had captured the gladiator's arrogance and physical splendor, but had missed the bleakness in his eyes, the despair hidden beneath a mask of cold, restrained power.

"Your lady has sent her maid for you," Sertes said. "Be at the delivery door at dawn." He left them.

Atretes' mouth tightened, and his eyes moved and narrowed on the small, slender slave girl looking at him. She wore a fine, cream-colored tunic that reached her ankles and was belted with a striped cloth that matched the shawl covering her hair and shoulders. He looked directly into her eyes, expecting to see what he usually did: adoration or fear. Instead, he saw a quiet calm.

"I will show you the way," she said. Her voice was low and gentle. He swung his cloak about his shoulders and covered his blond hair. The only sound he heard was the soft pad of her sandaled feet as he followed her. The guard opened the door for her without a word and watched her pass by, barely taking note of Atretes. The heavy gate of the ludus slammed behind him, and Atretes breathed more easily.

"You're a Jew," he said, coming to walk beside the girl.

"I was born in Judea."

"How long have you been a slave?"

"Since the destruction of Jerusalem."

"I knew a Jew once. Caleb, from the tribe of Judah. He had thirty-seven kills to his credit." She said nothing. "Did you know him?"

"No, I didn't," she said, although she had overheard Octavia and Julia talking about him. "The strongest and most handsome men of Jerusalem were taken to Alexandria with Titus and transported to Rome for the games. I was among the last captives who marched north."

"He died well."

Something in the flat emotionlessness of his voice made Hadassah look up at him. His handsome face was hard, but she sensed something deeper, something buried beneath the cold, ruthless face of a trained killer: beneath it all lurked a sorrow that tortured him.

The slave girl stopped. He was surprised when she took one of his hands between both of hers. "May God turn his face to you and give you peace," she said with such compassion that he could only stare down at her.

She resumed walking, and Atretes didn't speak to her again. He slowed his pace to match hers, following whatever course she took.

He knew he was in the richest section of Ephesus. Finally, Julia's strange little maid turned up a marble stairway. At the end of it was a door that opened into a passageway, most probably used by delivery men. When they reached the end of it, the girl opened another door into a storage room. "Please wait here," she said and left him.

He leaned against a barrel and looked around with growing distaste. Julia had undoubtedly stroked Sertes' palms with gold in order to have him brought to her. Brought like a whore to serve the rich girl's passions.

His proud anger evaporated the moment the door opened and he saw her. "Oh, I thought you'd never get here," she said breathlessly, and he knew she had run to him. She flung herself into his arms, digging her fingers into his hair as she raised herself on tiptoes.

With Julia Valerian in his arms, Atretes could think of nothing but the taste, feel, and scent of her. Only later did he remember his pride—and the shattering cost of an illusive sense of freedom.

Hadassah went to John at her first opportunity. A man who was past his prime, a fact that did not lessen the impact of his compelling eyes, answered her knock. He greeted her kindly and introduced himself as one of John's followers. Then he brought her to the quiet lamplit room where the apostle was writing a letter to one of the struggling churches in the Empire. He looked up and smiled warmly. Setting his quill aside, he rose to take her hands and kiss her cheek. When he drew back, she didn't let go.

"Oh, John," she said, hanging onto his hands as though they were her only lifeline.

"Sit, Hadassah, and tell me what lies so heavily upon your heart." She clung to his hands, not wanting to ever let go. Jesus had been crucified years before her birth, but in John, as in her father, she saw the Lord. In John's dear face she found infinite compassion, love, the glow of fierce conviction, the strength of true faith. Strength like her father's. Strength she so lacked.

"What grieves you so?" John said.

"Everything, John. Everything in this life," she said in misery. "My faith is so weak. Father went out into the streets when the zealots were murdering people and gave his testimony. But I'm afraid to even speak the name of Jesus aloud." She wept, ashamed. "Enoch bought me for the master because he thought I was one of his people. A Jew. They all still think I'm a Jew. Except for Marcus. He found out I was meeting with other Christians in Rome and forbade me to see them again. He said Christians are subversives who plot the destruction of the Empire. He said it would be dangerous for me to associate with them. Sometimes he asks me why I believe, but when I try to tell him, he never understands. He just becomes angry."

The words came flooding out.

"And Julia. Oh, John, Julia is so lost. She's done such terrible things, and I can see her dying inside, little by little. I've told her every story Father ever taught me, stories that built my faith. But she doesn't really hear. She just wants to be entertained. She wants to forget. Once, just once, I thought perhaps her father began to understand . . . " She shook her head. She let go of John's hands and covered her face.

"I know fear, Hadassah. Fear is an old enemy. I gave in to it the night Jesus was in the garden and Judas came with the priests and the Roman guards."

"But you went to his trial."

"I only went close enough to hear. I was safe among the crowd. My family was well known in Jerusalem. My father knew members of the court. But I will tell you, Hadassah, I never knew real fear until I watched Jesus die. I have never felt so alone as I did then, and it didn't change until I saw the empty grave clothes in the tomb and knew he had risen."

He took her hand. "Hadassah, Jesus told us everything and we still didn't understand who he was or what he had come to do. James and I were zealous, proud, ambitious, intolerant. Jesus called us Sons of Thunder because we sought to call down the wrath of God on men who were healing in his name, but who weren't following him. We wanted that power reserved only for us. We were such proud, blind fools. We knew Jesus was the Messiah, but we expected him to become a warrior king like David and then we'd reign beside him. It was impossible for us to believe this man who was God the Son had come to be the Passover Lamb for all of mankind."

He smiled sadly and patted her hand. "It was Mary of Magdala—not James, not me—whom Jesus chose to be the first to see the risen Christ."

She couldn't see through her tears. "How can I have your strength?"

He smiled tenderly. "You have whatever strength God has given you, and it will be enough to carry out his good purpose. Trust in him."

30

Phoebe found Julia's visitor impressive and disturbing. The woman spoke pure Latin, denoting her class, and though she appeared young, she carried herself with an elegant poise that bespoke worldly experience far beyond Phoebe's own years. And the visitor was stunning, not because of the perfection of her features, for they were far from perfect, but because of the arresting quality of her dark eyes. Their intensity was almost unnerving.

Phoebe knew Julia had once considered this woman a close friend. It seemed strange, for they were so different. Julia was passionate about everything; this woman was cool and controlled.

Speaking softly to one of the servants, Phoebe told the girl to come to the doorway the moment Julia returned. While they waited, Phoebe served refreshments and carried on polite conversation. When the servant appeared and gave a subtle nod, Phoebe excused herself and went to speak with her daughter. Perhaps, Julia wouldn't want to see this woman.

"Julia, you've a guest waiting in the peristyle."

"Who is it?" Julia removed the soft veil from her hair and tossed it to Hadassah, waving her away with a graceful lift of her hand.

"Calabah Fontaneus. She arrived an hour ago and we've had a very interesting conversation. Julia?" Phoebe had never seen such an expression on her daughter's face. She touched her lightly. "Are you all right?"

Julia turned haunted eyes to her. "What did she say?"

"Nothing really, Julia." The conversation had centered around the beauty of Ephesus, the long voyage from Rome, settling into a new home. "What is it? You look pale."

Julia shook her head. "I never thought I'd see her again."

"Don't you wish to?"

Julia hesitated, wondering if she could make some excuse: she had a headache from too much sun, she was weary from shopping, she had to get ready to attend Marcus' feast this evening. . . . She put fingertips to her temple. She *did* have a headache, but she knew she couldn't make excuses today. She shook her head. "I'll see her, Mother. It's just that I can't see Calabah without thinking of Caius."

"I didn't know you still grieved him. You've seemed more yourself the last few months." She kissed her lightly on the forehead. "I know you loved him very much."

"I loved him madly." She bit her lip and looked toward the doorway that opened into the corridor and peristyle beyond. "I'll see her alone, if you don't mind."

"Of course," Phoebe said, relieved. Calabah made her uncomfortable. She wondered what her young daughter had in common with such a worldly woman.

Calabah was sitting in the shadows of an alcove, waiting. Her very presence seemed to fill the peristyle. Even the sunlight retreated behind a layer of clouds, casting the courtyard into soft shadows. Julia gathered her courage and walked sedately toward her, forcing her lips to curve into a smile of greeting.

"How delightful to see you again, Calabah. What brings you to Ephesus?"

Calabah smiled faintly. "I grew tired of Rome."

Julia sat down with her. "When did you arrive?" she said, trying desperately not to show how she shook inside.

"A few weeks ago. I've used the time to get to know the city again."

"Again? I didn't know you'd visited Ephesus."

"It was one of many cities I visited before I married. I feel more at home here than anywhere else."

"Then you'll stay? That's wonderful."

Dark eyes probed. "You've learned to dissimulate since I last saw you. The smile you wear looks almost sincere."

Shaken, Julia didn't know what to say.

"You left without a word, Julia. That was cruel."

"It was Father's decision to return to Ephesus."

"Ah," Calabah said, nodding. "I see. You had no time to say good-bye to friends." Her mouth curved again, faintly mocking Julia this time.

Julia blushed and looked away.

"You said good-bye to Octavia," Calabah said, her tone revealing nothing.

Julia looked at her beseechingly. "I couldn't face you after Caius died."

"I understood that," Calabah said gently.

Shuddering, Julia admitted, "I was afraid."

"Because I knew," Calabah said. "Did you never stop to think? Darling, I knew *everything*. You shared your torment with me. I knew what Caius did to you for his own pleasure. You showed me the marks on your body. And we both knew what Caius would've done in anger. Julia, who else other than I could have understood what you were going through and the difficult decision Caius forced upon you? You should have trusted me."

Julia felt weak before the stare of those dark, fathomless eyes. Calabah covered her hand. "Ours is a true friendship, Julia. I know you as no one else knows you. I know what you've done. I know who you are. I know what you're capable of doing. You are very special to me. We are bound together."

As though drawn by a power stronger than her own will, Julia leaned into Calabah's embrace. "I'm sorry I refused to see you in Rome." Calabah stroked her gently, whispering encouragement. "I felt you had some hold over me. It made me afraid. I know better now. You're the only real friend I have." She drew back slightly. "I think Caius knew what I was doing toward the end."

Calabah's mouth curved. "All should bear the consequences of their failings."

Julia shivered. "I don't want to think about it. Not ever again."

Calabah ran cool fingertips over Julia's forehead. "Then don't," she said soothingly. "Remember what I taught you, Julia. Caius was merely an episode. You have many things yet to experience as you grow into the person I know you will be. Everything will be revealed to you in time."

Julia forgot all the reasons she had avoided Calabah and talked with her freely as she had in Rome. Calabah's voice was so melodious and soothing.

"How do you like your life in Ephesus?"

"I would enjoy it more had I my freedom. Father has turned everything over to Marcus to manage. I have to beg him for every sesterce."

"It's unfortunate women leave themselves at the mercy of men. Especially when it's so unnecessary."

"I had no choice."

"There's always a choice. Or perhaps you enjoy your dependence?"

Pride smarting, Julia tipped her chin. "I do as I please."

Calabah looked cool and amused. "And what pleases you? A love affair with a gladiator? You degrade yourself like Octavia."

Julia's lips parted. "How do you know about Atretes? Who could have told you?" she said in a hushed voice.

"Sertes. He's an old friend." She laid her hand over Julia's again. "But I must tell you, Ephesus is already abounding in rumor that a daughter of one of the wealthiest merchants in the Empire has taken Atretes as her lover. It will only be a matter of time before everyone in the city knows your name."

Furious, Julia cloaked herself in hauteur. "I don't care what people say!"

"No?"

Julia's expression fell. "I love him. I love him so much I'd die if I couldn't be with him. I would marry him if he were free."

"Would you? Would you really? Is it love, Julia, or his beauty, his brutality? Atretes was captured in Germania. He's a barbarian. He hates Rome with a passion beyond your understanding. And you, my dear, are every inch a Roman."

"He doesn't hate me. He loves me. I know he loves me."

"Caius loved you, too. It didn't stop him from using you for his own purposes."

Julia blinked.

Satisfied, Calabah rose. "I must go. I'm very relieved and pleased we're friends again." She smiled. Her visit had been most gratifying. "Primus invited me to accompany him to your brother's celebration of the proconsul's birthday this evening," she said and lightly brushed Julia's cheek with the backs of her fingers. "I didn't want to upset you by arriving unexpectedly."

Julia was distracted. "I've met Primus. He's one of the proconsul's advisors, isn't he?"

"He's well versed on foreign manners and customs."

"He's handsome and amusing."

Calabah laughed softly, her dark eyes veiled. "Primus is many, many things."

Julia saw her to the door. When she closed it, Phoebe spoke from the stairway. "Is everything all right, Julia?"

"Everything is fine, Mother, just fine," she said and tried desperately to believe it.

31

Decimus was losing his battle. Immediately upon his return to Ephesus, he had paid homage at the temple of Asclepius, the god of healing. After consulting with the priests, he spent hours along a colonnaded pool, among the snakes. The fear and revulsion he felt as the writhing, slithering reptiles moved over his body should have driven out whatever evil spirits were causing his illness, but it didn't.

When the snakes failed, Decimus consulted physicians who theorized that cleansing within would be a curative. He underwent emetics and purges and bloodletting until he was weak unto death. Still the illness progressed. Despondent, Decimus lapsed into a state of lethargy and hopelessness.

Phoebe suffered with him. Seeing him ashen from treatments and in such pain was agony to her. She bought drugs to ease his pain, but the poppy and mandrake left him half-conscious. Sometimes he refused to take them because he said he wanted to be aware of what went on around him.

As word spread about Decimus' wasting illness, medical experts approached Phoebe with various theories and treatments, all guaranteed to bring the return of good health. Everyone wanted to help him get well. Everyone had a suggestion, a theory, a better physician or herbalist or healer.

Columbella, a spiritualist, convinced Phoebe that physicians shouldn't be trusted; she claimed that they used patients they couldn't cure to perfect new methods of treatment. Columbella said nonscientific methods would restore Decimus' vitality and recommended her own potions and herbs, which had been passed down through the centuries. Health, Columbella insisted, was a matter of balance with nature.

Decimus drank her foul brews and ate the strange bitter herbs she prescribed, but they didn't harmonize and balance the energies within his body as Columbella claimed they would. They neither harmed nor healed him.

Marcus took him to the baths to soak in the cleansing waters and introduced him to Orontes, a masseur reputed to have the healing touch. Orontes claimed massage could heal. When this, too, failed, Julia came to Decimus and said Calabah had told her he could heal himself if only he would tap into the resources of his own imagination and mind. She held his hand and encouraged him to concentrate and visualize himself in perfect health and it would be so. He almost wept at her unconscious cruelty, for by her words she blamed him for his illness and for being too weak to overcome it, when he had fought against it with every ounce of his will.

With each visit, he saw in his daughter disappointment and subtle accusation and knew she believed he lacked whatever "faith" it took to cure himself. "Try this," she said one day and put a carnelian crystal around his neck. "It's very special to me. It vibrates in harmony with the energy patterns of the gods, and if you can give yourself up to those vibrations, you will receive healing." Her voice was cool, but then her eyes flooded and she lay across his chest weeping. "Oh, Papa . . . "

Her visits became less frequent and more brief after that.

Decimus cast no blame upon her. A dying man was depressing company for a beautiful young woman who was so full of life. Perhaps he had become a grim reminder of her own mortality.

Why couldn't he die and have done with it? A dozen times he contemplated suicide to put himself out of pain. He knew his family suffered with him, Phoebe most of all. Yet when it came down to carrying out a decision to kill himself, he found that he clung to life instead. Every moment, no matter how filled with pain, became precious to him. He loved his wife. He loved his son and daughter. Selfishly, perhaps, for out of love, he should release them—but he found he couldn't. And he knew why.

He was afraid.

Long ago he had lost faith in the gods. They were no help, they were no threat. But what Decimus saw ahead was darkness, obscurity, an eternity of nothingness, and that terrified him. He was in no hurry to enter into oblivion, and yet it pulled at him. With the passing of each day, he felt a little more of his life slipping away.

Phoebe saw and was afraid as well.

Watching over him constantly, Phoebe sensed his inner struggle and suffered with him. She'd sought every expert and method there was and now had to stand by helplessly and see how he fought against the ceaseless pain, fought for life itself. Lacing his drink with strong doses of poppy and mandrake, she tried to give him what ease she could. Then she'd sit and hold his hand until he slept. Sometimes she'd go and sit in one of the alcoves where others wouldn't notice her, weeping until she had no tears left.

What had she done wrong? What could she do to make things right? She prayed to every god she knew, gave offerings with an open hand, fasted, meditated. She cried out within her heart for answers and still she had to watch the man she'd loved since having glimpsed him as a young girl—the man who'd given her children and love and a wonderful life—die slowly, in agony.

Sometimes, in the stillness of night, when the silence was so heavy it rang in her ears, she lay as close beside Decimus as possible, holding him. And she prayed desperately, not to her own gods, but to the unseen god of a slave girl.

Atretes rose from his stone bench as his cell door opened and Hadassah stood in the torchlit corridor. They left the ludus together, both silent. Atretes felt the anger begin to grow within him. Where had Julia arranged for them to meet this time? In an inn? In the storage chambers of her brother's villa? At a feast, where they could steal a few minutes together in a private room? His mouth tightened.

Each time she summoned him in this manner, another piece of his pride was chipped away. Only when he had her in his arms, begging for him to love her, did he feel his pride return. Yet later, in his cell, when he had nothing to do with his time but think, he hated himself.

Sertes had told him yesterday that the games celebrating Liberalia would take place in two weeks. An elimination match had been planned. Twelve pairs would start; the survivor would be given his freedom. Atretes knew time was catching up to him, and this opportunity might be the last and only hope he'd ever have.

Atretes decided if he lived through the match and gained his freedom, he would never be brought to Julia again. Julia would come to him! He'd buy a villa on Kuretes Street and send a servant to bring her, just as she now sent Hadassah to bring him.

Over the past three years he had amassed enough money to live well in Ephesus or to buy passage back to Germania and take his rightful place once again as chief of the Chatti. Six months ago, there would have been no question in his mind what he would do. He wouldn't even have thought of remaining in Ephesus. But now there was Julia.

Atretes thought of the rude longhouses of his people and compared them to the marble halls of luxury in which Julia had been reared, and he wondered what to do. As his woman, she'd have a prominent position of respect in the community, but could she adjust to life such as he had known?

Would she be willing to adjust?

Hadassah brought him up an unfamiliar street. She walked more slowly than usual, and her expression was troubled. She paused at a winding marble stairway to a villa set into the hillside. "She awaits up there," she said, and, after pointing the way, withdrew.

"Obviously, this isn't another inn. Is this one of her brother's villas?"

"No, my lord. The villa belongs to Calabah Fontaneus. My lady believes her to be her closest friend."

There was something unspoken in the way she explained it. Atretes looked at her curiously.

"You enter through the lower door," she said before he thought to ask any questions. Eager to be with Julia, Atretes dismissed his unease. He went up the stairway.

The door stood open. He entered and found himself in a service corridor, with storage rooms off to each side and a stone stairway at the end. It reminded him of another meeting with Julia; she'd been waiting for him then.

This time another woman stood in the shadows of the stairwell. He strode toward her, feeling her critical assessment with every step he took. She stood three steps from the bottom so that she was on eye level with him when he stopped before her. Her eyes drifted over him and she came down one step. She lifted the amulet he wore. Holding it in her open palm, she looked at it and then up at him, her mouth curving into a sardonic smile. "Ah," she said, and Atretes looked into the coldest eyes he had ever seen.

He brushed her hand away. "Where's Julia?"

"Awaiting her pleasure." The woman laughed softly. The sound grated. "This way," she said and turned her back on him.

Eyes narrowed, Atretes followed her to the second floor. "Wait here," she said and opened a door. He clenched his teeth in anger as she went in and he heard her say, "Julia, your gladiator has arrived," in a tone so saturated with contempt that hot blood rushed into his face. Julia said something he couldn't hear, but her tone was filled with agitation rather than excitement and expectation.

Calabah came out again. "She's not ready for you. Wait here and she'll summon you when she is." She raised one brow. "See that you serve her well," she said and walked down the hall.

Atretes glared after her with black fury, then exploded into action. He banged the door open and saw Julia sitting at a vanity table covered with vials of makeup and perfume. Two maids were fussing with her hair, both of whom froze at his entrance. "Out," he said, jerking his head toward the door. They fled past him like mice escaping to their holes.

Julia sat staring at him with dismay. "I wanted to look absolutely perfect before—"

Atretes pulled her to her feet and yanked her into his arms. When she opened her mouth to protest, he covered it with his own. Her hair came loose beneath his fingers, and pearled pins dropped and scattered on the floor.

Julia struggled. "You're ruining my hair," she gasped when he allowed her an instant to catch her breath.

"Do you think I care about your hair?" he said roughly. "Except to do this." He dug his hands into it, clenching it in his fists as he kissed her again.

She pushed at him. "You're hurting me. Stop it!" When he let her go abruptly, she withdrew angrily, touching at her hair and then turning on him in anger. "Do you know how long I had to sit there while they worked on it just so I would look beautiful for you?"

"Wear it down then," he said through his teeth. "Like the women they send to my cell."

Her eyes flashed. "You're comparing me to a common whore?"

"Are you forgetting how we met?" he said, still fuming that she had commanded he wait in the hallway. Who did she think he was? *What* did she think he was?

Her own temper was roused. "Maybe we should wait for another time when you're in a better mood!" she said, turning away. She waved her hand as though to dismiss him from her presence.

Temper exploding, Atretes spun her around. "Oh no," he said through his teeth. "Not yet." After a few minutes, she was pliant and trembling, clinging to him. "Maybe you're right," he said with a sneering smile, suddenly letting her go so that she staggered backward. "Another time."

"Atretes! Where are you going?" she cried, feeling bereft and abandoned.

"Back to the ludus."

She reached him before he opened the door. "What's the matter with you this evening? Why are you acting like this? Why are you being so cruel to me?" She caught his hand as he reached for the latch. "Don't leave me." She put her arms around him and clung to him.

He caught her arms and freed himself. "You pay Sertes and summon me like a harlot!"

She looked stunned. "I don't mean it like that and you know it! It was the only way I could find to be with you again. I've given Sertes half of my jewelry to be with you. I would give it all to him if that's what it took. I love you, Atretes. Don't you know that? I love you." She pulled his head down and kissed him. "You love me, too. I know you do."

His desire rose swiftly, matching hers. "Don't make me wait again," he said, loosening the reins on his passion.

For an hour Atretes was able to forget everything but what it felt like to be with Julia Valerian. But in the quiet that followed, he felt empty.

He had to get away from her. He had to think.

"Where are you going?" Julia asked.

"I'm going back to the ludus," he said shortly, defensive because she had never looked more beautiful than she did at that moment. He was still captivated by her, but somehow, perhaps even unknowingly, she only fed his inner hunger rather than fulfilled it.

"But why? You can stay with me until near dawn. It's all been arranged."

"Not with me," he said coldly. He looked around the luxurious bedchamber and thought of the foul, arrogant woman who owned this house. "I won't come here again."

Julia sat up. "But why not? Calabah said I could use her house whenever I want. This is the perfect meeting place for us!" She recognized the banked anger in his eyes and the stubborn set of his jaw. He was going to be unreasonable. "Where do you suggest we meet, Atretes? Do you expect me to come to your vile little cell?"

He gave her a sardonic look. "Why not? It might be a new and exciting experience for you."

"Everyone in Ephesus would know by morning."

A muscle locked in his jaw. "So that's the way of it." He took up his belt and put it on.

Julia saw that he was insulted. "No, it isn't! You know it isn't. My family wouldn't approve of us. My father and brother hold very important positions in the community. If either of them found out I'd taken a gladiator as a lover, they'd put me under guard to keep you from me. Can't you understand? Atretes, they'd marry me off to some rich old man at the far ends of the Empire. They did so once before!"

"And if I were free?"

She blinked. The possibility had seemed so remote, she had tried never to think about it. "I don't know," she stammered. "It would change everything." She frowned slightly.

Atretes' eyes narrowed. He could see her mind working on all the possibilities. His mouth curved into a cynical, bitter smile.

"Atretes," she said as though speaking to a child, "it'll be years before you earn your freedom and you know it. We can't wait upon that hope. We have to enjoy every minute we have with each other."

Atretes put on his sandals. The pounding in his head was like a drum he used to hear in the forest.

"Don't go," Julia said, sensing that something was very wrong between them. When he straightened, she held out her hands. "Stay with me. Why are you being so stubborn? You know you want to stay."

"Do I?"

She dropped her hands into her lap and clenched them, hurt that he was being so cavalier. Cloaking herself in pride, she tipped her chin. "Shall I contact Sertes later in the week, or would you rather be left alone?"

His mouth curved sardonically as he opened the door. "I always forego women before I fight in the games," he said.

Fear gripped her at his careless words. "What games?" she said, panicking with the knowledge that she might lose him. He walked out the door. "Atretes!"

He strode down the lamplit corridor and took the stairs three at a time. "Get out of my way," he said to a burly guard in the main hallway and went straight out the front door. He heard her calling out his name. When he reached the bottom of the stairway and stepped onto the street below, he stopped to fill his lungs with clean air. Glancing back, he saw she hadn't cared enough to follow him into the street, where she would be seen.

He looked around, uncertain where he was, and swore violently. All he had thought about on the way here was being with Julia again. He should have paid more attention to the route.

Soft footsteps made him swing around instinctively, ready to counter any attack. The slave girl stood near the gate, looking up at him. "I'll show you the way," she said.

"Not before I've had time to walk."

He knew she followed, but he didn't slow his pace. Others were there in the darkness to watch him as well, others sent by Sertes to guard his investment. He could have called to them to show him the way. A galling thought. Take me back to prison. Put the chains on again.

He saw the temple of Artemis, but some hand seemed to turn him away from it. Instead, he found himself following a road that led to the arena. When he reached it, he stood for a long time, looking up at it, hearing the echo of screams, smelling the blood. Closing his eyes, he wondered why, with the few hours of solitude and freedom he had, he would end up here.

He wandered among the deserted stalls beneath the spectator stands, where all manner of debauchery was sold. He found an entrance and went up the steps. Moonlight filled the stadium, and he found his way easily to the box where highly honored Roman officials sat. Sailcloth rippled above him. One awning had come loose; the others had been rolled back and secured, leaving the platform open to the sky.

Atretes looked down on the sand. Soon Julia would be sitting here where he stood now, watching him fight for his life. Watching him take life. And she'd enjoy it.

The little Jewess stood beside him.

"We both serve Julia, don't we?" he said, but she didn't answer. He glanced at her and saw she looked around the arena as though she'd never been in one before. She was visibly trembling, shaken to be in this place of death.

"I'll fight down there in a few days," he said. "Sertes scheduled me for the elimination match. Do you know what that is?" She shook her head without looking at him, and he explained. "It would seem Artemis has smiled down upon me," he said dryly and looked away. "This time next week, I'll either be dead or a free man."

Atretes looked down at the sand again. It was like a white moonlit sea. Clean. Yet he remembered the stain of blood from every man he had ever killed. "Maybe death is the only freedom."

Hadassah took his hand. "No," she said softly.

Surprised, Atretes looked down at her, amazed that she had touched him at all. She held his hand as though one of them was a child.

"No," she said again and, turning to face him, she held his hand firmly between both of her own. "It's not the only freedom, Atretes."

"What other freedom is there for a man like me?"

"The freedom God gives."

He took his hand from hers. "If your god failed to save Caleb, he won't protect me. Better that I put my trust in Artemis."

"Artemis is nothing but dead stone."

"She bears the symbol of Tiwaz, the spirit god of the Black Forests of my homeland." He lifted the amulet he wore around his neck. His talisman.

She looked at it sadly. "A goat is used to lead sheep to slaughter."

His fist closed around the amulet. "So I should become a Jew?" he said sardonically.

"I'm a Christian."

He let out his breath sharply, staring down at her as though she were a dove that had suddenly sprouted horns. Christians were fodder to the arena. Exactly why, he'd never understood; what threat to Rome were people who wouldn't fight? Perhaps that was it. Romans prized courage, even in their victims. Cowardice drove them to frenzy. Christians were fed to the lions because it was a shameful thing, reserved for the worst criminals and the lowest cowards. The only death more humiliating than that was to be hung on a cross.

Why had she told him she was a Christian? Why had she taken the risk? He could tell Sertes, who was always looking for victims to serve up to a hungry mob; he could tell Julia, who spoke freely of her contempt for Christians.

He frowned, aware Julia couldn't know her personal maid was of this deviant cult. "Better that you keep this to yourself," he said.

"I have," Hadassah said. "I've kept it to myself for too long. This might be the last chance I have to speak with you, Atretes, and I fear for your soul. I must tell you—"

"I have no soul," he said, cutting her off. He didn't know what a soul was. He wasn't sure he wanted to know.

"You have. All have. Please listen," she pleaded. "God lives, Atretes. Turn to him. Cry out to him and he'll answer. Ask Jesus to come into your heart."

"Jesus. Who's Jesus?"

She opened her mouth to speak.

"Be silent," he said suddenly, sharply, and she, too, heard the guards coming. A paralyzing fear swept through her as she glanced up and saw the Roman soldiers a few rows above them, watching like birds of prey. She remembered the screams of the dying in Jerusalem, the forest of crosses outside the broken walls, the suffering survivors. Her mouth went dry.

"Time to return, Atretes," one said. "Dawn's coming." The others stood ready should he refuse to obey.

Atretes nodded. His eyes flickered to meet Hadassah's, and he frowned slightly. "You were foolish to tell me anything," he said so only she could hear.

She tried not to weep. "I was foolish not to tell you everything sooner."

"Say no more," he commanded and saw her eyes glisten with tears.

She put her hand on his arm. "I will pray for you," she said, and her hand tightened as though to hold him there and make him listen. "I pray God forgives me my fear and grants us another chance to talk."

Atretes frowned, perplexed and strangely touched. He turned away and went up the steps, the guards falling in around him, hedging him in. When he reached the opening into the corridor that led to the stairs out, he looked back. Hadassah was still standing there.

He'd never looked into such eyes before, eyes so full of compassion that they pierced through the hardness of his heart.

"He said he's fighting in the games again," Julia said, upset that Calabah had stopped her from going after Atretes.

"Well, of course he's fighting in the games. He's a gladiator."

"Don't you understand? He could die! The only games scheduled are in celebration of Libernalia, and Sertes is planning an elimination match. Marcus told me yesterday. Atretes won't be fighting just one man or two." She pressed her fists against her temples. "I was such a fool, such a fool. I never even thought what it might mean. What if I lose him? I couldn't bear it, Calabah. I couldn't."

"And what if he lives?" Calabah said in a strange tone that made Julia glance at her.

"Sertes would have to free him."

"And what then? What would he expect of you?"

"I don't know. I'd marry him if he wanted."

"You would be so foolish?" she said disdainfully. "He's worse than Caius, Julia."

"He's not. He's nothing like Caius. He was angry with me because I left him standing in the hallway."

"I'm not speaking of his violence, though there is that to consider. I'm speaking of the way he *controls* you. His pride gets a little bruised and he leaves. And what do you do? Do you bide your time and wait for him to come to his senses and apologize? You should have seen yourself, Julia, running after him. It was embarrassing to see you behave so badly."

Julia blushed. "I wanted him to stay."

"Anyone in Ephesus could've seen how much you wanted him to stay," Calabah said. "Just who is it that controls this relationship?"

Julia looked away, remembering Atretes' cutting remark about abstaining from women before the games. Did he have others when he wasn't with her? She hoped she was the only woman in his life, but what if she were just one among many?

Calabah tipped her chin back and looked into her eyes. "This gladiator owes you respect. Who does he think he is? The proconsul of Ephesus? Why do you allow him to treat you like a woman of convenience?" She took her hand away and shook her head. "You disappoint me, Julia."

Hurt and shamed, Julia became defensive. "Atretes is the most famous gladiator in the Empire. He has over a hundred kills to his credit. They make statues in honor of him."

"And these things make him worthy of you? You're a Roman citizen, the daughter of one of the wealthiest men in the Empire, a woman of substance. This Atretes is nothing more than a brute animal capable of fighting in an arena, a barbarian who lacks the least refinement. He should be honored that you chose him to be your lover—and grateful for every moment you spare him."

Julia blinked, staring into Calabah's dark eyes. "I hadn't thought of it that way."

Calabah put her hand over hers, squeezing lightly. "I know. You think too little of yourself. You've allowed yourself to become his slave."

Julia looked away again, further ashamed. Was she his slave? She remembered how she had pleaded with Atretes to stay and then run after him. It hadn't stopped him. She had humbled herself, and he had turned his back on her.

"You must put him in his proper place, Julia. He's the slave. Not you."

"But he could earn his freedom."

"I understand why you're thinking this way, but think some more. Did you know that barbarians kill wives who take other lovers? They drown them in a bog. What if this gladiator did earn his freedom? What if you married him? Perhaps you'd be happy for a little while, but what if you tired of him? If you dared even look at another, he could kill you. In Rome, a husband has the right to kill an unfaithful wife, though few are so hypocritical as to ever do so. This man wouldn't think twice about killing you with his own hands."

Julia shook her head. "I'm not like you. I love him. I can't help myself. I can't give him up because of what I'm afraid might happen."

"You don't have to give him up at all." Calabah rose from the couch.

"What do you mean?"

Calabah stood thoughtful for a long moment. "You could marry another man, a man you could trust implicitly. A man who would allow you complete freedom to do as you please. Under those circumstances, Atretes could remain as your lover as long as you wished. If you tired of him, there would be no harm done. Give him a token gift to salve his pride and send him on his way back to Germania or wherever else he might want to go."

Julia shook her head. "I've been married before and hated it. Claudius was worse than my father. And Caius. You know what Caius was."

"You'd have to pick the man very carefully."

"The only man I've ever trusted is Marcus."

"You can hardly marry your brother, Julia," Calabah said dryly.

"I didn't mean that," she said, her mind agitated by the thoughts Calabah threw at her. She pressed her fingers to her throbbing temples.

"Do you still trust your brother so much?"

"Of course. Why wouldn't I?"

"I wondered why you came to me for help with Atretes instead of him. Since you trust him, I assume he knows of your love affair and approves." Tilting her head slightly, she studied Julia's averted face. "He doesn't know? What would he do if he did know?" Her sweet question held a tinge of mockery. "Your father has been very ill lately. Has Marcus loosened the reins or tightened them?"

Julia pressed her lips together. She couldn't deny Marcus was becoming difficult. In fact, he was becoming all too much like Father. At the last feast she had attended, Marcus had almost dragged her from the room by the arm. He'd swung her into a private chamber where he had accused her of being *excessive*. When she demanded to know what he meant, he said her behavior among his guests reminded him of Arria. Clearly, he hadn't meant it as a compliment.

Just thinking about it stirred her anger again. What was wrong with making every man in the room want her? Besides, wasn't that why Marcus had wanted her as his hostess in the first place?

"First your father, then Claudius and Caius," Calabah said. "And now you allow yourself to be ruled by your brother as well as a gladiator, a man who's nothing more than a slave of Rome. Oh, Julia," she said wearily. "When will you learn that you have the power within yourself to control your own destiny?"

Julia sat down, defeated by Calabah's reasoning and her own turbulent spiraling desires. "Even if I knew a man I could trust enough to marry, I'd have to have Marcus' consent."

"No, you wouldn't. You've heard of marriage by *usus,* haven't you?"

"Simply move in with a man?"

"An agreement could be drawn up between you and the man you chose, if you desired, though it wouldn't be necessary. Marriage by usus is very simple and as legally binding as you wish it to be. Binding enough to regain control of your own money."

Julia looked up.

"Many women use it to protect their estates," Calabah said. "Let's take an example. If this gladiator were free and did want to marry you, do you think he would allow you to control the money you would bring into the marriage? Do you think you could do as you wish? I've only met him once, but it was enough to see he would choose to dominate. If you were married to someone else by usus, he couldn't exert that kind of control. You would have both your money and your freedom in your grasp, and there would be no way he could wrest either one from you. On the other hand, if you married him, everything you have becomes his."

"And if the man I married by usus wanted to exert control?"

"You just walk out the door. It's as simple as that. As I said, Julia, this kind of marriage is only as legally binding as *you* will it to be."

The idea had appeal to Julia, but there was a problem. "I don't know anyone with whom I could live."

After a long, heavy silence, Calabah said quietly, "There's Primus."

"Primus?" Julia thought of the handsome young man Marcus frequently invited to his celebrations. Primus was well connected politically. He was handsome, charming, and often amusing—but there was something about him that repulsed Julia. "I don't find him attractive."

Calabah laughed softly. "It's highly unlikely he'd be attracted to you either, my dear. Primus is in love with his catamite."

Julia blanched. "You're suggesting I marry a *homosexual?*"

Calabah looked impatient. "As usual, you think as a child, or one so mired in traditional thinking that you fail to see the benefit of anything else. I'm merely presenting you with an acceptable alternative life-style. You're in love with this gladiator of yours, but you know if you married him, you'd have less freedom than you have now. With Primus, you could do as you want. Atretes could remain your lover, and you would have your money and your freedom. Primus is the perfect husband for you. He's wonderful to look at, intelligent, entertaining. He's a close friend of the proconsul. With Primus' connections, you'd enjoy mingling with the highest levels of Roman and Ephesian society. Best of all, Primus is very easily managed."

She sat down beside Julia again and laid her hand over hers. "I suggested Primus because any other man would expect certain predictable favors from you, favors you may not wish to grant to anyone but this gladiator. Primus would make no demands on you."

"He would surely expect something in return."

"Financial support," Calabah said.

Julia rose. "I don't need another man like Caius depleting me of every resource I have."

Calabah watched her, feeling satisfied. Julia was walking along the path she had planned for her long ago in Rome. Excitement tingled along her nerves at the power she had, a power Julia didn't even recognize. Not yet. But soon.

"You needn't worry about that, Julia," she said smoothly, her melodious voice almost hypnotic. "Primus doesn't gamble, nor would he throw money away on lovers. He's faithful to his companion, who adores him. Primus lives simply, but he would like to live well. He rents a small villa not far from here. You could move in with him there until you regained control of your money. He has an extra bedchamber. Once you established legal right to your estate, you could buy a larger villa in a better area of the city. Closer to the temple, perhaps." Her mouth curved mockingly. "Or closer to the ludus, if you like."

Julia stood silent for a long moment, emotions flickering across her beautiful face. "I'll think about it," she said.

Calabah smiled, knowing she'd already made up her mind.

32

Hadassah was drawing water from the well in the peristyle when one of the slave girls came and said she was wanted in the master's chambers. Phoebe stood behind the couch on which Decimus reclined, her hand resting on his shoulder. His pale cheeks were sunken, his eyes enigmatic and watchful. Phoebe's gaze flickered to Hadassah's small harp.

"We didn't summon you to play for us, Hadassah," she said solemnly. "We have questions to ask. Please sit." She gestured to a stool near the couch.

Hadassah felt the cold chill of fear rush through her blood as she sat before them. Back straight, hands clasped on her lap, she waited.

It was Decimus who spoke, his voice roughened by pain. "Are you a Christian?"

Hadassah's heart fluttered like a fragile bird taking wing within her. A single spoken yes could mean her death. Her throat closed.

"You have nothing to fear from us, Hadassah," Phoebe said gently. "What you tell us will go no further than this room. You have our word. Please. We only want to know about this god of yours."

Still frightened, she nodded. "Yes, I'm a Christian."

"And all this time I thought you were a Jew," Phoebe said, amazed that Decimus had been right about her.

"My father and mother were from the tribe of Benjamin, my lady. Christians worship the God of Israel, but many Jews did not recognize the Messiah when he came."

Decimus saw his son enter through the adjoining study. Marcus stopped when he saw Hadassah, a muscle moving in his jaw.

"Messiah?" Phoebe said, not noticing him. "What is this word *Messiah?"*

"*Messiah* means 'the anointed one,' my lady. God came down in the form of man and lived among us." Hadassah held her breath and then said, "His name is Jesus."

"*Was,"* Marcus said and entered the room. Hadassah tensed

when he spoke. He saw her cheeks bloom with color, but she neither moved nor looked up. He gazed at the gentle curve of her neck and the soft strands of dark curling hair that lay against the nape of her neck. "I've done some investigation on this Jewish sect over the past few weeks," Marcus said roughly.

He had paid men to research the cult, and they had brought him the name of a retired Roman centurion who lived outside Ephesus. Marcus had ridden out to talk with him. He should have been pleased with what he learned, for it could shatter this faith Hadassah had. Instead, he had been depressed for days, avoiding the moment when he would speak with her again.

And now she was spreading this cancerous story to his own father and mother.

"This Jesus the Christians claim as their messiah was a rebel crucified on a cross in Judea. Hadassah's faith is based on emotion rather than fact, on a desperation for answers to unanswerable questions," he said, directing his statements to his parents. He looked down at Hadassah then. "Jesus wasn't a god, Hadassah. He was a man who made the mistake of defying the powers in Jerusalem and paid the price for it. He challenged the authority of the Sanhedrin as well as the Roman Empire. Just his name was enough to cause insurrection. It still is!"

"But what if it's true, Marcus?" his mother said. "What if he is a god?"

"He wasn't. According to Epaenetus, a man I've met who saw what happened back then, he was a magician of some repute who performed signs and wonders in Judea. The Jews were hungry for a savior and were easily convinced he was their long-awaited messiah. They expected him to expel the Romans from Judea, and when he didn't, his followers turned on him. One of his own disciples betrayed him to the high court. This Jesus was sent to Pontius Pilate. Pilate tried to free him, but the Jews themselves demanded he be crucified because he was what they termed a 'blasphemer.' He died on a cross, was taken down and entombed, and that was the end of it."

"No," Hadassah said softly. "He arose."

Phoebe's eyes went wide. "He came back to life?"

Marcus swore in frustration. "No, he didn't, Mother. Hadassah, listen to me." He knelt and turned her roughly to face him. "It was his disciples who said he arose, but it was all a hoax planned to further the spread of this cult."

Hadassah closed her eyes and shook her head.

He shook her slightly. "*Yes*. Epaenetus was in Judea when it happened. He's an old man now and lives near us outside the city. I'll take you to him if you don't believe me. You can hear the truth for yourself. He was one of the centurions at the tomb. He said the body was stolen in order to make people believe that there had been a resurrection!"

"He saw this?" Decimus said, wondering why his son was so determined to shatter the slave girl's precious faith.

Marcus saw nothing change in her eyes. He let go of her and stood. "Epaenetus said he didn't see the body taken from the tomb, but that was the only logical explanation."

"Right from beneath the noses of Roman guards?"

"Do you want to believe this ridiculous story?" Marcus said angrily.

"I want to know the truth!" Decimus said. "How is it this Epaenetus is still alive if he was a guard at the tomb? There's a death penalty for neglecting duty. Why wasn't he executed for failing in his?"

Marcus had asked the same question. "He said Pilate was sick of being used by the Jewish factions. His wife had been tormented by dreams before this Jesus was brought to him, but the Sanhedrin and Jewish mob forced him to hand this messiah of theirs over for crucifixion. Pilate washed his hands of the whole matter. He wanted no further involvement with these religious fanatics and wasn't about to sacrifice good soldiers over the missing body of one unimportant dead Jew!"

"It seems to me it would have been important to all concerned to make sure the body stayed *in* the tomb," Decimus said.

"He arose," Hadassah said again, calm before Marcus' harangue. "The Lord appeared to Mary of Magdala and to his disciples."

"Who probably lied to keep the story of this messiah going," Marcus retorted.

"The Lord also appeared to more than five hundred others at one time," Hadassah went on.

Marcus saw his mother's desperate hope for anything that might help his father. She had put her faith in gods and goddesses, in physicians and priests, in spiritualists and healers, and all any of them had done was sap his father's strength.

"Mother, don't put yourself through this. It's a lie perpetuated by self-serving men."

Hadassah turned slightly on her stool and looked up at him. Her father self-serving? John and all the rest? She thought of her father going out into the streets of Jerusalem to speak the truth. *Why?* She had cried out to him. *Why?* And now as she looked at Decimus, Phoebe, and Marcus—and saw suffering, despair, and disillusionment—she knew how wrong Marcus was about everything. "What reason did they have to lie?" she said gently.

"Money, power, the esteem of men," Marcus said, thinking he might finally break through to her and open her eyes. "Those are reasons for many men to lie."

"Do you believe I would lie to you?"

He softened. He wanted to kneel down and take her hands and tell her he was sorry to hurt her. He wanted to protect her. He wanted to love her. He wanted her for himself. But her faith in this nonexistent god stood between them. "No," he said bleakly. "I don't think you'd lie to me. I don't think you are capable of lying to anyone. I think you believe every word of this wild story because you were raised to believe it. It was drummed into you from the time you were born. But it's not true."

She shook her head. "Oh, Marcus," she said sadly. "You're so wrong. It is true! Jesus arose. He's alive!" She pressed her clasped hands to her chest. "He's here."

"He's dead!" Marcus said in frustration. "Why won't you listen to the facts?"

"What facts? The word of a guard who saw nothing? What did the men who followed Jesus gain? Not money or power or the esteem of men. They were reviled as the Lord was reviled. James was beheaded by King Herod Agrippa. Andrew was stoned in Scythia. Bartholomew was flayed alive and beheaded in Armenia. Matthew was crucified in Alexandria, Philip in Hieropolis, Peter in Rome. James the Less was beheaded by order of Herod Antipas. Simon the Zealot was sawn in two in Persia. And none of them recanted. Even in the face of death, they still proclaimed Jesus the Messiah. Would they all have died like that to preserve a lie? My father told me they were all afraid when Jesus was crucified. They ran away and hid. After Jesus arose and came to them, they were different men. Changed. Not from without, but from within, Marcus. They spread the Good News because they knew it was true."

"What is the good news?" Phoebe said, trembling.

"That the Lord came, not to condemn the world, but to save it, my lady. He is the resurrection and the life. Whoever believes in him shall live even if he dies."

"On Mount Olympus with all the other deities, I suppose," Marcus said scathingly.

"Marcus," Phoebe said, embarrassed by his mockery.

Marcus looked to his father. "Hadassah's right about one thing. Speaking of this messiah does bring suffering and death. Her own if she persists. This Jesus preached that man answers to god alone and not to any Caesar. If she helps to spread this religion, she'll end up in the arena."

Hadassah was deathly pale. "Jesus said render unto Caesar that which is Caesar's, and to God, that which is God's."

"And by your own words, everything you are, everything you do is in service to this god of yours! Isn't that so? He *owns* you!"

"Marcus," Phoebe said, disturbed by her son's intensity. "Why do you attack her so? She didn't come to us to speak of her god. We summoned her here to ask her for ourselves."

"Then leave well enough alone, Mother. Leave her god unseen and forgotten," he said. "Her faith is based on a god who doesn't exist and on an event that never happened."

Silence fell over them. Hadassah spoke into it, like an echo in the canyons of their minds, a flicker of light in the darkness. "Jesus raised my father from the dead."

"What did you say?" Phoebe whispered.

Hadassah raised her eyes. "Jesus raised my father from the dead," she said again, no waver in her voice this time.

"But how?"

"I don't know, my lady."

Decimus sat forward slightly. "You saw this happen with your own eyes?"

"It happened before I was born. In Jerusalem."

"Hadassah," Marcus said, trying to curb his exasperation, "you only have it on the word of others that he did such a deed."

Hadassah looked up, all the love she had for him revealed. "Nothing I can say will ever convince you, Marcus. Only the Holy Spirit can do that. But I *know* Jesus arose. I feel his presence now, here, with me. I see the evidence of his Word every day. From creation forth, the whole world is witness to God's plan revealed through his Son. From the beginning, he prepared us. In the passing of the seasons; in the way flowers spring forth, die, and drop seeds for life to begin again; in the sunset and sunrise. Jesus' sacrifice is reenacted every day of our lives if we but have the eyes to see."

"But can't *you* see? That's simply the natural order of things."

"No, Marcus. That's God speaking to all mankind. And he will return."

"Your faith is blind!"

Hadassah looked at Decimus. "If you stare into the sun and look away, you see the sun, my lord. If you stare at death, you see death. Where does hope lie?"

His eyes flickered. He leaned back slowly. "I have no hope."

Marcus turned. He saw the dullness in his father's eyes, the pain etched into his face. Marcus was suddenly filled with deep shame. Maybe he had been wrong. Maybe it was better to have false hope than no hope at all.

"You may go, Hadassah," Phoebe said, stroking Decimus' shoulder in futile comfort.

For the first time, Hadassah did not obey a command. She knelt beside the couch and broke every unspoken law by taking her master's hand in both of hers. Then she did the unforgivable by looking straight into Decimus' eyes and speaking to him as an equal.

"My lord, to accept God's grace is to live *with* hope. If you but confess your sins and believe, the Lord will forgive you. Ask and he will come to dwell in your heart, and you will have the peace you crave. You only have to believe."

Decimus saw love in her eyes, the kind of love he had always longed to have from his own daughter. Her plain features and brown eyes were alight with a warmth that came from within, and for a moment he saw the beauty his son wanted to possess. She believed the incredible. She believed the impossible. Not with stubbornness and pride, but with a pure, childlike innocence the world had been unable to mar. And without thought of the risk to herself, she offered her own hope to him if he could accept it.

He might not believe anything of what she said—he might not be able to believe in this unseen god of hers—but he believed in her.

Smiling sadly, he laid his other hand against her cheek. "But for Julia, I would set you free."

She squeezed his hand tenderly. "I am free, my lord," she whispered. "You can be free, too." She rose gracefully and left the room, closing the door quietly behind her.

Atretes stepped up into the chariot and braced himself for the *pompa,* or opening ceremonies, to begin. His gold and silver chest armor and helmet were heavy and hot, even though it was early morning. He flipped the red cape back over his shoulders and shifted so he could see the other gladiators making ready for the presentation. There were twenty-four in all; he'd have to kill five to earn his freedom.

Sertes had arranged for a broad mix this time. The chariots lined up carrying *dimachaeri,* men armed with daggers; Samnites with gladii and shields; *velites,* gladiators who fought with javelins; and *sagittarii,* those armed with bows and arrows. There were four *essedarii,* combatants who rode in their own decorated two-horse chariots, followed by another three *andabatae,* who were astride powerful, trained war horses, and who wore helmets with closed visors—which meant they basically fought blindfolded. In the chariot just behind Atretes was an African retiarius, his trident and net displayed. The mob would be pleased by the menagerie.

"The priests are coming out," Atretes' driver said, looping the reins expertly between his fingers. Atretes had seen the priests, dressed in white tunics and red scarves, leading in a white bull and two rams with golden headdresses for the sacrifice. They read the entrails to be sure this was a good day for the games. Atretes' mouth curved cynically, knowing that any day was a good day for the games. No priest would dare call them off, no matter what bad omen he saw in the bloody viscera.

Trumpets blared and doors opened. "Here we go," the driver said as he drew into line behind the Roman officials and promoters, who financed the games. Sertes was just ahead of Atretes.

The mob screamed wildly. Atretes heard his own name cried out over and over, as well as the names of half a dozen others. His fame was not as great in Ephesus as it had been in Rome, but he didn't care. He focused all thought on what lay ahead, counting the other gladiators and assessing their merit as he was driven around the arena for the spectators to see. Only once did his attention wander. As he passed by the box where the proconsul sat, he glanced up and scanned the guests with the politician. Julia was among them. She was wearing the red palus she had worn to the temple of Artemis. His heart quickened at the sight of her and then he looked away. He would not look at her again until the games were over.

The chariots made several more circles about the arena and then drew up in a line before the proconsul. The gladiators stepped down and paraded, some removing their capes, and others, to the delight of the crowd, removing everything. Atretes did neither. He stood, feet planted slightly apart, his hand on his sword, and waited. When the others finished their preening for the mob and joined the formation, Atretes drew his gladius and held it up with the others.

"Hail, Caesar! Those who are about to die salute you!"

The proconsul began a brief speech. Atretes kept his eyes from Julia, looking instead for the strange little slave. She was in attendance. The crowd roared in approval as the proconsul officially opened the games. Atretes and the others stepped up into the chariots again, and the drivers laid on the whips until the chariots raced one last time around the arena and then sped out the gate to the wild shouting of the mob.

In the holding room, it was cool and deeply shadowed, and the smell of lamp oil was strong. Iron-grated windows were high in the stone walls. No one spoke. Atretes removed his fancy armor and donned a simple brown tunic. It would be hours before any of them fought.

At the feast the night before, Sertes had read to them the *libellus,* the program listing the coming events. The pompa would be concluded by the proconsul dedicating the games to the emperor. Following would be a grand parade opening and speeches; then acrobats and trick riders would perform; followed by the dog races. Next, two robbers would be crucified, and Molossian hounds would tear them down from the crosses. Then hunters, or *beastiarii,* would hunt Nandhi bears from the Aberdare Mountains of Kenya, followed by prisoners being fed to a pride of European lions.

Sometime near the middle of the day, a brief hour-long respite from the carnage would occur, during which the arena would be cleared and fresh sand brought in. Food would be distributed, lottery tickets sold, and bedroom farces performed. However, these entertainments always palled swiftly on a mob hungry for the narcotic of violence and blood.

The big match was planned for late afternoon.

Fear coiled in Atretes' belly. Twelve pairs of gladiators . . . the most men he had faced in a single day had been three. Today he would have to kill five, one right after the other, if he were to survive.

However, none of the men he would face worried him so much as the long wait. That was his worst enemy, for it was during the hours before the fighting that every hope and every fear rippled through his mind, until he thought he would go mad.

Julia's palms perspired, and she had trouble concentrating on what the proconsul was saying. She wasn't interested in politics or economics; all she could think about was Atretes and the fact that he might die today. She hadn't seen him since their argument a week before. She had wanted to send Hadassah to bring him to her, but was afraid he would still be angry and refuse. So she had waited, hoping he would send word to her. When he hadn't, she had swallowed her pride and gone to the temple, hoping for a glimpse of him. He hadn't come.

When he had entered the arena for the pompa, her heart had raced at the sight of him. As the gladiators had drawn up before the proconsul and he stepped down, she'd waited for him to look at her. She had spent hours preparing herself and knew she looked more beautiful than ever before. But not once had she seen his head turn in her direction. He had stood still, head high, while the others strutted like peacocks before the crowd.

"See how he ignores you," Calabah had said disdainfully. "With all these others screaming for him, why should he care that he's broken your heart?"

"Atretes! Atretes!" Men and women cried out, tossing flowers and coins down to him.

The memory refueled her hurt and jealousy, and Julia pressed her lips together, her thoughts poisoned by Calabah's taunt. Primus lounged nearby, evaluating the gladiators they had seen with the skill of a connoisseur. "I'll wager on the German," he said and popped a round purple grape into his mouth.

"Five hundred sesterces on the African," another man said, indicating a tall, powerful-looking veles.

"Ha! Neither will have a chance against an essedarius. What good is a sword against a chariot?" someone else retorted.

"Surely they won't pit an essedarius against a Samnite," Julia said in alarm.

"Not to begin with, but don't forget this is an elimination

match," Primus said. "They'll pair what's left. Laquearius against Samnite, andabata against retiarius, Thracian against mirmillo. You saw that they have some of each type here for the games. The best in each class. That's what makes it exciting. Those trained to face the sword may be forced to face a javelin instead. The victor is less predictable that way."

Heart pounding, Julia felt sudden fear for Atretes. In silence she beseeched the gods to let him survive. She willed herself to relax and enjoy the refreshments and conversation. Primus was quite amusing and seemed intent upon entertaining her.

She grew annoyed watching the robbers hang on their crosses. "Why don't they set the Molossians loose on them and have done with this? It's taking too long."

"Such a thirst for blood," Primus said, amused. "Come, Julia. I'll take you down to the booths and we'll see what catches your fancy."

Restless and tense with waiting, Julia swiftly agreed. She went up the steps, her hand on Primus' arm. Hawkers shifted by them, carrying boxes laden with fruit, sausages, bread, and skins of wine. "Persian peaches, succulent and ripe!" Their staccato shouting mingled with the rolling thunder of the mob. "Spicy sausages. Three for a sesterce!"

Other spectators, bored with watching men hanging from crosses, milled around under the stands, looking for excitement. With Primus beside her, Julia wandered by the booths of astrologers, fortune-tellers, souvenir and food vendors. Soon they came to stalls where more lewd and unusual entertainments were taking place. Small painted boys with tunics hitched up above their buttocks moved among the milling customers. Primus watched them grimly. "Prometheus was such as these until I rescued him."

Uncomfortable at the mention of Primus' catamite, Julia remained silent. She stopped to watch Moorish dancers undulating to the primitive beat of drums and cymbals.

"Calabah has spoken with you about my offer," Primus said, half questioning.

"Yes," Julia said bleakly. "I've given it much thought."

"Have you made a decision?"

"I'll tell you when the games are over."

"It's time," Sertes said, and a hot rush swept through Atretes' blood, accelerating his heartbeat and heating his skin. He pulled the *manica,* a leather- and metal-scaled glove, over his right arm. "I'd have preferred owning you a few more years to having you wasted like this," Sertes said grimly.

"Perhaps the goddess will smile on me today and I will gain my freedom," Atretes said, pulling the *ocrea*, another protective covering, over his left leg.

"For a gladiator, freedom is another word for obscurity." Sertes handed him his *scutum,* a simple shield.

Atretes slipped his left arm into the metal braces at the back of the scutum and stood with his arms extended outward and his legs splayed. A slave rubbed his exposed body with olive oil. "Obscurity is preferable to bondage," Atretes said, staring coldly into Sertes' eyes.

"Ah," Sertes said, "but not to death." He held out the gladius.

Atretes took it and held it up before his face in a salute of respect. "Either way, Sertes, today I leave the arena victorious."

A laquearius, on foot and armed with his rope, was matched against an essedarius in his chariot. The essedarius sent the chariot careening past the laquearius several times. Though he failed to run his opponent down, he did manage to dodge the lasso. On the eighth pass, however, the laquearius looped his rope over the essedarius, then set his feet and catapulted the man straight off the back of the speeding chariot. The essedarius hit the ground and his neck snapped, drawing a groan of disappointment from the crowd. Without the chariot driver, the animals kept running and the chariot went round and round the arena.

Several slaves were sent out to capture and calm the stallions, while a man dressed in a close-fitting tunic and high leather boots danced out onto the sand. He was representative of Charon, the boatman who ferried the souls of the dead across the Styx to Hades. As he approached the victim, he spun and leapt across the sand, holding a mallet high in one hand. The beaked mask he wore resembled a bird of prey. Another man dressed as Hermes, another guide for the souls of the dead, brandished a red-hot caduceus with which he prodded the fallen essedarius. When the body twitched, Charon leaped in and brought the war hammer down on the man's head, spraying a crimson stain across the sand and assuring Hades of its prey. The *libitinarii,* as the two guides were called, quickly bore the corpse through the Gate of the Dead.

A dark sound moved like a wave through the thousands of spectators. They grumbled that the match had ended too quickly. They felt cheated. Some booed the victor. Others threw fruit at him as he held his hand up to the proconsul in salute. He received the signal to withdraw, but didn't depart quickly enough, for spectators began shouting for him to be matched with the tall African veles.

"Let's see what a laquearius could do against a man with a javelin!"

Sensitive to the whim of the mob, the proconsul raised his hand slightly to the editor of the games, and the African entered the arena before the laquearius could leave. They circled one another for several minutes, during which the laquearius tossed his rope several times and missed. The veles jabbed at him with the javelin, but kept a cautious distance. The crowd yelled in anger; things were going too slowly. Hearing the spectators' discontent and recognizing it as a threat, the laquearius threw his rope again and hit the veles across the chest. Swiftly, the African caught hold of the rope, looped it around his arm, then threw his javelin, sending it straight through his opponent's abdomen. The laquearius dropped to his knees, hunching over the spear. Tossing the rope aside, the African strode toward him to finish him off when given the *pollice verso,* thumbs down.

The proconsul glanced around and saw thumbs turning down everywhere he looked. He put his hand out and turned his thumb down as well. The veles yanked the javelin from the laquearius' abdomen and rammed it through his heart.

"They aren't getting what they want," Sertes said to Atretes from where he watched. "Listen to them. If it continues like this, they'll want the proconsul thrown to the dogs!"

The veles triumphed over the fish man, or mirmillo, but fell to the sagittarius' bow and arrows. The sagittarius fought well against an andabata, who was on horseback, but lost his footing when he wounded the rider, and fell beneath the pounding hooves of the war horse. Charon dispatched both of them, and the mob roared its approval.

"Bring them all in at once!" someone shouted at the proconsul, and the cry was taken up by others until it became a chant. "All at once! All at once!"

Responding to the whim, the remaining eighteen gladiators were paired off and sent into the arena. They spread out and raised their weapons to the proconsul. The spectators went wild, shouting the names of their favorites.

Atretes was matched against a swarthy, black-eyed Thracian, who was armed with a scimitar. Grinning arrogantly, the Thracian swung his weapon around in a theatrical sword play. He twirled his sword from one side of his body to the other and over his head, and then stopped, feet spread.

Standing in a deceptively relaxed pose, Atretes spit on the sand.

The crowd laughed. Enraged, the Thracian charged. Atretes ducked the deadly swing of the scimitar, rammed his scutum into his opponent, brought the hilt of his gladius down across the side of the man's head, then plunged it into the Thracian's breastplate. Yanking the gladius free, he let the already dead man fall back.

Turning, he saw a retiarius using his trident to spear a fallen secutor, whose fish-crested helmet offered him little protection. Atretes strode toward the victor purposefully, aware of the swelling sound of his followers. The retiarius yanked his trident free and tried to retrieve his tangled net before Atretes reached him.

Atretes charged, and the retiarius managed to block his first and second blow. But without his net, Atretes' opponent had only the trident to defend himself, and the German's years of experience with a framea gave him the advantage. With brute force, Atretes battered the retiarius with scutum and gladius until he found an opening. He took it.

The crowd screamed wildly, and his name sounded like a drum beat. But in Atretes' own mind, the cry was, "Freedom . . . freedom . . . *freedom!*"

Before the retiarius had fallen, searing pain burst along Atretes' side as a dimachaerus' dagger glanced off his rib cage. He stumbled back, blocking a frontal attack with his scutum. Regaining his balance, he uttered a cry of pain and rage. No foul little back-stabber was going to take this chance from him! He swung his gladius with all his strength and bent the dimachaerus' shield in half, knocking him to his knees. Dropping the now useless scutum, the man scrambled to his feet and ran, knowing his dagger was no match against a gladius. To the glee of the crowd, Atretes ran after him. As he did so, he bent and snatched up the fallen retiarius' trident, took a hopping step, and hurled it with the skill he had learned in using a framea.

The mob went wild when the trident hit its mark. Men stood and pounded on those in front of them, women screamed in mad abandon. Some fainted, overcome with excitement, while others tore at their clothes and hair and jumped up and down. The earth beneath the stadium trembled.

"Atretes! Atretes! Atretes!"

Atretes caught their bloodlust and let it reign. He cut down a mirmillo and attacked a Samnite. He unleashed his rage against Rome, allowing hatred to pump through him, sending the strength he needed surging through his wounded body. Knocking the scutum from his opponent's arm, he gutted him like a fish.

Turning, he looked for whoever stood between him and his freedom. Thousands of spectators were on their feet, waving white banners and chanting. It was a moment before Atretes' mind cleared and he realized what the mob screamed so loudly: *"Atretes! Atretes! Atretes!"*

He was the last man standing.

Julia trembled violently as Atretes walked toward a gateway that opened to the stairs he would climb to the platform where the proconsul waited to award the victor. She was torn between jubilation and fear. She loved him and was proud of his triumph, but she knew his newly won freedom would jeopardize her own liberty.

As Atretes walked toward the stairs, he stumbled and fell to one knee. The crowd gasped and grew quiet, but he used his gladius and pushed himself up again. The crowd cheered wildly as he reached the gate to the victor's platform, where a soldier opened it for him and drew back in respect as he ascended the stone steps. The proconsul was waiting, a laurel wreath of victory, an ivory pendant, and a wooden sword in his arms.

Julia scarcely heard what the proconsul said as he placed the laurel wreath on Atretes' head. Then the politician's daughter looped the small rectangular ivory pendant proclaiming Atretes' freedom around his neck. Jealousy swept like a hot flood through Julia as the girl pulled Atretes' head down to kiss him full on the mouth. Women screamed ecstatically around her, and Julia wanted to press her hands over her ears and turn away. Sertes handed Atretes the wooden sword, proclaiming his triumphant retirement from the arena, and two soldiers deposited a chest of sesterces at Atretes' feet.

The proconsul raised his hand to the cheering masses. Within a moment, the stadium was quiet. Thousands craned forward to hear what reward would be given the triumphant victor next.

"We have one last honor to bestow upon our beloved Atretes for his victory today!" the proconsul called out. He turned dramatically and took a scroll from Sertes hand. "I bestow this by order of Emperor Vespasian," he called out and extended the scroll to Atretes, who accepted it mechanically. The proconsul put his hand on Atretes' shoulder and turned him to face the thousands, proclaiming, "Atretes is hereby made a citizen and defender of Rome."

Atretes stiffened briefly, his face going pale and taut with violent emotions. Julia saw his fist clench at the proclamation.

"See how he hates Rome," Calabah said, leaning close to Julia as the mob cheered in adoration. "He would throw that proclamation in the dust if it didn't give him everything he wants." Calabah's words blended with the cries of the mob as they began shouting his name again and again. "He stands an equal with your father and brother now."

Atretes turned his head, seeking Julia out among the proconsul's guests. He looked straight into her eyes, his own blazing with promise, which made her heart race. For one terrifying moment, she thought he meant to claim her right then and there. Instead, Sertes and several Roman guards escorted him down the steps, across the arena, and to the Door of Life, inside which his wounds would be tended.

Primus helped Julia to her feet. "You're shaking," he said with a knowing smile. "But then, I imagine every woman in this stadium is trembling at the sight of him. He is magnificent."

"Yes, he is," she said, remembering the look in his eyes. Now that he had his freedom, what was to keep him from trying to make her his slave? Her mouth went dry.

Primus lifted her easily into the canopied litter so that she could be borne aloft by six of his slaves. Before he drew the curtains closed, he tipped his head and gave her a faint, but charming, smile. "So, what have you decided?"

Julia's stomach tightened until it hurt. When she spoke, her voice was flat. "I'll sign the agreement this evening and have my things brought to your villa tomorrow morning."

"How very wise of you, Julia," Calabah exclaimed from behind Primus, her eyes gleaming. Primus took Julia's hand and kissed it.

As he drew the curtains closed, she leaned back and closed her eyes, wondering why she suddenly felt so desolate.

33

Julia's announcement that she was leaving home and moving in with Primus burst with the force of a volcano upon the Valerian household. Marcus was furious, Phoebe appalled.

"You can't do this, Julia!" her mother said, fighting to retain control of her emotions. "What will I tell your father?"

"Don't tell him anything if you're afraid it'll upset him," Julia said, closing her ears to her mother's appeal and giving in to her own emotions.

"Upset him!" Marcus gave a sardonic laugh. "Why would he be upset to find out his daughter is moving in with a homosexual?"

She turned to him angrily. "It's my life and I'll do as I please. I'm moving in with Primus and there's nothing you can do about it! If Primus is so abominable, why have you invited him to your feasts?"

"Because it's politically expedients."

"In other words, though you despise him, you use him," she said.

"As he'll be using you if you enter into this ridiculous farce you claim will be a marriage."

"The marriage will be mutually beneficial, I assure you," she said haughtily. "I want a full accounting of what's mine by the end of the week, Marcus, and from then forward, I'll handle my own financial affairs. And you needn't look at me like that! My money will remain mine. Primus can't touch it." She glanced briefly at her mother's stricken face. "If you don't like any of this, Mother, then I'm very sorry, but I have to do what will make me happy."

She went into her room, Marcus close on her heels. "You'll go through everything you have within a year," he said. "Who put this foolishness in your head? Calabah?"

Julia glared at him. "Calabah doesn't think for me. I think for myself. I'm not the fool you think I am." She ordered one of the servants to bring a cart around while the others took her trunks out to be loaded.

"I never thought you a fool, Julia. Not until now."

Julia's chin jerked up, her dark eyes blazing. "My jewel box, Hadassah," she said in trembling fury. "We're leaving now."

"Oh, no," Marcus said, losing his temper further. "Hadassah isn't leaving here unless I say so."

"Just what *is* Hadassah to you?" she demanded with chilling softness. "She's my slave, though it appears you want her for yourself."

"Don't be ridiculous," Phoebe said from the doorway.

"Am I being ridiculous, Mother?" Julia's dark eyes burned as she looked between her brother and Hadassah. "Take the box downstairs, Hadassah, *now*. And wait for me at the sedan chair."

"Yes, my lady," Hadassah said softly and obeyed.

Marcus jerked Julia around to face him and held her there. "You've changed."

"Yes," Julia agreed. "I've changed. I've grown up and developed a mind of my own. My eyes are open, Marcus, wide open. Isn't that how you always encouraged me to be? Wasn't it you who introduced me to all the finer things the world has to offer? Wasn't it you who told me to watch out for people who would betray me? Well, dear brother, I've learned my lessons well. Now take your hands off me!"

Frowning, Marcus let her go and watched her walk out of the room.

"Julia, please," Phoebe said, following her. "Think what you're doing. If you enter a marriage like this, you'll be sullied."

"Sullied?" Julia said and laughed. "Mother, you've been locked behind Father's walls so long, you know nothing of the world. I'll be considered a woman of independent means, a woman of substance. And you know why? Because I won't have to crawl to my father or my brother to beg for my own money. I won't have to account to anyone for anything I choose to do."

"Do you despise me so much?" Phoebe said softly.

"I don't despise you, Mother. I just don't want to be like you."

"But, Julia, you don't love this man."

"I didn't love Claudius either, did I? But that didn't stop Father and you from forcing me into marrying him," she said bitterly. "You can't possibly understand, Mother. You've done exactly what was expected of you all your life!"

"Explain to me then. Make me understand."

"It's quite simple. I won't be a bondservant to any man, be he father, brother, or husband. Primus won't dictate my life as Father has always dictated yours. I'll answer only to myself." Julia kissed her mother's pale cheek. "Good-bye, Mother." With that, she left Phoebe standing in the corridor.

Primus greeted Julia with a chaste kiss on the cheek. "Only one little slave and a box of jewels?" he said. "It was bad, wasn't it? I've found Marcus intolerant about certain things. He's never allowed me to bring Prometheus to one of his feasts. I suppose he tried to stop you from moving in with me."

"I thought he would understand."

"Dear Julia. Your brother isn't the man he appears to be. Beneath that epicurean mask he wears beats the heart of a traditionalist." Primus petted her hand soothingly. "Give your mother and father time, and they'll accept things." He smiled faintly. "What else can they do if they ever want to see their beautiful daughter again?"

Just then, a young man of no more than fourteen entered the room. "Ah," Primus said, holding out his hand. The boy took it and allowed himself to be pulled forward and presented to Julia.

"This is my beloved Prometheus," Primus said, watching proudly as the boy bowed respectfully to Julia. "I'll be with you shortly," he said, smiling at the boy, who bowed again and left.

Julia felt an unpleasant sensation curling in the pit of her stomach. "He is quite charming," she remarked politely.

"Yes, he is, isn't he?" Primus said, pleased.

Julia forced a smile. "If you don't mind, I'd like to be shown to my chambers. My things should arrive shortly," she said.

"Of course. I'll show you the way." He ushered her through the archway into the sunny peristyle and then up the marble steps to the second floor. Her room was next to his own.

As soon as he left, Julia sank down wearily onto the couch. "Put my jewel box here," she told Hadassah, indicating the small table beside her. Hadassah set it down carefully. Julia opened the lid and dug her fingers into the baubles and necklaces. "The first thing I'm going to do when I have my money is replace the things I've had to give to Sertes." She closed the lid with a bang.

She rose and wandered around the room. "Prometheus looks just like those effeminate boys who rode with Bacchus." Fingering the wall hanging, she remembered the wild celebrations in

Rome, when a drunken man rode through the city streets on a flowered cart that was pulled by a leopard.

"My lady, are you sure you want to remain here?"

Julia let go of the Babylonian tapestry and turned to face Hadassah. "So you disapprove as well," she said with dangerous softness.

Hadassah went to her. Kneeling, she took her hand. "My lady, you're in love with Atretes."

Julia snatched her hand away and stood. "Yes, I love Atretes. Moving in with Primus doesn't change that. Primus is free to live however he pleases, and so am I."

Hadassah stood, eyes downcast. "Yes, my lady," she said softly.

Julia pushed her doubts away, focusing her mind on material things. "It's a lovely room, but too small. And I don't like the murals with all those little boys. As soon as Marcus releases my money, I'll buy another villa, bigger than this one, one grand enough for me and Atretes. Primus can have his own floor."

She stepped out on a narrow terrace and looked back toward the center of the city. She wanted to fill her lungs with clean air. She could see the temple in the distance and wondered if Atretes was giving offerings to the goddess for his triumph in the arena. Her eyes smarted. If only everything had stayed as it was. If only Sertes hadn't entered Atretes in the elimination match.

The servants arrived with her things and Hadassah took charge of the unpacking. "Leave that to Cybil," Julia ordered. "I want to speak with you." Hadassah came out to her on the terrace. "I want you to find Atretes and tell him I've arranged for a permanent residence where we may be together as often as we want. Don't tell him anything about Primus. Do you hear me? He might not understand. Not yet. He's still very uncivilized. It's best if I explain everything when I see him. Just tell him he *must* come to me now. I need him."

Hadassah's heart was heavy. "Will he still be at the ludus, my lady?"

"I don't know, but go there first. If he isn't there, Sertes will be able to tell you where he is." They went back inside, and Julia opened her jewel box. Frowning, she ran her hand lightly over a necklace of pearls. She passed over it to a gold brooch set with rubies. Weighing the piece in her hand, her mouth tightened. She liked the brooch. Why should she have to part with it? Atretes was free now. She shouldn't have to pay to have him brought to her. A word from her should be enough to make him come of his own free will.

She dropped the brooch back into the box and closed the lid firmly. "Tell Sertes I've sent you with a message for Atretes. He'll either tell you where Atretes is or live to regret it." She walked with Hadassah to the door, speaking softly so the other servants wouldn't hear. "Deliver the message exactly as I've given it to you. Nothing about Primus. Do you understand? I'll tell Atretes about Primus later."

As Hadassah turned to do her mistress's bidding, she wondered how Julia, who had spent so much time with Atretes, could not know the man at all.

Even while Atretes lay on the table having his wounds stitched and salted, offers were brought to him from high Roman officials inviting him to be a guest at their villas. "Get them out of here," Atretes growled at Sertes.

"As you wish," Sertes said. It hadn't been his decision to have Atretes fight in the elimination match. The proconsul had demanded it after receiving word from the emperor that the barbarian was to be included. Sertes had been unable to refuse, and although the proconsul had paid him enough to reimburse him for Atretes' purchase price, housing, and care, Sertes saw future profits go down the sewers. Either way, dead or free, Atretes would be out from under his control.

But Sertes was no fool. There were other ways to make money off of Atretes if the goddess but smiled on him.

Atretes returned to the ludus, where he intended to stay until he decided what he was going to do with his freedom. Sertes gave him a large chamber connected to his own and shrewdly treated him with the respect of an honored guest.

As Sertes expected, a crowd gathered outside the main gate of the ludus the next morning. Most were amoratae waiting for a glimpse of Atretes, but many others were businessmen who had come with money-making ventures for Atretes to consider. Sertes had the latter brought into a large meeting room, then informed Atretes that he had esteemed guests. The men clamored around the German as he entered, growing louder and louder as they tried to out shout one another with their propositions. Sertes stood aside and watched.

One man wanted to paint Atretes' image on vases, trays, and

cameos. Several wanted to sell him villas. Another wanted him to become half owner of an inn. Still another wanted him to endorse his chariots. Sertes let the confusion mount.

"I will give you the most elaborate chariot I build, as well as two matched horses from Arabia to go with it!" the chariot builder offered.

Atretes had the look of a cornered lion about to pounce. He glanced at Sertes as though silently demanding that he do something. Sertes made a vow to place a large offering before Artemis, then pressed through the crowd. He took his place beside Atretes.

"Your offer is ridiculous," he said to the chariot builder. "You know what profit you'll make with Atretes' name, and yet you make such a paltry offer?"

"I'll add a thousand sesterces to my offer," the man said quickly.

"Ten thousand and he might consider it," Sertes said contemptuously. "You will excuse us." He turned Atretes away and leaned close, speaking softly. "I can handle these negotiations for you if you wish. There's no reason for you to be here. I'm experienced in business dealings and know how to make them raise their offers. My fee will be a meager 35 percent of what you make. Everything will be presented to you for final decision, of course. I'll make you a very rich man."

Atretes clamped a hard hand on Sertes' arm. "I want a villa of my own."

Sertes nodded. "Whatever you want, you've only to say. I'll arrange it." He would milk Atretes' fame for as long as it lasted.

A servant entered the room and made his way to Sertes. "That little Jewess is here, my lord. She said she has a message for Atretes."

"Take me to her," Atretes ordered, ignoring the protests of the men who had waited hours to see him.

Sertes raised his hands. "Enough! Atretes has more important matters at hand. Prepare your proposals and make your offers to me. I will discuss them with Atretes at his convenience and notify you of his decision. That will be all!" He nodded to one of the burly guards. "Get them out of here. I have a ludus to run."

Atretes saw Hadassah waiting just inside the closed gate of the ludus. "Leave me," he said to the servant and strode across the sandy compound toward her.

Her face filled with warmth when she saw him. She smiled and bowed low. "Praise God for his bountiful mercy," she said. "You are alive and well!"

He smiled down at her, remembering the night in the stadium and her promise to pray for him. Her kindness filled him with a warmth he hadn't felt in years. Had it been prayers to her god that had kept him alive? "Yes, I am alive and well. I am also free," he said. "You've brought word from Julia?"

Her demeanor changed subtly. She lowered her eyes from his immediately and delivered the message. Atretes listened, and each word burned his pride. A muscle locked and then worked in his jaw.

"*Must?*" he said coldly. "Tell your lady it will not be as before. *I* will send for *her* when *I* am ready." He turned away and headed back for the barracks.

"Atretes," Hadassah said hastening after him. "Please. Don't turn from her now."

He glared down at her. "Remind your lady that I'm no longer a slave to be summoned at her whim and for her pleasure."

She looked up at him beseechingly. "She loves you, my lord. She means no offense."

"Ah, but it's the Roman way to give offense! And she is Roman, isn't she? Born and bred upon pride and arrogance."

Hadassah laid her hand gently on his arm and smiled sadly. "Pride and arrogance are not limited to Romans, Atretes."

Surprisingly, his fierce anger evaporated. His hard mouth softened into a half smile and he gave a bleak laugh. "Perhaps not," he said ruefully. She was a strange little woman with fathomless eyes that were so gentle they had the effect of a calm sea.

"Speak with her gently, Atretes, and she will do whatever you ask." Hadassah knew this was the truth. A gentle, loving word from Atretes, and Julia would even turn away from the terrible path she was now following.

"I vowed never to be summoned by her again," he said flatly. "And I hold to that vow." He nodded toward the high walls of the ludus and said, "Nor would I dishonor her by summoning her here." He looked down at Hadassah. "Tell your mistress I'll send for her when I have a house and can take her into it as my wife." So saying, he strode away.

Hadassah turned away sadly, seeing only tragedy ahead for them both.

"Where is he?" Julia demanded when Hadassah returned to Primus' villa alone. "Didn't you tell him I wanted to see him? You didn't, did you? What did you tell him?"

"I gave him your message, my lady, exactly as you said."

Julia slapped her. "You deceitful little Jew. You told him about Primus, didn't you?" She slapped her again, harder.

Hadassah drew back from her, afraid. She put a trembling hand to her stinging cheek. "I didn't, my lady."

"If you said nothing to him about Primus, he would be here!"

"He said he would send for you when he had a house and could take you into it as his wife."

Julia went still, her face blanching. She stared at Hadassah, then sank down onto her couch, suddenly unable to stand. She closed her eyes. She'd known what to expect, but somehow hearing he had said it so openly made her weak inside, weak with confusion and longing.

Hadassah knelt before her. "Please, Lady Julia. Return to the house of your father and mother and remain there until Atretes sends for you."

Julia felt a moment of uncertainty—but then Calabah's warnings rose in her mind, clear and logical. If she married Atretes, he would take her into his house and never let her out again. He would be worse than Claudius and Caius put together.

"No."

"Please," Hadassah pleaded softly. "Don't stay here."

The momentary confusion on Julia's face cleared. "If I go back now, I'll look like a fool. And nothing would change. Marcus wouldn't approve of my relationship with Atretes any more than he approves of this one with Primus." She gave a weak laugh. "Atretes might be proclaimed a Roman citizen, but he's still a barbarian at heart. Marcus might not even allow me to see him."

"Marcus wants you to be safe and happy."

Julia raised her brow at the familiar way Hadassah said her brother's name. She glared down at her for a long, still moment as the deep seed of jealousy, planted by Marcus himself, began to grow. "You only want to be close to my brother, don't you?" she said coldly. "You're just like Bithia and all the rest." She rose and moved away. "No, I won't listen to you. I'm staying right here. Once I've spoken with Atretes, he'll understand. I'll make him understand."

She would remind him of how he had hated his slavery and

demand if that was what he expected of her now. A wife was a slave, someone at the mercy of her husband. This way, they were both free. Nothing had to change between them. They would continue to be lovers just as before. It would be even better. She wouldn't have to pay Sertes. Atretes could come whenever she sent him a message. But even if all her reasoning didn't work, she knew one thing that would make him listen.

She would tell him about the child she was carrying.

Hadassah went to John and wept over Julia.

The apostle listened and then took her hands between his own. "Perhaps God has given Julia over to the lusts of her heart so that she may receive in her own person the due penalty of her errors."

Hadassah looked at him, her cheeks streaked with tears. "I've spent hours singing psalms to her and telling her stories of David and Gideon, Jonah, and Elijah. So many stories, but never once the greatest story of all. When I'm with Julia, the name of Jesus freezes in my throat." She took her hands from him and covered her face.

John understood. "We all know fear at some time, Hadassah."

"You're not afraid anymore, though. And my father was never afraid." She remembered her father being carried into the upper room by Benaiah, his beloved face beaten almost beyond recognition. And still he had gone out again and again and again, until the last day of his life. *They're throwing bodies over the wall into the Valley of Hinnom,* Mark had said the day he was killed, and in Hadassah's mind, she could see her father lying there among the thousands of dead cast over the temple wall and left rotting in the Judean sun.

"As I have told you, I have known fear well," John said. "When they came and took the Lord away from the Garden of Gethsemane, a Roman soldier grabbed for me, and I ran. He was left holding a linen sheet, which was the only thing covering my body, while I escaped, naked." His kind eyes were shadowed with remembered shame. "But fear is not of the Lord, Hadassah."

"I know that in my mind, but still my heart trembles."

"Lay your burden before Jesus."

"But what if your burden is not only fear, but love? I have a love for Julia as though she were my own sister."

His eyes filled with compassion. "We sow in tears that we might harvest in joy. Be obedient to the Lord's will. Love Julia despite what she does, that through you she might come to know Christ's surpassing grace and mercy. Be faithful, that she and the others might be sanctified."

"But will they be sanctified if they refuse to believe? And what do I do about Calabah?"

"Nothing."

"But John, she exerts greater and greater control over Julia. It's as though Julia is being transformed into her likeness. I have to do something."

John shook his head. "No, Hadassah. Our struggle isn't against flesh and blood, but against the powers of darkness."

"I can't fight Satan, John. My faith isn't strong enough."

"You don't fight him. *Resist* evil and be strong in the Lord, Hadassah, and in the strength of *God's* might. He's given you armor for the battle. Truth, his righteousness, the gospel of peace. Faith is your shield, the Word your sword. Pray with perseverance in the Spirit of the Lord. Then stand firm, that the Lord might go out before you."

"I'll try," she said softly.

John took her hands and held them firmly, his warmth and strength surrounding her. "God doesn't fail in his good purpose. Trust in him, and in his time he'll open your mouth and give you the words to speak." He smiled. "You are not alone!"

Reclined on one of the couches in the triclinium, Julia selected a delicacy prepared by her new cook. Primus was telling her another of his ribald stories, this one about a Roman official and his unfaithful wife. She'd learned very quickly that she had an insatiable appetite for his stories, an appetite Primus was only too willing to satisfy.

"I know who you're talking about, Primus," she said. "Vitellius. Am I right?"

He raised his goblet in salute to her shrewdness, smiling at Prometheus, who was leaning against him. "You know I never break a confidence," he said drolly.

"You can call him by whatever name you like, but you imitate his lisp so well, it leaves me in no doubt whatsoever. Vitellius it is. Fat, pompous, lisping Vitellius."

"He'll never trust me with another secret," Primus said ruefully, then frowned in annoyance as Hadassah entered the triclinium with another tray. Prometheus stiffened slightly and drew away from Primus, who gave an irritated sigh. "Set the tray there and leave us," he ordered tersely and glanced at Julia. "Tell her, Julia." She nodded, and Hadassah silently went from the room. "I don't like her," Primus said, glaring toward the empty doorway.

"Why not?" Julia said, selecting a honeyed hummingbird tongue from the platter.

"Because every time she enters the room, Prometheus becomes agitated. Why don't you sell her?"

"Because she pleases me," Julia said and poured herself more wine. "She sings and tells stories."

"I've heard some and I don't like them, either. In case you hadn't heard, Calabah has a healthy dislike for your slave, also."

"She's told me." Julia gave him an impatient look and sipped her wine. She knew she was getting drunk, but she didn't care. It was better than suffering from depression. She'd had no word from Atretes or Marcus or her mother. Everyone had deserted her. She saw Prometheus' eyes flickering nervously toward the archway and felt a malicious satisfaction.

A servant entered. "My lady, your brother is here to see you."

She sat up, spilling wine on her new green palus. She set the silver goblet down hurriedly and put her hand against her swimming head. "Bring him to me," she said and pressed cold hands to her warm face. "Do I look all right?" she asked Primus.

"As lovely as a sea nymph rising from the foam."

Marcus entered the room and seemed to fill it with his presence. He was so handsome, she swelled with pride looking at him.

"Marcus," she said and held out her hands to him.

He took her hands and kissed her cheek. "Little sister," he said affectionately. Then he straightened and glanced at Primus. "I wish to speak to my sister alone."

Primus' brows rose mockingly. "You forget where you are, Marcus. This is my villa, not yours."

"Leave, Primus," Julia said testily. "I haven't seen my brother in weeks."

"And we know why, don't we?" he said, watching Marcus' face as he took Prometheus' hand. "Come, Prometheus. We'll leave these two to talk over their differences."

Marcus glared after him. "How you can sit and see how he acts with that boy is beyond me, Julia."

Defensive, she retaliated. "Perhaps I'm more tolerant of others.

And who are you to judge Primus? I saw you more than once with Bithia."

"There's a vast difference."

"Indeed there is. Primus is more faithful to Prometheus than you ever were to Arria or Fannia or a dozen others I could name. Besides," she said airily, sitting down again, "I find Primus extremely sensitive. He was rude because you've hurt his feelings." She reached for her wine again, feeling in need of it.

"No doubt he gives you your way in everything. You are paying all the bills, aren't you?"

"And what if I am? It's my money to do with as I like. I chose this villa, by the way. It's beautiful, isn't it? And in the most affluent section of the city. I chose the furnishings, too. That's more than I've ever had to say about anything in my life."

Marcus knew he had to quiet his temper. "You're happy living this way?"

"Yes. I'm happy! Happier than I was with a repulsive old man obsessed with his studies or a handsome young man who was cruel beyond words. Caius would've run through all my money with his gambling if he hadn't died." Her voice cracked and she quickly drank more wine. Her hand was trembling, and she took a breath to calm herself. "Primus asks for very little, Marcus," she said more quietly. "He's no threat to me. He listens to my problems and encourages me to do whatever will make me happy. Besides, he makes me laugh."

"I'd be careful what I told him, little sister. Primus has a very cutting wit, and he collects rumors like a dog collects fleas. It doesn't take much to get him scratching and spreading everything. His penchant for gossip is what's kept him in money for years. People pay him *not* to talk."

She stretched out on the couch again. "Sit down and have something to eat, Marcus." She waved an elegant hand over the laden trays. "It may improve your disposition."

Marcus noted she was wearing several new rings, and the platters of food displayed an expensive array of delicacies. He made no comment. What was the use? Perhaps it was the rich food that accounted for her thickened waist, but he doubted it. He was fairly sure she was pregnant again, and he knew by whom.

"Primus isn't in a position to hurt me, is he?" she said, smiling cynically. "But if you're worried, I'll ask him to overlook your deplorable behavior."

"Don't ask him to overlook anything!"

"Why did you come?" she said wearily, and her mask of haughty disdain slipped enough for him to see his vulnerable little sister beneath it.

He sighed heavily and came to her. "Julia," he said gently and took her wine goblet from her, setting it aside. "I didn't come to argue with you."

"It's Father," she said, her eyes flickering with fear. "He's dead, isn't he?"

"No."

Her body relaxed. "Did Mother tell him why I left?"

"She said you were visiting friends. He seems content with the letters she reads to him."

"What letters?"

Marcus looked at her in surprise for a moment, then let out a soft breath of comprehension. Poor Mother. "Apparently, the ones she writes in your name."

Julia got up and moved away from him, wanting to escape her guilt.

"We had a visitor this morning," Marcus said. "A guard who had been instructed to bring you safely to Atretes."

Julia swung around and stared at him. "Atretes sent for me?" She came back to him and clutched his hands. "Oh, Marcus. Where is he? You didn't send him away, did you? If you did, I'll kill myself. I swear it." Her eyes welled with tears.

Marcus could feel her trembling. "I told him you were away and asked where his master could be reached when you returned."

She let go of him and began to pace nervously. "I didn't know what happened or where he went. You can't imagine how unhappy I've been. I love him so much, Marcus, but when I sent for him, he refused to come to me."

"How long have you been involved with this gladiator?"

She stopped and tipped her chin. "I don't like the way you say *gladiator.* Atretes is a free man now and a Roman citizen."

"How long, Julia?"

"Six months," she said finally and saw his gaze move slowly down over her body.

"So, it's his child you're carrying."

Julia blushed and covered her abdomen defensively. "Yes."

"Does he know?"

She shook her head. "I've had no opportunity to tell him."

"Obviously he doesn't know about your marriage to Primus, either, or he wouldn't have sent his guard to me to have you brought to him."

"I planned to tell him about all this weeks ago, but I didn't know where he was!"

"With very little effort, you could've found out. How are you going to explain Primus to him? Julia, I spoke to his guard. Atretes bought an estate a few miles outside Ephesus. He expects to marry you."

She kept her face averted, and Marcus stood and went to her. He turned her around to face him and saw she was crying. "You don't betray someone like Atretes," he said softly.

"I haven't betrayed him!" she cried, shaking free. "You don't think I'd sleep with Primus, do you? I don't! I don't sleep with anyone."

"I hope Atretes will listen long enough to let you explain that. You can't toy with a man like this one, Julia."

"I moved in with Primus before Atretes was freed," she said, not meeting his eyes.

"That's a lie, and you and I both know it. You moved in with Primus *after* the Ephesian games."

"Well, Atretes needn't know that! It's only a matter of one day's difference."

"One day." His eyes narrowed. "Did you know you were pregnant when you moved in with Primus?" He knew when she looked away that she had. "By all the gods, why did you move in here if you're in love with Atretes?"

"If I'd told you about him, you wouldn't have allowed me to see him again and you know it."

"Possibly," Marcus conceded. "But then you probably wouldn't have given me any more say about that than you have with Primus. Listen to me," he said, striving for control. "Right now, I'd approve anything over this unnatural arrangement you are in. I'll take you to Atretes myself, right now if you wish it."

"No. I moved in with Primus for all the reasons I told you."

"Then you don't love Atretes."

"I love him, but I could never marry him. Think about it, Marcus. He doesn't think like a Roman. In fact, he hates Rome, hates it absolutely. What if we grew tired of one another, and I fell in love with someone else? Would he let me be happy? No. He's a barbarian. They drown unfaithful wives in a bog. And what if he wanted to go back to Germania?" She gave a harsh laugh. "Can you see me living in a filthy longhouse, or whatever it is that barbarians live in? But he could make me go, couldn't he? Just because I was his wife!"

Marcus listened to her in disbelief. "Do you really think Atretes will come to you now and be your lover when you're involved with another man?"

"Isn't it the same thing as Arria?"

He frowned. "What are you talking about?"

"You knew about her affairs with various gladiators. She used to tell you about them, don't you remember? I asked you why you permitted her to be unfaithful to you, and you told me Arria was free to do whatever she wished. And you were free to do the same."

"I never intended you to fashion your life after Arria!"

"I didn't. I fashioned it after you."

Marcus stared at her, stunned into silence.

Julia kissed his cheek. "Don't look so surprised. What would you expect from a sister who adores you? Now, tell me where Atretes is." When he told her, she sat down. "I'm tired," she said, drowsy from all the wine she had drunk. She lay back against the cushions and closed her eyes. "You can tell Mother about the baby if you want." Her mouth curved in amusement. "Maybe she'll think better of Primus."

Marcus leaned down and kissed her forehead. "I doubt it."

She caught hold of his hand. "Will you come back?"

"Yes. Maybe I can undo what I've done."

She kissed his hand. "I don't think so." She smiled, thinking he was teasing her as he always had, not hearing the hard tone in his voice.

As Marcus went out of the room, he saw Hadassah sitting on a bench, her hands folded loosely in her lap. Was she praying? She lifted her head and saw him. She arose gracefully, her gaze lowering from his in respect. Marcus crossed the room and stood before her. It was a moment before he could speak. "Mother and Father miss you."

"I miss them, too, my lord. How does your father fare?"

"He's worse."

"I'm sorry," she said softly.

He knew she meant it, and her sincerity filled him with inexplicable pain. He reached out and let his hand glide down her arm. "I'll find a way to bring you home," he said huskily.

She withdrew from his touch. "Lady Julia needs me, my lord."

He let his hand drop to his side. She stepped past him. "I need you, too," he said softly and heard her stop behind him. He turned his head and saw she was looking back at him with tears in her eyes. She turned away again and went into the triclinium. To Julia.

At the soft scraping sound of sandals above him, Marcus glanced up sharply.

"We'll see you again soon, won't we, Marcus?" Primus said, smiling down at him. He puckered as though to kiss him and then grinned. "Oh, yes, I'm sure we will."

As Primus' soft mocking laughter floated down into the peristyle, Marcus turned and strode angrily toward the door.

Atretes grasped Julia's wrists and yanked her hands down from around his neck. Shaking with murderous rage, he thrust her from him. "If you weren't with child, I'd kill you," he said through clenched teeth and walked out of the room.

Julia ran after him. "It's your child! I swear it! I haven't betrayed you. Primus is nothing to me. Atretes! Don't leave me! Listen to me! Listen!" she cried out, weeping. *"Atretes!"*

Leaping onto his chariot, Atretes grabbed up the reins and shouted. The matched white stallions lunged forward into the street. Shouting again, he took the whip and drove them harder until they were racing with all their strength. People dove out of the way, shouting curses after him.

He reached the edge of the city and raced on. The wind in his face didn't cool his rage. The villa he had bought rose ahead of him on a green hillside. A guard saw him coming and opened the gate. He raced through and turned the chariot, showering the entryway with small rocks. Throwing the reins out of his way, he stepped down and left the lathered animals to prance nervously as he strode up the marble steps into the house.

"Get out of my sight!" he shouted at the slaves who'd been preparing for the arrival of their new mistress. Giving a savage cry, he swept the feast from its long table. Silver and gold trays crashed to the floor, goblets slammed into the wall, chipping the mural that was painted there. He kicked the table over, smashed the murrhine glass, and heaved the Corinthian bronze vases.

Yanking the Babylonian hangings down from the wall, he ripped them in two. He overturned couches and destroyed the Oriental silk cushions.

Striding through the archway, he went into the chamber that had been prepared for Julia. Kicking over the ornate braziers, he scattered hot coals beneath the big bed and into the soft canopy of netting that draped over and around it. It caught fire quickly. As the bed began to burn, Atretes swept a large box from a beautifully hand-carved table and scattered pearls and jewels across the marble mosaic floor.

As he came out of the room, several of the young women he had bought to attend Julia stood nearby, wide-eyed with terror. "You're free," he said, and when they only drew back a few steps, looking at him as though he had gone mad, he shouted, "Get out!" They ran from him.

He went into the inner courtyard and leaned over the open well. Scooping up some water, he splashed his face. Breathing heavily, he leaned down, intending to put his whole head in the water, when he saw a rippling reflection of himself.

He looked Roman. His hair was cropped short, and there was gold about his neck. Grabbing the front of the gold-embroidered tunic, he ripped it from his body. He snatched off the medallion of a saluting gladiator and flung it across the courtyard, then threw back his head and cried out in savage rage, the sound of it rising and growing until shepherds heard it on the hillsides.

34

Phoebe sent word to Marcus and Julia to come immediately, that their father was dying. She told the servant who went for Julia, "Be sure she brings Hadassah with her."

Marcus arrived first and went in to his father. When Julia arrived, Phoebe was relieved to see Hadassah beside her. Julia went in, but stopped when she neared the bed. It had been weeks since she'd seen her father, and the devastation of his illness shocked and repulsed her. With a strangled cry, she fled the room. Phoebe quickly caught up with her. "Julia!"

She turned and spoke as she walked backwards. "I don't want to see him like this, Mother. I want to remember him the way he was."

"He asked to see you."

"Why? To tell me I've disappointed him? To curse me before he dies?"

"You know he wouldn't do that. He's always loved you, Julia."

Julia put her hand over her abdomen, distended from her advanced pregnancy. "I can feel the baby moving. It's not good for me to be in there. I mustn't get upset! I'll wait in the peristyle. I'll stay there until it's over."

Marcus came out and saw his sister on the verge of hysteria. He put his hand on his mother's shoulder. "I'll talk to her," he said.

Phoebe turned away, looking at Hadassah and holding her hand out to her. "Come with me," she said softly, and they went in together to Decimus.

Hadassah felt an overwhelming compassion for her master. A skillfully woven blanket of white wool was drawn up over his emaciated body. His arms lay limply at his sides, blue veins standing out against the whiteness of his thin hands. There was the smell of death in the room, but it was the look in his eyes that made her want to weep.

Marcus brought Julia in. She had gained control of herself, but the moment she saw her father again, she began to cry. When Decimus turned his sunken eyes on her, she cried harder. He lifted his hand weakly. When she hesitated, Marcus gripped her shoulders and pressed her forward. He pushed her down into the chair beside the bed, and she covered her face with her hands and bent forward, weeping profusely. Decimus laid his hand on her head, but she shrank from his touch. "Julia," he rasped and reached out to her again.

"I can't," Julia cried out. "I can't bear this." She tried to push past Marcus.

"Let her go," Decimus said weakly, his hand falling limply to his side. He closed his eyes as Julia hurried from the room. They could all hear her weeping as she ran down the corridor. "She's young," he rasped. "She's seen far too much of death already." His breathing was labored. "Is Hadassah here?"

"She's gone to be with Julia," Phoebe said.

"Bring her to me."

Marcus found her in a small alcove in the peristyle, comforting his sister. "Hadassah. Father wants to see you."

She took her arms from around Julia and rose quickly.

Julia's head came up. "Why does he want to see *her?*"

"Go," he commanded Hadassah and then turned to Julia. "Perhaps he needs more comfort than you do, and he knows he can get it from her," he said, unable to keep the edge from his voice.

"Nobody understands me," she said bitterly. "Not even you." She started to cry again. Marcus turned away and strode after Hadassah. "No one knows what I have to bear!" Julia called after him shrilly.

Hadassah entered and went to stand at the foot of the bed where Decimus could see her. "I'm here, my lord."

"Sit with me a while," Decimus rasped. She came around the bed and knelt beside it. When he lifted his hand limply, she took it gently between her own. He sighed. "So many questions. No time left."

"Time enough for what's important," she whispered. She pressed his hand gently. "Do you want to belong to the Lord, master?"

"I must be baptized . . . "

Hadassah's heart lifted, but she had seen enough death in Jerusalem to know there was no time left to carry him into his own baths. *Oh, please, God, give me your wisdom, forgive my lack of it.* She felt a flooding warmth and an answering assurance.

"The Lord was crucified between two thieves. One mocked

him. The other confessed his sin and said, 'Jesus, remember me when you come into your kingdom,' and the Lord answered, 'Truly I say unto you, today you shall be with me in paradise.' "

"I have sinned greatly, Hadassah."

"If you but believe and accept his grace, you will be with the Lord in paradise."

The troubled look left Decimus' eyes. His trembling hand took hers and placed it on his chest. She spread her hand over his heart. "Marcus . . ." His breathing rattled in his chest. Marcus leaned down on the other side of the bed.

"I'm here, Father." Marcus grasped his father's other hand.

Decimus took his son's hand weakly and placed it over Hadassah's. He put both of his hands over theirs and looked at his son.

"I understand, Father."

Hadassah glanced up as Marcus closed his hand firmly around hers.

Decimus gave a long, slow sigh. His face, so tensed and marred by years of pain, relaxed gently. It was finished.

Marcus' fingers loosened, and Hadassah quickly drew her hand free, but as his mother came forward, Marcus raised his head and looked straight into her eyes. Heart leaping, she clenched her hand against her chest and stepped back from the bed.

"He's gone," Phoebe said. She gently closed her husband's eyes. Leaning down, she kissed his lips. "Your suffering is over, my love," she whispered, and her tears wet his peaceful face. She lay down beside him and put her arms around him. Resting her head on his chest, she gave in to her grief.

"Of course, it was too much for you," Primus said, pouring Julia more wine. "It was cruel of them to expect you to sit and watch your father die."

"I went to an alcove and waited there."

Calabah took Julia's hand and kissed it tenderly. "There was nothing you could do, Julia."

Vaguely discomforted by Calabah's kiss, Julia jerked her hand free and stood up. "Perhaps my presence would have comforted him."

"Would your presence have changed anything?" Calabah said softly. "Was your father even coherent at the end?"

"I don't know. I wasn't there," Julia said, fighting tears, knowing Calabah saw them as weakness.

Calabah sighed. "And now you've let them make you feel guilty. Isn't that right? When will you learn, Julia? Guilt is self-defeating. You must use the power of your own will to overcome it. Focus your mind on something that pleases you."

"Nothing pleases me," Julia said miserably.

Calabah's mouth turned down. "It's this pregnancy that's made you so emotionally fragile. A pity you didn't have an abortion sooner."

Julia's fingers whitened into a fist. "I won't have an abortion at all. I've told you that before, Calabah. Why do you keep suggesting it?" She glared at her, her hand resting protectively on her swollen abdomen. "It's Atretes' child."

Calabah's eyes widened in mock surprise. "You don't still hold any hope that he'll come back to you, do you?"

"He loves me. Once he's thought things over, I'm sure he'll come back."

"He's had several months to think things over, Julia, and you have heard nothing from him."

She turned away. "I've sent Hadassah to him. She'll make him see the child is his."

"And you think that will make any difference?"

"I'm surprised you trust that treacherous little Jew," Primus put in, full of hate for the slave girl.

"Hadassah isn't treacherous," Julia snapped. "She knows I was never with another man after I was with Atretes. She'll tell him. Then he'll come back and beg me to forgive him."

"She'll probably try to steal him from you the way she's trying to steal my Prometheus."

"Hadassah isn't the least bit interested in your catamite!" Julia said in disgust.

"You don't think so? I saw her sitting in that alcove with Prometheus, and she was holding his hand! Tell me now she's innocent!"

Calabah smiled faintly, her dark eyes glowing with feral pleasure. "Perhaps the boy is tiring of you, Primus," she said, fanning his jealousy into hotter flame. "You did find him when he was very young, before he had yet tasted all this world has to offer him."

Primus' face paled.

"The suggestion is ridiculous," Julia said haughtily. "Hadassah's a virgin and will stay that way until she dies."

"Not if your brother has any say about it," Primus said.

Julia stiffened. "How dare you!"

Undaunted by her anger, Primus leaned back, fully satisfied with the impact of his words. "Open your eyes, my dear Julia. Do you think Marcus comes to see you? He comes to see your slave."

"That's a lie!"

"You think so? That first day, when he came to tell you Atretes had sent for you, do you remember? Perhaps not, as you'd had a little too much wine. As you dozed unaware, I saw Marcus come out. Your Jew was standing right over there, waiting for him beneath that arch. He took her hand and, I can tell you, the look on his face was a sight to behold."

"Didn't you say your father asked for her?" Calabah said with calculated curiosity. Julia looked at her, her lips parting.

Calabah cast a glance at Primus and shook her head. "And still the child trusts her," she said. She looked up at Julia again, her dark eyes full of pity.

"You've sent a viper to your lover," Primus said viciously. "Do you know what she'll do? She'll do exactly what she's done to my Prometheus. She'll sink her fangs into Atretes and fill him with poisonous lies."

Julia was trembling violently. "I won't listen to you. You talk like a spiteful *woman,*" she said and turned her back to them.

"You tell her, Calabah," Primus said in frustration. "She'll listen to you."

"I don't need to tell her," Calabah said calmly. "She knows for herself already. She simply hasn't developed the courage yet to do anything about it."

Hadassah stood in the burned-out ruins of the villa Atretes had purchased for Julia. "He's not here," a man standing nearby told her. "He's out there in the hills somewhere, completely mad."

"How do I find him?"

"If you're wise, you'll leave him alone," the man said and left her there in the rubble.

Hadassah went out and prayed to God to help her find Atretes. She wandered about the hills for what seemed hours before she saw him sitting on a hillside, staring down at her. His hair was like a mane, and he wore a loincloth and bearskin cape.

A deadly looking spear was in his hand. His blue eyes glared at her coldly as she came up to him.

"Go away," he said in a chill, dead voice.

She sat down beside him and said nothing. He glared at her long and hard, then turned his eyes from her and stared out over the valley, back toward the great city. For hours he sat that way, unspeaking, cold and hard as stone. Hadassah sat beside him in silence.

The sun descended and the valley fell into darkness. Atretes rose, and Hadassah watched him walk along a worn pathway that led into a cave. She followed. Entering, she saw he was laying wood for a fire. She sat down against the wall.

Grabbing up his framea, he pointed it at her. "Get out of here or I'll kill you!" She looked from the framea up into his eyes. "*Get out!* Go back to that harlot you serve!" She didn't move, nor did she seem afraid. She simply looked up at him with those beautiful brown eyes so full of compassion.

Atretes drew back slowly and lowered the framea. Glaring at her, he turned his back and hunkered down before the fire, determined to ignore her.

Hadassah lowered her head and prayed silently for help.

"She expects me to come back, doesn't she? She still thinks she has a hold over me."

Hadassah lifted her head. His back was to her, and he was bent over the flickering flames. She was filled with sorrow for him. "Yes," she answered truthfully.

Atretes came to his feet, his body taut with the power of his rage. "Go back and tell her she's dead to me! Tell her I swore to Tiwaz and Artemis that I'd never look upon her face again." He went to the opening of the cave and stood staring out into the darkness.

Hadassah rose. She stood beside him and looked out at the starry night. She remained silent for a long while and then said very softly, "The heavens tell of the glory of God, and their expanse declares the work of his hands . . . "

Atretes went back inside the cave and sat down. He raked his fingers through his golden hair and held his head. After a moment, he took his hands down and looked at them.

"Do you know how many men I've killed? One hundred and forty-seven. *Recorded.*" He gave a harsh laugh. "I probably killed fifty men before that, Roman legionnaires who marched into Germania thinking they could claim our lands and make us slaves without a fight. I killed them with pleasure, to protect my family, to protect my village."

He turned his hands over and stared at his palms. "Then I killed for Rome's pleasure," he said bitterly and made fists. "I killed to stay alive." He raked his hands into his hair again. "I can remember the faces of every one of them, Hadassah. Some I killed without the least regret, but there were others. . . ." He closed his eyes tightly and remembered Caleb kneeling and lifting his head for the final death stroke. And his German countryman. Atretes remembered driving the framea through the young clansman's heart.

He opened his eyes again, wanting to blot out all the faces from his mind, knowing he never could. "I killed them because I had to. I killed them because I wanted to earn my freedom." He gritted his teeth, and the muscles stood out in the line of his hard jaw.

"*Freedom!* I have it now, written on an official document. I have it hanging around my neck." Grasping the ivory pendant in his fist, he broke the gold chain and held his proof of freedom out toward her. "I can walk where I want to walk. I can do as I please. They threw offerings at my feet like I was one of their gods and made me rich enough to live in a villa next to the proconsul of Rome! I'm *free!*"

He gave a harsh, mirthless laugh and flung the ivory piece and gold chain against the stone wall of the cave. "I'm not free of anything. Their yoke is still around my neck, choking me. I'll never be free of what Rome has done to me. She used me for her pleasure. She adored me because I set her blood on fire. I fulfilled her lust. She had only to command, and I performed." He looked up at Hadassah standing at the mouth of the cave, her face so gentle, and smiled bitterly. "Rome. Julia. One and the same."

Hadassah saw the inner agony etched into Atretes' hard, handsome face. "'Out of the depths I have cried to You, O Lord; Lord, hear my voice! Let Your ears be attentive to my cry for mercy. If You, O Lord, keep a record of sins, O Lord, who could stand? But with You there is forgiveness.'"

She saw how he frowned and came inside. She knelt beside him. "Life is a journey, Atretes, not our final destination. You are captive to your bitterness, but you can be set free."

He stared hopelessly into the fire. "How?"

She told him.

Atretes shook his head. "No," he said firmly and stood up. "Only a weak god would forgive those who nailed his son to a cross. A god with power would obliterate his enemies. He would wipe them all from the face of the earth." He went to the mouth of the cave again.

"It's hatred that keeps you a slave, Atretes. Choose forgiveness and love."

"Love," he said contemptuously, his back to her. "As I loved Julia? No. Love doesn't set you free. It takes hold of you and weakens you. And when you're most vulnerable, when you feel hope, it betrays you."

"The Lord won't betray you, Atretes."

He glared back at her. "You can have your weakling god. He did Caleb no good. Tiwaz is my god. A god of power!"

"Is he?" she said softly and rose. She walked to the mouth of the cave and looked up into his eyes, which still burned with anger. "Is he powerful enough to give you the peace of mind you need?" She put her hand lightly on his arm. "The child is yours, Atretes."

He jerked his arm away from her touch. "If Julia laid it at my feet, I'd walk away and never look back."

Hadassah saw he meant it. Tears filled her eyes. "May God have mercy on you," she whispered, then she walked out into the night.

Atretes watched her follow the narrow pathway down the hill. His gaze never left her, even after she reached the road that would lead her back to Ephesus.

Julia turned at Marcus' request and looked at him strangely. "You want to see Hadassah?"

"Yes. It concerns a matter of some importance."

"What matter?" she said, seeming only curious.

"A personal matter," he said, annoyed at being questioned. "I'll answer your questions after I've spoken with her. Is she here or have you sent her on an errand?"

"She just returned from an errand," she said strangely and clapped her hands. The sound was like a violence in the peaceful stillness of the peristyle. "Send Hadassah to us," she told one of Primus' servants. She looked at her brother again and smiled. She asked about their mother, but hardly seemed interested as he told her she seemed to be handling her grief with surprising serenity.

At the sound of soft footsteps approaching, Marcus turned and saw Hadassah. She came beneath an archway into the sunlight and walked toward them with a humble grace that made him ache. She didn't look at him.

"You wanted me, my lady?" she said, her head bowed.

"No. My brother wants you," Julia said coldly.

Marcus glanced sharply at his sister.

"You're to go to the bedchamber on the second floor, and wait for him there . . . "

"Julia," Marcus said, his temper rising, but she ignored him.

"Wait until he comes to you, then whatever he wants you to do, you will do it. Do you understand?"

Marcus saw Hadassah's face become a mask of confusion and fear, and he wanted to strike his sister. "Leave us, Hadassah." She stepped back uncertainly, looking between the two of them as though they'd both gone mad.

"You conniving harlot!" Julia screamed suddenly and came at Hadassah, hand raised to strike her. Marcus caught his sister's wrist and jerked her around to face him.

"Leave us *now!*" Marcus commanded Hadassah harshly. When she was gone, he shook Julia once. "What's the matter with you? Has this pregnancy driven you mad?"

"What Primus told me is true!" Julia said, fighting him.

"What did Primus tell you?" he demanded, his stomach sinking.

"He said you came to see Hadassah rather than me. I said he was being ridiculous! My brother, in love with a slave? Absurd! I told him you came to see me—*me!* And he said I should open my eyes and see what's been going on around me."

"Nothing's been going on. You've been drinking Primus' poison," Marcus said tautly. "Don't listen to him."

"If it's not true, why do you come asking to speak to Hadassah?"

"For personal reasons that have nothing to do with you or Primus or anyone else."

Her smile was unpleasant. "'Personal reasons,'" she said with disdain. "You won't answer, will you? You can't without admitting that you care more about her than you do about *me!*"

"Your jealousy is out of place. You're my *sister!*"

"Yes. I'm your sister and I deserve your loyalty, but do I have it?"

"You know you have it. You know you've always had it." Recognizing her fragile emotional state, Marcus took her hands. "Julia, look at me. By the gods," he said and jerked her again. "I said look at me. What I feel for Hadassah has nothing to do with my love for you. I adore you as I've always adored you."

"But you love her."

He hesitated and then let out his breath. "Yes," he said softly. "I love her."

"She's stealing everyone from me!"

He let her go. "What are you talking about?"

"She stole Claudius."

He frowned, wondering what was going on in her mind. What dangerous truths had Primus and Calabah twisted into foul lies, playing on Julia's jealous nature? "You didn't want Claudius," he reminded her bluntly. "You sent Hadassah to him, hoping she'd divert him from you."

"And she did, didn't she? She diverted his interest completely. Did you know he never once asked for me after I sent Hadassah to him?" She'd never thought about that until Calabah had asked her about it, and then she had realized the truth. "And he spent hours with her, hours she should have been serving me."

"She *was* serving you. She did what you demanded of her. You wanted Claudius distracted, and he was. He questioned Hadassah about her religion."

She looked at him coldly. "How would you know that unless you asked him?"

"Of course, I asked! You'll remember I was furious with you for sending her in your place."

"I remember," she said, eyes blazing. "You were angry that I'd given her to him. I thought it was concern for me, concern for my marriage. But that wasn't why, was it?" Her voice was thick with bitterness, and she shook her head and turned her back to him.

"I've been so blind!" she said with a bleak laugh. "I look back now and see it all so clearly. All those times when I thought you came to be with me because I needed you." She turned to him. "It wasn't like that at all, was it, Marcus? You didn't come to Capua for me. You didn't move back into the villa in Rome or come to Ephesus for me. You came for *her.*"

Marcus turned her around. "All those times, I did come to be with you. Don't let anyone make you think otherwise." It hadn't been until later, much later, that he had realized Hadassah mattered to him in ways no other woman ever had. Julia had been his first concern. Until now.

Julia looked away from his wrath. "I wonder what she said to Atretes all those times I sent her for him at the ludus, things that have poisoned him against me."

"What happened with Atretes has nothing to do with Hadassah," Marcus said angrily. "You can't cast the blame on her for your own foolish actions. You drove him away, not Hadassah."

"If she told him the child is his as I commanded her to, he would have come. And he hasn't! She probably went to him and sang psalms and wove her stories instead." She broke down, weeping. "If she'd done what I told her, why hasn't he come to me? Why this hateful silence?"

"Because you thought you could have him on your own terms," Marcus said. "And you can't." Full of pity for her, Marcus sighed and drew his sister into his arms. "It's over, Julia. Some things you can't put back together again."

Julia leaned against him and gave in completely to tears. When she finally regained her composure, she drew back and sank down onto a cold marble bench in the small alcove. Marcus sat with her. She looked at him bleakly.

"Why is it that love burns so hot you think you'll be consumed by it, and then, when it's over, there's nothing left but the taste of ashes in your mouth?"

"I don't know, Julia. I used to wonder that myself."

"With Arria?"

"With Arria and others," he said.

A small frown flickered across her pale face. "But not with Hadassah. Why?"

"She's different from any woman I've ever met," he said softly and took his sister's hands. "How many slaves would give their lives to protect their mistresses? Caius would've killed you if not for Hadassah. She's served you faithfully, not out of a sense of duty like Enoch and Bithia and the others, but out of love. She's something rare and beautiful."

"'Something rare and beautiful,'" Julia repeated dully. "But she's still a slave."

"Not if you free her."

Julia glanced up at him. "I need her," she said quickly, feeling a sudden, inexplicable sense of panic. "I need her now more than ever."

Marcus looked down over her swollen abdomen and nodded. "Then I'll wait," he said softly, "until after the baby comes."

Julia didn't respond. She merely stared at the floor, and Marcus felt a strange chill come over him at the emptiness he glimpsed in his sister's eyes.

35

After a long and difficult labor, Julia gave birth to Atretes' son. The midwife handed the squalling infant in his womb coat to Hadassah. The child was beautiful and perfect, and Hadassah felt a sweet joy fill her as she washed him carefully and rubbed him with salt. She wrapped him in warm clothes and came to place him beside his mother. "Your son, my lady," she murmured, and smiled as she bent down to give him to her.

Julia turned her face away. "Take him to the temple steps and leave him there," she rasped. "I don't want him."

Hadassah felt as though Julia had struck her. "My lady! Please don't say such things," she whispered pleadingly. "You don't mean it. He's your child."

"He's Atretes' son," she said bitterly. "Let him grow up a temple prostitute, or a slave just like his father." She glared up at Hadassah. "Even better, put him on the rocks to die. He should never have been born."

"What did she say?" the midwife asked, her hands pausing as they wrung out a bloody cloth in cold water. Hadassah drew back from Julia, stricken.

"She said to put it on the rocks," a voice spoke from the darkness.

Hadassah instinctively drew the child closer.

The midwife protested. "But there's no flaw in this child. He's perfect."

"And who are you to say? It's for the mother to decide what happens to the child, not you." Calabah came from the shadows of the room, where she had been waiting for the ordeal to end. "If Lady Julia doesn't want a man's issue, so be it. It's hers to discard or keep as she wishes." The midwife shrank back at her advance. Calabah turned her cold, soulless eyes on Hadassah.

Hadassah bent desperately to Julia. "Please, my lady, don't do this! He's your son. Look at him. Please. He's beautiful."

"I don't want to look at him!" Julia cried out, covering her face with her white hands.

"You don't have to, Julia," Calabah said soothingly, her gaze still fixed and burning on Hadassah.

"My lady, you will regret—"

"If Atretes didn't want him, neither do I! What is he to me that I should be made miserable every time I have to look at him? It's not my fault I got pregnant. Must I suffer forever for a mistake? Get rid of him!"

The child wailed pathetically, tiny arms flailing, his tiny mouth open and quivering.

"Get him out of here!" Julia screamed hysterically.

Hadassah felt the cold bite of Calabah's fingers and felt herself thrust toward the door. "Do as you're commanded," Calabah said. Frightened by what she saw in Calabah's eyes, Hadassah left.

She stood outside the door, her heart racing, sickened and horrified, the child crying in her arms. She remembered the other babe buried in a Roman garden, no marker to even tell of his brief existence. "What do I do, little one?" she whispered, holding the child closer. "I can't keep you here. I can't take you to your father. Oh, God, what do I do?"

She closed her eyes tightly, searching her mind for words that would instruct her, and the Word came. *"Slaves, be obedient to those who are your masters according to the flesh, with fear and trembling, in the sincerity of your heart, as to Christ; not by way of eye service, as men-pleasers, but as slaves of Christ, doing the will of God from the heart . . . "*

But did that mean she must obey Julia? Did that mean she must put Atretes' son on the rocks to die?

The will of God from the heart. Her mind stayed firmly on that beacon of light. God's will, not Julia's. Not the dark will of Calabah Shiva Fontaneus. Not even her own will. God's will be done.

Hadassah quickly took the baby to her sleeping mat and wrapped him until he was tight and warm in her shawl. Then she took him up in her arms again and left the house.

The night air was cold and the baby cried pitifully. She nestled him closer and spoke softly to comfort him. Her destination was some distance away, but, even in the darkness, she didn't waver once from her path. When she came to the house, she knocked and the door was opened.

"Cleopas," she said, recognizing the man from gatherings she had attended. "I must see John." She knew if anyone learned that she had brought the child to him, John would be in danger. So would anyone else who aided her in disobedience to her mistress. Romans believed they had the right of life and death over their children. But Hadassah answered to God, not to Rome.

Cleopas smiled, his eyes shining with an excitement she didn't understand. "John said you were coming. We've been praying since this morning, and the Lord answered. Come. John is with Rizpah."

Hadassah knew the young woman whose husband and infant son had succumbed to one of the many illnesses plaguing the Empire and gone to be with the Lord. She followed Cleopas to the steps as he brought her to the upper room of the house. John was sitting with Rizpah, their heads were bowed, their hands clasped as they prayed together. As Hadassah entered, John spoke softly to Rizpah, let her hands go, and rose.

"I'm sorry to intrude, my lord," Hadassah whispered in grave respect. "She wanted him left on the rocks to die. I couldn't do it, John. It's not God's will that a child be left to die, but I didn't know where else to bring him."

"You came where God led you," John said and took the child from her arms. Rizpah stood slowly and came to him. Her eyes rested tenderly on the child. "A mother without her child, and a child without a mother," John said.

Rizpah held her arms out and John placed Atretes' son in them. Rizpah nestled him close in the crook of one arm and touched his face. His tiny hand flailed, searching. She brushed his tiny fingers and he grasped one and held tight. His crying stopped. Rizpah laughed joyously. "Praise the Lord! God has shown mercy upon me. My heart magnifies the Lord, for he has given me a son to raise up for his glory!"

Marcus received word from Primus that Julia had given birth. He waited several days to give her time to rest, and then went to her.

"I don't know if you've heard," Primus said, "but the child is dead."

"How?" Marcus demanded, discomforted.

"The will of the gods. If you love her, don't ask her anything about it. She's very depressed and the last thing she needs is to discuss what's happened. Let her forget."

Marcus wondered if he had misjudged Primus. Perhaps his relationship with Julia wasn't purely selfish. "I will take great care with her," Marcus agreed and went into Julia's chamber.

Hadassah was removing a tray. She glanced at him once, bowed respectfully, and went quickly from the room. A muscle locked in his jaw as he watched her go, then he approached the bed. Though pale, Julia smiled and held out her hands to him.

"Help me to sit up," she said, and he propped cushions behind her to make her more comfortable. "I have so much to tell you," she said, and for the next hour she repeated Primus' embellished and humorous stories of well-known personages in the Empire. She held Marcus' hand tightly. She laughed.

Not once did she mention her child.

Yet, for all her pretense that everything was normal, Marcus saw something had gone from her . . . some spark, some part of her life . . . perhaps a part of life itself. He didn't know. All he knew was that some of the light had gone out of her eyes, and a hardness had taken its place.

"Why are you looking at me like that?" Julia said defensively. "And you've hardly said a word."

Marcus laid his hand gently against her cheek. "I just want to know my little sister is all right."

She searched his face and relaxed. "Yes, I'm all right," she said wearily and leaned into his touch, placing her own hand over his. "What would I do without you? You're the only one who ever understood me."

But had he, Marcus wondered. Did he?

Julia drew back slightly. "Even Hadassah doesn't understand me anymore."

"Why do you say that?"

"I don't know. She just makes me feel uncomfortable." She shook her head. "Never mind. It'll all pass away, and everything will be the way it was."

When he left, he saw Hadassah sitting on the marble bench. She didn't raise her head or look at him once, and he did not risk approaching her and giving Primus more fuel for his rumor mill. Another week or two and Julia would be well enough to release her. Then he would take her away with him and marry her.

On Marcus' second visit, Julia was in the triclinium with Primus, reclining comfortably on one of the couches and laughing at one of his salacious jokes.

"Marcus, you must sit with us," she said, delighted to see him.

"Have something to eat." She waved her hand toward a platter of expensive delicacies. "Primus, tell him the story you just told me. It'll make him laugh. And Marcus needs to laugh. He's been so serious lately."

"Well, Marcus? You used to like my stories," Primus said and poured himself more wine, "but they no longer amuse you. Why is that, I wonder?"

"Perhaps it is that I now see them for what they are," he said frankly. "Half-truths woven into vicious lies."

"I've never lied about you."

Marcus ignored him and directed his attention to his sister. "How are you feeling, Julia?"

"I'm well," she said lazily. Ever since Calabah had introduced her to eating lotus, she had stopped having bad dreams and drifted on a calm sea of cloudy sensations. She giggled at his frowning look.

"Poor Marcus. You used to be so much fun. What's happened to you? Is it because you've been worried about me? Don't be. I feel better than I've ever felt before."

"Words to delight his ears and mine," Primus said and raised his goblet. His mouth curved. "Give him what he wants, Julia. Give him your little Jewess."

"Hadassah," she said with a sigh. "Sweet, pure little Hadassah." Julia knew her hesitation played less on Marcus than on Primus, who claimed Hadassah's presence disturbed the entire household. He said it was as though there was a fragrance about her wherever she went; to some it was sweet, but to him it was a stench in his nostrils. He said if she were gone, Prometheus would act like himself again.

"I don't know if I can part with her," Julia said and saw Primus' face tighten.

"Julia," Marcus said, his voice taut with annoyance. He didn't have to remind her that she had already agreed to relinquish Hadassah, nor that he wanted no part of her byplay with Primus.

"Very well. Just promise me you'll send her back to me when you tire of her."

Marcus strode from the room and went in search of Hadassah.

"He's hungry for her, isn't he?" Primus said mockingly. "He can't wait to feast upon her purity. I wonder if he'll come away unscathed."

Julia suddenly rose from her couch and spoke in a low voice

that was filled with fury—and threat. "If you speak one word about my brother, I'll make you sorry. Do you understand? No one laughs at Marcus. *No one!*" She went out of the room.

Cursing her under his breath, Primus emptied his goblet.

Hadassah had known Marcus would come for her. She had known it from the moment Decimus had taken her hand and joined it with his son's, from the moment Marcus had looked at her. Every time he was near she trembled, torn between her love for him and her knowledge that they couldn't be together, not as things were now. Night after night she went down on her knees and pleaded with God to soften Marcus' heart, to turn him to the truth. "And if he will not turn, Lord, turn him away from me," she prayed, afraid she wouldn't have the strength to turn from him herself.

But when Marcus entered Julia's chamber, Hadassah knew she was going to go through the fire. He looked at her and the purpose of his presence burned in his eyes, searing her with her own desire for him. He came to her and cupped her face, his hands shaking. Gently, he kissed her, and his touch made a sweet longing sweep through her body. "You're mine now," he said, his voice low with emotion. "Julia has released you. As soon as the documents can be drawn up, you'll be free, and I can marry you."

She uttered a soft gasp, her heart crying out to God.

"I love you," Marcus said huskily. "I love you so much." He dug his fingers into her hair and kissed her again.

Hadassah melted against him. Like a flood, his passion poured over her and carried her with its hot, rushing tide. She forgot Marcus didn't believe in God. She forgot she did. All her senses focused on Marcus, the sound of his breathing, the feel of his racing heart beating beneath her palms, the strength of his arms around her. Drowning in sensation, Hadassah forgot everything she had ever known and clung to Marcus.

Shaken, he drew back and looked at her, his hand cupping the back of her head. "I want you," he rasped. "I want you too much." The look in her eyes filled him with elation. "Oh, Hadassah," he said, trying to get his breath, "I thought I knew what love was. I thought I knew everything about it." He touched her features, loving them, tracing them with his fingers, trying to regain control of his raging emotions.

"I want you," he said again huskily, putting her away from

him. "So much that I hurt. But I remember the last time I let myself lose control with you, and I won't let it happen again. Not like that."

At his words, Hadassah gave a small, broken gasp, the fog of passion washed away in the clarity of what she faced. Trembling, she went back into his arms.

Marcus misunderstood. "If we made love now, I'd never regret it," he told her, holding her away from him. "But you would. Purity until marriage. Isn't that one of your god's laws? Religion doesn't matter to me. It never has. But it matters to you, and because of that, I'll wait. All that matters to me is that I love you. I want no regrets between us."

She closed her eyes. *Your* god, he said—and she knew God hadn't answered her prayers. "Oh, Marcus," she whispered, heartbroken. "Oh, Marcus . . . " Her eyes blurred with tears. "I can't marry you."

He frowned slightly. "Yes, you can. I just told you Julia has consented to give you to me. Father gave his blessing. So has Mother. We'll be married as soon as I can arrange it."

"You don't understand." She drew back from him and covered her face. "Oh, God, why must I choose?"

Marcus saw her torment, but didn't understand it. He gripped her shoulders. "Julia has released you. She doesn't need you anymore."

"I can't marry you, Marcus! I can't!" She turned away because she was afraid to look at him, afraid she would weaken and give in to him instead of obeying God.

Marcus turned her around roughly. "What do you mean you *can't?* What's to stop you? Who's to stop you? You love me, Hadassah. I feel it when I touch you. I see it in your eyes."

"Yes, I love you," she said. "Maybe that's it. Maybe I love you too much."

"Too much? How can a woman love a man too much?" And then Marcus thought he understood. "You're afraid my peers will say I married a slave. Is that it?" Her concern for others had always come before her own needs. "I don't care, Hadassah. Let them say what they will."

Marcus knew he had been contemptuous of a man once who had freed his slave in order to marry her, but he hadn't known then how love could break down the barriers between master and slave. He hadn't known then how much a woman could matter to a man.

She shook her head. "No, Marcus. It's not because of that. I can't marry you because you don't believe in the Lord."

Marcus let out his breath in relief. "Is that all that's worrying you?" He tucked a strand of hair behind her ear and smiled slightly. "What difference does it make? It's not important. What I believe or don't believe doesn't change how much we love each other. It makes no difference."

"It makes a great difference."

"No, it doesn't." He touched her face tenderly, loving the feel of her skin and the way her eyes softened. "It's a matter of tolerance and understanding, Hadassah. It's a matter of loving one another and allowing there to be freedom within a relationship. My father never made an issue of my mother worshiping gods and goddesses he didn't believe in. He knew she found comfort in them, just as I know you find comfort in yours. So be it. Worship your unseen god. I won't stop you. You'll have the protected privacy of our home to do as you wish."

"And what of you, Marcus? Whom will you worship?"

He lifted her face and kissed her. "You, beloved. Only you."

"No!" she cried, struggling free. She turned from him, tears spilling down her cheeks.

Marcus put his hands on her shoulders and kissed the curve of her neck. He felt her racing pulse beneath his lips. "What can I say to assure you it will be all right? I love you enough to tolerate your religion."

"Tolerate. Not believe." Hadassah turned and looked up at him. "How can I make you understand?" she said bleakly. "When two oxen are yoked together, they must pull in the same direction, Marcus. If one pulls to the right, and the other to the left, what happens?"

"The stronger wins," he said simply.

"And so it would be with us. You would win."

"We're not oxen, Hadassah. We're people."

She struggled within herself. She wanted to be with him, to feel his arms around her, to have his children and grow old with him—but she heard the warning of the Lord, and she had to heed it. "If I yoked myself to you in marriage, if I became flesh of your flesh, pleasing you would become the most important thing in my life."

"And isn't that as it should be? The husband leads and the wife follows."

"You would pull me away from the Lord," she said.

The Lord, he thought, anger rising up against her unseen god. *The Lord. The Lord.* "I just said you could worship whatever god you chose."

She saw his anger, and it only confirmed her fear. "At first, you'd allow it. And then it would change. You wouldn't even know when or how. Nor would I. It would just happen in small ways that seem unimportant and, little by little, day by day, you'd pull at me until I was walking in step with you and not following the Lord."

"Would that be so wrong? Shouldn't a wife put her husband above all else?"

"Not above God, never above God. It would mean death to both of us."

His temper rose. "No, it wouldn't. Loving me instead of this god of yours would mean *life,* life as you've never experienced it. You'd be free. No yoke on you." When she closed her eyes, he uttered a curse. "Why must we always come back to this god of yours?"

"Because he *is* God, Marcus. He is *God!*"

He gripped her face tightly. "Don't turn away from me. Look at me!" When she obeyed, he knew she was slipping away from him, and he didn't know how to hold on to her. "You love me. You said you did. What do you have with him? A yoke of slavery. No husband. No children. No home to call your own. And a future, stretching on and on, of nothing but the same." His hold gentled. "And what would I give you? Freedom, my love, my children, *my passion.* You want those things, don't you? Tell me you don't, Hadassah."

The tears came, slipping down her pale cheeks as she tried so desperately to stand firm. "I do want those things, but not if it means compromising my faith, not if it means turning away from God. And that's what it will mean. Don't you see, Marcus? If I provide for this life and turn away from the Lord, I am wise for a moment, but lost forever." She put her hands tenderly over his. "And so are you."

Marcus let her go.

Hadassah saw the look on his face: hope gone, pride shattered, defensive rage rising. She wanted to reach out to him. "Oh, Marcus," she whispered brokenly, hurting and afraid for him. What if they did marry? Would her faith justify him? Her resolve weakened. "Oh, Marcus," she said again.

"It's a pity, Hadassah," he said sardonically, fighting the emotions choking him: love for her, hate for her god. "You'll never know what you threw away, will you?" He turned from her and strode out of the room.

Blind to everything around him, Marcus went down the corridor, taking the stairs two at a time.

Julia watched him go from where she was standing just outside the door. Her hand balled into a fist. She had heard Hadassah reject him. A slave had turned down her brother! She felt his humiliation. She felt his rage. She shook with it.

Looking into the room, she saw Hadassah on her knees, bent over, weeping. Julia watched her coldly. She had never hated anyone so much in her life. Not her father, not Claudius, not Caius. No one.

She had been blind to what Hadassah was. Calabah had seen: "She's salt in your wounds." Primus had seen: "She's a thorn in your side." Only she had been fooled.

She returned to the triclinium.

"Is Marcus gone?" Primus said, clearly getting drunk.

"Yes, but Hadassah is remaining here for a while longer," she said, trying to keep her voice steady and not give her feelings away. Primus was far too shrewd, and she didn't want him weaving mortifying stories to shame her brother. "I told him I'm not ready to part with Hadassah yet," she lied.

Primus swore to the gods. "When will you be ready?"

"Soon," she said. "Very soon." She stood at the archway and looked up. Hadassah came out of the room, carrying a wash bucket, going about her duties as though nothing had happened. "Didn't Vitellius invite us to a feast celebrating Emperor Vespasian's birthday?" she said.

"Yes," he said, "but I declined for you." His mouth twisted mockingly. "I told him you lost our baby and were bereft with grief over it."

The mention of her child sent a dull pain through her. She would not let him see his words had struck their mark. "Send word I'll be attending."

"I thought you loathed Vitellius."

She turned and gave him a disdainful smile. "Indeed, but I find I have use for him."

"And what use would that be, dear Julia?"

"You'll see, Primus. And I think you'll enjoy the play as it unfolds."

Phoebe heard Marcus return. She came out eagerly from her chambers and saw him climb the marble steps. Her heart sank when she saw his face. Sensing her presence, he glanced up.

"Hadassah will remain with Julia," he said and walked into his room.

Distressed by his countenance, she followed. "What happened, Marcus?"

"Nothing I shouldn't have expected," he said blackly and poured himself some wine. He lifted his goblet in a toast. "To her unseen god. May he take pleasure in her faithfulness!"

Phoebe watched her son drain the goblet dry and then stare at it bleakly. "What happened?" she asked again, softly.

He set the goblet down hard on the tray. "I forsook my pride and she threw it back in my face," he said in self-contempt. "That's what happened, Mother." Marcus went out onto the terrace, and Phoebe followed him. He gripped the railing. Her hand slid gently over his.

"She loves you, Marcus."

He jerked his hand from beneath hers. "I offered to marry her. Would you like to know her answer? She said she didn't want to be yoked to an unbeliever. There's no reasoning with a faith like hers. There's no compromise. One god! One god above all else! So be it. Her god can have her."

He turned away, his knuckles whitening on the rail again. "It's over, Mother," he said grimly, determined to put Hadassah behind him. An evening at the baths would help him forget her. If not, Rome had many more exciting pleasures to help a man obliterate his frustrations.

36

The Ethiopian dancers moved with increasing violence to the beat of drums as Vitellius' guests supped on ostrich and pheasant. Julia's heart beat in time to the drums, faster and faster, until she thought she would faint. Then, *boom,* the dance ended, the drums stopped, and the half-naked dancers adorned with colorful plumes flew from the room like frightened exotic birds.

The moment had come. Her breathing still quickened, Julia raised her hand slightly, summoning Hadassah. No one noticed the small Jewess; she was just another maid among the dozens who served their masters and mistresses. Julia dipped her hands into the bowl of warm water that Hadassah held for her, and wondered how long it would be before Vitellius noticed the sash around her maid's small waist.

Hadassah knew something was wrong. She had been glad of Julia's command that she attend her at Vitellius' feast. Primus had always insisted one of the other maids attend Julia. This evening, though, he hadn't quibbled about Julia's decision . . . and now Hadassah sensed that Julia had another, darker purpose for her insistence that she be present. As she stood, holding the bowl of water, people began staring at her and whispering. Hadassah felt a warning prickle on the back of her neck.

Julia slipped the towel from Hadassah's arm and dabbed at her hands delicately.

Primus leaned close to her. "Do you know what you're doing, Julia?" He forced a smile, pretending a nonchalance he was far from feeling. "Vitellius is glaring at us as though we carried the plague into his house. Send Hadassah away. Send her away now."

"No," Julia said and lifted her head slightly, staring straight into Hadassah's eyes. A cold smile curved her lips. "No, she's going to stay right here."

"Prepare yourself, then. Vitellius is coming over and he looks greatly offended. If you will excuse me, my dear," Primus said, rising, "I will share a story with Camunus and leave you to explain yourself to our host."

The guests grew quieter as Vitellius made his way to Julia.

"Put the bowl down, Hadassah, and pour me some wine," she said.

Hadassah felt Vitellius' presence without raising her head; his hatred was like a tangible presence surrounding her. Her throat went dry, her heart beat like a trapped bird. She looked at Julia in appeal, but her mistress was smiling up at her host in greeting. "Vitellius," she said, "you lay a most impressive table."

Vitellius ignored her flattery and stared with loathing at the striped sash around Hadassah's waist. "Of what race is your slave?"

Julia's eyes widened. "Judean, my lord," she said and those nearby fell silent. Frowning, she glanced around her in apparent innocence. "Is something wrong?"

"Jews murdered my only son. They besieged Antonia Tower and broke in to slaughter him and his men."

"Oh, my lord, I am so sorry. I didn't know."

"A pity you didn't," he said, his dark gaze still fastened on Hadassah. "Mad dogs, all of them. The spawn of scorpions. Titus should've exterminated them from the face of the earth."

Julia rose and placed her hand on his arm. "Hadassah isn't like those who took your son's life. She is loyal to me and to Rome."

"Do you think so? Perhaps you are too kind and naive to understand the treachery of her race. Have you tested her?"

"Tested her?"

"Does your maid worship at the temple of Artemis?"

"No," Julia said slowly, as though the admission caused her to think.

"Has she burned incense to the emperor?"

"Not publicly," Julia said, and Hadassah's heart sank at her words. As though sensing her silent plea, Julia looked at her, and it was then Hadassah knew. Julia had brought her to this deliberately.

"Test her as you desire, Vitellius," she said smoothly, a dark triumph glowing in her eyes.

"And if she refuses to proclaim Vespasian a god?"

"Then do to her as you see fit."

Vitellius snapped his fingers and two guards came and stood on either side of Hadassah. "Stand her over there for all to see," he commanded, and they took her arms. She went with them without resisting. They stood her in the center of the marble floor where the Ethiopian dancers had just performed and turned her to face Vitellius.

"Put the emblems before her."

The guests gathered closer, curious and eager to see what she would do. They whispered among themselves. Some laughed softly. The emblems were brought in and placed before Hadassah. She knew she had only to proclaim Vespasian a god, light the slender reed, and put it to the incense as an offering to him, and her life would be spared.

"Do you see how she hesitates?" Vitellius said, and the frightening promise in his tone made Hadassah tremble.

Lord, you know what's in my heart. You know I love you. Help me.

"Take up the flame, Hadassah," Julia commanded.

Hadassah reached out slowly, her hand trembling violently. She took a slender reed and placed it to the flame.

Oh, God, help me.

And the Word came to her, filling her. *"I am the Lord your God, and there is no other."* She took her hand from the reed and watched it curl and blacken in the flame. Guests began whispering.

The soft voice whispered through her mind. *"Take up your cross and follow me."* Hadassah put her hand over her heart and closed her eyes "God, forgive me," she whispered, ashamed that she had almost given in to fear. "Don't forsake me."

"Lo, I am with you, even to the end of the age."

"Take up the flame!"

Hadassah raised her head and looked at Julia. "The Lord, he is God, and there is no other," she said simply and clearly. Astounded and angered, everyone spoke at once.

"Strike her," Vitellius said, and one of the guards struck her hard across the face.

"Vespasian, he is god," Julia said. "Say it!"

Hadassah stood silent.

"Didn't I tell you?" Vitellius said coldly.

"She'll say it. I'll make her say it." Julia went to her and slapped her. "Speak the words. Speak them or die!"

"I believe that Jesus is the Christ, the Son of the Living God."

"A Christian!" someone whispered.

Julia struck her again. "The emperor is god."

Hadassah looked at Julia through a blur of tears, her face

laced with pain, her heart breaking. "Oh, Julia, Julia," she said softly, wondering if this was how Jesus had felt when Judas kissed him.

The desire to avenge her brother's broken pride had set Julia on this path, but it was her own jealousy that made her erupt into violence. Uttering a feral scream of rage, Julia attacked Hadassah. The guards stepped back as she beat the girl with her fists.

Hadassah took the blows with soft cries of pain, but made no effort to defend herself. Julia stopped when Hadassah was on the floor, unconscious. "You can have her, Vitellius," she said and kicked her in the side.

"Haul her up and take her to Elymas," Vitellius ordered, and the guards obeyed. "He pays five sesterces per victim for his lions."

Atretes came awake with a deep, guttural cry and sat up. His body was drenched in sweat, his heart galloping. Panting, he raked shaking fingers through his hair and stood. He strode to the entrance of his cave and looked back toward Ephesus. The Artemision was there, glistening like a beacon in the moonlight. It wasn't in flames.

He wiped the beads of sweat from his face and went back inside the cave again. He knelt down and covered his head.

The dream had been so real, he could still feel the power of it. He wanted to shake himself free of it, but it came, night after night, bits and pieces of it clearer until he knew he would never be free until he understood its meaning.

And he knew the only one who could tell him the meaning was the one who had come to him the night before the dreams had begun.

Hadassah.

The guard of the lower dungeon threw the bolt. "What are the odds on Capito surviving against Secundus, Atretes?" he asked, eager for tips on how to bet at the games. Atretes didn't answer. And after a look at the German's hard face, the guard asked no more questions.

The sound of the Roman's hobnailed sandals sent Atretes back to Capua. As he followed the guard, the smell of cold stone and human fear made the sweat break out on his skin. Someone cried out from behind a locked door. Others moaned in despair. Then, as they kept walking, Atretes heard something coming from the far end of the dank environs—a sound so sweet that it drew him. Somewhere in the darkness a woman was singing.

The guard slowed, tilting his head slightly. "Have you ever heard a voice like that in all your life?" he said. The singing stopped, and he walked more briskly. "A pity she's going to die with the rest of them tomorrow," he said, pausing before a heavy door. He threw the bolt.

A sickening stench hit Atretes as the door opened. The cell was on the second level, and the only vents into the chamber were from another level above it, rather than from the outside. The air was so close, Atretes wondered how anyone could survive in it. The foul smell was so overpowering, his gorge rose and he stepped back.

"Bad, isn't it?" the guard said. "After five or six days, they begin dying off like flies. It's no wonder some prisoners run into the arena. They crave one last breath of fresh air before they die." He handed Atretes the torch.

Breathing through his mouth, Atretes stood on the threshold and looked from face to face. A single torch flickered in the mount on the side wall, but those in back were cast in shadows. Most of the prisoners were women and children. There were less than half a dozen old bearded men. Atretes wasn't surprised. The younger men would have been saved for the fighting, pitted against men like Capito and Secundus . . . men like himself.

Someone said his name and he saw a thin woman in rags rise from the mass of filthy captives.

Hadassah.

"Is that the one?" the guard said.

"Yes."

"The singer," he said. "You there! Come out!"

Atretes watched her as she picked her way across the room. People reached up to touch her. Some took her hand, and she smiled and whispered a word of encouragement before she passed by. When she reached the open doorway, she peered up at him with luminous eyes. "What are you doing here, Atretes?"

Unwilling to say anything before the Roman guard, he took her arm and drew her out into the corridor. The guard closed the door and set the bolt. He opened another door across the corridor and lit the torch.

"Leave us," Atretes said when the guard remained just outside the door.

"I have my orders, Atretes. No prisoner leaves this level without written authorization from the proconsul himself."

Atretes sneered. "Do you think you could stop me?"

Hadassah put her hand on his arm and turned to look at the guard. "You have my word that I will not leave." The guard looked from Atretes' murderous anger to her gentle eyes. A frown flickered across his face. He nodded once and left them alone.

Atretes listened to the sound of the hobnailed sandals on stone and clenched his fist. He had vowed never to enter a place like this again, and here he was, by his own choice.

Hadassah saw his distraction. "Did Julia send you?"

"Julia sent word you were dead."

"Oh," she said quietly. "I had hoped—"

"Hoped what? That I'd been sent to free you?"

"No, I hoped Julia would have a change of heart." She smiled sadly and then looked up at him with a faint frown. "But why would she send you word about me?"

"Because I sent for you. After the first message, a boy came to me. He said his name was Prometheus and that you were his friend. He told me Julia had sold you to Elymas. I went to Sertes and he made inquiries and found out you were being held here."

Hadassah came closer and placed her hand gently on his arm. "What troubles you so much that you would go to such lengths to find a mere slave?"

"Many things," he said without hesitating or asking himself why it was easy to trust her. "Not the least is the fact that I can't get you out of here."

"That doesn't matter, Atretes."

He turned away, anger filling him. "Julia should be the one in this place," he said harshly, looking around at the cold, stone walls of the dank chamber. "She's the one who should suffer." How many hundreds had waited within these walls to die? And for what? The pleasure of the Roman mob. When he had come to the gates of this place, he had almost turned back from the black memories. "She should be the one waiting to die. Not you."

He hated Julia so much he could taste the bile of it in his mouth, feel the rush of it heating his blood. He would enjoy killing her with his own hands if it wouldn't mean he'd end up back in this place, waiting to fight in the arena again. And he would take his own life before that ever happened.

Hadassah touched his arm, pulling him out of his murderous thoughts. "Don't hate Julia for what she's done, Atretes. She's lost. She's frantically searching for happiness, but she's drowning. Instead of grabbing hold of the one thing that will save her, she grasps at flotsam. I pray God will yet be merciful to her."

"Merciful?" Atretes said, looking at her in stunned amazement. "How can you pray for mercy on the one who sent you here to die?"

"Because what Julia did has given me the sweetest joy of all."

Atretes searched her face. Had confinement driven her mad? She had always had a strange look of peace about her, but now there was something more. Something that surprised him. In this dark place, with a horrifying death facing her, she looked changed. Her eyes were clear and luminous—and filled with joy.

"I'm free," she said. "Through Julia, the Lord has set me free."

"*Free?*" he said bitterly and looked pointedly at the stone walls.

"Yes," she said. "Fear was my constant companion, from as far back as I can remember. I'd been afraid all my life, Atretes, from the time I was a small child visiting Jerusalem, right up to a few days ago. I never wanted to leave the safety of the little house where I grew up in Galilee or the friends we knew. I was afraid of everything. I was afraid of losing those I loved. I was afraid of persecution and suffering. I was afraid of dying."

Her eyes glistened with tears. "Most of all, I was afraid that when the time came and I was tested, I wouldn't have the courage to say the truth. And then the Lord would turn his face from me."

She spread her hands. "And then it happened, the very thing I feared most . . . I was stood before people who hated me, people who refused to believe, and I was given a choice: recant or die. And the cry came from within my soul, a cry the Lord gave me through his grace. I chose God."

Tears ran down her cheeks, but her eyes were shining. "And the most amazing, miraculous thing happened to me in that moment, Atretes. Even as I was speaking the words, proclaiming Jesus is the Christ, my fear fell away. The weight of it was gone as though it had never been."

"Had you never said the words before?"

"Yes, among those who believed, before those who loved me. Where there was no risk, I spoke them willingly. But in that moment, before Julia, before those others, I surrendered completely. He is God and there is no other. To not tell them the truth would have been impossible."

"And now you'll die for it," he said grimly.

"Unless we have something worth dying for, Atretes, we've nothing worth living for."

He felt an aching sadness that this gentle young woman would die such a foul, degrading death. "You did a foolish thing, Hadassah. You should have done what was expedient and saved your life." Just as he had done, and countless others before him.

"I gave up what I can't keep for something I can never lose."

Looking upon her, Atretes felt an aching hunger for a faith like hers, a faith that could give him peace.

Hadassah saw his torment. "You must hate this place," she said softly. "What brought you here to me?"

"I've had a dream. I don't know what it means."

She frowned slightly. "I'm not a seer, Atretes. I have no prophetic abilities."

"It has to do with you. It started the night you came to me in the hills and it hasn't stopped since. You *must* know."

She felt his desperation and prayed God would give her the answers he needed. "Sit with me and tell me," she said, weak from confinement and days without food. "I may not know the answers, but God does."

"I'm walking through blackness, a blackness so heavy I can feel it pressing against my body. All I can see are my hands. I walk for a long time, not feeling anything, and then I see the Artemision in the distance. As I come closer to it, the beauty of it amazes me, just as it did the first time I saw it—but this time, the carvings are alive. They're writhing and uncoiling. The stone faces stare down at me as I enter the inner court. I see Artemis, and the symbol she wears upon her crown glows red."

"What symbol?"

"The symbol of Tiwaz, the god of the forests. The head of a goat." He knelt down before her. "And then the image of Artemis begins to burn. The heat is so intense I move back from it. The walls are crumbling, the temple falling in on itself until there's nothing left but a few stones."

Hadassah touched his hand. "Go on."

"Everything is black again. I walk on, searching for what seems forever, and then I see a sculptor. And before him is his work, a statue of me. It's one like those they sell in the shops around the arena, only this one is so real it seems to breathe. The man takes a hammer and I know what he's going to do. I cry out for him not to do it, but he strikes the image once and it shatters into a million pieces."

Shaking, Atretes rose. "I feel pain, pain like I've never felt before. I can't move. Around me I see the forest of my homeland and I'm sinking into the bog. Everyone is standing around me, my father, my mother, my wife, friends long dead. I cry out, but they all just stare at me as I'm being sucked down. The bog presses around me like the blackness. And then a man is there, holding out both hands to me. His palms are bleeding."

Hadassah watched Atretes sink wearily down against the stone wall on the other side of the cell. "Do you take his hand?" she asked.

"I don't know," he said bleakly. "I can't remember."

"You awaken?"

"No." He breathed in slowly, struggling to keep his voice steady. "Not yet." He shut his eyes and swallowed convulsively. "I hear a baby crying. He's lying naked on the rocks by the sea. I see a wave coming in from the sea and know it'll sweep him away. I try to get to him, but the wave goes over him. Then I awaken."

Hadassah closed her eyes.

Atretes leaned his head back. "So tell me. What does it all mean?"

Hadassah prayed the Lord would give her wisdom. She sat for a long time, her head bowed. Then she raised her head again. "I'm not a seer," she said again. "Only God can interpret dreams. But I do know certain things to be true, Atretes."

"What things?"

"Artemis is a stone idol and nothing more. She has no power over you but what you give her. Your soul knows that. Perhaps that's why her image burns and her temple crumbles." She frowned slightly. "Perhaps it means more. I don't know."

"And the man?"

"That's very clear to me. The man is Jesus. I told you how he died, nailed to a cross, and how he arose again. He's reaching out to you with both hands. Take hold and hang on. Your salvation is at hand." She hesitated. "And the child . . . "

"I know about the child." Atretes' face tautened with barely controlled emotion. "He's my son. I thought about what you said to me that night you came to the hills. I sent word I wanted the child when it was born."

Seeing Hadassah's startled look, Atretes stood abruptly and paced restlessly. "At first, it was to hurt Julia, to take her child from her. Then I truly wanted him. I decided I'd take the child and return to Germania. I waited, and then word came. The child was stillborn."

Atretes gave a broken laugh filled with bitterness. "But she lied. The child wasn't stillborn. She ordered it left on the rocks to die." His voice choked with tears, and he raked his fingers through his hair. "I told you if Julia laid him at my feet, I'd turn and walk away. And that's exactly what she did, isn't it? Placed him on the rocks and walked away. I hated her. I hated myself. God have mercy on me, you said. God have mercy."

Hadassah rose and went to him. "Your son is alive."

He stiffened and looked down at her.

She put her hand on his arm. "I didn't know you'd sent word you wanted him, Atretes. Had I known, I would have brought him directly to you. Please forgive me for the pain I've caused you." Her hand fell limply to her side.

He took her arm. "You said he's alive? Where is he?"

She prayed God would make right what she had done. "I took your son to the apostle John and he placed him in the arms of Rizpah, a young widow who'd lost her child. She loved him the moment she looked upon his face."

His hand loosened and fell away from her. "My son is alive," he said in wonder, and the burden of pain and guilt fell away from him. He closed his eyes in relief. "My son is alive." His back against the stone wall, he slid down it, his knees weakened by what she told him. "My son is alive," he said in a choked voice.

"God is merciful," she said softly and lightly touched his hair.

The light caress reminded Atretes of his mother. He took Hadassah's hand and held it against his cheek. Looking up at her, he saw again the bruises that marked her kind face, the thinness of her body beneath the ragged, dirty tunic. She had saved his son. How could he walk away and let her die?

He stood, filled with purpose. "I'll go to Sertes," he said.

"No," she said.

"Yes," he countered, determined. Though he'd never fought lions and knew there was little chance he would survive, he had to try. "A word in the right ear, and I'd be in the arena as your champion."

"I have a champion already, Atretes. The battle is *over.* He's already won." She held his hand firmly between her own. "Don't you see? If you went back into the arena now, you'd die without ever fully knowing the Lord."

"But what of you?" Tomorrow she would face the lions.

"God's hand is in this, Atretes. His will be done."

"You'll die."

"'Though He slay me, yet will I trust Him,'" she said. She smiled up at him. "Whatever happens is to his good purpose and for his glory. I'm not afraid."

Atretes searched her face for a long moment and then nodded, struggling against the emotions raging within him. "It will be as you say."

"It will be as the Lord wills."

"I will never forget you."

"Nor I you," she said. She told him where to find the apostle John, then laid her hand on his arm and looked at him, peace in her eyes. "Now, go from this place of death and don't look back."

She went out into the dark corridor and called to the guard.

Atretes stood with the torch as the guard came and unbolted the cell door. As he opened it, Hadassah turned and looked up at Atretes, and her eyes shone with warmth. "May the Lord bless you and keep you, the Lord make his face shine upon you and be gracious to you. May the Lord turn his face toward you and give you peace," she said with a gentle smile. Turning away, she entered the cell. A soft murmuring of voices greeted her, and the door was closed with a hard *thud* of finality.

37

Hadassah picked her way carefully among the other prisoners and sat again beside the little girl and her mother. Raising her knees, she rested her forehead upon them. She thought of Atretes, a prisoner of bitterness and hatred, and prayed for him. She prayed that Julia would turn away from the path of destruction she had chosen. She thanked God for Decimus, for his entry into God's kingdom, and she prayed that Phoebe would find her way to the Lord, too. She prayed that God would open a way for Prometheus' escape. She prayed that God would show mercy upon Primus and Calabah. Through the rest of that night, she prayed.

And, finally, Hadassah allowed herself to think of Marcus. Her heart cried out in pain as hot tears came. "Oh, Lord, you know the desires of my heart. You know what I want for him. I humbly beseech you, Lord, open his eyes. Open his eyes that he might see the truth. Call his name out loud, Lord, and let it be written in the Book of Life."

The torch sputtered and someone cried out. "I'm afraid," a woman said, and a man answered, "The Lord has forsaken us."

"No," Hadassah said gently. "The Lord has not forsaken us. Never doubt in the darkness what God has given us in the light. The Lord is with us. He is here now. He will never leave us."

She began to sing softly and others joined in. After a moment, she bowed her head again, using what little time she had left to pray for those she loved. Marcus. Phoebe. And Julia.

When morning came, the door opened and the young guard who had come with Atretes entered.

"Listen to me," he commanded, staring straight at her. "You will die today. Listen to what I tell you that it may go quickly. Lions that have been starved aren't necessarily vicious. They're weak and easily frightened, especially when the crowd starts yelling. You'll be strange prey to them. Now, do this. Stand quiet. Spread out. Move your hands and bodies slowly so the lions will know you're alive and no threat to them. If you do this, they'll charge. The end will come swiftly that way."

He fell silent for a moment, still looking at Hadassah. "They're coming for you."

She rose. "May the Lord bless you for your kindness."

He turned away. Everyone rose and began to sing praises to the Lord until the cell filled with the sound. Other guards came. They shouted and shoved the prisoners along the darkened corridor and up the narrow stairway and finally to the gates. Hadassah could hear a heavy sound like rolling thunder from outside. Sunlight reflected off the raked sand, blinding her.

Metal screeched against metal as the gates were opened. "Move out into the middle!" the guards shouted again, pushing at them. "Hurry up! Get moving!" A whip cracked, and someone gave a cry of pain and stumbled against Hadassah.

She took hold of the man's arm and helped him walk to the gate. Then she smiled at him, let him go, and walked out onto the sand. The others followed.

After days of darkness, the sunlight made her gasp. She put her hand up to shield her eyes. Jeers and insults rained down on her and the others. "Call on your god to save you!" someone shouted, and mocking laughter resounded.

"They look too thin to tempt a lion!" another called out, and rotten fruit and vegetables and picked bones were flung down at them. "Send in the lions! Send in the lions!"

Hadassah looked up at the mass of people, drunk on cruelty, screaming for blood, *her* blood. "God have mercy on them," she whispered, her eyes welling with tears.

At the roar of lions, a familiar coldness coiled in Hadassah's stomach. Her throat closed and her mouth went dry. Her old enemy closed in on her, but she knew how to fight now. Standing firm, she called upon the Lord.

"Oh, Jesus, be with me now. Stand by me and give me your strength that I might glorify you," she prayed. The calmness came upon her again, washing away the fear and filling her with joy that she would suffer for the Lord.

More gates were opened and the crowd cheered wildly as a dozen lions were driven into the arena. Terrified by the screaming mob, the beasts hugged the walls, paying no attention to the group of ragged prisoners standing in the middle of the arena.

"Mama, I'm afraid," a child whimpered.

"Remember the Lord," her mother answered.

"Yes," Hadassah said, smiling. "Remember the Lord." She separated herself from the group, walked calmly toward the center of the arena, and began to sing praises to God.

The mad screaming of the crowd rose. Slaves jabbed dull spears at the beasts who still hugged the rim of the arena, driving them away from the walls. They turned toward the center nervously. One lioness turned toward Hadassah and crouched low, advancing cautiously. Still singing, Hadassah lifted her arms from her sides and spread them slowly. Seeing she was alive and no threat, the beast charged, and the mob screamed wildly. The animal covered the distance with astonishing speed and leapt, claws spread, jaws open.

Julia laughed and tossed grapes at Marcus. "You're a terrible tease, Marcus," she said, reclining comfortably as he laughed.

"Would I turn down such a heart-wrenching plea from my beloved little sister?" he said, leaning back comfortably, his foot resting on a small stool. "You sounded desperate for my company."

"Who else ever made me laugh as you do?" she said and snapped her fingers. "Pay attention, girl," she said, and her new maid moved the large fan again. Marcus smiled faintly, his gaze flickering briefly over the girl's lithe body. "A new acquisition?"

"I'm glad to see you're your old self again," Julia said, amused. "She's pretty, isn't she? Much prettier than Hadassah," she said, watching him surreptitiously.

Marcus gave a cool laugh and turned his attention to the gladiators as they paraded before the spectators. He didn't want to think about Hadassah today. He had come to the games to forget. The bloodletting would be a cathartic release for his pent-up frustration. "Capito and Secundus fight today," he said, aware Julia was watching him. She was pensive and he wondered why.

"So I read. Who will win, do you think?"

"Secundus."

"Oh, but he's so boring. He plods around the arena like a tired old bull."

"His plodding is what keeps him alive," Marcus said. "He waits for his opportunity and strikes." The pompa completed, the chariots sped from the arena. The trumpets blared loudly, announcing the beginning of the games. The noise of the crowd rolled and swelled, restless and hungry. Marcus stood.

Julia sat up. "Where are you going?"

"To buy some wine." He glanced up at the cloudless sky. "It's getting hot already. The awnings aren't going to do much good."

"I have wine, plenty of it, the best quality. Don't leave. The games are beginning."

"There's nothing of interest at the beginning. Just some criminals being fed to the lions. There's plenty of time before the real blood matches begin."

Julia reached out. "Sit down, Marcus. We've hardly talked at all. Primus can go for whatever we need, can't you, Primus?"

"Of course, my dear. Whatever your heart desires."

"Sit here, Marcus," Julia said, patting the seat closest to her. "Please. It's been so long since we attended the games together. It was never as much fun as when I attended with you. You've always had an eye for what was coming. You always pointed things out to me that escaped my attention."

Marcus sat down beside her. He felt her tension. "What's wrong, Julia?"

"Nothing's wrong, except that I want things to be the way they used to be between us. I want to go back to the way things were in Rome, before I married Claudius, before anyone came between us. Do you remember the first time you brought me to the games, Marcus? I was so excited. I was such a child. You laughed at me because I was squeamish." She smiled at the memory.

"You got over it quickly enough," he said with a rueful grin.

"Yes, and you were proud of me. You said I was a true Roman. Do you remember?"

"I remember."

"Things will be the way they were, Marcus. I promise you. After today, we'll forget everything that's happened between then and now. We'll forget everyone who's hurt us."

Frowning slightly, Marcus touched her cheek. He thought of Caius and Atretes. She never spoke of either, but he knew both had left scars, deep scars that she kept hidden even from him.

"Do you love me, Marcus?" she asked, her eyes intent.

"Of course, I love you."

But not the way he once had, she knew. His expression became guarded, pained. All that would change soon. Today would wipe away the past and avenge his wounds—and hers. "You were always the one person I could count on, Marcus," she said and took his hand. "You were the one person I knew would always love me no matter what I did. And then others got in the way and made things change. We let them get in the way. We shouldn't have done that."

"I never stopped loving you, Julia."

"Perhaps you didn't stop, but things changed between us. People made them change. I'd see the way you looked at me sometimes, as though you didn't know me anymore. But you do know me, Marcus. You know me as well as you know yourself. We're so much alike, peas from the same pod. Only you've forgotten."

Her hand was cold and strong. "What's wrong, Julia?" he asked again, concerned.

"Nothing's wrong," she said. "Everything is right. Or will be. I've made sure."

"Of what?"

"I have a surprise for you, Marcus."

"What surprise?"

She laughed. "Oh, no. I'm not going to tell you. You'll just have to wait and see. Won't he, Calabah?"

Calabah smiled faintly, her eyes cold and black. "The games have begun, Julia."

"Oh, yes," she said eagerly, her hand tightening on his even more. "Oh, yes, they have. Let's watch, Marcus. You'll see what I've done for you."

A chill of premonition swept through him. "What have you done?" he asked, willing his voice to be calm and steady.

"Look!" she said, extending her right arm, pointing. "The gates are opening. Do you see them? Foul stinking wretches. They deserve death. Everyone of them. Look! Do you see? *Christians!*"

Heart pounding, Marcus saw the prisoners stumble out into the sunlight.

Oh, gods. . . .

Even at this distance, he recognized Hadassah. His heart stopped. "No!" he said, his voice a hoarse whisper, trying to deny what his eyes could see.

"Yes! Hadassah," Julia said and saw how white his face was. "She's getting what she deserves."

He stared as Hadassah led the group out, walking calmly. "What have you done, Julia?"

"I heard what she said to you! I heard her throw your love back in your face. She preferred her god over you, and you said her god could have her. Well, now he shall."

"You arranged this?" His voice was filled with desperation

and loathing. He tore his hand from her, wanting to strike her. "You did this to her?"

"She did it to herself. I took her to Vitellius' feast."

"You know Vitellius hates Jews!"

"Yes, he hates them, and with good reason. They're the most miserable race on the face of the earth! Full of pride. Guilty of rebellion from the womb. She wouldn't recant. I knew she wouldn't. I knew it! She just stood there, looking at me with those pathetic, soulful eyes, as though she pitied *me.*"

"She saved your life once! Or have you forgotten Caius almost killed you? And yet you sent her to her death?"

"She's a slave, Marcus. When she protected me, she only did what she was supposed to do. Should I be grateful for that? Her life means nothing."

Marcus felt desperation rise within him, making it almost impossible to breathe. "Her life means everything to me! *I love her!*" he cried.

Suddenly the crowd screamed wildly, and Marcus turned to see that the lions had entered the arena. He surged to his feet. "*No!* She's innocent! She's done nothing wrong!"

"Nothing?" Julia rose with him, clutching at his arm. "She put her god above you. She put her god above Rome! She's a foul stench in my nostrils. She's a thorn in my side, and I want her plucked out, destroyed. *I hate her!* Do you hear me?" She looked back at the arena. "Yes! Drive the lions from the wall!"

"No!" He shook Julia off. "Go back, Hadassah! Go back!"

"Drive the lions out!" Julia screamed again, more wildly.

"*No!*" Marcus tore his sister's hands from him. "Go back, Hadassah!"

The sound of the screaming mob rose as Hadassah walked calmly toward the center of the arena. The lioness crouched. Hadassah lifted her hands slowly, spreading her arms as though to welcome the beast as it charged.

"*No!*" Marcus cried out again, his face convulsing as the lion hit her. He turned his face away as she went down—and something inside of him died.

"There," Julia said triumphantly. "It's finished."

The sound of ecstatic pleasure rose as spectators cheered wildly. More lions roared. Screams of fear and pain rang out, and someone laughed near Marcus. "Look at them scatter now!"

Another hooted. "Look at those lions fighting over the carcass of that first girl!"

And in that instant, God answered Hadassah's prayer.

Marcus looked back, and his eyes were suddenly opened as he stared down at Hadassah, lying crumpled on the sand, her tunic shredded and bloodstained. Two lionesses were fighting over her body, ripping at one another. One bit into Hadassah's leg and tried to drag her away. The other attacked again.

"I paid her back for what she did to us," Julia said, clutching at Marcus. "We can forget her now."

"I'll never forget her," he said hoarsely and grasped Julia's wrists tightly, looking at her as though she were something foul and hateful. "But I will forget *you.*"

"Marcus," she said, frightened by the look in his eyes. "You're hurting me!"

"I'll forget I ever had a sister," he went on, pushing her away from him. "May the gods curse you for what you've done!"

She stood staring at him, her face white, her eyes wide with shock. "How can you say such cruel things to me? I did it for you! *I did it for you!*"

He turned from her as though she hadn't spoken, as though she didn't exist. "You want her, Calabah?" he asked, his voice low, filled with loathing.

"I've always wanted her," Calabah said, eyes glowing with black fire.

"You can have her." And Marcus turned his back on Julia, pushing his way past Primus, who was just returning with the wine bags. "Get out of my way!"

"No!" Julia cried out. "Stop him! Marcus, come back!"

Calabah caught hold of her hand, her grip strong and unrelenting. "It's too late, Julia. You've made your choices."

"Let go of me," Julia cried, weeping hysterically. *"Marcus!"* She struggled to go after her brother. "Let go!"

"He's gone," Calabah said, satisfaction in her voice.

Julia looked back at Hadassah on the bloodstained sand. A great emptiness opened within her as she looked at the still form. Gone, too, was the salt that had kept her from complete corruption.

"Marcus!" Julia screamed. *"Marcus!"*

Desperate to get out, to get away, Marcus shoved past screaming spectators. The sound of the mob swelled around him in wanton passion, drunk on human blood and suffering, craving more, frenzied. Fighting his way through them, Marcus reached the top of the steps and fled down the other side. He ran through the gates out into the open, tears blinding him. He didn't know where he was going, he didn't care. He ran to get away from the sound, the smell, the sight that was branded into his mind. He ran to get away from the image of Hadassah crumpled on the sand, the beasts fighting over her body as though it was just another piece of meat.

His lungs burned as he ran harder. He ran until his strength gave out, then stumbled aimlessly along a marble street lined with marble idols that couldn't help him. The city was almost empty; most of the citizenry was at the arena enjoying the games. Legionnaires stood at each corner, preventing looting. They stared at him as he passed.

Leaning heavily against a wall, Marcus looked up at the writing brazenly announcing the games. Staring at it, Marcus remembered the countless times he had sat in the stadium, watching innocent blood be spilled and thinking nothing of it. He remembered the times he had laughed as people fled for their lives, or shouted profanity when a blood match took too long. He remembered sitting, bored, as prisoners were fed to beasts or nailed to crosses.

And as he remembered, he saw his part in Hadassah's death.

Marcus heard the familiar rumble in the distance . . . unsated humanity. He covered his ears, and a sound came up from deep inside him, a cry of pain and despair, a cry of remorse and guilt. It tore from him and rose, echoing down the empty street.

"Hadassah!"

He fell to his knees. Hunching over, he covered his head and wept.

EPILOGUE

"But the eyes of the Lord are watching over those who fear him, who rely upon his steady love.

"He will keep them from death. . . ."

Psalm 33:18

The story isn't over!

Don't miss the exciting and moving conclusion of the story of Hadassah, Marcus, and Julia in Book Two: *An Echo in the Darkness*.

An Echo in the Darkness

CHAPTER ONE

Alexander Democedes Amandinus stood at the Door of Death waiting for the chance to learn more about life. Never having enjoyed the games, he had come reluctantly. Yet now he was transfixed by what he was witnessing, amazed in the deepest part of his being.

The mad intensity of the mob had always filled him with an instinctive unrest. His father had said there was release in watching violence done to others, and Alexander had seen, on occasion, an almost sick relief on faces among the crowd as they observed the destruction of the games. Alexander frowned. Perhaps those who sat watching the horrors were, in some sense, thankful that it was not they who faced the lions or battled a trained gladiator—or fell victim to some other more grotesque and obscene manner of death.

It was as though thousands came to find a catharsis in the bloodletting, as though this embracing of planned mayhem somehow provided a buffer between each of the spectators and their increasingly corrupt and arbitrary world. Yes, terrible things were happening in the Empire, but—for this brief moment—they were not happening to the elite, to the faithful, to those who truly belonged to Rome. Alexander smiled wryly, aware that few who sat in the stands noticed what was obvious to him: that the stench of blood on the sand was no less strong than the stench of lust and fear surrounding everyone in the Empire. It was in the very air they breathed.

Today, though . . . today, something startling had happened. Something that had moved the young man as he'd seldom been moved before. And now he turned his eyes toward the fallen young woman and felt an inexplicable sense of triumph.

His hands gripped the bars as he looked out upon the sand where the woman now lay dead. She had walked out apart from the others, calm and strangely joyful. Alexander remembered how his attention had fastened on her immediately. As an aspiring physician, he had been trained to notice anything unusual, anything different in a person, and he had seen in her something extraordinary . . . something that defied description.

And then she had begun to sing, and the sweet sound had pierced through him.

The screams of the mob had quickly overwhelmed the sound of her voice, but she had continued forward, walking across the sand serenely, heading straight toward where Alexander stood watching. He could feel again the way his heart had pounded with each step she had taken. She had been rather plain in appearance, and yet there had been a radiance about her . . . an aura of light that he had felt rather than seen. It had been as though her open arms would reach out and enfold him.

The lioness had hit her with a sickening *thud,* and Alexander had felt the blow himself.

He closed his eyes, a shudder running though his body, then he looked at her again. Two lionesses were fighting over the still body. He winced as he watched one beast sink its fangs deeply into the young woman's thigh and attempt to drag her away. The other lioness sprang, and the two rolled and clawed at one another, fighting over the kill.

Just then, a screaming child ran by the iron-gridded gate where Alexander stood, a jewel-collared lioness in pursuit. The young man gritted his teeth and leaned his forehead against the cool bars, his knuckles whitening with the intensity of his inward struggle. The sight of so much suffering and death assaulted and nauseated him.

For as long as he could remember, he had heard the arguments in favor of the games. Those sent to the arena were criminals, he was told, deserving of death. He knew that the people who were on the sand now belonged to a religion that encouraged the overthrow of Rome.

Yet he could not help but wonder if a society that murdered helpless children should not be undone.

When the child's terror-filled screams were suddenly silenced, Alexander let out his breath, hardly aware he had been holding it. The guard behind him laughed harshly.

"Hardly a mouthful in that little one."

Alexander made no response. He wanted to shut his eyes, to close out the carnage before him, but the guard was watching him now. He could feel the cold glitter of those hard eyes as they observed him through the visor of the polished helmet. Alexander would not humiliate himself by showing weakness. If he was to become a good physician, he must learn to overcome his emotions. Phlegon had warned him often enough that he had to harden himself if he was to succeed in his life pursuit. After all, Alexander's learned teacher had told him, death was a part of a physician's lot in life.

Alexander drew a calming breath and forced himself to look out at the sand again. Without the games, he knew he would have no opportunity to study human anatomy. Phlegon said Alexander had gone as far as he could in his studies with scrolls and illustrations. Now, if he was to learn what he needed to know to save lives, he must perform vivisection. Recognizing Alexander's aversion to this fact, the old physician had been adamant, closing the younger man in a net of reason. How could he hope to perform surgeries without firsthand knowledge of human anatomy? Charts and drawings were not the same as working on a human being. And in Rome there was only one way to do that.

Silently, Alexander cursed the Roman law that forbade dissection of the dead, thus forcing physicians into the grisly practice of working on those who were near death. And the only place one could do such a thing was at the games, where the injured were criminals.

Now, one by one, the victims went down, until the horrific sounds of terror were replaced by the relative quiet of feeding lions. Then another sound informed Alexander that his time was at hand: the sound of the crowd's growing boredom and discontent. The contest was over, their entertainment at an end. Let the beasts gorge themselves in the dark interiors of their cages rather than tax the spectators with their tedious feasting.

The crowd's wishes were quickly heeded by the editor of the games. Gates swung open and armed handlers approached the animals, who dug in their claws and teeth more fiercely to protect their downed prey. Right behind the handlers came a man dressed as Charon, the guide who ferried the souls of the dead over the river Styx. As Alexander watched the costumed actor dance from one body to the next, he prayed that there might be a flicker of life in at least one of the victims. If not, he would have to remain here until another opportunity presented itself.

Alexander's gaze swept across the sand, searching for any survivors, yet holding little hope of finding even one. He glanced again at the young woman. No lion was near her, and he found that curious as she was far from the men driving the animals toward the gates. Eyes narrowing, he scanned her still form, then felt a shock of excitement. Had he seen a flicker of movement? Leaning forward, he peered intently against the glare of the sun. Her fingers did move!

"Over there," he said quickly. "Near the center."

"She was the first one attacked. She's dead," the guard responded flatly.

"I want to take a look at her," Alexander insisted.

The guard shrugged. "As you wish," he said, stepping forward and giving two quick sharp whistles. Alexander watched as Charon leapt and turned toward the fallen girl, then leaned down slightly, his feathered, beaked head turning as though listening intently for some sound or sign of life. He waved his mallet around in the air theatrically, prepared to bring it down if judgment had not been done and the victim was still alive. But, seemingly satisfied that the girl was dead, he grabbed her arm and dragged her roughly toward the Door of Death.

Suddenly, a lioness turned on the handler who was driving her toward a tunnel. The crowd in the stands rose to its feet, shouting in excitement. The handler barely managed to escape the animal's attack, using his whip expertly to drive the enraged beast back toward the tunnel to the cages. The guard took advantage of the distraction and swung the gate wide.

"Hurry!" he snapped at Charon, who ran, dragging the girl into the shadows. The guard snapped his fingers, and two slaves hurriedly grasped the girl by the arms and legs and carried her into the dimly lit corridor.

"Easy!" Alexander said angrily as they tossed her up onto a dirty, bloodstained table. He pushed the slaves aside, sure that even if the girl had been alive, these oafs had finished her off with their rough handling.

The guard's hard hand clamped firmly on Alexander's arm. "Six sesterces before you cut her open," he said coldly.

"That's a bit high, isn't it," Alexander asked, raising an aristocratic eyebrow.

The guard grinned. "Not for a student of Phlegon. Your coffer must be full of gold if you can afford his tutelage." He held out his hand.

"It's emptying rapidly," Alexander replied dryly, opening the pouch at his waist. He didn't know how much time he had to work on the girl before she died, and he wasn't going to waste time haggling over a few coins. The guard took the bribe and withdrew.

Alexander returned his attention to the girl. Her face was a bloody mass of torn flesh, and her tunic was drenched in blood as well. There was so much blood, he was sure she must be dead. Leaning down, he put his ear near her lips and was amazed to feel the soft, warm exhalation of life. He didn't have much time to work.

Motioning to his own slaves, he took a towel and wiped his hands. "Move her back there, away from the noise. *Quickly!"* The two servants hastened to obey, as Troas, Phlegon's slave, stood by watching. Alexander's mouth tightened. He admired Troas' abilities—the slave had assisted Phlegon many times during the past and knew more about medicine than most practicing free physicians—but not his cold manner.

"Give me some light," Alexander said, and a torch was brought close as he bent over the girl who now lay on a slab in the dim recesses of the corridor. Alexander had come for one purpose: to peel back the skin and muscle from the abdominal area and study the organs that were revealed. Stiffening his resolve, he untied a leather case and flipped it open, displaying his surgeon's tools. He selected a slender, razor-sharp knife from its slot.

His hand was perspiring. Worse, it was shaking. Sweat broke out on his forehead, and he could feel Troas watching him critically. He did not have much time; he had to move quickly and learn all he could.

He wiped the sweat from his brow and silently cursed his own weakness.

"She will feel nothing," Troas said quietly.

Clenching his teeth, he cut the neckline of the bloodstained tunic and tore it to the hem, laying it open carefully in order to assess the damage to the young woman's body. After a brief moment, Alexander frowned. From breasts to groin, she was marked only by superficial wounds and darkening bruises.

"Bring the torch closer," he ordered, leaning toward her head wounds again, reassessing them. Deep furrows were cut from her hairline down to her chin, and then from her collarbone to her sternum. The young physician's gaze moved slowly down, noting the deep puncture wounds and broken bones in her right forearm. Far worse, however, were the wounds in her thigh where the lioness had sunk in her fangs and tried to drag the girl.

Alexander's eyes widened as he realized that the girl hadn't bled to death because sand clogged the wounds—probably the result of being dragged—effectively stanching the flow of blood. Alexander's breath caught in his throat. One swift, skillful slice and he could begin his study. One swift, skillful slice . . . and he would be the one to kill her.

Perspiration dripped down his temples, his heart pounded heavily. He watched the rise and fall of her chest, the faint pulse in her throat, and felt sick.

"She will feel nothing, my lord," Troas said again. "She is not conscious."

"I can see that," Alexander said tersely, flashing the slave a dark look. He stepped closer again and positioned the knife. Just the day before he had worked on a gladiator. He had learned more about human anatomy from those few minutes than in hours of lectures. Thankfully, the dying man had never opened his eyes, but his wounds had been far worse than those of the girl lying before Alexander today.

He closed his eyes, steeling himself. He tried to focus on what Phlegon had taught him when he'd watched the physician work once. "You must cut quickly. Like this," his teacher had said as he sliced expertly. "They are nearly dead when you get them, and shock can take them in an instant. Don't waste time worrying about whether or not they feel anything, for the moment the heart stops you must withdraw or risk the anger of the deities and Roman law." The man Phlegon had been working on had only lived a few minutes before bleeding to death . . . yet his screams still rang in Alexander's ears.

He glanced now at Troas. "How many times have you overseen this, Troas?"

"More times than I care to recount, my lord," the dark-skinned Egyptian said, his mouth tipping sardonically. He read the younger man's surprise and hardened. "What you learn here today will save others tomorrow."

The girl moaned and moved on the table. Troas snapped his fingers and Alexander's two slaves stepped forward. "Take her by the wrists and ankles," he ordered, "and hold her still."

She uttered a rasping cry as her broken arm was drawn up. "Yeshua," she whispered, and her eyes flickered open.

Alexander stared down into dark brown eyes so filled with pain and confusion that he suddenly couldn't move.

"My lord," Troas said more firmly, "you must work quickly."

The girl muttered something in a strange tongue, and her body relaxed. The knife dropped from Alexander's hand and clattered onto the stone floor. Troas took a step around the slab table and retrieved it, holding it out to him again.

"She has fainted," he said, glancing from Alexander to the girl.

"Get me a bowl of water."

Troas frowned. "What do you mean to do? Revive her?"

Alexander glanced up at the mocking tone. "You dare question me?" he demanded imperiously.

Troas looked at the young, aristocratic face. The line had been redrawn, and he dared not cross it, regardless of his own experience or skill. Swallowing his anger and pride, he stepped back. "My apologies, my lord. I only meant to remind you that she is condemned to die."

"It would seem the gods have spared her life."

"For *you*, my lord. The gods have spared her that you might learn what you must know to become a physician."

"I will not be the one to kill her!"

"By command of the proconsul, she is already dead! It's not your doing. It was not by word of your mouth that she was sent to the lions."

Alexander took the knife from him and tossed it back among the other surgical tools in his leather case. "I'll not risk the wrath of whatever god spared her life by taking it from her now." He gestured angrily. "As you can clearly see, her wounds have damaged no vital organs."

"You would rather have her die slowly of infection?"

Alexander stiffened. "I would not have her die at all!" His mind was in a fever. He kept seeing the young woman as she walked across the sand, singing, her arms outspread, as though to embrace the very people who screamed for her death. "We must get her out of here," he spoke with a fierce determination.

"Are you mad?" Troas hissed.

Alexander didn't seem to hear him. "I don't have what I need to treat her wounds or set her arm," he muttered. He snapped his fingers, issuing hushed orders to his servants.

Troas watched in disbelief, then, forgetting himself, he grasped Alexander's arm. "You cannot do this!" His voice was low, restrained, and he nodded surreptitiously toward the guard who was, at this moment, watching them curiously. "You risk death for us all if you attempt to rescue a condemned prisoner!"

"Then we'd all better pray to her god that he will protect us and help us get her out without detection. Now stop arguing with me and remove her from here immediately. Take her to my home. I'll handle the guard and follow as soon as I'm able. *Move!*"

Troas saw there was no arguing with him and gestured quickly to the others. As the Egyptian whispered further commands in a low voice, Alexander tucked his surgical blade back into its slot and rolled the leather carrier, tying it casually, aware that the guard was watching them intently now. Alexander picked up his case and tucked it beneath his arm. Taking up the towel, he wiped the blood from his hands as he calmly walked toward the guard.

"You can't take her out of here," the soldier said, his eyes narrowed with suspicion.

"She's dead," Alexander lied casually. "They're disposing of the body. I'm sure you don't mind not having to touch her." He smiled sardonically at the guard, then leaned against the iron-grated gate and looked out at the hot sand. "She wasn't worth six sesterces. She was too far gone to be of any use to me." He looked at the guard pointedly.

The man grinned. "That's the chance you take."

Alexander pretended interest in a pair of gladiators who were locked in battle. "How long will this match last?"

The guard assessed the opponents. "Thirty minutes, maybe more. But there will be no survivor this time."

Alexander frowned as though disappointed. He paused, then tossed the bloodstained towel aside. "In that case, I'm going to buy myself some wine."

As he walked along the torchlit corridor, he forced himself to walk slowly—but his heart beat more quickly with each step. As he came out into the sunlight, a gentle breeze brushed his face.

"Hurry! Hurry!" He heard the words clearly, as though someone whispered urgently in his ear. But no one was there.

His heart pounding, Alexander turned toward his home and began to run, urged on by a still, small voice in the wind.

GLOSSARY OF TERMS

amorata (pl. amoratae): a male or female devotee, or fan, of a gladiator

andabata (pl. andabatae): a gladiator who fought on horseback; *Andabatae* wore a helmet with the visor closed, which meant they fought blindfolded.

Aphrodite: Greek goddess of love and beauty, identified with the Roman goddess Venus

Apollo: Greek and Roman god of sunlight, prophecy, music, and poetry. The most handsome of the gods

Artemis: Greek moon goddess. Her main temple was in Ephesus, where a meteor fell (the meteor was then kept in the temple), supposedly designating Ephesus as the goddess' dwelling place. Although Romans equated Artemis with Diana, Ephesians believed she was the sister of Apollo and daughter of Leto and Zeus and viewed her as a mother-goddess of the earth who blesses man, beast, and the land with fertility.

Asclepius: Greco-Roman god of healing. In mythology, Asclepius was the son of Apollo and a nymph (Coronis) and was taught healing by a centaur (Chiron).

Athena: Greek goddess of wisdom, skills, and warfare

atrium: the central courtyard of a Roman dwelling. Most Roman houses consisted of a series of rooms surrounding an inner courtyard.

"Ave Imperator morituri te salutant": "Hail, Emperor. Those who are about to die salute you." A perfunctory phrase spoken by gladiators before the Roman games began.

baltei: the circular walls of the Roman arena. There were three walls, formed in four superimposed sections.

Batavi: a clan from Gaul that fought with the Chatti and Bructeri against Rome

beastiarii: "hunters" in the Roman games. Wild animals would be let into the arena, and the beastiarii would hunt them down as part of the games.

bibliotheca: library room of a Roman dwelling

brassard: an armor piece that covers the upper arm

Bructeri: a Germanic tribe that fought with the Chatti against the Romans. The Bructeri apparently warred with the Chatti before being united with them against Rome.

caduceus: the herald's staff carried by Hermes. It had two serpents twined around it and wings at the top.

caldarium: the room in the baths that was nearest to the boilers and thus was the hottest (probably similar to a Jacuzzi or steam room of today)

catamite: a boy used by a man for homosexual purposes

cavea: tiers of seats in the Roman arena

cena: Roman name for dinner or a main meal

Ceres: Roman goddess of agriculture

Charon: In the Roman arena, Charon was one of the *libitinarii* ("guides of the dead") and was portrayed by a person wearing a beaked mask and wielding a mallet. This portrayal was a combination of Greek and Etruscan beliefs. To the Greeks, Charon was a figure of death and the boatman who ferried the dead across the Rivers Styx and Acheron in Hades (but only for a fee and if they had had a proper burial). To the Etruscans, Charun (Charon) was the one who struck the deathblow.

Chatti: one of the Germanic tribes

cisium: a fast, light wagon that had two wheels and was usually pulled by two horses

civitas (pl. civitates): a small city or village

coemptio: bride purchase—a form of Roman marriage that could be easily dissolved (i.e., the couple could be easily divorced)

confarreatio: a form of Roman marriage that was binding

consul: a chief magistrate in the Roman republic. There were two positions, which were elected annually. An honorific title under the emperor.

corbita: a slow-sailing merchant vessel

cuisse: an armor piece that covered the thigh

curule chair: the official chair of the highest civil officers of Rome, who were the only persons privileged to sit in them. The chair was similar to an upholstered "camp stool" of today and had heavy, curved legs.

Cybele: Phrygian goddess of nature worshiped in Rome. In mythology, Cybele was the consort of Attis (the god of fertility).

Diana: Roman goddess of childbirth and of the forest, usually portrayed as a huntress

dimachaerus (pl. dimachaeri): "two-knife man"—a gladiator who fought with a short sword in each hand

Dionysus: Greek god of wine and revelry, more commonly known by the Roman name of Bacchus

Eros: Greek god of physical love; equated with the Roman god Cupid

essedarius (pl. essedarii): "chariot man"—a gladiator who fought from a chariot that was pulled by two horses and usually decorated

fanum (pl. fana): a temple that was larger than a shrine but smaller than the regular temples

far: meal, grain

framea: a spear with a long, sharp head, used by the Germanic tribes. It could be thrown like a javelin or its shaft wielded like a quarterstaff.

frigidarium: the room in the baths where the water was cold

gladiators: male prisoners who were forcibly trained to "compete" in the Roman gladiatorial "games." Their prison/school was called a *ludus;* their trainer, a *lanista.* There were several types of gladiators, each of which was identified by the weapons he was given to use and the role he was assigned to play in the games. Except in unusual situations, gladiators fought until one of them died.

gladius: the standard Roman sword, about two feet long.

gorget: an armor piece that covered the neck

gustus: hors d'oeuvres served at beginning of a feast

Hades: Greek god of the underworld

Hera: Greek queen of the gods. In mythology, Hera was the sister and wife of Zeus and was identified with the Roman Juno.

Hermes: In Greek mythology, Hermes guided departed souls to Hades. He was also the herald and messenger of the gods and was known for his cunning. In the Roman arena, Hermes was one of the libitinarii and was portrayed by a person carrying a red-hot caduceus, with which he prodded people to make sure they were dead.

Hestia: Greek goddess of the hearth; identified with the Roman goddess Vesta

insulae: huge, Roman high-rise tenements, each of which filled a city block

Juno: Roman goddess, comparable to the Greek goddess Hera. Juno was the goddess of light, birth, women, and marriage. As wife of Jupiter, Juno was the queen of heaven.

Jupiter: The Roman supreme god and husband of Juno, Jupiter was also the god of light, sky, weather, and the state (its welfare and laws). Jupiter was comparable to the Greek god Zeus.

kaffiyeh: a headdress worn by Arabs

lanista: a trainer for gladiators. The head *lanista* at a *ludus* was held in both esteem and disgrace.

laquearius (pl. laquearii): "lasso man"—a gladiator armed with a lasso

lararium: part of a Roman dwelling. The *lararium* was a special room reserved for idols.

libellus: the program listing the coming events of the Roman games

Liber: Liber and Libera were Roman gods of fertility and cultivation. They were both associated with Ceres (Roman goddess of agriculture), and Liber was also identified with the Greek god Dionysus and was thus considered a god of wine growing. At the festival of Liberalia, boys who had come of age were first allowed to begin wearing the *toga virilis,* the clothing of a man.

libitinarii: the two "guides" of the dead (Charon and Hermes from Greek mythology) at the Roman games. They were in charge of clearing the dead bodies from the arena. At the games, Charon was portrayed by a person wearing a beaked mask and wielding a mallet, and Hermes by a person carrying a red-hot caduceus.

locarius: an usher at the Roman games

Ludi (plural): refers to the Roman games: "*Ludi Megalenses*"

ludus (pl. ludi): prison/school where gladiators were trained

lusorii: gladiators who fought with wooden weapons to warm up the crowd before the deadly games began

maenianum: the sections of seats behind and above the *podium* in the Roman arena. The knights and tribunes sat in the first and second maenianum to watch the games, and the patricians sat in the third and fourth.

manica: a sleeve/glove that had leather and metal scales

Mars: Roman god of war

megabuzoi: eunich priests in the temple of Artemis

melissai: virgin priestesses consecrated to service of the goddess Artemis

mensor (pl. mensores): a shipyard worker who weighed cargo, then recorded the weight in a ledger

Mercury: in Roman mythology, the message carrier for the gods; identified with the Greek god Hermes.

metae: cone-shaped turning posts in the Roman arena that also served to protect the *spina* during races. They were twenty feet high and had pictures of Roman battles carved on them.

mirmillo (pl. mirmillones): from *mirmillo,* a type of fish. A gladiator who was armed in Gallic fashion with a helmet having fish-shaped crests, a sword, and a shield. A *mirmillo* was usually paired against a *Thracian.*

Neptune: Roman god of the sea (or water), often accompanied by seven sacred dolphins. The Greek, Poseidon.

ocrea: an armor piece that covered the leg

paegniari: mock fighters at the Roman games. Like the *lusorii,* who came after them in the games, they were used at the beginning of the games to warm up the crowd.

palus: a cloaklike garment worn by Roman women over a *stola*

patrician: a person of (Roman) aristocracy

peculium: an allotment of money given to slaves by their owner. Slaves could treat *peculium* as their own personal property, but under certain circumstances their owner could take it back.

peristyle: a section of a Roman dwelling (often a secondary section) that enclosed a courtyard and was surrounded by columns on the inside. Often located in the *peristyle* were the bedrooms of the family, the domestic shrine (*lararium*), the hearth and kitchen, the dining room (*triclinium*), and the library (*bibliotheca*). In wealthier homes, the courtyard in the *peristyle* became a garden.

plebians: the common people of Rome

podium: the section of seats closest to the arena where the Roman emperor would sit to watch the games

pollice verso: at the Roman games this was the signal of approval to kill. It was usually a "thumbs-down" sign.

praetor: a Roman magistrate who ranked below consul and whose role was chiefly judicial in nature

Praetorian Guards: Roman imperial bodyguards

proconsul: a governor or military commander of a Roman province, who answered to the Senate

pullati: the highest (and least desirable) section of seats in the Roman arena

quadrans (pl. quadrantes): a bronze Roman coin

raeda: a heavy, large wagon with four wheels, usually pulled by four horses.

retiarius: "net man"—a gladiator who would try to trap or entangle his opponent with a net and then dispatch him with a trident. A *retiarius* wore only a short tunic or apron and was usually paired against a *secutor.*

sacrarii: shipyard workers who carried cargo from wagons and dropped it on a scale

sagittarius (pl. sagittarii): a gladiator whose weapons were a bow and arrows

sagum: a short protective cloak worn by the German tribesmen during battle. It was secured at the shoulder with a brooch.

Samnite: a gladiator who used the national weapons—a short sword (*gladius*), a large oblong shield, and a plumed helmet with a visor

sburarii: shipyard workers who unloaded cargo from ships and put it into wagons

scimitar: a saber (sword) made of a curved blade with the cutting edge on the convex side

scutum: an iron shield covered with leather, used by German tribesmen

secutor: a gladiator who was fully armed and considered the "pursuer"—that is, he was supposed to chase an opponent down and kill him. A *secutor* was usually paired against a *retiarius.*

sesterce: a Roman coin, worth one-fourth of a denarius

spina: a long, narrow platform area in the middle of the Roman arena that was both a monument area for Roman gods and the location of an elaborate and ornate fountain. It dimensions of approximately 233 x 20 were dwarfed by the much larger chariot track that surrounded it. The *spina* was protected from the chariots by cone-shaped turning posts called *metae*.

stola: a long, skirtlike garment worn by Roman women

stuppator: a shipyard worker who balanced on scaffolding to caulk ships when they docked

tepidarium: the room in the baths where the water was warm and soothing

Thracian: a gladiator who fought with a curved dagger (or scimitar) and used a small round shield (often worn on the arm). A *Thracian* was usually paired against a *mirmillo*.

Tiwaz: the war god of the Germanic tribes (Chatti, Bructeri, Batavi), symbolized by the head of a goat

toga virilis: the toga was the characteristic outer garment worn by Romans (although its use was slowly abandoned). It was a loose, oval-shaped piece of cloth draped about the shoulders and arms. The color and pattern of a toga were rigidly prescribed—politicians, persons in mourning, men, and boys each had a different toga. Boys wore a purple-rimmed toga, but when they came of age, they were allowed to wear the *toga virilis,* or man's toga, which was plain (see also Liber).

triclinium: the dining room of a Roman dwelling. The *triclinium* was often very ornate, having many columns and a collection of statues.

trident: a three-pronged spear

urinator (pl. urinatores): a shipyard worker who dove after cargo that was accidentally dropped into the sea during unloading

usus: the least binding form of marriage for Romans. It was probably similar to what we might today call "living together."

veles (pl. velites): a gladiator whose weapon was a javelin

Venus: Roman goddess of eros, love, and beauty; identified with the Greek goddess Aphrodite

Way, the: a term used in the Bible (the book of Acts) to refer to Christianity. Christians probably would have called themselves "followers of the Way."

Yeshua: Hebrew name for Jesus

Zeus: Greek king of the gods and husband of Hera; identified with the Roman god Jupiter

DISCUSSION GUIDE

Dear reader,

We hope you enjoyed this story and its many characters by Francine Rivers. It is the author's desire to whet your appetite for God's Word and His ways—to apply His principles to your life. The following character study is designed for just that! There are four sections of discussion questions for each of the four main characters:

- Character Review—gets the discussion going
- Digging Deeper—gets into the character
- Personal Insights/Challenges—gets you thinking
- Searching the Scriptures—gets you into God's Word

When writing this story, Francine had a key Bible verse in mind: "In the same way, let your good deeds shine out for all to see, so that everyone will praise your heavenly Father" (Matthew 5:16). Our deeds, be they words, actions, or the lack thereof, define our character and allude to our motivations. With this in mind, let me encourage you to get together with some friends and discuss your favorite scenes, characters, and personal insights from this novel. May your insights never end, and may your discussion "runneth over"!

PEGGY LYNCH

HADASSAH

Character Review

1. Choose a favorite moving or disturbing scene and discuss the elements that caught your attention.
2. Compare Hadassah leaving Jerusalem to Hadassah in the coliseum. What events caused the change?

Digging Deeper

1. Describe Hadassah's internal conflict.
2. In what ways did Hadassah rely on God's unfailing love?
3. How does God's unfailing love motivate you?

Personal Insights/Challenges

1. In what ways do you identify with Hadassah? And how are you different?
2. Do you think Hadassah's faith was realistic? How does your own faith compare?
3. "Without wavering, let us hold tightly to the hope we say we have, for God can be trusted to keep his promise" (Hebrews 10:23). What is the basis for unwavering faith?

Searching the Scriptures

As you think about Hadassah and decisions she made as a result of her faith in God, read the following Bible verses. They may reveal her motivations and even challenge you in your own life decisions.

> *If anyone acknowledges me publicly here on earth, I will openly acknowledge that person before my Father in heaven. But if anyone denies me here on earth, I will deny that person before my Father in heaven.* Matthew 10:32-33

> *For if you confess with your mouth that Jesus is Lord and believe in your heart that God raised him from the dead, you will be saved. For it is by believing in your heart that you are made right with God, and it is by confessing with your mouth that you are saved.* Romans 10:9-10

> *In the same way, let your good deeds shine out for all to see, so that everyone will praise your heavenly Father.* Matthew 5:16

> *But the Lord watches over those who fear him, those who rely on his unfailing love.* Psalm 33:18

MARCUS

Character Review

1. Select a favorite scene with Marcus and share insights about his personal character.
2. Contrast Marcus, the aristocrat, with Marcus, the man interested in Hadassah. What are the subtle differences?

Digging Deeper

1. How did Marcus perceive himself?
2. What kind of friends did Marcus keep, and what influence did they have on him?
3. In what ways have other people influenced you? How have you influenced them?

Personal Insights/Challenges

1. How do you identify with Marcus? How are you different?
2. How do you think Marcus perceived himself when Hadassah was led into the arena? What had changed?
3. "We can gather our thoughts, but the Lord gives the right answer" (Proverbs 16:1). When soul searching or heart stricken, who do you turn to for right answers?

Searching the Scriptures

In looking at Marcus' life and the decisions he made as a result of not knowing God, read the following Bible verses for possible insights into his motivations—as well as finding challenges for yourself, too.

> *People with integrity have firm footing, but those who follow crooked paths will slip and fall.* Proverbs 10:9

> *People may be pure in their own eyes, but the Lord examines their motives.* Proverbs 16:2

> *Good people enjoy the positive results of their words, but those who are treacherous crave violence.* Proverbs 13:2

ATRETES

Character Review

1. In your opinion what is the most memorable scene with Atretes and why?
2. What do you consider to be "outstanding" about Atretes?

Digging Deeper

1. What events brought Atretes to the coliseum?
2. In what ways did Atretes become sidetracked? What were some consequences?
3. What sidetracks you and why?

Personal Insights/Challenges

1. In what ways are you like Atretes? How are you different?
2. Discuss Atretes' anger and how it affected his decisions.
3. "There is a path before each person that seems right, but it ends in death" (Proverbs 14:12). What kind of path was Atretes on? What path have you chosen?

Searching the Scriptures

As you discuss Atretes and the decisions he made as a result of anger, read the following Bible verses and see what may have motivated him or what motivates you.

> *A hothead starts fights; a cool-tempered person tries to stop them.* Proverbs 15:18

> *Mark out a straight path for your feet; then stick to the path and stay safe. Don't get sidetracked; keep your feet from following evil.* Proverbs 4:26-27

> *Above all else, guard your heart, for it affects everything you do.* Proverbs 4:23

JULIA

Character Review

1. Which one of Julia's relationships stands out to you the most and why?
2. Compare Julia to her brother, Marcus. In what ways did Julia's family influence her?

Digging Deeper

1. How did Julia deal with conflict?
2. In what ways did her pride lead to arguments? What were some consequences of those arguments?
3. What draws you into arguments? How has pride misguided you?

Personal Insights/Challenges

1. In what ways do you identify with Julia? How are you different?
2. Contrast Julia with Hadassah.
3. "Do not withhold good from those who deserve it when it's in your power to help them" (Proverbs 3:27). How did Julia withhold good from Hadassah, and what was the result?

Searching the Scriptures

As you think about Julia and the decisions she made out of stubbornness and pride, check out the following Bible verses. They may reveal her motivations and challenge your own discernment.

> *Blessed are those who have a tender conscience, but the stubborn are headed for serious trouble.* Proverbs 28:14

> *Pride leads to arguments; those who take advice are wise.* Proverbs 13:10

> *A prudent person foresees the danger ahead and takes precautions. The simpleton goes blindly on and suffers the consequences.* Proverbs 27:12

BOOKS BY BELOVED AUTHOR FRANCINE RIVERS

The Mark of the Lion

- *A Voice in the Wind*..............................ISBN 0-8423-7750-6
- *An Echo in the Darkness*........................ISBN 0-8423-1307-9
- *As Sure As the Dawn*............................ISBN 0-8423-3976-0
- Boxed Set ....ISBN 0-8423-3952-3

The Atonement Child

- Hardcover...ISBN 0-8423-0041-4
- Softcover..ISBN 0-8423-0052-X

The Scarlet Thread

- Softcover..ISBN 0-8423-3568-4
- Living Book ....ISBN 0-8423-4271-0

The Last Sin Eater

- Hardcover ....ISBN 0-8423-3570-6
- Softcover ....ISBN 0-8423-3571-4

Leota's Garden

- Hardcover ....ISBN 0-8423-3572-2
- Softcover ....ISBN 0-8423-3498-X
- Audio ....ISBN 0-8423-5211-2

The Shoe Box ....ISBN 0-8423-1901-8

A Lineage of Grace

- *Unveiled* ....ISBN 0-8423-1947-6
- *Unashamed* ....ISBN 0-8423-3596-X
- *Unshaken* ....ISBN 0-8423-3597-8
- *Unspoken* ....ISBN 0-8423-3598-6
- *Unafraid* ....ISBN 0-8423-3599-4

Visit www.francinerivers.com